KU-613-800

JUDITH PARIS

The Herries Family

Judith Herries, *afterwards Judith Paris, daughter of Rogue Herries and Mirabelle*

Georges Paris, *her husband*

Adam Paris, *her son*

David Herries, *son of Rogue Herries*

Sarah, *his wife*

Francis *m.* Jennifer Cards ⎫
Deborah *m.* Squire Withering ⎬ *their children*
William *m.* Christabel Carmichael ⎭

John ⎫
Dorothy ⎬ *Francis' children*

Walter, *William's son, m.* Agnes Bailey

Uhland ⎫
Elizabeth ⎬ *Walter's children*

Deborah Sunwood, *daughter of Rogue Herries*

Rev Gordon Sunwood, *her husband*

Reuben ⎫
Humphrey ⎬ *their children*

Sir Pomfret Herries, *son of Sir Raiseley Herries, m.* Rose Dymock

James ⎫
Rodney ⎬ *their children*

Cynthia, *Pomfret's sister*

Carey Bligh, 2nd Lord Rockage

Maria, *his wife*

Carey *m.* Cecily Fowler ⎫
Phyllis *m.* Stephen Newmark ⎬ *their children*

Madeline, *Rockage's sister*

Jeremy Cards, *son of Humphrey Cards*

Prosper Cards, *son of Henry Cards, m.* Amelia Trent

Jennifer *m.* Francis Herries ⎫
Robert ⎬ *Prosper's children*

Morgan Cards, *Prosper's brother, m.* Ruth Ormerod

Montague, *his son*

Warren Forster, *great-grandson of Humphrey Cards*

Also available in Pan Books

ROGUE HERRIES

Coming Soon

THE FORTRESS
VANESSA

CONDITIONS OF SALE

This book shall not, by way of trade or otherwise, be lent, re-sold, hired out or otherwise circulated without the publisher's prior consent in any form of binding or cover other than that in which it is published and without a similar condition including this condition being imposed on the subsequent purchaser. The book is published at a net price, and is supplied subject to the Publishers Association Standard Conditions of Sale registered under the Restrictive Trade Practices Act, 1956.

HUGH WALPOLE

JUDITH PARIS

UNABRIDGED

PAN BOOKS LTD : LONDON

First published 1931 by Macmillan & Company Ltd.
This edition published 1971 by Pan Books Ltd,
33 Tothill Street, London, S.W.1

ISBN 0 330 02585 6

*This book is copyright to all countries which
are signatories to the Berne Convention*

*Printed in Great Britain by Cox and Wyman Ltd,
London, Reading and Fakenham*

FOR
J. B. PRIESTLEY

I have kept my faith, though faith was tried,
To that rock-born, rock-wandering foot,
And the world's altered since you died,
And I am in no good repute
With the loud host before the sea,
That think sword strokes were better meant
Than lover's music — let that be,
So that the wandering foot's content.

W. B. YEATS

A PREFATORY LETTER

My dear Jack,

There is in general no reasonable excuse for burdening a novel with a Preface or any sort of statement; a novel should show in itself its purport without outside emphasis. But, after the publication of *Rogue Herries*, I saw that with the next 'Herries' volume there must be a note of explanation. And for these reasons:

First: when a reader sees another instalment of Herries history he may think it necessary that he should read the first in order to understand the second.

Secondly: after *Rogue Herries* had made some friends it was in some places assumed that '*now*, of course, I would write a sequel'.

And thirdly: the principal criticism of *Rogue Herries* was on the ground of its diffuseness.

I must explain then that, firstly, the story of *Judith Paris* may be followed without any knowledge of her father or curiosity as to her descendants. Then, far from considering a sequel to *Rogue Herries* for the first time *after* its publication, I must here confess that I had, more than twenty years ago, the plan of writing the history of an English family that should cover two hundred years and that should have, throughout, the same English scene for its centre. This was, I think (although Mr Galsworthy may correct me), before the later Forsytes were thought of, or any suspicion of Sagas hung in the literary air.

Thirdly, I hope that when any who are interested realize (possibly with dismay and indignation) that there are to be, in all, four volumes of Herries history, certain details and characters will not seem so unnecessary, nor certain scenes so diffuse.

I would like, very modestly, to defend the fact that I write, and must write, from my own point of view. I can see that the Herries family offers, in its history, subject-matter for every kind of historian. But my view of the Herries in these volumes is frankly a romantic one.

Every historian, whether of a country or a family, is compelled by his temperament to his own individual vision. I can see that there is a Herries history that is realistic, one that is comic, one that is scientific. Any of these might be more broadly convincing than my own, but I must mix my own colours and stand by the result.

As to diffuseness, compression in such a scheme as this is not easy. I might have written a novel, a long one too, only about Jennifer. Even with Judith I have been compelled to squeeze ten years of her life into one chapter. Those ten years could well be the subject of another novel. The Rockages at Grosset fascinate me, but my theme compels me to keep them minor. And how much more I know about Georges Paris in London or Charlie Watson in Watendlath than I have space to tell!

Every scene and character has been deliberately chosen by me because of the book's continuous theme. At the awful word 'Theme', however, I feel that I am growing altogether too serious and solemn.

My intention is simply to record scenes from the life of an English family during two hundred years of English change and fortune, and beyond that to pay a tribute to a part of England that I dearly love.

Judith Paris may be read as a quite independent novel, but the four books are seen together in my mind as a piece of gaily-tinted tapestry worked in English colours.

Affectionately yours,
HUGH WALPOLE

Contents

Part One

Part Two

Part Three

Part Four

MOTHER AND SON

JUDITH PARIS

Part I

Rogue's Daughter

FORECHAPTER

THE OLD WOMAN and the newborn child were the only living things in the house.

The old woman, Mrs Henny, had finished her washing and laying-out of the bodies of the child's father and of the child's mother. She had done it alone because she had been afraid to leave the house with no one alive in it save the newborn child. Now she was exhausted and, in spite of her labour, fearfully chilled, for the snow, although it fell now more lightly, was piled high about the doors and windows as if, with its soft thick fingers, it wished to strangle the house.

She was very cold, so she drank some gin, although it was not as a rule her weakness. The bodies of Mr and Mrs Herries lay, the eyes decently closed, the pale hands folded, each in its proper bed.

A fine heat burnt through Mrs Henny's old body. The gin was good. Then her head fell forward and she slept.

The old house rattled and squealed in the wind that was rising up now that the snow had almost ceased to fall. Feet seemed to creep up and down the stairs, fingers were at the windows, but the dead and Mrs Henny slept on.

Then, in the room where the old woman, the child, and its mother were, from the window a piece of glass, very old and dark green like weeded water, was loosened with the wind and fell tinkling to the boards. The snow blew in like a live thing and the room was icily chilled.

The child that had been sleeping felt the cold and began to cry, a shrill cry on one note. But Mrs Henny heard nothing, the gin holding her fast.

Squire Gauntry – little Tom Gauntry – riding along the Borrowdale path just below the house on the farther side of the little bridge, heard the cry. It was strange that from so weak a creature the cry should be so clear. He heard it, and he pulled up his horse; the six hounds who were with him stopped also. The snow had but just ceased to fall and for the first time that day. It was so unusual in that country for there to be so heavy a fall that he halted and looked about him in wonderment. The roofs of Rosthwaite, all the hills, the fields, were buried in the white smooth covering, and now, for the first time, light began to break through. The grey stuff of the snowy sky was torn and a faint green field spread over the dim hills, and the snow began shyly to sparkle. The wind blew the top of the snow into little smoking spirals. Some rooks flew, like black leaves, cawing, breaking the sacred silence. The green field spread.

Herries, the house, raised on its little hill, to Gauntry's right, seemed to be overwhelmed by the snow, huddled, shapeless, helpless, and out of that white shapelessness this thin, desolate, tiny cry continued.

Gauntry was eager to be home; his high black riding coat was heavy with snow, he was weary and chilled, but there was something in that cry that moved him. A hard-bitten little man, leading always his own life and telling everyone else to go to the devil, nevertheless he was sentimental too: so he turned his horse, crossed the bridge over the stream, and, followed by the six hounds, guided the animal through the snow, and, striking with his whip on the gate of the courtyard, holloaed three times.

There was no answer at all. The silence settled down again. There was no sound but the thin persisting cry. He hesitated as to his next step. He had met Herries once and again, but had no intimacy with him. Indeed, no one had. He was said to be a queer customer, one not easy to deal with, one who would not thank you for uninvited interference.

Gauntry was just like that himself, and, for that very reason, had always felt a sympathy with Herries. He liked a man who told the world to go to the devil: it was what the world was meant for. Nevertheless, he was tired, cold, thirsty. Why should he put himself about for a man who would only curse him?

Then something about the stillness of the house hit his attention. The place was but a ruin in any case; under the snow he could fancy how the boards creaked and the chimneys rocked.

He dismounted from his horse, pushed wide the old, grumbling gate, the snow falling thickly from it, then, followed in silence by the hounds, crossed the courtyard.

The house door was unbarred. The iron handle turned easily. He entered, to be met by two rusted suits of armour stationed at the foot of the stairs. Still there was silence everywhere, save for the lament of the child.

How cold the house was! He shivered, drawing his cloak tighter about him. Then again he holloaed. No answer. Where

the devil were they hiding? Not a sound, not even a clock-tick.
Up the creaking stairs he went, the dogs padding after him.

He came to a room hung with faded brown tapestries; there
was a portrait of a wicked-looking old man in the dress of
Elizabethan times, dead ashes in the stone fireplace, remains of a
meal, bread, a mutton bone, on the table.

He called again: 'Herries! Herries!' but this time softly.
Something in the place constrained him. Lord! how cold the
house was!

A narrow wooden stair led higher, so on he went, the hounds
following, crowding one another on the stair but making no
sound.

At the stairhead there was a room. He pushed the door,
entered, then stood there looking.

First he was aware that the snow was blowing in through a
broken window, and then that a child lay in a wooden cradle.
It was the child's cry he had heard. Then he saw that in a chair
near the bed an old woman was asleep, and at her side was a
bottle, tumbled over, spilling its contents on the floor. Then,
stepping forward, he saw farther. On the bed a woman was
lying. He saw at once that she was dead. Her red hair was spread
about the pillow, her eyes were closed, and in her face there was
a look of great peace and contentment.

Mrs Herries! He had heard of her many a time, but had never
seen her. She had been a gipsy girl when Herries married her.
She had run away from him, and then returned. Herries' second
wife, the only woman, they said, whom he had ever loved.
Gauntry bent forward and touched reverently the cold, thin
hands. Yes, she was dead. Where, then, was Herries? Roughly
he shook the old woman by the shoulder, but she would not stir.
Only her old head rolled. He called softly 'Herries!', then went
to the cradle, and the infant, who must be but newly born, at
once ceased to cry.

He went to the door and listened, then seeing a room close
by pushed softly into it. Herries himself was lying in bed there.
Going closer Gauntry saw that he, too, was dead – an old man,
his face scarred, but he, too, seemed to smile in great contentment and happiness.

Both, then? Both dead? He turned back to the other room,
again shook the old woman, but saw that the drink held her
fast. He stood there wondering what he should do, while the
hounds sat on their haunches by the door and watched him.

Through the dusk the snow sparkled like diamonds, and

somewhere a solitary bird began its chirping. The infant did not cry, but seemed to watch him.

'Old woman!' he cried. 'Wake up! Wake up!'

But she would not wake. What must he do? The child must not be left here in this bitter cold: he could see that it was very warmly wrapped. Every preparation had been made for its coming. Poor woman! Poor Mrs Herries! Died in childbirth maybe, and Herries himself dying in the next room. Strange end to a strange life!

A tenderness seized him as he looked at that thin childish face, those thin delicate hands! What lovely hair she had! Herries had loved her, they said, almost to madness.

Well, someone must be told. Herries' son, David Herries, at Uldale must be told. Someone in Rosthwaite village must be fetched. But he could not leave that child there to start its melancholy cry so soon as he was gone. No, he could not. Very delicately for so dried and rough a little man he picked up the child, wrapping round it its warm bedding. Were it warm enough it would not suffer. They were hardy children in Gauntry's world. He was pleased that the child did not cry, but lay there in his arms contentedly.

Then he went out, down the stairs, across the courtyard, led the horse with one hand, and so, followed by the hounds, crossed the little bridge.

He knocked on the first cottage door in Rosthwaite. An old, wrinkled woman opened it. He told her of what he had found. She exclaimed something incoherently of witches and warlocks; another woman came, they chattered together. Two men joined them.

After many wonderings, forebodings and murmurs they started off up the hill to the house, in a group together as though they were afraid.

He stood there, considering. He did not wish to leave the child. It would be late when he was home. He would take it to his own place, Stone Ends, that night, and the family at Uldale should have it in the morning.

Yes, he did not want to leave it. Poor baby; it trusted him and seemed to watch him lest he should go away. Both dead in the one hour! He was helped to his horse, the child lifted to him by a village girl, then he called to the hounds and rode away. The infant, warm under the thick wrapping, uttered no sound.

LIFE AT ULDALE

IN THE AUTUMN of the year 1785 David Herries was sixty-six years of age, his wife Sarah forty-seven, his children, Francis twenty-five, Deb twenty-three and Will fifteen; his little half-sister, Judith Herries, was eleven.

They all lived at Fell House, Uldale. Uldale is on the farther side of Skiddaw and looks over the moor to the Solway Firth. The sprawling flanks of Skiddaw spread between Uldale and the town of Keswick.

In 1785 Marie Antoinette was playing hide-and-seek with her ladies in the gardens of Versailles, William Pitt was Prime Minister of England, Jane Austen was ten years old, and a Keswick boy of sixteen had just been hanged for stealing a leg of mutton. Nevertheless, this is a poor way of reckoning history, especially at Uldale, where the crops mattered and cock-fighting mattered and old Mrs Monnasett had only this very moment died.

History, of course, begins anywhere and everywhere. For Judith Herries it began, perhaps, when little Tom Gauntry found her squealing under the closed and lifeless eyes of both her parents. She never reckoned it so; she reckoned that it began on this autumn day when, after looking at Mrs Monnasett's corpse, she was whipped by her half-brother David.

This at once shows the ludicrousness of her position. She was eleven years old, and yet was sister to David Herries, who was sixty-six, and, yet more absurd, aunt, or at any rate half-aunt, to Francis, who was twenty-five, and Deb, who was twenty-three.

To make the matter more complicated yet and surely most improper, she was in love with her nephew Francis. For excuse you may say that she loved and hated alternately everyone around her a hundred times a day.

One of the disgraceful colours to this first notable event in Judith Herries' life was that Mrs Monnasett was but just dead and lying in state in the Blue Room. It was, indeed, because Mrs Monnasett lay there that the trouble began.

Fell House was a pleasant building, square-shaped, its brick rose-coloured, a walled-in garden, many fruit trees, the farm buildings with all the animals and the odours, a Gothic temple beyond the lawn, pigeons in the loft, swelling downs stretching almost to the sea, Skiddaw against the windows, and the road where the coaches ran not so far away that you could not hear the horses.

Life for Judith should have been agreeable there. They all wished to love her, and there was nothing in the world that she liked better than to be loved, but it had all been spoilt for her from the very beginning because she preferred so infinitely the life at Stone Ends, where Uncle Gauntry drank, hunted, beat her, loved her, taught her to ride, to hunt, to prepare the birds for cock-fighting and to learn everything there was to learn about men and women.

She was only eleven, but she knew more, far more, about everything than her half-niece Deb, who was twenty-three, or that other Deborah, her half-sister, who was married to a clergyman at Cockermouth and had two grown sons.

Uldale was by far too tame for her, and yet she loved them all and yearned for them all to love her. She knew, though, even at this age (she had known it long ago), that they could not really love her, for her mother had been a gipsy woman taken by her father off the fells and married by him when he was already an old man. She knew that David and Deborah, his children, had been ashamed of this marriage and had despised him for it. (They had not despised him for it. She would learn that one day.) Oh yes, they could not love her at Uldale, because she was the daughter of a gipsy who had been found one day dancing naked on the roof and could swear most horribly. But at Stone Ends they did not mind whose daughter she was and allowed her to do whatever she pleased.

Now on this afternoon in October they had but just finished dinner, Mrs Herries, Deb, Will, and Judith. Mr Herries and Francis had ridden to Newlands to see about a piece of land. Mrs Monnasett was to be buried the following day. The house was quite still. Mrs Herries went to the China Room to write a letter to her sister-in-law, Mrs Sunwood of Cockermouth. Deb was for the dairy, Will away on some secret purpose of his own. No one needed Judith. She stood, listening to the stillness of the house, halfway up the staircase, her fingers in her lip, considering. She was an odd little creature, even as odd little creatures go. She was very small, although made in excellent proportion, save that her red hair, which hung in ringlets, seemed weighty for her head. Her complexion was pale and would always be so: she had the horse-features of all the Herries, prominent nose and cheek-bones. She was, in fact, no beauty, but there was very much character in her bright and challenging eyes, the resolute-ness of her mouth. When she smiled she could be very winning. She could also look exceedingly impertinent, and, when angry, with her red hair, her pale face, and perfectly balanced, lightly swinging body, she could seem a flying fury. She had tiny hands and feet; of these already she was boastfully proud.

She was dressed in a red bodice with silver buttons and a small orange hoop. She wore red shoes. This was her best dress, bought for her in Carlisle on a birthday by David Herries, who alternately loved and hated her. She was supposed to wear this grand dress only on very special occasions; she put it on most days of the week, but although she wore it so often it was as fresh as when it was new. She had, from the first, that gift of being clean and spotless in all her circumstances as a piece of china. That was a dirty age, but Judith had always a passion for washing; no water was too cold for her; she was so hardy that nothing ever ailed her. One out of every three children at this time died before it was four years of age. Judith had never known an ache or pain. They said that it was because Tom Gauntry had carried her on the very day that she was born through all the snow and ice from Borrowdale to Stone Ends. If that hadn't killed her, nothing would.

She stood, swinging a red shoe, sucking her thumb, and considering. She had intended to go to the corner of the road and watch for the return of Mr Herries and Francis. She loved Francis madly, passionately, although he was her nephew. She loved his thin delicate body, his pale austere face with the dreaming eyes, the soft gentle voice. He should have been a woman, people said, and that was why so few understood him, but Judith understood him and she would willingly (she thought) die for him. She would not, of course, in reality die for anyone, having now and always a fierce and tenacious hold on life. But she fancied that if he said (in his soft dream-ing voice) 'Judith, pray jump from yonder window and break all your bones', she would jump. The fact that he con-sidered her very little, scarcely ever thought of her, made no difference. She loved him only the more fiercely. He and Uncle Gauntry were the gods of her fiery, agitated, dramatic world.

As she stood there the stillness of the house forced itself ever more upon her attention. She had intended to go to the road, but what an opportunity this was to creep in and look at Mrs

Monnasett! She had seen dead people before. There was the boy in Bassenthwaite village who had been beaten by his master and had suddenly (most ungratefully) died; she had been walking with Will and they had come on him lying against the Cross on the Common. There had been the beggar who came to their door one summer night to ask for food, and he had fallen dead while walking away up the hill. She was no stranger to death, and thought, in a general way, little of it. But Mrs Monnasett was different. Judith had known her all her life. She had been nurse and tyrant and friend to all the children. She had been there for years, ever since Francis and Deborah were born, and what a strange woman she had been, with the hairy mole on her cheek, the strange stories that she used to tell, the songs that she used to sing, the ghosts she had seen and the witches she had known, and, more than all, the little gold box that she carried with the charm of a snake's skin and the queer-smelling foreign root; would she have that little box with her yet, even though she were dead?

Judith had thought that the charm would prevent her from ever dying. She would live for ever. But no, she had not. She was dead now and the worms would eat her. Had she the little box yet with her? Judith considered. She and Will had been forbidden to go near the room, but that forbidding only made the matter more charming. She would have a whipping, but she had had many, and when David Herries whipped her she had only to sob in a certain strangling way and he was always sorry for her and would kiss her and let her have a pinch of snuff out of his box. Yes, the risk was nothing. Softly she stole up the stairs.

As it happened, Mrs Sarah Herries was at that same moment writing of Judith to her sister-in-law, Mrs Deborah Sunwood. She sat in the China Room, pleasant and sunny, the low windows looking across to Skiddaw. The room was handsomely furnished with some pagodas and vessels of Chelsea china, in which were set coloured sprigs of artificial flowers. The walls were hung with a Chinese wallpaper and, to quote an old Herries journal, 'A looking-glass, enclosed in a whimsical frame of Chinese paling, stood upon a Japan table over which was spread a coverlet of the finest chintz.' Yes, a pretty room, burnished now with the last orange glow of the setting sun, for it was after five, and Sarah Herries must light the candles.

She stood there a moment watching the trembling flame, a handsome woman in a rose-coloured hoop, wearing her own hair, a fine bosom, and the face stout a trifle but kindly, good-humoured and patient.

She was thinking, perhaps, as she held the snuffer in her hand and glanced at her broad figure in the looking-glass, that her life had been cast in pleasant places since that day so many years ago when David had snatched her out of Wasdale and fought her uncle on the Stye Head Pass.

She was thinking of that and of her Will, whom she adored, and her Francis, whom she adored not quite so much, and of her fat good-natured Deborah, whom, because she took a trifle after herself, she loved a little less . . . yes, ever so little less. And then her thoughts turned, as they always did were they given any freedom at all, to her beloved, worshipped David, the fire, the heat, the passion of her happy life, still the most handsome of all human creatures although he might be stout now, still the best of all humans although he might on occasion drink himself under the table or lose at faro with Squire Osmaston and the others the money that he had put aside for the purchase of Brandon's field. Her eyes were wet a trifle, the candle flame danced mistily as she sat herself down in the dark Irish Chippendale chair to write to her sister Deborah.

There was nothing in the world that she liked better than to write to Deborah, for she understood so precisely the importance of everything that Sarah thought important, was interested in all the cures that Sarah practised on the children, thrilled to the heart when she heard that wicked Cousin Pelham, now nearly seventy and old enough to reform (but he never would), had sent Sarah all the way from London by coach and carrier a Chippendale bookcase with a Gothic design in the cornice and rosettes on the lower panels.

Yes, Deborah understood everything, and most especially did she understand about Judith.

This, then, was the letter's first part, the candle flame trembling, the China paper dancing, the outer world fading to a silver star and the white tone of the climbing road.

MY DEAREST SISTER – I hope that you were not disappointed of your lodgings in Kendal and that the boys took care for you. I can give but little account of these last days for, as you know, we have had Kate Morris' children with us while the house in Keswick was set to order. Their visit had like to have been fatal to me for they not being acquainted with the Semblance of Manners nor trained indeed to any-

thing but having their own Way perfectly in all things that
were bad enough without our Judith's added wickedness to
excite them.

There is also now Mrs Monnasett dead in the House and
last Tuesday the new Coachman that we had from Mr
Newsom of Newlands was drunk returning Home from
Penrith and the postillions also and like to have overturned us
on a gallop against a Post coming through Threlkeld.

However, dearest Deborah, you are aware that my Nature
is both Tranquil and Harmonious and that if I might but be
sure that the Beneficient Creator is not on occasion busied
with His Attention in other more interesting Directions I
would not trouble for drunken Coachmen or anything else.

Mrs Monnasett is to be buried tomorrow forenoon.

I am happy that I consider nothing more disagreeable than
Learning in a Female for Mr Huxtable the Tutor of Kate's
children has been here a week and found us all Savages save
Francis.

With him he must talk Greek and all the Indian Languages
and has Mr Young's *Night Thoughts* at his Finger End and
Mr Pope's *Essay on Man* sprouting from his Eyeballs – a
Man heavy of figure and such a Comedy on a Horse that it
would do you good to see. But Judith who must always carry
everything too far put a Cracker under his Chair and a Mouse
in his Wig for which David whipped her, but not I fear so
severely as she merited. But Mr Huxtable showed no Impatience, reminding us that Alexander the Great and Diogenes
were Characters alike for their indifference to Trifles, the one
holding the World as his Tub, the other his Tub as the World
or some such Nonsense.

And now in Seriousness, my dearest Sister, I have been
so gravely disturbed over Judith that last Tuesday I was
blooded and on two occasions my throat has been excoriated.

For the Child has a Devil that there's no exorcizing. She is
now high and now low and not altogether bad; David indeed
swears that she is not bad at all and has as good a Heart as
anyone in this house, which may be in Truth enough save
that if she has a Heart she has also a Temper and a Disposition
to Evil that I swear poor child is as great a Trouble to Herself
as it is to Us.

I have no doubt as I have often said to you before but that
it had its commencement in Mr Gauntry's love for her as a
Baby. We have forbidden her his Place for the Present. I have

no Need to tell you, Sister, of the scandalous Conduct now
current in Stone Ends. It is the Talk of the Countryside. The
last Time Judith was there they had been wanting to make
her drink with him and I must not be ingreateful to the Squire
when I acknowledge that he will not have her contaminated
and in any Case she can, with a marvellous Discretion for a
child of her years, manage the whole Establishment at Stone
Ends that she has under her little finger. It is Managing that
she is always after and has been from a Baby. All the satisfaction that I have is that she has not yet learnt the Fashion
of managing me nor ever will, but to see that Chit of a Child
with her red hair and Herries Nose giving orders to my Will
and Deb is so Unnatural as to be only partly Decent. Monnasett could deal with her and would have it that her Temper
was from her Consciousness of and Uneasiness at her unlikely
Parentage, but I have not seen her so Sensitive but have found
again and again a brutal insensibility to the wants and opinions
of others.

For the present she is in a Pretty Tantrum because she is
forbidden Mr Gauntry's and if we do not watch her she will
be over there in a trivet. She has found out, I fancy, that I am
not to be feared although I am not yet assured that she has
found out that I am to be loved. But am I indeed? She is too
odd a changeling for either David or myself to be certain of
our Hearts towards her. It was the same with her mother, poor
Mirabell, who as you will well remember, dearest Sister,
never loved me because I was too Settled a Wife and Domestic
a Woman for her. And this Child also could be in her turn
Domestic when she wished. She is in fact of a Mixture so odd
that it needs a more perceiving Woman than myself to fathom
her, only it is Plain enough that she must have her Way in
everything and Dominate all those around her. Then,
granted her Desires, she will let her Heart speak and has a
Generosity that is not to be checked. Nevertheless I am filled
with Fears for the future. As she grows her Nature becomes
more clear with every hour and this house is in a Turmoil
over her . . .

As to your Complaint, gentle purging is to be advised;
no vomits but if your stomach flags four to eight drops of
Elixir of Vitriol is excellent and if feverish three spoonfuls of
a decoction of the bark by boyling one ounce and a half in a
quart of water to a pint. I must tell you, dearest Deborah,
that since the days that Cupid set Hercules to the distaff he

has not had a nobler conquest than mine over the straightening
of the cupboard room in the new . . .

The remainder of this letter has nothing for our purpose.

It is Herries history, however, that at the moment when Mrs
Sarah Herries was doing her best to place Judith upon paper,
the same Judith was with the utmost gentleness and caution
opening the door of the Blue Room where Mrs Monnasett
was lying.

Entering, she was both pleased and sensually alarmed by the
dim candle-fluttering light that hung about the room, making the
blue pagodas on the wallpaper, the high tallboy, seem of infinite
mystery, and the blue tester hangings and overlay of the bed
sway in some dimly felt stirring of the breeze. Not that she was
frightened. Judith did not know now, did not, for many years,
know what it was to be afraid. The day would come, and in a
room not unlike this present one, when, hearing her beloved
Francis enter the hall below, she would know, but that was not
yet.

She approached the bed; it was one that had always most
especially attracted her with its reeded and fluted columns,
delicately carved with acanthus leaves. There were very few
things, even at this early age, that she did not notice. The candles
were standing at the bed-head, and Mrs Monnasett, very yellow
against the white of the pillow, her black hair spread, her large
strong hands neatly folded, lay there, her lips curved in a
sardonic smile. So, Judith reflected, often in real life she had
smiled as though she knew more, far, far more than anyone
around her. And so, indeed, Judith was very sure that she did.
If she had not been an actual witch she had been as near to it
as not to matter. Judith had known that all the domestics and
hands about the farm had thought her one. Yes, she had known
everything, and now what did she know? Did Death tell you
anything more? She looked as though, behind those closed
eyelids, she was seeing a thousand things. A fire burned in the
room. It was hot, and there was a faint cloying smell of cor-
ruption. Judith came very close, stood on her toes because
the bed was high, and touched with her warm fingers the dead
hand. It was not only cold like iron but hard like iron. Where
was Mrs Monnasett now? With God? Asking God questions?
Telling Him, perhaps, things that He did not know. But, above
all, had she the little gold box with her? Judith did not intend
to steal it, only to see whether they would bury it with her.

She looked about the dim dark room, sniffing the faint decaying odour like a little dog. The heavy curtains at the windows fluttered, the blue pagodas on the wall seemed to run a race, the fire crackled and sputtered, mice would be behind the wainscot, but none of these disturbed Mrs Monnasett, who lay there, growing surely with every moment more yellow, and the mole black upon her cheek, smiling her secret smile because of the things she knew that others didn't. But had she the little gold box with her? Had she? Had she? Judith must know.

She stood at her tallest, leaned over and, with a shiver of excitement at her daring, felt with her hand, under the clothes, in the hollow of Mrs Monnasett's breasts.

She had scarcely touched that chill flesh when there was a voice at the doorway, a voice of horror and disgust.

She nearly lost her balance and, half tumbling, started away from the bed to see Mrs Herries, holding high a lighted candle, in the doorway. The child assumed at once the attitude that she always had when she was set for trouble. She flung her head back, held her hands behind her and waited.

'Judith! Come out of here.'

She followed Mrs Herries from the room. In the passage she stood by the door like some small wild animal ringed about with enemies.

'What were you doing there?'

'Nothing.'

'Nothing! That is a lie!'

'I wasn't doing anything.'

'You wicked child! You had been forbidden to enter the room.'

'Yes, ma'am.'

'You confess your disobedience?'

'Yes, ma'am.'

'And at the bed you were touching—' Sarah Herries' voice broke in her disgust and revulsion.

'I wished to look at Mrs Monnasett – and bid her farewell.'

Sarah Herries sighed. This strange child! But there was feeling there, tenderness. The child had heart. And all would have been well had not that odd impulse to absolute honesty that would, throughout Judith's life, force from her such inconvenient avowals burst from her now:

'I wished to see whether Mrs Monnasett had yet with her the gold box with the charms.'

'You wished to see – what?'

'Whether she had yet the little gold box with the charms.'

'You would see . . .' Mrs Herries broke off. Her nature was kindly, wise, tolerant, but she did not understand this child any better than in the earlier days she had understood the mother. And just as then elements would arise that sickened some sound English normality in her, so now with Judith there would be often moments when she hated this child, in reality hated her so that she wished her out of her house and her family, a thousand miles away, never to return.

She felt this revulsion now, a sort of sickness. To search the corpse for a gold box – a child of eleven. She was afraid of what she might do, so she said: 'Go to your room and wait there until I come to you.'

Judith, without a word, turned and went.

Her room was a small one under the roof. From her window she could see the road, the hills, the woods that stretched towards Bassenthwaite. Here she had her treasures – a candle-stand that Francis had given her, a china jar, old and cracked, but with lovely orange flowers on it, that she had begged from Mrs Monnasett, two 'babies' – rag dolls from her own babyhood – a fox's brush that Tom Gauntry had sent her, a piece of China silk, a faded and stained battle-piece in a black frame that she had found in a cellar, a treatise on cock-fighting, and a Bible that Reuben Sunwood had presented to her last Christmas-time. Here she would sit on a small oak-panelled armchair and watch from the window the outside world that she so desperately loved.

Now she banged the door behind her, kicked off her red shoes and stood scowling. She hated Fell House and everyone in it save Francis. She knew that she had been wrong to go and look at Mrs Monnasett, and more wrong still to touch her. Her immaculate honesty forbade her to blame Mrs Herries for any injustice. She had been right to be angry, the punishment that would follow would be just. She was so much wickeder than all the others, as she very well knew. Here was no portrait of a poor, ill-treated little girl. They tried to love her; it was her own fault that they could not. But with every breath that she drew she was longing for Tom Gauntry – the odd, rambling, ill-shaped house with the smell of dogs and horses and drink and dung and cooking food and musty curtains, with the noise and laughter and songs, with the freedom and airy indulgence as though all the doors and windows were for ever open – that was her life, that the place into which she had been taken on the very first day of her existence, and Uncle Tom with his twisted brown face and twisted brown body, his funny bow legs and his hoarse whisper and his cry to the hounds and his oaths and angers – *he* understood her as no one else in the world did ... And then, cutting across that picture, as so often it did, was another one, quite opposite, that made her understand the Herries decency of Uldale, made her, in certain moods, finely handy about the place, in the store cupboards, the dairies, so that she could sew and bake and clean with the best of them, and understand too when Will (for whom she did not really care) would tell her, with all the gravity of a grown man, of how he would advance the Herries family and have money in all the banks and buy land everywhere – all this she could understand and believe in.

Yes, but at this precise moment she was a little girl of eleven in one of her hellish tempers, one of her incoherent rages, so that she could swear in proper Cumberland just like any of the girls or men about the place, so that she was mad to be out of the house and over the fells, sniffing the peat, hearing the water of the mountain streams run and the tug of the sheep at the grass and the sharp bark of the sheepdogs ...

She turned, her eyes furious and her little feet stamping, at the sound of the open door. Francis Herries had come in.

At the sight of him she forgot for a moment all her trouble. He was still in his riding clothes. He must have come straight to her after his arrival. His face was so beautifully peaked and serious under his brown wig, his legs in their riding boots so handsomely shaped and his eyes so far away, so mysterious ...

She drew her breath sharply as she always did when she saw anything that seemed to her beautiful. How she loved him! And he, from his great height, looked down gravely to the odd little figure with the defiant mouth and the red hair and rebellion in every inch of her.

He slapped his whip against his thigh.

'Father is coming shortly to beat you. I thought I'd best prepare you.' Then he smiled, a lovely winning smile which, in anyone more self-conscious, must have been artificial. But Francis Herries, as he never thought of himself, never thought of his smile either.

'I know.' Her eyes devoured him. 'I don't care as long as you've come.'

'What have you done, you little devil? Why can't you be good?'

'I can't be good,' she answered defiantly, 'because my father married a gipsy. And I'm happy he did,' she added.

This was an old familiar statement of hers. She was always dragging in the gipsy. It seemed to Francis to be in bad taste, so he said again:

'What have you done this time?'

'I went in to see Mrs Monnasett.'

The thought and image of death, so familiar as to be less than nothing at all to the men and women of his time, always affected Francis Herries with a queer tremor of mystery and horror. It seemed to him revolting that this child should have been in Mrs Monnasett's room.

'Why must you do that?' he asked.

'To see if she had her little gold box.'

'What box?'

'A box of spells that she had.'

He said nothing and turned to the door.

With a little tremor in her voice she said: 'Please punish me.'

He turned back. 'Punish you?'

She broke out passionately, an unusual passion for so young a child.

'I didn't know that it was wrong, but if you had told me not I would never have gone. Punish me and you will see. I will do anything you tell me, stand in icy water or let the rats in the cellar gnaw me or sleep in the stable.'

He looked at her, met the intense absorbed devotion of her eyes, and was greatly touched. When he could come out of his dreams and notice human beings he loved them, loved all humanity. He was humble also, and found it strange that anyone should care for him. This small child, standing there in her stockinged feet and coloured hoop, adoring him, moved him. They were friends from that moment, although neither realized that it was just then that their long alliance was formed. He spoke lamely enough:

'Punish you? No. Why should *I* punish you?'

They could say no more because at that moment David Herries came in. He carried a riding whip, was in his riding clothes, looked exceedingly sheepish. He had been always of great size and immense strength. Now, at sixty-six, he was beginning to be corpulent, had a red face and something of a belly, but looked very much the same kindly, obstinate, unimaginative boy who had, nearly thirty years before, carried his Sarah away from the dark house in Wasdale.

He looked sheepish because he hated this business. Francis
went out. Judith bent over the chair and he whipped her.
Neither said a word until it was over. She replaced her little
clothes, then stood, her lip trembling, because she was very
near to tears but would not cry, near the window.

Her stockings were crooked, which seemed to David very
pathetic, and without knowing it she had her hand on her back
where it was sore.

He filled the room with his great bulk, and his red face was
creased with kindliness. He scratched his bare head, pushing his
wig a little awry. He talked because he saw that she was near
to tears.

'Now, Judith, why must you do such a thing? 'Tisn't decent
to be in the death-chamber, and it was against all orders, as you
very well knew. Now, then, it is over, isn't it? Never to be
spoken of again . . .'

He went and picked her up and kissed her. Had he known it
(and it had been always one of David's weaknesses that he was
not clever at perceiving things), this was, of everything that he
could do, the thing that she detested most.

To be picked up, like a tiny baby, to be dangled in the air,
to be held close to this huge man and feel his bristly cheek and
smell the odour of liquor and horses, to have her neck pricked
by the sharp buttons of his coat, and, worst of all, to have his
great heart hammering in her ear, this was the final ignominy!

She stayed passive, only when he would kiss her mouth she
turned her head aside. He put her down with a grunting sigh.
She was a problem, this child, just as her mother Mirabell had
been before her. He did not understand her at all.

He looked at her, smiled an awkward, clumsy smile, muttered,
'We shall say no more about the thing,' and stumped away.

She stood there, considering. She did not want to see any
of them ever again, save Francis. Somewhere a clock sounded
six. A cart rattled down the Fell road. She went to the window
and looked out. It was almost dark; the hills were shadows
against shadow.

Then she smiled.

She knew what she would do.

STONE ENDS

SHE WAS SO made that once a plan came to her nothing in the world was going to stop her, and every pulse of her body beat to that one purpose.

She flung back the narrow diamond-paned window, found a cloak and a shawl, left the red shoes for thick country ones. No time was wasted, and as she worked for her purpose her small mouth was set, her chin was out. Nothing was to stop her in such a mood. She didn't think of consequences (she was never to think of them as she should do), recked little that this second disobedience in one evening meant trouble for her more serious, perhaps, than any that she had yet encountered.

She had been out of that window before. There was still light enough for her to see the old crooked water pipe that jerked an arm round the farther end of her casement, then there was the water butt, then the stone passage leading to the stable. But she had a long descent on that pipe. She clung to it with hands and feet, her chin and nose rasped by its casing. Her small legs trembled, the shawl blew against her face, she felt (or imagined that she felt) spiders' thread in her hair, then her feet found the water butt, she held her body together and jumped.

She fell on her hands and knees, and the black cat, Solomon, ran from under her very feet, scrambling up the monkey-tree. Her knees were bleeding, her hoop under her cloak was torn. But she stood, holding her breath like a proper conspirator, to hear whether the noise had made any stir. There was no sound but the owl hooting. It seemed that a breath of light had blown back again into the sky. Over the garden wall, the Caldbeck fells were outlined as though a row of candles were lit behind them.

It was the moon; later that moon would strengthen, and the freshening wind would blow the stars up. All the garden scents were crowding the night air. She was very cheerful indeed, and, pulling the cambric tight about her face again, stepped across the irregular paving of the yard, called very softly, 'Barnabas! Barnabas!' At once the little black horse with the white star on his forehead put his head over the paling. In another moment she had unbarred the door and was leading him out, stroking his nose.

Barnabas understood perfectly what she wanted. She mounted

the black outside the gate and, her legs spread very wide, her hair flying, was away up the road. A mile later, the first delirium of freedom passed, she began to consider ghosts, witches, and warlocks. She was not afraid, but there was the man with the face like a rat, the woman with two heads, the lost soul of Judas that whimpered like an infant, the old woman with a rat on her shoulder, the lovely lady on the skeleton horse, the old woman with three beards, the soldier who had lost his head in the wars and carried it in his handless arms, the coach with the eight devils and the fiery horses, the lady of Caldbeck who walked searching for the child that she had murdered.

And worse, perhaps, in actual fact, than any of these, the highway robber who had been hung in chains on the path between Thistlebottom and Whelpo, although there were now only his bones remaining.

She was not afraid of any of them, but she repeated aloud to herself the Lord's Prayer and so much of the Creed as she could remember, and then the names of the places near her home – Ireby, Snittlegarth, Binsey, Aughertree, Nevin Tarn, Orthwaite, Over Water, Braefell, Branthwaite. It comforted her that Barnabas trotted comfortably along as though he knew precisely his destination, but it comforted her yet more when she met a cheerful gang of pack horses, the bell-horse first with his pleasant noise. They were carrying peat from the moors in halts, old-fashioned wicker baskets that were very soon now to give way to carts.

Judith called out to the men as she passed them, waving her hand, and they talked that night about the witch that had greeted them (on a black horse) and had waved in the air hands shining with flame.

Stone Ends, Tom Gauntry's place, was a mile beyond Caldbeck. She made no further encounter. The clock of Caldbeck Church struck seven as she trotted through the deserted little street.

On the dark road beyond Caldbeck she met two drunken soldiers who stood in the road and waved at her. They had a lantern; one had a wooden leg. She leaned forward on to Barnabas' mane and cursed them in good Cumbrian. She called them 'Hulkers' and 'Lubbers' and 'Dummle-heads'. She told them that they gave her 'a nasty dwallow taste in her mouth' and that they'd better 'jump up and knep a daisy'. She must have astonished them, perched on the horse, her red hair flying about in the uncertain circumference of the lantern that waved in their

drunken hands. At any rate, they did nothing, and stood aside
to let Barnabas by.

So she arrived at Stone Ends. This was a rough-cast building
of no height, with an outside gallery and stair. There were
mullioned windows, great trees overhanging the mossy slates and
round thick chimneys. There was a garden with a clipped hedge,
the fells everywhere beyond, a rough plot of flowers, some out-
buildings, a sundial, a little stream.

Lights burnt in the windows, but Judith did not need a light.
This little place had been familiar to her since her babyhood,
her only true home. She tied Barnabas to the gate and went
cautiously to the porch. She was not certain how she would be
received. Old Gauntry was not always the perfect host, especially
when taken unawares. Riding Barnabas so soon after the beating
had not improved the soreness of her seat. She did not want
another whipping, nor to be sent directly back to Uldale again.
So, with her ear to the heavy door, she listened. Little listening
was needed. The chorus of revelry was clear enough. They
would have been hunting, she decided, and were now in process
of becoming drunk as soon as possible. *That* did not frighten
her. She had heard often enough: 'Now this is a fine fox we've
killed and it munna be a dry one.' The important thing was to
ascertain the *stage* of drunkenness at which they had arrived.
She knew that between the first and second hour they would
all be in a state of exceeding friendliness.

She was, however, given no time to consider. The door opened
and Wull shoved his hairy head out. Wull (or William Flint as
was his proper name) stood to Tom Gauntry as the Fool stands
to his King. Judith would never forget the agitation with which
she had first beheld him. In her babyhood she had been told
that he was the Hobthross, the Brownie who lurks in old houses –
works all night for the family to whom he has attached himself,
stretches himself before the fire, churns the milk for the girls,
and can be heard singing at his tasks. A kindly spirit, but wild to
look at, with his shock of hair, his broad ugly face, his mis-
shapen limbs. Just so was 'Wull', and when she was an infant
he would love to pull faces at her until she howled with rage.
She was never frightened of him, but only angry. Later he became her friend, then her warm ally. He poked his ugly head out
at her now.

'Wull! Wull!' she whispered.

Sometimes he was a complete fool, sometimes most intelligent. He would tell her about himself with a broad grin: 'Ah'm

nobbut a bit goffish.' It was probable that he was not 'goffish'
at all, but knew exactly what he was doing. When he saw who
it was he let her in. The house-place was filled with dogs and
smelt like a midden. Judith did not mind the smell in the least.
The dogs were everywhere; every kind of dog. They ran at her
when they saw her, barking and tumbling all over her. Some of
the hounds were bigger than she. They all knew her. One, a
spaniel bitch, Clara, adored her, had followed her once almost
all the way back to Uldale.

When Clara saw her she was in an ecstasy of happiness, springing up and down, yapping on a shrill high note, her beautiful
large eyes beaming with joy. Judith asked Wull how many
gentlemen there were in there. He didn't know; about twenty
maybe. They had had a grand day's hunting and had killed over
by High Hesket. He cuffed the dogs and quieted them, but the
noise had been heard. The room door opened and Tom Gauntry
came out. He stood with his funny crooked legs straddling. He
was fairly drunken. When he saw Judith he gave a loud 'Yoicks!
Yoicks! Tally-ho! Tally-ho!' and they came crowding to the
door. Judith recognized a number she knew – young Osmaston,
Squire Watson, old Birkmyre, Statesman Peel – also two
ladies.

Gauntry came over to her and picked her up and carried her
shoulder-high into the room where they were dining. Oddly
enough, what she hated in David Herries she liked in Uncle
Tom.

'And why the hell have you come ?' he asked her.

'Because I wanted,' she answered.

From her height she looked over the scene, which was for
her no new one. The room was not large. They were crowded
about the round table upon whose shining surface the candles
guttered grease. Food was piled everywhere – mutton, beef,
puddings; wine was spilt on the table, and almost the first
thing that Judith noticed was the naked head of old Dunstable,
robbed of its wig, lying forward in a puddle of wine. He had
succumbed already.

Most of them had not. Sitting now, sharp-eyed, on a chair
beside Uncle Gauntry, she saw very quickly that there were
two boys there, boys of about her own age. It was not unusual
that boys should be there, and one of them she knew, little
Johnny Peel, two years younger than herself. It would later
be said of him that he was 'lang in the leg an' lish as a lizard',
and someone in the *Gentleman's Magazine* was to record that 'he

seems to have come into this world only to send foxes out of it'.
He was of Caldbeck village, but there was no hunt already that
he wasn't attending within any radius from Penrith to Cockermouth, Cockermouth to Carlisle. It was said of him already that
he could do thirty miles in the day and not be tired of it; later
on it was to be fifty. But Judith knew that boy before; he didn't
interest her. The other was another matter. She had not hitherto
allowed her young life to be much encumbered with boys. On
the whole she despised them; of late, especially, her real worship
of Francis Herries had veiled her sight.

But this boy struck through to her deep consciousness. How
often afterwards she was to look back to this moment when, as
she sat perched up on the chair beside Tom Gauntry, her little
sharp eyes flashed across to the table to the equally sharp eyes
of that small, black-haired, bullet-headed urchin, who was
grabbing any food that he could see. Very characteristic that
Judith's first vision of him should be of greedy rapacity! But
(also how characteristic of him!) it was not merely greed. While
he snatched at meat and bread and the thick pastry of the beef
pie his little black eyes were flashing about him, humorous,
contemptuous, but as alive as fire-balls!

'Who's that?' Judith asked of Gauntry. He was, as she had
hoped, at the cheerful side of his drinking, singing a catch,
shoving food into his mouth, exchanging bawdy stories with all
and sundry.

'That!' he laughed, following her eyes. 'That's the Frenchy!
There's his mama!' pointing a chicken bone at a lady farther
along the table. There were only two women here, one of them
the wife of young Squire Osmaston, a flaxen-haired, broad-
bosomed, opulent lady at the moment chucking Sam Newton
under the chin. This other was different. She sat upright like a
maypole and was black as a raven. Marvellous black eyes, she
had, a lovely shapely bosom, and silver ornaments in her dark
hair, which was her own and unpowdered. You could see,
Judith decided, that she was the little boy's mother. They would
be French then. Judith had heard of Paris, where silks and
brandy came from. She had seen a print of the French Queen
dancing in a great hall lit with flambeaux. This lady looked as
though she could be a queen were she given the opportunity.

The noise and confusion now were very great. Old Dunstable had slipped beneath the table.

Wilson of Ireby was standing on his chair proposing healths;
fat Dick Conyngham of Penrith and a thin young man with a

crooked nose were embracing. Voices rose and fell, then suddenly the chorus, everyone joining together:

> Then chink and clink your glasses round
> And drink to the Devil below the ground.
> The more you drink the better you be
> And kiss the lasses upon your knee.
>   Chink, clink!
>   Chink, clink!
> The Devil himself can't drink like me.

Then young Drayton of Keswick, whose sweet tenor was famous for miles around, stood up and sang the song of 'Beauty Bathing':

> Beauty sat bathing by a spring
>   Where fairest shades did hide her;
> The winds blew calm, the birds did sing,
>   The cool streams ran beside her.
> My wanton thoughts enticed mine eye
>   To see what was forbidden:
>
> But better memory said, fie!
>   So vain desire was chidden:
>   Hey nonny nonny O!
>   Hey nonny nonny!
>
> Into a slumber then I fell,
>   When fond imagination
> Seemèd to see, but could not tell
>   Her feature or her fashion.
> But ev'n as babes in dreams do smile,
>   And sometimes fall a-weeping,
> So I awaked as wise this while
>   As when I fell a-sleeping:
>   Hey nonny nonny O!
>   Hey nonny nonny!

The beauty of the words, of the voice, seemed for a moment to sober them.

> Hey nonny nonny O!
> Hey nonny nonny!

they sang, and down the fat cheeks of Dick Conyngham drunken
tears were coursing.

No one appeared to think it strange that the child should be
there. Most of them knew her; she seemed to belong to the place,
and for many of them that happy time was now approaching
when nothing anywhere seemed strange, when the candles on
their silver stalks swam like gold roses in a shimmering haze,
and the moon, now delicately rising beyond the uncurtained
windows, was quadrupled in its pure serenity; now, through
the open door, the dogs were coming in to pick up what trifles
they might from the scattered floor, and a thousand clocks were
ticking their friendly chatter on a thousand walls. No one
thought of the child, not even Gauntry himself; only Clara,
the spaniel bitch, coming in with the rest, had found her and
was sitting behind her chair.

Judith ate very little and drank nothing. It was no unusual
thing at that time for a child to be drunk. The children of the
poor lay in the gutter drowned with gin. In the back parts of
Keswick town Judith herself had seen them. But something in
her, connected possibly with her immaculate personal cleanliness, had made her, so long as she could remember, detest
liquor. When she was only a baby some friend of Gauntry's
had tried to make her drink Madeira, and she had screamed,
beaten his face with her hands, torn his nose with her nails.
She didn't like the smell of it very much, but in a scene like
this the stench of wine and heat and unwashed human bodies,
dogs and horses, candle grease and cooked meats, was so
familiar to her that she never thought of it.

What she did think of, though, was that when the drinking
and rioting had reached a certain pitch she would leave them,
for they were then no longer of any use to anybody.

It neither shocked nor distressed her that they should lie
about the floor with their heads in puddles of wine. She preferred in fact the rough-and-tumble riot here to the orderly
drunkenness at Fell House, and she had on several occasions
watched while Wull and Andy and Matthew had stripped Uncle
Gauntry and laid him in his naked bed. What she did mind was
that they were all so stupid when they were 'gone'. She was
quickly developing that passion, afterwards to be so strong in
her and so irritating to her acquaintances, of hating to waste a
single moment! Her restless energy was, later, never to leave
her for an instant alone. They were a waste of time, these stupid
hours when they all lay about, dribbling and drabbling, with the

moon high, the wind fresh, blowing the stars about the sky.
She might as well be in her bed, which was where, indeed, she
would be had she remained at Uldale.

Her bright eyes searched the room. She saw one thing, that
the French lady was absorbed by Mr Drayton, who had sung
'Beauty Bathing'. He was a good-looking man, Mr Drayton,
slender and straight, with yellow hair like a blazing candle,
and he wore a beautiful flowered waistcoat. There were gold
buckles on his shoes. The French lady liked him, that was plain.
They stood, the handsome pair of them, gravely by the window,
away from the litter, noise and mess; quite suddenly Mr Drayton
took the French lady's hand. Now was the time, then, for Judith
to speak to the little French boy.

She stepped off her chair and, followed by the spaniel, came
round to where the French boy was sitting. She touched his
shoulder. He turned round and smiled at her.

'Come out,' she said.

He came at once, making a last grab at a handful of raisins
before he went. They ran hand in hand, as though they had
known one another for ages, into the dark hall, where the fire
was blazing, and the dogs, as though they owned the house and
everyone in it, were moving about, snapping at one another,
yawning, lying down to sleep, climbing the stairs, gnawing
bones, scratching for fleas.

The two children sat close together beside the fire.

'I know. You're French,' Judith said.

He spoke without an accent, as though he were English. He
gave her, rather reluctantly, some raisins. The truth is, she took
them.

'I was born in London,' he told her.

'Oh, I want to see London!'

'Is your hair in truth that fine colour?' he asked, pulling it.

She slapped his face, not lightly but with genuine feeling.
He got up, his eyes blazing. He stood there, his sturdy little
body trembling with anger. It seemed that he would kill her.
But he thought better of it. His hand to his cheek he sat down
again.

'Because you are a girl I won't hurt you,' he said.

'Hurt me!' She was indignantly scornful. 'No one can hurt
me!' Then she went on: 'I was whipped this noon.'

They were friends again. She, taking more of his raisins,
asked him how it was if he were French he had never been
in France.

'My papa and my mama are French born,' he told her.

She asked him his name.

'Georges.'

And his other name.

'Georges Paris.'

'But Paris is a town.'

He told her there were people called Paris too. He told her then (he always from the very earliest time loved to talk about himself) that his father was dead, that his mother liked England to live in, that they lived for the most part in the village of Hampstead, near London. Hampstead was on a hill, and at night you could see all London lit up from their window. Judith wanted to tell him something about herself. Her name was Judith Herries, her mother had been a gipsy, she lived with her half-brother at Fell House in Uldale. She could ride and swim, had a horse called Barnabas (it wasn't in fact her horse at all, but it made it grander to say so), could stand on her head, train a bird for fighting, and so on, and so on. Mrs Monnasett was dead and would be buried tomorrow. She had run away and would be whipped on her return.

But he wasn't interested. He could do nothing but look at her hair. He had never seen anything like it in his life before.

Then her mind ran away from him. The place where they were was lovely to her, with the leaping fire, the moonlight, the dogs. She thought of Statesmen and farmers and boys and horses – all friends of hers. She liked to hear the men singing in the distance. All her troubles were far away; tomorrow, the whipping, Fell House. In an impulse of general happiness that had little to do with the boy she put her arm round his neck, drew his head towards her and kissed him. He did not mind that at all and pulled her hair – but gently. And she did not, this time, smack his cheek.

Dreamily she went on: 'Maybe when I'm grown I shall marry you. But I must have dogs and horses, and we must have our house near to this. But you must not be drunken.' Then, pushing his head away from her, she asked sharply: 'But what shall our children be – French or English?'

'French,' he answered her quickly.

'No, they shall not. English.'

'French.'

'No, English.'

'Then I'll not marry you.'

She pinched him in the place where it hurt the most. In

another moment they were fighting, rolling on the floor, all the dogs yelping. But they were interrupted by a greater agitation, for the door suddenly swung open, there was a shout and clatter, and into the hall came fat Dick Conyngham riding Judith's Barnabas. Poor Barnabas was in any case overweighted by the huge body that rode him; he was frightened also. He came kicking into the hall, the dogs setting up an infernal din.

'The stairs! The stairs! I'll ride him to the attic!' and Conyngham drove the little horse towards the staircase, waving his fat arms like a madman.

They all came pouring in out of the other room, those of them who could stand, to see Barnabas kicking with his hind legs and Judith raging like a mad thing.

She rushed to little Gauntry, catching him by the arm: ' 'Tis my Barnabas . . . He has no right . . . He'll break his knees!' and Gauntry, who had been singing the tail-end of some chorus, was suddenly, in the manner of drunken men, in a terrible rage and rushed at Conyngham. The fat man drove the horse at the stairs, but in a moment they had him on the floor and were kneeling on his stomach.

Barnabas, wild now with the lights, the dogs, the fire, began to prance madly hither and thither; and Judith, fearing nothing, had caught him, was carried off her feet as she hung to his mane, crying 'Barnabas! Barnabas! Dear Barnabas! They shall not touch you!' The little horse knew her hand and voice. He snorted, pawing the wood floor with his hoofs; he looked wildly around, then he suffered her to lead him away.

She took him this time to one of the outhouses. She stood there in the soft moonlight wondering whether after all she would not ride home again. Not far from her was the lower end of the garden that held a little pond with a statue of an armless lady. The little pond was like a curved shell of ivory, and the lady was green in the moonlight.

A moment later they all rushed past her, a shouting and singing rabble. Fat Conyngham was to be ducked in the pond for that he had taken a lady's horse without her permission. They were not like men at all, but shadows that the moon had made. They were stripping him; a moment he escaped and ran, a ridiculous pink figure, bald-headed, across the grass. They chased him around the sundial, caught him; there was a splash, and she could see a spray of water dazzle the air.

She rubbed her nose in Barnabas' mane. Should she go home? She was lonely, a little frightened. They had never been so wild before in this place. The house did not seem to be her friend any longer, only the quiet fells that stretched beyond it, with the boggy peat, the sheep cropping, the eternal sound of running water.

It seemed of a sudden comforting to have Sarah Herries' arm around her. She was a child again. She was not *truly* frightened. She had never been frightened. She would not be frightened now. But in absolute truth it would be pleasant to be in her bed with the cherry curtains, to hear the owl hooting and Deborah Herries snoring not too far away.

Then, because she would never grant to either God or Man that she could be afraid of anyone or anything, she threw up her head defiantly at the moon, stroked Barnabas on the nose, whispered to him that she would not be long away and went back to the house.

They were still dancing and singing round the pond. The garden had a fantastic air like a witches' sabbath. The house was now deserted and empty. The dogs were for the most part away, the moonlight stained the floor, the fire was low. No sign of the French boy, no sign of anyone. She peeped through the door, and there were two men, asleep, with their heads on the table. The candles guttered.

She herself felt a fearful weariness. She was aching for sleep. She staggered on her little feet. Her shoes hurt her, her beautiful dress was torn, the place where she had been whipped was smarting. She would find the room upstairs that was generally hers. The thought of sleep was so delicious as to be incredible.

She sat down halfway up the stairs, and with her head in her hand dreamily considered herself. She had learnt to do this early in life, because, observing things and people, she had realized that if you do not consider yourself no one else is going to. But when she began to think of herself it was always to her mother and father that she was led.

Years ago she had persuaded Tom Gauntry to take her, pillion-fashion, to see the house where she was born. They had ridden into the heart of the valley of Borrowdale, and there, on a little hill above the village of Rosthwaite, was standing this strange tumbledown house. She could not credit her own sharp eyesight when she saw it. They had tied the horse to the gate and walked in the grass-grown courtyard. It was late April, and the smaller daffodils were blowing under the wind. A storm was coming up over Glaramara, and flashes of sun glittered in cold sharp gleams and were gone again. Under the wind and the hurrying cloud the house looked desolate enough. Judith, used to the noise and vitality of Stone Ends, the luxury and comfort of Uldale, could not believe that this was where her father had lived for so many years. Some peasant lived there now. Two very dirty children, sucking their thumbs, lurked in the doorway. Behind the house a waterfall glistened against rock. There was the sound of running water everywhere. It looked as though one 'fuff' of wind would blow the place down.

That day 'Uncle Tom' told her to the smallest detail of how he had found her, the snowstorm, her wailing cry, her father and mother dead. But he would never tell her enough about her father. He had not known him, he said. Neither would David and Sarah tell her much, although he had been David's father, and so David must know everything. David would tell her only the grand things, how passionately through many years he had loved her mother, how tall he was and strong, how noble he was, and went his own way whatever people might say. 'Whatever people might say—' Judith nodded her head over that. People had said a good deal, no doubt. She only wished that she could have been there, standing at her father's side, to tell those people what she thought of them. To tell those people what she thought of them— Her head was nodding, and had not the moon been shining straight into her eye she would have fallen into deep slumber. As it was she was suddenly awake. She would find the room and the bed . . .

She climbed the stairs, looked out of the window on to the outside gallery and the fell beyond, pushed back a door. She stood there. Her heart seemed to stop its beating. The almost bare room, with only the yellow-curtained bed, two chairs, a chest, was sunk in moonshine. In the middle of the moonlit pool the French lady was standing quite naked. Behind her, her clothes were piled on the boards. She stood, her legs together, her arms raised above her head, her black hair loosened about her shoulders. Her breasts were full and firm. She was smiling.

At her feet, clad only in his shirt, young Drayton was kneeling, his hands about her naked waist, his eyes raised in an ecstasy to her face.

They never spoke nor moved. Judith saw that something glittered sharply in the light – the diamond buckle of her shoe, lying on top of her clothes.

Then the child heard him speak:

'Oh, how beautiful you are! Oh, how beautiful you are!'

But the French lady only smiled.

Judith turned away. Her shoes made clop-clop on the boards. She sat down on the top of the stairs.

What had she seen?

Something that she would never forget, something that hurt her.

She began to cry very softly, lest anyone should hear her. She cried and cried. She wanted to go home. She wanted someone to care for her.

Huddled up, now only a baby lost and bewildered, crying and sobbing, there with her head against the banister she fell fast, fast asleep.

SUNWOODS IN COCKERMOUTH

DEBORAH HERRIES, the daughter of Francis Herries, sister of David Herries and half-sister of Judith, married, early in 1761, the Reverend Gordon Sunwood, a clergyman who lived in the town of Cockermouth. Mr Sunwood had no particular cure, but after his marriage published two admirable works – one *A Treatise on the Magnificat*, the other *The Hope of Grace to Come*, or *Sinners at the Feet of Jesus*. This second work had a very real sale throughout the North of England. He was in considerable request as a preacher. In 1765 his aunt, Miss Mercia Sunwood, died in the town of Exeter, bequeathing him a very reasonable fortune.

They had two boys, twins, born in the year 1763, Reuben and Humphrey.

Deborah Herries had been always, unlike her sister Mary and brother David, of a quite unambitious disposition. For the first half of her life she had lived quietly with her father at Herries in Borrowdale, perfectly content to care for him and offer him as much love and affection as he was willing to accept.

After his second marriage, however, which occurred when he was well on in years, she considered that she was no longer needed by him (which was perfectly true), left him and married her clergyman in Cockermouth. She had loved Mr Sunwood from the first moment of seeing him at a ball in Keswick, and he was indeed exactly suited to her, being as kindly, well-disposed, unenterprising and equable as she. She differed from him greatly in her perceptions; she had a good deal in her of her father's poetry, very much more than had her brother David, who had, however, been always much closer to their father, She had been kept from her father by a sort of terror of him. being never very comfortable with persons who were scornful or sarcastic, or liable to sudden temper or indignation.

Mr Gordon Sunwood had been a rest and refreshment to her after her life with her father, for, as his rotund body, snow-white hair and kindly rosy face portended, he could with the greatest difficulty be angry with anyone or anything, and then only for a moment at a time. Methodists, Wesleyans, Quakers, Dissenters of any kind – these were almost the only animals who could rouse him to any sort of genuine indignation.

Marriage with Deborah excited him to a kind of mild ambition, and it is quite certain that he would never have written or, having written, would never have published his two books had she not stirred his faculties.

Having published them he exhibited a natural pride very evident in most authors, who have, from time immemorial, found it difficult to conceive that theirs are not the only shining fish in the literary ocean.

When Deborah's twins were born the cup of her joy was full. And, as is not the case with all optimistic parents, her joy continued, for as the boys grew in physical stature so also they grew in kindliness of nature and obedience to their parents.

They were, one is happy to record, by no means angels, but their vices were mild ones, and their faults just sufficient to keep them properly human. Humphrey had by far the easier disposition of the two. Tall, slender and flaxen-haired, life was for him one long adventure. He was as restless as he was merry, so popular at the Cockermouth school that it was entirely to his credit that he should wish to be constantly with his parents.

Everyone spoke well of him, and it is not, perhaps, altogether to be wondered at that his charm became his principal asset and an easy substitute for hard work and diligence. His parents succeeded in affording him his residence at St John's College, Cambridge, and, if he did nothing there but secure the pleasant good wishes of his fellow-men, that was more than many others succeeded in securing.

After Cambridge the question was what should be done with him. He would hear of nothing but London, and to a lawyer's office there he went. On this bright afternoon in early November of the year 1785 his proud mother was excitedly occupied in reading his first letter from the Metropolis.

Humphrey's twin brother Reuben had quite another history. They had only small resemblance to one another whether in character or in physical appearance. And yet the bond between them was almost fantastic. From their first conscious moments they had been all in all the one to the other; theirs, indeed, was a love that nothing in life would be able to influence. Humphrey, volatile, restless, and woman-lover as he was, yet knew no emotion so unyielding and passionate as this for his brother. For Reuben, Humphrey was always and ever in a world apart. Reuben was unlike Humphrey in that he was stout, clumsy and plain. He was not uncleanly in his person, but his clothes never fitted him, nor could he be brought to consider the practical details of daily life. His eyes were good and faithful, his mouth, although too large, kindly and tolerant, but his nose was ludicrously ill-shaped, his hair wild and of a dingy colour, his limbs uncouth and ill-disciplined. From his very early years he had been of an intensely religious mind. It had been always understood that he would be a clergyman. At the age of sixteen he joined the religious society of St Bees, but was there for a year only, finding that he could not come to the same mind with the authorities.

He returned to his parents' house in Cockermouth, and to their considerable grief had in the last five years shown little progress in anything; his favourite occupation was to walk the hills for days on end by himself, and he could be seen striding along the roads, talking aloud and snapping his fingers in the air.

He was devoted to his parents, amiable and docile. There had, however, been strange rumours of late concerning him, not of any immorality or cock-fighting, or gambling, but of something that was, in his father's eyes, very much worse: a suspicion that he was concerting with the Methodists. A well-known Wesleyan itinerant, Mr Jeremy Walker, had been seen in his company. There was a rumour that he had taken part in some sort of outdoor meeting. His father had not yet dared to ask him whether there was any sort of truth in this. He knew well his son's honesty, but Mr Sunwood was grievously disturbed in his mind.

Their home on the outskirts of Cockermouth was a pretty place, looking out to the fields and woods, having a garden filled with sweet-williams and pinks and hollyhocks in their due season, and an arbour and a trellis for roses. In the parlour there was a rosy chintz and some fine pieces of mahogany, in Mr and Mrs Sunwood's bedroom a grand four-poster and a dressing-

chest with a lattice of Chinese decoration. At the corner of
the stair there was a round-faced clock of Irish Chippendale.
There were spindle-backed chairs, a Bury settee and a fine
Turkey carpet in the dining-room. These things were the very
pride of Mr and Mrs Sunwood's hearts. There was a maid-
servant called Rebecca, a cat, Timothy, and a boy, who worked
(when he felt inclined) in the garden, named Jacob. Deborah
herself cared for the preserving, pickling and daily cooking.
She and Rebecca kept the little house as clean and shining as a
new saucepan. They were, both of them, so proud of it that
they dreamt of it at night.

Deborah had but seldom any time for rest and reflection; she
did not, indeed, desire it. On this particular afternoon, however,
she was expecting her sister-in-law, Sarah Herries, and some
members of her family to dinner at four o'clock; they would
remain for the night and return to Fell House on the following
day. Everything was ready for them, the Guest Room prepared,
the dinner preparing. All day she had had with her Humphrey's
letter. Only now was she free to settle herself and read some of
it. Her excitement was as intense as though Humphrey himself
had made a sudden unexpected appearance.

Mr Sunwood came in from tending a pig, who led (unwitting
his destiny) a greedy and contented life in a sty at the back of
the house; close together on the settee, his hand resting often
on her plump shoulder, they read the letter. Humphrey began
with loving messages to everyone. Then he had many things
to tell of London: the eating-house where he had paid a shilling
for his dinner of meat and pudding, the Thames with its fine
bridges and noble arches, the hackney coaches, the dangers
of the streets where the coaches and carts crowded so closely
that there was scarcely room to move, and the noise so fierce
that you must step into the quiet of a shop if you wanted to
converse with a friend, a ship on land near the Tower that was a
trap for pressing simple people into being sailors, the signs
outside the shops with 'Children educated here', 'Shoes mended
here', 'Foreign spirituous liquors here', the general drunkenness,
so that the common people were always far gone in gin and
brandy. He had visited Vauxhall with the son of his master,
Mr Hodges, and had much to say about the paintings and statues,
the rotunda and the orchestra therein.

The most exciting news to his parents, however, was that
he had taken dinner with his mother's cousin, Sir Pomfret
Herries, who had a fine house in Kensington: Pomfret was the

son of Deborah's first cousin Raiseley, who had once owned a
fine house in Keswick but was now with God. Deborah's memory
flew back to her cousin Raiseley, a sickly and arrogant youth
who had been for ever at war with her brother David. It had
seemed that there would be a family feud there, but when
Raiseley had in later years moved to London, and the Keswick
house was sold, communication had altogether dropped.

It seemed, however, that this child Pomfret, whom Deborah
remembered as a little stout boy beating David's big black
horse with a toy whip, now a man of thirty-four or so, had done
well for himself in the City, married a clergyman's daughter,
and begotten of her body two healthy children.

Well, feud or no feud, Pomfret Herries had been kind to her
boy, and for that she would forgive him all old scores. Young
Humphrey described the splendour of the Kensington house,
the garden with its fountain and statues, the many servants,
the rich food and wine. Cousin Pomfret was large and stout
('like his poor grandfather before him,' sighed Deborah, with a
sudden desire to go somewhere and be kind to that poor old
man with his red face and pimples, suffering so sadly from gout,
sitting alone and deserted in the Keswick house by the Lake).
And now there was this new Pomfret with his children and handsome wife sitting in his grand Kensington house, forgetting
no doubt that he had ever had a grandfather. Time flies, thought
Deborah, and this is a modern world that we are in. Those old
days are gone for ever! There was indeed a certain moment's
melancholy in this excited acceptance by her son of this new life.
She had lost him! – he who only a moment ago had been rolling
naked on this Turkey carpet while she turned the tunes in the
music box – and, her eyes a little tearful, she placed her chubby
hand on her husband's chubby arm that she might feel securely
that he, at any rate, was still with her.

Mr Sunwood loved his son, but so confusing is this modern
life that there were four things in his head all obscuring and
dimming the things that Humphrey had to tell him. That was
the worst of these days: you never had a moment's peace. There
was his friend Mr Forster, who wanted a midshipman's place
for his boy, and hadn't Mr Sunwood some interest; there was
his own wickedness in sitting up almost all night at cards two
days back at Mr and Mrs Donne's, and although he had lost
but a shilling in all it was a habit that must not grow on him;
and there was the funeral of Mrs Hardacre tomorrow and he
must see that his black silk hatband had its proper white love-

ribband; there was their own dinner, too, this very day. Sarah and David Herries were accustomed to good fare. Deborah had told him that there would be a couple of rabbits smothered in onions, a couple of ducks roasted and an apricot pudding. He himself had seen to the wine, punch and beer. And what was that that Deborah was reading to him? 'A girl staying in the house, Nancy Bone, has a lovely figure, and we laughed and joked much together. I sat beside her when we played Forfeits, and I have bought her today a purse made of Morocco leather. For dinner we had a turkey roasted, a boiled chicken, blancmange, tarts, a damson cheese . . .'

Deborah, her eyes shining, said: 'If it should be a match between our Humphrey and this Nancy . . .' upon which, throwing to the wind all the other concerns that had been plaguing him, and realizing only her, the best wife God had ever given to man, he put his arm around her broad shoulders, kissed her on the lips and pinched her ear for an audacious matchmaker.

He was about to ask 'And where is Reuben?' when they heard the clatter of the horses on the cobbles. A moment later and there in the doorway were Sarah, David and their youngest boy.

Everyone was very happy; they were sitting in the parlour, and little Rebecca, looking her best in her fresh cap and ribbons, was offering wine and cake, and Jacob was caring for the horses.

Mr Sunwood, although he would acknowledge it to no man, was always a little shy of his brother-in-law, David Herries. He was always hoping that this hesitation would shortly be conquered and had even prayed to God about it, but on every fresh occasion the shyness was there. For one thing David Herries was now a great man in the county, his influence everywhere felt, and men said that one of these days he would be knighted. Mr Sunwood could never feel perfectly assured that David had not a little despised his sister for marrying a simple clergyman. Then David was a great man physically too, enormous he looked now as he spread about the settee with his snow-white wig, which he still occasionally wore, his round red face, his full-skirted blue coat and silver waistcoat, his immense thighs and legs in their riding boots, his silver spurs.

But no one could have been kinder than David was to his brother-in-law. There was no condescension in his heart to anyone, he had no pride anywhere in his heart save that he was a Herries and had done something to raise his branch of the

Herries family in the world. It was strange indeed to see how
the moment that David and Deborah his sister were together
again, the Herries family feeling was suddenly everywhere.

The house, the furniture, the cake, the wine, Rebecca and
the cat, little Mr Sunwood himself, all became adjuncts of the
Herries Family, whether they would or no. That was a way that
the Herries people had.

Nevertheless David and his brother-in-law discussed the
affairs of the nation in quite a broad general spirit. David had a
great deal to say about the recent rejection of Pitt's Reform Bill.
He was glad indeed that it had been rejected. If ever there was a
true Tory in the world it was David Herries, and Mr Sunwood
agreed with him, being as Tory in Church as David was in
State. David's voice had a way of rising to a regular boom when
his feelings were roused, and they were roused now. He could
not himself see that there was anything wrong with Parlia-
mentary Representation. He would have things left as they were.
For all that he could see, this was nothing but a plot on the part
of the Yorkshire freeholders to put a check on the authority
of their good and wise King. He shook his great head over
these new times. Why couldn't we leave things as they were?
This discontent of the lower orders boded no good. What was
this chatter about their Rights? When he had been a boy they
had had no Rights and were contented enough. He recalled
the admirable behaviour of a servant his father had had, Benjamin he had been called. The more you whipped him the better
he was pleased, and he had died in his father's arms. David never
perceived the incongruity of his remarks in that he himself
could never beat anyone and was notorious for over-indulging
his servants. Mr Sunwood, however, agreed cordially and sighed
over these new times, and was afraid that there were many
fresh changes coming.

Sarah and Deborah meanwhile were talking together as
eagerly as any two women will who are very old friends, and
have not seen one another for a while. Sarah, although she did
not at present declare it, was paying this visit because, above
everything, she wished to discuss with Deborah the urgent
matter of Judith. Deborah, on her side, was longing for the
moment when she might begin about Humphrey's letter and
his visit to the Pomfret Herries.

Sarah had the greatest opinion of Deborah's sound common
sense. Judith's escape to Tom Gauntry's on the evening of her
whipping had had most momentous consequences. David had

ridden over to Stone Ends and brought her home. From then until now her nature had changed. She was obedient, docile, with flashes of fiery temper, strange impetuous affections; Sarah, whose nature was equable and always under control, could not understand her at all: she felt, too, that she was alone in this, for David had not the art of understanding temperaments. Francis could do what he liked with the child, but would not, so there you were . . .

Meanwhile one member of the household was in his attic room drumming with his fingers on the window. This was Reuben. He could not decide to go down. He had seen them arrive. The one of them that interested and touched him most was not there – Judith. She came in his heart after his brother and his mother, and so warm, so almost passionate, were his affections that she would have been surprised indeed had she known of them. As yet she never thought of him; she had seen him but seldom, and he was no figure to appeal to a child, with his lanky hair, his stout ill-shapen body and his untidiness.

But if she had been there he would have come down. He would have endured his awkward distrust of himself before his grand uncle and his discomfort before the sharp critical eyes of young Will his cousin. Had Judith been with them he could have sat and looked at her lovely hair, and perhaps done her some little service.

But he knew what they thought of him. He could hear his uncle ask why he was not at some work, saving his parents their charges. He had seen his uncle stand by the horse, giving his riding coat to Jacob, revealing the splendid clothes. Why was he never to be like that? Why was everything in him just so turbulent and disordered, as though he heard from a great distance some Call to the obeying of some Order, and yet could not distinguish what that Call might be – and why, oh, why, was something driving him now towards a step that must enrage his father and make his brother grieve?

It had been only a year ago that Mr Walker had given him an ill-written, exceedingly ill-printed *Life of John Wesley*, and this book had been for him, since then, almost his Gospel. Everything related in it had seemed to grow into his own nature. When he read that Wesley wore his hair flowing loose upon his shoulders to give the money that would be spent in caring for it to the poor, that seemed to him a divine action. When he read Wesley's words: 'I would as soon expect to dig happiness out of the earth, as to find it in riches, honour, pleasure (so called) or indeed in the enjoyment of any creature. I know there can be no happiness on earth, but in the enjoyment of God, and in the foretaste of those rivers of pleasure which flow at His right hand for evermore. Thus by the Grace of God in Christ I judge of happiness. Therefore I am in this respect a new creature': his soul thrilled within him; it was almost as though he saw God Himself standing before him and the light of His Countenance shining upon him.

When he read of how Whitfield on the afternoon of Saturday, February 17th, 1739, stood upon a mound, in a place called Rose Green, his 'first field pulpit', and preached to the Kingswood colliers, he felt that he would have given all that he had might he but have stood at his side on that great occasion.

He read how Wesley preached at Gwenap, in Cornwall: 'I stood on the wall, in the calm still evening, with the setting sun behind me; and almost an innumerable multitude before, behind and on either hand. Many likewise sat on the little hills, at some distance from the bulk of the congregation. But they could all hear distinctly while I read "The disciple is not above his Master", and the rest of those comfortable words which are day by day fulfilled in our ears.'

Oh, those comfortable words! Why had he not too been there on that beautiful evening, following that great man's counsel?

Above and beyond all, there was the necessity for the New Birth. 'One will ask with all assurance, "What! Shall I not do as well as my neighbour?" Yes; as well as your unholy neighbour, as well as your neighbours that die in their sins; for you will all drop into the pit together, in the nethermost hell. You will all lie together in the lake of fire, "the lake of fire burning with brimstone". Then at length you will see (but God grant you may see it before!) the necessity of holiness in order to glory, and, consequently, of the new birth; since none can be holy, except he be born again.'

None can be holy except he be born again! So he was not holy. No, indeed, he was not. He was filled with a loathing and hatred of himself, of his body, but far more of himself, his character and true person. He knew himself for a glutton, a coward, an idler, filled with vanity, sensual thought, ingratitude.

But it was worst of all that he should not know which way he should go. He had seen during the last year something of Mr Walker and his friends; he had been to some of their meetings and was not happy there. There was something of his father in him, more than he knew; something perhaps of the Herries blood of his mother. The violence and hysteria in the meetings repelled and silenced him. And they, too, felt that he was not with them. What he wanted he could not tell, save that he must serve God, and must in himself bring about some entire change. Poor Reuben! He was just now the loneliest young man in the world.

He leaned from his window and listened to the sounds of the little world about him. Some horse was impatiently pawing the cobbles, a pedlar sharply cried his wares, a flock of sheep came hurrying under the window, pressing together with their wide, startled, stupid eyes; the shepherd, an old man, with a white shaggy beard, wearing a wide black hat, called shrilly and with an absent mind to his sheepdog. Beyond these movements the wood lay in dark shadow, motionless as though painted on the silver sky. Every fibre in him responded to this lovely world. He must get out into it. He would not go down to his aunt and uncle. He would see them later in the evening. Had little Judith been there—! And at the thought of her, although he had no sensual feeling for her (was she not, ludicrous thought, his aunt ?) he became quite suddenly disturbed by consideration of women. They flocked, like a covey of bright shining birds, about him, settling on his head, his shoulders, his hands, ruffling their feathers, crimson and silver and gold, with their sharp beaks pecking at his cheeks, smiling at him out of their hard, bright eyes. His body was burning, his heart roughly beating. The Devil himself was with him in the room, which had become hot and airless. The sun was sinking, and the wood, as though stricken by the hand of God, was ebony. The silver sky was a camping-ground for tents of crimson; shadows of approaching evening stole across the brightness of the field. His room was evil and filled with temptation. Not realizing that he was hurrying to the turning-point of his life, he hastened softly down the stairs, along the passage, into the path before the house.

The little town was embraced by the rosy light of approaching evening. Fresh breezes from the sea ruffled the hair and wigs of the citizens; not far away the kindly hills caught the light. The streets were narrow, ill-paved, and of a certain odour, but it was the time when the labours of the day are drawing to a close, many were at their dinner, children ran playing from door to door.

At the door of Jacob Hilton's Library young Mr Clementson, flour-dealer, was having a pleasant word with Mr Fletcher of the

'King's Arms', and here was the Carrier coming in from Workington.

They all knew young Reuben Sunwood well enough and greeted him kindly, but he had the sense (perhaps with some truth) that they regarded him oddly and avoided too plain a recognition of him for the Methodist company he was keeping.

So he turned off the main street up a dark and narrow way, thinking of his own troubles, his evil temptations, his loneliness, his perplexed opinions, and found himself, almost without knowing it, in the coachyard at the back of the 'Black Bull'.

He had been attracted here, it might be subconsciously, by the shouts and laughter of a pushing, pressing crowd. He was among them before he knew. He stood there watching. In the middle of the yard there was a cleared space, and in the cleared space a post. Chained to the post was an old, ragged and exceedingly weary bear. Near to the bear, held in the arms of two stout young men, was a small brown-faced man, his forehead streaked with blood. It seemed that he was a foreign pedlar of some kind from his long black hair, his brown complexion, a torn jacket of crimson with a silver chain. It was soon clear that he was a foreigner, for he jabbered ceaselessly in a strange tongue, words pouring from him in a tangled, agitated flow. Once and again he would raise his little body as though he would break away, and then his voice jumped into a shrill scream of protest that roused bursts of laughter from the onlookers.

Kneeling on the ground were two men who held in leash a bulldog and a small terrier, and these two dogs were madly straining to be free that they might get at the bear.

Everyone was hurling bets into the air, and close to Reuben a short thick-set man sucking a straw was taking bets down in his book. The excitement was intense; it was months, a tall farmer near Reuben told him, since there had been a bear to be baited.

Above the hubbub and bustle, clouds of saffron sailed tranquilly over the sky that was now white as moonlit water. Two children hung between the balusters of the inn balcony, laughing at the little pedlar.

At first it seemed to Reuben that he was not concerned in the matter. The bustle and noise, the friendly stomach of the large farmer against which he was pressed, the general air of goodwill and happiness was a relief to him after his own silly and selfish perplexities. There was very much of the child in him, and he liked above all to have happy people around him. To see animals baited was no fresh thing to him; he had been accustomed to such sights since he was a baby. The cruelty of his time was natural to his time and so was no cruelty. He pushed himself forward that he might see the better.

Then he encountered the face of the bear. An encounter it was, as though the pale sky, the crowd, the inn buildings had been swept into lumber and only he and the bear remained. The bear raised its old sad wrinkled face and looked at him. Age was there, bewilderment was there, but what was there, beyond all else, was Reuben himself. Reuben looked at Reuben.

The bear was fastened to the post by a rusty chain that went round his middle and his foot. His body was chafed in a number of places, where life had been hard on him. The long brown shaggy hair of his body was tangled with mud and dirt, and above his left eye there was a deep cut from which blood dripped.

It was this that Reuben first saw, how he raised his paw clumsily, slowly, as though he were resolved to be cautious, and wiped the blood that trickled down his nose. From under his thick tangled brows his eyes looked out, melancholy, slow and brooding. It was these eyes that seemed at first to be exactly Reuben's own. He knew how often his gaze had been fixed upon himself and the world in which he moved with exactly that same perplexity and sadness. The bear's loneliness was his own loneliness.

Then the bear began quietly to realize that he was in the middle of his enemies. Carefully, with that same caution, he moved his head to look for his master, and when he saw him held with his coat torn and his brown breast bare he began to be angry. (Just, Reuben thought, as he would himself slowly, in the middle of his enemies, begin to be angry.) But with his anger there rose also slowly his sadness and his bewilderment. He shuffled with his feet; his paw rose and fell again. He began to roll his head. Then he tried to break from his chain, and when he found that he could not, he jerked his head towards his master. Then again rubbed the drops of blood from his nose.

Something very grand entered into him, the grandeur of all captured and ill-treated things. He lifted his head and stared from under his jutting brows at the crowd, and was at once, with that single movement, finer than all of them. He was no longer Reuben. Reuben had been left behind and was now one of the crowd.

Then a large fat man without a hat, his hair tied with a brown ribbon, in red faded breeches, strode forward and undid the chain. Everyone shouted. The bear, bewildered, hesitating, rubbed his nose again, then, like a man in bedroom slippers, shuffled towards his master.

At the same moment the two dogs were loosed. Everyone began to shout together. It seemed to Reuben that it was towards himself that the dogs were running.

The bulldog instantly attacked the bear, caught his leg and hung on there. The smaller dog stayed back, whining.

The world was pandemonium. Men were laughing, yelling, moving, so that the crowd rocked like a wave. But the bear stood doing nothing; he only raised his paw and stroked his nose. He was a very old bear, who had been travelling for an infinity of years; he was very weary and did not understand why things were as they were.

The bulldog loosed his hold, sprang at the bear's throat, missed and rolled over. The bear sank on all fours, and, rolling his head with a blind gesture, seemed to be asking of them all what they were about.

It was then that Reuben, pushing violently his way, broke into the centre and ran to the bear. Then everything happened swiftly and, for the crowd, comically. A bear or a man, it was the same to the crowd. The bulldog bit Reuben's leg. Something struck his face. There were shouts and cries. Lightning broke from heaven, and the multitude of men, faces, heads of hair, hands, rose in a swirl like a shifting canopy of black flies and carried him sky-high. Then he fell, fell into a pit that was black, that had the mouth of a fish, opening, shutting, opening again. But as he fell somewhere, triumph, joy, freedom – things that he had never known – broke like silent fireworks in his heart . . .

Many generations after, he was sitting in a chair in the parlour of Mr Candlish the bellman. He knew him well, a short pursy fellow with a wart on his nose. Mrs Candlish had bound his head. One eye was closed. A little crowd in the doorway surveyed him. Someone held a candle. He smiled feebly on them all, climbed to his feet, found that he could walk, although his body ached and blood trickled from under the bandage.

He said that he would go home now, thank you. No one stayed him. They were silent when he limped past them, and stared after him in silence as he hobbled down the street. He did not know at all why he was happy, but he was.

He had not far to go. Every step was an agony. He opened his house-door and pushed into the parlour, where they were at dinner. With his one eye from under his bandage he saw his Uncle David, shining in splendour, his father pouring wine, his mother – her face suddenly springing into terror at the sight of him – his aunt, and his little cousin Will, who watched everything and missed nothing that anyone said.

He saw the table piled with food, the candles that danced in their silver holders and the harpsichord in the corner. Someone cried out; he swayed in the doorway, tried to ask for some wine, could not, fell fainting at his mother's feet. As he tried to catch her hand he smiled.

He was the bear, and none of them knew it.

FIREWORKS OVER THE LAKE

FOR THE EVENING of June 23rd, 1787, Mr Joseph Pocklington of Vicar's Island announced that there would be fireworks discharged from his own ground *if* the weather were fine.

If the weather were fine! How that phrase beat its anxiety in a thousand hearts, for not only was it a question of the fireworks, but the band, organized by Mr Peter Crosthwaite, of Crosthwaite Museum, would play airs from Haydn and Mozart, and there would be dancing in Crow Park, to say nothing at all of the boats that there would be on the Lake itself, the Chinese lanterns, and the dark recesses of the water hidden from the inquisitive glances of the moon.

Would there be a moon? Yes, there would be a moon. Mr Crosthwaite himself, who, after serving his country for twenty years in the Navy, had but recently returned to his native place with a most interesting collection of curiosities, promised that there should be a full and lustrous moon.

It mattered little where you went on that early morning of June 23rd. Every riser had the same idea; nightcap after nightcap might be seen hanging from the window, sniffing the weather. From the windows of the 'Royal Oak' and the 'Queen's Head', from John Powe's where the Old Club for so many years held its meetings, from the attics of the 'Shoulder of Mutton', from the Excise Officer at the 'George and the Dragon', from Abel Graves the hairdresser's and Mr Lancaster the pattenmaker's, from the toll-gate at Brown Top – yes, and much farther afield than these . . . right around the Lake; from Stable Hill and Burrow and Low Low Door, High Low Door and Grange, Borrowdale Common and Manesty Nook, Mutton Pye Bay and Branley, House End and Water End, Finkle Street and Portinskill. Yes, and beyond these again, from Newlands and Rosthwaite, Stonethwaite and Watendlath Braithwaite and Bassenthwaite, even to Buttermere and Uldale and Caldbeck and Threlkeld – even to Penrith and Grasmere, to Patterdale and Ambleside, the news had run and the nightcaps were at all the windows, whether of mansion or Statesman's farm, of shop, of meeting-house or humble cottage.

For these nights on the Lake, *if* only the weather were fair, were nights to stir the poets to song, and they *did* stir the Keswick poets to song. Are not those poems to be found in Keswick archives to this very day ?

Mr Pocklington himself loved to give pleasure to the people of Keswick, and the people of Keswick loved to have pleasure given them. And was not Mr Pocklington a fine man, seeing that he owned so much land around the Lake and had his place on Vicar's Island and at Ashness and at Fall Park, and had set up a wonderful Druid's Circle in the pleasantest imitation of the real one above Keswick ?

If only the sun would shine, everyone and everything was in favour. And the sun *did* shine. It rose above a curtain of mist that cut the Lake into half, turned the islands into clouds of emerald, touched Skiddaw with rose and the sharp edges of Blencathra with ebony.

All the gardens of Keswick – and at that time Keswick was filled with gardens – glittered in the sun. Then, as now, no gardens in England could grow sweet peas and pinks and stock better than the Keswick gardens. On a summer day, such as this one, Keswick smelt of flowers, save only in the slums, behind Main Street, where the odour was quite another one. But here dwelt only gipsies and whores and smugglers from St Bees and Ravenglass, and they didn't matter to anyone.

So the day lengthened; the air was balmy, Mr Crosthwaite took out his flute and tuned it; Miss Evins the schoolmistress practised her dancing steps privately in her bedroom; the 'Royal Oak', the 'Queen's Head', the 'Shoulder of Mutton' prepared for an infinity of custom; all the children were beyond human discipline; Mr Pocklington's gardeners guarded the fireworks, and from distant silent valleys the horses had set out, the ladies riding pillion as happy as though there were not a heartache in the world. All the Herries would be there. It was a proud day for the Sunwoods, for their Reuben was but just returned from France, where he had been these last two years; and all the Herries from Uldale – David and Sarah, Francis, Deborah, Will and Judith – rode out in the forenoon and had dinner in state at the 'Royal Oak'.

William Herries, now seventeen years of age, small, short, spindly-legged, an arrogant nose in the proper equine Herries style, a thin rather tight mouth that could, and often did, break into a very charming smile, and clothes neat, correct and most unobtrusive, this William Herries was, as he always had been, exceedingly old for his age.

He himself knew that this was so; he had realized for the last ten years at least that he was quite the oldest of them all. Without any sense of condemnation, without any outward show of superiority, he had long felt a very real contempt for all the other members of his family – for his mother because she was jog-trot, his father because he was conservative, his brother Francis because he was a dreamer (here was his severest contempt), and Judith (could she be reckoned as one of the family) because she was mad and had no control of her emotions. (Strangely, though, here he recognized in Judith some spirit of mastery closely akin to his own.)

He recognized that he was superior to every member of his family but chiefly in this: that he knew so exactly what he wanted to do with his life and how he would do it.

His father, poor man, had a kind of notion that Will would follow himself in his trading business, would work in Liverpool for a while, travel in the East for a while, and finally, having doubled the value of everything, settle down as Squire of Fell House.

Some of this prophecy was, indeed, correct. Will *would* follow his father in the business, would in truth double it and more than double it, but *not* from Liverpool. It was in London that Will Herries intended to make his career. It was not at all that Will objected to business; that was not the kind of snob that he was. Now, with all England's glorious foreign conquests, with the India Trade, the China Trade and the rest, now was the very time to make a fortune. But it was to be a fortune made in the grand manner, made in the very heart of the universe, made against the very strongest opposition, and made – here was the fount and crown of the whole ambition – made for the HERRIES' glory.

Will was nothing if he was not Herries, and Herries practical, material, of the earth earthy. He was sentimental about nothing; he was most certainly not sentimental about this. He did not know in what distant childish dreams this ambition had not had its birth, to make a fortune and with that to take his place at the head of the Herries family. So that men everywhere might say: 'That is a Family, that is. It has houses and barns, gardens and fields, ships and horses and sheep and cattle. *That* is what a Herries can do.'

He saw neither poetry nor romance in this ambition. It seemed to him a perfectly practical logical plan. He would not mind if, at the end of it, one day he returned to Uldale as its master. He cared for this North Country if he cared for any country at all. There was something in its bleak spaces, its coldly blowing winds, its little stone walls running like live things about the fells, its glancing, shining waters, its cleanliness and strength and honesty, that was akin to his own strong unfaltering purpose.

He had, of course, the defects of his qualities like all of us, and it was one of his defects that he made no allowance for the poetic, incalculable quality in human nature. He thought, even now at the young age of seventeen, that he could always calculate with perfect safety. He knew exactly what his father and mother would do and say. His father with his large hearty good-nature, his simple laughter; his ability for seeing what was under his nose, and his stupidity in thinking that that was all that there was; his common sense that stopped just short of real knowledge; his sentimentality (Will, like many another practical man and woman, mistook for sentimentality quite deep and genuine feeling); his boisterous physical life, love of food, of drink, of hunting, of horses, of cock-fighting and card-playing and wrestling and football; his kindliness and satisfaction with small material things. Will knew that most of the business was now left to Mr Metcalfe and his son, his father's partners in Liverpool, and he despised his father for so leaving it. He had a good-natured regard for his father and he despised him thoroughly.

He really loved his mother; it was perhaps the strongest human feeling that he had, and this was chiefly because he thought that she managed the house very well, ruled the servants and had everything in order, but she was always doing what seemed to him silly sentimental things.

For his elder brother Francis he felt a contempt that was almost savage. Francis stood for everything that he despised; he did nothing, but hung in idleness about the house, reading, dreaming, saying absurd, ridiculous things, seeing poetry in everything, liking to be alone, simply cumbering the ground. He had not even the natural passions of drinking, wenching, gaming. He was nothing, nothing at all.

From them all, with a self-control that argued well for his future success in the world, he completely hid his scorn. To them all, he appeared a quiet, obedient, studious boy, who did what he was told and gave no trouble.

Francis possibly had some suspicion of the iron will and determined purpose that was developing there, but no one knew what Francis thought about anything. The only other person who had any accurate knowledge of Will was Judith. His own attitude to Judith was a peculiar one. He had to confess that Judith perplexed him. He had to confess regretfully enough that to sum her up as wild and foolish was not sufficient. She was, it was true, all of these things, but she appeared to be something else besides.

The relation between them was exceptional. Judith was now approaching thirteen years of age. She, like himself, was older than she looked, except that, at times, she looked old enough to be eighty. She had all the colour, all the oddness, all the uncertainty, irresponsibility, that he distrusted and condemned. It was natural enough, he considered, when you thought of her mother. But besides this was her desire to dominate everyone with whom she came in contact, and this was like his own desire except that she wanted it for other reasons. She wanted power because of *people*, he wanted it because of *things*. He had sensual feeling like anyone else, and had had already two experiences. She had sensual feeling too, but it was quite different from his, because whenever she cared for anybody (and she cared for fifty different people a week) she threw herself into it as though this were the only affection of her life, while he always knew that people were nothing, that no one ever cared for anyone else very long.

And he told himself this, although right before his eyes were his own father and mother who had loved one another for so many years and would do so to the end. But his father and mother had so much ridiculous Sensibility – and very little Sense at all.

Nevertheless it remained to him puzzling, this relation of his with Judith. Defensive or offensive? She wished to dominate

him as well as the rest of her world. It amused him sometimes
to allow her to think that she did.

So he remained, this young man of seventeen, watching,
waiting, calculating all his chances.

The night was enchantingly warm. They went down to the
Lake in a body – David in his fine rose-coloured coat, wearing
his own hair clubbed and powdered (an increasing fashion);
Sarah in a fine hoop of silver with little roses; Deborah, red in
the face with pleasure and happiness ('blowzy', Will thought
her); Judith, a fascinating little hat on the side of her red hair
and a little hoop with silver ships painted on it; Will, very
soberly dressed in brown, demurely in the rear; Francis, slim,
aloof.

Mr and Mrs Satterthwaite of Bassenthwaite village walked
down with them. Mrs Satterthwaite's talk was all of servants;
a new one, Mary Benson, recommended by Mrs Blane, five
pound a year, tea twice a day, good at cookery and understanding
her needle. Well, we hope, don't we, that it will turn out for the
best? But they begin so well, don't they, up so early, ready to
milk the cow, and then, where are you? A month later, already
in child from the cowman or drunk on the parlour floor. Yes,
where are you? All the sky, milky now with golden fleece
before the sun's setting, is crowded with maids flying like witches,
mocking their mistresses, and men, bare as they were born, down
the wind after them. Do what you will, it is all Nature, and what
do you say to Mr Bradby, the new schoolmaster in Keswick?
A sensible and good-natured man, unmarried – and at once
Mrs Satterthwaite's two daughters, single and plain, poor things,
always left to their own thoughts at every dance in the neighbourhood, staying in Carlisle at this very instant with an aunt
to see whether *she* couldn't do something about it, filled the
scene and checked the conversation.

Not for Judith. She was so happy that she must dance along
the path as she went, chattering to Francis, although she knew
that he was listening to nothing that she had to say.

Everywhere, on every side of her, people were moving forward
to the Lake, and all of them as happy as she. She loved that
people around her should be happy; she was to love that as long
as she was alive. If only they were happy and *also* did what she
told them, she asked nothing more of life.

And tonight, everything was perfection. She had had her
own way in everything, was wearing the clothes that she wanted,

there would be dancing under the trees and they would be in a boat on the Lake, the moon would rise, and then, best of all, there would be Fireworks – Fireworks, of all things in life that she loved best! Could she have seen Mr Joseph Pocklington, she would have flung her arms around him and kissed him. She did not mind what she did when she was happy. Her soul and body surrendered then completely to the emotion of the moment. Nothing existed for her except that moment.

Even Will, who thought it foolish, indeed, when you were a little short thing with a pale face and so many people around you, to dance along so that all must notice you, was forced to acknowledge to himself that her happiness was infectious. He himself hoped to have his arm around some feminine waist before the evening was over.

When they gained the lakeside it was beautiful indeed. The Lake, whose waters scarcely moved, only a trembling shudder of pleasure once and again mysteriously stirring, had caught flakes and scatterings of gold from the last rays of the sun as it fell behind Cat Bells. Vicar's Island lay like a dark hand upon the water. Under the trees there were booths with many things to buy. Someone was playing a fiddle. Everywhere boats floated, and the oars plashed like music through the air.

Happiness? Happiness? Where is it? Where is it? Here, now, this very moment, with the movement of the people under the trees, the fiddle and the soft distance of the orchestra on the Meadow, before one's eyes the silver stretch of water spreading to the hills that lay like friendly elephants (thought Judith, who had never seen an elephant) humped against the sky. Yes, here is Happiness, because here is Mystery and promise of Adventure. One cannot quite see who is moving beneath the trees. One step and whom may one not encounter?

Two boats were waiting for the Herries family in the charge of old John Blacklock, who was so broad in the waist and thick of the leg that he was like one of the sights at the Fair, two bodies with one head. This head and face, too, were so thickly covered with hair that his eyes shone out like a friendly animal's from a bush. Judith always talked Cumberland to him.

She greeted him now with: 'Noo than what, John?' which pleased him greatly. In his opinion she was a 'gay fewsome lass'. When the weather was bad, he would come out to Uldale and work in the garden for a week or more.

But there was at once a real excitement for her, because Reuben was there. They were waiting for them – little Mr

Sunwood, very neat in his best parson's clothes; Deborah, always so kind and comfortable; and Reuben, a trifle neater for his two years' sojourn in France, but otherwise very little changed. She liked Reuben, in part because of the power she had over him, in part because of his modesty and warm-heartedness. She even understood his shyness, although it was so far from anything in herself. It was, indeed, part of her character that she should care more for Francis and Reuben, so unlike her in temperament, than any other of her relatives.

And at once her power for having things as she wanted them was apparent. A child of less than thirteen, she was in five minutes seated under an oak tree, the Lake spread in front of her, and settled around her were Reuben, Francis, and Will. It was true that they were there to take a breath and look about them before the activities of the evening began for them, and were scarcely conscious, perhaps, that Judith was there, or it was Reuben only who was conscious. Will, as usual, had his sharp eyes fixed on everything at once and was absorbed in considering how he should turn things to his own advantage, and of what Francis was thinking no one could tell, but very quickly Judith had fastened her personality upon all of them and was taking the lead.

So they talked, the background of the fading evening, the faintly rustling trees, the moving people, voices, music forcing from all of them a gentle comfort and well-being that drew them all together in general friendliness. In after days these voices of the lost and ghostly past of this moment would visit them again.

For Judith, as she sat perched on the bole of the tree, a cloak over her shoulders, her shoes shining in the dusk, it seemed to her, as it had seemed to her a thousand times already, that life was at this very moment beginning. She was so happy that she should have been afraid, but she was never afraid when she was happy.

'Reuben, tell us about France. Did you see the King and Queen?'

But Reuben had very little to tell about France. Something about Lourdes, where there was a castle on a rock; State prisoners were sent there by *lettres de cachet*. Here they died of despair and misery. At Pau he had been shown the cradle of Henry IV, which was the shell of a tortoise. At Bordeaux he had seen Dauberval the famous dancer. He had visited Versailles and had seen men walking in rags of the direst destitution. There was a wonderful botanical garden there. In the Castle at Chambord he had been shown the room where Marshal Saxe had died. It was said that he had been run through the heart by the Prince of Conti in a duel. And so on. And so on. Little things, unalive, related by him in his shy, hesitating voice so that, Will thought impatiently, he turned everything to dullness. But how could it be other? How could he, in this quiet homely comfortable scene, tell them of the things that had been burning in his heart – the filth, oppression, cruelty, suffering? Tell them of the man whom he had seen in Tours beaten to death before his eyes, because he had taken a log from the Seigneur's wood, or the two girls ravished by the son of the Lord of the Manor, one of them within a week of her wedding, or of the horde of starved creatures that he came upon on the road outside Paris, scarecrows, their bodies shivering in the bitter wind? The bear again, lodged now close in his heart, he the protector of it; how could he speak of that to Will or Francis Herries? So his voice died away, and he felt the scornfulness of Will's eyes.

'When I am grown,' Judith cried, 'I shall go to France. I shall see the French Queen and dance in Versailles. I shall see India and China and the savages of the West Indies. What will you do, Will?'

He smiled. It was always his way to be courteous and friendly to everyone. Besides, nothing in the world interested him so greatly as to think of what he would do when he grew up, a time that was very near to him already.

'I shall build the Herries fortunes,' he said in that voice, a little mocking, a little ironical, so that if anyone objected to what he said he could declare that he had never meant it. 'I shall have a larger fortune than any other Herries, and then, when I have accumulated it, I will tour the globe and return to make another fortune.'

'And will you not marry?' asked Judith greatly interested.

'I shall marry,' said Will gravely, 'and so increase the Herries stock. I shall have six children,' he added mockingly.

To their surprise an angry voice broke on the scene – surprise because it was the voice of Francis, who seemed never to be disturbed nor to wish to join in their childish conversations. But he was disturbed now, and at the sight of his disturbance two fish-shaped clouds above Vicar's Island joined hurriedly together the better for self-protection.

'There, Will; that's your fancy. It's you, yourself. Moneybags, children, more money-bags. God, what ambition!'

It was a sharp interruption and rather frightened all of them.
Francis was twenty-seven years of age and so in another world
from their own. He had never mingled with them; he was like a
ghost to them with his thin, handsome face, his cold blue eyes
that could on a sudden so strangely burn, the severe suit of
grey and silver that he so generally wore. Will might despise
him, but there was fear mingled with that scorn.

And now suddenly he was standing, all shadows around him,
his voice that had been always so chill and reserved beating
with emotion.

'You shall have your money-bags if you want them. What is
easier? And getting them you will have nothing. And is that all
life is to you? Are you so blind that you can see no ghosts
behind the money-bags and ghosts behind them again? Have
you only your physical parts to cram food into your swelling
belly?'

('I have no swelling belly,' Will thought complacently. 'I
have an admirable figure.')

Francis went on, coming close to them, standing over them.
His anger was gone as soon as it had come. He spoke now
gently.

'When I was small I had a dream of a grand white horse
breaking from an icy pool and breasting the rocks, tossing its
mane. I have not dreamt that for a long while, but I know that
that dream is more real to me than all the chairs and sofas,
the mutton pies and shoe buckles. How can you not tell that
that only is real in this world, that vision of ice and strength
breaking it, and if we have not seen that we have seen nothing?
Who can tell what is Reality? But this at least I know, that I shall
never know happiness until I have seen more than you will
ever see, Will, my young brother.'

'Thank you for nothing, Francis,' Will answered, looking up
at him and smiling. 'I prefer my money-bags to your white
horses.'

'Aye, I know what you think,' Francis broke out passionately.
'What you all think. That I loaf at home and take what my
father gives me ... Wasting ... wasting.' His voice broke.
'Our grandfather was so. He was searching all his days and
never found anything ... Forgive me, I have been absurd. This
world itself is absurd to me, but behind it ... behind it ...
there are Wonders. Forgive me ... forgive me,' and to their
utter surprise he turned and vanished into the trees.

For a moment they were all in a great discomfort. It was so

agreeable an evening. They had not the slightest notion of Francis' meaning and they did not wish to spoil his pleasure. Judith, who loved him, would have wished to have run after him, to have taken his arm and comforted him. But to have comforted him for what? She could not tell.

And at that moment, fortunately, the first fireworks broke like a sigh in the darkening heaven. Everyone said 'Ah!' and then 'Ah!' again, just as a hundred years after, and a hundred years after that again, they would sigh with pleasure and strain their eyes upwards. So now they gazed. Everywhere they were gazing, in the little flower-scented streets of Keswick, lovers waiting among the Druid stones, shepherds on Blencathra, watchers by the Watendlath Tarn, children gathered by the cottages in Newlands and under Castle Crag and by the waving reeds of Bassenthwaite.

A star broke into a silver cluster, another into points of blue, another showered drops of gold. In the hills the echo called and answered. For a flash all the faces were lit with a white radiance, the dancers paused in the Meadow, the trees on the Island were fiery and then the darker for their flame.

For Judith it was a moment of sheer ecstasy. She sat, her head back, her hat behind her neck, her legs uptilted, and at every rush as of wings, at every gentle crackle of sound, at every fresh miracle of blue and gold she murmured, her hands tightly clasped. She forgot everything and everyone in that beauty. A star burst, and showers of silver flecked the sky.

She sprang up and ran to the Lake edge. Others were crowding there, and she stood with them, her head bare, gazing upwards. Three rockets burst together, and the sky was scattered with stars. 'Bravo!' 'Bravo!' 'Bravo!' everyone shouted. She clapped her hands; everyone was clapping with her. Again the hills called and answered. Then the pause came, a sudden deep and mysterious silence. The Lake was now infinite. Far, far away, where the hills were packed together, a faint radiance was gathering, the coming moon. Real stars began to twinkle.

Out of this dark lovely world a voice spoke to her: 'It is better in a boat.'

She knew the voice well; in the last two years she had thought of it very often. It was the French boy of Tom Gauntry's.

The lanterns had been lighted and were swaying from the trees. She could see him quite plainly. He was just the same, only taller, in a very grand coat and breeches with gold braid. Under his hat his hair was as black as ever, and his eyes as

black. His mouth was just as impudent. She grinned at him, a
childish grin.

'Fetch me a boat then.'

What would Sarah think? It would mean perhaps another
beating. She had been ordered not to go near the boats until
they told her. The thought of being alone with the French boy
was most exhilarating. She watched him while, without another
word, he was in a boat, had pushed it towards her and, like a
grown man, with fine ceremony, handed her in. As she stepped
in she glanced about her to see whether any of the family were
near. No sign of any of them. She fancied that she heard Sarah's
voice, and in a sudden panic pushed from the shore. Many other
boats were now moving, and, in the distance, they were singing.

'Quickly,' she cried, with delight, 'or they will see us.'

They floated away: the oars touched very gently the water
as though they were whispering to it their pleasure in the evening.
As they moved, the shore behind them came out, with all the
dark figures, the lights like jolly smiling faces among the trees,
and shadows dancing on the Meadow to a thin faint tune that
was reedy like wind through wallpaper.

'Where have you been?'

'In London with an uncle.'

'And your mother?' She saw the room, the beautiful naked
woman, her arms raised, the diamond buckle shining.

'My mother is dead.'

'Dead?' And at the moment a firework broke in the sky again,
this time a circle of fierce rasping flame that whistled with the
hiss of an angry cat.

Dead? Judith shivered. Then for these two years the picture
that had transformed her, that had changed her from a thoughtless baby into something, something very different ... that
picture had been for nothing, of a dead woman.

'Why did she die?'

'What is it? I cannot hear.' He had leaned forward on the
oars.

'Why did she die?'

'She died of the smallpox.'

'When was it?'

'A year back.' He spoke quite indifferently.

'Did you not care?'

'No. She was unkind to me.'

'She must have been very gracious; a beautiful lady. Her hair
was so dark.' Judith shivered again. She wanted to return to the

shore, to be with her own people. And, surprisingly, something else dominated almost every other feeling, that she wanted to kiss the French boy. Hateful, when his mother, his beautiful mother, had for her, at any rate, only this moment died.

'How old are you now?' he asked her.

'Twelve – nearly thirteen.'

'I am sixteen.'

'What are you doing here? Why are you not with your uncle?'

'My uncle is in Carlisle. I am with Gauntry until he fetches me. I like this country. Soon I shall come to live here.' Then he added, laughing: 'Is your hair yet the same colour? I have thought of your hair often.'

Because she wanted to kiss him and because she mustn't, because she was only twelve and he sixteen, she flipped water in his face. He laid down his oars in the boat, moved near to her and roughly kissed her, cheeks, eyes, mouth. She pulled her head free and smacked his face just as she had done two years before. But he did not move. He sat quietly beside her, his hand at her waist. She did not move either. Fires were burning now on Vicar's Island, the set-pieces of the fireworks. A trellis-work of flame ran like live things from tree to tree. All the Lake near the Island glowed, but in the distance it was very dark, with a smoky sheen on it, the first fore-shadowing of the moon.

She sat there in perfect happiness. She hoped that he would kiss her again. He did so. Then she returned his kiss.

'I shall be whipped if they know about it.'

'My mother whipped me, but my uncle dare not. When my mother was angry she could kill a man.'

'Was she long ill of the smallpox?'

'No. A month. I was glad when she died. Do you love me?'

'No.'

'Later you will. You are only a baby. In two years I will write you a letter, and perhaps you will come to London.'

'Will you want to marry me?'

'Perhaps. You have such beautiful hair.'

Judith considered. In two years she would be nearly fifteen. She could marry soon then and leave Fell House and live in France.

'If I married you should we live in France?'

'Maybe.'

'Will you have money and a house and horses.'

'Yes. Of course.'

'And we will have children?'

'Yes. Of course.'

'We will have six children, and I want to see the French Queen dance in Versailles.'

'I want to live in this country and have dogs and horses.'

'But will you not take me to France for a visit?'

'Maybe.'

They kissed again. She kissed him like a child, just as she kissed Francis. Then quite suddenly she knew that she must return to the shore. At once, at once! She was afraid of him and of the Lake that seemed dark now because the fireworks had died away.

She told him to take her to the shore.

'No. We will stay here.'

Then he saw another Judith. She stepped from him, and, the boat rocking under them, went to the oars and began to row. She could do anything with a boat or a horse.

'If you leave me now I will never see you again,' he said to her fiercely. She made no answer, and a moment later had scrambled over the boat's edge and had landed.

That was the last she saw of him, standing up very dimly against the dark water.

She ran in to the trees and, quite breathless, tumbled straight into Reuben and his mother.

'I was lost,' she said. 'Where are they?'

She put her hand under Reuben's arm and smiled at him so sweetly that he was enraptured. She looked such a baby with her pretty hat crooked, a little breathless.

'We will go and find them,' he said.

THE FUGITIVE

HOW DOES A house first know that changes are coming to it? or does a house know? Are we not attributing to it emotions, fears, agitations that are not its real property? The answer depends on yourself. What you see, hear and feel is for yourself alone.

It is certain in any case that in that winter of 1788–9 Sarah Herries, just arrived at her fiftieth birthday, knew that some change was at hand. It was the first unhappy winter for her since

- since when? Since she had lived with David at Herries.

Had she cared for wider issues she might have realized that
the change was not only here, but in all the civilized world. She
did not, however, care for wider issues, had never done so.
It had never meant anything to her that the American rebels
had thrown tea into Boston Harbor, that old Chatham had the
gout, that Fox made an unholy alliance with North, that young
Pitt pored over *The Wealth of Nations* at Cambridge, that men
were trampled to death by the horses of noble carriages on the
roads outside Paris, that Necker sat up all night biting his
thumbs over the impossible business of turning twice-two
into five. If she had known of these things she would not have
cared.

But she did perceive that nothing now went right in the house,
that doors swung on their hinges and refused to close, that the
Chinese figures in the Blue Room tumbled, through nobody's
fault, and were broken to pieces, that the cows gave no milk
and the horses went lame.

Twenty years earlier she would have hunted for witches. Now
she could only discover that David was becoming an old man,
that she herself was fifty and that everyone in her family was at
odds. She was a sensible woman, who refused to surrender to
superstition, but things were going wrong, and as she lay at
night awake in the big four-poster beside David she could hear
the wind come whispering down from Skiddaw and must listen,
do what she would, to a hundred steps creeping about the stairs
and mysterious voices behind the curtain.

But there were unhappy evidences more material than steps
and voices.

The first trouble was on the day after the firework evening
on the Lake. At dinner Will had suddenly said to Judith:

'Well, miss, you enjoyed, I trust, your pleasant trip in the
boat last night.'

No one knew why he said it. He did not care for Judith,
but he bore her no especial malice. He did not himself, perhaps,
know why he said it. It came no doubt from his deep restless
love of power. He was only a boy, but he could turn them any
way he wished.

All might even then have been saved had it not been for
Judith's implacable honesty.

'You were in a boat?'

'Yes, ma'am.'

'With whom?'

That she would not say: with a gentleman, yes. For a brief period, to see the fireworks better. David beat her. The child said nothing, only afterwards alone with Will she told him that she would not forget his kindness.

'I wanted to see how it would go,' he told her quite honestly. He admired her then, such a little thing, standing on her toes to make herself seem taller. She bore him apparently no grudge.

'It shall not be for long,' she said, nodding her head like a woman of forty. She turned on her toes, pirouetting. 'I'll be a woman very shortly.'

But for the moment, as the consequence of this indiscretion following many others, she was in great danger of the one and only thing that she dreaded – of being sent to Miss Macdonald's Academy at Carlisle.

She had heard something of this school from Margaret and Hetty Worcester of Threlkeld, who attended this place for a time, and she did not like what she had heard. They rose at six winter and summer, ate a piece of bread and then had an hour's schooling. Then there was 'Punishment Hour', wherein, it seemed, the Misses Macdonald indulged in an orgy of whipping, six stripes of the rod for a small offence, and a 'proper whipping' meant that you fetched the rod, kissed it, and then, before the school, were stripped, 'mounted' on another girl's back and beaten till the blood came. Hetty Worcester gave an admirably detailed description of it. Judith knew well that before she suffered that ignominy there would be a murder done. Not that Hetty thought much of it, for in her home everyone was whipped, the maids and the grooms, the dairy girls and even the tutor. Nevertheless, Judith knew that a week in Miss Macdonald's Academy and she would be a vagrant loose upon the world, and for that she was not yet ready.

While her fate hung thus in the balance the relations between Sarah and Judith developed uncomfortably. Judith bore her sister-in-law no grudge, she knew herself to be a difficult ill-disciplined child, but the difference between their ages was so great and their characters were so ill-suited that, as Judith grew, trouble was bound to come.

Sarah in her heart cared for nothing at the last resort but David. She loved her children, but David was her adoration. She could not endure to see him vexed, even for a moment, and now she realized that Judith was constantly vexing him. He understood her as little as did Sarah. He was too kindly-natured to exercise his authority sufficiently. Judith was for ever escaping him. After all she was not his child, but his half-sister. There were many times when she seemed to him her mother come alive again.

He was a great deal at home now; went to Liverpool very seldom. He trusted the Metcalfes for everything, and soon Will would be in Liverpool. Therefore he was much at Uldale. He loved every stick and stone of it, and he could be seen, his body casting a vast shadow, pottering over the sunny lawn, looking up as a great hurrying cloud flung its shadow over the Fell, examining the horses, watching the maids working in the dairy, going over accounts with Mr Matcham the agent, or simply leaning on the stone wall and gazing across the white road at the low sprawling shape of Skiddaw.

So, being at home thus, he was always tumbling upon Judith and Francis; Judith, her ringlets flying, riding Barnabas or sliding down the banister of the great staircase, or, in another mood altogether, standing motionless, watching, waiting – what was the child about and why did she look so damnably like her mother?

Or Francis, twenty-eight years of age now, always so slim, elegant, apart, silent – and doing nothing. Twenty-eight and doing nothing! For you could not call reading Cowley or Milton or Shakespeare anything, or roaming aimlessly the countryside (and greeting no one as he went) anything. His father would catch him writing in a book and when he would ask him of it he would close the book and, secretly, deep in himself, would answer the question by saying:

'Nothing, sir.'

Once David lost his temper, and only once.

'I'll not keep you here idling.'

An hour later Francis came down the stairs in his riding coat, Andrew the boy carrying his valise. He was going away, and David knew that it was for ever. David found then how deeply he loved him. Afterwards he pleaded with him: why were they drifting so far apart? Could they not open their hearts to one another? And Francis answered: 'Oh, sir, would to God I could! Something silences me. I will work, father, anywhere you place me . . . in your Keswick office . . . I will do all I can.'

What an echo of ghosts was here! For had not David's father once, in the dead years, said the same? For a moment Francis Herries the Elder stood there, that same ironical twist to his lip that his grandson had.

So Francis went to work in the Keswick office, and he was

useless. All he cared for was to read poetry and philosophy. Poetry and philosophy! So, loving one another deeply, they drifted further and further apart.

But Judith was a greater mystery for poor David, who would sit back in his armchair before the fire, his legs spread, his great bulk at ease, but his honest friendly face twisted with perplexity.

He wanted to do what was right by the child. She was his own father's daughter; but the truth was that neither he nor Sarah felt that she had anything to do with him at all. At one moment she was a child of her proper age, at another almost a woman, ordering the men and maids in the place as though she commanded it. She had a good heart, he could tell that, but when she couldn't get her own way she was a devil, not raging nor crying but her sharp, pale, little face cold and savage under her red hair. And he sometimes thought that she hated Sarah. They didn't forbid Gauntry's to her any more. What was the use? She would simply go there, and one day, if they were not careful, she would never come back, and what a scandal that would be! Besides, there was no harm in little Gauntry, and he loved the child like his own daughter.

So David went over all his perplexities, feeling perhaps, as Sarah did, that changes were coming. When things were too difficult for him he would ride over to Worcester's or Osmaston's and play cards all night or get drunk and be carried up to bed.

Meanwhile he clung to Sarah, his wife, ever more deeply. She was his real friend, had always been. He loved Deborah, his daughter, but in his heart found her a little dull; he was a little afraid of Will, who always knew better than he himself did; Francis, whom he loved best of his children, was a mystery. So he stayed with Sarah and was only truly happy when she was by.

In March of the new year they decided that Judith should pay a visit to the Sunwoods in Cockermouth. Maybe they would manage her. Judith was very happy to go. She was very happy to go, but never dreamt before going that when she was there she would be so happy to stay.

She had visited a number of times at the little house, but had had no notion that it would suit her so perfectly to live in it. It was the very size that she liked, small, compact, comfortable. Everything in it went on under her very nose; she could have her fingers in every pie, in Deborah's cooking and preserving, sewing and cleaning, in the dealings with the pig, in all the little affairs of the town, the gossip, the tea parties, the expeditions on fine days, the cosy conferences round the fire on wet ones. In five minutes she had Mr Sunwood entirely under her control, he would read his sermons to her, she would listen to his accounts of his Quadrille parties, enjoy by proxy the first piece of roasted swan that he had tasted at a grand party at the Castle, and even advise him as to the right time to take a good dose of rhubarb.

But the element that made this visit so enchanting was her quite unexpected friendship with Deborah. Deborah was nearly sixty-six years of age and Judith only fourteen, yet the difference in their ages seemed to make no division between them at all. Judith was hungering for affection with all the ardour and excitement of her temperament. She was separated from Francis and also (although of this she tried to prevent herself thinking) from Georges, the French boy. So she was ready, in any case, to throw herself upon Deborah and Reuben. But she soon discovered that she had never been brought into contact before with anyone at all like this stout, soft-eyed, soft-voiced, gentle-hearted woman. The people whom she had hitherto known had not (save for Reuben, and he had been two years away) been gentle-hearted – not Gauntry, nor Sarah, nor Will, nor even Francis.

The first thing that drew her to Deborah was that Deborah let her do anything that she wished, and the second thing was that Deborah told her so much that was new and exciting about her father.

They sat together beside the fire, Deborah sewing and Judith leaning forward, her chin cupped in her hands, and Deborah recovered for the child her own childhood. This gave Deborah herself a surprising happiness and pleasure. No one in her own family had asked her questions about those days. It was her husband's belief that he had rescued her from some wild sort of savagery and the less said about it the better, and her sons had never shown any curiosity. But this strange child, with her ardent, eager, impetuous spirit, brought her father back to her as though he were with them in the room. *Her* father! *Their* father! And at the thought that they had, both of them, she nearing the end of her life, the child only beginning hers, the same father, a bond of affection was formed and remained. She soon discovered that she herself loved to recall that long-ago time, the wild Borrowdale valley, so cut off and remote, the old house rocking to every wind, the death of her mother and her own fear at being left alone with her father, although she

loved him. Her devotion to her brother David, such a wonderful
boy, the strongest boy and man in the valley (different, she was
forced to confess, from the stout, rather lazy monarch of Uldale),
the old witch, Mrs Wilson, who lived with them and was drowned
in the Derwent by the villagers, her own lonely thoughts, love
of natural things, shyness – then the ball in Keswick and the
little clergyman coming to sit beside her and make love to her,
her father's strange marriage to Judith's mother, and then the
unhappiness of that odd woman, her flight, her father's loneliness and madness and search, and always the tumbledown house
and the isolated valley behind and through it all.

She let Judith ask as many questions as she wished and answered all that she asked. Judith recovered the personalities
of her father and mother as she never had done before. They
became alive to her. She saw Francis, her father, the scar
marring his face, tumbling the villagers down the stairs after
the wedding. She saw Mirabell, her mother (it was part of her
oddness that she should have a man's name), breaking her heart
because the man she had loved had been murdered under her
eyes in Carlisle. She saw Francis, her father, setting out in
search of her, wandering over England looking for her, at last
capturing her again, and then the two of them dying together in
that lonely house.

Something grew in her as these two ghosts were drawn to her
side. *Her* ghosts and only hers. No one alive in the world had
the right to both of them as she had. She was never, after this,
to lose the fancy that all her life long there were three of them
moving about together through the world.

'Oh, if but I had been there,' she cried. 'I could have made
them so happy!'

And Deborah, in her turn, recovering thus her young days,
felt her heart warm in her for her dear, lost father. Only she
and David in all the world thought of him any more – and now
this child. How could she not but love her?

Judith was easy enough to love in such a case. She asked nothing better than to love and be loved in return: it was only when
someone was an enemy, or she thought was an enemy, that her
fierce hostility flamed out. Even then she could be generous and
large-hearted. She wished Will no evil because he had betrayed
her about the evening on the Lake. She could not be mean nor
spiteful about little things.

They were both large-hearted, she and Deborah.

Then something more drew them together. Judith discovered

that Deborah was very unhappy. For eight months she had had
no word from her son Humphrey. Mr Sunwood pooh-poohed
the whole business. The boy would write when he had leisure;
the Post was a very uncertain affair; he, himself, would soon
make a journey to London and see the boy.

But none of this could comfort Deborah. They had heard
nothing, either, from his master. The last news had been a year
ago. At first the boy had written frequently. He had been last
home a year and a half ago and had been well and merry, but,
even at that, she had fancied that he had said too little about his
work. It was all his pleasure, his visits to Vauxhall, how he had
seen the good King and Queen, been to a picnic in Twickenham,
travelled down the river with the Pomfret Herries, and so on,
and so on. But of his work very little. And that was a year and a
half ago.

As Judith listened to all this her impatience leapt into flame.
But why didn't someone go to London? Why didn't Mr Sunwood or Reuben? She would go herself. Why should not she
and Deborah go? It was a shame to leave it in this uncertainty
... She jumped up and ran about the room, tossing her red
ringlets in the air.

But Deborah, smiling, shook her head. It wasn't so easy to
go to London, a very long journey. Mr Sunwood felt no alarm,
why should she? Reuben had his work at Mr Stele's the solicitor's. Oh, it was all right. She was sure that all was well. Humphrey was such a good boy. Any day there would be a letter. And
she would look across the room at the little bottle-green
window and shake her head, and her eyes would swim in tears.

So Judith went to Reuben. Reuben was changed by his two
years in France, more remote. He was tidier, but alas! little
cleaner. It was not at that time important that you should be
clean, and Judith was peculiar in wishing for cleanliness.
When Mr Sunwood came in from attending to the pig he was
not very clean and would sit down to his dinner without thinking of it. But Reuben's linen, his small-clothes, oh, they
wanted a deal of attention! His hair was not brushed and fell
untidily about his shoulders. His shoes were often caked with
mud. In his attic there was always a close stuffy smell, terrible
untidiness, his bed where he used to lie, his hands behind his
head, looking up at the attic roof, staring and thinking, sadly
tumbled. Judith never came into the room but she longed to set
about it with a scrubbing brush and a pail of water. But she
loved him none the less, his fat loose body, his kindly, large,

wondering eyes. He was generous and soft-hearted like his
mother, but so often like something that had lost its way. He
moved at times as though he were blind. He was a dreamer
like Francis, but what an incongruous comparison he made with
that slim, elegant, severe figure! And he had told her once that
if he were afraid of anyone in the world it was of Francis.

Then one evening she came up to his attic and found him
lying on his bed, his coat off, his shoes off, his stockings halfway down his legs, and he was talking to himself, while a long
drunken candle guttered on a chair beside the bed.

She herself held a candle. She stood for a moment listening to
him:

'Oh, Lord! Oh, Lord!' he was saying, 'I am a sinner. I have
no courage in my heart. I am a poor wretch. Oh, damnation!
Damnation! I long in my heart after women and go the way I
should not! Oh, Lord, Lord! . . .'

She stopped this peroration by crying in a very solemn voice:
'I am the Devil and have come for your soul, O Reuben!' and
he, hearing her, jumped from the bed and stood blinking at her
like an owl.

'Do you truly long after women?' she asked him a little later,
when they were both sitting on the bed close together, the candles
throwing great shadowy shapes on the wall.

'Yes, I do.'

'Well, then, you should marry.' She nodded her head, swinging her little legs and wishing for the thousand-thousandth time
that they were longer.

'No woman would have me.'

'No, not while you are so untidy in your clothes. Why don't
you brush your hair and have a new ribbon for it? And there is
a hole in your stocking.'

'I hate Mr Stele and his office,' he said suddenly. 'I was so
happy the day I saw the bear. That was a sign, and I did not
follow it.'

'They sent you away to France,' she said, 'because of the
bear.'

'Yes.' He nodded his head. 'And one day in the road beyond
Tours – a hot glaring day – I saw Jesus Christ standing there.
He stood right in my path; the sun was shining in His hair.
He looked at me so kindly and said: "Reuben, feed my Lambs."
And I have done nothing, nothing.'

'For how long did He stay there?' she asked. She had a very
practical mind and no sense of religion at all. She could not

help that. She wished to have it, but she found it very difficult to believe in anything that she did not see.

Reuben pulled up his stockings. He was always aware that she disliked his untidiness. She herself looked so neat now in her little orange hoop and brown shoes.

'He did not stay long,' Reuben sighed. 'It was the second time. He came to me once at St Bees.' He put his hand timidly and took one of hers.

'Judith,' he said. 'You are so brave. Show me what to do.'

'Yes, I will show you,' she answered, coming close to him. 'Go to London and see Humphrey.' She felt him tremble.

'I dream about Humphrey,' he answered her, 'every night. I know that he is in great trouble. One of us always knows when the other is in trouble. I know that Mother also is grieving, but I am afraid to go to London. I am afraid of everything. I would not know how to behave in London nor what to do. They would all laugh at me, and I cannot bear to be mocked. London is so vast, and there is so much noise there . . .' He broke off, plucking with his fingers at his clothes.

'No, but you must go,' she answered. 'I will never speak to you again if you do not. It is your duty to your mother. Do you love me, Reuben?'

'Of course.'

'Then go to London or I will never see you again.'

She began then eagerly to speak of what he would do and just where he should go. She seemed to know everything about London, although she had never been there. His cheeks kindled, there was light in his eyes. Yes, he would go. He would ride into Kendal and take the coach there. He would speak to his father . . . And then he shrank back. But all the people, so many strangers, the lighted streets, he would be lost.

'Well, if you do not go, I am finished with you.'

She stood in the middle of the floor, her head up, scorning him. And at that moment some of her strength entered into him, entered into him never to leave him again. He went to the window and looked out across the darkness. Then he looked back into the lighted room and saw her standing there. He cried out in a kind of frenzy:

'I'll go! I'll go! I'll go!'

How often in other places, in later times, he remembered that scene! And then she danced about the room like a mad thing, caught his hands and made him dance too. She ended by tying his hair with a new ribbon and finding another pair of stockings for him. She hoped that he would find a woman in London to make him happy, and she also hoped that he would not, because she wanted to have him all to herself.

Howbeit, events moved faster than Reuben. Before he could speak to either his mother or his father something very terrible occurred.

Years and years afterwards Judith would remember that March afternoon and its sudden storm sweeping her off her feet into an adventure that would have its consequences for all her life.

She and Deborah had been shopping in the town. It was market day and proper March, with a sky that was here pale green, there pale blue, while little busy clouds like torn sheets of grey paper flew and scattered under cross tugs of wind. The sky was swept with streams of light that flooded out into glory, throwing sheets of pale silver colour on to field and wood.

It was one of those days when everyone in the little town was conscious of the near neighbourhood both of the mountains and the sea. The wind had begun with little anticipatory gusts, as though it were trying its forces to see whether they were strong and sound, then, as everything went well, it increased its power, began to find pride in its strength, and soon, doubtless, would be bellowing with vainglory. You could see in your mind's eye Ennerdale, that was not far away, ruffling into little flakes of foam, its waters chocolate-coloured, while the sky above the hills was all busy with its traffic, sending clouds hither and thither, flashing light now on, now off, under order of the March gale. All the hills, black and grim, gathered like conspirators close about the waters. On the other side of the town there was the sea, the wind tugging at St Bees Head, and all the shipping tossing maliciously in Whitehaven Bay.

The booths of the market were creaking and cracking, cloths blowing about, the pedlar forced to cover his wares, ropes straining, doors rattling, everyone clinging to their hats and wigs.

Then with a shriek of whistling fun the wind and the rain came, driving straight up the street, sweeping the trestles and boards away, carrying the whole town with it as though it would toss it into Ennerdale.

Judith and Deborah went scurrying home, hats, wigs, pieces of cloth, fragments of wood, dogs, cats, shrill voices, laughter, all hurrying through the air, it seemed, with them.

Safe in the little house again, panting for breath, wet, blown, laughing, they looked about them, while the rain rattled on the

windows crossly because they had escaped it. They stared under
wet eyelashes about them, and the first thing that Judith saw
was a letter, lying innocently on the table: it was addressed 'Miss
Judith Herries'.

She snapped it up.

'A letter?' asked Deborah.

'Yes.'

'From Uldale, I warrant.'

'Yes,' said Judith. It was not a lie because she had not yet
looked at it. It lay warm in her wet hand. She thought it would
be from Sarah, summoning her home. Who had left it there?
Had David perhaps ridden over, or Francis? It might be that
they would spend the night. But she wouldn't go back to Uldale.
She was too happy where she was. She wouldn't go back until
she had seen Reuben safely away to London ... She had got
thus far. She was climbing the stair to her room. She saw what
it was. It was from Georges Paris. He was in Cockermouth. He
asked her to meet him in the parlour of the 'Greyhound', five
o'clock that evening. He would wait until six.

Her first thought was of his impertinence, then that he should
have the spunk to leave the letter at her very door where anyone
might read it, then that she wouldn't go, nothing should induce
her, then that she would greatly like to see him again just to tell
him what she thought of him, then that she would take Reuben
with her (it would be so amusing to see Georges' face of disappointment), then that this would be the first time of seeing
him since the evening on the Lake, then that she would not
go but would send a letter by Reuben, then that perhaps she
would go just to see what he was like now ...

By this time she was in her room and laughing at the thought
of an adventure. For it *was* an adventure. Georges was always
an adventure. She would wear her orange hoop ... But in this
weather with the streets swimming in water! She heard the
maid calling her to dinner. Three o'clock. There would be
plenty of time before five ...

By the end of the meal she was uneasy. She was always uneasy
when she thought of Georges. She determined that she would
take Reuben with her.

Behind the parlour there was a little room with nothing much
in it but a large yellow globe, a powder-stand and a shaving-
table. It could be turned into a guest room at a crisis. She pulled
Reuben in there after her. The little windows looked out on to a
narrow crooked path that ran through fields to a shaggy wood,

on fine days a pleasant prospect, but this afternoon you could
see nothing but the storm that swung in sheets of rain across the
scene, the drops on the panes in the windows rattling like little
pellets from a shotgun. From a side door of this room there was a
short passage and another door opening on to the field.

When she had Reuben in the room with her, she suddenly
thought – no, after all, she would not tell him. Why should she
not go alone? Georges could not harm her. They would be in a
public place. She was not afraid to smack his face again if need
be. She was not afraid of Georges nor of anyone. So when she
saw Reuben, still wiping his last draught of ale from his mouth
and smiling in that uncertain way that he had when he was not
sure how she was going to use him next, she burst out laughing.

'Reuben—' she said, and then she paused.

'Yes,' he said obediently.

'It's raining.'

'Yes,' he said again, wondering.

'But I am going out into it.'

He said nothing.

'And no one is to know. I shall go by this door.'

He looked at her in perplexity. She could always do as she
liked with him, but after all she was but a child. Her small
stature and something innocent in her wide-open eager eyes
always made her younger than her age, just as the resolved
dominating lines about her mouth made her older. Nevertheless,
she was young to be going out into the town alone, and in this
weather, and what could she be going for but to see a man?

At the thought his heart beat thickly, his stout cheeks coloured,
he plucked at his coat.

'You shall not go alone,' he said. 'I shall accompany you.'

'Oh no, you will not!' she answered laughing. 'You shall stay
here and keep them quiet. If they ask where I am you shall say
I am busy working – and so I shall be.'

'Busied at what?'

She stood on her toes, pulled his head down, and kissed him.

'Never you mind. I am your aunt.'

'I shall accompany you,' he said firmly.

She looked at him. Would it be better perhaps, after all, that
he should? She was *not* safe with Master Georges. She remembered a moment in the boat, when, in an instant, at a touch of his
hand, she had been warned.

Many visits to Stone Ends had acquainted her with life.
Children were not children for long in those days. *Should* she

take Reuben with her? And it would tease Georges so that he should be there. And Reuben was so strong, so safe, so devoted. A sudden impulse of great affection for him, one of those impulses that were often all through her life to rise in her, straight, unalloyed, from her heart, influenced her now. She put her hand on his arm.

As she did so they both heard, quite clearly through the slashing and angry rain, a rap on the window. Her hand tightened on his arm and they turned. The rap came again, urgent, imperative. They stared and at first could see nothing. In any case there would have been only a pale, fading light, but now with the storm all was darkness. Reuben hurried to the window and pressing his face against the pane stared out. He could see a shadowy form.

'There is someone there,' he whispered to Judith, then, hurrying through the little passage, opened the outer door. The wind almost blew the door to, but holding it firmly he looked out.

'Who's there?' he called softly.

A moment later his fingers were grasped by a cold hand, he had been drawn back into the passage, a figure soaking with wet was pressed close to him, and his brother Humphrey's voice was in his ear, nay, at his very heart.

'Reuben . . . for God's sake – no sound . . .'

'Humphrey!'

'Yes. Is there anyone there?'

'Only Judith.'

But Judith, hearing the whispering voices, had come into the passage. Humphrey, pushing past them, had peered into the little room, seen that there was no one there, hastened to the door and bolted it, then turned to them both:

'No one must know. Not Father nor Mother. No one. Get me something to eat. Oh, God, I am so weary!'

He sank into the only chair in the room, murmuring again, 'Food. Food, and secretly.'

Reuben didn't question. It was, as it always was with his brother, as though this were part of himself, soaked with rain, fugitive, in some frantic plight, hiding from the world. He moved as though hurrying to save himself, undid the bolt and was gone.

Judith bolted the door again. Her heart was moved at once to eager pity and a desire to help. When she had last seen Humphrey he had been so young, so handsome, so self-confident, so sure of himself and his ability to manage any situation in life; now another man was there, utterly weary, exhausted, his head back, the water dripping from the capes of his coat, his hair long and matted, his face pale, haggard, and his eyes that had been so gay and happy now restless, hunted, brimming with despair.

He seemed to her to be years older, older than himself, older than Reuben, and he seemed, beyond that, to be mysterious, a man from some world that she had never before realized, a man who should, by right, speak to her in a strange language.

He wasted no time, did not ask her why she was there, did not consider her except as an agent of assistance for him.

'I have been an age outside. I could not see clearly who was in the room. I had to risk something. Thank God, it was Reuben!'

His words came in gasps. His hands moved ceaselessly.

'I've had no food for two days. I have tramped from Kendal . . .'

She was intensely practical, as she always was in a crisis. 'You must take off your coat. It is dripping. You must have dry things.'

He got up from the chair and she helped him to take off the shabby soiled riding coat. His body was trembling; he was wet through to the skin. The thing that moved her most was that his eyes were never still, searching the globe, the powder-stand, the dull green portrait of some old Sunwood ancestor, the dark bulging window against whose panes the rain, falling now gently, pressed.

She did not stop to ask him why he was there, nor what catastrophe had plunged him into this disaster, but his fear infected her. She was not in the least afraid, but she listened, as he did, to any outside sound. She realized that whatever else happened his mother must not now see him. She did not know the reason, but she understood that he was bitterly ashamed to see his mother, that, beyond any other possible disaster, that was the one he dreaded.

Her sense of this made him still more mysterious to her and touched her heart yet more deeply. Towards anyone pursued she was always to be sympathetic, although there was some true Herries in her that placed her also on the side of justice. In herself she was to be always both pursued and pursuer.

Reuben scratched on the door and came in, not clumsy nor shy any more, but swift, silent, efficient. He was acting for the stronger part of himself. He closed the door very gently behind him, bolted it softly. He had half a cold mutton pie, bread, cheese, ale.

Humphrey drew to the little table, devoured the food frantically. He seemed just then like an animal, his ears pricked, his eyes everywhere, his hand curved close about the meat.

'Mother is with Father,' Reuben whispered, 'listening to his sermon.'

'He is wet to the skin,' Judith answered. 'He must change everything.'

Reuben went out again. She stood by the door, letting him finish his food. Life was like this. She had seen it already countless times. Mrs Osmaston's maid had stolen stockings, had fled and been caught in Keswick, jailed there; a pedlar had murdered a woman in Keswick for a shilling, he had been chased by a crowd of men and boys to Threlkeld and stoned there to death . . .

'Yes,' said Humphrey, speaking quite clearly out of the half-light illumined only by one blowing candle. 'And now I must get to the coast. I am so weary. God, if I could sleep for twelve hours.'

'What is it?' she asked. 'What has happened?'

His face, pale, drawn, the hair shaggy on his forehead, looked up at her. She felt as though he were her child.

'I killed a man in London. Over cards.'

'Have you any money?' she asked him.

'Nothing – now. It is all gone.'

She came over to him and stroked his hair back from his forehead. With a gesture of infinite weariness he leaned his head, wet with rain as it was, back against her childish breast.

'I shall sleep,' he murmured. 'How soft your hand is!'

Reuben knocked; she unbolted the door. He came in with clothes on his arm. At once, as though a desperate hurry were now his accustomed state, Humphrey jumped up and stripped. Judith helped him. This was no time for maidenly modesty, and she had seen many a man naked before.

When he was finished he sat there holding Reuben's hand in his. The three of them began a quick whispered conversation. On the one thing he was determined, that his father and mother shouldn't know. Nothing would shake him in that. He told them very little of what had happened. Things had been going badly for a long while. Some fierce love-affair he had had with Nancy Bone: Pomfret had forbidden him the house. After that Judith had a picture of some dark underground London, gutters running with water, sudden flares of light, gambling, little rooms in crooked inns, life by the river, curious interludes of some great man like Mr Fox or Mr Burke, a struggle up again to larger rooms, then down again, fights in that same gutter, swinging shop-signs, a narrow street crowded with carriages, a woman looking from a window, a fight, some fat man with a wound in his breast, and all the while it seemed to be rain and fog ... She was to have this queer picture of London for years until the reality gave her another one.

But the one thing that stood out clearly was that he must escape from England. Some port ... Whitehaven ... It was then that she had her idea. With a flash of inspiration she thought of Georges Paris. She had long known that young Georges with other friends of Gauntry's had dealings with some sort of traffic on the Cumberland coast. Some kind of smuggling perhaps. She had been too much of a child for them to take her into any kind of confidence, but her last time at Stone Ends there had been a Captain Barnett, a thin green-faced man like a nettle, who had praised young Georges for his enterprise in some Whitehaven or St Bees expedition.

She did not doubt but that that was what brought Georges into Cockermouth this afternoon. He would do anything for her; he should help to get Humphrey out of the country. Once again in a moment she took the situation into her hands. She acknowledged without a tremor to Reuben that it had been this Georges Paris whom she had been going to meet. Was he to be trusted? Of course he was to be trusted. He was her friend. She had known him for years. He would do anything that she told him. They followed her. What else? Something had to be done at once. They must not stay in this house. There was no other plan.

Only Reuben said one thing that often afterwards she was to remember: 'If he does this for you, are you under some obligation to him?'

Feverishly eager to be off, as she always was when she had a plan, she tossed her head. She did not even answer, but almost pushed them both in front of her, through the little passage and out of the door.

That brief journey from the house to the 'Greyhound' was the most exciting thing that had yet happened in her life. She was in charge of the expedition; the men followed meekly. That sense of power, the strongest sense in her, drove her like a charm. Without her, Humphrey, all of them, would have been lost. Now she would direct the affair like God Himself. The rain had ceased; the little cobbled streets were gloomy and deserted. They left Humphrey in the shadow of the yard of the inn and went quickly up the wooden staircase to the parlour. No one was about. In the parlour, a small panelled room, a little sea-coal fire was smoking and two candles guttering. Someone came forward. It was Georges, almost hidden in the capes of his riding-coat. She saw at once that he was angry because she was not alone. She felt herself forty years of age at least as she took his hand, introduced Reuben. He had never seen her so beautiful. Indeed he had never thought her beautiful, only strange, un-usual, in some antagonistic way appealing to his senses. Now, in the half-lit smoky room, in all her colour, her small hat with a feather, her hair, her little face ivory-coloured and in expression mischievous, kindly, proud, all together, she seemed to him for the first time a woman. He put his riding whip on the table, clasped his hands behind him. He longed to kiss her. Who was this big clumsy oaf of a fellow with her?

Very quickly Judith explained, keeping him greatly at a distance, very lofty, commanding rather than requesting.

And she saw, a moment later, that he found an opportunity in all this. It was the first real request that she had ever made of him. He asked no questions about Humphrey. A relation of hers in distress ... He must get to sea swiftly and quietly ... Had he a friend? ... Was there a boat? ...

By chance he had a friend. He paused and looked at her oddly.

'If I do this for you—?' he broke off. They had both, con-cerned in their own personal drama, quite forgotten Reuben.

He forced her eyes. She would not be brow-beaten by him, so stared proudly back at him, at his dark eyes, black hair, thin, proud, restless face.

She said nothing. He, as though satisfied, nodded his head.

'Where is the gentleman?'

They passed to the staircase. As they went down she whis-pered to Reuben: 'Have you any money?' He nodded his head: 'I had thought of that.'

They had found Humphrey in a panic of nervous anxiety. How strange it was to Judith to see what circumstances could do to a man! He had been so easy, gay-hearted, confident. Her whole being ached for him. She would have liked to go with him, share his adventure wherever it might be, see that he was not cold, hungry, lonely. As they hurried down a dark side street, stumbling over gutters, holes in the road, refuse, she put out a hand and caught his. For a moment she held it, hot, dry, quivering ...

They stopped before a door below the pavement; a little flight

of steps went down to it. Georges went ahead of them and
knocked. While they waited, a man, swinging a lantern, passed
them. He did not look at them, but Judith felt as though it were
the whole town staring. Then the door opened a little way, a
head peered out, some words were exchanged. They all went in.
The place was a large cellar, a lantern hanging from a hook,
some farming implements in corners, a pile of hay, and, seated
on an overturned barrel, a man of an enormous corpulency. His
coat was open at the neck to allow room for his three chins. His
cheeks were purple above a yellow beard and his nose had been
slightly flattened on one side in some fight, but his eyes were
large, clear and merry. His hand was a roll of beef and his
thighs so huge that it was a wonder any breeches could ever
contain them. He rose to receive them, and standing, his legs
wide, he was like a vast amiable monster at home in its cavern.
He smelt of oil, fish and whisky, but it was plain that he admired
Judith immediately, hanging over her with a merry possessive
look as though at any moment he would pick her up and slip
her into his deep coat pocket.

It was clear also that he knew young Georges Paris very well
and understood immediately what was wanted. He never looked
at Humphrey, who had slipped into the shadow, nor addressed
a word to him. His name, it seemed, was Captain Wix. His voice
was deep, rolling, and had the same kindliness as his eyes. Those
eyes scarcely left Judith. Straddling on his legs he kept looking
at her while Georges quickly whispered. He nodded his head
several times, took a great chequered handkerchief from his
pocket and blew a blast on his nose.

'It will be good enough for charges,' he rumbled to Georges.

Judith who was adoring this adventure, the dark close cellar,
the straw, the swinging lantern, and the sense of having arranged
the whole affair, spoke then and said that they had money with
them.

'Keep it, lady,' growled Captain Wix. 'Tis no matter.' He
became gallant and was inexpressibly comical. 'I have a ship,'
he informed her, 'like a daisy. An' you come for a trip in her
you shall be as safe and trim as in your mama's parlour. I'll
have the cabin done up special for you.' He bent towards her,
beamed at her with the greatest kindliness: 'Now what do you
say to a piece of fine lace? A present from a friend who knows
the coast of France like his own hand. What do you say now to a
little trip?'

But here Georges intervened. He drew the gigantic creature

aside, speaking to him very seriously rather as a king speaks to his subject. The matter, it seemed, was concluded. They were to leave Humphrey in Captain Wix's charge.

Reuben went to his brother. When he rejoined them there were tears on his cheeks. Judith then kissed Humphrey.

He spoke with sudden desperation. 'My mother mustn't know . . . I will beat them yet . . .' Then fiercely, catching her hand: 'There's no God . . . Naught but injustice, no mercy . . . I shall find my way yet.'

Captain Wix kissed her hand.

When she went up the little steps again with Georges she felt suddenly helpless, very tired, six years old, and so cross with him that she did not thank him, only said 'Good night' quickly and walked up the street.

Georges, before he went downstairs again, looked after her, smiling. He felt very important, very wise, a ruler of men.

DEATH OF DAVID

THE JULY HEAT bathed the little town in its ardour, but breezes, stealing from the Lake, from the higher woods, from Skiddaw forest and Blencathra shallows, carried the scent of flowers everywhere. The town slept. Some sheep wandered dreamily down Main Street, the dust blew in little spirals between the hedges toward Crosthwaite Church, the post-chaise waited outside the 'Royal Oak', two young men, with nothing whatever to do, lounged up against the wall of Mr Crosthwaite's Museum. A little way up the street a small group waited for the arrival of the Good Intent post-coach from Kendal. It was five minutes past four of the afternoon, and nine out of every ten of Keswick's citizens were still discussing their good liquor and digesting the day's dinner.

Francis Herries came down the sunny street, riding from Penrith. He was, in this July of 1789, twenty-nine years of age and as handsome a bachelor as the counties of Cumberland and Westmorland contained. He was, however, as awe-inspiring as handsome. No young lady anywhere, not even the pretty daughters of Mrs Herring of Bassenthwaite, reputed the most daring young women in the whole of the North of England, had ever attempted a flirtation. He was immensely clever, they said, was for ever reading. It was true in any case that he had no close friend – now, riding down Main Street, he seemed alone with his own shadow.

He may have been half asleep, may have been deeply lost in some speculation, when he felt a hand laid on his bridle. He looked down and saw little Mr Summerson the Surgeon, short, stout, very gay in a purple coat, looking up at him.

'Have you heard the news, Mr Herries?' he asked.

'No,' answered Francis. 'What news?'

'The Bastille in Paris has fallen.'

Francis straightened himself. 'The Bastille?—'

'Yes, sir. Fallen to the Revolutionaries. I know no more. I had it from Mr Jobling, who has just ridden in from Kendal. The news is quite certain.'

Francis smiled. 'Thank God, sir. Thank God. This means a new world.'

Little Mr Summerson looked as though he were not so sure, but Francis did not wait to hear what he had to say. His heart triumphant, as though it were by his own agency that this great deed had been brought about, he passed along the road to Bassenthwaite now like a conqueror.

The Bastille fallen! The Bastille fallen! It must be true. Summerson had been certain of it, and if it were indeed so, then all the secret wishes of his heart were gratified. Secret indeed, for there had been no one in whom he could confide. The secret history of his mind had been born with him perhaps; he had always, to his own thinking, been different from all the others, but its first real mature food had been the treatise of Helvétius on 'Mind' and 'The System of Nature' of Holbach. Holbach's work especially had seemed to explain the whole of life to him; its system of metaphysics had exactly suited his speculative untrusting nature, his instinctive cynicism, and its eloquent ardour for physical science had become his ardour also.

Voltaire's scepticism and good sense, the absence of all fanaticism and mysticism had carried him yet further. He delighted in his clear ideas, his ironical banter, and his determination to make the world a wiser place so that ultimately it might become a better one.

His education had then been completed by the influence of Rousseau. The *Contrat Social* seemed to him the Bible of the new world. This sentence of Rousseau's, 'The moment the Government usurps the sovereignty, the social compact is broken, and all the simple citizens regaining by right their natural liberty are forced, but not morally obliged, to obey' became his gospel.

Had his youth been spent in a larger and more varied society much of the effects of these doctrines might have been worn away in contact with older and more experienced minds. But there had been few with whom he could discuss anything. His nature was in any case reserved; some inherent shyness forbade confidences; his father had views utterly divorced from these; his father was conservative absolutely in religion, politics, agriculture, everything. Will's mind was quite selfish and practical, his mother was not interested in ideas. Judith was only a child.

He made no friends among the gentlemen of the neighbourhood; there were very few gentlemen to make friends with. He knew that had any of them seen into his mind they would have regarded him as traitor to everything in which they believed.

At Penrith there was a certain Mr Frederick Moore, an elderly man, a retired Army officer, who thought as he did, but went much further. Mr Moore was, indeed, a fanatic, and in that displeased the reasonableness of Francis' mind, a strange man, solitary, embittered, intensely dogmatic. But he lent Francis books and pamphlets, and they had many talks together.

Rousseau was Mr Moore's god, and he very quickly became Francis' also. They would neither of them see that Rousseau himself recoiled from many of his own opinions and conclusions. Passionately they out-Rousseaued Rousseau. They disregarded such sentences as: 'If there were a people of gods, they would govern themselves as a democracy. So perfect a form of government is not suited for men' and 'The best and most natural order is, that the wise should govern the multitude, provided that one is sure that they govern it for the profit of the multitude and not for their own'.

But Francis, although he thought continually about Government, had only the simplest notions of the matter. Had he been a fanatic like Mr Moore he would have gone further, but just as his nature held him back from extravagance so also it prevented inspiration. He felt that he was fortunate that he was born to be a citizen of a new world, but in cruel fact he was neither the child of the old world of reason nor of the new world of feeling. He had the misfortune to sympathize deeply with the unhappiness of a vast multitude of human beings, who were only now growing conscious of their rights, but he was an aristocrat by instinct although a democrat by reason – and was too reserved, too lonely,

too self-suspicious to venture into any kind of demonstrative
action.

He had followed, as well as news-sheets, pamphlets, books,
and Mr Moore permitted him, every movement in France –
the doctrines of the Economists, who contended for the in-
violability of private property, the shameful consequences of
the stupid despotism of Louis XV, the iniquitous taxes, the
brutalities of the upper class, the exemption of the nobles from
taxation, Necker's poor attempts at reform in 1780, the monstrous sale of offices, the increase of tyrannies that followed
Turgot's fall, Necker's failure in 1781, and after that the growing
incompetence of everybody and everything: the luxury and
ostentation of the Court of Versailles, the unpopularity of the
Queen, the amiable weakness of the King, the Assembly of
Notables by Calonne, their dissolution – until at last he had
felt that he was almost a personal witness of the most dramatic
of the recent events, the *coup d'état* of May of last year, the
convoking of the States-General by Brienne, the strength of the
Third Estate, the gradually rising tide of disorder, the flood of
revolutionary pamphlets, the bad harvest of '88, and the fearful
winter that succeeded it, the freezing of the Seine, the promin-
ence of Mirabeau and Sieyès, of Barnave and Dupont and Bailly,
the Oath of the Tennis Court on June 20th.

The Oath of the Tennis Court was the last absolute news
that he had had until today; for the last month he had been
living in a ferment of expectation and feverish excitement. He
could not understand that the men and women around him took
so slight an interest in these events. If they spoke of outside
affairs at all it was, at the most, in a late day, of the King's
sickness, the possibility of a Regency, some new gambling
scandal of Charles Fox or the eccentricities of Mr Pitt. The small
business of the countryside contented them all.

So he had moved, poor Francis, as though he carried a bomb
in his breast. There were times when he thought that he would
cross to France and take part in the great crisis that was developing there, but his self-distrust, his natural love of England and
his home (cherished passionately in his heart, unguessed at by
anyone save possibly Judith) held him where he was.

This great news today released him! The world was free!
The strongholds of all the tyrants had fallen! This was to be a
symbol that would stand to all the world for the new freedom!

These may seem empty phrases enough set down upon paper,
but in Francis' heart they were flames and torches. In very

truth, as he rode now under the July sun beside Bassenthwaite, he felt as though every constriction, every doubt of himself, every shyness and stupid caution were now released.

France would lead the way for all the world. He saw Louis with his fat good-natured face, Marie Antoinette with her gay beauty, seated grandly on their thrones by the will of their people. He could almost hear, beside these quiet sparkling waters, the wild cheers, the frantic shouts of joy that must fill the Paris streets. And now all men would hear them, and would be ashamed of their lethargy, their shameful lazy injustice and indifference.

He was indeed ashamed of himself. As he rode along he felt born again; his life had been most selfish. It should be so no longer. At any cost to himself he would take part now in forwarding the new justice and uprightness that was come into the world. As he rode he could have sung his happiness aloud.

He did not doubt but that his father, with all other men, would see the grandeur of this event. His father was a just man, although an obstinate. He loved his father dearly (who could help but love him?), although he was shy of him. How this new era in France would bring them together, would bring all men together and would lead to a new era in England also! As he turned up the lane to Fell House his eyes were dim with tears of joy.

And at once, so characteristically, he was checked by contact with his fellow human beings. A maid, coming from the dairy carrying buckets, Will's tutor seated reading on the lawn, his mother stepping down the staircase as he entered the house, all these drove him at once to silence.

His stout good-humoured sister met him at the turn of the stairs. He had nothing at all in common with Deborah. She had all the good-natured domesticity of a thoroughly contented Herries. So absolutely satisfied was she with herself, her family, all the little circumstances of her surroundings, that in all her twenty-six years she might be said never to have suffered an ache of a pain, whether of body or of soul. She was handsome in a large-boned Herries fashion, was never irritable, never excited, never curious about the nature of other people, always ready to do anything for anyone.

How ridiculous to say to her: 'Deb, the Bastille has fallen!' It would be to her exactly as though you had said: 'Deb, the cat has kittened!'

Having washed, brushed, changed his linen, he came downstairs

again, walked into the garden and discovered Judith mocking the tutor. Mr Langbridge was shortly leaving them. Will
was now nineteen and did not need a tutor. Mr Langbridge
was long, gaunt, perpetually hungry, brilliantly founded in the
classics (which was of no use at all to Will), hoping to be a
clergyman, of a fanatically serious mind. He understood no
sort of humour, and it delighted Judith to hold long conversations with him, asking him gravely about his health, his studies,
and his home in Dorset. For he detested the North, with its
dark clouds, its rain, the savagery of its people, its bare strong
hills. He was a perpetual exile. She stood in front of him now,
her hands behind her back, her eyes twinkling, but her expression very serious.

Francis, coming upon her, realized quite suddenly that she
was a woman. She was old for her fifteen years in her self-
possession, young in her childish impulses. He knew that she
adored him, just as she had always done; it had been a long
faithful service on her part for which he had made little return.
There was something about her small stature, pale face, and
almost savage unlikeness to the average Herries order that
frightened him, and yet he had long ago realized that she was
the only one in this family who ever remotely understood him.

He realized it again now, for as she turned to him he saw that
she immediately recognized him to be under the power of some
very strong excitement. Mr Langbridge pulled his long lanky
body together, rose, very solemnly bowed to Francis and stalked
away.

She looked at him, half roguishly, half with that affection
that she could never keep from her eyes when she was with anyone of whom she was fond.

'Dear Francis,' she said, dancing about the lawn on her very
small feet, 'you have got a secret. I can see that you have. And
none of the family is worthy of it.'

She turned towards the house and they both saw David,
followed by Will, coming towards them. The whole scene, the
rosy brick house with its chimneys and gables and pigeon-loft,
the dairy and stables behind it, the moor that was like a heaving
green curtain moved with the intensity of the sun, the blue sky
without cloud, the lawn so brilliant in colour that it hurt the
eye, the trimmed hedge, the Gothic temple, the sprawling
shadow of Skiddaw, the figures in their gay clothes, David in
purple, Judith in green, Francis in silver, this moment of heat
and colour would be remembered by all of them for ever.

David, carrying a riding whip, moved heavily.

'Well, Francis,' he said, 'what news in Penrith?'

'Great news, sir,' Francis answered.

'What! has Pitt a fresh plan for the franchise?' David asked with good-humoured scorn. All Francis' notions seemed to him those of a child. But it was a half-sneer on Will's superior face that drove Francis on.

'No, sir,' he answered. 'The Bastille has fallen to the People of Paris.'

They all stayed, rigid, transfixed. David said at last:

'Where did you have the news?'

'Mr Summerson told me in Keswick. He had it quite surely from Kendal.'

David raised his head and looked at everything, the buildings, the walls, the garden, as though assuring himself that they were all still there, safe and secure. Then he said slowly: 'If this is true it is terrible news.'

'I think,' Francis broke out, 'that it is the grandest news the world has ever had.'

Judith, who cared nothing for the fall of the Bastille in comparison with the immediate dangers of the scene, saw David's broad hand tremble about his riding whip.

'Then you advocate rebellion,' he said slowly, 'murder, revolution . . .'

'Yes,' Francis answered hotly, 'if these things are to bring justice back into the world.'

'Justice!' David's whole body trembled. 'Justice for the dirtiest mob of cut-throats that ever fouled a country. Justice for ingratitude, for disloyalty to a worthy King . . .' He half turned towards the house, then, his face swollen, it seemed, with anger, he came nearer to Francis. 'You are not my son if you find this foul rebellion glorious.'

'Then I am not your son,' Francis cried. 'I have long suspected it. For years I have watched your blindness to the way the world was going. For how much longer do you think a million men will suffer at the orders of one, and of one weaker, more selfish, more tyrannous than they could ever be? Thank God, men are to be free at last, free from tyrants, free . . .'

'From tyrants like myself?' David cried, his anger now quite uncontrollable. 'A fine thing for a son . . .'

'Take it as you will,' Francis answered, his words biting on the air. 'There is tyranny everywhere, here as well . . .'

Some long accumulation of small persistent differences,

always unsettled, mingling with the heat of the July day and their deep love, always checked, always running into perverse courses, combined to produce in them both a furious anger.

'By God, for less than that . . .' David cried.

'If your pride is hit,' Francis answered, 'it is by your own will. It is time that your eyes were opened.'

'I'll have no rebellion here,' David shouted. 'No rebellion here. Your gutter-friends may for the moment have their way in Paris. I am yet master in this house.'

'No more!' Francis cried. 'Many masters are falling.'

David raised his riding whip and struck Francis on the cheek. They were silent then, and the cooing of the pigeons ran like water through the air, the only sound. Francis bent his head. David dropped the whip.

'Francis,' he began in a thick low guttural, turned a step and fell, like a log, to the grass. He was carried in. It was a stroke. Mr Summerson the Surgeon was fetched from Keswick. David was bled. Consciousness returned to him, but he could not speak, and his left side was paralysed.

Francis went about the place with his head up, his features cold and severe, and agony in his heart. No one, except Judith, knew that he felt anything. His mother would not speak to him. That moment, running out on to the sunlit lawn at the sound of a cry, had changed Sarah Herries from a cheerful normal woman of her world into a creature of one impulse and one impulse only. Nothing now was alive for her in the world save David, her house meant nothing to her, her children meant nothing to her, she meant nothing at all to herself. She would not speak to Francis. She looked through him as though he were not there. She regarded none of them very intently. They were shadows to her. She seemed in one half-hour to become of a thinner, straighter figure; the colour left her cheeks, her eyes held a steely radiance, her voice a hard metallic ring. Something masculine that had been perhaps always in her personality came out now very queerly, save when she was in David's room; there she was soft, gentle, maternal. David had always been her child; now her love for him burnt with twice the earlier intensity because he was altogether dependent on her. He lay there, a huge bulk, beneath the clothes, only his eyes moving.

Judith watched all this with an acute perception, but in the first weeks her thoughts were all for Francis. She longed to tell him what she felt; at last she had her opportunity.

One evening, a cold wet August night drawing on, at the turn of the stairs on the upper passage beyond her room, she ran into him in the half dusk. His hands held her in the first shock of contact. She could feel how they trembled. And at once, deeply moved by that trembling, she began, not weighing her words nor thinking of anything but that she must comfort him:

'Don't go. Don't go. I have been wanting to speak to you for these weeks past. I know that you have always a little mocked at my affection for you – indeed I have mocked at it a little myself – but it gives me a right, after all these years, to tell you that I am the only one in all this house who understands you. Don't grieve about him, Francis dear. It was not your fault, indeed, indeed it was not. You had to say what you believed that day, and I know that he admired you for that behind his anger. The stroke must have come in any case – Mr Summerson says so. And his heart, too, has been weak these years past. So soon as he is better he will send for you and tell you that he loves you—'

'My mother will not allow me to see him,' Francis interrupted her.

'She cannot prevent you if he wishes it. As soon as he can speak he will ask for you. I know that now he is sorry and is grieving for you.'

His voice shook. 'No, I must go and never return. I have been a curse to this place. Only I can't go without a word from him. I am waiting only for that—'

'Yes. He is better today. Mr Summerson thinks that in a week or so he will be able to speak a little. The paralysis is only on one side.'

They were in the dark together; neither could clearly see the face of the other, but Judith knew that Francis was crying. Half a child, she was greatly inclined to cry, but she only stood close to him, her hand on his arm.

'You have always been the best friend I have had here,' he said at last.

'And I will be,' she answered.

Afterwards she could not but reflect that she was always better with anyone who was in distress or desired her help. She liked above everything to feel that she was needed, and yet she had a strong contempt for any weak-willed person who was for ever relying on others. What she liked was to assist or direct those who normally were quite able to assist themselves. What she would have done now to have helped Sarah had Sarah

but invited her! But Sarah needed no one's help, and least
of all Judith's. She allowed Deborah to do things for her, and
very remarkably Deborah began to develop under this crisis,
but Judith she completely disregarded.

This, again, was why Judith had no sort of contact with Will.
Will relied on no one but himself and took no one into his
confidences. He gave the impression that he was watching every
move, every phase of the situation, weighing it all that he might
turn it in the best way to his advantage.

The house very quickly suited itself to the new circumstances.
Everything turned now around the room where David was lying.
He had been always greatly popular with his servants; unlike
many men of his time he had always seen them as separate
individuals, was constantly inquiring about their families and
circumstances, had a jolly, natural, healthy interest in all of
them. He had been the one of the family for whom they cared,
who stabilized their loyalty. His simple animal health and boyish
pleasure in little things had always pleased them. He had been
an indulgent but not a foolish master; they were very sorry now
for his misfortune.

David rose with infinite slowness and caution from a sea of
darkness. Wearily he pushed aside fold after fold of heavy clinging cloth that hindered his sight. Then, tired out, he lay back
to resist no longer, and saw swaying above his head a gold
rose set in a green cloud. He heard, a little after, from an infinite distance a voice speaking to him. Someone touched him,
and he sank instantly back into the dark sea whose waters,
smooth like oil, lapped him round and lay upon his eyes and
mouth. Aeons later he saw again the gold rose on the green
ground, and once again heard the voice, and knew that it was
Sarah his wife who was speaking to him.

He raised very slowly his right hand and touched the chill
flesh of his breast beneath his shirt. Then he would raise his
other hand, but he had no other hand. His perceptions moved
with infinite slowness. After, as it seemed to him, a lifetime of
patient watching he realized that the gold rose was fixed in
its place above his head, and that there were other gold roses.
Then, after another infinity of time, he knew that these
gold roses belonged to the tester of the bed in which he was
lying.

His wife's voice was often in his ear. She made a noise like a
bird, like a mouse; the noise came and went and came again.
He was immensely susceptible to light. A wave of light would

slowly sway in front of him, would be withdrawn and then return with greater intensity.

There came a time when he wished to speak about this light but he could not. He could speak no more than a dead man. But he was not dead at all. An urgent pulsing life began to beat within him. This life was connected with nothing that he saw or heard. It had a wild riotous time of its own within him: it laughed, it sang, it wept, it sighed, but it was imprisoned, and it longed to get out. His eyes began to take everything in – the room with the purple curtains, the piece of green tapestry, the crooked legs of the chairs, Sarah, Deborah, the maid, once and again Will. He saw and recognized them all, but he could not speak, nor had they anything to do with the wild life inside him. When he knew this he pitied himself and them; tears, helpless tears, rolled down his cheeks, and his wife wiped them away.

He knew now all the things that they did to him – the things the surgeon did, how it was when they turned him in bed (he was a very heavy man and it was not easy), and when they put a new shirt on him, washed his face. Sarah kissed him, and he touched her cheek with his right hand.

He was never by himself. At night candles were burning, and Sarah sat there, sometimes sewing, sometimes reading a book, her eyes continually going to meet his eyes. He was ashamed at some of the things she must do for him, but she was his wife, he had lain with her in his arms; he would lie there staring at the gold roses and think of how often he had buried his hands in her hair.

He was glad that she was always there, because he was lost in that wild turbulent life within himself, and she was all that there was to call him back. Then one night he was far away. He was standing on a deserted beach beside a lonely sea. Someone was beside him, a man, and quite suddenly this man raised a stick to strike him. He seized this stick, broke it in half and flung it into the sea. After that this man never left him. He was very tall, thin of face, and he had a scar that ran from eye to lip. The man stood beside him on a green lawn, and this time it was he who had the whip; he raised his hand and struck; as he did so the man changed. He was young, and after he was struck he bent his head.

David lay there for a long while striving to reconcile these two figures. They were the same and were not the same. At one time they seemed to be himself; then they were separate, then together again.

One grey ghostly morning he awoke and knew everything. The man who had wished to strike him was his father; the man whom he had struck was his son. He knew everything. He had been ill, and was lying now in his bed, while beyond the window a bird sang, and near him the candles were almost burnt out, and Sarah sat in a high chair, her head forward, asleep. He passed then, struggling all alone, hours of terrible agony. His left side was dead; there was no feeling nor motion in it. His heart bled for his son. He could think of nothing but that. He must see his son. He must see his son. He raised his right arm: he tried to shout and to shout again. No sound would come. His father and his son. He must ask them both to forgive him; until he had done that there was no peace for him.

At last the door opened; someone came in, carrying something. Sarah woke and came to the bedside. His eyes besought her. He raised his hand. His agony of mind was terrible, for he could not reach her. How strange that he could not reach her! After all these years together, their love, their intercourse, their friendship. She was the mother of his children, and he could not reach her. Strange low mutterings came from his mouth. His eyes implored her, begged of her.

The light, grey, webbed, hung like a film about the room, and in this film she moved. At length she bent down to kiss him, and as she did so, his eyes were so near to hers that she must have seen the agony in them. He made sounds that seemed to him explicit prayers, but she could understand nothing.

It was three hours later that the surgeon understood sufficiently to send for a paper. Then David wrote in a large sprawling hand the word 'Francis'. Francis came. They were alone in the room together, and David spoke the first word since his illness. 'Forgive.' His voice was strange, cracked, with a slur in it, but Francis understood and knelt beside the bed. David, with his trembling right hand, stroked his hair.

After that he could not bear to have Francis out of the room, so that the two of them, Francis and Sarah, were there together. But Sarah would not speak to her son nor look at him if she could help it. David began then the slow business of seeing that two and two make four. There were some things that he could not understand at all. He did not know why he had struck his son with a whip, nor why he was sometimes there quite clearly in the room with his wife beside him and at other times he was in the little dark house in Borrowdale, following his father, hearing his father's voice, and behind the voice the wind rustling the tapestry, and the noise of water falling down the rock.

He slept a great deal, and in his dreams he climbed the rocks, ran across the springing turf of the Fell, stood on the Pass with Sarah in his arms, watching his enemy climb the road towards him.

At times again he would be dreadfully unhappy. Tears would roll down his cheeks; he would wipe them feebly with his hand. But why he was so unhappy he could not tell.

But at these times an infinite pity for himself overwhelmed him. 'Poor David. Poor, poor David. Poor, poor David.' Was there ever anything so sad as poor David – and, from a great distance away, he watched this poor David and sympathized so deeply with his loneliness, his helplessness, the injustice of his state.

After a time words came back to him. He could say 'Francis. Sarah. I don't want. Goodnight.' He mumbled them; his mouth was twisted.

His brain conceived a new map of the world for him. There was the room where he lay. Pieces of furniture became alive and personal to him. A china table, a tea-kettle stand, chairs with faces. He liked especially a ribband-back chair covered with red morocco, a real friend of his, that would smile and wave his leg at him. The tapestry on the wall, its subject Susanna and the Elders, was also his friend. He liked Susanna's kindly breasts and her shining thighs. He was glad that he had not allowed Sarah to make the house in the Gothic style, as she had once planned to do, after Horace Walpole or some other London absurdity. He had an honest scorn for artists and writers. She had wanted a wallpaper printed in perspective, windows with saints in painted glass, and even arrows, long-bows and spears.

Poor Sarah! What a good woman, how wonderful a wife she was to him! He liked her to sit beside the bed and be near to him. He would smile a crooked twisted smile and murmur her name. Yes, all this was real enough. Summerson with his hour-glass, the basins and glasses, old Ballard the manservant with his handsome white wig, Will, Judith, and, above all, Francis. Deborah too, good girl. She had a genius for moving quietly, big woman though she was: no hand so soft as hers, and – best of all – she breathed good-humour. He wanted no sad faces about him; in Sarah's eyes he detected sometimes a look of terror and that he would not have because it made himself afraid . . .

Yes, all this was real enough. But beyond the room he could not be sure where he was. The landscape was the landscape of

his young life, and although in this room he was tied to the
heavy four-poster, once he was outside the room he could move
where he wished. Every part of Borrowdale was open to him.
All the old places: beloved Stonethwaite, with its tumbling
stream, the springing turf of Stake Pass, the swinging birds above
Honister, hundreds more; the wrestling bouts, the high room
of old Peel's with its blazing fire and broad rafters, the taste
of the dried salted beef and mutton, the oatmeal puddings, the
bull-ring in Keswick, when on a grand day in the market place
you must sit on an adjoining roof to get a view, the shearing days
with the chairing and the bell-ringing, Twelfth Night when the
lighted holly tree was carried from inn to inn – all had departed
from him so long, long ago, killed by the later modern times, but
now he was back in them again, all his health and vigour were
returned, he was the strongest man in all the valley, and every
hill knew him, Glaramara smiled on him, Eagle Crag was his
brother, Sprinkling Tarn his sister, Sea Fell his lover . . .

He lay there, motionless, smiling, his blue eyes fixed on the
gold rose. They thought that he was imprisoned there, a helpless
hulk. Little they knew! He was free again, as he had not been
for many a year.

His father now accompanied him everywhere. His father
digging that intractable ground, riding with him to Ravenglass,
sitting beside him at the old stone fireplace in Herries, his hand
on his thigh, his father and Mirabell, his father and Deborah,
his father who had been always closer to him than any other
human being.

They wished to pull him back from this happiness, this freedom, this strength of body, and cold running air of the fells,
smell of the bracken, sound never stilled of running water. The
sheep moved, the sun glistening on their fleecy sides, the shepherd whistled to his dog, the clouds rushed out and covered the
sun that yet escaped them, mocking them and flashing a shield
of light upon the distant brow . . .

'Hold on to me, Father. They are dragging me back. I will
catch your arm. They shall not separate us . . .'

It was time for him to be washed, to be turned in his bed.
The smell of the sick-room was there, the chair with the red
morocco, Susanna with her breasts, Sarah's grave face and that
look of terror in the eyes. Only Francis and Judith knew his
father. That child with her pale face and red hair, hair like
Mirabell's. Poor Mirabell . . . but no, she was not to be pitied,
for she loved his father at the last . . .

His mouth crookedly formed the word 'Judith'. She came to the bedside, not frightened like Sarah, smiling, standing on her toes to be level with the bed. He took her hand in his. It lay there warm and soft.

'Judith.' That was the last word that he spoke.

For he was swung away in a great torrent of light. He flew on the air, kicking his limbs free, his head up, his hair tugged at by the wind. Away and away, over Borrowdale and Stonethwaite, over Sea Fell and the Langdales, over Waswater, black like ebony . . . What freedom, what happiness!

He shouted; 'Oh, hoi! Oh, hoi! Oh, hoi!' He came swinging down until the turf sprang beneath his feet. He was leader in an immortal chase. 'Oh, hoi! Oh, hoi! Away! Away!' The scent of the bracken and the falling leaf, the touch of the stone of the little running walls! He had caught a cloud and swung into the dazzling sun. Old Herries was at his side, the moulded shoulders of the Tops were beneath his hand, the ruffled water of the Lakes spun to the swirl of his great strength.

'Follow! Follow! Away, away!'

His father and he, masters of the air, friends of every hill, laughing with every twist of tarn and river, raced towards the sun . . .

Watching the bed, they saw his body lie motionless: the eyes stared.

Sarah's scream brought Deborah running into the room.

QUARREL AND FLIGHT

JUDITH AWOKE TO a sudden consciousness of distress. She had been very happily asleep curled up in the corner of the settee with the green Chinese dragons. These dragons had pursued her very pleasantly in her dream, large amiable creatures with green scales; from their bodies flakes detached themselves (as they ambled along) and lay like green pennies on the hot dry sand.

It was so hot, this sandy country, that she woke with a start to find the warm spring sun shining in through the window on to her face. She looked about her, bewildered, on to the Sheffield-plated candlesticks and the blue and white china in the corner cupboard. With the final release from her dream she pushed a large, fat, beery, and most affectionate dragon away from her and sat up, listening. What she heard was Sarah, in the room across the hall, talking to herself.

Sarah was not talking to herself, she was talking to David. Judith knew exactly how it was; Sarah was walking quietly up and down the room and was begging David to return, was telling David that she could not endure life without him, was asking David how he could have left her.

These outbursts were becoming rarer with Sarah, but they were still constant enough to fill the house with uneasiness. She had been for years the happiest, most normal of women. One man's death had changed her from that into this suffering remote figure, who was battling, who had been battling for months, to recover her security. Soon she would be armoured again safely against life, but the old Sarah was dead, vanished for ever, and happiness was, for the time, gone from that house.

It was part of Judith's character that she had no patience at all with nerves or hysteria. It was a period when women enjoyed and fostered all the artificialities that might give them an important place in a world designed entirely for men. 'Vapours' were the order of the day for the majority of God's females. If they could not rouse attention by one manoeuvre they would rouse it by another.

Judith had never had the 'vapours' nor would she ever have them. Nevertheless, she was near sixteen, and had the understanding, in many things, of a grown woman. Her education in life had been, thanks to Tom Gauntry and his friends, early and thorough. She realized that this was no nonsense nor affectation on Sarah's part. David's death had simply taken away from her all the ground on which for years she had been standing. She was fighting to regain her sure footing; she would regain it. Meanwhile she would allow no one to help her.

Now, as Judith listened to that murmuring voice, she longed to go and help her. She knew, if she did go, the kind of treatment that she would receive. The only person in the world who could assist her now crossed the hall and went in to her. Deborah's soft comforting voice could be heard. A little later the two women passed out into the garden together.

It was one of Judith's deepest chagrins that in all this crisis she had been of no use at all. It was Deborah, of all people, who had saved the situation, stout dull Deborah who was suddenly the principal figure in the house, was kind and tactful with everyone, managed the servants, entertained the local gentry, kept the accounts, prevented Will (when at home) and Francis from open quarrel and understood Judith, it seemed, better than anyone had ever done. This had been that quiet woman's chance and she had seized it.

In the year that followed David's death the situation had demanded exactly such a woman as Deborah. She had always seemed slow, unobservant, uninterested; now it was apparent that she observed much and was never uninterested. She was greatly assisted by limiting her horizon to her own affairs. That France was in revolution, that her mother was in hysteria, these were not her business. She had loved her father as well, possibly, as any of them, but her father was dead, life must go on, the cows must be milked, intercourse with neighbours resumed. She quietly assumed direction of the house.

Had Will been there her domination might not have so quickly succeeded, but Will was in Liverpool, forming new contracts with Mr Metcalfe. Francis also was away for days at a time. The house became the abode of the three women, and had it not been for Deborah, catastrophe would have rent it from attic to cellar. For Sarah, in the strange unnatural world that she now inhabited, had a fierce and unresting grudge against Judith. Judith's name had been the last word on David's lips, it was into Judith's eyes that David had looked before he turned his head on the pillow and passed. Judith was to Sarah still the strange unaccountable child that she had been ten years ago. At that time a girl of sixteen was often a mature woman, but Judith was for Sarah still a rebellious intriguing child, born of a gipsy. These things are mysteries, but beyond question there mingled now in Sarah's feelings about Judith something of her old uneasiness with Mirabell. Mirabell, Judith's mother, had never liked her, had indeed refused her kindliness and friendliness. Here was Mirabell born again.

But Judith was not Mirabell; she was fiercer, more readily hostile and resentful, far more dominating. She would not let Sarah hate her without making some return for it. It was not her fault that David had said her name before he died. If anyone wished to make a friend of her she was ready, but she was ready – oh, exceedingly ready – for anyone who wanted her as enemy.

Deborah disregarded all this. She was loving to Sarah, loving to Judith, loving to Francis, to whom even now, after these many months, his mother would not speak. Deborah took the situation and kept it, for the moment, safe. She could not keep it safe for long – it was charged with violence and danger – but

what she could do she did. She indulged also her own fancy.
Her fancy was, and had always been, for social amenities. She
loved tea-drinkings, card parties, evenings, when some neighbour 'put up' four or six couples for a dance, expeditions of a
moderate kind to some interesting site or historic building, and,
above all, the chatter that circled around love-affairs and interesting engagements.

She had now entirely her own way in this, for Sarah was
living altogether in her own world. When a decent interval had
passed since David's death, neighbours came and went at
Uldale with an easy frequency unknown for some time past.
There were the Redlands of Thornthwaite, the Darlingtons
from Whelpo, the Berrys of Roseley, the Carringtons of Forest
Hall. It was suddenly a woman's world, and a world that seemed
to Judith ridiculous in its obsession with trifles and incredible
in its indifference to all outside events.

Deborah's principal friends were the Redlands of Thornthwaite – Squire Redland, his stout pleasant wife, and the two
handsome Miss Redlands – and the two Miss Berrys of Roseley.
The elder Miss Berry was the great gossip of the district. She
found everything amusing and left everything scandalous. The
Miss Redlands, dark, big-boned, handsome women, were the
flirts of the district. Their thought was only of men. Mrs Redland had a genius for the arrangement, in other people's houses,
of teas and suppers, parties at cards and little musical occasions.

Hours – and for Deborah most enchanting hours – would be
spent in the discussion of social combinations and permutations.
Mrs Redland had the talent of making any house in which she
happened to be visiting appear instantly as her own. She was
massive, enjoyed bright colours and had a laugh like a trooper.
She would arrange herself on the settee with the green dragons
and instantly begin:

'But, my dear Miss Berry, we must not be too nice. Invite
them all. Why not? They are a standing example of good humour and amiable intention, and I am sure Mr Frank Fuller,
although he may be the oddest creature in the world, is a
gentleman, which cannot be said for Mr Beaton, who has a
store of underbred finery quite amazing.'

And little Miss Berry, with her sniff that suggested an eternal
cold, would observe:

'Mr Beaton is a coxcomb as everyone knows. But there is
nothing to be ashamed of in being a coxcomb. What he enjoys
the most is an evening of noisy entertainment, and for my part

there are times when noisy entertainment is the thing. Ask Mr Beaton by all means. That will make six couples exactly.'

'And this time,' Mrs Redland would say, looking about her, 'we will make the dining-room of use by shifting the pianoforte. Last time there was not room for anyone to have real enjoyment.'

And Judith, listening, would wonder that Deborah had the patience to submit to these ladies who ordered the house as their own. But, indeed, she herself was not at all popular with them. They wondered why this sulky sarcastic girl was there. Was she 'out' or was she not 'out'? Was it true that she was the love-child of some peasant courted in the ditch by that old ruffian of a Herries, who had died in a hut in Borrowdale?

David was only a year dead, and they were dancing in his house. But if Sarah made no objection to it had anyone else a right? Sarah's face was now a mask. She sat in her upstairs room, looking from her window. There were some days when no one came to the house at all, and then, so eerie was the silence, so threatening the atmosphere, that Judith understood why Deborah encouraged her sociabilities.

But with every week the inevitable crisis drew nearer. Francis was absent during all that summer. Will came and went, but in November, two days after Judith's sixteenth birthday, Francis returned – and life was permanently changed for them all for ever after.

His return was innocent and quiet enough. There was a storm of rain. Skiddaw was hid in purple shadow and over its head an ebony lake of cloud hung like a reflection. Beyond it, towards the sea, faint strips of blue sky showed that it was but a shower. The rain fell like thunder. Mrs Redland and one of her daughters, the two Miss Berrys, Deborah and Judith sat in the parlour and waited for the rain to pass. A dance – arranged entirely by Mrs Redland – was to take place in the following week at the Darlingtons'. The Darlingtons were lazy, but good-natured. They did not mind at all that Mrs Redland should consider their house as hers so long as she did all the work for them. She was now in high feather. All the invitations had been successful. There were to be eight couples.

Mrs Redland was pretending to be angry with Miss Berry's imitation of old Miss Clynes, whose teeth clicked in her head like castanets. 'For shame, Miss Berry, you shall not mimic her! And as to young Mr Clynes, he is perfectly satisfied with his sheep and his farm.'

'Yes,' cried Miss Berry in an ecstasy of enjoyment at her own

sense of fun and humour, 'and they say that coming in the dark
into the house one day he took his aunt for one of his sheep that
had been straying all the afternoon. "Shoo! Shoo! Shoo!" he
cried. And you know how the good lady, when she is but half
awake, baas for anyone who is close to her ... Well, well, I've
no doubt but the young man will make a match of it with Jane
Bastable. Poor thing. She missed the dancing master last year,
although she trudged into Keswick twice a week and oftener ...
"Baa, baa!", and it wasn't until the young man lit a candle that
he saw how things really were.'

Miss Berry's imitation was most lively, and they were all in a
roar of laughter over it when the door burst open and Francis
Herries, the capes of his riding coat dripping with water, stood
there, glared fiercely for a moment, and was gone.

Judith, who had been sitting by herself in the window
watching the black cloud above Skiddaw shred into a dozen fish-
tails, hating Mrs Redland and Miss Berry, wondering what end
all this unhappiness in the house could have, seeing him, sprang
up and went out.

She saw him standing in the hall, that was dark with a kind
of smoky reflection of the rain, as though bewildered. He looked
at her, and without a word turned into the little room that had
been always David's sanctum, a cold and cheerless little room
now; here were cases with old books that David had never read,
but his chair was there, a table with some of his papers and the
prints of Derwentwater, Keswick, Borrowdale that he had dearly
loved.

Judith followed Francis there. He had flung off his cloak and
turned to her, his face working with anger and impatience.

'The house is changed,' he said bitterly. 'It is no home for
either of us any more ... Where is my mother?'

'In her room. Oh, Francis, I am so glad that you have returned!'

'I have come back with a purpose. This cannot continue.
My mother must speak to me for there are things that must be
settled. This silence has lasted a year, and I will have no more
of it.'

He looked so unhappy, so desolate, as he stood there that her
heart ached for him, and the anger that had been piling up all
these months at the treatment of both himself and her reached at
that moment its crisis. She felt that the time had come for a
settlement, and she was glad of it.

'Oh, Francis, isn't it the strangest thing! She loved you so.

She was always so kind and so good. I have thought that it was a sickness that would pass, but you are right; it must be brought to an issue . . .'

She recollected in that instant the scene in the cellar at Cockermouth, when Humphrey Sunwood, outcast and fugitive, had said farewell to her. Now she and Francis were outcast and fugitive: for no fault of theirs. She thought, standing in that room, of David's kindliness and benignity. Were his ghost with them now he must grieve at these circumstances. Oh, if he were only here, if he were only here!

'You do not know,' Francis went on rapidly, his voice trembling with emotion, 'that two weeks ago from Penrith I wrote to my mother. I said everything in that letter, of my love for my father, of my great unhappiness, that I was the cause of his sickness, that I would never, never, so long as I lived, forgive myself for that, but that I loved her too, that I loved her the more for my own fault, that I had borne patiently all these months her silence and that I had well deserved it, but that this must have some limit because I loved her, because I loved our home . . .' His voice broke. He turned, leaned his head on his arms against the fireplace. For a little the only sound in the room was the driving rain. When he looked up and spoke again his voice was stern and resolved.

'She did not answer my letter. I have waited these two weeks. So now it must end. I must know one way or another.'

'Yes, it must end,' Judith answered. 'For all our sakes . . .'

'I am going to her now.'

He left the room. She stood there, heard him mount the stairs. In a little while the rain had stopped. She heard the ladies come out, chatter, laugh, depart. Deborah came past the open door, but did not look in, and moved slowly into the servants' part of the house. Still there was no sound from upstairs. Then, quite sharply, Francis' voice rang out, one word cutting the air like a snapped stick. Judith, driven by an impulse that was entirely beyond her governance, ran up the stairs, stayed for a moment, then, her face hardening into resolve, walked down the passage.

She pushed Sarah's door open and went in. The room that Sarah had chosen for herself after David's death was a small bare one. Over the fireplace was a highly coloured, badly painted picture of David. It had been done by some travelling artist some ten years before, and showed David complacent in full wig, a crimson coat and flowered vest, red-cheeked, exceedingly amiable.

He grinned down at Sarah, his wife, who sat in a chair of crimson morocco; her hair, her face, grey, her dress black, a ghost of desperate anger and unhappiness. It was the unhappiness that Judith, standing in the doorway, first saw, then, a second later, she was engulfed in the anger as though she had to push up her head to avoid drowning in it. She closed the door.

'I will not speak either to him or to you!' Sarah cried, her hand trembling on her chair.

Francis, in entire command of himself, was by the window. He came forward.

'I am glad you have come, Judith,' he said. 'I would have a witness to this. After twelve months my mother has at length addressed me . . .' He went close to her. His voice was tender and full of affection. 'I cried out at what you said, Mother, but you have a right to say what you wish. You have told me to go and never to come back. I will go, but not before you have heard me.'

She did not look at him, but, half rising in her chair, spoke to Judith.

'I know that you are on his side,' she said, 'but that is no new thing. Ever since they brought you to this house as a baby you have made nothing but evil here. You have never belonged here, and it is quite fitting that you should take the part of the son who killed his father, leaving us all desolate.'

Even as her face was a mask hiding some real woman under it, so her voice was not her own. Judith had a queer perception of the old, rather tired, very quiet woman that Sarah would be after this sickness was over, as unlike the woman that she had once been as this present woman was unlike. She had a strange conviction, as though someone spoke to her, that throughout this scene she must keep that old tired woman in her mind, so she would be kinder and more just.

No one could be more just or more decent than Francis.

'Listen, Mother,' he said. 'You *shall* attend to me, for later when you look back you will be glad that you heard me. You loved Father. God knows I did also. My love is something; you cannot take it from me. But I could not deny my nature, neither for you nor Father nor anyone. That nature has always put me by myself, alone. I tell you now so that you may remember it after, that I would change it, God knows how I would change it, if I could. And is it not enough that I must carry with me all my life the knowledge that it was my insane obstinacy that killed Father; is not that some punishment for a man? Did he not himself forgive me? Was he not the most generous-hearted of men, and can we not now, who both loved him, find some ground in his generosity and make a peace? Mother—'

He approached her. She drew back violently, almost pushing the chair over. Then she rose, swept by him as though he were not there, and went to the window.

'Very well,' she said, 'if you wish it you shall hear me. I was a happy woman; you have made me an unhappy woman. I had a home, a husband whom I loved; I have nothing any more. You say it was only your nature. Very well, I am an enemy of that nature. I was your mother. I am so no more. I do not know you. You may remain in this house if you will. You have the right. I believe the house is now yours. I will leave it if you wish. But understand, if you stay and I stay I do not know you. We remain as strangers.'

She beat her hand against her black dress, her fingers scraping the silk as though her control was almost exhausted. Yet her eyes, looking beyond them both into some mysterious distance, seemed to say: 'I am imprisoned here. These words are not mine. I do not know who is the speaker.'

Francis turned to Judith with a gesture as though of despair.

'No,' he said, 'I will not go like that. I am no stranger to you whatever I have done. You have borne me, suckled me. I have lain on your breast. Things cannot be ended . . .'

'Listen then,' she interrupted quickly. 'I was once a girl, very unhappy. Your father came and rescued me, fought for me, married me. From the first moment that I saw him I worshipped him. I bore him three children. Now I have but two. Can you understand *that* then? That . . . That . . .'

But Judith, furious with what seemed to her the theatrical falseness of a woman hugging with a sort of selfish joy the self-inflicted tragedy, broke in:

'I have something to say in this. I am a woman, Sarah, as you are a woman. I am a child no longer. What right have you to fancy your grief is yours alone? For a year and more you have walked by yourself, hugging your wrongs, and you have hugged them so long that you are a comic figure, not real at all. We have all endured your nonsense long enough. Oh yes, you can order me to go. I know that I have no place here any more. I am going. But Francis is another matter. For a whole year, with absolute patience, he has endured your tantrums and bewailings. He is offering you now your last opportunity. Lose it, and when you

come to your senses again you will whistle for him back and
whistle to empty air. If I were your daughter I could show you
something. You adore David, yes, but you allow the house to be
filled with chattering women, and Mr Finch comes with his
fiddle from Keswick, and the pianoforte is moved to have room
for another two couple, and—'

She paused for breath. She was in one of her rages, almost
dancing on the Turkey carpet.

Sarah broke into her pause.

'No, you are right, Judith. You are no child of mine. Thank
God for it. We, at least, have been strangers always. I see no
kind of reason for you to intervene in this. Francis is the master
here now. If he wishes you here I have no say. If you think me a
comic figure, that also is of no importance. I did not ask you to
come and wrangle here. I may be allowed, perhaps, another
room where I may be by myself. When you have finished, if
you wish to stay here, I will go.'

Then Francis turned to her, his face lit with a most noble
generosity and kindness.

'Mother, listen. Why should you cut yourself off? You have
been angry with me long enough. Were Father here he would
laugh at all of us. There are never so many in the world who
are our own stock, our own flesh and blood, that we should
separate ourselves from those we have. I have told you that all
my life long I shall carry with me the burden of my father's
death. But life is not over for that. Would my father wish us,
because he is gone, to spoil our lives for him? He would be the
last, the very last in the world, to tolerate it. He loved life, every
piece of it, and he loved friendship and fellowship and the
forgetting of injuries. He never grudged an injury his whole life
long. You know that he did not. He has forgiven me, although
I cannot forgive myself. Dear Mother, in his name, forgive me
too. Let me be your son again; come out and make this house
real. I will be as true a son to you—'

She broke in: 'No. No. Never! You, both of you together, do
you think I cannot see into your hearts? Do you think this
treachery is a new thing to me? Make no mistake. I know you –
and now, perhaps, you will allow me to find another room.'

Judith cried: 'You shall not go like that. Listen. You say
that I have been false to you all my life long. I know that I
haven't been good. I have always found discipline hard; not *your*
discipline, Sarah. Any discipline. But I think, looking back, that
you were always very kind to me. You never saw that I was

always older than I should be, that I was disgraced by my own impulse to be for ever making new resolutions that I couldn't fulfil. There was no more evil in it than that. The greatest kindness you could ever show me was to let me have my own way that I might quickly discover how foolish my own way was. But there was no more wilfulness than that. I have always cared for you, Sarah, and now when I leave you, as I shall do this very night, I want you only to remember afterwards that I would tell you truths while I can and wish you well.

'And it is for that, because I wish you so well, that I beg you not to lose Francis. He is right. David's death is no reason for any separation. Keep him with you. His situation should secure your compassion, not your anger—'

Francis broke in: 'Judith, you are not to go.'

But Sarah was already at the door: 'Our worlds are separate, Francis,' she said, more quietly than she had hitherto spoken. 'You have thought me comic, Judith, in my selfishness. There you are doubtless right. Only I pray God that you may never know the unhappiness that I know. I did not think there could be such an unhappiness in the world and anyone live with it.'

She opened the door and went out.

Judith stared at the picture of the rubicund and complacent David.

'When he was alive,' she said, 'Sarah was quiet enough in her affections. She loved him, but not to any desperation. Francis, I hate women with their exaggeration and sentiment. There is something rotten here like a poison.'

He sighed wearily, stroking his forehead with his hand.

'No. There is a reality in it somewhere. I always knew that we were nothing to her compared with my father. He filled her whole vision, and now she is lost.'

'I will never be that for a man,' Judith answered sharply. 'Mark you that, Francis. Never, never, never!'

She went up to him, stood on tiptoe, kissed his forehead.

'Dear Francis, goodnight.'

He did not attempt to stop her, but stood there, lost in his own problem.

'Even he,' she thought, 'does not want me here.'

Indeed, when she reached her room, she felt more desolate than ever before in her life. She belonged now to exactly no one at all.

She must go at once, this very night, but she had no doubt at all as to what this going meant. She was going now once and for ever. This place was never again to be her home, or so at least she thought, being no witch to see in a glass her future.

She looked about her little room that had been the same ever since her babyhood. There was the oak-panelled armchair, the tallboy, the bed with the faded cherry-coloured hangings.

She got out of the drawer her childhood treasures: the fox's brush from Tom Gauntry, the book on cock-fighting, the china jar with the orange flowers, the two rag 'babies' and, best loved of all, the Bible with the wood-cuts that Reuben had given her.

She smiled when she looked at them, but smiled quite without sentiment. Her childhood was over, quite finally, for ever. And she was not sorry. It had been a mischancy ill-fitting time. Yes, that was one thing, but this sudden exile into a vast uncanny world was quite another. Suppose Tom Gauntry didn't want her? He was growing old now and was uneasily under the domination of his cook, Emma Furze . . . Oh, well, if he didn't want her, there were other places. She could work; she wasn't afraid of anyone.

Then, quite unaccountably, she wanted to cry. Indeed, indignantly, she brushed some tears from her eyes. How she wished that Reuben was here! He loved her, and only he in all the world. Poor clumsy, fat-faced, kindly Reuben. She hadn't seen him for six months. Deborah Sunwood, too, was altered since Humphrey's troubles, not the same bright tranquil woman as before, and Reuben was so restless that he might be away from Cockermouth any time.

Something had happened to them all, just as it was happening to the larger, outside world, breaking up all the old moulds, busily forming new ones that would be, no doubt, very like the old ones when they were settled.

But the thought of the change and of some movement in the world very much larger than her own little trivial affairs stirred her to action. There were no tears any more. She would go to Stone Ends tonight, and if they did not want her there she would move on. What of London? There were Herries there, who would help her. After all she *was* a Herries, whatever they might say. And at that she thought suddenly of Georges Paris. She had seen him once and heard from him twice since the adventure with Humphrey in Cockermouth. The time she had seen him had been at Stone Ends; they had not been alone, had had few words, but there had been something in a kind of mocking proprietary air that he had had that had not altogether pleased her. Nevertheless, he had grown extraordinarily handsome, slender, dark, with a sort of sword-like sharpness and brilliance. He shone among all those befuddled squires and hunting men at Gauntry's like a prince in disguise. Oh no, she was not romantic about him. She knew his selfishness and conceit and laziness well enough, but when he was near to her, looked at her, touched her, he stirred her blood, and she liked her blood to be stirred. She liked anything, any risk, any danger, rather than stagnation. That Georges Paris *was* a danger she never disguised from herself for a single moment.

Well, she must be moving. She wanted to get away from the house, away from Sarah's sickness, from Francis' unhappiness, from Deborah's chattering women, as quickly as might be.

She began to turn everything out, her possessions, clothes, hats and shoes, until they lay all over the room. Then she decided to take nothing with her. She would ride over on the cob to Stone Ends and send for her things.

She smiled as she remembered the time when, years ago, after David's whipping her, she had climbed out of the window and ridden away.

It should not be so dramatic an exit this time.

But, in honest fact, when at last she walked out of the house she heard no sound, she met no one. It was as though she were going out of a dead house.

Out of a dead house into life.

MADAME PARIS

SHE WENT ALONG on her horse – clop-clop, clop-clop – and with every ring of the road she was more surely leaving everything behind.

She saw nothing, thought of nothing outside herself. The separate strains fighting for order in her mind slowly, by a kind of reluctant agreement, as though they were obeying commands against their will, sulkily settled themselves.

'I have left everything behind me, and I am going out into nothing – or perhaps everything. Everyone with whom I have had to do has been showing Sensibility about something, even Will. But I wish to show Sensibility about nothing. I have only myself to consider. Even Francis does not need me. I am nearer to my dead father and mother than I am to anyone else. But

there also I will not show Sensibility. They are dead and dead
for always. I shall never see them or speak to them. I may have
feeling in me that comes from them, but they cannot help me.
They will not weep if I come to disaster. They will not answer
if I call. Who is in my life? David is dead. Sarah has just thrown
me out, Will and Francis think of themselves, Deborah is
nothing, Deborah Sunwood has her husband and is grieving
for Humphrey, Reuben thinks about God, Tom Gauntry to
whom I am going is old and loves his cook, Georges – Georges
wishes to kiss me when he sees me. Otherwise I am nothing to
him. There is nobody at all who needs me. So far as I can tell,
I have not a penny in the world, although Francis would, I
suppose, give me some money if I asked him. I shall not ask
him. I have no friends, no money, no work.

'I am sixteen years of age, with fine hair, a poor complexion,
a nose too large, and ridiculously small stature. I have no
especial intelligence, but I know when persons are speaking to
me and I remember something of what they say. I have never
been afraid of anybody or anything, but I have not as yet met
anybody or anything to be afraid of.

'I have never had a lover, but am very ready to have one. I
am curious about love. I expect that love itself is nothing very
fine, but I could care for somebody very deeply. I would wish to
have children that I might care for them. Is this Sensibility?
I do not mind whether it be so or not.

'I know nothing as yet about the outside world, but I am
extremely inquisitive concerning it, nor do I believe, like Mrs
Redland or Miss Berry or Deborah, that it spreads no farther
than Kendal. I would be interested to see many countries, and
the Revolution in France is a very exciting event. I would like
to see Mr Pitt and Mr Fox and the King and Queen (although
they do not appear to be interesting).

'I fancy that I have no very good Disposition. I have a violent
temper and dislike to be opposed in anything, but when my
affections are roused there is nothing I will not do. Is this
Sensibility? I fancy that it is.

'I am not a child any more but a woman. When did this
change come to me? I think that day in Cockermouth with
Humphrey. I had no concern that day as to what happened. I
knew that whatever happened I could master it.

'I love this part of England. This is undoubtedly Sensibility,
but I do not mind if it is. I do not wish ever to live anywhere
else, although I wish to see other places. I would like to marry

a man here, and have children here close to where I was born . . .

'Because of my father I am very proud to be a Herries. I would like to meet all the different Herries, although I am sure that I should not wish to be with most of them very long. I find that it is in my nature to hate people very much and to love people very much, and also to laugh at everybody and also myself when I am very angry.

'I do not think that there is a God or that Reuben saw Him on the road outside Tours. If there is one He is stupid because He has so much power and makes very little of it. Neither Francis nor Georges thinks there is a God.

'When I have some money I shall be very good at managing it. I am very good at managing anything if no one is in my way. I am not sorry for Sarah as I should be. She likes to be miserable, because she has never been miserable before. It is a new feeling for her. I am sorry for Francis, because he will remember all his life about David, which is a sad waste of time. I am resolved to make my life very amusing.'

With this she discovered that she was outside the gate of Stone Ends. The house was dead. A thin quarter moon hung like a wisp of pale rag over the end of a dirty silver-edged cloud, and, washed by ghostly mist, the house showed nothing human. She tied the horse to the gate and walked up the irregular stone path to the old worm-eaten door. At the sound of the banging knocker all the dogs in the house set up a fearful yelling and barking.

There was a pause, and Judith felt desperately cold and frightened. Suppose the old man didn't want her? He had been always good to her, but now he was aged and ailing, and under the thumb of his cook, people said. Suppose he didn't want her? And the wind, blowing sharply from Skiddaw, rustled all the plants in the weedy neglected garden in melancholy echo. One thing she noticed. The fountain was no longer playing. That had been Tom Gauntry's great pride, and his boast was that, however badly things went, he would always have enough water for the fountain. An owl hooted.

'You see,' said the owl, 'we haven't water enough any longer.'

There was a great unrasping of bolts from within, and then the door slowly opened. Old Tom Gauntry, holding a blowing candle, stood there, and a comical figure he looked. He was in a nightdress, black stockings and dingy slippers, and he wore a very long nightcap with a red worsted tip to it. Over his nightdress he had flung an old riding coat. He peered out, shivering, his old wrinkled face like an anxious monkey's. When he saw who it was he gave a cry.

'Judy. By God, 'tis Judy!'

He looked so comical, with his nightcap, his nose dripping, his unshaven chin, that she couldn't help herself. She began to laugh, and then the cold and her own most uncertain situation in some strange way forcing her, once she had begun to laugh she couldn't stop. She pushed past him, to get in out of the cold, and then laughed and laughed and laughed.

'Judy! For Almighty sake shut the damned door. I've a cursed cold on me.'

'I must go and look after the horse first,' she said. 'Where's Wull?'

He began calling 'Wull! Wull! You devil, where are you? Wull! Wull!,' and all the dogs began to bark.

While she was standing there she could take in the scene, which was certainly funny enough. The old hall stank of dogs, drink, damp. Dogs as usual were all about the place, scratching, sleeping, suddenly lifting up their heads and howling. In the stone fireplace a great fire was roaring up the chimney. In the ingle two old men, one in an untidy wig, one bald-headed, were sitting. On a table near them was a large bowl with a ladle in it, and, her head resting on the table, slept Emma Furze, a tall woman, snoring lustily.

'Hush!' said Judith. 'You'll wake her.'

'The last trump won't wake her,' cried Gauntry. He was rather drunken, but not badly so. 'Wull! Wull! Where the hell are you?'

Wull appeared, yawning, scratching his untidy head, his shirt hanging out over his breeches.

'Take Miss Judith's horse to the stable.' He put his old horny hand on her arm. 'Come to the fire and get warm, my pretty.'

She came to the fire and was introduced to the old men.

'This is my ancient friend, Mr Jeremy Cards. He's a relation of yours. And this is Joe Twisset, he's a relation of none but the devil.' He kicked and cuffed the dogs, who, however, knew Judith and jumped about her, licking her hand. She went to the fire and stood in front of it roasting herself. She smiled on the two old men.

She was suddenly happy. She was at home here. The dogs, the smells, the old men, they were all right. She could manage it all very comfortably.

Gauntry was delighted to see her. She was, as he explained to the two old men, his especial pet, his pride, his joy. And although he was rather drunk he meant it all. The two old men were rather drunk too, but blinked their eyes in the firelight, rubbed their hands and looked happy.

'But why, my pretty, have you come so late? You should be abed, a child like you.' Sniff, sniff, sneeze, sneeze. 'I've a hell of a cold, a damnable hellish cold, and I'm not as young as I was.'

Judith explained that she had left Fell House for ever. She said very little about it. She had taken off her hat, and her hair burnt in the firelight. The old men looked at it admiringly.

'Yoicks! Yoicks! Hurray for ever!' Gauntry was delighted. 'Didn't I know it was coming? "Wait a bit, you old devil," I said to myself. "She'll be coming to you. Just be patient a trifle." This is your cousin,' he added, pointing to the old man in the wig, 'and it's certain he's delighted to see you. Aren't you, Jeremy?' he shouted in the old man's ear. 'This is Judy Herries, daughter to Francis. She's your cousin, you old bastard!'

Old Jeremy Cards rose on his trembling legs and made a low bow.

'I knew your father, my dear, and a fine grand man he was. I was born in 1712, I was, and I'm seventy-eight years of age and got my full sight and everything, but my hearing's failing a trifle. My right ear's the one for you to speak into if you'll be so good. It was in 1763 I saw your father last in the town of Kendal, and I remember like yesterday . . .'

'Well enough, well enough,' Gauntry broke in. 'You must drink something, my pretty, and then we'll find a bed for you. Before she wakes,' he added, suddenly dropping his voice. 'Better get settled before she wakes. Although I can manage her, mind you. She's afraid of me, she is, but she's a good soul when she's sober, and an old man like me can't be expecting young beauties at his time o' life. Down, Roger, get out of it, Trixie . . . The dogs know you well enough. So they should. This is your proper home, my dear. Didn't I find you when you were not a day born? By God and I did! Have something to warm you, my pretty.'

She was glad enough of the hot strong drink. Wull came in to say that the horse was stabled. The old kitchen clock rivalled Mrs Furze's snores. All was cosy and comfortable.

Judith told the three old men about the scene at Uldale, and they nodded their sympathy, but old Jeremy Cards was galvanized to an extraordinary life by the very mention of the

Herries family. So David was dead! Aye, aye – a pity, a pity! He'd
known him as a fine young man who could cross-buttock anyone
in the country. When would that be now? Aye, 1742, just before
the Jacobite troubles, he'd seen David wrestle a man in Newlands, a great bullock of a man he was too, but David was the
prettiest lad stripped – and there came before Judith's eyes a
David whom she had never known, young, fresh, strong-
limbed. Behind him were other Herries, old Maria who had
lived to be almost a hundred, Pomfret and Jannice in Keswick,
little Harcourt at Ravenglass, and Jeremy's own people, his
father Humphrey, who had been born in 1687, and his mother
Charlotte, who loved dancing and was a Beauty in the days of
Queen Anne. The old man went rambling on, putting his skinny
finger to his bare poll and wiping his eyes, that the smoke
made to run, with a large yellow handkerchief. The logs fell to
crimson ruin in the fire, and all the dogs slept.

Old Jeremy sighed: 'All dead, buried, and the worms have
eaten them. But the family goes on. I daresay there'll be Herries
sitting in this same spot a hundred years from now.'

He seemed, Judith thought, a brave old man, because he was
quite alone in the world and hadn't a penny. He stayed about in
the district, in any house that would keep him. He didn't want
much, a drink, a bite, and the fire to sit beside. As he told them,
most of his days were now swallowed by dreaming. 'It's hard to
tell what's a dream.' Yes, that was true. It was hard to tell.

It occurred to Gauntry that the girl might be hungry. She
acknowledged that she was, and the old men all said that they
were hungry as well, so the host scuttered off in his clop-clop
slippers to find them some food. He returned with a mutton
ham and a piece of a pie. Some of the dogs woke up and came
sniffing round; then Emma Furze woke also. She raised her
head slowly from the table, stretched her arms and yawned.
Then she saw Judith and stared as though her eyes would burst
from her.

'This is little Judy Herries, Emma,' said Tom Gauntry
nervously.

She stood up. She was a big woman. She had large black eyes,
a fine bosom, and she stood with her legs spread like a trooper.

The old man looked at her apprehensively.

'Oh, is it?' she said.

Judith rose and held out her hand. But Mrs Furze was uncertain as to whether she saw two Judiths or three, so, to avoid
any silly mistake, she walked off a little unsteadily.

'She will be most agreeable,' said Gauntry, 'in the morning. She has a totally different nature in the morning.'

The mutton ham was extremely good.

In the morning, indeed, Mrs Furze shed tears upon Judith's shoulder. She arrived in Judith's room before Judith was awake and sat for a long while moodily observing her. Judith, before many weeks were out, was to know all Emma Furze's history, was to know, too, that there was much merit in her if also some melodrama. Emma was to play an important part in Judith's story. But for the moment, Judith, after a most healthy sleep, awoke to see this big woman balanced on a small chair and tears rolling down her nose. Tears, whether male or female, had always an instant effect upon Judith's heart, so now in a moment she was out of bed and, in her thin shift, was kneeling on the bare boards by Emma's side, imploring her to tell her trouble.

What, now as ever, was not Emma's trouble! At present it was difficult enough to disentangle. Emma, as Judith soon heard, had been an actress, and fine words were her pleasure. Words poured from her like the water from Lodore after heavy rains, and out of all the confusion nothing was immediately to be gathered. There had been a villain somewhere, 'a villain of uncultivated manners and corrupt heart'; there had been 'a smiling innocent babe'. She had been 'tossed on the waves of a sea of sorrows' and so, 'washed up' on Tom Gauntry's 'shores', had consented to be both his cook and his mistress.

Her tale was so lengthy, so incoherently mingled with tears, the boards of the floor were so hard, that Judith was compelled to rise, whereupon Emma also rose and, folding Judith to her bosom, embraced her very warmly, told her that she would 'worship her for ever' and, becoming instantly practical, asked her what she would have cooked, with what clothes she might supply her; stated that, in fact, she was her servant for life. She was very quickly of the utmost cheerfulness, laughing and plunging about the bare room. It was thus, in this ridiculous manner, that Judith made one of the principal friendships of her life.

The next occurrence was, of all amazing things, the appearance of Will Herries. Two days after Judith's flight he appeared on a grand calm morning when the grass was still silver with frost and the scent of the Fell was stung with the breath of icy running water. The grass of the little tangled garden was crisp and crackling under Judith's heels. She looked up and saw Will, sitting there very stiff and reserved on a fine coal-black horse. She had not seen him for a long while. She thought he was in Liverpool. He looked older, thinner, better pleased with himself than ever, and he had all the pursed-up solemn air of a man who finds himself immensely important.

Their conversation was short. He did not come down from his horse, but was quite friendly. She stood near him, her hand on the bridle, looking up at him and often smiling. He seemed to her so very pompous.

'Where are my things, Will?'

'Your things?'

'My handsome possessions, my marriage portion, my liveli-hood. There is a dress and a cap, two pairs of shoes, a cracked china jar, the brush of a fox, a Holy Bible . . .'

He looked severe. 'You must ride back with me, Judith.'

She laughed. He couldn't but feel that she was a lively attractive little thing, standing there in the crisp morning air with the Fell and the old house for her background. He saw, too, with surprise that she had become in the course of a night or so a woman.

'Ride back? Is that your mother's wish?'

He leant over towards her confidentially. He always prided himself on his diplomatic gifts.

'Now, Judith. These are women's quarrels. You know well enough that my mother has been a sick woman since my father's death.' (He said *My* Mother and *My* Father as though they had been his own most especial private property.) 'A sick woman . . . But it will pass. It is already passing.'

'Has she spoken of me?'

'No. She has kept to her room.'

'Has she spoken to Francis?'

Will's upper lip, that was thin and tight like whipcord, was sharp.

'Francis is greatly to blame. He is my brother, but I cannot acquit him of fault.' (He said *My* Brother as though, rather reluctantly this time, he owned him.)

Judith broke out fiercely:

'He is *not* to blame . . . David's attack would have followed whether Francis were aggravating or no. You know well what the surgeon said. And after David's death Francis did every-thing that was possible. Sarah hugs her misfortune. She is not alone in losing a husband.'

Will said severely: 'You forget that she is my mother.'

'I forget nothing at all. Least of all do I forget that I never belonged at Uldale, Will. This is an old shabby place, and there are only old men in it, but it has always been my home more than the other. A poor taste, but my own. And so long as Sarah is living we can never be under the same roof. No, here is my place and here I stay.'

Will looked sternly about him as though he were making a quick businesslike survey of the house, grounds, view, and found them of exactly no value at all.

'You know of Gauntry's bad repute ?' he asked.

'Oh, Will,' she answered lightly, smiling at him. 'Who shall cast stones ? There is not one of us without his detractor—'

This made Will uncomfortable. He looked for a moment as though he were going to ask Judith whether she had heard anything about himself. He had all the sensitiveness to personal reputation that belongs to very selfish men. However, all he said was:

'You yourself are a Herries, Judith, and in this part of the country the Herries have a reputation.'

She interrupted him laughing. 'There's another Herries in the house here already – Jeremy Cards. He knew my father.'

Will's expression was as though he had smelt some strong odour, which, indeed, as they were not far from the midden, he might have done.

'I have heard of him. A disreputable old man . . .' He saw apparently that there was nothing to be done. He was relieved, perhaps, that it was so. 'So you will not come ?'

'No, Will. I am happier here.' She asked him: 'Are things going well with you ?'

He looked at her kindlily. He liked anyone who took an interest in his affairs.

'Well enough . . . I am to go to London very shortly.' (He said London as though it were *His* London, just purchased by him.) 'I'm glad. They say there's a deal of money there.' He nodded very seriously. 'Liverpool is too small a place,' he told her.

He shook her hand, was minded to pat her head, but refrained. Then he rode off, she calling after him:

'Remember that my things must be sent.'

He turned in the saddle, nodded gravely and disappeared.

She went in to find Tom Gauntry huddled in an old bed-gown over a grumbling fire, dogs spread all around him. He looked up at her smiling, but his old face was wrinkled with pain. Her heart ached for him.

'That was Will Herries,' she said cheerfully. 'He asked me to return to Uldale. I say nay, like the girl in the ballad, and that is the end of that.'

'That is the end of that,' whispered the coal in the fire. 'Are you sure that you are wise?'

He put out his dry bony hand and took hers: 'Here has always been your home, and so long as I'm alive it shall be. But maybe that's not so long. My back aches and my head's like a turnip. There's a hunt today, Threlkeld way. Hunting's over for me. And I'll never be on a horse again neither . . . Strange, strange! I've lived my life on horses . . . But it's been a long life. Emma likes ye, my pretty. She's got a heart, Emma has, poor silly soul. She'd skin herself for anyone she's fond of – *has* skinned herself a hundred times, poor girl. It's mortal cold this morning. And yet I'm hot in the head, as though there were coals of fire blazing away. It's the devil to be an old man – better go while you're active.'

She nodded her head. 'I think,' she said, 'I could deal with whatever came. I feel that way on a fine crisp morning. Uncle Tom, what am I to do today? There are a thousand things – I'll ride over to Bassenthwaite village. There's a woman there a marvel with herbs. David had her once for his leg . . .'

The old man rolled his head. 'Nay, nay, I'm past everything but dreaming, damn my bones. Don't you worry, my pretty. When you've had a pain in your leg a long while it's a kind of friend.' Then he added quite casually as though he were saying nothing at all: 'Georges may be riding over from Whitehaven today.'

Her heart began to hammer. 'Georges Paris?'

'Aye. He's grown a fine young man, but he'll burn his fingers one of these days. He's in with a lot o' rogues. I've told him, but he don't listen. Thinks he can manage them. Very confident young man is Georges.'

Before she could say anything or even reason with herself about her foolish excitement Emma Furze joined them. Judith saw that she had smartened herself. She had a black hoop and a silver band in her dark hair. She looked really handsome as she stood there. There was something both foolish and good in her face; her black eyes were large and always brimming with emotion; at the slightest excuse her breast would heave and swell. She looked at Judith with a childlike smile of pleasure.

'I saw a fine man on a horse and said to myself, "He's come to take her away." I was tortured by the anxiety, my dear.'

'You need be tortured no longer. No fine gentleman shall take me away.'

With a sigh of relief Emma sat down beside them. How pleasant it was for Judith in the fresh quietness of the morning, no sound in the house but the old clock ticking and a mouse scratching behind the wainscot!

Judith asked Emma some questions, and out her history tumbled in an overwhelming flood – some of it at least. As Judith was to discover, there were endless, endless chapters to it; she had led, it seemed, a thousand lives, and was yet, according to her own account, but two and thirty.

Her first part had been that of the Duke of York in *Richard the Third* at the Birmingham Theatre, then Cupid in *The Trip to Scotland*, then Prince Arthur in *King John*, then Bath, where Mr Palmer gave her five shillings a night. Her first girl's part was Sukey Chitterling in *Harlequin's Invasion*. She drew from her bosom a packet of papers, yellow with age and greatly torn; she read to them with every possible dramatic gesture some of her notices.

'On Tuesday night Miss Pomeroy ("My name at that time, my dear") made her appearance in *Isabella*; and, although the audience went with such strong prejudices in favour of the fashionable Melpomene, yet never did Mrs Siddons draw more genuine tears from an audience. It is impossible to conceive what a high-fashioned picture this lady gave of Isabella's woes, and how nearly she arrived to nature in almost every scene. There were no studied pauses, to purchase, by vacancy of time, the approving hands of the audience, and yet the house echoed with repeated marks of approbation. Her shriek at the discovery of Biron had a good effect, but was rather that of terror without amazement, than of terror and amazement mixed. When the public consider that this Miss Pomeroy is that Miss Pomeroy who performed Cowslip . . .'

Old Jeremy came stealing down the stairs to join them. He was blinking his eyes and yawning, for he was only now awake, but Emma's dramatic voice, the great rise in it as she came to the word 'terror', her sudden declamation of Isabella's most moving lines, soon stirred him. It was as good, he declared, as being at the Theatre and with nothing to pay. The dogs barked, Wull came to the door and listened, and Judith, who had never seen a play, was entranced.

Very early in the afternoon the light vanished behind the hills,

and the house was a place of shadows. Judith riding in from
Caldbeck, and, chilled to the bone, hurrying to the fire, saw
Georges Paris standing in the firelight. No one else was there.
It was the same as when they had run, that first time, from the
supper-room, and she had smacked his cheek.

She would not smack his cheek now. He had grown a man,
slim and tall in his riding coat and riding boots, his black hair
tied in a queue, his handsome self-confident face bright with life,
fun, energy, adventure.

He saw, too, a changed Judith. From the child whom he had
left there had grown a child-woman, charming in her small
buoyant independence, throwing her hat beside her and shaking
her red curls just as she used to do, holding out her hand to
him at once in their old friendship.

'How d'ye do, Georges? I'm happy to see you again.'

'By heaven,' he thought, 'she's somebody . . . I'm glad I came.'

For he had been in two minds about it. Stone Ends was in
no sort of way the place it had been. Gauntry was ill, only old
men there, flea-bitten dogs, and the strange woman, half cook,
half play-actress, in command. Georges was profoundly convinced that he could live but once and must waste no time. Had
he been present when Gauntry needed he would have helped
him to his last shilling, for he was impetuously generous, but
he was happy in living for the moment and in finding the moment
always exciting.

And now this Moment was Judith. He had not expected to
find her here and certainly not supposed that she would, at
his very first glimpse of her, affect him so strongly. He had
thought of her, forgotten her, thought of her again. He lived
for excitement, and only accepted the things and people that
could contribute to that. Since he had seen her he had had
adventures enough – on the Cumberland coast, on the Solway,
in Holland, in London – to satisfy, he thought, any man. What
he did not recognize – as we never recognize the truest things
about ourselves – was that all these adventures had been
scattered with a thin second-rate dust, as though, with everything that he touched, he robbed it of a degree of fineness.
He had first-rate moments and a great quality of happy fearless
adventure when things went well, but he had second-rate
ambitions, second-rate vision, second-rate reactions. He was a
fine young man with a soul, through no fault of his own,
inevitably shabby. Was it perhaps in Judith's power to raise
him into a finer world? He did not think so, because he was

convinced that no world could be finer than the one he was in;
and she did not think so, because she never, all her life through,
saw herself as a moral agent in anything. She never thought
at all about moral qualities in the abstract.

At any rate, simply as a factor in the intricate course of
Herries history, it must be recorded that on that afternoon,
November 24th of the year 1790, Judith Herries and Georges
Paris, standing beside the fire in the hall of Stone Ends, fell in
love with one another.

Judith knew at once what had happened to her. She was
always extremely clear-sighted about herself. Now if he attempted to kiss her she would not smack his cheek. But she did not
intend that he should kiss her. She was in fact very cool to him
indeed.

He had intended to stay the one night at Stone Ends and
then ride on to Penrith, where he had business of an especially
interesting nature. He was by present occupation a smuggler and
just now a prosperous one. But his intention was to find a
little place somewhere in the district, a rather remote place if
possible, and make it his centre. This was not only a business
ambition. He had a true love of the country, possibly the truest
thing in him; he liked nothing better than the old life of hunting,
fishing and the rest that he had had in the earlier days at Stone
Ends. Sensuous enough, he nevertheless vastly preferred men
to women as companions. He had long pictured to himself a
small farm somewhere that could be the centre both of his
business and his pleasure. Now that he was in funds was the
time to purchase such a place. He certainly would not be in
funds for ever.

So, at the very first instant of seeing Judith walk across the
floor towards him, in a flash it had come to him: 'Here is the
woman you want.' He had always considered her, even as a
child, a most sensible capable person. There was some hard
common sense in Judith that had always roused his keenest
admiration. She knew this country and liked it. She would run
a house well, would manage men with authority. She had no
ties. She had pluck and courage and, he surmised, would not
trouble herself too deeply about transgressions of the law. Now
that he beheld her again he remembered how greatly he had
been impressed in Cockermouth by her decision and resolution.
She was not strictly a beauty, but there was something very
attractive to the senses.

When he wanted anything he always, in five minutes,

concluded that it was his. He wasted no time at all; before they had been half an hour together he was making ardent love to her.

Emma Furze was in her room that night imploring her to be careful.

'He is not for you – no, never, never!' She held Judith's hand and spoke as though the fate of nations were in danger.

'What have you against him, Emma?'

'He has no character, no fine feelings. I have known men and been betrayed by them too. They are all false, and this young man is French as well.'

'They are not all false,' said Judith, thinking of Francis and Reuben. 'But you must recollect, Emma, that I am acquainted with Georges Paris since I was a baby.'

'Yes, but now you are in love with him. You were not and now you are. Love blinds poor women. Men are never to be trusted for a single instant. They are filled with cruelty and caprice. On the most vain and frivolous pretexts, whenever their temper is in the least ruffled, they cast you aside. They behave with propriety only when it is to their advantage.'

'Well, my dear, you need not fear. I know myself.'

But did she? She lay in bed looking at the moonlight washing the door. She was in love – and for the first time. Did she know that? Her cheek was hot as she fell asleep. And her dreams were of a fiery splendour and a happiness that she had never touched before.

It was plain enough to everybody next day that Georges remained at Stone Ends only because of Judith. He carried on his courtship with an impatient ardour that had a great deal of very real passion in it. He was ruthlessly selfish about everyone else. Gauntry he patronized, the two old men he disregarded, Emma Furze he detested. Like many sensual men nothing exasperated him more than having to be in the company of a woman who was most unattractive to him. Emma exasperated him by her apparent vagueness. She seemed to him to live entirely in a world of make-believe. He declared that she did not know where France was nor that Paris was the capital of that country: neither politics nor money meant anything to her at all. She lived entirely in a world of the passions, except when she was cooking. (She was a very excellent cook.) She was vague and ignorant and absent-minded except when someone for whom she cared was in question; then she was as sharp as a needle. He knew at once that she was his enemy so far as Judith went, and he loved her none the better for that knowledge.

So things moved swiftly. Judith was in a strange state. He caught her when she was isolated from all her claims and associations. Everything played into his hands. When her things arrived from Uldale, with them came a letter from Reuben. It was very short.

DEAREST JUDITH – I am going with Humphrey to France. There is the centre of all the movement for the Betterment of Mankind. I shall learn there in that New World how to help Mankind. I shall think of you so often, dearest Judith. I love you with my whole Heart.

REUBEN SUNWOOD

France! It had taken Reuben as it had taken Francis. And now it seemed that it must take her too. But what a different France hers! For Georges seemed to care nothing for his parents' country, save that he got lace and brandy from it, nor did it concern him at all that there was a Revolution there. What was Georges in reality? Did she know him? Did she see him as he was? Was Emma in the right about him? But, as the days went on, she could not think any more. She had never been in love before. She had not known that it would be this strange fiery heat, mist before the eyes, all the outside world sounding dim to the ear.

The house, the old men, Emma, all grew faint and unreal to her, and Georges was ever more clear. He seemed to her most beautiful, and now, because he also was in love, he was most tender.

In these chill frosty December days he was at his very best. There were in him somewhere noble instincts; he wanted her so fiercely (as he wanted anything withheld from him) that his very desire brought him close to her and he caught some of her fineness. He had been in love again and again since he could remember, but now three things were united that had perhaps never been before – desire, perception of character, and practical advantage. There was wisdom in his choice of her, although the very thing that now attracted him, the strong domination of her will and purpose, would be, when passion had died, the last thing that he would want in her.

She held out against him so long as she could, but he was too strong for her. It seemed to her that this had been foreshadowed since her sharp farewell to him in Cockermouth. He had looked at her then as though he knew that one day she would come to him.

But she was never less assured about him than at the moment before she submitted. Coming down the stairs she saw him standing in the hall that was lit by a blazing fire. He was dark black, standing motionless there, as though he were waiting for her. She paused on the stair, and the thought struck her heart: 'This man is my enemy.' Then she came down, and a moment later she was in his arms.

Afterwards he was speaking in all sincerity when he said:

'My dearest, I will care for you with my whole heart. You can make me noble and fine. This is a new beginning. There is nothing you cannot make of me.'

Lying in his arms she was wildly happy with that fierceness of intensity that was always hers in everything that she did. But she had never surrendered herself before to anyone save the ghost of her father. No one had held her and loved her and stroked her hair and kissed her with passion. She did not know that it could be so sweet. What vows she made of service and devotion! How she would work now that she had someone to work for!

She did not ask him where he would take her, whether he had money to keep her! She could work for them both; at what she did not inquire.

Her cheek against his, she stayed in a trance. Perfect happiness had come. How could she ever have thought that she did not know him? She knew him utterly. She had always known him as she knew herself.

She was so very young.

Part II

Watendlath

FRANCIS RIDES OVER

THIS BOOK IS the history of a country, England (not of course, the whole history); of a family, Herries (nor the whole history of that); and of certain members of that family especially – Judith Paris first, then, after her, of Reuben, Will and Francis (and not, of course, their whole history either).

But the Herries are English, and Judith, Reuben, Will and Francis are Herries. At the heart of this family there is a struggle and in each of these individuals a struggle. The history of that struggle is the history of this book, is the history, perhaps, of every book that has ever been written.

The history of any country and the history of any family is continually presenting strange underground movements of ebb and flow, and to these movements members of the country and of the family are for ever responding, although they may themselves be quite unconscious of it. Moreover, the actions of one individual will often permeate the whole body of which he or she is a part; even slender characteristics may affect it as the shape of Cleopatra's nose swung Egypt, Napoleon's passion for hot baths France, and Mrs Fitzherbert's virtuous tenacity England.

So the determination of Will Herries' prominent chin affected just now the fortunes of the whole family of Herries. They may be said to have swung upwards upon it.

In 1791 Will Herries moved to London and married there a Miss Christabel Carmichael, a young woman with a fine waist, something of a fortune, a doting father; against these benefits must be set a slight cast in one eye and a rather hysterical temper. Will cared nothing for the first and soon dominated the second. He was determined to get on, and, as in this life everyone gets what he wants if only he wants it hard enough, he did get on, and speedily.

He was soon known in the City as a man of prudence and enterprise nicely commingled. His business was especially in Indian trade, tea, silks and spices. He had a pretty house in the village of Chelsea, and in February 1792 Mrs Will Herries gave birth to a son, Walter, who, with his opening shout to the world, proclaimed that he also meant to get on and to waste no time in doing so.

It would, however, be an exaggeration to say that at this time
any other members of the Herries family were at all aware
that they were about to swing upwards on the point of Will's
chin. As was always the Herries characteristic, there was perfect
self-confidence everywhere until disintegrating imagination
broke in and threatened it. The Family was at this moment
divided, unlike Gaul, into four parts. There were the Herries
of Uldale, Sarah and her children, Francis and Deborah; the
Pomfret Herries of Kensington, with whom poor Humphrey
Sunwood once on a time visited; the Cards of Bournemouth,
Prosper Cards who married Amelia Trent and had offspring,
Jennifer, born in 1770, and Robert, born in 1771; and, fourthly
(but in their own opinion absolutely firstly), Lord and Lady
Rockage of Grosset Place in Wiltshire. Judith Herries, sister
to Raiseley and first cousin to David, had, many years before,
bewildered into matrimony the Honourable Ernest Bligh, who
in his gout-ridden and exceedingly ill-tempered old age had
become Lord Monyngham, then Viscount Rockage. Of them
had been born three children, Frederick, who died, Carey in
1755 and Madeline in 1756. Carey, now Lord Rockage, had two
offspring – Carey the younger, born in 1780, and Phyllis, born
in 1782.

Lord and Lady Rockage, his sister Madeline, his children
Carey and Phyllis, lived all in penniless grandeur at Grosset
in Wiltshire, where the rain trickled through the roof, the trees
creaked and wailed, and the cold of the stone passages carried
rheumatism into the bones of all who suffered it.

Lest these family branches should seem confusing it may be
said that the Uldale family stood for Country Life, Pomfret's
family for London, the Cards in Bournemouth for Social
Intercourse, and the Rockages for the Ruling Classes; yes, and
more than that, for two strong elements of the Ruling Classes
at the end of the eighteenth century in England, namely the
arrogance of a dominating Aristocracy and the narrowness but
courage of Methodism.

This book is not, however, in the main the history of the
Rockage fortunes. There is a story there, in that odd proud
group of the family, that should command a book of its own.

To have suggested to either the Rockages or the Cards of
Bournemouth at this time that Will Herries was an important
relation would have been to invite derision. But Will's time was
approaching.

Possibly Francis, up in Uldale, had more foreknowledge of

it than any other. He knew his brother. Indeed, very often, Francis, who was without any personal conceit, felt that he knew everything about his own immediate relations, that he knew too much for anyone's happiness. He had in fact a very special quality of psychological penetration. He was now grown very handsome for those who did not find his figure too slender. His features were sharp but delicate, his colour fresh and gentle; he carried himself with a strongly reserved dignity, was always clothed with perfect simplicity but in absolute taste.

He wore an air of melancholy, no pose of the period, but very real indeed. These years were, in fact, very unhappy.

They might well be so. Uldale was, at this time, no cheerful place. He held himself there because he thought it his duty. A bailiff managed the farm, but Francis managed the bailiff – and everyone else as well. He had far more authority than cheerful stout David had ever had; he was the friend of no one, and would have been unpopular in his remoteness had there not been a very proper pride in him. He was the Aristocrat of the district, and everyone was pleased that there should be an Aristocrat. His melancholy reserve lent not only the house but all the district an air. Unlike his sister Deborah, who was in and out of all the houses of the neighbourhood with her giggle, her two little dogs and her passion for gossip, he went nowhere and entertained only with reluctance.

But it was on his relations with his mother that the whole house hung.

Sarah Herries was now an aged and shrunken woman. In the spring of 1792 she was fifty-four years of age, but she looked another ten. Her hair was white; she dressed always in the deepest black, her shoulders a little bent as she walked slowly, leaning on an ebony cane. Her eyes were scornful, as though she said always to the world: 'You took from me the only thing for which I ever cared. What do you expect of me now?'

Now that her features were more slender there was a resemblance between herself and her son. The stout and chattering Deborah seemed to have no relationship with either of them.

Sarah had not, of course, forgiven Francis; she would never forgive him. She would never forgive him, but she surrendered to his influence. She allowed him to do what he would with the house and everyone in it. She found indeed no interest in either contemporary life or persons. She sat, either in her own upstairs room or in the temple in the garden on a fine day, staring in front of her, at the bad blowzy painting of David or the china figures or across the sunlit lawns to the sweep of Skiddaw or the Scottish hills. Her lips moved; her thin pale hands beat together a little on her lap. She was in no way deranged. Any question asked of her she answered sharply and with a certain shivering impatience.

She allowed Deborah to chatter to her for so long as she would, and Deborah flattered herself that but for her jolly brightness and good-nature the house would fall into ruins. But Deborah also abandoned everything to Francis. She paid visits with increasing avidity among the neighbours. She was a great player of cards, a passionate gossip, surely a destined old maid. But Destiny does not always work to pattern.

Francis behaved to his mother with unfaltering courtesy and an unflinching patience. But it seemed to him that life could not continue for very much longer like this. His real life was imprisoned within him like a fire within an ivory bowl. The bowl would crack, and the fire burn the hand that held it.

He was thirty-two. His life was passing. And a day came when his endurance broke.

In the evening he sat opposite his mother in the China Room, while a thin coal fire whispered grumpily between them. The curtains, with their stamped pagodas and blue tilted bridges, were drawn. A small King Charles spaniel bitch lay at Francis' feet. He realized quite suddenly, with that premonition of coming events, always his special gift, that some crisis was approaching. Everything in the room seemed to share his knowledge.

On his lap, as he was always afterwards to remember, was a copy of Burke's *Reflections on the Revolution in France*. His mother spoke. She had a fashion, when they were alone together, of speaking, as it were, to herself, so that when he answered her it was as though he were addressing the wall behind her or a picture or a chair. But now she looked at him directly.

'Francis,' she said, and her eyes wandered over his face as though she were seeing him for the first time. 'Why do you stay here? It is not, I know, to give yourself pleasure.'

'Yes, ma'am,' he answered. 'I am happy here.'

'No, you are not. I know exactly why you stay. It is from a sense of duty. You think that you did me a wrong and repay it by this attention to us. That is your duty.'

He made no answer. His heart beat thickly.

'Well, it is no duty. You have your own life to be lived. Will is working in London, but there is money sufficient for you to travel. Herman is honest enough and will see that everything goes smoothly here.'

Herman was the bailiff. The reference to Will was no new one. The inference was that Will was working hard at making money in London while Francis idled . . . No new inference.

But Francis, tried by much practice, only nodded his head.

'If you wish me to go, ma'am.'

'I wish! I wish! Who cares what I wish? . . . I am a dead woman.' Then a surprising thing happened. She turned to him almost eagerly, as though they were, for an instant, friends. 'You didn't know, did you, that one person can die and quite another take her place within the same skin? That other woman would have long forgiven you had she lived. Besides, she was your mother. She was gay and happy, foolish possibly in her trust of events, but she was only a child, although she bore children . . . But this other woman here is not your mother, was not even when she was alive. You have often felt her unjust, I know . . .'

'No, ma'am,' he answered her.

'Oh, but you have, you have! And rightly . . . Only I am not sorry at any injustice. That belonged to your mother.'

As always a strange mingling of irritation and pity rose in him. He hated a sort of melodrama and extravagance in her speech, and yet he knew that at the heart of the extravagance there was a real cankerous sickness.

He felt deeply sorry for them both, so gently he answered:

'I do not want to go, Mother, unless you wish it.'

She got up, felt for her cane, walked towards the door, then turned and said roughly:

'I do wish it. We can have no life together, you and I.'

Then she went out.

He stayed there alone in a kind of impotent fury. So that was all he got for his years of faithful service! He had always had a sharp, keen sense of reality and also a kind of hunger for it. He felt now that ever since his father's death this house had been completely unreal, and it was his mother who had made it so.

Tonight, his mother's last words in his ear, he was moved to a passionate sense of rebellion. He paced up and down the little parlour, the spaniel following his movement with soft anxious eyes. Yes, if she wished him to go he would do so! No word of thanks for all the drudgery of these years! Here he had lamed his life at its most active and promising period to serve her, and all he received was a contemptuous reference to Will. Will, who had never, in all his days, thought of anyone but himself or of anything but his own advantage!

Poor Francis was one of those who are confident about ideas but doubtful about the human race. That Liberty, Equality, Fraternity must ultimately flourish, he was convinced, but he was hurt, with pitiful ease, by any act of human injustice. He found it difficult to believe that human beings were egoistic, jealous, cruel, niggardly, and yet on every day of his life he was injured by proofs that they were.

He *could* not credit that all his years of service went for nothing. They did not go for nothing. Did he but know it, it was his mother's acute knowledge of her own injustice that aggravated her bitterness. But ... 'Herman will do as well.' Herman, the stout, red-faced bailiff, who was honest only because he was stupid and faithful, only because he was without imagination.

Tomorrow, then, he would go. He would show them— He stopped abruptly. Wiser councils were prevailing. First he would ride out to Watendlath and see little Judith. She would help him. She was now, he sighed, his only friend. The spaniel came to him as he sat down by the fire, put her paws on his knee and gazed into his face.

Next morning he rode out. He took a magnificent white mare, Juno, his especial favourite, who knew the country so well that she could find her way over almost trackless paths and climb precipitous hills like a young pony. He was a fine figure in his purple riding coat with the high collar, his head up, like a king. But he didn't feel like a king. There was something surreptitious in his departure as he turned down over the fell towards Bassenthwaite.

He told no one where he was going. Mention of Judith to the Uldale household was a great deal worse than useless. He had seen her three times in the fifteen months since her marriage, once in Keswick, twice at Watendlath. Watendlath was an exceedingly remote little valley lying among the higher hills above Borrowdale. It could indeed be scarcely named a valley: rather it was a narrow strip of meadow and stream lying between the wooded hills, Armboth on the Grasmere side and King's How and Brund Fell on the other.

It was utterly remote, with some twenty dwellings, a dark tarn and Watendlath Beck that ran down the strath until it tumbled over the hill at Lodore.

Georges Paris had found here exactly the place that he wanted, an old house once a Statesman's but now belonging to a farmer, Ritson, who, owing to a ne'er-do-well son, now dead, was at money odds, but owned two farms. Paris bought one farm from him, but kept him there to maintain both. And here he deposited Judith, while himself, for much of the year, was engaged on all kinds of doubtful adventures on the coast, even in Holland and Scandinavia.

Francis had not seen Judith for some months, but at his last sight of her had been amazed by the happiness that radiated from her. He had regarded the marriage with that ragamuffin Frenchman as most certainly disastrous, had not had spirit even to contradict the self-congratulatory 'I-told-you-so's' of his mother and sister. When he heard that Judith had been banished to Watendlath, disaster seemed even more certain. But when he saw her he found her confident, assured, triumphant. It was true that it was then still the first year of her marriage and for most of that Georges had been away. But she had had six months in Watendlath alone – and had flourished on it. When he rode out there on the last occasion it had been veiled in rain and storm. It had seemed to him simply the end of the world. With the rain lashing his face and the gale tugging at his hair he had looked back to see that small indomitable creature laughing goodbye to him in the narrow doorway. Indomitable, yes! But the happiness was real. It was not assumed to reassure him. His heart was touched, and he loved her more than ever.

He thought, as he rode on this March morning of flushing sun and hovering cloud through Keswick and then beside the Lake water that now tumbled with a shiver of grey and then swam into straths of gold, that she was the only human being now in all the world whom he did love.

In old days, when she had been a child and told him insistently that she adored him, his own shyness and sensitiveness of taste had held him back, but, after his father's death and her flight to Gauntry's, he had realized to the full the courage, fidelity, warmth of feeling in her, yes, and her egotism and passion for power as well. How could that passion for power be satisfied in this lonely place where there were scarcely a hundred souls ? He himself, who had no passion for power, but only for justice, could not be quiet there. No, he thought, sighing, as he turned Juno away from the Lake up the Fell path, nor anywhere else.

Where in the world now was Equality, where was Freedom ?

He, who had killed his father with his joy over the fall of the Bastille, must now in this March of 1792 begin to tremble at the things that his Frenchmen were contemplating. After the Flight to Varennes his sympathies, always so easily swayed by human misfortune, had begun to turn towards that unhappy King and Queen. Then the news in December of the ultimatum to the Elector of Treves had moved him again towards this brave country beset by so many external, as well as internal enemies, but the latest news of the quarrels between Delessart and Brissot in the Assembly caused him the bitterest disappointment.

He was afterwards to recollect that it was on that March day of cold sunshine, riding out to Watendlath, that he foresaw something of the cruel confusion that led to the September Massacres.

As he rode into the higher air and crossed the little bridge above the running stream he shook his shoulders with a sort of indignant despair. He had never before felt his life to be so lonely, so aimless, such a failure. He looked about him, and as always the beauty of this beloved country fell on him like a balm. Only a few days before there had been a March snowstorm in the upper dales. He could not yet, riding among the trees, see the rising Fell, but he could scent the snow in the air. He knew that if the snowfall had been deep the shepherds would be anxious for the sheep. He felt suddenly a touch of their anxiety and with that kind of shame for bothering about unreal things like politics when there were such real things as sheep close at hand. Soon he would be clear of the trees for a while and see how the sheep were faring.

He had reached now the spot where Watendlath Beck tumbled into Lodore, and as always when he was here he must stop and breathe in deeply that perfect beauty. This was surely one of the loveliest places in all England – English, too, in its qualities of old imperturbable age, a kind of wistful tranquillity, a cosiness of beauty mingled with an almost fierce suggestion of force. Here Vikings had stood, here two hundred years later his descendants would stand, and at every time the cataract (when the rains had fallen) would fling clouds of mist above the turning flower-like whiteness of the water that leapt and fell and leapt again between the thin brown stones. The dark bare stems of the larch and oak stood sentinel on either side, and exactly framed by the delicate pattern Derwentwater lay, in colour now snow upon steel, a thin shadow of stainless white hovering over the silver grey. Skiddaw and Blencathra seemed to sway under the chang-

ing passing cloud. Every colour – white and grey and brown –
although so delicate, seemed to hint at the coming Spring;
there was a promise of saffron and primrose in the stems of the
trees, in the leaping water of the Fall.

Francis felt for a moment that here was the answer to all his
unrest. With his hand on Juno's back, his eyes leaping with the
water, he swore to himself that he would be true to this fragment
of English soil, and that so long as he was so no other disappointment, whether in God or man, could deeply touch him. Here
was his proof that there was something lovely in the world that
made his life worthwhile.

He rode then higher on to the Fell, Juno picking her way on
an almost trackless path, and could see now the sheep gathered
into dark groups feeding on the loads of hay that the farmers
had sent to relieve them. The whole sweep of the Fell was
flooded with thin sunshine, and little rocks stood out in it like
islets of ebony. The snow, on the farther Fell, was more scattered
and lay in streaks like marking on a tiger's back. The sheep
moved in black sequence against the running stone walls. There
was silence everywhere, except for the rhythm like a humming
voice of the distant falls.

He rode on, through forest again. As he approached Watendlath in his purple coat on his great white horse, the distant white
fells, like pummelled pillows, shining down on him, he might
have been some knight-at-arms riding into the Forbidden Land.
He seemed to be more and more withdrawn from the world.
He was high up among the hills, and yet this meadow and stream
had the quality of a mysterious valley that would later on be
rich with flowers and enchanted with the voices of birds. But
today ice and snow and rock ringed him inexorably round.

Soon, looking down, he saw the odd dumpy shape of John
Green House, Judith's home. A queer little place indeed,
crouched into the soil as though it feared a blow, its narrow
windows peering blindly on to Armboth Fell that here was split
to allow a beck to tumble down the hollow. There was the
chattering of the beck, the bark of dogs, the lowing of a calf,
but before he had reached the door Judith had seen him, had
run out, had almost pulled him off his horse in her eagerness,
flung her arms round his neck and dragged him into the house.

John Green House was L-shaped with a double porch. From
the 'hallan' or passage there were three doors, one that led into
the 'down-house', now used for farm purposes, baking, brewings
and the rest, the second that led to the garden, and the third

to the 'house-place' or 'house', a beautiful room with lovely views, surrendered now entirely to Judith; beyond this room was a smaller panelled one, Judith's bedroom. A small staircase led upstairs to rooms that had been formerly open to the rafters but that were now ceilinged.

Judith took Francis into the 'house-place', shining now in the pale March sunlight. The walls were plastered. There was a stone mantelpiece over an open hearth; there was a settle, some carved chairs and a large oak table.

There were signs of Judith's passionate cleanliness every-where. Everything gleamed and shone; china, candlesticks of beaten brass, an old spit with many hooks and a dripping-pan. Some early daffodils were in a china bowl on the oak table.

She stood back and stared at him.

'Now, let me look at you! Oh, how handsome you are, Francis! I had forgotten. You are more beautiful every day!' She stood on tiptoe, pushing back the high hard collar of his riding coat that she might see the white fall of his neck cloth and the beech-coloured waistcoat with the stamped silver buttons.

'I always put on my best when I come out to see you,' he said, laughing, and taking off his riding coat.

'That's more than I can do for you,' she answered.

She was wearing the country clothes, an upper-dress of undyed duffel like a man's and a skirt of native wool woven into a sort of serge – wool of the black sheep mixed with red and blue. Her stockings were of blue homespun, and she had clogs of uncurried leather. They were lined with straw to keep her feet warm.

Francis thought she looked extremely well, with her pale excited face and the pile of red-gold hair on top of it. She was, as always, immaculate from head to toe. She had an air of virginal purity as though the wind, the rain, the unchecked sun had cleansed her with an austerity of their own. In fact she was neither austere nor remote. She was wild with excitement at seeing him, could not keep still, went dancing about the room, touching first one thing and then another, talking all the time. Of course, she was yet a child, only seventeen, while he was thirty-two. But it was true what she said, suddenly turning to him and crying: 'You know, Francis, I've always loved you – from the moment that I was born!'

She had to have someone to love, and she had to have some-one to dominate too. It amused him to see how at once she took charge of him, telling him where he must go and what he must do. It would soon be the dinner-hour, but first he must see everything, and she danced in front of him, taking him along the 'hallan' into the farmhouse of the Ritsons. He was aware of a great fire roaring in the open fireplace, of a spit turning, of sacks of corn, hams and sides of bacon hanging, the oak settle screened by the 'heck', the 'rannel-balk' or great wooden beam across the chimney, and a chain with hooks for cooking utensils hanging. The big room seemed filled with men and women, all busied with affairs, but he noticed in especial one magnificent old man with a snow-white beard like a patriarch. Judith introduced him. This was Robert Ritson, the head of the Ritson family, a man of seventy-four, who, in spite of his many troubles, financial and others, was yet above the world, above it and removed a little from it, with that touch of remoteness and austere reserve that is in all true Cumbrians.

Then they went out. She led him over the boulders and the foaming beck down the hill above the meadow to the Churn. The Churn was filled just now with water from the snow off the fells and toiled and tossed and seethed, an odd spot of turmoil above the quiet silence of the long meadow. Judith said a strange thing as they were looking into it.

'If Georges were to leave me I'd throw myself into it,' she said. Then laughing: 'No, I would not. I would stick a knife in his back.'

'Do you love him then so much?' asked Francis.

'I do.'

'And does he love you?'

'He loves no one at all but himself,' she answered.

Then they went and stood by the Tarn in front of the stone wall of the house. All was very grey and silent. The hills streaked with white, thick with naked trees, looked down on them while quilts of wadded cloud rolled heavily across the sky. Francis shivered.

'It's a black piece of water,' he said.

She told him that it could be every colour, that it had so many moods that she could almost believe that it was alive, as Mother West, the witch, said it was.

'Have you a witch then in this small place?' he asked her.

They had, but a good and kindly one who gave the girls love potions and the men cures for the rheumatism. 'She is an immense woman, like a whale.' Then, as they walked back into the house again, Judith told him about all the families in the

place, the Ritsons, the Wilsons, the Tysons, the Morrows, the
Blythwaites, the Gibsons, the Robsons.

Judith knew everyone and, as Francis soon perceived,
governed everyone. She was Mistress of Watendlath, knew it and
triumphed in it.

But it was not until after their dinner that they truly talked.
For dinner they had oat-bread baked on the girdle, a broth of
onions and savoury herbs, and a goose pie that had been made at
Christmas. To drink there was ale brewed in the 'down-house'.

When dinner was over they sat over the fire, while the logs
hissed and crackled and spat and threw out tongues of flame
against the blackened stone. He asked her first whether she were
happy. As she replied, telling him everything in her mind with
her accustomed honesty, he watched her. She had changed but
little, and he thought to himself that her real struggle with
Georges was yet to come.

She had all the audacity and self-confidence that she had
always had. Nothing in life had frightened her as yet then. She
had a woman's knowledge and common sense.

'This Georges of yours,' he said. 'You'd stick a knife in his
back if he left you. But he's always leaving you. How long has
he been away this time?'

'He has to be away on his business.'

'What is his business?'

'Oh, smuggling, stealing, anything bad. But when he has
made money he will settle down here.'

'Such a man settle down?'

'Oh yes. You cannot know him, of course. I often think no
one knows him but myself.'

'How much has he been here in the fifteen months of your
marriage?'

'Three months. Three months and a half. There was the
first month – oh, that was grand! We did nothing but make love
to one another. I was new to him. It couldn't stay ... One
morning he knocked me down, and before I was myself again
he was gone. But he wrote me a beautiful letter from Whitehaven. He was away then six months. He came back one forenoon without any warning and then we loved one another again
– two weeks or more. Then he was away five months, and the last
time he was here we were good company, not lovers. He had a
woman in Whitehaven.'

'You knew all this,' he asked her, 'and didn't care?'

She looked at him with bright eyes. 'Most certainly I cared.

Night after night I cried myself sick; then if I made a noise he would go and sleep with the farming men. He has no heart. He is quite cold. When I saw that, I stopped crying.'

'And you love such a man?' he asked, disgusted.

'Certainly. He wants me to love him. And I find him charming. He is the most elegant company in the world. When he is here at home we laugh and laugh for hours together. If I am in love with him and troublesome, he is either in love, too, or he is drunk and doesn't care, or he goes away. He certainly cares for me more than anyone in the world, but not for me very much. He says it is the fault of his mother, who was a bad woman and beat him. Did I ever tell you, Francis,' Judith dropped her voice a little, 'how when I was little and ran away to Uncle Tom's I looked through a door and saw Georges' mother naked and a young man in his shirt kissing her knees?'

'No,' said Francis, 'you never told me.'

'Well, that was the beginning of it.'

'The beginning of what?'

'Of my love for Georges. I love him because he is beautiful and witty and cares for nobody. But one day I will make him think of me so that he can never get me out of his mind. It is almost so now. He is always writing to me ... and when he has stolen enough money from other people, we shall go to London and steal some more.'

Francis was aghast.

'But, good heavens, child, do you approve of stealing?'

'I would not steal myself. I wouldn't steal a halfpenny. But no one will ever stop Georges from stealing. It is in his blood. He steals my things all the while – and from the Ritsons too. But one thing about Georges – he never tells a lie. If I ask him whether he has had women in Whitehaven he always says Yes. He tells me all about the smuggling. He tells me everything. You cannot change people's natures. Isn't that what your Mr Rousseau said? I have read the *Nouvelle Héloïse* and find it too full of sentiment. Well, I love Georges and I cannot change him. He had a bad mother – so what would you?'

'And he beats you?'

'No longer. After the last time I said next time I would kill him. Perhaps I would. He knows my father was mad and my mother a gipsy. That is one thing he cannot understand – that I am so *practical*.' She said the word twice with immense satisfaction. 'And on the other side so wild. I tell him that is the Herries blood; what makes them so interesting a family.'

'But,' cried Francis, still greatly distressed, 'there will be some terrible scandal. He will kill someone or be killed or be put in gaol or be hanged for a thief . . .'

She nodded her head. 'Georges says he will never die in his bed. I would be for ever anxious while he is away if I were not – what is it? – a fatalist. That's what I am, Francis, a fatalist. What will be will be, and nothing shall beat me.'

Then she went on eagerly. 'I want to go to London. London must be fine. I want to see all the Herries, my relations. Will lives there now, and they say his wife is as proud as a peacock and has a cast in her eye. Georges heard about them. And there is Pomfret, old Raiseley's son . . . Oh yes, and there are the Rockages in Wiltshire. It was the greatest fun, Emma Furze saw them.'

'Who is Emma Furze?'

'She is my greatest friend. She was Uncle Tom's mistress, and after he died she went back to the theatre again. She had a season in Salisbury, and Lady Rockage had a meeting about the wickedness of the theatre. Emma went, and she says Lady Rockage is like an old pincushion and has two children at her heels, and they have a house always in the rain—'

'It can't always be raining,' Francis interrupted, laughing. Then he asked: 'But how can you endure it so long here alone?'

'I am never alone,' she answered indignantly. 'Never for a moment. I shall prove it to you. I keep a Journal.'

She ran, pulled out the drawer of a cabinet and brought back to him a book bound in dark-green leather with heavy clasps.

He opened it at random and read, in her sprawling childish hand, entries such as these:*

Nov. 3rd, 1791. Mrs Ritson had a Haunch of Venison this morning from Mr Crosthwaite of Keswick. Obliging of him but I think he has an eye on Mary Ritson. While I was in at Tom Blythwaite's this morning their cousin Nancy B. from Mardale was taken in Labour being only a quarter gone and had a Miscarriage. No doctor nearer than Grange and he not arriving till late afternoon.

Nov. 7th, 1791. The Carrier, Ned Wilkinson from Keswick, round this forenoon. 2 Sauce Ladles pd twenty shillings. Poor Rate from Lady Day to Michlms pd 1.5.2½. Oh I forgot bought also of Ned Wilkinson a pair of Garters 0.1.0. To

* Judith Paris' *Journal* is still Herries property. See *An Old Border Family*, published by Houghley & Watson, 1894.

Poor Travelling Woman walking over from Grasmere o.6.o.
Mrs Mary Robson's little Boy by me for an hour while his
Mother baked.

Nov. 23rd, 1791. Mrs Watson of High Head Grange sent
us 2 Tubbs of Geneva. Very kind. The Robsons and Braith-
waites – John, Hob, Anne, Henry, came in last evening and
we had a Grand Feast. I gave them Pease Broth, boiled Leg
of Mutton and Caper Sauce, Mince Pye. After supper we
had Quadrille at which I lost 1d per fish – 1.0.0.

Dec. 4th, 1791. Mr Bletson rode up from Rosthwaite –
said he wished he could have driven up his new Curricle to
show me. Very smart painted Green with Red lines. Walked
down to Rosthwaite with him, he leading his horse. Walked
back through Snowstorm. Very heavy over the Langdales.
Fine Show of Sun betweenwhiles above Armboth. Pd 1.0.
per yd for 6 yds of white Cotton for Lining.

'Yes,' said Francis, looking up from the book to her eager
face. 'You're not dull – and you *are* practical.'

'It is to show Georges,' she answered, 'if he were ever to ask
where the money goes. But he never does. I have enough from
the farm, even though,' her voice lowered, her face grew dark,
'Georges were never to return again.'

'Then you don't know ... whether he comes, when he
comes—?'

'No; even though he writes he never says. A while ago I had
a letter, and from it you might fancy he would be here any
moment. My eye is always on the road by the Tarn. One day
without a word he will be coming along.'

She came closer to him, sitting curled up at his feet, her hand
on his knee. 'I think so much of my father. I fancy that I am
the only person left alive who gives him a thought. Already
he has gone so far back for everyone else, but not for me. His
house, you know, was just below here at Rosthwaite. It is
tumbling down. Poor Father! Everyone thought him too mad to
be real, but I understand how he felt. He is alive in me still,
Francis. Perhaps none of us ever die.'

'Better the dead than the living!' Francis broke in so fiercely
that Judith turned to stare at him. 'Put no trust in anyone alive,
Judith – not in your Georges nor in me nor in your friends here.
The dead are faithful, but the living change with every breath.
What was my mother ten years back, Judith? You knew
her. No one kinder or more generous ever breathed; but now,

although I may break my heart serving her, she can only say that Will is making money in London or that the bailiff manages better than I . . . I am going away from Uldale. I can endure it no longer.'

She could feel his whole body heaving with his distress. She thought that in a moment he would break into tears.

'Nay, nay, it is not so bad. I mustn't speak of Sarah because, God forgive me, I never loved her, but it will be good for you, Francis, to go to London for a while. Perhaps I shall follow you with Georges.'

'Everything has left me,' he murmured. 'I am quite alone. I am not a man to make friends readily. Even Moore, with whom I had an intimacy, has gone too far for me in this French business. And now – my mother, my sister—'

She kissed him passionately. 'I will never, never leave you, Francis. After Georges I love you most in the world. Do you remember years ago when I crept in to look at Mrs Monnasett after she was dead and your father beat me, how you came and comforted me? I ever *adored* you!'

'And do *you* remember,' he said, holding her close to him, 'one evening when there were fireworks on Keswick Lake, how we sat together – you and I, Will and Reuben – and talked of our future, how Will said that all he cared for was to make money, and I talked like a ninny, and Reuben—'

He broke off.

'And where is Reuben now? I have not seen him these two years. Someone told me he was an itinerant preacher.'

Judith nodded. 'Yes . . . He preaches in the hills to anyone who will listen. They throw stones and mud at him and set dogs on him from the villages, but he says that he is happy now, and so I hope he may be. Poor Reuben! Francis, will it not be terrible for him if there is no God, and when he is dead he has had all the stones and mud for nothing?'

'There can be no God,' Francis answered. 'This world is too unjust and bitter. No God could suffer Himself to witness it, and it is His own doing . . . And yet I dream sometimes of a fine Heaven, all mercy and charity, where all men are free and there are no tyrants . . .' He sighed, rubbing his eyes with his hands. 'Certainly a dream – further from this world every day . . . But you, Judith, Will, Reuben and I – we are a mixed lot of Herries. All Herries is in us together. From a study of all of us you would get the Herries quality. All obstinate, all proud, all English, but in nothing else alike. But you are right. You have told me what I came to ask. I will go to London. And yet I doubt that I will be happy there. I love this piece of country like none other in the world.'

She would have answered him, telling him, too, how she loved it; but he saw that she suddenly stiffened. She rose slowly from his feet, straightening her small body as though under a spell. Her eyes were fixed on the window.

He followed her gaze and saw coming on the rough path above the Tarn a group of people.

'It cannot be! It cannot be!' he heard Judith mutter, and then, a moment after, she had broken from him with a cry, had rushed from the room, and, her red hair tumbling, had started down the path.

Standing at the window, he saw then a figure detach itself from the group and run ahead of the rest. The figure met Judith, raised her in the air, hugging her.

'This must be Georges,' thought Francis with a quick sensation of sadness and loneliness. It was right that Judith should run to him. It must be marvellous for her after so long an absence, but why must the fellow come just now and spoil the only happy hour that Francis had known for many months?

Judith cared for him, Francis, but at the sight of her husband she could forget him as though he had never been. So it was with him always. Everyone had someone else. He was first with no one. Well, what of it? Had he not courage enough for that rôle? He shrugged his shoulders and went out.

Standing in the little wind-swept garden, he could see that others had been attracted by the noise and had come to the doors. In front of a cottage not far from him stood an enormous woman, yes, like a whale. That must be the witch of whom Judith had spoken.

A wind blew up the little stream that tumbled from the tarn. Some fat Herdwick sheep wandered like sleep-walkers towards the Fell. The group was near enough now for him to distinguish them. The leader was a slim, handsome, dark fellow, Georges Paris. He had an arm round Judith, who was looking up, talking eagerly. In the other he swung carelessly a gilt bird cage that contained a bright crimson bird.

Behind were two pack horses laden with boxes; there were sheepdogs, some young men, a stout laughing girl with a red ribbon in her hair. Georges Paris was wearing a handsomely cut riding coat and a broad hat with a silver cord round it. The colours of the gilt cage, the crimson bird, the red ribbon, stood

out sharply against the dark Tarn ridged now with the wind
like a gridiron, the snow-streaked hills, the heavy grey sky.

The air quivered with excitement; there were the voices,
dogs barking; everyone was laughing. A group of the Ritsons
came out eagerly from the farm.

He felt that he could not bear to meet them. He slipped away,
found Juno and rode off. No one noticed him. Within a week
he had departed for London.

THE CRIMSON BIRD

GEORGES PARIS, running forward to meet Judith, did not
know and would not have cared had he known that with those
very steps he was influencing the future form and shape of
branches of the Herries tree.

He was gay, he was honourably fatigued, he was hungry and
thirsty, triumphant with physical health and money in his
pocket. He hadn't seen his dear little Judith for many months.
He was going to remain with her now and make her happy and
make himself happy; but even as he greeted her he was able to
notice that one of the Ritson girls, advancing now towards the
little bridge, had grown uncommonly pretty while he was away
and had exactly the figure that he preferred.

Judith, too, running forward to meet him, was unaware that
she was running forward into the first chapter of her mature
life, and that when he caught her up, putting the bird cage for a
moment on the stones, and hugged her and rubbed his cheek
against hers, this was the opening of a battle that would form
her nature and mould it, affecting through her the whole future
stock and texture of the Herries family.

That moment when Judith was caught up and felt Georges'
arms about her and his mouth on hers was her last of peace.
She did not at the time realize that. She was to have weeks now
of happiness. But looking back long afterwards she saw clearly
that that was so. The steps from that were so gradual, so silent,
but the movement was sure. So, to the end of her life, she remembered that heavy grey sky, the snow-flecked hills, the ruffled
water of the Tarn, the crimson bird beating against the bars of
the cage on the wet shining stones, and that warm amused
murmur of Georges' voice.

'My little darling . . . And is your hair still so lovely ?'

Afterwards she thought perhaps that she got what she deserved, because in all her excitement she forgot entirely Francis, never all that afternoon remembered him, sank into her husband's arms that night without a thought of him.

It is of no use, however, to be too solemn about it, for that day and many days after it were exceedingly happy for both Judith and Georges. Georges wanted only for himself to be happy, and if he was happy, why, then, he was charming to everyone. It was only when he began to be less happy that others began to suffer.

And Judith wanted only that Georges should be happy. She could not have believed that the world could be so lovely as it was in the weeks after Georges' return. They were still children, both of them, in their capacity for happiness. They could be happy at a moment's notice and over nothing at all, a bird's cry, a gooseberry pudding, a dance in the road, the sun on the Tarn.

The sun shone during those weeks. All the valley was illuminated. Nor was it ever a constant sun, whose glow can be wearisome. Not in this country. It was a sun attended by flights of happy clouds, and it shone upon all the running streams with the endearing tenderness of a passing hand, glittered in the heart of the bogs of peat and struck fire from the streaming rocks.

For the first weeks Judith had no conception but that she was going to be happy for ever. She knew that Georges was selfish, grabbing, thoughtless of others, a liar and a thief. On the other hand he was delightful to look at, a charming companion when he was pleased, and, although a liar about his deeds, quite honest about himself. But beyond these things she loved him. She loved him with all her being, and when one says that of Judith one means it.

She loved him maternally, because she knew that he was an evil small boy, who had not reached any age of discretion. She loved him physically. She loved him as a comrade. She loved him quite selflessly, never thinking at all of her own advantage in anything, but in her heart she was determined one day to dominate him. She could not help that in herself. It was so in her with everyone whom she met. She must *want* to dominate them.

But she loved him behind and beyond these ways, as only women can love – that is as though she had made him herself. She did not like altogether some of the things in him that she

had made, but it was her work. So she loved him with deep
tenderness and care, but also with the proprietary pride that a
craftsman has for his beautiful creation.

She knew that he did not love her in any sense of the word
as she understood it, but she did not want him to love her in
her way. She wanted him simply as he was. Well, she got him
as he was, and the first trouble came when he showed her a
little of what he was. This was in March 1793.

The suddenness of that first trouble took her breath away.
They had had a merry evening. They had had a 'rocking-night'
in the Ritsons' great kitchen, the women spindling while everyone told tales. Wonderful stories were told, stories of the 'Wise
Man' and 'Hobthross', sovereign remedies against witchcraft,
stories of the hunting of the 'hiding' men after the '45.

Suddenly Judith was aware that no one there liked her
husband. The Cumbrian can hide his true feeling better than
any other of God's people; there is no sober reticence anywhere
in the world so dignified, so impenetrable as his if he wishes.
Judith knew these people; they were her friends; they had taken
her in and made her one of them, and when the Cumbrian does
that you are safe. They had not, however, taken Georges.

How did she know it? She could not tell, unless perhaps it
were something that she saw in the bright unswerving eye of old
Ritson, seated in the settle, his body high and taut, his white
beard a prophet's. His eye rested on Georges, and Judith was
suddenly frightened. They did not like Georges. They none of
them liked him.

Later that night she was lying beside Georges in bed. They
could hear the tumbling water beyond the house. No other sound.
Driven by her queer uneasiness, she began to ask him questions,
questions about his life in Whitehaven; he kept always a dark
cloud over all his life away from her. It had always been understood between them that she left that alone. But if she asked
him anything he must answer her truthfully. As his answers
always hurt her she had learnt not to ask.

But tonight she was uneasy. Why did her friends here not like
him? He felt strange to her, as though she had never touched
him before nor heard his voice. She was very young and knew
nothing yet about marriage.

So she said a very foolish thing.

'Next time that you go to Whitehaven, I shall come with you.'

He laughed gently. He put up his hand and buried it in her
hair. 'Then I would kill you and throw you into the sea,' he said.

'But when you go to London you say you will take me with you.'

'Yes, I shall need you there.' He tugged at her hair.

'Don't, Georges. You hurt me ... But perhaps you need me in Whitehaven.'

'I neither need you nor think of you in Whitehaven.'

'You don't think of me?'

'But why should I? I have quite another life there.'

'But you write letters to me.'

'Yes. Suddenly you come into my mind ... Your smallness, your hair, how you laugh when you are amused. Then I write.'

She sighed with satisfaction.

'Then you do belong to me. I can make you do what I say.'

This was the instant of transformation. He sat up in bed and shook her until her head was, it seemed, separated from her neck. Then he pushed her out on to the floor.

She got up slowly, rubbing her hands in her eyes and staring at him in amazement. Then he jumped out of bed and chased her out of that room into the next. He caught her, dragged her by the hair and threw her on to the floor again. He was trembling with anger. She could see him only dimly in a pale-green moonlight that shadowed the sky and the room. But two stars quivered with laughter above the dark stern trees.

'Never you say that again!' he shouted at her. 'I'll beat you! That you own me! Never you say that again! You miserable! I'll whip you. By God, I shall show you!'

He was dancing with rage. She got up and stood against the wall, staring. She was too angry to speak. She sat all night in a chair under the green moonlight. She was bitterly cold. She couldn't think at all; she was so utterly surprised.

Early in the morning he came to her, kissed her feet and her hair, said that he was so sorry, so very, very sorry. Then he carried her to bed and warmed her cold body. She said not a word. She had never in all her life been so completely surprised.

All that day she was silent, going about her duties with a grave set face, and all day in her eyes there was that look of surprise. But she was not a fool, and she had the great gift that was to serve her again and again of seeing straight in difficult crises. When the situation was sentimental she was unsentimental, as indeed most women are. She was not in the least sentimental now, and when, in the evening of that day, Georges, made very uncomfortable by her silence, explained himself, she listened gravely, not thinking at all as to how she could snatch compensation from him for her wounded pride, but simply as to whether what he said really explained what had happened.

But in the middle of the explanation, Judith, looking up, saw the crimson bird, a cockatoo, in the gilt cage hanging from a nail. The bird had its head on one side and, with its beady eyes shining, listened attentively to everything that Georges said.

'I am bad,' he began. 'I always told you that I was. I have never had – what do you say? – any fine sense of morality. I am not at all like your Sir Charles Grandison. I despise the sentiments; they are for women. I have the devil of a temper and I have never tried to check it. My mother had it also. For myself I think that if you understand my temper it is very agreeable. It makes a change.'

'Do you love me?' asked Judith suddenly. She asked not at all from sentiment, but because whether he did or not was a practical question of importance.

'No,' he said. 'No, Judith, I do not. I love nobody. I don't know what it is to love anybody if by love you mean to be in a fever, to give up what you want, to run hurrying to the feet of the beloved. I have never been in a fever about any person except to sleep with a woman, and then it is quickly over. No, I do not love you.'

'I see,' said Judith.

'No, but you must understand. I do not love you, but I care about you more than anyone except myself. I am bad and worthless. Not that I am ashamed. Why should I be? It is the colour I was born, that is all. But I am nearer having virtuous feelings when I am with you than at any other time. I have always thought that I had no heart as my mother had none. The French people are not famous for their heart. But at times I suspect that you are giving me a little. For example, I have been unhappy today because I hurt you, and I have never before been unhappy about hurting anybody. I always want to come back to you when I have gone away, and I feel now that if ever I bring everything down about my head – as I shall one day – it is only you in the whole world that I want to come to. You are a wonderful woman, Judith. You have more strength and courage and sense than I have ever seen in a woman. I don't really care for women except for a moment. I prefer greatly men, and that is what I like, to be in danger, to be against the law. More than anything in life I like to be against the law. I cannot bear that anyone should say to me "Do this!" or "Go there!" I am like a bird in a cage. That was why last night, when you said that you could make me do what you wished, I hated you and wanted to kill you. I am no good, Judith, but I do not care. If I want to be in a rage I am in a rage, if I wish to steal I steal. Life is not important, not in the least. You and I are not important. No one is important.

'Only to break the law, to beat someone who plays against you, to take what isn't yours and make it yours, that for a short time is amusing. But I hope my life will not be long.'

After all this Judith nodded her head. 'I think I understand you,' she said. 'You are very honest with me, Georges, and it would be an easier matter if I did not love you. There is no reason for loving you that I can see, but I do. Only I must protect myself. You must not beat me nor drag me by the hair. That is stupid and sentimental. It is like Emma Furze acting in a play.'

He agreed that it was. They were reconciled and were good friends again.

But when two people live together, every struggle between them, however handsomely it is ended, alters the relationship. Judith was now on her guard. She watched Georges, even as the crimson bird watched her. Yes, the crimson bird was very like Georges. It was charming when it wished, and twisted its neck to be scratched and rubbed its beak against your finger. But it surrendered, for no very obvious reason, to the most frantic tempers, screaming its rage and rasping its claws against the cage; it was very proud of itself and its feathers, and its spirit was undaunted, which was also one of the fine qualities in Georges. Judith had no intention of surrendering to Georges; he should not dominate her, but he was now a little distance removed from her. She must be close to him without his knowing it. She thought that she was clever enough for that. But it is difficult for any woman who has a very tender heart and no sentimentality. She is for ever tempted into situations that seem to her foolish. And therefore she keeps back so much that she feels.

As the summer came nearer Georges began to grow very restless.

He was not restless with the place. In his fashion he cared for it almost as deeply as Judith did, and it did not worry him at all that the people did not like him. Ever since he had first come to Cumberland as a little boy, the Cumbrians had disliked and suspected him, and it had never disturbed him at all. That it did not was one of the things that in the old days amused Tom Gauntry about him.

Watendlath was the wildest piece of land that he had yet known. The fells towards the Langdales appeared endless, and their mingling of peat and heather, ancient rock, strange tumuli in human shape, and sudden streams rushing through the soil as though on some secret mission enchanted his lawlessness. On the other side there was Keswick. All England just then was gambling crazy, and Keswick had its little share.

Georges was a born gambler; one day he was a genius at cards and on another he would be so wild and reckless that he would lose all his advantage. Like Mr Fox and the superior gentlemen in London he would bet on anything, the fall of a leaf, the approach of a woman round the corner, the wax of a guttering candle. There were plenty of men, from gentlemen like Mr Osbaldistone and Mr Kenrew down to ostlers at the 'George' or broken-down wasters like Tom Fawcett, who, in Keswick, would oblige him. At first, after his return from White-haven, he was well in funds. Then less and less so.

Judith sometimes rode with him into Keswick. She had a few friends there; a Mrs Pounder who had come from Bath; a rather blowzy red-cheeked lady, who knew Emma Furze, had a warm heart but an uncertain moral code; a Mrs Dunn and her husband Henry Dunn, kindly people, crazy about dogs and horses; one or two more. But on the whole Judith did not care for Keswick and would have given thirty of it for one of her beloved Watendlath. What really distressed her as the weeks passed was that Georges might in a gambling fit rid himself of her adored farm. That he was capable of it, in one of his excitements, she well knew.

For her own expenses she needed almost nothing at Watend-lath. She shared with the Ritsons food and shelter. She was scrupulous in her record of expenses, chronicling every penny; Georges never looked at her laborious accounts. At first he was ready to shower money on her. He bought her scarves and dresses and shoes and bonnets. She didn't need them in the least. Now he was less ready. She didn't care. There would always be food and shelter for him at the farm.

But if one night he should suddenly tell her that the farm was gone?

On the other hand, she shared with him his excitement about London. She would like to experience that adventure. They were not so cut off in the North as they had been. There was plenty of talk about the old King, the Regent, Mrs Fitzherbert and the rest.

Beyond this she had a strong Herries feeling. The Pomfrets in Kensington, Will and his ambitions, the Rockages in Wiltshire, she wanted to see them all and maybe, herself, play some part in the Herries fortunes. Half of her was sober Herries – she could understand Will's ambitions – the other half was wild English, born of her mother and father, belonging altogether to these hills and lakes and streams. One half of her looked at the other half of her, partly in mockery, partly in wonder.

By the month of July, which was hot and green with no wind, she knew that a crisis was approaching. Even the crimson bird seemed to know it, for it rapped its nails no longer on the bars of the cage, nor fell into violent rages. It perched, with its head on one side, and listened.

And the crisis came. But before it came, she had a moment with Georges that she would never forget, one of the happiest of her life.

He rode in from Keswick, up the little rough path above the beck that was now thin and placid like a child asleep. The evening sun was deep and fair over all the landscape, and gold-dust was in the air. He came and sat beside her in the window-seat, took her hand, put his arm around her and drew her to him. These gestures were so rare in him that she knew that something critical had happened.

She sat there, her heart trembling lest in his next words he should tell her that he had gambled the farm away. But he did not. He told her nothing, and she, wise through much experience, asked no questions.

They sat in the golden silence for a long time. The little stream that ran down the break in Armboth was only an amber line now after the dry weather.

'Judy, you funny little thing, how can you stay here month after month and be happy?'

'Because I love the place. My father lived below the hill in Rosthwaite, and he was there without moving for years and years.'

'Yes, but your father was crazed.'

'Maybe I'm crazed as well.'

'No, but you're not. You have more sense than anyone in Keswick. I'm proud of you, Judy.' Then after a pause he asked her: 'Do you not hate me for riding into Keswick and gambling, leaving the business in Whitehaven to tumble?'

'No,' she answered. 'I could never hate you.'

'Why not? Cannot you hate?'

'Oh yes, I can hate very well.'

'I could almost love you,' he said, 'if I were quieter. Some-times I dream of making a handsome fortune, and we have a big house with dogs and horses, and you have all you want . . .'

'I have all I want.'

He drew her closer, held to her as though someone would tear her away. She did not dare to let him see how happy she was. Wild ideas ran through her head that perhaps always life would be like this now. He would give up his dangerous ventures, they would improve the farm, sometimes they would go to London for a holiday, perhaps there would be children. She would be a hostess, as Sarah used to be in Uldale; on occasion she and Georges would escape from everyone up into the hills, Eskdale or Patterdale, away from everyone . . .

'How old are you now, Judy?'

She told him. Nineteen in November.

'I should not have married you so young. Indeed, I should never have married you at all.'

She drew his head close to her childish breasts. She sat on the window-seat clutching him to her. She saw her feet dangling. How she wished she were taller! Of course, he could not love her, so small and insignificant. Then as she looked at his dark head and felt the warmth of his cheek against her thin dress she thought that she was as good as another, better than many. But she would love him all her life long, even though she lived to be a hundred. He was worn out. 'He was playing cards all night,' she thought – and he slept there, his head on her breast.

It was her last quiet hour for many a day.

The crisis came a week later, and the cause of it was, of all people in the world, Reuben. She had seen Reuben but thrice since her marriage, once at his mother's house in Cockermouth (little Mr Sunwood had died a year and a half ago of a chill), once in Keswick, and had once listened to his preaching in Borrowdale beyond Rosthwaite. Poor Reuben! On that last occasion her heart had ached for him. He wandered, so she understood, from place to place, belonging to no especial ministry or sect, simply preaching Christ and His message. Yes, simple enough in intention, but involved in every possible sort of loneliness, hostility, ostracism. Reuben had not even, Judith thought, the gifts or personality of a preacher. He looked clumsy, ill-shapen, in his awkward, ill-fitting black coat, and he had what no public orator must have, lack of confidence in his own gifts, and so he bred lack of trust in his audience. He gazed anxiously around, and, save when he was caught up on the wings of his devotion and imagination, he hesitated for words and moved restlessly on his feet. On the day when she heard him there was a gathering of farmhands, women, boys, who listened, some with a mild, some with an angry, interest, and before the end he had been driven away with mud and stones. She had hurried after him, but had not found him.

Now, on a lovely summer's day, Mrs Ritson ran in to say that there was an itinerant preacher on the nearer side of Brund Fell and that they were going to hear him. It might, Judith thought, be Reuben. Georges was away at a farm bargaining for a horse.

Indeed, it was Reuben. She saw him at once, standing in his black coat bathed in sun, while all about him the rough tumbled fell wore that rather sinister look that this country has in brilliant sunlight – something too naked and bold, as though the real country were only present in cloud and mist and had given way to some flaunting and scheming intruder. Reuben looked the more helpless, the more dishevelled in the glare, and Judith, her heart always instantly touched by anything at odds, longed to go and stand beside him. He had by now, however, his supporters. Since she had last seen him he had collected apparently a little band of strange and incongruous figures – a large stout woman in a man's jacket and a bedraggled green skirt, two rheumy old men who were so nervous of their audience that they could scarcely stand on their rickety legs, two girls and a boy. Reuben was stouter of body, Judith thought, but younger than ever in face, his eyes wide and anxious like a baby's, his cheeks plump, his chin indeterminate.

A crowd had collected, it had followed him from Seathwaite, Rosthwaite, Grange. It was a rough-looking lot of men, women, children and dogs, some there in evident sympathy, but for the most they were, Judith thought, strangers to the district. She had noticed of late a certain class of foreigner in Keswick and surroundings. There was much distress abroad. Food prices were high, work in many parts scarce. Transportation, too, was so much easier than it had been. This little world was no longer isolated from the older one. The days of its extreme remoteness were over for ever.

Reuben was speaking when Judith, Mrs Ritson, and two other women drew near. He spoke with a shrill, rather piercing note that dropped suddenly to a low bass. There was something ludicrous about this that almost at once set some of his audience laughing. As he talked he waved his hands in the air and rolled his eyes. Every once and again the little group round him would break into singing with a wavering and unsteady tone. Judith became with every moment more uneasy. He began a passionate evocation of the character of Jesus Christ, speaking of His charity, His unselfishness, His courage. Behind his uncertain voice there was a piercing sincerity, but he had not the power to evoke for others what he himself saw. Judith had the strange notion that the hills, the rocks, the peat seemed to understand him better than the people around him. She fancied that the sun was a little veiled, the colours a little milder. But he could not catch his audience; they were not fish that day for his net. Some of the more scornful men began to laugh. One of the dogs began a fight with another dog. When the quavering voices were raised other voices joined in derisively. And as the opposition grew, Reuben's voice was ever more shrill, and his eyes wandered more beseechingly to the heavens.

Then someone threw a stone, pretending that it was aimed at one of the dogs. Other stones followed. Two men had been drinking gin from a bottle and began to quarrel; a moment later they were rolling on the ground atop of one another. The dogs were barking, the women screaming, figures were running down the hill. Clods of peat were thrown, more stones; something cut Reuben's cheek. His little band clustered close together, and then, as the scene was wilder, the two old men and the stout woman started away quickly over the brow of the hill.

Reuben stood there, his hand on his bleeding cheek, as though he did not quite know what to do. Judith went up to him and put her hand on his arm.

'Reuben dear—' she said.

He started, at first seeming not to recognize her. The crowd was streaming away down the hill.

'Come and rest at the farm,' she said.

He followed her quite passively, like a child. She felt his arm trembling under her hand. Then when they had gone a little way he began to speak.

'They think it finer not to listen ... to throw mud ... I cannot hold them. You may laugh, all of you may laugh, but the day is coming when the spirit of the Lord will descend upon me ... Stay a moment, Judith, while I fasten my boot.'

He was wearing faded and stained green breeches under his coat. He bent to tie the worn string of his boot. When he raised his head his forehead was bathed in perspiration and his cheek was bleeding again. But he was smiling.

'God has but just spoken to me and told me that I do well. He watcheth over me and will see that I come to no harm.'

'Where are you living?' she asked him; she had to take many quick little steps to keep pace with his almost running strides.

'Like the birds of the air—' Then he shook his head. 'I cannot remember, but I must always be talking in Bible phrases like the Methodists. But with you, Judith, that's folly. I live nowhere. I have no home unless I go to Mother. You know,' he began more excitedly, 'now that God is the only real thing in my life, roofs and walls are constricting. I am happier in the open.' She asked him to stay with them for a little while and be rested, but he shook his head. 'No, no . . . I must go on. There is so much to be done.'

While he was sitting beside the big open fire, she brought water, and he washed his face. He took off his coat and his shabby riding boots and his soiled neckcloth. He opened his shirt and bathed his breast that was smooth white like a woman's. His hands, too, were soft.

He became more collected and told her of his brother's death in France, how he had joined the first ragged French army and almost at once had been killed in some squabble on the way to the frontier. As he spoke Judith saw again the desperate hunted man in Cockermouth. It had been, it seemed, since that day that both for her and Reuben active consciousness of life had begun. After his brother's death, he told her, he had been always restless, and at last had begun to preach up and down the country, simply by himself, attached to no creed. He didn't know whether he did any good; it seemed to him that he did not. But he must go on. He was the Bear, ordered to play his part . . .

She realized that he had no great interest in her affairs. He put up his hand once and touched her hair, but he asked her no questions about herself, whether she were happy, how she lived here . . . Once he broke out about women. They were his great temptation, the temptation of the Devil. He tried to lead his life without them, but they were always breaking in. Often he could not sleep at nights, and in the towns, in the taverns and inns . . .

She kissed him. 'Reuben, stay here for a little. It is very pleasant here, and I will care for you—'

She broke off. Georges was standing in the doorway, looking at them. She realized at once the evil temper that he was in.

Things had gone badly with him over the horse. Reuben rose. His coat and vest were on a chair-back, his long muddy riding boots on the floor. He looked doubtfully at Reuben.

Judith said: 'Georges, this is Reuben.'

Georges began at once. 'Yes, and we want no canting preachers here. I have heard of your doings, sir. Whatever my wife may say, this is not the place for you.' He was in one of his black rages, trembling with anger.

Reuben at once hurried to pull on his boots, drag on his coat. He said nothing.

Judith burst out: 'Georges, you shall not. Reuben is my relation and my friend—'

'A fine relation. A canting humbugging preacher who steals the chickens and kisses the maids. A fox! A fox—'

But Reuben was clothed and stood for a moment with a very fine dignity. He kissed Judith's cheek. 'Goodbye, dear,' he said, then staying a moment before Georges, quite, as Judith was afterwards to remember, without any fear: 'Good day, sir; I do not steal chickens, and that I am a preacher is true and is God's will.'

She ran forward with a cry. 'No, no, Reuben—'

But he was gone. She could see him walking swiftly, but still with dignity, along the little path by the Tarn.

She stayed, watching, until he was out of sight, and then she was a proper termagant. Georges knew well that she had a temper, but he had never seen it like this, and had his own rage not been too fierce for him to be clear about anything he would have marvelled.

Although now they were close together, they shouted at one another as though they were at far ends of the valley.

'That is the last time! This is my place. He is my relation, like a brother. He came here weary, soiled—'

'A fine brother with his thieving.'

'You to talk of thieving—'

'Well, at least, I do it in the open. There's no hiding in women's cupboards.'

'You *shall* not! He is more noble than you can ever understand—'

'Well, go to him then! Tie a string to his tail and follow him round the countryside.'

She looked at him, then, moving back to the fireplace, drew her little body to its full height and in a small chill voice, speaking now very low, said:

'You are cruel. I have always known it, but how cruel, not until tonight.'

He came towards her, not for reconciliation. At that moment he hated her: to set up her will against his, and she had been bathing his cheek, that mean canting rat of a preacher – she – his wife—

'Aye,' he said slowly, 'when I have a ranting woman to discipline.'

'Now learn this,' she answered him, looking him in the face as though she had struck him between the eyes. In his rage he was not so angry but that he could see some dignity of anger in her that gave her a dominance he had never suspected in her. 'Learn this. I am not your woman to be disciplined. Here was one who came to me, my kinsman, weary, hungry, beset, and you drove him out with a curse. That I will never forget.'

'And I will never forget,' he answered as fiercely, 'what you have been to me this day. I am master in this place.'

'You shall never be master of me,' she answered.

'We shall see.'

He came towards her as though to strike her. She never moved. Then he remembered something. He was held. She was the elder at that instant as he stood there like an angry boy, his black hair ruffled and damp. He had on still his riding coat, and he carried a whip in his hand.

They exchanged a long defiant look. Then he turned on his heel.

'I have had enough of this,' he said, and he went up the winding stair.

She never moved. Later – she had no sense of time, but her anger bore her as though on a horse with bright wings, timelessly, through dry air – he came down, pulling after him a box. It bumped on every stair. He stood in the doorway, dark in an evening glow all saffron, with faint blue light in the upper sky.

'I shall never return,' he said.

Still she did not move. She heard him call to young Jacob Ritson. She heard them lead the horse out and its sharp stamp on the stones, very clear on that summer evening. Then she saw him ride off, the box behind him. She saw him climb the Fell beyond the Tarn. And still her anger was so hot that it held her high in fiery space.

Many hours later, at some early morning time, she woke, and her brain was quite clear and her anger all gone. She did not at first realize that he was not there. Half awake, she turned as she was accustomed to do, to settle her small body inside the curve of his arm. She would lay her head on his breast, even in her sleep seeing that her hair was not in his eyes, then her hand would fold inside his palm.

She stretched out her hand and touched only the cold bed. Then she was fully awake. She sat up to hear some bird calling its cry like slipping water beyond the open window. There was a pale light, like stealing smoke over the room, and in her ear as though a voice had called it from over the hill: 'I shall never return.'

She waited weeks for a letter. None came. He was gone; and he meant, no doubt, what he had said. It would be like him. She saw now that she had never had any real hold on him. He did not love her; he had very often told her so. He liked to tell her. She knew nothing about his life without her. She envisaged White-haven and the sea as a strange town, the houses running down to the sea-edge, figures moving on the foreshore, bales loaded in dark-ness, the firing of a pistol, or some woman, very opposite to her-self, tall and dark, coming softly in a candlelit room, drawing him towards her . . . and outside these scenes a sea always angry, grey and roaring, and some foreign coast, darkness again, men moving on tiptoe. That was what her imagination did for her, and it was to this land that he had returned. He would never come back.

She had great courage. She would show no one that anything had occurred. She went about all her daily business, her head up, poking her nose into every village affair, nothing too trivial for her, deciding always what was best to be done, hypnotizing them into believing that she was a woman, although she knew now that she was only a child.

Her business now was to cut out all the outside world. She would not think of Georges nor of anything beyond Watendlath Beck.

All the souls of the village she brought into her world and made them giant-size to fill the space better – old man Ritson, patriarchal, aloof, believing fiercely in God and His angels, whom he expected to descend from the skies at any moment, but practical, too, about money so that he knew where every penny went to; young Tom Ritson, deformed, with a crooked back, a marvel at any job with his hands; Mary Ritson, the beauty who loved some imaginary man of her dreams and would wear a lost faraway look when earthy young men courted her; Giles

Braithwaite the wrestler, famous in all Borrowdale already, though he was only twenty, later to be famous through all Cumberland and the North, at present a stupid young man who thought the French lived over Ullswater way; James Wilson, broad, brown-faced, kindly-eyed, the finest Cumbrian of them all, whose wife Jane gave him a child every year so that he now had fourteen; Mother West, the whale, the witch, perhaps at the last, when all was said, Judith's warmest friend in the place; the children, the babies, scattering like ducks, like chickens, like puppies in and out of the becks, the peat, the stony passages – all Cumberland, if you liked, held in this small space, among these few rocks and boulders. Nor so changed from today when the Herdwick sheep still pass from descendant to descendant, and the children still go, day after day, rain or shine, down the rocky path to school in Rosthwaite. They did not care that only a mile or two away by the sea the new Industrial England was beginning to show its dusky evil-stained face, nor that there was an old mad King in London. Here, between Armboth and Brund Fell, was, and is, the whole heart of England.

Soon, though, it was not enough for Judith. With all her resolve and courage, unhappiness crept closer and closer to her. She began to dread the waking moment of every day. She began to watch, against her will, more and more anxiously the path by which the carrier would come on his old fat horse from Keswick.

She realized for the first time for many years how lonely she was. These friends of hers in Watendlath were not enough for her. Reuben, even if she could find him, was not enough. Francis was in London. Deborah, Reuben's mother, was a widow in Cockermouth. Judith thought sometimes of going to visit Deborah Sunwood, but she shrank from it because it was there that she had one of her liveliest memories of Georges. She began to see, with a vividness that appalled her, that she had staked her whole life on Georges. She had not cared so much when he was away, because she had always known that he would come back. Like many another she discovered that true love is irreplaceable. There may be other later experiences as fine, but never *that* one again. There was no one else like Georges. There never would be. His very selfishness, ill-temper, childish reckless independence gave him his colour. And the fact that she had lost him made him twice as precious. She was growing through all this knowledge. Life taught her more now in these few weeks than in years before, but we do not thank life for teaching us *while* we are being taught.

She became more and more miserable. Sleep forsook her. She lay for hours, watching for the light, and when it came she watched the road. One evening she went to Mother West's dark smoky room that smelt of herbs and bacon, and made her tell the cards.

But the cards told nothing. Then one autumn afternoon her unhappiness was so deep that all her courage left her. She went out on to the peak of the Fell that looks down over Borrowdale and sat there, while the clouds rolled over Scafell in red and smoky splendour and all the bracken was gold. But she saw nothing. She sat there, her head in her hands, and cried her heart out. Only a stone's fall below her her father had lived, crazily alone for years.

'Oh, I cannot endure it any longer,' she cried as though to him. 'I cannot live without Georges. What am I to do?'

She dried her eyes and tried to be sensible. This was what she always despised others for doing, to have the vapours as the women in Keswick did, or to want a man who did not want them. Georges did not want her. Now, here on this hill, with only the sky about her, she must understand that he was never going to return. Her life with him was over, and she must make a new life for herself. 'No one can beat you but yourself.' She was young, strong, full of curiosity and eagerness to see the world.

Georges had never cared very much for her (but had he not always returned to her?), he was not a fine man (but was he not endearing with his dark hair and his sense of fun?), he was for ever in a temper (but was he not enchanting when things went well?), he would be hanged one day (would she not be proud to stand at his side when all the world was against him?), he was French, and the French were a bad nation (did she truly care *what* he was so long as he was with her?), she was an independent woman (who would live her life in her own way whatever men did). Perhaps (for queerer things happen in this world than facts allow for) an old man with a scarred face stood beside her then, his arm about her, he looking down through rock and stone to a little house tumbling to ruin.

So she went back over the Fell with her head up, and the first thing that she heard was that there was a letter for her. On the one day that she had not watched!

It was scribbled on some rough tea-paper and ran:

DEAR LITTLE QUEEN JUDY – I have got a Fortune and

We shall go to London to spend it. I am coming Home to fetch you – Your loving husband,

GEORGES

She allowed the letter to drop. She ran like a mad thing in to all the Ritsons, and she caught the Patriarch round the neck, crying, 'He's coming home! He's made a fortune! He's coming home!'

She danced like the child that she yet was, into the hallan and over the cobbles, and ran into the whale's parlour and danced all about between the stuffed birds and the snakes in spirits and the bottle with the baby's thumb.

The smoke blew out of the chimney, and old Mother West, smoking her pipe, nodded her head with pleasure, for she loved this child.

The crimson bird in the cage woke up and scraped with its talons on the wires.

HAPPINESS IN LONDON

THE ONLY PART of Georges Paris that was visible was his nightcap, white with a red tassel that lifted and fell above his nose with the rhythm of his breathing.

Through the open door in the larger room Judith Paris lay, also sunk in sleep, her hair loose about the pillow, and on her lips a happy smile, because she dreamt that she and Georges were alone in a chaise made of silver that drove swiftly through the clouds above Scafell.

All the cocks around Cheapside were crowing. Above London a heavy dark mantle was slowly lifted, and soon over all the mud and running water that clung to the toes of the red-bricked City the sun would ride with an especial triumph, because it had not been seen for so many days. It had rained for nearly a week, and Jackanapes Row and Blowbladder Street were running with water.

Had Georges looked out from his little window into the street below at the first cock-crowing hour, he would have encountered Cheapside at the single moment of either day or night when all life there was still, for the roisterers had roistered to their beds, the 'Charlies' had not yet started their policing day, the watch-men had completed their happy and far-too-easy duties. The cocks, calling from St Dunstan's in the West to the Strand, from Butchers' Row to the Poultry, were kings of the hour.

Then as the light grew stronger he might have seen one small figure, little Jack Robinson, youngest son of Mr Jack Robinson, shoemaker, whose premises were on the ground floor under Georges and Judith. Mr Robinson, senior, had four small boys, who worked on his behalf sixteen hours of the day, and twelve children, fruit of his own loins, so that he was accustomed to children. That Jack, his youngest, should at this moment be earning his wages as 'climbing boy' seemed to him but right and proper, so that there he was with shovel, scraper and brush, and in his cap a brass plate with his master's name and address. He had had some bad chimneys that night, and was so sleepy that he had found his way home as it were blindfold, with chimneys dancing by his side all the way. His lungs were half-choked with soot, his knuckles were in his eyes, but he was home. In another five minutes he would have rolled under the blanket with six other young Robinsons, pushing in among them like a little bird. He was awake enough, though, to see that it was a fine day and to rejoice thereat, for there was to be a cock-fight by Bath Street that afternoon, and there would be rich gentlemen to beg pennies of on a fine day.

You can almost see Cheapside sit up, rub its fists in its eyes, give a great yawn and, jumping out of bed, start shaking its rattle. A light air has sprung up with the sun. For days these piles of little red houses, lifted, like boats on a stormy sea, on heaving cobbles, open sewers, sudden little hills that run up and down in the middle of narrow thoroughfares simply for fun, have felt the mud rise higher and higher about their doors. But this is June, and even in Cheapside the country is not far away. You can smell hay and roses as well as sewage and stale cabbage and the offal of cows and dogs and horses. The river, too, is close at hand; you can hear the noise from the steam-engines in the factories of the soap- and oil-makers, the glass-makers and the boat-builders. Were you to stand on the roof above Georges' nightcap, you would see the Pool, a forest of masts, the ships at anchor, the lighters and the barges . . .

But Cheapside has its own noises, and soon, its face rosy with pleasure, is waving its rattle like the infant that it is, while the sun grows stronger and stronger and the churches are ringing their bells.

The noise is now rocketing about Georges' room. He hears nothing because he is well accustomed. But soon it is ten in the

morning, and Cheapside is going to make the best of the splendid
day.

First there are the milkwomen, then the baker ringing his
bell and calling out 'Hot Loaves', then the watercress men (three
bunches for twopence), then the old lady (at this time there were
two old ladies, one with a beard, who made Cheapside their
headquarters every day from ten to one) crying 'Baking or
Boiling Apples', charcoal stove and barrow attending them. And
now there is the man with bandboxes, carried on either end of
a pole (at this time in Cheapside and the neighbourhood a
giant Negro), then the brickdust man with his small sacks and
his donkey (the brickdust men are, after the lamplighters, the
great trainers of bulldogs). There are the rat-trap dealers and
the bullock-livers man, the basket man, the bellows man, the
chair-mender and the doormat man. All calling together they
are answered by the opening of high windows, the emptying
of pots and pans, the rumbling of the country wagons, the first
stir in the shops whose glass windows run round-bellied above
the cobbles, the barking of dogs, the lowing of cows, the ringing
of bells – such a hubbub that, although it is not yet mid-day, a
lady with her servant meeting another lady with *her* servant
must step into Mr Jordan's the silversmith's to exchange a
word or two and, once there, there are clocks to be seen and
necklaces, and there is a bull, they say, loose by St Paul's and
a crowd running really for the fun of the thing, because it is a
June morning with the sun shining, and here is an Italian with a
peep-show and a monkey, and a man caught robbing Mrs
Morris' fruitstall and no 'Charley' anywhere to be seen so that
Mr Benjamin Morris, fresh from a good night's sleep and fit
for anything, has given the thief two between the eyes and he
has tumbled into the gutter, and the little Robinsons, thoroughly
up and about now, throw choice pieces of dirt at him, and the bull
they say, is really mad, has trampled down two flower stalls and
a Jew's clothes-basket, and in the distance coming in veiled
harmonies through the summer air there are the strains of a
band, strains that mingle with the scent of the roses and new-
mown hay and make the young dandy in his blue and silver,
reading his paper in one of the Turk's Head Coffee Houses,
think of Apollo Gardens and St George's Spa.

All this before mid-day, and while Georges and Judith are
yet happy dreaming. The room in which Judith was sleeping
was a large one, Georges' little more than a closet. A shabby
place, Judith's room. The bed in which she was had over it

a very heavy mustard-coloured canopy, covered with faded red roses. The mantelpiece was tall and narrow, surmounting a wretched stove, semi-circular, with a flat front. There was a bowed fender of perforated sheet brass, a scarred table, and a large china jar filled with roses. There were two cupboards, a mean stand with a wash-hand basin. On one of the stiff high-backed chairs some of Judith's clothing. On another most of Georges'. The crimson bird hung in a gilt cage by the window, but there was now a green baize cloth over his head. The sun poured in through Georges' room into Judith's, lighting up patterns of dust and the bare boards of the floor and the bright green silk jacket over the chair and the silver sheen of Georges' white waistcoat with buttons of emerald. There were lying on the floor two masks, a child's drum painted brilliant red and yellow, and a bunch of artificial flowers.

So they slept, but not for long. A door burst open. A woman's voice (it was Mrs Robinson's, who was at the moment stumbling down rickety stairs, nursing a naked baby, devouring a slice of bread and ham) screamed: 'You can have it your own way, ma'am . . . You can have it your own way!'

In the doorway stood a lady of magnificent proportions, tall as a grenadier, as broad as tall, with a fine bosom, a grand impassioned eye, an air of ruling the world. How magnificently, too, was she dressed! Over her hair, arranged 'hedgehog' style and powdered a very light yellow, she wore a high-brimmed hat of dark beaver fur, adorned with splendid trimmings of purple silk. The dress that covered her noble form was a long caraco jacket of brown striped silk, a light corselet of black taffeta with white trimming. She carried a cane with an ebony top. She stood, her head high, her large face rubicund and jolly, her arm out resting on her stick in a fine theatrical pose.

Her eyes took in the room. Then she saw the bed and moved nearer to it. She stood looking down on Judith, smiling, her eyes sentimentally soft, for she was a most sentimental woman and had not seen her dear Judith for two years.

Then after a while she tiptoed across the room and looked in upon Georges, who was snoring lustily now with his mouth wide open. She looked out of window and had the pleasure to see a grand coach, wobbling along like a fat woman, stick in a rut between cobbles, little boys run up to the windows, a lady in a beaver hat very like her own push her head out, and a man have his fruit barrow overturned in the general excitement.

After five minutes of this, back to the bedroom again and

back to the bed. With a magnificent gesture that it was a thousand pities there was no one there to see, she bent forward
and gave Judith a smacking kiss on the forehead.

Judith woke, sat up, pushed her hair from her eyes, then saw
her visitor. With a cry she was out of bed and had her arms
around the other's tremendous waist.

'Emma! my darling, darling Emma!'

'Emma it is, my love! Thy Emma, whom Fortune has constrained, but the Heart—'

She could say no more, for Judith kissed her again and again,
while Emma's great arms enfolded her in her thin nightdress
with the excited fervour of an amatory bear.

'Oh, Emma. Where *have* you been? I assure you I think it
most ungrateful in you—'

But Emma would let her finish no sentence. Words poured
from her. She had been in Ireland. She had been in Dublin.
She had had the greatest success in the Irish theatres since Venus
and Minerva took human form. Especially in *The Irish Widow*
or, maybe yet more, in Dryden's *Rival Queens*. Tragedy,
comedy or farce, as Judith knew, it all came the same to her.
And there had been a gentleman in Dublin . . . Oh, a gentleman
in Dublin! 'Everyone who knew us spoke of marriage as a
speedy and certain affair, and I could have cried myself into
the vapours had I not Resolution and Character . . .'

'Well, and what prevented him?'

'An impudent little Toad with the morality of a – but I shock
you, my darling Judith.'

'Never fear,' cried Judith, jumping up and down on the floor
in her bare feet and the greatest excitement. 'I have stood a
good many shocks.'

'But how are you, my dear little love? and how does Mr
Georges?'

'Very well. Very well . . . we are all very well. But why have
you been so long away from me? Two years . . .'

All this in jerks, in exclamations, in frenzied pauses while
Judith laughs and Emma laughs.

'And he pursued me, the monstrous wretch, through three
streets and an alley-way until I was forced to run into a toy
shop and hope to have the fortune to meet with a chair!'

'But you are handsome now, Emma, so handsome! And so
grand. You have money. You have wealth.'

'I have a little. Just for the moment. All to spend upon you,
my darling. I am hoping to have an engagement at Drury Lane.'

'Georges and I, we too have money, just for the moment . . .'

'Your Georges, he detests me. I am terrified of him. He finds me impossible.'

'But Georges is changed, as you will discover. He is older, more serious. He has still some bad friends, but I have now a little influence, a very, very little influence. When he is not gambling at the "Salutation" or at Offley's he does very well with the money that he made two years ago; he started a business in Whitehaven with Captain Wix. You know Captain Wix? I forget. He is huge as a barrel, and his heart is as big as his belly. He is all heart. Even his liver is heart. But he is also shrewd, and they have made money . . . Georges travels from London there and back again . . . Yes, when he is away from his wicked friends, Mr Charteris, Mr Mandable, and there is a White-haven young man, Mr Stane. I like him the least of them all. His father owns a ship that trades to Holland. Georges has a share in it. But Georges is good now. You will see that for a Frenchman he is very well . . .'

'Oh, God, yes!' cried Emma, throwing her arms abroad in ecstasy. 'I can see that you are the happiest of women.'

'I am indeed, indeed happy,' Judith cried, 'now that you are come.'

They settled down more quietly after that, and sat down to-gether on the bed under the yellow canopy, Emma's arm around Judith, Judith's red head on Emma's bosom.

There was no insincerity in their affection; there was even a certain relief in their pleasure at being together again, for with neither of them had the success of their fortunes been quite so great as they gallantly pretended.

Emma had great qualities, and one of them was constancy to those whom she loved – for so long, at least, as they loved her! For Judith she had an especial care: there was something brave and reckless and good-humoured that exactly appealed to her. She liked a woman to have both spirit and heart, and a friend-ship with Judith that extended now over a number of years had proved her both dauntless and passionate.

When Emma had last seen the pair they had but lately descended on London, and their position was hazardous. She suspected, looking about the room, that it was still hazardous. Judith, she thought to herself, had been through something in these two years. She was prettier, her features were maturely formed, her assurance greater, her recklessness also, perhaps.

There was something individual in the dark flame and shadows of amber light of her hair. Emma had never seen any like it – and beneath it the pale vivacity of her small face was so sharply featured. Her body was lit with energy and independence. Covered as it was now with only the lightest of nightdresses, the June sun warming it, there was something virginal, untouched, in its fire and purity. Emma had once again the sense, that she had known before, that there was something in Judith remote and separate. And yet there could be no one more human, more normal in her passion for all the adventure, all the fun, all the experience that life chose to bring to her.

They had talked then, two years before, upon the great things that were to come from the descent upon the Herries relations. Well, what had come of it. How were they all?

Judith jumped off the bed, caught Emma's beaver hat, seized her cane. 'Look, Emma! Look! Now I'll give you Will! He's very tall, you know, very tall. Oh yes, extremely! And he talks like a war-horse. "Oh yes! Ha, ha! Well, well! Dear me! How are you, my dear?"' (Here Judith bent forward, very grand, almost to the ground and shook hands solemnly with an invisible midget.) 'Just as though, you know, we hadn't been brought up as children together. He's the City Man, but he's also moving up. Oh yes, very much up indeed! He can tell you all the latest about the Prince and his bride, and what poor Mrs Fitzherbert is doing, and why Lady Jersey chose the Prince *such* a plain partner and what Mr Fox lost last night at cards. He moves doubly, you know, Emma, darling. There's the Will of the moment and the Will of ten years hence – the Will there's going to be if he has any luck. And Christabel. Oh, Christabel! She's like this!' (Judith rolled her eyes, stood on tip-toe and made her face as vacant as a saucepan.) 'She's so stupid you can't believe it! She's for ever running herself down that you shall run her *up*! "I am but an old wife," she'll say. "I have my principles but nobody cares to bother with *me*!" And nobody does, you know. But she's kind, poor Christabel. She has a heart. She's all extravagances. "That's a *sweet* fellow," she will say. "Oh, a *sweet* fellow."' (And Judith gave her voice such a pitch of stupid ecstasy that Emma roared with laughter.)

'And then there are the Herries from Kensington, Pomfret and Rose and dear James and sweet Rodney. Pomfret's kind, but he loves the women, and Rose is so busy catching him that she can think of naught else. Pomfret's stout and dresses grandly. He and Rose are socially finer than Will and Christabel, but they haven't the money. No Herries have as much money as

Will, and the house in Kensington costs a deal. I like Pomfret.
Georges and I found him the other evening at Ranelagh, with a
lady all simpers and jewellery. Oh, it was the loveliest thing!
They had a chicken and a dish of ham between them, and he was
feeding her with the merrythought ... Mr James Herries puffs
himself like a bull when he walks. Like this.' (Here Judith gave
an admirable imitation.) 'His voice is all falsetto. He's at the
pimple stage.

'Then there are the Cards from Bournemouth. They come
every year to London for the Season. Prosper and Amelia and
the beautiful Jennifer, their daughter. Prosper is nearly fifty
years of age and is most distinguished. He wears a full-bottomed
wig, although it's the fashion no longer, and can tell you all
about the virtues of Bournemouth. He's so grandly dignified
that his knees won't bend, and he has buckles on his shoes as
large as saucers. Amelia's a little woman like a rabbit. But I like
Amelia. She'd be happier in a cottage with a sampler to work at.
But Jennifer, she's a beauty! She really is, Emma. Of the
dark kind! All cloudy splendour and proud as Helen of Troy.

'And then – oh, Emma darling, best of all there are the
Rockages. I've stayed there down in Wiltshire. Yes, twice.
Without Georges, you understand. Maria likes me – wherefore I
can *not* understand! But she does! She thinks I have a soul to be
saved, and so I don't doubt that I have. And what a place! They
haven't a penny between them, and the family coach has rats
in the straw, and they put buckets in the hall when it's raining
to catch the water through the ceiling. But Carey – that's Rockage – must have everything as grand as grand, although the footmen have holes in their stockings, and there isn't food to go
round. The last time I stayed there I half died of discomfort.
You know how it is in a country place where nothing is looked
after. Here it was the *extravagance* of neglect! All day long it
was nothing but pulling at bell-ropes that brought no answer or
always the wrong servant, or a pair of rusty tongs that let slip
a coal that is smaller than your head, or an asthmatic pair of
bellows, the coals always out, all the pencils with their heads
broken off, and *such* a mess of things in every room that was
lived in – phials, fiddles, books and knick-knacks, and the rooms
that weren't lived in as cold as tombs with all the family portraits
frowning from damp. And the gardens! Oh, Emma, the gardens!
All laid out in the ancient taste. You know – a mile's length of
clipped trees with spouting lions, fish ponds as round as a wheel,
with six or eight flights of neglected terraces and a summer-

house, all broken-down windows and decayed bluebottles.

'And the religion. Oh, Emma, the religion! Early morning, all the maids and the footmen with their patched heels in air, while Carey read a sermon, and trampling through the Wiltshire mud with Maria delivering tracts on the villagers, and Madeline, Carey's sister, mad with enforced virginity, talking to herself in the cupboard . . . And yet, Emma, it's there that I feel all Herries and want to feel so. Half of me is so Herries that I understand Will's ambition and Carey's pride and am proud of Jennifer's beauty because she's Herries like myself. But the other half of me . . . that's with Francis and Reuben and Georges and is lost in Cumberland peat. That's from my father, Emma, and I doubt it will ruin me in the end. But when I'm at Grosset or Kensington or Will's place I'm *all* Herries, and I would run all the establishment and see how the butter's used and where the beef bones go to and how every penny fares. Were it not for Georges I'd be mistress of Will's place by now, and Comptroller at Grosset, but they're afraid of Georges. They think he may be hanged any day, and they don't want a hanging relation.'

'Well,' said Emma reflectively, 'I'm glad that there's plenty of money. Money! Money! Judy, my darling, I'd sell my heart and lungs for money. I've never enough.'

'To tell you truth, neither have we,' said Judith, dropping her voice. 'I was speaking a trifle out of order, maybe, when I said that Georges' business was admirable. It might be if he'd attend to it, but we've been put to some odd straits, and it isn't twice or thrice only he's been in the lock-up.'

'But not today!' cried Georges, laughing. They looked up. He was standing in the doorway with his nightcap still on his head, a quilted blue bed-gown wrapped around him, rubbing his eyes and yawning.

This was an uneasy moment for Emma. In spite of her size she was a deeply shy woman, ready to burst into tears at any moment from sensitiveness. In the bad old days Georges had hated her; moreover, she was uneasy with anyone who had known her in the raggle-taggle times when she had been poor old Gauntry's mistress. Two years ago Georges had been polite to her and that was all.

Now, however, his regard was amiable. He was stouter than he had been, she reflected, but still very handsome. She was no trivial observer, and at once she realized that Judith's influence over him was now a very real one. Their relations had changed.

He was more good-natured, less self-willed, a little lazy, some
of his earlier energy dissipated. All this she realized in the next
half-hour, and with it her attitude to Judith insensibly altered.
Judith had a new power. She was somebody now. Emma
surrendered to her, but resisted her too, a mixed attitude that
Judith would rouse out of many of her later companions.

They spent the happiest hour. Both Georges and Judith were
of a ravenous hunger. In the cupboard there was a cold pie,
a rice pudding, beer and cheese. They had everything out on the
shabby table and ate as they were, Judith in a yellow jacket,
her nightdress, and Emma's hat still on her head. Georges was
kind to Emma. He had won money the night before over the
contest between Battling Ginger and Monty Punt. He was right
now for a day or two. He scattered his winnings on to the table
among the pie and the rice pudding, and let Judith take what
she wanted. Emma, encouraged, was able to come out with her
project, which was that they should both accompany her to the
'Elephant and Castle' at Newington for supper. She had, she
told them, a young friend, a Mr Audley, and the young friend
had a coach, and he would drive the three of them, through the
fields, to Newington. They should drive back under the moon
with the hedges smelling of flowers; at the 'Elephant' there were
sheep and cows and on a June night country dances on the
Green.

So they all gave themselves up to being happy. They had a
fine natural capacity for happiness, all three of them, and being
in one degree or another all adventurers, happiness brought no
kind of obligation with it. Georges dressed there in front of
Emma, and there was no false modesty on either side. The
bells of St Mary le Bow had struck three by the time that everyone was ready.

The usual dining hour was anything between three and four,
but they would wait now until they could enjoy their supper
under the trees of the 'Elephant'.

Georges, when dressed, was a dandy, and Emma sighed
romantically, as she always did at thought or vision of a handsome man.

His stoutness, not yet pronounced, added to the impressive-
ness of his foreign good looks. He was a man now, not a boy,
a man with a reckless air, a good-natured mouth, a roving and
humorous eye. A man to be trusted? Emma thought not. A
man for a woman to love? Of course. A man for Judy to love?
Oh, Emma hoped so, but could not be sure. They made a fine

pair. The colour of Georges' coat was dark cinnamon, no collar
to it, single-breasted; the waistcoat fully seen, of light blue
satin cut low under the pockets, under which, as well as down
the front and at the bottom, was a border of rosebuds, jonquils
and heart's-ease. He wore a lace frill, called a Chitterling, the
ends of his white cravat trimmed with lace, and the ruffles at his
wrists the same, his hair powdered, no curls, but brushed back
from his face and hanging in a black bag with a rosette behind.
Judith wore a jacquette of pale silver-coloured silk and the bodice
and underdress were of dark wine colour. Her red hair was unpowdered and fell down behind with curled ends, and perched
on it she wore a hat of light straw, also of pale silver. Her shoes
had silver buckles.

Judith thought the clothes that she and Georges wore on
this day important, for she describes them in her Journal
minutely, and at the top of the page has written in a hand that
is still very childish: 'The Happiest Day of My Life.'

Mr Audley's chariot-chaise was to be met in Holborn so they
engaged a hackney-carriage and drove there, Judith with her
head out of window for there was so much to see on this very
fine day. They rattled along with a great deal of bumping,
jerking in and out of holes, climbing little hills and running
down the other sides again, along Blowbladder Street, past
Butcher Hall Lane, Bath Street – sacred to the memory of
Charles II – Ivy Lane, where Dr Johnson had his Club, under
the ancient gateway beside Giltspur Street, up Snow Hill, past
Cock Lane, Cow Lane, Fleet Market, then a steep climb up
Holborn Hill, when they moved so slowly that little boys looked
in at the windows, a gentleman with silver rings in his ears
wanted Judith to buy a green parrot, the Bishop of Ely's Palace
with his gardens, Thavie's Inn, Staple Inn and so to Holborn.
Here, at a corner of Whetstone Park, was Mr Audley with his
coach.

Judith had already asked Emma to tell her all she could about
Mr Audley, but Emma could not tell her very much. It seemed
that Mr Audley was a young man with a very rich City father
(here it was Georges who pricked up his ears), that he was a
great admirer of Emma's ('A passion for the Play, my dear. He
was in Salisbury at the time, buying a horse, and he saw me in
Othello. I am free to confess that Emilia is not so splendid a role,
most especially in the version that we were playing, which was
one with music, and Othello, Mr Barnstaple, had a fine tenor
and played the flute in the third act, but I was wearing white

satin, and poor little Miss Huxley, who was playing Desdemona, was a chit of a thing that you could fit into a nutshell. To be honest, my dear, he liked my size. He was heard to say loudly in the pit that the Furze was his style and – well, we were friends very shortly after. He is a nice young fellow with most agreeable manners.')

He flushed with pleasure when he saw them. His coach was very smart, of a bright bay colour with silver ornaments on the harness. He was attended by a stout driver in a blue and yellow striped waistcoat who, as they approached, was engaged from the box in a sharp and apparently rather bitter discussion with two gentlemen and a fruit barrow.

Everything and everyone was very lively, including the June sun, the shopmen standing in their doorways, the glittering glass of the shop windows, an old man with a fiddle to whose tunes several children were dancing, a stout lady with a bell who was selling pinks and roses, and a church near by ringing peals as though it were mad with joy.

Mr Audley was introduced, they all climbed in and started off. Judith gave herself up to complete enjoyment. Everything was as she would have it, except that she would have preferred a chaise to a coach, because in a chaise she could see more, but in a chaise there would not be room for them all.

Mr Audley was exceedingly attentive to her, so attentive that she was afraid lest Emma should be jealous. His method of attention was to ask innumerable questions, to which, however, he appeared to expect no kind of answer. He had a foolish expressionless face, but his questions were for the most part educational, concerning literature and the drama. Judith soon conceived a feeling of maternal care for him, as though he were an infant or a puppy. He seemed to her so very eager, inexperienced and untutored.

'Pray, ma'am, you have read *Evelina*, of course. Do you not find the Branghtons too amusing? Is it not laughable where the Captain throws Madame Duval into a ditch? Is not the close inexpressibly touching? Is London not dull in June – no Covent Garden, only the Little Theatre? Pray, ma'am, have you been to the Tower lately? Are not the tigers and lions fine? I saw recently Foote's play *The Minor*. It is all against the Methodists. I laughed myself into hysterics. I was at the Pantheon the other evening. It is never the same since it was burnt. I was at a Masquerade there, as mean as ever you saw. But the fireworks at Marylebone! Have you seen the fireworks at Marylebone? I hope you find this coach easy. I have a phaeton, bought only last week, but Mrs Furze told me that friends might accompany her. I trust you are comfortable.'

It was his way, she assured herself, of courtesy and politeness. She need not listen to his questions if she did not wish. She had once and again, an uneasy feeling that Georges was watching Mr Audley with a growing conviction that he would, a little later, be an easy friend to win money from. She pushed that from her. She did not care just now to consider that side of Georges' character. Yes, she surrendered herself completely to happiness. There had been many days in the last two years when she had been, it seemed to her, living on the very edge of irretrievable disaster. One touch and she and Georges would both tumble over into a bottomless pit, and no one in the world care that they had gone. She knew Georges so well now that the black side of the account of her life with him was fearfully familiar. But slowly, slowly she was influencing him. Month by month he was less drunken, attended more steadily to his Whitehaven business, submitted to her will.

By a constant good humour, a perpetual check on her fears and alarms, a refusal to be astonished at any sudden calamity, a trained restraint on her own nerves, temper, moods – by all these things she had gradually governed him, he not knowing that he was governed. The odd thing was that, although she knew now by heart all the iniquities of which he was capable, all his tempers, his violences, his infidelities, his shadiness, she loved him more than ever. He was still her created work, although she was wise enough now never to show him that it was so. And there was, when all was said, somewhere in his strange character, a strain of sweetness, of loyalty, of liberality, of boyish candour, that made him to her, with reason, endearing. But, when all was said, she loved him, had always loved him, would always love him. There could be no one else for her.

It was enchanting when, after crossing the river, they left the town behind them and passed into the open fields. The blue sky was cloudless. Everything was painted with a shining lustre, and the trees were dark at the heart of their green foliage. They were at the 'Elephant' almost before they knew it.

Here, indeed, there was liveliness! In the centre was the stout signpost with its four pointers, and round and about it all the world was on the move. There was a countryman on a donkey driving two other donkeys in front of him, two shouting peasants with whip and dog, urging their stupid but amiable cows, two coaches drawn up at the inn door, and another, loaded with people, nearly riding down a little collection of barrows piled with flowers, fruit and vegetables. There was a private coach crammed with six people, and led by four horses, chariots, hackney-coaches, groups of country-people stood about enjoying the lovely afternoon, a party of very fine ladies and gentlemen, moving as though they were creatures of another planet, brilliant in their colours of red and purple, children outside the gardens playing at ball, dogs everywhere, and a superb solitary gentleman riding his horse, his servant riding behind him on another. Judith's heart beat with ecstasy when she saw all this life. She put her hand through Georges' arm and walked as proud as a duchess with him into the inn.

Here everything was in a bustle with the arrival of the two coaches, so, very soon, they crossed the road to the Gardens on the other side. These were simple Gardens, not like Marylebone or Bagnigge Wells, but they were what Judith preferred. There were 'Chinese' benches, rough wooden tables, very childish amusements with a pillory for a gentleman to sit in until he was liberated by a kiss from a lady, a maze in which lovers might be lost and a peepshow rather the worse for wear and weather. But soon, Judith was attending to none of these things, for sitting on the bench, her mouth open with excitement at all the things and people to see, her legs swinging, her eyes shining with delight, she was aware that Georges, of his own volition, had come to sit beside her, had his arm around her, was pressing her to him. All the world was forgotten in the heart-beating discovery of that moment. He had come of his own will, there in the public view, he who was so shy of demonstration, of anything that could attract general attention.

Wise from experience she showed no great responsiveness, only moved a little closer to him. But her heart was beating, and within herself she was thinking: 'I must keep this in memory. Whatever comes in the future nothing can take this away!'

All she said aloud was: 'Oh, how hungry I am! It is almost six, and we have eaten nothing all day long.'

'There was the cold pie,' he reminded her; then he whispered in her ear: 'Judy, do you love me?'

'A little,' she answered.

'Are you happy?'

'Yes – but when I have eaten I shall be happier.'

'I think you are charming. I am seeing you today with fresh eyes.'

'Your old wife!' She turned round to him, her eyes dancing. 'After so many years you can find that she has charm?'

'You are better. You are vastly improved. You are a woman now and yet you are still a child. Life has taught you something.'

'Marriage with you has taught me something,' she answered, laughing. 'Striving to alter you—'

'I doubt your capacity to amend me,' he said. 'Nobody enjoys better spirits than I – at times. Today when the sun is shining and my French blood is warmed and you, my little wife, are beside me, and we are in fine clothes and have money . . . Then I think heigh-ho! how virtuous I could be! But soon it will be Mr Moss and cold mutton and flying down side-streets to avoid creditors and the fog and rain—'

'Meanwhile,' she cried, 'let us be happy now. We have a happy day. We must enjoy it.'

'We must enjoy it,' he repeated after her. His eyes lighted as he saw Mr Audley coming towards them.

'Sir,' he cried. 'I would have a wager with you. Guineas that the next person through that gate yonder is a female.'

Mr Audley looked rather nervous. Judith saw that he was no gambler by nature.

'Why, surely,' he agreed in his silly fluttering voice. 'Guineas it is, sir.'

They watched the gate. Judith saw, with an odd mixture of tenderness and chagrin, that Georges was watching with an eager excitement worthy of some great hazard. His body was tingling with his suspense. For a moment no one came. Then a stout man in a high beaver hat, very solemn in his claret-coloured coat, marched in through the gate.

'Damn!' cried Georges. 'It is against me! But double or quits, Mr Audley, that the next is a female.'

'No, no,' Judith broke in. 'For shame, Georges. I am famished. Food I must have . . .'

She saw his brow clouding. He would, in another moment, have forgotten all his recent affection for her had not, fortunately, Emma been seen arriving and with her a serving-man.

She was now in her proper and most happy element, arranging ceremonies that had to do with food and drink. They were to have their meal under a large spreading chestnut. They would have veal cutlets, a small green-goose and asparagus, a damson pie . . .

Judith was long afterwards to remember that scene, the soft warm air, the cool green benignity of the great tree, the children

playing on the sward near to them, the noise of the coaches and
the carriages, the voices, sheep bleating – all beyond the gate;
the laughter of lovers happily lost in the maze near to them, her
own happiness as she sat beside Georges, her hand once and
again resting on his knee.

They were all so happy, Mr Audley so proud of his entertaining, and Emma in her tall hat at almost bursting point with
pleasure at the food, the cheerfulness, the general sense of security. Poor dear! Her life did not provide her with so many
secure moments!

She complained, of course, of the cooking as in duty bound,
being herself so great a connoisseur, but hugely nevertheless she
enjoyed it. She shouted orders to the waiters, and herself, at one
moment, hurried forward to inspect the green-goose on its
way through the gate from the inn opposite.

Then, as the sun sank beyond the garden walls and everything
was suffused with a pale shadow of gold, the dark friendly
patterns growing lengthy on the grass, a silver star or two
winking through the trees, a fiddler drew near and with him a
woman, who had a strong sweet voice. She sang:

> 'Beauty clear and fair,
>   Where the air
>   Rather like a perfume dwells:
>   Where the violet and the rose
>   Their blue veins and blush disclose
>   And come to honour nothing else;
>   Where to live near
>   And planted there
>   Is to live, and still live new;
>   Where to gain a favour is
>   More than light, perpetual bliss –
>   Make me live by serving you!
>
> 'Dear, again back recall
>   To this light,
>   A stranger to himself and all!
>   But the wonder and the story
>   Shall be yours, and else the glory;
>   I am your servant and your thrall.
>
> 'Dear, again back recall
>   To this light!'

Oh, that this moment might last for ever, never to change. This voice, this shining light, enclosed in this garden . . .

Georges, too, must have felt something of it for he rose impetuously and pressed money on the fiddler, then turned back to them a little shame-faced. But he kissed Judith before he sat down. The dusk came; candles were lit. There was dancing on the green.

But, alas, when it was time to go it was found that the coachman was perilously drunk. He greeted them all with a warm and most appreciatory affection. He would have embraced Emma, quarrelled with a little gentleman near by, who had, he fancied, insulted her.

Mr Audley was greatly ashamed and not of much value in the situation. He twittered like a bird whose nest is in danger, looking at Emma as though to implore her not to like him the less for this accident. Georges was of excellent practical use. It was just the situation for his temperament. He helped to hoist the man on the box, frightened away the interested spectators, quietened the horses and threatened the coachman with such dire penalties were there an accident that for the moment he was sobered. So they started off down the road under the stars. There was a moon, and everywhere a radiant peace.

But not for long. After a while the coachman began to sing; the horses took fright; the coach rocked and rocked again. Georges attempted, with head out of the window, to bring the man to his senses. There he was with throat uplifted, singing to the moon. A moment later there was a fearful heave, and the coach was on its side in the ditch. Georges climbed through the broken door, ran to the horses' heads. The others, uninjured except for a shaking and a bruise or so, climbed painfully after him and sat in the hedge. The coachman, his singing silenced, was perched skywards, fallen almost on to the horses' backs, his thick legs dangling. Georges assisted him down, and he at once began to snivel, his fist in his eyes like a schoolboy's.

The shafts and one wheel were broken. The other wheel raised in mid-air made a fantastic gesture.

At length Mr Audley and the coachman, still snivelling, set off for the nearest village to find some other conveyance. Emma, Judith and Georges sat in the hedge over a ditch, and a network of fiery stars shone down upon them. There might be highwaymen, an added adventure, but it seemed not; for the whole world was still, holding its breath under the moon.

In the shadow of the fantastic coach with its clamant wheel
Georges and Judith sat close together. He seemed to be, in the
spirit of that beneficent night, a transformed creature. He
declared his love as though this were the first night that he had
met her. She held her breath, catching the divine moment that
it might be with her for ever.

'Judith, I love you tonight. I have never told you that before.'

'No, never – and I have wanted it so.'

'It has grown in me. Through all my vagaries it has been
ever drawing closer to me. *You* have been drawing closer to me.'

'And I love you, Georges. I always shall.'

'Perhaps this is the beginning of a new life for us.'

She shook her head humorously.

'No. Things will be up and down again as they have always
been, but I am very happy for this moment.'

She was in a transcendent happiness. The two different
strands of her life were suddenly united in one common glory –
her practical daily Herries life, and the dream, that which
separated her from the rest of her kind. Love had for a moment
united them.

The fantastic wheel of the coach against the sky seemed to
promise her something:

'Trust this moment.'

And to threaten her something:

'This moment is already almost gone.'

'Oh, let me keep Georges!' was her unuttered prayer. And
if in the sequel her prayer was denied her, it was also granted. Her
whole nature in that half-hour was fulfilled.

In the hedge, bathed in the warm flower-scented air, for a
brief while they were completely united.

THE HERRIES BALL

MAY 17TH, 1796

JUDITH WENT TO the famous Masquerade at Will Herries'
house, given there in the month of May of the year 1796,
dressed as her mother.

She had never seen her mother, who had died in giving birth
to her. She had seen no picture of her; nevertheless it was a

link in the strange sequence of events that once there should have been a child sheltering in its mother's skirts at a Christmas games in a Borrowdale farm, that then there should have been a woman crying over her lost lover in Carlisle streets, that again there should have been a weary woman knocking at the door of Herries in Rosthwaite, that now Judith, dressed as a ragged gipsy, her red hair loose about her head, should be waiting in an almost breathless excitement for the coach to take her to another Herries house.

There were to be many consequences from the Masquerade on this night, consequences as important to the whole Herries family as the quarrel that rose out of this occasion, consequences that helped to make Judith's life afterwards what it was, and from that to affect generations and possibly the colour of England itself. For if, on that night, Judith had not been dressed as a gipsy, would the beautiful Jennifer have snapped the ivory stick of Mrs Will's fan – that famous fan!

It is still in dispute as to whether the mandarins painted on it were clothed in blue or silver. A letter still extant, written on the day after the Masquerade by Rose, Pomfret's wife, speaks of 'Christabel's *blue* Fan'. On the other hand, in Judith's own Journal, there are these words: '. . . And so, scarcely knowing what she did, so angry was she, she snapped one of the sticks of Christabel's Fan with the Silver Figures that had been lying on the Table at her side . . .'

We may go back, too, and ask History whether if Francis Herries, senior, had not sold his mistress at a Keswick Fair, would Jennifer Cards have recollected the fable of old Maria and her spaniel, and, if she had not . . . Of all the things of which we are uncertain in this world – and there are more every day – we can at least be sure that History has for one of its subjects the ultimate importance of trifles. A coin rolled on a table, a verse by Mr Pope, a cabbage grown in a stubborn garden, a foggy night in Carlisle, a players' booth in Penrith, scattered snow reflected like feathers in a lake – such things were the landmarks in the life of Francis Herries of Herries. Such things were to mark the life of his daughter also. And it is in the chronicle of such things that the history of the Herries family finds coherence.

Judith and Georges were ready dressed waiting for the hackney-coach, Judith as her mother and Georges as Mephistopheles. Four of the Robinson children, thumbs in their mouths, stood inside the doorway, wondering at the splendour, and a moment

later there was Mrs Robinson herself, a baby in her arms, to
announce that the coach had arrived.

Georges was superb and was well aware of it. He wore scarlet
shoes, black silk hose and doublet, a crimson cloak, a red peaked
hat with a black feather. His costume, tight-fitting, displayed
his figure to splendid advantage. He knew that his ankles, his
thighs, his chest, could suffer any display. He would, if he did
not take care, soon be too stout, but that was not yet.

Judith's dress was orange colour, trimmed with silver; it was
ragged a little, showing her neck and arms. She had a wreath
of flowers in her hair. She looked a child of ten; her excitement
gave her a colour of eager expectation. But although her excitement was great, she was yet able to be practical. She had her
anxieties. Georges was in one of his wild moods. They had,
during the last three months, been living very precariously. She
was not sure – he would not tell her – but she fancied that he
had been losing heavily at cards. Young Mr Stane (whom she
hated) had arrived three days before from Whitehaven; in his
sinister and complimentary politeness she had imagined threats
and bad omens.

She was in the difficult position of attempting to protect
Georges, but not knowing from what to protect him. He had
been in his most cynical, mocking, restless temper, treating her as
though she were a helpless child, assuming for himself an air
of profound wisdom (which was, as she well knew, quite un-
justified). She could only control or have any influence over
him by asking him no questions. She would not ask Henry
Stane anything. The lovely intimacy of that wonderful June day
at Newington had never returned. She had been wise to tell
herself that day that she must treasure it, for there would not be
many like it. Her anxiety over him only made her love him the
more, but she was working in the dark, fearing she knew not
what, dreading some awful disaster. She never saw Henry Stane
without knowing her fear increase. And she was not yet twenty-
two years of age.

However, it was her nature to be concerned with the happiness
of everyone who came near to her, and, before they started, she
was busy with all the Robinson children. They were a dirty little
group, as, indeed, necessity forced them to be. Judith, with her
passion for cleanliness, had kept her place as decent as she might,
but the rest of the house, although some of the rooms were let to
gentlemen of means, was a pig-sty. Many of the window-frames
were black with soot, windows were stuffed with paper and rag;

in one room eleven members of an Irish family slept in two beds; a drunken tailor on the floor above Judith kept a pig in his apartment.

Mrs Robinson had enough to do with her lodgers, her family and her husband's apprentices. She was not a bad-natured woman, and she had a deep admiration for Judith because she kept her room so clean, was always in a sensible mood and was connected with fine families. She had intended binding out her eldest girl Fanny, a child of eleven, to a tambour-maker, but very reluctantly, for she knew well enough the cruelty that these apprentice children must suffer. And Fanny was a bright, pretty child. But Judith had persuaded her to keep her at home, had even herself employed the child and paid her a wage. Then there was the little chimney-sweep (already out on his work this evening), who was falling into bad ways. Judith had been looking after him a little, letting him come into her room in the early afternoon when he had had his sleep out and was ready for any mischief. He was a funny old little boy and regarded Judith as just of his own age ...

So now she pinched the cheek of one child, patted the verminous head of another, smiled at the harassed mother and then, followed by her splendid Mephistopheles, picked her way down the filthy staircase.

Chelsea was a great distance in the coach, and they had plenty of opportunity for conversation. Avoiding any display of sentiment as she always did when she wanted to get at the truth, she challenged him at once as to the position: things were bad? He shrugged his shoulders. He had been unlucky. He was always unlucky now. Henry Stane had come down from White-haven with his usual complaints. Henry Stane – she shivered. Why had he so much to do with everything now? Well, he wanted to be a partner with Wix and Georges. He was ambitious. Because his father had once been a simple fisherman, he thought it fine to have risen in the world as he had; now he wanted to rise still further. Judith, trying to think connectedly in the jolting coach, had an impulse to implore Georges to free himself from Stane, buy him out, do anything. She did not know why she dreaded him as she did. Her mind flew back to the night in Cockermouth when she had helped to save Humphrey. That dark cellar, the fugitive, they were connected in some way with Stane and his ambitions ... But she said nothing. After the night of that quarrel in Watendlath she had determined not to question Georges about his Whitehaven affairs unless he wished.

'Don't sell the farm,' was all she murmured, as much to herself as to him.

'The farm?'

'Watendlath. You said once that if all else failed you could be
happy there, in the life . . .'

'By God, I could! It's strange, Judy, but when you speak of
it I could leave this London and the coin and the stinking
candles – all shut up, closed – I'd give a fortune to see that water
now tumbling over the stones and watch those smutty-nosed
sheep pushing up under the stone wall . . .'

She, too, had for a moment a vision – the cut in Armboth Fell,
the Tarn when the wind played on it, the ridge of the Fell
looking over Borrowdale.

But with his French impatience and eagerness for practical
things he drove all that from him. He had now an immense
confidence in her common sense and a respect for her judgement. It had grown in him through the years. So he began to
outline the schemes that he had for making use of all the Herries
connexions. This was an old topic with him. He often blamed
her for not making more of all her Herries family. They liked
her. Those old Rockages would do anything for her. Will was
like her own brother. Will Herries was becoming a very rich
man. Everyone talked of him. Why could they not give up this
hand-to-mouth existence? Why should she not get Georges some
place in Will's City business? Tonight would be a fine time to
work something. Will would be in great feather at having so
grand a Ball in his house. Judith would be able to do anything
with him.

Judith sighed to herself. This was an old, old topic. Georges
always raised it when things were going badly. When things
went well he loudly despised Will and his business, and that
he wouldn't be tied in the dirty City for all India's wealth. It
was only when he was in a corner that he thought of it. Yes,
Judith sighed. The omens were bad. Georges must be desperate.
And she could not tell him what was the truth – that all the
Herries family regarded Georges as a wild adventurer, almost as
a vagabond. That they would not have Georges, this little gambling Frenchman from nowhere, into any intimate connexion
with them, not if you offered them all China! It was bad enough
with the country crowded with French refugees as it was . . .

Georges went on. How clever Will had been about all this
French War that was ruining so many men, and he had managed
to make his profit out of it! There were rumours that he had been

lending the Prince money. Everything that he touched seemed
to turn to gold! And Georges was just the man for him! They
were much of an age. Will could not be more than twenty-six or
so. So young a man must need partners.

'He has partners,' Judith remarked. 'He is the youngest in
his firm.'

Well, young or not, he was the lively one. What would he not
be at forty? And he had been in the City for so short a time!
Georges *must* make some association with him! Surely Judith
could manage it. Judith had an impulse to turn to him: 'It's
your own fault that I can't – you with your tempers and sudden
idleness and bad company and gambling and the rest!' But she
might as well have said: 'You, Georges Paris, because you were
born Georges Paris.'

Their coach was going very slowly now, for they were approaching Ranelagh and there was much traffic. The road (that
had been but a few years before all country, but now buildings
were springing up) was crowded with chairs, private coaches,
hackneys, boys running with lights, families walking – so much
noise of wheels and shouting that Georges and Judith could not
hear one another speak. Now, as always, she surrendered at once
to all the excitement. She forgot all troubles, financial, domestic,
thought only of the Ball and all the fun there would be.

Will's house stood in its own ground. The whining purr of
the violins could be heard coming, as it were, from the heart of
the trees. Above the wide staircase the long ballroom glittered
under the wavering flutter of the candles that blew gently in
their hanging silver lustres.

Will had taken a bigger house than his present needs when, at
a moment, Sir Frederick Cottenham must sell at a ridiculously
low price because of a night's loss at cards. Servants were so
cheap as to cost almost nothing, except for mouths to be fed,
and although, because of the French War, food was more costly
every day, here there seemed to be always an abundance. It
came from somewhere, Christabel herself scarcely knew whence.

But the events of that strange evening began for Judith
not as she stood masked watching the fantastic medley of Turks,
Nuns, Punchinellos, Italian Ladies of the Renaissance, Devils,
Monks, Columbines and the rest, but rather at the sudden sight
of Francis, disguised only by his mask, wearing otherwise a
plain suit of black and silver. She would have moved at once to
his side, but she must first speak to Will and Christabel. They
were the only two unmasked in the room. There was something,

Judith felt at once, a little pathetic in Will's sense of triumph. She had a divination (how utterly surprised he would be if he knew!) of what this glorious moment would mean to him, and of the jealousies, hatreds, contempts that his very success would rouse up against him.

Yes, even now, this very room would be seething with them! The Herries who were here would be resenting his power, but resolving to make use of it, and those who were not Herries would be scorning him for a City merchant who was pushing into Society. And yet the Herries were as ancient and well-rooted a family as any in England. But it was new, this pushing upwards of the merchant by power of his wealth, this very Ball the symbol of the reluctant yielding of the old world to the new.

Will would have no sense of any of this. She realized, looking at his thin stiff body, marked with the sharp horse-bones of the Herries, his eyes lit with a cold, nevertheless animated pride, that he could feel nothing but his success. He might well be proud. Little more than a boy, he yet had arrived at this power. But Judith felt that in Christabel there was a real uneasiness. In an ugly dress of a pale yellow, her hair done too high for the present fashion, she seemed almost to be expecting sneers and insults. Judith saw that this evening had been both her proud expectation and anxious dread for months before. She was in a state of nervous tension that might lead to anything. And, in fact, at this time moods, tempers, resentments, wild pleasures were very near the surface. There was in the London of that moment much social etiquette, but little social control. The world was turning over, and everyone's foothold was a little insecure.

Neither Will nor Christabel had at that moment very much time for Judith, and after a while she was free to find Francis. A minuet was in progress. The coloured masked figures stirred in the candle-shine like fragments of a pattern moving towards a perfect arrangement. The moment when that arrangement was achieved – would the world stop ? But on every occasion something prevented perfection. Tall high windows were covered with curtains of silver brocade. On the distant gallery the musicians played. Judith could see, above the clouded colour that was veiled with a kind of dim smoke, one fiddler, very thin, his arm raised like a stick, a sharp-pointed nose that seemed almost to be directing the whole room . . .

She found Francis and touched his arm.

'Sir,' she said, 'a word with you,' as though they were strangers. Then she laughed. They stepped back into the curve of the windowplace. They had not seen one another for six months.

Francis had, the year previous, made friends with a Mr Samuel Rogers. This gentleman was a poet, who had become famous with a piece entitled 'The Pleasures of Memory'. He lived at Stoke Newington, and Francis had stayed with him there. In January of this same year he had been involved in some of the troubles connected with what was known as the White Terror, the suspicious and terrified reaction in England of the Terror in France, and Francis had been able to show him some assistance during this anxiety. He was, from Francis' account, a sharp-tongued little man, bitter in speech about every-one, but of great active kindliness in deed. Francis, at least, seemed to understand him, and in his company lately had met many interesting people. Rogers had London rooms in Paper Buildings, and Francis had had wonderful evenings there with men like Horne Tooke, Parr, Sheridan, and even the great Mr Fox himself. Francis had taken to a sort of sporadic journalism, the political variety. He also had published essays in the *Gentleman's Magazine* under the pseudonym of Peter Mountain.

But he seemed tonight to have but little interest in his own career. He was making a new life for himself; but Judith soon saw that it was no more the life that he wanted than the earlier Cumberland one had been. He was as alone here in this sound-ing, moving gaiety as he had been beside the silence of the Watendlath Tarn.

He seized upon Judith with a kind of feverish thirst. His need tonight was for someone who could give him some sort of re-assurance. Behind his mask his loneliness seemed for a moment to darken the candles, the coloured clothes, to put out all the splendour. She had her own excitements, her own anxieties, but as always when she was with anyone whom she loved she forgot her own life in her eagerness to benefit the other.

'Judith, let's escape together thousands of miles away – to some island where there are no people.'

'Only the savages,' she answered him, laughing.

'Well, we Herries are savages. I hate us in the mass. Behind the masks you can scent Herries a mile away. There, in that silly black costume, that's Maria Rockage, and near her in the red and gold that's Rockage. There to the right, the Punchinello, that's Montague Cards; there's Amelia, dressed as a Nun, dancing. We are a horrid family, so pleased with ourselves. For ever casting someone into outer darkness. "Oh, he's mad." "She's lunatic." "That's an atheist." And for what are we proud?

Because we are English, because we are Herries, as though you said: "Because I'm a cow." Judy, there was old Maria. Have you ever heard of Maria? She died in '45. She lived almost to be a hundred, within a month or two. When she failed her century Herries were angry all over the country. That is a record of the sort that they value. I have heard my father tell how your father visited them in Keswick after old Maria's funeral and found them all at odds. But her dog was there, the only thing that cared for her, and your father said that the scorn of them all in that dog's eyes . . .' He broke off. Looking at her half quizzically, he added: 'You know you have no right here, you and Georges. You are vagabonds. And I am one also.'

'I know,' Judith answered. 'And I had the whim to dress as my mother. I never saw her. But I fancied her at this Ball. What they would all say, if she came in from Borrowdale with the mud on her shoes! But I feel Herries as well, Francis. I would like to be the head of the family, very wealthy, telling them all what to do.' Then, catching his arm: 'Why, see, that must be Jennifer! Did you ever see anyone so lovely?'

Francis turned, looking more closely into the room.

'Do you know,' he said, 'I have never seen Jennifer? My lovely cousin . . .'

But he broke off. Quite close to them a beautiful girl was passing. Jennifer Cards was, in that year when Francis first saw her, twenty-six years of age. Francis Herries was thirty-six. That first sight of her was one of the more important moments of Herries history evolved on that eventful evening. She was dressed as Catherine de' Medici in a magnificent robe of slashed crimson, and behind her lovely head a stiff high collar of silver. Ropes of pearls were in her black hair. She was tall, carried herself superbly, her skin had the whiteness of a white rose. She walked lazily as though half asleep. Francis stared. He could not speak. It was as though, after all these years, his dream had been, by some favouring magician, created into fact for him.

'Her dress suits her nobly,' Judith said. But he did not hear her. He stood like a man lost.

Like a man lost! It was from that moment, perhaps, that Judith began to have the sense that this whole affair was a dream, and a dangerous dream too. Her excitement did not leave her, but the happy element in it. She began to feel that there was something evil in the air.

The dance had stopped, and the dancers broken up. A sort of wildness crept into the house. Not far away, in Ranelagh, down

the dark alleys, couples were standing in the shadow, body
strained against body in deep embrace. Although the music in
the room had ceased it still seemed to linger in the trees, and
little companies of wanderers gathered at the garden gates,
watching the house so brilliantly lit, heard the lean fiddler. Was
he seated among the chimney pots? Was it some strain from the
Ranelagh musicians? Or an old beggar fiddling wildly down the
road?

Judith saw that she had lost Francis. He cared no more what
she said to him. And then she saw another thing. She saw
that her own especial Mephistopheles was attracted just as
Francis was. But he was more active. His eyes fixed on the lovely
lady, Georges waited until he saw her a moment detached, alone.
He went up to her and spoke. How exactly Judith knew what
the tone of that voice would be, the softness, the charm! His
mother's! She saw again, as she often did when she was with
him, that moment of her childhood when in the bare room the
young man had knelt to the naked woman! Mother and son.
Ah, but he had charm when he spoke like that, when his body
seemed to tremble behind his voice. She could fancy how his
eyes would shine behind the mask! He spoke. Jennifer turned.
She looked at him and laughed. He spoke again. She smiled, and
they both moved away together, she leading, he following.

Judith shivered. She was cold there in the window. Francis
and Georges, the two whom she loved best in the world, they
would both leave her at any moment for a fine woman. She had
done so much for Georges, but at any instant he forgot her.
Indeed, it seemed that no one remembered her. She seemed to
be as alone in that crowd as though she were by herself on Brund
Fell. Her gipsy's dress, how shabby it was beside all these
splendours! And her mother would have been shabby, too, had
she been here. Once again she knew that sharp pang of alarm
at her own insecurity in this harsh, indifferent world. She
had no one but herself. Only her own pride to keep her. No one
would care if this moment she vanished for ever. Not Georges?
No, not Georges. Emma, perhaps, and at the thought of that
large, comforting women the tears stung her eyes, were damp
behind the mask. Then she pulled herself up. What did it matter
if she *were* alone in the world? So her mother had been, so
her father. Oneself was enough. She was aware then that a Mask,
dressed as Punchinello, stood motionless at her side. He had been
there perhaps for a long while. She turned, and as she did so
he spoke:

'You would not expect to find me here,' he said.

She knew at once the voice. It was young Stane. How was young Stane here? She thought he did not know Will. Georges had not brought him. He was always to her uncanny, and his presence now only increased her sense of the strange wildness of the evening.

She said coldly: 'I did not know that you were acquainted with Mr Herries.'

'Yes. You would not know. I had said nothing to Georges. But I have known Mr Herries – for some time.'

She might have guessed that he would. It was like him to make use of every advantage, but to tell no one of what he was doing. He would go far. He was not now more than twenty-five. Ten years back on naked feet he had been selling fish in Whitehaven. Georges had told her of his father, a huge man with a white beard, always reciting the Scriptures, who worshipped this his only child. She turned and looked at young Henry Stane. He had large black eyes behind the mask. He was black-haired, sallow like Georges, but tuned, she knew at once, to a far greater determination. He would eat Georges up! She saw at once how Georges' laziness, good-nature, bad temper, self-indulgence, all these would be simply easy material for Stane's advancement. He was an adventurer too, but he was resolved not to remain one.

Meanwhile she had never hated anyone so much; instinct, fear for Georges, and her own innate repulsion. She was not at her best when she hated anyone. She showed her feeling too readily. She showed it now.

'I congratulate you, Mr Stane,' she said. She saw (and it was to explain very much to her afterwards) that his most maddening quality was his imperturbability. Nothing could touch him. That would infuriate Georges just as now it was angering her. Then his next words amazed her:

'Pardon me. I know how you regard me. All is love or hatred with you. I admire so much your sincerity. But although you dislike me so very much, would you not perhaps allow me to say a word about your husband?'

'No,' she answered.

'Very well. But you have much influence with him.'

'What is it, then?'

'Only that he is making a great mistake to neglect his business so constantly. It is a good business, but it needs attention. He has a good head, Georges, but no discipline.'

She hated the familiarity in his voice. From behind her mask she looked at him.

'I know quite well what you feel about my husband. You wait only to climb over him into his place.'

'No, I assure you, madam—'

'Oh yes, I know very well—'

'Then there is nothing more to say. I meant it civilly.'

As he went it was as though another little Punchinello leapt out of him and sat on his shoulder, its small, puckered, malicious face laughing back at her. How insulting of him! — but there was truth, too, in what he said. And Georges was whispering somewhere in Jennifer's ear.

She had not for many years felt so miserable, so lonely, lost, deserted. Again and again the hot tears gathered behind the mask, and she beat them back. She felt as though some influence separated her from everyone there. She had expected to be so happy, but now that sense of slipping on the very edge of some disaster frightened her so threateningly that all she could do was to start off in search of Georges, to be sure that he was safe. No, she did not care whether he were with Jennifer or no, so long as he were safe.

She was soon caught into the throng. She realized that everything was growing very wild. Couples whirled madly together, colliding with others. Both men and women were elated with their freedom. Many were unmasking. The fiddlers seemed to be playing mad, discordant tunes as though they were drunk.

She had an odd thought as some stout Cardinal tried to catch her by the arm. 'It's because in their hearts they despise Will that they do this. It would not be like this in a really grand house.' She suspected that any of the 'really grand people' who had come had left already.

She was confirmed in her suspicions by having thrown almost into her arms poor Maria Rockage. Maria and Carey had, she knew, come to the Ball with a great sense of condescension. For one thing, Will was young enough to be their son; for another, he was a City man; for another, nothing in London anywhere was so fine and superior as Grosset. So they had come with condescension, with Methodist suspicion, and with kindliness of heart. Judith, young though she was, knew every motive in Maria Rockage's brain, her poverty, so that often at Grosset there was not food enough, her passion for her offspring, her confused Methodism, her muddled benevolence and her real warmth of heart. It was on this last ground that the two of them met.

But now Maria was frightened. She could not find Carey. She *must* find him for they must leave at once. Even the servants downstairs were drinking. There was a little black boy on the staircase eating pie out of a dish. The whole affair was tumbling out of control. She must find Carey and take him home, back to their rooms in Berkeley Square. As a matter of fact, Judith knew that the rooms were not in Berkeley Square, but up a mews in Brick Street. Young Phyllis (safely asleep at Grosset) was for ever betraying her mother's tactics. Maria's terror rose. She especially resented that Jennifer Cards should be the belle of the evening. She disliked and condemned the Bournemouth branch of the family. Moreover, her own rather shabby black dress had been, in intention, a Catherine de' Medici. It had a stiff high black collar. 'She paints shockingly high. How Amelia permits her . . . But Amelia wishes to sell her to the finest bidder, and for all they were so grand when Carey stayed at Bournemouth last year, the rain came into the coach and the straw was soaked . . . and I'm sure that Robert (Jennifer's brother) is an effeminate young man as you'd find among the silks and gauzes at a dressmaker's. Judith, *where* is Carey? Oh, help me to find him! This is, indeed, pandemonium.'

Almost everyone now had unmasked, and the scene had a strange phantasmal beauty.

In the brilliant dusty light, figures moved now to country dances. One followed another, the 'top couple' always 'calling the dance'. There were Chain Figure, Allemand, Triumph, Swing Corners, Poussette and many more. The dancers kept their places, observed their decorum. It was beyond them, in the alcoves, up and down the stairs, in the hall, that the coloured figures, devils and monks, courtesans and milkmaids, Columbines and sea-captains tumbled and laughed, whispered and embraced. Silver and purple, cinnamon and orange, grey and crimson broke, melted, formed, as though from the gilt ceiling with the pink naked cherubs a figure solemn, sad-faced, remote, hiding a gigantic yawn, absent-mindedly pulled the strings.

In any case the Herries strings were pulled that night. By a kind of fate the little Herries figures were drawn together and with disastrous consequences.

For Christabel Herries the evening had become a torture. She was only a girl in years, although tall and gawky of figure. Will's wealth had come suddenly. Of the many persons invited she knew herself not half, and their masquerades made them only more mysterious to her.

At that time in London it was a very general complaint that
many persons came to private Balls and Masquerades who were
quite unknown to their hosts and hostesses. It was the increasing
licence of these London seasons that led to the strict etiquette of
Bath and other watering-places. With the divisions at Court,
the uncertainty of the war with France, the consciousness of a
lower class slowly but increasingly vocal, the new importance
of the business man from the City, the advancing licence of
Vauxhall, Marylebone and the many lesser resorts, no hostess
during the last years of that century but knew alarms and terrors
that would have horrified her grandmother. No smaller hostess,
in any case – and Christabel was a very new hostess indeed. It
is an old and very true axiom that nothing can harm a party
save the anxieties and alarm of the host and hostess themselves.
All would have been well on this especial evening had Christabel
been able to command herself. Unfortunately, when the crisis
arrived, Will was elsewhere. He in fact saw nothing the matter
with his Ball. It would have taken a great deal more than a few
riotous spirits to upset his complacent equanimity. He had also
enjoyed no small quantity of his own wine, which he thought
excellent; he congratulated himself on acquiring it cheaply from
a Jewish gentleman in the City. He was dancing the Triumph
with a lady quite unknown to him, but, in his eyes, of an especial
fascination, when Christabel so desperately needed his support.
There were to be many occasions afterwards when he would
have given half his wealth had he only been there that he might
have prevented what occurred.

Many times in the records of any family it must seem that
the stage has been set with especial and malicious purpose.
Had Will's house not been an old one of Queen Anne's date
there would not have been the small ante-room leading
from the ballroom itself, and had there not been the small
ante-room . . .

It happened that Rose Herries, Pomfret's wife, from Kensington, began the trouble. Rose Herries was a woman thinned
and raddled by incessant jealousy. By birth the daughter of a
small Worcestershire clergyman, she had been amazed when the
handsome young Pomfret Herries had proposed for her in
marriage. Pomfret's father, Sir Raiseley Herries, had married
the sister of David, the son of old 'Rogue' Herries, but there had
been an old boyhood feud between Raiseley and David that
David's sister had certainly done nothing to heal. It was because
of the proximity to David's family at Uldale that the Raiseley

Herries had moved from Keswick to London. Raiseley, Pomfret's father, had always been delicate and ailing. When Pomfret
had been around twenty-five years of age, Raiseley had moved
for a summer into Worcester because of some doctor or other,
taking his two children with him. It was here that one fine
morning young Pomfret had seen the lovely Rose walking down
a country lane. He had fallen in love with her on the spot.
He had been often in love before, but never considered matrimony. Now he did consider it, and six months later was married.

Rose had never recovered from the shock of it. The most
that she had ever expected was a local squire, but now to be a
baronet's Lady, to have a grand house in Kensington and, above
and beyond that, to be married to a man whose figure was
everything that her most romantic imagination could have
designed for her! Sir Pomfret was an amiable fellow, contented
with all that came his way. He was as good a husband to her as
was in his nature. But, after the first month, he was unfaithful,
nor was he either then or later able to conceal his infidelities.
And, so evilly does fortune arrange, Rose was designed to be
jealous. She was made for it. The more jealous the more she
loved, and the more she loved the more jealous. Pomfret learned,
as all husbands learn, to conceal more skilfully his private life,
but the less Rose knew the more she guessed. She was frankly a
plague both to herself and to him. A Masquerade such as this was
designed to torture her.

Sir Pomfret's stout figure (he had come to the Ball as Henry
VIII) soon escaped her vision. She told herself, as, poor woman,
she had told herself a thousand times before, that 'she must
permit him his pleasure'. For five minutes she knew a sort of
unhappy nobility. She was being fine, generous, the true wife;
but the five minutes were as long as a lifetime, and soon, her
long thin neck craning (she was dressed in a watery green and
considered herself a Naiad), she looked for him everywhere. She
had come to the Ball happy and expectant; Pomfret would
stay by her side, he would dance with her and then, very
handsomely, she would say: 'Now be off. You don't want your
old wife at hand all the evening.' But he had left her so quickly;
he had given her nobility no opportunity.

It is another of the signs that Providence had its long finger
crooked in this affair that the men were all of them absent,
Will dancing, Rockage talking of his place in Wiltshire to an
elderly baroness, Pomfret making love to a very young but very
worldly Nun, and Georges . . . Well, Georges, his head singing

with Jennifer's beauty, was betting with some young men on the
staircase as to the number of young women's feet you could see
moving across the ballroom floor.

So the men were away. This was a woman's affair. Rose Herries
met Christabel by chance behind the bronze-coloured curtains
that portioned off the ante-room from the ballroom. It was
comparatively quiet here: the music, the voices came like water
flowing up, ebbing away again. The room had been cleared of
furniture; the walls had a blue and white paper recommended
to Christabel within the last month as the very latest design.
On it were depicted over and over again the sorrows of Werther,
an elongated Werther watching a gigantic Lotte beside the spring.

It was unquestioned that Christabel did not, by this time,
know what she was doing. It seemed to her that the whole thing
was a devastating, world-shaking scandal. Tomorrow all London
would be speaking of it. She and Will would be disgraced for
ever. The scandalous Herries Ball ... She had been always a
delicate woman. Child-bearing had but shaken her nerves the
further. Her stupid, wondering features, pale but strangely
streaked as though with the marks of someone else's fingers,
were puckered and childishly distressed above her ill-fitting
yellow dress.

She had convinced herself that it was Jennifer Cards who had
disgraced the Ball. She had always disliked Jennifer, always distrusted the Cards branch of the family, who, she was well aware,
looked down upon Will and herself. She did not like Rose and
Pomfret, the Kensington branch, very much better. Little Judith
was the one she especially cared for. She would have liked to
have her always with her. It was a thousand pities that she must
live up in that rough Cumberland and be married to a scamp
of a rascally Frenchman. Poor little Judith! Christabel knew that
she would come to some catastrophe. But she liked her; Judith
was kind and considerate, despised no one, understood one's
troubles. How she wished that Judith were here now! Then she
saw her with Maria Rockage and at the same moment Rose, in
her ugly green dress, peering about among the crowd.

The four women drew together as though by instinct, standing
just inside the ante-room as bathers, soaked with the sea, gather
together on a rock for a moment's pause. They were all nervous
and uneasy – Christabel because of her social anxiety, Rose
because of her errant husband, Maria because she could not find
Carey, Judith because the whole evening had been a failure for
her.

The big room was thinning. The candles were burning low. The music had lost its vigour. In the distance a crimson Cardinal pursued a Dairymaid, who ran with little screams of pleasure across the shining floor.

'That Baddeley,' said Rose Herries scornfully. 'There is some resemblance to mankind in him. That is as much as you can say . . .' She was speaking of a Mr James Baddeley, an acquaintance of Pomfret's.

'It is scandalous,' said Maria Rockage, 'that Jennifer should be so monstrously without a chaperon all the evening. When I was a girl, to leave one's chaperon for an instant, except to dance with an acceptable young man—' She broke off. She thought of her daughter Phyllis at Grosset, and how she could not afford to buy her the dresses . . . that flaunting crimson with the silver collar . . . 'But, of course, the looseness of these Masquerades . . .'

Christabel felt at once that this was a criticism of her Ball. All over London tomorrow . . . Her long fingers closed and unclosed about her fan. (The famous fan. Were the figures painted on it of blue or of silver ? Who will ever know ?)

'I admit . . . 'Tis a failure, a monstrous failure . . . I am distracted . . . And Will has assisted me in nothing at all . . . I have had all the burden myself . . .' She did not mind now what she said. She was on the verge of tears.

The others were surprised. They had not been thinking of the Ball. They had not thought it out of the way. Everyone knew what these Masquerades were. Once you wore a mask . . .

'Why, Christabel,' Maria said amiably (for when she could rise above her own worries she was a kindly woman), 'the Ball is well enough. A very fine Ball. A Masquerade must always have a certain licence.' (But nevertheless she thought 'This is a pandemonium.')

Judith, who had been standing looking into the outer room, wondering where Georges was (she could not see with her small stature over the head of the dancers), thinking that at least he might *once* that evening have sought her out, felt an instant desire to take Christabel in hand, to reassure her, to persuade her that everything was well, to make her happy again (and behind that she was still wondering about Georges, thinking that her love for him was a sort of poison in her blood, a poison that she would never, never be rid of).

'Yes, Jennifer has no modesty,' Rose said, bending her long neck. (Was *that* Pomfret laughing with that girl in white, there near the window in the farther corner?) 'Her father permits her to do as she pleases. Amelia has been playing cards instead of doing her duty. I never liked the girl: swollen with self-approval. They say that at Vauxhall the other week . . .' She broke off, for Maria Rockage's hand was on her arm. Jennifer was standing quite close to them, alone, looking into the ante-room.

It must be understood that the girl was elated with her triumph. She had not been so very much in London, and Bournemouth's triumphs were not very satisfactory. This was her first *real* Ball, and, more than that, it was in the very heart of the family. Although the Rockages had been there, yes, and the Herries from Kensington, it was she who had been the evening's sensation. She knew that socially the High World had not been represented here. But Jennifer was true Herries in that. Although she disliked all the other Herries except her own family, yet she thought them as good as anyone in the world – as good as the Pope or the Prince or Queen Charlotte or Lady Jersey. She wanted nothing more than to be the acknowledged Herries Beauty, and that not at all for the outside world but simply for the Herries world.

So here she was, panting with triumph, her mask in her hand, her marvellous dark blue eyes glittering with success and pleasure, her magnificent bosom half bare above the crimson, her carriage superb, her youth, vitality, self-confidence all alive and shining – and she glanced for a moment into the ante-room to see whether her mother were there. She looked and saw the four women, three of them, to her, untidy old frumps, and the fourth that strange girl Judith Paris, whose force of personality she felt. The girl had marvellous hair. She had character too. She didn't like her.

She might in fact have passed on had Judith's gipsy dress in some odd way not challenged her. Judith in her ragged dress with her unpowdered hair was unlike anyone else at the Ball. She had had, Jennifer knew, a vagabond for her mother and a vagabond for her father. Jennifer's grandfather had known 'Rogue' Herries.

So Jennifer stayed. She had not intended to look scornful. She was too happy. But there was an element of cruelty in her. She looked at Christabel's pale face and ugly yellow, at Rose's thin bones and ill-chosen green, at Maria Rockage's untidy hair, and before she moved away, she smiled.

Then she asked:

'Is my mother at cards?'

The smile was, for Christabel, a statement of the whole
evening's failure. Her voice trembling, she answered:

'No. But wherever she is, you should be with her.'

Jennifer came forward a little into the room. She wanted these
old women to have a full sight of her youth and her beauty.
Christabel was her own age, and yet how elderly, how worn, how
awkward she seemed! And perhaps Christabel thought: 'This
is what I should be! The Ball would have been a success tonight
had I been!'

Jennifer stood there, swinging her mask between her fingers.

'Christabel,' she said, 'I must congratulate you on the evening.' She meant a compliment. She had no sense of irony there.
But Christabel saw it as only ironical.

'I do not need your compliments,' she answered, 'and least
of all when they are not intended. I know what you have felt
this evening. I must tell you that you have failed entirely if you
wished to conceal your feeling.'

With a shock of surprise Jennifer realized that Christabel was
in a hysterical rage. The three girls were standing near to one
another, the two older women farther apart. Maria, who wished
that everything should be peaceable, but that at the same time
she might satisfy a little her own sense that her daughter had
not fine clothes and that the evening had lacked decorum, said:
'You should have been more with your mother, Jennifer, or your
mother more with you. Chaperons are still in fashion, my child.
Yes, your mother is at the card table. Pray give her my love.'

'Oh,' cried Jennifer, 'so that is what my sweet relatives have
been settling with one another. That I need a chaperon!' She
curtsied to them, and Judith thought that she had never in her
life before seen anyone so beautiful. ('But,' she also thought,
'what a temper! My God, what a temper!')

'But for my own part,' Jennifer went on, addressing Christabel
as though no one else were there, 'it appears ridiculous ostentation to me! At a Ball like this—' She paused, staring Christabel
in the eyes. She had always hated Christabel, she thought, the
mean pudding-faced thing, proud only because her husband
had made money as a merchant, a vulgar City merchant.

'And what at a Ball like this?' Christabel whispered. They had
come close together as though they were discussing some very
intimate secret. Rose interrupted. She was aware that there was
a very dangerous element here, something that threatened
everyone's comfort. 'There!' she cried, laughing nervously.
'Why, I am certain that Jennifer meant nothing. The Ball is very

fine. We have all enjoyed a most handsome evening. Jennifer
had no intention—'

'But I had an intention,' Jennifer interrupted hotly, looking
only at Christabel. 'If you fancy that I am to have my manners
taught me – and my mother her manners also. There is a shabbi-
ness here that one might have expected. Manners learnt from
Great-Aunt Maria, I don't doubt, who learnt them at the Battle
of Naseby . . .'

'Manners!' cried Christabel, beside herself with weariness,
hysterical exhaustion, jealousy, loneliness. 'Manners from you!'

She moved forward. Jennifer turned aside and, resting her
hand on a small table beside her, without knowing what she did,
picked up Christabel's fan that was lying there. She raised her
head contemptuously; her fingers tightened about the fan, and
one of the sticks broke with a little crack that sounded in
Christabel's ears like a pistol shot. It was her favourite fan, one
of her finest possessions.

She stepped forward and smacked Jennifer's face.

And this, exactly, was the true history of one of the most famous
and momentous quarrels in all the Herries history, so long as
events have been recorded.

THE HANGING

JUDITH SAT FACING old Montague Cards. He was not old in
years, being but twenty-nine. He was the only son of Morgan,
brother of Prosper and uncle of Jennifer, and was, therefore,
the lovely Jennifer's cousin. He was a bachelor and plainly
designed from the beginning for that character. He was thin
to emaciation, never varied in his dress, a bag-wig, a suit of
black silk. His nostrils constantly heaved in a sort of simpering
protest, as though he were offended by a bad smell. But he was
not. It was a sort of inner nasal irritation. His voice was affected
and often rose to a shrill note, but behind these absurdities he
was in reality a kindly, nervous, generous soul, who longed to be
liked but did not know how to set about it. He had a horror of
being made love to by women, although he liked their company,
for he adored gossip.

He was tyrannized by his manservant and his manservant's

wife. He had been, until Will's sudden rise, the wealthiest of all
the Herries. His grandfather had left him money, and he, by
careful investment, had increased it. He was very cautious and
reputed to be miserly. This he quite certainly was not, but he
found the reputation useful. Like all the other Herries he
thought there was no other family in England so fine and so
grand, but he quarrelled with individual members of it. He had
not, for instance, spoken to either Carey or Maria Rockage for
years until today. This cleavage was the result of the bursting
of a damaged water pipe upon him in the middle of a winter
night when he was staying at Grosset. He complained that the
Rockages thought it an honour to receive the contents of a burst
water pipe at any time, in any place, were it a Grosset water pipe.
He liked to stay with other Herries in the country. Visits saved
expense. At once, however, on hearing of the family crisis, he
had offered his rooms in Berkeley Square as an unprejudiced
meeting-place. The Ball had not, as Christabel had feared, been
the subject of any general scandal. It had in fact, in the outside
world, made absolutely no mark whatever, but among the Herries
themselves the effect had been terrific.

Judith, looking now at the various Herries seated in the fine
brocaded chairs round Montague's panelled room, saw, from the
barely concealed sentiments of pleasure in the various faces, that
here at last was the family battle for which they had all for long
been aching.

Carey Rockage, as someone outside the dispute and the titled
head of the family, was in charge of the conference, and delighted
he was. It had been no easy matter for the Rockages, economic-
ally, to be compelled to stay in London an additional week, but
their rooms in the Mews were cheap, and young Carey and
Phyllis would be living on short rations for many a week after
their return to Grosset.

Rockage had a round baby face with dimples. His suit was
rusty with age, his hair shabbily powdered, and one stocking
had a hole above the heel. But he was a real Herries. There was
dignity and discipline there. He could command men, and there
was a certain sweetness in his nature, as there was also in his
wife's, which had, in spite of their narrowness and Methodism,
long ago drawn Judith to them. Maria, his wife, was sitting near
to him, and in her excitement it was all that she could do not to
be speaking all the time. She hated so intensely the beautiful
Jennifer, jealous of her loveliness, the advantages she had over
her own dear Phyllis, but in the main thinking, quite honestly,

that the beautiful creature represented all the whoredoms of
Babylon.

Jennifer herself was not present. It was thought more fitting
that she should not be, but her father and mother, Prosper and
Amelia Cards, were there in very truth; it would not be too
much to say that their rage and sense of insult was as fine and
pure an emotion as ever a Herries had known.

Prosper, in spite of his forty-eight years, was, by far, the finest
figure in the room. His suit of crimson and silver, his elaborate
wig of shining whiteness, the splendid ruffles at his throat and
sleeves only served to emphasize his magnificent physique. He
had the chest and neck of a bull, but his features were not common. They had, as Amelia was proud to emphasize, a classical
correctness. He was not fleshy as Pomfret Herries was; his
frame was gigantic. He carried on the Herries' physical tradition
of David, Will's father. Curiously enough he was not proud
of his beauty; he had been so, maybe, once, but now he had
transferred it all to his lovely Jennifer and it was in her that the
whole of his life – physical, material, mental – and his ambitions
were centred. She was to marry a Duke. Nothing on this earth
was too good for her. And that she should have been struck in
the face . . .

He sat there outwardly calm, his splendid legs in their silk
stockings stretched in front of him. Outwardly calm. But, if he
lived to a hundred, as he and all the other Herries felt it their
right to do, he would never forget this insult. Amelia, his wife,
in a dress of canary silk, seated at his side, had the subdued and
colourless appearance of a woman who has, her life long, played
second to a splendid husband. She was not, however, as he
knew, so colourless.

The round shining table between them, on the farther side
of the room sat Pomfret, fleshy, unserious, gay in spite of himself; Rose, his wife, thankful that she had Pomfret secure at her
side for an hour at least, eagerly excited at the human possibilities
of the situation; Will, very stiff, trying to be grand, feeling
desperately young, aware at one moment that he was richer
than them all, at another that his wife had slapped the face of a
guest in her own house, trying to calculate the social and family
consequences of the incident, rather as a financier will balance
his probabilities; Christabel, gauche, awkward, knowing that the
whole family, save possibly Judith, was against her, a sort of
rough obstinacy rising to support her, warmed too by an almost
frantic hatred of Jennifer; a little farther from them again

Francis, elegant, aloof, looking out of window as though he were thinking of something else – and Judith.

She had not intended to come. It was only because Christabel herself, coming all the way to Judith's lodging in a coach, had persuaded her.

Christabel, bursting into tears, had protested that all the world was against her: even Will had scolded her, had told her that her temper had put back his affairs a dozen years at least. True, she had slapped Jennifer's face, but was she to endure impertinence from anyone who offered it her? Rose and Maria had been with her in that. But now – who knows? They were under the thumb of their husbands ... Judith must come and support her.

Judith had her own private troubles – worse, she could not but think, than anything that Christabel had to suffer. In the week since the Ball, disaster had crept nearer, and now, for these last two nights and days, Georges had not been home.

He was attempting (how well she knew it!) to repair desperate fortunes with some desperate remedy. At every occasion when he left her she did not know but that she might never see him again. Maybe he was even now at the Thames bottom with his head battered or his throat cut. She thought, sitting in that room warm with the May heat, smelling the scent of the lilac bloom that came up from the Square below, hearing the cry of some vendor in melancholy tuneful cadence, 'Oh, if he would only come. Nothing else matters! It is strange how I love him!'

She had left word at the lodging if he should return there while she was away. Did any of those in this room love anyone as she loved Georges? She clasped her small hot hands together, smoothed her dress, and heard Prosper Cards' deep stern voice come to her as though from the heart of an abysmal pit:

'I am not indicting Mrs William Herries for anything,' she heard him say. 'That is too strong a word. There must be, however, an apology in writing.'

'Come, come, Prosper, my friend,' Pomfret's easy genial voice interrupted. 'Is there not altogether too much ado about a trivial matter? Nay, nay.' (He raised a fat white hand.) 'We are all one family here. It is among relatives. Jennifer and Christabel are young, life is beginning for them, they had both an intemperate moment. For my part I like a little hot blood ...'

'Yes, Pomfret, we know you do,' Prosper answered dryly, crossing one splendid leg over the other. 'But I do not consider it a trivial matter, nor does my wife. We demand an apology in writing.'

Will's voice broke in. It trembled a little and was more human than Judith had ever heard it. 'If one apology is necessary, then so is another. My wife has already agreed that her action was hasty and undisciplined. The more reason that the affair was under her own roof. But what of the cause? Your daughter, sir, used words of gross discourtesy and in her temper destroyed one of my wife's most cherished possessions . . .'

'Cherished possessions!' broke in Amelia Cards. 'Fiddlesticks! A fan, and no extraordinary one either!'

'Fiddlesticks!' Will cried, now very hot and red in the face. 'Is that a word for a lady? . . .'

But Rockage interrupted, the dimples on his cheeks deepening so that he looked like a laughing cherub:

'Ladies! Ladies! Gentlemen! Gentlemen! You have invited me to preside over this conversation, simply, it was understood from the first, a friendly conversation that the little incident may be closed finally. It was with the wish of everyone that we met. Let us all part friends. The matter is surely clear enough. There was regrettable temper on both sides. The evidence has proved it. Mrs Will Herries has stated her own regret. It only remains for my friend Prosper on behalf of his daughter—'

'Not a whit! Not a whit!' answered Prosper, slapping his silken thigh. 'I must have an apology in writing. There is no evidence that my daughter showed temper.'

'She did! She did!' broke in Christabel, on the edge of tears. 'She spoke most insultingly, comparing me with old Great-Aunt Maria of Naseby Battle, and making a play of our entertainment, and all for no reason but her own vanity, because she thought that she was the beauty of the evening—'

'As indeed she was,' Prosper said with deep satisfaction. 'No one within a mile's race of her.'

The lilac, rich, warm, pungent, floated in through the open windows, bathing Judith's eyes with its lovely odour. Oh, why must they squabble about this silly business and her own life on the knife-edge of ruin? She was here, a grown woman, to help her cousin, to aid in the family councils, but she did not feel like a grown woman. She felt like a little girl, shut in a dark room expecting she knew not what terrible entry. What did they, these comfortable, well-fed Herries, know of the struggle that these last years had been for Judith and Georges, the scrapes for money, the taming of landladies, the corners of Coffee Houses, the night hours when Judith in her shift, her arm around Georges, had again and again persuaded him that all would yet be well? What did they know? ...

Then Rose's introduction of her own name caught her attention.

'There can no no question about the impertinence offered. Ask Judith Paris.'

All eyes turned to her. Her head was confused. Her own personal anxiety pressed upon her heart like a hand closing down on it, and the hand seemed to crush lilac bloom in its fingers; lilac swinging through the sky, while the tops of the green trees in the Square flamed on the iridescent air.

She heard Prosper Cards' deep arrogant voice: 'Well, what has little Miss Judith to say?'

Years after, when she looked back and wondered at the sudden temper that she showed now (temper that had immense consequences), it seemed to her that everything rose together to influence her. Just as, had Christabel's fan not been on the table, there would have been no family crisis, so had there been no warm day, no lilac, no anxiety for Georges, nay, even no dimples in Carey Rockage's cheeks, and, most certainly, no 'little Miss Judith' from Prosper, why then there would have been no temper, no such public taking of sides, binding her, she often afterwards felt, to a whole lifetime of consequences. 'Little Miss Judith' indeed! There was certainly something insufferable about this Cards family!

She heard her own voice, rather shrill, not like her voice at all:

'I think that Christabel had aggravation. Contempt was shown for her Ball, not too civil in a guest who had been so kindly entertained. Christabel should not have slapped her face, maybe ... but I would have slapped her. I would indeed. One's own guest ... Oh, there was certainly cause!'

She realized with some satisfaction the surprise that everyone felt. For a moment she forgot even Georges, for she was doing what she loved to do, influencing a situation, a group of persons, above all, a group of Herries! She could feel how Rose Herries was thinking, 'Well I never; who'd have thought it!' and would wonder whether Judith's boldness might possibly titillate Pomfret's sensual side: how grateful Christabel would be, and even Will; how furious Amelia, Jennifer's mother; how scornful Prosper (but in his slow grandeur and handsome pride he would never forget it nor forgive it).

She stole a glance at Francis, who still was staring out of window, staring at the trees that shimmered like green glass in the sun. And what was *he* thinking of? She knew at once by a sort of inspired divination. He was thinking of the lovely, lovely Jennifer – had been thinking of her all day. Years later she was to know that her divination was true.

Meanwhile she had to fight to maintain her position. Prosper was regarding her through his large liquid brown eyes with a patronizing indulgence.

'Come, come, Miss Judith,' he said. 'Why so unkind to my daughter? How has she offended you?'

'She *has* not offended me!' (Judith thought – does he not know that I'm married, the great pompous ox? Oh, how once again she wished that she were larger, her legs longer, her brow more imposing!) 'I have nothing against your daughter, sir, I was present, and must say what I think. In my advice it would be more seemly for nothing more to be said of the matter on either side. There was temper shown both ways. It was a late hour, and everyone was weary.' She was surprised at the firmness of her voice. Her personality counted; she knew that they were all impressed with it.

Perhaps Prosper felt that also, for he said, his voice a little more angered than it had been:

'Why do we waste our time? I should be in the country by now. My wife and I are not here for some child's play. I demand from Mrs Will Herries an apology in writing.'

Will, his face pale with anger, the horse-bones of his cheeks emphasized with his passion, answered:

'It is clear enough from the evidence ... I also demand an apology in writing.'

Then everyone began to speak at once:

'No apology on either side.'

'Great rudeness.'

'For my part I'd have a public apology.'

'And what could you know of the matter? If you'd been beside your daughter as you should have been—'

'Most certainly she insulted me. She laughed at my entertainment and broke my fan—'

'I demand an apology in writing ...'

'After all, they are both young. Who should mind a slap in the face? ...'

'I would call you out, Cousin Prosper, for less.'

'Call me out then. I'll make mincemeat out of you!'

'Pomfret! Pomfret!' (This, shrilly, from Rose.) 'What are you about? And at your age . . .'

And then a contribution from Cousin Montague, who had said no word until now, had been completely forgotten by everyone:

'The weather is so warm. There are refreshments in the parlour. The other room has a cooler outlook—'

Then from the hubbub, the decisive authority of Carey Rockage. Strange, the dominance of that shabby baby-faced man!

'Friends, friends! This is a family affair. About nothing so outrageous neither. Mrs Will has agreed that she will offer an apology. As to writing, I am sure, Prosper, that your good-nature will insist—'

'Good-nature be damned!' Prosper interrupted. 'My daughter has had her face slapped and publicly. My wife is with me in this. For the hundredth time – there must be an apology in writing.'

'And I say there shall not!' cried Will suddenly jumping up and tipping his chair over. 'This is our last and final word. My wife has expressed her regret for her hastiness. We expect the expression of similar regret from Miss Jennifer Cards. Otherwise there is an end to any possible intercourse between this branch of the family and the Bournemouth part of it. Greatly to be regretted – but this is final.'

The boy, for he was little more, glared across the room at the magnificent Prosper. It was a little, Judith thought, David defying Goliath. But she was proud of him. She saw now – perhaps for the first time – why it was that he was making himself a solid figure in London.

Then came the real surprise of the occasion. For Francis, who had hitherto been silent, spoke. 'I should wish to say,' he interjected, 'that I am dissociated from my brother in this. I hold that Miss Jennifer deserves an apology in writing.'

'Oh no, Francis – oh no,' Judith whispered under her breath. She realized with an actual pang of apprehension that this silly dispute about so trivial an affair was going much deeper than she had ever supposed. Her memory spread before her in an instant of vision, scene after scene – Uldale in the old years, Sarah and David, Francis and Will; Francis hardly more than a child, staring at Skiddaw, turning and picking Will up from the long orchard grass, smoothing some fancied hurt; Francis and Will bathing and running naked from the stream; Francis, Will, Reuben, herself, watching the fireworks at the Lake's

edge. But Francis must be possessed by this Jennifer! That he
should so defy his brother, so publicly . . .

And it was the last straw for Will. He caught Christabel by
the arm, dragging her from her chair.

'No apology!' he shouted; 'neither now nor ever!' He shook
his fist across the room. 'You can carry your Bournemouth
manners back with you! I wish you good day.' At the door he
turned. 'And your own betrayal of me, Francis, I am not likely
to forget.'

He pulled Christabel through the door with him. Everyone
broke into confusion. Judith could hear Montague urging:

'It is the warm weather . . . refreshments . . . a cool parlour.'
And Prosper's measured tones: 'Young puppy! I'd call him out
for a penny!' And Maria Rockage: 'Oh dear, oh dear! . . . That's
a pity, and Carey so wonderfully discreet.'

Well, the thing was done. Judith sighed, turning away from
Francis, who stood with his back to the company, looking out
of the window down into the Square. It seemed, Judith thought,
as though the beautiful shadow of Jennifer hung over all the
room.

A moment later she had forgotten them all, for there, standing
just within the door, looking at them all, a half-defiant, half-
apologetic smile on his face, was Georges!

He was neat and tidy, in a brown suit, holding his hat in his
hand, but – she saw at once – infinitely weary. His round face
was ashen. He held himself as though at any moment he might
fall.

Rockage knew him. Rose and Pomfret spoke to him. A moment
later Judith was tugging at his arm.

'Georges, you had my note. I have waited two days . . . Where
have you been ? . . . What ? . . .'

'I came to fetch you,' he said, looking at her with a great
kindliness that caught at her heart. 'We shall talk better outside.'

She took his arm. He bowed to the assembled company. One
last impression she had (that was to seem to her afterwards like
the closing note on all her old life) of Francis, turning from the
window and very gravely regarding them both. Then they were
out of the room and down the stairs.

The Square was quite deserted and beautifully still in the
dusty golden sunlight of the hastening summer afternoon. They
walked along, she still holding his arm.

He spoke very rapidly, but still with a great and considering
kindness.

'Listen, Judy . . . Everything is up. I have been a fool these
two days, just as I have been a fool all my life. But worse now,
much worse. Listen to what I say. I must be off this instant.
There's a boat I know at Greenwich; away tonight for Copen-
hagen—'

'But what have you done?'

'I've played two nights and a day. Once I was handsomely to
the good, then lost it all again. But that's not the thing. There
was a scuffle this morning at Jonathan's. I stuck a ninny – no,
he's not dead – but they are out against me and several more.
London's closed to me for a time at least.'

'And I?' Her mind was active with a thousand possibilities.

'Go back to Watendlath and wait for me.'

They stood at the Square corner, and now she had actually
just above her head a thick bush of purple lilac that leaned towards her as though it would brush her cheek. A Negro boy,
with a silver turban and leading a spaniel by a thin chain, passed
them whistling.

He spoke to her most urgently. 'Judy, I know you are brave,
and most sensible. I'm sorry indeed that I have brought you
to this pass, the more that these years in London have made us
friends. I have no friend in the world like you. You've tamed me
because you caught my admiration and kept it . . . Judy, I
think I could love you for long now, were we quietly in Cumberland . . .'

At the word 'Cumberland' she broke out: 'Oh, why could we
not go there? Both of us. No one would look for you in Watendlath.'

'No,' he answered sharply. 'I must be out of England. I've
come to think that they hate me here. They turn on me and hunt
me like dogs a hare if they have the slenderest reason. I'm a
man of no country. I'd rather be on the sea than on the land
anywhere. Except for you I'd go to sea and never touch land
again . . . But I always have to come back to you, and will come.
Go to Watendlath. Be patient there. I shall write and send
money if I have any. But you can manage in any case. You have
a man's head on you. There's money enough in the lodging –
the drawer by the fireplace. Here . . . the key. That will carry
you North. I should pay the woman and leave tonight. Stay
quietly there. Answer no questions if they ask you. One day,
perhaps soon, you'll see me walk up the road. I *must* come back
to you. There's no one and nothing else in the world draws
me . . .'

She asked no questions. She hated people who asked tiresome questions at an urgent crisis.

He caught her by the shoulders, as he sometimes did when he was pleased, lifting her a little from her feet. He kissed her.

'Now – goodbye,' and he had turned the corner swiftly and was gone.

She stood there, looking up into the lilac, but not seeing it. Not from sentiment but because she knew that in the future it would often please her to remember, she repeated some of the things that he had said.

'I think I could love you for long now . . . Except for you I'd go . . . You have a man's head . . .'

And so she had. She wanted to commit some panicky folly like running down the street to find him and then insisting that wherever he went she would go with him, but she must be practical and do exactly what he had asked her.

She was glad that she must leave London. As though to be in tune with the urgency of her own affairs, the day was clouding. Thunder was behind the houses. She walked on, thinking how, with ease, she could catch the night coach to York. From there across country she might share a post-chaise if she were lucky. The very thought of Watendlath made her heart beat with pleasure. The cool breeze slipping down the mountain-side, the water, green-clear, tumbling into the Punchbowl, the Tarn, mirroring one white cloud, while the Fell looked down to Rosth-waite; the Ritsons, the children, the dogs, the smell of the peat, the dung, the Cumberland bracken (now there would be new fresh fronds springing up, curling above the stem) and, most lovely of all, the eternal running streams, so reassuring, so friendly . . . Why had she left it? Although she was only a step from Berkeley Square all the members of the Herries family, with whom she had so lately been, seemed unreal and unalive.

She hurried on, for her mind was set now on the practical business of doing what Georges had told her – leaving London and catching the night coach.

Soon she was in the poorer streets that hung like spiderwebs about Charing Cross. The heavy day was dark now above her head, and the noise of the traffic on the street, the stench of the gutter, the projecting windows and the roughness of the cobbled road held and confused her.

When she stood it seemed that almost at once people closed in upon her. She was in a narrow street that opened out until it became almost a small cobbled square hemmed in with uneven and overhanging houses. She was aware then that her own thoughts had hindered her from noticing that some event was going forward. Before she knew it or could resist it she found that a mixed and very evil-smelling crowd was pushing her on; then, looking about her, saw that beside a butcher's shop that had above it a large swaying sign a platform had been erected and on the platform a gibbet.

The sight of the gibbet sickened her; it had in its very rough newness and sharp angles a sense of torture and pain about it. She turned as though to go back, but found now to her dismay that the crowd behind her was too thick for her to pass through.

She had heard at one time that malefactors were sometimes hanged by the place of their crime, and she supposed that unwittingly she had tumbled upon some such scene. The odd mixture of emotions in her breast at that moment – her passionate feeling of love for Georges, the excitement of the recent family squabble, the sense of the exceeding importance that she should do at once what Georges asked her – threw her into a special state of nervous apprehension. Her first thought was that she must at once get away from where she was. She realized that in her abstraction she had moved into a crowd that must have been waiting there for a considerable period. All the windows of the neighbourhood were open and were crowded with figures. Boys were clinging to the lamp-posts, and along one side of the street a platform of boards had been arranged on barrows and tubs, and this was thronged. Above the roofs the sky was dark, and she fancied that she could hear distant rumbles of thunder. Whatever happened she must escape, so she turned to go back the way that she had come, but she was at once obstructed by a large man carrying an empty tray round his middle, and a group of women who, so soon as they saw that she wanted to pass them, with laughter prevented her.

'No passage this way,' one woman, who had a huge bosom and her skirt tucked up almost to her knees, cried.

'I beg you,' Judith began. 'It is an urgent matter – if you please.'

'If you please – if you please!' the whole street seemed to echo her. 'Only one thing urgent here, and that is a jerk with the rope and, lady or gentleman, it's all the same, we all go to heaven!'

She was so small that she had no hope of asserting herself. She looked about her to see whether some face were likely to help her, but she thought that she had never seen so many

coarse mouths, bright hard eyes. There was in the look of everyone a flutter of the animal – the animal allowed for an hour a
little freedom, to prowl into a larger cage and taste handsome
food. The sense that she had had for a long time in London
that times were changing, that the people themselves were now
more actively conscious of possible power and were moving
towards it, held her now. For the first time in her life she was
afraid of people. She had never before been aware of what a
crowd was. Her individuality was lost. If she were not careful
she would be trampled down, not her body but something much
more real and vivid than that.

She hated any public scene; her reserve and dignity came to
her rescue. She turned back and found that she could move
forward more easily. She might escape at the broader street-
end. But when she had gone some way, jolted, pushed, with
much unpleasant contact with clothes and hot breath, legs and
arms, she came to a stop again. She saw to her great distress that
she was almost under the platform where the gibbet was. Here
was a thick ring of people, mostly women; she thought of France.
It must have been often like this in France, the women knitting
and singing, their ears straining for the rattle of the tumbrils.

She felt faint with the heat and the smells and the noise.
Scarcely knowing what she did, she caught at an arm to steady
herself and found that she was holding on to a little thin man in
a large hat and a rusty black suit. He smiled at her kindly.

'Can you help me out of this, sir ?' she asked gently.

He shook his head. 'I fear not, madam. It is best to stay where
you are. The crowd grows thicker every moment.'

'Oh, but I don't wish to stay. I have a most urgent appointment.'

He pointed with his finger. She looked and saw that escape
was now impossible. The crowd had in the last five minutes
flooded in. She could see the shining hats of the 'Charlies' at
the crowd's edge.

'Is someone to be hanged ?' she asked.

'A young man.'

'What had he done ?'

'Stolen three shillings from his master's till – the butcher's
there.'

She was a woman of her time, she did not feel the injustice
of it as a woman of a later day would do, but it was as though,
in that moment, looking anxiously into the little man's mild eye,
pressed in on every side, stirred perhaps by the drama of her

own personal circumstances, she received some especial consciousness, ahead of her time, a sense of cruelty and persecution that pierced her very heart.

'Oh, poor boy . . . I don't want to see . . . Please cannot you assist me ? What are all these people here for ? If he must die it should be by himself alone. Oh, help me, please! . . .'

She saw herself the hopelessness of any escape. He was very kind. He put his arm very courteously round her. 'There is no way out. You can see for yourself. It will be over soon now. It was to be at five o'clock. We shall have a storm if they are not quick.'

Something compelled her to look around her. The people near her were decent enough, quiet, grave-faced. They waited indifferently, as though it were a peep-show they had come for. Two women close to her were chatting about their own affairs. A hush spread slowly over the crowd, as though a hand had been laid upon them all. A man, burly and broad, carrying a cane, mounted the steps to the scaffold. He went to the gibbet and felt the rope. A flock of pigeons flew from one side of the street to the other, and a sudden clap of thunder, as though someone had fired a gun, startled them. They rustled their wings like a shower of falling paper.

It seemed to Judith that this was her own personal tragedy, that all her life she would be affected with her memory of it. She was forced now to watch; indeed two opposite impulses seemed to fight in her, one that she should hide her face, the other that she should see every slightest thing.

The crowd was very still in the vicinity of the scaffold, but beyond that, there were laughter and singing and beyond that, in a great distance, all the noisy traffic of the day. The atmosphere was strange, very dark above their heads, but pale beneath with the flat colour of sunlight. The shops were like pale faces staring from darkness, and the thunder muttered like an uncertain drum.

She saw all this with a sickness of anticipation. She really felt sick, as though it were Georges or Francis or Reuben – someone who was very close to her – who was going to suffer. The silence grew and seemed to spread to the farther distance. She saw individuals – a woman's face with a wart, an old gentleman in a shabby brown wig, a girl with a sharp nose who lifted a child that it might see better, a man, a foreigner surely, wearing a bright green turban – and all these individuals seemed to belong to her, to know all about her, and to have arranged to come with her to see this sight.

Then, as though obeying some signal, a little procession mounted the steps. There was the stout fellow with the cane, a long thin man bare-headed, three officers in uniform, a clergyman with parson's bands carrying a book, and, last, between the officers, a boy with his hands tied. At once she could not remove her eyes from the boy. He was broad and short and ruddy-faced, like any strong country boy. His hair was cropped, he had large blue staring eyes that, Judith saw, were now mad with an ununderstanding terror. But his mouth, which was a child's mouth, uncertain and tremulous, was trying to be resolved and manly.

She was, against her will, so terribly close that she was forced to see these things; she fancied then (she knew afterwards it could have been only fancy) that as soon as he was on the platform the boy's eyes were seeking hers. What he was doing was searching the crowd, the houses, the sky; a wild animal at bay looking for escape, although he knew that there was none. But Judith fancied that she could help him. Raising herself on her toes she nodded and smiled and nodded again; even (although she did not know it) her lips were forming words: 'Be brave! I'll help you! I want to help you! Be brave!'

Indeed he tried to be, poor lad. Things moved very quickly. The parson, who looked shabby and had mud on his stockings, read from a book. The boy came forward. He was in his shirt and breeches; the shirt, open, had slipped from one shoulder and showed his breast. His face was ruddy in spite of his fear; he looked as though he should have been caught robbing an orchard.

He came forward and began to speak bravely enough. Now an absolute silence froze the scene. Carts could be heard rattling on the Strand cobbles very far away.

'Good people,' he began (his voice was fresh and very young), 'I am told to bid you all farewell and to beg you to stay in peace with God. Good people, it is very true that I took the shillings from the till – I never for an instant denied it. I was tempted by the Devil, good people, for I am very weary of the Town and was hungering for the country again. It was but an instant's temptation, and here I am, so that, good people, all learn by me to resist—' He had begun bravely, held up, perhaps, by the importance of the attention given him by the listening crowd, but suddenly it seemed to come upon him that he was really going to die, that, in a few moments, he would be fighting for breath . . .

He broke off, his voice rising to a shrill terror. 'No, no . . .

I must not die . . . I must not die . . .' He moved as though he would throw himself from the platform. The officers caught him, and then began a dreadful struggle. He was young and strong. The three officers wrestled with him all over the platform. His shirt was torn from him and he was bare to the waist. He cried again and again, 'No, no . . . I will not . . .' and other words that no one could distinguish, some private name that sounded like 'Nancy'. Then they had him. His arms were bound behind him; his naked chest, white and shining with sweat, pushed forward, his head, turning, twisting, turning like an animal's in the pen before execution. An agonized whisper came: 'Jesus! Oh, Jesus Christ!' Just before they had the rope round his neck his eyes seemed to find Judith's, blue, staring and asking some question.

Then he was swinging, his legs twisting as though with independent life. The body heaved, then his head hung and he was still.

'Now, madam,' said the little man from an infinite distance, 'I can assist you.'

Judith nodded her head. Reuben had been right. Until the Bear was safe from persecution nothing could be well in the world.

THE CLIPPING

SARAH HERRIES, widow of David Herries and mother of Francis, Deborah, and Will, died on the 3rd of July 1796, suddenly, at the age of fifty-eight.

She was walking in the garden with her daughter Deborah, wrapped in one of her strange and brooding silences, when she cried out suddenly in a proud and joyful voice: 'Davy! Davy!', ran forward, her arms outstretched, and fell down on the green sward.

Her heart had failed her, and she was mercifully relieved of a life that was only a torment and distress to her. Judith went from Watendlath to the funeral. Will and Francis naturally could not arrive from London. The distance was too great and the time too short. Deborah Sunwood, now an aged, white-haired, and very quiet little woman, long a widow and never the same since the death of her son Humphrey in France, came from Cockermouth, and she and Judith had a very loving meeting. Deborah

Herries, a stout, large, rosy-faced, cheerful woman, was now left in sole charge of Uldale and its affairs. She begged Judith to come to her whenever she wished. They had a friendly regard for one another, but nothing whatever to say, and Judith knew that Deborah, who loved social events and decent behaviour, regarded Georges in her heart as a rogue and a vagabond, which indeed he was.

The night of her return from the funeral Judith had wild and fantastic dreams. It was a hot airless night, very still, and the streams, thin though they were, seemed to leap in through the open windows and chatter about the room. She had been sleeping badly for a long time past. Wise though she was and determined always to be sensible, a foreboding of distress and misfortune grew on her day by day, as though a cloud with every hour grew heavier and darker above her head. She had had one letter from Georges since he left her in London. It was addressed from Bergen in Norway, very short, sending his love, telling her that he was busy and would return when he could. She thought that she read between the lines a new sense of care and longing for her, but that, with her usual good sense, might be a willing imagination.

The nights were the bad times. During the day she was surrounded with friends in whose affairs she took ever a more active and dominating interest, but at night she was alone, and that part of herself that she could least easily control – her wild and restless part – seemed to have full power.

On this particular night she suffered especially from the thought of Sarah. Her loving heart could not endure that she had never been reconciled to Sarah. When she was a child she had not thought that she cared for Sarah at all, but as she grew, so she perceived that there was some deep loyalty and submission in her feeling.

She had always been too proud to go to Sarah and ask her forgiveness; besides, she did not think that Sarah had anything to forgive, but she had supposed that some accidental meeting would bring them together again. Now it would never be.

At least, if there was another conscious life, Sarah was now with David, was happy again and understood everything. But this supposition, a very doubtful one, as it seemed to Judith, was poor comfort. She tortured herself, on the ride back from Uldale, with the thought of all the lonely years that Sarah had endured. She could never bear that people could suffer, and especially that they should suffer through her fault, and now there occurred to her a thousand ways in which, with a little courage, she might have approached Sarah and done something for her.

Her dreams that night were wild, entangled and desperate. She was again in the London street, where the boy was to be hanged. Pressed in, tossed about by a wild and revengeful crowd. But it was Georges who was to be hanged. She could do nothing to save him, but must stand there helplessly and watch. The sky was black, the houses ringed with flame, and from a high window Christabel, Will's wife, leaned out and cried that her fan was broken and Georges must suffer for it. Then Georges came sailing towards her in a little boat; waves, hot and angry, with cruel white tongues, filled the street and beat about the scaffolding. Young Stane was in the boat, and Georges suddenly caught him, held him in the air, then flung him into the waves while all the people cried.

She woke, trembling, damp with sweat. At first the deep quiet of the room with only the sound of the singing streams soothed her. She lay there and listened to her heart as it slowly diminished its terrible beating. How good that it had only been a dream! From her bed she could see, in the faint morning light, the shadows of the homely, familiar things, and beyond the open window the friendly breast of the rising hill.

She was in her own house with friends on every side of her. Since her return, although she had said very little to anyone, they had all understood, it seemed, that Georges was in some trouble. They did not like Georges, but with that wonderful silent sympathy that is perhaps the Cumbrian's finest gift, they had closed in around her, showing her their affection and loyalty. She had never been so near to them before as she was now.

Yes, but she wanted Georges. She wanted him with a fierce hunger that was an experience quite new to her. She was doing what he told her, staying here and filling her life with little daily interests, but, in the back of her mind, there was always the fear that after a while, if he did not return, waiting would be too hard for her, and she would run off to Whitehaven and search for news of him.

To conquer her desire for him she lay there, as the new light flowed about the room and a cluster of sharp steel-glittering stars faded out above the black hill line, saying over to herself, aloud, the names of places that she loved, and the names of people whom she loved. She said, as though she were addressing the shapes, with every moment less dim, in her room:

> '*Stonethwaite, Honister,*
> *Gavel, Watendlath,*
> *Rosthwaite, Uldale,*
> *Bleaberry, High Seat,*
> *Armboth, GreyKnotts,*
> *Glaramara*—'

They had sung her almost to sleep again, mingling with the streams that ran about the boards of her room when, with a sharp stab of awareness, she was conscious of an odd thing – that with every day she was becoming more frightened of leaving her own square of ground.

It was as though someone had told her that did she step over a certain line, something terrible would befall her. She had noticed at the funeral that she had to force herself to face people, even good friends like Deborah Sunwood. It was as though she expected that anyone at a moment's notice would cry: 'I have news for you. Georges—' The people here around her she could trust. They were her own people – the Ritsons, the Wilsons, all the children and the dogs. And her new great friend, Charlie Watson.

Watson had a farm, New Hope, towards Armboth. He had come there in the last year; he was from the village of Strands, near Wastwater.

He was a Cumbrian of the Cumbrians; that is, he was silent, often churlish, sharp, a marvellous shepherd and utterly loyal. She had met him one day coming up from Rosthwaite. He had two dogs with him. She had been startled by his looks, for he was broad and massive and his hair was of so jet a black, his cheeks of so warm a colour, that at first he seemed a foreigner. He had a short, sharply cut, black moustache that was not like the neighbours'. He was so broad of shoulder and thick of thigh that his height seemed moderate, but he was of good height nevertheless.

He would be thirty-five years of age. They began to talk. You would have said that all he thought of at that time was sheep, that or any time. He thought of other things later, though. He was proud, sensitive, suspicious, and hated foreigners till he knew them. He had worked in Liverpool five years in his youth. He was single; preferred sheep to women, he told Judith once. True enough then – not true later. On their first meeting he said little more than 'Aye!' He looked at her as though he disliked her. He stood, his legs wide apart, striding the fells.

He told her that his sister looked after his comfort, that it was a dry month, that he didn't hold with politics – Regent or King, it was all the same to him, but we'd better not take after the Frenchies.

Judith said: 'My husband's French.'

He said: 'Aye,' looking at her meditatively and without a hint of apology. Then abruptly, still looking at her, he remarked: 'You'll be Mrs Paris. I mind hearing of you.'

'Nothing bad, I hope,' said Judith.

'For t'matter o' that – nay,' he said, suddenly smiling a slow deep smile. He strode away, not looking back, his dogs after him.

After that first meeting they were always encountering one another. He was a friend of old man Ritson's, but it seemed to her soon that he came to the farm very much more often than he had done.

Once or twice, without any conceit of self-flattery, she wondered whether he were in love with her. He seemed to seek her out so directly, with a simplicity that might elsewhere have caused gossip. But, in a week or two, she realized that the Ritsons and the rest knew just what his feeling for her was. He was sorry for her, but without hurting her pride. They said of him that he was mighty tender with all animals and rough with women and off-hand with men. It seemed that he thought that she needed protection as an animal might. He made himself her protector. There was no sentiment between them. They made a curious pair, he so large and she so small, and she could have disappeared, she used to fancy, into the outer pocket of his coat. He was an unusual man with his intense depths of feeling unexpressed. One day they were standing together near the Tarn, and three strangers, two ladies and a gentleman, rode up on horses. They were sightseers, the first 'tourists', perhaps, that Watendlath ever beheld. They called Watson 'my good fellow' and, when he had given, very curtly, some information, the gentleman threw him a shilling. The ladies, very grand and speaking with affectation, looked at Judith, who was dressed like Mrs Ritson or any of the people of the place. When they were gone Watson threw the shilling into the Tarn. He was trembling with anger.

'I'll tell them if 'tis t'right road. If they come again without biddin' they maun stay a bit . . . I'll settle him.'

She laughed and said that she supposed that anyone had a right to the place.

'Nay, they havena . . . the man's a lump of mutton off an auld tup.'

She didn't laugh any more, when she saw how deeply moved he was. It was as though these people had soiled the landscape for him.

Judith went one day and called on his sister. Then one evening, sitting in his kitchen, she told him everything: about her father and mother, her childhood in Uldale, her life at Stone Ends, her marriage with Georges, her time in London, her present distress and ever-growing anxiety, her love for Georges that seemed to grow ever deeper and deeper. He took her hand in his huge one.

'Aye, you want someone to look after you.'

From that evening it seemed to her that he was always at hand, although there were days when she didn't see him. Indeed he was a tremendous worker, had no time for idling with females. But he was behind her and beside her. The thought of him infinitely comforted her.

As, lying there, she considered him, his silence, his tenderness, her fears thinned away. It seemed that it was her fate to have these figures guarding her, protecting – Tom Gauntry, Emma, now Charlie Watson. The strange thing was that she did not want anyone to protect her. She was quite well able to protect herself. But she liked to have friends. She loved to be loved – that is, by the people whom she wanted to love her.

The sun flashed above the purple ridge of the hill. The sky was pale green like the wing of a young paroquet.

The Ritsons had their 'Clipping', and it was a grand day. The hot weather had lasted for over a fortnight, and this was the hottest day of them all. The sheep panted fit to burst their sides. Armboth Fell shone like a brazen shield and was so slippery dry beneath the bracken that it was flaming ice to the feet. The Tarn was shadowed with an ebony mist under a sky clouded with heat.

The clipping was perhaps the grandest day of the year for the Ritsons. They were farmers in a small way, but very popular. Neighbours came from miles, first to help in the clipping, then to eat of the feast and dance in the Ritson kitchen.

Charlie Watson came. He was the best clipper in Cumberland maybe; a Master. Then there was Tommy Blunden of Smoke, Robert Tyndale of Cardale, Will Bennett of Axholme, Roger

Perry of Thunder. They, their wives, their children, their dogs.

Judith was happy again. The night was far behind her. But the thundery weather distressed her; it had been ominous to her ever since that last day in London, and now, in the middle of helping with the great joint of beef, with the huge pease-puddings, with the arranging of the long table, she would go to the porch and look out over the Tarn to the hills and listen. Perhaps it was Georges, also, for whom she was listening.

In the kitchen there was tremendous noise and confusion. Old man Ritson was too aged now to move about, the rheumatism had him fast, and sometimes the pain was so bad that someone inside him yelled loud enough to bring the roof down, but the yell never passed his inside. He sat, his grand head high, his gnarled hands on his knees, watching and saying nothing. His daughters, his grand-daughters and a great-grand-daughter (in a cradle by the window) were all around him. A sea of femininity. But he said nothing. He sat there thinking of his youth, of fighting a man bare-skin in Whitehaven and throttling him, of tending sheep on the hills above Coniston Water, of the fugitives in '45 from Butcher Cumberland and his father hiding one up the kitchen chimney, of sheep and sheep, cows and cows, fine weather and bad, of women whom he had loved, his children and their ways, Armboth and Brund Fell and Glaramara that were live creatures to him, Gods maybe, carrying on their gigantic forms the rocks and tarns and streams that were their splendid properties. Yes, he had plenty to think of. And he sat there, looking straight in front of him, while the pains at his hip made him bellow inside.

When the table was laid, Judith, to escape the kitchen heat, went out to watch the clippers.

As the weather was so grand the clipping could be in the open air instead of in the barn. All the sheep had been brought in. There were eight hundred sheep and five hundred lambs.

Beyond the house in a grand half-circle were fifteen clippers striding the sheep stools, and each clipper held a sheep, shorn, half shorn, about to be shorn. There was a tremendous noise, for the gate of the farmyard was packed by five score of wooled sheep penned against it. They would be caught, one after another, by one of the boys, who, in a wild, excited pack, tumbled and fought and shouted, having the day of their lives. The sheep bleated and their lambs on the fell-side or in the fields bleated as well. The dogs barked and even horses neighed. It was strange to feel, beyond this excited whirlpool of sound, the glazen silence of the Tarn, the road, the hills, pulsating through the shimmering heat, but silent, as though holding their breath for the first peal of thunder that would release them from this spell.

Judith first looked for Charlie Watson, and a splendid sight he was. His shirt was open at the neck, and sweat beaded the thick black hair of his chest. His arms, red-brown to near the elbows then snow-white, bulged with muscle; his legs planted wide to hold the sheep between them seemed to be rooted in the ground; every once and again his head went up and his mouth parted, showing his teeth white under the short thick black moustache. (His perfect teeth were a phenomenon in the dale, for most men lacked one or two.) His short, thick hair had almost a metallic gleam in its blackness.

As always when at work, his dark eyes shone, his parted lips seemed to cry aloud his energy, his body worked in harmony with the fell, the running water. He worked with rhythm, as though the whole of English nature and the wheel of the brazen sky moved, back and forth, with the pulse of his blood; and he handled the sheep as though he loved them.

Tom Ritson was in charge of the clipping; an old man called Benny Held – with two fierce questioning white eyebrows and a face like a wrinkled turnip – kept the pitch pan heated and held the marking iron and the rudd stick. Young Roger Perry of Thunder, a lad nearly as thick and broad as Watson, held the animals while old Benny applied the marking.

Judith forgot her anxieties and trouble for the while. Now there came out in her all her passion for management. She could not be present at a scene like this without burning to 'arrange things'.

She looked fifteen years of age, with a high sunbonnet tied over her red hair and her legs bare as the other women's were, stamping about in her clogs. Her cheeks were flushed, her eyes shining. Her Cumberland blood exulted in the scene. This was the heart of England and so the heart of the world. Everything was right for her – the scent of the bracken, the still waiting expectancy of the hills, the sun shining on the little stone walls that ran up into the edge of the sky, the rough voices that had a sort of grumbling humorous note in them, the jokes and oaths and laughter, the bleating of lambs and sheep, the strange help-less whiteness of the sheep after they were shorn – knowing that they were so different, so changed that their own lambs did not recognize them – the life of this little community centred here in this circle of fells, so remote from the world but strong,

independent, asking nothing from any man (as for centuries they
had asked nothing, so for centuries more they would ask
nothing), and all of them looking at her, speaking to her as
though she were one of themselves (which, indeed, she was), the
sun slipping over the sky and, as the afternoon drew on, shadows
staining every hill with a different dye; Armboth saffron as
though sunlight had soaked into its very heart, Brund Fell
orange-red, then sinking, with almost an audible sigh, into a
gentle silver-grey, and beyond them the farther hills, violet
cloths spread before a sky white with evening haze, and, with the
evening, a breeze springing that had every scent of coolness in
it, young grass, water over shining stones, and the wet wavering
mosses that shadow the Tarn's edge. The sea also was not far
away.

Ale was brought out in pots, and there were hunks of fruit
pie. Then the sky was green, and the first star winked at a silver
moon half full. The fleeces were tied in small bundles, the loft
door was closed on them, and everyone moved indoors to the
feast.

There were rounds of beef and oat-bread, pease-puddings,
gooseberry pies, puddings 'touched' with rum. Soon everyone
was very merry. Benny Held had brought his fiddle. Robert
Tyndale, who had a fine tenor, sang Ewan Clark's 'Happy
Bachelor':

> *'A bachelor life of all lives is the best;*
> *No cares matrimonial disturb his calm rest;*
> *No lectures called* Curtain *shake sleep from his eyes,*
> *When tir'd he can rest, and when tir'd he can rise.'*

and 'Wey, Ned, Man!':

> *'Wey, Ned, Man! Thou luiks sae down-hearted,*
> *Yen wad swear aw thy kindred were dead;*
> *For sixpence, thy Jean and thee's parted –*
> *What then, Man, ne'er bodder thy head.'*

Then, Charlie Watson, shy but determined, sang in a deep
bass: 'What charms has fair Chloe':

> *'What charms has fair Chloe!*
> *Her bosom's like snow!*
> *Each feature*
> *Is sweeter,*

Proud Venus, than thine!
Her mind like her face is
Adorned with all graces,
Not Pallas possesses
    A wit so divine.

'*What crowds are a-bleeding*
While Chloe's ne'er heeding:
        All lying
        A-dying
    Thro' cruel disdain:
Ye gods, deign to warm her
Or quickly disarm her;
While Chloe's a charmer,
    Your temples are vain.'

He sang without any expression whatever, and a disdainful
look on his face as though he despised the song and himself
for singing it, but, when it was over, and the applause had been
terrific, he flushed with pleasure and looked down the long table
to see whether Judith had approved.

Then the tables were cleared, Benny Held struck up his fiddle
and everyone was dancing. Stamp-stamp-stamp, clamp-clamp-
clamp along the kitchen floor, the dust rising, faces flushed,
bodies a little unsteady with the ale, whispers and protesting
laughter, kissing, and hugging, and old Ritson, sitting in his
chair, looking straight before him, thinking of the time when he
had taken the girl of his heart out of the hot room into the cold
of the valley and wandering down to the Tarn's edge had kissed
her for the first time. He fancied that now, although she had
been dead so long, she was standing just behind the hallan, her
eyes taunting him . . .

Charlie Watson asked Judith to dance. He clamped round the
room with her, staring over her head, saying nothing. He trod
on her toes, bundled her about, and his arm held her like an
iron rod.

They stayed by the door, and he was about to speak to her.
Alice Ritson, the only unmarried Ritson girl remaining, for
Mary had died two years before, ran in from the garden path,
waited an instant, looking at the crowded room, then went up
to Judith, caught her arm and whispered: 'Judith, 'tis Mr
Georges. He's coom back. He's there, in your own place.'

For a moment the room with its figures and haze of heat

swayed, in movement, almost it seemed, to the fiddler's tune.
She remembered afterwards (looking back as she did so many,
many times) that Charlie Watson put out his arm and for a
moment held her. She felt (she knew afterwards, although at the
time she did not notice it) the beating of his heart against her
cheek. What an agony of joy, anticipation, and fear!

'It is my husband,' she said, looking up into his face: then
she ran out.

Georges was standing in their living-room, near the staircase,
down which he had once bundled his box. She ran to him, and
at once knew by the way that he held her that something terrible
had happened to him. He had never held her like that before,
as though his only safety lay in his contact with her.

'I thought that I would never be here,' he said. He lifted her
off her feet and looked into her eyes. Then he put her down and
went to the door, which he closed, slowly, surely; then stood
for a moment with his back to it. They could hear through the
wall the scream of the fiddle and the tramp-tramp-tramp of the
dancing figures.

'Will you come down to the Tarn?' he asked her.

'But you must eat.'

'I had food at Keswick.'

'Where's your horse?'

'I've tethered him. He had his corn. He can stay.'

'But here ... You must be so weary. I can make all comfortable.'

'No, no, no. I must be outside. Away from the music.'

Taking his hand, looking up at him, she said: 'What is it?
Are you in trouble?'

'Yes,' he answered. 'I'm in trouble.'

She nodded her head, asking him no more.

They went out together, and the evening was sweet with all
the summer scents. One lamb in a fold bleated incessantly; as
soon as they came down the hill the music faded to a murmur
like a voice in the Fell. The Tarn had a broad path of moonlight
that quivered with little shudders of gold.

'Will you be cold?' he asked her. 'If you've been at the dance.'

'No. The air is warm.'

He put his arm around her; she was pressed close against
his thigh, and they walked up and down.

'Judy, I've murdered Stane.'

She shivered, and he held her close. When she could steady
herself she thought, at once: 'Now he will need me. He shall

want me always. He is mine to the end,' and directly afterwards:
'Are they searching for him ? I must get him away.' It was odd,
but she thought of Humphrey Sunwood and how sensible she
had been then.

She asked him at once: 'Are they after you for it ?' She had
always hated Stane. She didn't care that he was dead.

'No. It was two weeks back. Off Bergen. No one knows.'

'How was it ? Was it in a fight ?'

'No. Not a fight. I murdered him deliberately. I took him out
in the boat to do it.'

'And no one saw ?'

'It was evening. A storm got up. After I had drowned him I
turned the boat over and swam to land. But do you not shrink
from me ? First, before all else, I must know that—'

'No. I love you. How could I shrink from you ?'

'Because I shrink from myself. It was deliberate, Judy.
Planned. Intended. Not a drunken scuffle, not a hand-to-hand
struggle. I took him by the throat and squeezed it till I thought
my fingers would break. Then I toppled him over. The rain was
coming down in torrents, and there was a wild sea. I thought
I should myself drown, and I would have been glad of it, but
nothing can drown me nor hang me nor stab me . . . I shall live
for ever, Judy, with Stane around my neck – like a dead bird,
clammy, with talons scratching my skin.'

His hand was fiery hot in hers. She remembered afterwards
that in all her bewilderment, her determination to be sensible,
her tenderness for him, her hatred of Stane, which seemed now
to be double what it had been, was amazement at this new
Georges. He was like a man whom she had never seen before;
she loved him as deeply as the other Georges, nay more, because
he needed her, which the other Georges had never done. But
his French indifference, callous humour, self-sufficiency . . .
Where were they ? Was this man a coward ?

He seemed to know her thought. He drew a deep sigh of relief.

'Now it is better. If you are with me we will beat that damnable ghost. For he's been a ghost, Judy, keeping step with me
all the way. Afterwards it was like a spell. In Bergen they believed every word. His body was beaten on to the rocks the
day following, his face disfigured. It seemed natural that his
neck was broken. Three days after I set back to Whitehaven. In
Whitehaven I saw his father . . .'

He broke off.

'His father – a giant old man with a beard to his waist. He

had a mad worship for his son. You know it. I've told you. I
thought that he must suspect, caring so much . . . But no. He
stood there without moving. He went blind, groping with his
hands. Then he caught me round the neck and kissed me. He
thought I was Stane's best friend. There was water lapping
up against the room where we were and a man came in with a
sword. I thought young Stane would slip from beside me, catch
the sword and stab me with it. I would offer no resistance. But
when later old Stane called his son, running up the staircase
after him, shouting his name in the rooms, there was no one
there.

'But he would not let me go. All night he sat there holding
my hand.'

'But how did it come?' Judith asked. 'Stane's death, I mean.
What made you do it?'

'You know how it was. You felt it as I did. Stane and I always
hated one another. I've been bred in England, Judy. I speak like
an Englishman, walk like one, in my behaviour am like one – is
that not so?'

'Yes,' she said, but she knew in her heart that it was not
so. He had never walked, talked or behaved like an Englishman.

'Yes, but there are times when I am French through and
through, when I loathe England and the English. And some
Englishmen I hate from the beginning. So I did Stane. So satisfied, arrogant *and* ignorant. That mixture of conceit and ignor-
ance that is in all your relations, Judith – the most obvious thing
in the English. And he was clever, too; he saw at once how I was,
my laziness, excitement, that I was unable to stay with anything
for long. He judged me well, truly – that was partly why I
hated him. And he meant to supplant me. He saw that the others,
Wix and the rest, were dissatisfied. He manoeuvred me to
London and then worked on them . . . My God, Judy, he was
clever! And I a fool! Holy Heaven, the fool I was!'

The words broke from him in a despairing cry such as she
had never heard from him before. It seemed to be echoed from
the hills. She was afraid lest someone should hear.

'Hush, hush!' she said, leaning up and stroking his cheek as
she might with a child. 'Not too loud. And then—?'

'Well, he came to London to work his way into Will Herries'
counsels. You saw him at the Ball that night. He gave a black
account of me to Herries, worked promises out of him and then
returned to Whitehaven to show them that he had power in the

City, while I diced and drank . . . Oh, it was true enough! Every word was true . . .

'Then when I had fled from London to Christiania he knew all of it. He must have been spying into every corner. I started some business in Bergen. Not much, but something. It was doing fairly, and I meant to return to Whitehaven, show them my steadiness, make all well again. For I knew Wix cared for me in his heart . . . I hadn't heard that Stane had told him all the London affairs, my debts, the scuffle in the Coffee House, everything. He came over to Bergen, Stane, I mean. He pretended that it was an accident, but I knew well what it was.

'We met in an inn room above the sea. He was victorious. He had a letter from Wix to say that they were ended with me in Whitehaven, that I had best never return to England. Stane was triumphant. It was the moment for which he had been working so long. His face was lit up. He had a wart on his right eyelid. Behind his head on the green wall there was a map of China and the Indies. I can tell you, Judith, that I all but killed him there, drove his head into that yellow map, there, just where China was. But there were men about, a street with traffic, boats knocking with the tide against the wall.

'I waited. I waited two days. I was most friendly. I licked his hand, asked that I should be the clerk. Then he boasted, how his father had once been a common fisherman and he himself had sold cockles barefoot. And he went further. He paid for my drink and told me how easy I had been, what a simpleton, and then he said something about you, Judy—'

'I always hated him,' she said.

'Yes, but he wanted you. You were his size, he said. He liked small women – and he was haunted by the wish to plunge his hands in your hair—'

She said nothing, only came closer to him.

'So I made my plan. I said I would row him across an inlet to a house where there were paid women – drink, women, dancing. He could be lascivious. Contemptuously he permitted me. As I strangled him he called out for his father thrice. That was his only decency. Physically he had no strength; I could have broken him anywhere.'

He stopped and said hoarsely: 'I have a fearful thirst. My mouth is dry every hour.'

'We will go home,' Judith said, laying her hand for an instant on his brow, 'and sleep.'

THE OLD MAN OF THE SEA

JUDITH AWOKE, AS now she was accustomed to do, to find
Georges standing on the floor wrestling in his sleep with his
implacable enemy.

She could see only his shadow. The October night was dark;
clouds hid the stars. The words came from him thick and fast:
'No, no. Leave me. I have done with you. That was to end it.
Struggle then, and the water's cold ... Sharp, sharp. I'll not
touch you again. Keep off me. No, no. I'll listen to no whisper.
It is useless. Oh, God, keep me free!'

The last was a whisper of intense and gasping weariness. He
sank to his bare knees. She knew that he was kneeling on the
floor, his head in his hands, while his body trembled.

She got out of their bed, went to him and very gently put her
arms round him. He stayed there trembling against her. Then
slowly he woke.

'Where am I?' he asked.

'Here with me.' She led him back to bed, he docile as a child.
They lay down together, hand in hand. Almost at once he was
asleep again. But she remained for a long time awake, wondering
what it was best to do.

This was October. He had returned in July – July, August,
September, October, and there seemed to be no end to it, no
frightening away of the ghosts, no helping him to overcome
them. For the first time in her life she wished that she were
older – older and wiser. In the immediate weeks after his return
her great fear had been lest in an instant of indiscretion he
should confess to somebody what he had done. He never rode
into Keswick but she waited in an agonized terror for his return.
She never saw him talking to the Ritsons or walking with Watson
(for whom he had conceived a great liking) but she expected the
end of the talk or the walk to be some terrible revelation. But
now, especially when she was weary or lying awake at that time
of the early morning when fears are most pressing, she sometimes wondered whether it would not be better that he should
confess to someone. The burden of sharing it alone seemed often
more than she could bear.

She was not subtle about it. She was not made for subtlety.
He had killed Stane, who had tried to bring him to ruin. That

seemed to her fair. She would herself kill, if need be, anyone who threatened Georges. She would lie in bed, clenching and unclenching her hot little hands, with such a hatred of Stane in her heart that she would almost swoon of it. He had tried to kill Georges, to kill in Georges' life everything that was of any value in it: he would have taken from Georges his livelihood, his friends, even his wife. Well, then — what crime had Georges done ?

No one had seen. No one guessed. It was over. What then possessed Georges ? It was perhaps the hardest part of her task now that this Georges was another man from that careless, wild, courageous, casual Georges, whom she had married and loved. And yet they were the same! She saw dimly how the one had become the other. She could trace back a thousand times when, in the past, he had been afraid of his deeds and then, because he was afraid, had recklessly covered the old fault with the new one. He had never had any stability. He had refused to dig deep into life. She had seen that in him again and again, and now, when he had tumbled into reality, it had been *too* deep for him.

His kindly casualness had always made him live for the moment, but from his childhood — although he would never confess to it because of his pride — he had had an anticipation of fear like a child who is safe only while the lighted candle is in the room.

She did not analyse this. Women of her day did not analyse natures and motives, but she understood him at last.

The irony of it was that now at length she possessed him as she had always longed to do, but as so often when in life we are granted our desires, her gratification was tragic. For, although she possessed him, she could not help him. He relied on her now for everything. He did nothing without asking her. He hated that she should be out of his sight.

There in the half-dark, he uneasily sleeping at her side, she was teased by the odd mixture of her feelings. If she had killed Stane she would see to it that she was not haunted by his ghost. Once done well done! There was impatience in her love for Georges. He must get some work to do: that would worry his ghosts! The farm was theirs and the next farm the Ritsons', both worked by the Ritsons. That just sufficed them for their immediate needs, but she could not endure to see Georges standing about, leaning against a stone wall watching the sheep or the clouds or walking on the uneven stone path beyond the farm outhouses, his hands behind his back, his head down, as though he were a prisoner. His only healthy days were those when he went off on the fells with Charlie Watson.

She was beginning to 'manage' him as she 'managed' old Ritson's rheumatism, Mrs Ritson's bad clumsy sewing, Tom Ritson's carelessness about money, young Alice Ritson's love-affairs; and like all managing people she always a little despised those who succumbed to her management. It was part of Watson's power over her that she couldn't manage him anywhere.

But her real anxiety was that she did not herself know which way she would go. Part of her — her father's part — shared Georges' terrors to their depths. She knew how real that ghostly world was, how dark its valleys, how awful its inhabitants. But for the other part of her all ghosts were unreal, fantastic, just as her father had been altogether unreal and exaggerated for many people. As though, indeed, someone had said to her about her father: 'Fielding would not have drawn such a character.' No, but there were ghosts outside the books of Mr Fielding and Mr Richardson. But were there? Was it not merely the colic? How real were Georges' terrors? 'Very real,' whispered a shadow by Rosthwaite. 'I spent my life in fighting them.' 'Balderdash,' said Will Herries and all the Herries.

But if only she herself could go one way or another! At one moment she wanted to shake Georges by the shoulders, to wake him thoroughly from a silly dream; at another she had only to close her eyes, and young Stane, the wart on his eyelid, his mouth curled contemptuously, his clothes wringing wet, crawled from the Tarn and slipped up the field towards her. Two events showed her very sharply the division between her two worlds. One was an unexpected letter from Francis. He wrote from Bournemouth saying that he had intended to send her a letter 'weeks back' but had been so closely occupied ... Closely occupied in Bournemouth?

He was staying with Prosper and Amelia Cards. He had been there for some weeks. Judith, remembering the Ball, whispered to herself: 'Jennifer.'

... At first, dear Judith, I will be honest and confess that I found the country so desolate that I could have drowned myself. But there have been ameliorations, and now I find myself hanging on when the season is inclement and London calls. Moreover, my conscience tells me that I should come

North and assist poor Deborah and see my darling Judith. Not that yourself are my conscience, dear Judith, but rather my pleasure. However, I am kept here and by what I will one day tell you.

('By whom rather,' thought Judith.)

The Town is a nest of old women who drink nauseous water and talk gossip by the bushel. We have also had a Menagerie with two Lions and a Bear. I tasted the waters but once. Do you remember how once for a punishment my poor mother gave us a pint basin of thin gruel with a spoonful of salt in it for a week and how it tasted? Well, that's for these waters. I fear that the Dispute that had its commencement with that accursed Ball of Will's shows no abatement but only an increase. Brother Will will have nothing to do with me, and there is indeed now a Division in our family starting with Brother Will and Cousin Prosper and spreading into many directions.

I am myself deeply sorry for it. What a stupid affair to start with a Broken Fan! I console myself with the friendliness of my relations here and especially with my cousin Jennifer.

I fear that yourself, dear Judith, are held here to have taken sides most decisively, and that Amelia, at least, is not to be reconciled to you. Cousin Prosper in his cups is reconciled to all the world, but out of them – well, he has enough family pride for Sir Charles Grandison. I have been entertained by Godwin's *Enquiry concerning Political Justice*. You should read it, for if we are going the way of France, which is none too unlikely, there are wise words for us here. I am myself engaged on a paper answering some points in Paine's *Age of Reason*. We were never, I am convinced, in all our National History, more at the parting of the ways than we now are. All Europe is in an uproar. The People's Voice is making itself felt everywhere and splendid extravagances at Brighthelmstone are not sufficient satisfaction for such a heavy rise in prices.

You know, Judith, that I was always more Dreamer than anything. Now more than ever I dream my dreams. I am thirty-six years of age and have done nothing with my life. See Will, who is adding pound to pound with every breath he draws. Dare I venture into matrimony, little Judith?

Is there any woman would be fool enough to take me if I asked her ? . . .

'Any woman ?' thought Judith. 'Will Jennifer ?'

The thought struck her with an added pang of loneliness and difficulty. If Francis married Jennifer, then he was lost to her, Judith, for ever. And with Francis gone it seemed to her that she would be, indeed, alone. But Jennifer would not have him. She was to make a far finer match than a poor North Country cousin ten years her elder.

Putting the letter down with a sigh, the world contained in its pages slipped into incredibility. How unreal, beside her present actual trouble, seemed that little pasteboard quarrel of the fan. Will's city life, Bournemouth's waters, Paine's *Age of Reason*, Jennifer's beauty, Prosper's pride and the rest. There *were* two worlds, and the secret of living was to know both to be real! But it was a problem. So she went out and rubbed old Ritson's back with ointment, looked at Tom Ritson's bull that he had bought in Keswick, advised Alice Ritson against young Humblethwath of Rosthwaite and stood, shading her eyes against the October sun, to see Georges ride up the path with Watson.

What she did see was incredible.

Georges was walking along the rocky path leading his horse and beside him was walking – Reuben! Reuben, as she could see, talking, gently, kindly, smiling, and Georges was smiling too.

At the first sight of them she had to recall that last time when she had seen Reuben, proud, master of himself, but driven from the house . . . and now, Georges was walking with him as though he loved him!

Reuben had been often in her mind. She was always thinking of him, but she had never seen him again since that day. Now, as she turned towards them, she loved him for being kind to Georges, and she loved Georges for being kind to Reuben. It was the first time she had had comfort since Georges' return. She met them and kissed them both. They stood there, the three of them, looking down at the Tarn, which was ruffled with little grey bird's feathers that ran in flocks under the pale sun, making the whole sheet of water quiver with life.

Reuben was different. He was far surer, more in command of himself and of everything. He was stouter but harder too. He was wearing black knee-breeches and stout black shoes and a broad black hat, but he was clean and neat; his white stock was

clean and the white bands at his wrists. His voice was quiet
and assured like his carriage. He moved and spoke like a man
who had discovered how to rule himself.

They all went into the house. Reuben said that he would stay
with them the night. He had come from Wasdale. Tomorrow
he had to preach in Mardale. He had walked from Waswater
over the Stye Head and up from Rosthwaite.

That evening they had a strange conversation that Judith
was never to forget. Oddly now Reuben dominated them both.
He had never dominated Judith before, he had always been subservient to her, but now, although he was as loving to her as
ever, being with her as though they had never been separated,
he had a new power that set him apart. Soon she knew where his
power lay. He was no longer afraid of anybody or anything.
She saw that Georges submitted to him like a child to an elder.
They sat, the three of them, close together by the wood fire
that blazed with a sharp exulting power in the hearth. Judith
sat at Georges' feet, her head against his thigh. She caught his
hand in hers and felt its pulse leap wildly against her palm.

She was always saying to him now with every movement,
'Don't be afraid, I'm here.'

Reuben had not very much to tell them about himself. He
went about, just as before, preaching everywhere, anywhere.

'What do you preach?' Georges asked suddenly.

'Jesus Christ,' Reuben said.

'I do not wish to be offensive,' Georges went on slowly. 'May
I say what is in my mind with honesty?'

Reuben smiled. 'Yes. If you will.'

'Well, then, Christ is a figure to me who died long since. A
Jewish rebel. The times needed a new religion. This was offered
them and they took it. I cannot believe in any God, or that Christ
was more than a brave man, mistaken . . . This life is all that we
have, and, by God, it is a poor one!' His hand trembled in
Judith's.

'I do not think so,' said Reuben. 'I know Jesus Christ. I
have talked with Him.'

'But these are words,' said Georges. 'My mother was heathen
and her father before. My grandfather was an atheist, famous in
his day, in the town of Toulouse. It is true that I was always
taught that the Christian influence was a false one, but that has
not formed my mind. I have observed men and their actions,
and I find that there is no sign of a God in the world.'

'Then life is meaningless.'

'Yes, meaningless.'

'It is a question,' Reuben said quietly, 'that every man must decide by his own experience. Here we are, two men in the world. You are certain of your experience and I of mine. But if I had been to China and seen the Emperor and you had not, you would permit my right to my certainty, would you not?'

'Yes,' answered Georges impatiently. 'But the Emperor of China exists. Many people have seen him. The Christ is a fable.'

'You must permit me my experience. I know that God is in the world.'

'And I know that He is not.'

'Are you as certain,' asked Reuben, 'that He is not, as I that He is?'

Georges raised his eyes, haggard and restless, to Reuben's face.

'Then if He is, how can He permit this cruelty, this pain ...' He broke off. His whole body was trembling.

'When I was a lad in Cockermouth,' Reuben said, 'I saw one day a bear baited in the street. I suffered torture from its helplessness. Now I know from my own life that all experience adds to one's riches. And pain possibly gives the most.'

'Was the bear the richer?' Georges broke out passionately.

'If the bear knew his gain. This is not the end,' Reuben said. 'Or so I believe. I have an immortal part, and Jesus is my friend to show to me that I have.'

'This world is enough,' Georges cried. 'A vile world in which we have no chance and are buffeted by a hidden enemy.'

Reuben was silent. He bent forward and gazed into the fire.

'Ah, but I have two worlds,' he said at last, 'and there I am richer than you. I must deny neither. I am citizen of both. In the one I am very young, an infant, but with the Grace of God I shall grow. In the other I eat my bread and pay my tax, but my body dies, my tax is paid and I go through the door, out of it, at any time.' Then he added, smiling to himself: 'The great lesson of life is patience.'

'Patience!' Georges broke out. He started to his feet. 'I swear to God, if there be one, that I have no patience. That I refuse to delay. I want my judgement. For my sin ... for my crime ...' He stood over Reuben, bent forward, shaking the other's shoulder.

'Reuben! Your sins, if you've committed any, do they stay with you? In your other world that you speak of, will you be punished for ever? Will there be no release?'

Reuben nodded his head. 'Yes, there is release for sin – after repentance.'

'But I do not repent. I have done no wrong. He merited his death. He . . .' Georges broke off, seeing what he had admitted. There was an intense silence between the three of them. Judith, whose guard over Georges was constant, turned to Reuben with some of her old ferocity, as though she would defend Georges with her claws. But there was no need. Reuben looked down at the floor; then, glancing up, he said:

'What I tell you must seem like empty folly to you. I can only warrant you that nothing is final; there is no end to experience – and there is no sin too large to keep Christ Jesus from your life.'

He rose and went over to Georges and put his hand on his shoulder. 'Pay for your sin – good worthy coin. Then travel on.'

He went up to his bed.

After he was gone they sat close, hand in hand. Georges said desperately: 'Judith, there must be ghosts. It is true, although I never thought it. He will not leave me. At every corner I think to see him, and now it is months since I broke his neck and he drowned.'

Then after a little he added: 'There must be some end coming to this. I can *feel* it coming. If I could fight someone with my hands, stand my trial, be hanged by the neck – yes, anything rather than this stealthy silence. I, all my life I have never cared what I did nor minded what I did, and I am young and have everything before me. And he's dead and no one knows. It is sentimental imagination, this fancy I have – but I can't be free of it. I can't! I can't! I can't!' He walked desperately about the room. Then he stopped sharp in front of Judith. 'Judith, do *you* think there's a God?'

'I don't know. No one knows.' (But she thought to herself: 'What he said about the two worlds is true. That is the way *my* life is going.')

But she rose and then, bending forward, said:

'I shall tell you what I think, Georges. That you are lazy. That you must go somewhere to work and forget Stane. Why should you think of him? If he were here and he had tried to hurt you as he did, and I were strong enough, I should strangle him with my two hands. He was our enemy, and you slew him fairly. Shake off your imagination! Go farming with Charlie Watson for a while. He'll teach you things. He has no business with ghosts—'

Georges looked above her head to the farther wall.

'Stane's father,' he said. 'His heart was broken.'

She herself felt a pang then. Yes, the consequences went, as always, beyond the act. But she faced them ... Stane, his father, all his relations – she'd face them all. Let them attack Georges and they attacked her too. But to fight for Georges, she now saw, needed more than physical combat.

A week later Judith lost her temper in the good old fashion of her childhood, and this loss of her temper led to an incident.

There was a man just then, Larry Tod, who was helping Tom Ritson with his cattle. He was a waster, this Larry, no good at all, and he wandered about the district doing odd jobs hither and thither and not much good anywhere. He was famous, though, as a wrestler. He was big, carroty-haired, broken-nosed. He liked to strip to his shirt and drawers and show a chest like a board, and, to quote the old description of the famous French wrestler, Le Bœuf, 'a stomach like a bale of wool'. He was very proud of himself, very sly, up to any mean trick, the right sort of figure for the villain in a wrestling bout. And that, on this occasion, because of Judith's temper he was.

On this day, an October afternoon of driving black cloud when the fells looked twice their natural size, Judith coming into the yard saw Tod bending down and twisting the tiny arm of young Walter Ritson, who was yelling his loudest.

Tod straightened himself when he saw Judith. He was always dirty with manure and mud and the rest. Now he wiped the back of his hand over the flat of his broken nose and said something about the child's laughing at him. Young Walter, the tears drying on his cheeks, stared up at them both in interested amazement.

Judith's temper was fine to see. She enjoyed it herself. She had been living in half-shadows with Georges for months back and she needed a change. Then she hated the huge oaf with the surly eyes, the tangled hair that seemed like a parody of her own. He was a sort of ogre personification of all that threatened Georges. She told him her notions about him. Slowly his brow darkened. What he would have said or done no one will ever tell, for Charlie Watson came by. Tod turned his rage in that direction. He hated Watson anyway.

A minute later Watson was stripping his coat. It was to be a wrestle. The news went round as though a bell had been rung. Everyone came flocking, and the match was moved to the green mound above the farm.

All the little village was there – men, women and children.

A ring was formed, Watson and Larry Tod stripped to shirt and drawers. Both men were open at the neck.

It was to be the best of three throws. The little crowd held their breath, while the sky tossed cloud after cloud as though there were some giant juggler over the hill, and the Tarn, black as ink, lay insolently below them.

In the front of the ring, squatting on the grass, was young Walter Ritson, the cause of the trouble, with his mouth open. He hated Larry, but he feared him too, and if Larry won he fancied that there would be trouble for him. Perhaps the others felt the same. Larry Tod had been prominent in the little place these last weeks, and with every day he was becoming more sure of himself and more insolent. And for Judith and Georges, also watching, although neither confessed it to the other, the result of this seemed like an omen. Let the red-haired ogre win, Georges thought, and he was pushed a step farther into his prison.

The men shook hands and got into holds. Larry tried at once the back heel, the simplest and oldest of all 'chips', for all the wrestler has to do is to lay his foot behind his antagonist's heel and bend him over it. But you must be strong to do it. Larry was strong, but so was Watson, who at once slackened his hold and moving his beautiful firm body with the most delicate grace, turned his side. Watson tried then for a buttock, but Larry's immense strength prevented him. Watson tried to get under him to lift him over his back. Then, when that failed, he stepped away and there they were again, their arms at one another's necks. They began slowly to step round. The little crowd drew their breath. This was to be an even match.

For Georges it was an agony. In his strange, over-nervous, harassed state everything was exaggerated. The dark furry clouds hung low, as though with an especial sinister message for himself. When the sun suddenly struck out from them with bright splinter-like rays, flinging the dry bracken into patches of amber light as though there were a secret flame beneath the soil, that, too, seemed to point the finger at him. Why was he thus persecuted? Could he not bring his mind to order? It was true what Judith had said, that Stane deserved his death. It was only his imagination that dragged with him everywhere the accompanying scene, the rain hissing on to the boards of the boat, the sudden consciousness in Stane's eyes of Georges' intention, the cry lost in the storm, the whip, whip of the wind.

The women were shouting. Watson had tried the right-leg trip, making Larry swing sharply towards his left. With a mighty straining of muscle, his thighs and buttocks forced to their uttermost strength, he lifted Larry up, hoisting Larry's left leg up with his right and – to a great shout of all and sundry – landing the ogre with a fine bump on his back.

First throw to Watson.

The two men stayed a moment, wiping their brows. The crowd were silent. Did they feel, perhaps, that there was some-thing concerned here more deeply than the personal encounter ? The women were all on Watson's side, and yet he was aloof from them. He had never tried to make love to any of them. There was a little feeling that he was 'a bit above himself'. Larry, when he was dressed up and had washed his face, was a great figure of a man and knew what love-making was. One and all, though, in their hearts, they loathed him and perhaps, like little Wallie, feared him too.

At any rate he looked now a man to be feared. As he stood there waiting, scowling between his sullen eyes, he looked as though he would kill Watson had he the chance.

When they came together again Larry tried the hitch-over, that is, he attempted to turn his left side to Watson, curl his left leg round Watson's right and, while Watson was standing on his left leg, cross-buttock him. But Watson was too quick for him, and soon they were moving round, slowly, cautiously, trying for some advantage.

You would not tell from looking at Georges, standing straight and grave, his rather round cheeks composed, his black eyes sombre and still, that his soul was in torment. If he had one! If he had one! That preacher, Reuben Sunwood, with his confidence in his Christ, his quiet happy assurance . . . Ah well, that was not for Georges! His life had gone for nothing, one silly mistake and foolishness after another! He had begun life with a sense of adventure, with a kind of bravado, as though he could dare the world and bring it tumbling to his feet. But the world had snapped its fingers at him. He had got nothing out of it. Nothing save Judy!

He half turned and looked at her, standing on tiptoe, her mouth a little open, her hair blowing, all excitement like a child. A child! But how courageous and independent! How she had held by him – from the first, through everything, her loyalty never for a moment wavering. If he could but get rid of this present burden and dread he would show her that at last he realized her worth. He had been a long time coming to it, through slow selfish stages, but he knew it now, that he had had the luck of the devil to get her – yes, luck far better than he deserved.

He heard the deep indrawing breath of the women beside him and saw, with a beat of excitement, Larry Tod turning his back suddenly, getting right under Watson and, with a great heave that had also in it a lightning quickness, sending Watson flying over his back. He had buttocked him. Buttocked him, fair and square.

Second throw to Tod.

Then, indeed, Georges' whole life and purpose seemed to be in the match. Watson must win; he must, he must! The very sight of Larry Tod strutting about there like a flaming peacock, pushing out his chest, stroking his arms, throwing glances from his narrow eyes to heaven as though he expected the clouds to acclaim him, that was indeed too much. If Watson lost now all was lost. It was as though Tod with his coarseness and his evil had been sent as a messenger to Georges threatening him with some low, vile dominion for ever.

Watson stood there quietly, no expression in his eyes, waiting. Above them the clouds were stripping the sky, which began to be flooded with a white pale glow. The Tarn, beneath them, was white like the peeled inside skin of an orange; all the houses of the village were black.

The men took hold again. First Tod, setting his teeth, tried the swinging hips, but this, if it is to succeed, must be a swing of great quickness, and Watson was too strong for him. Then Watson, in his turn, tried the chip, getting his knee behind his opponent's so that Larry might lose his balance. It seemed that Watson would succeed. Larry raised his head to the white sky, his teeth clenched, his eyes closed; you could feel that he thought that he was going. But his strength was too much for Watson. He escaped, and suddenly, a moment later, was clicking Watson's right leg with his own right and his left with Watson's left. The struggle now was fearful. Both men put out their uttermost. Watson resorted to the outside click to save himself from falling, placing his leg as near the ground as possible. The two men swung and strained; Watson's neck and upper chest were soaked with sweat. Then Larry's little eyes were triumphant; he crossed both Watson's legs quickly with his own, cross-buttocking, and with a shout, his huge frame seeming to double its natural size, he had Watson on the ground.

He stood there, smiling.

Georges turned. His fate was sealed then. He walked away down the hill. Coming to the little rough bridge he saw someone standing there, someone with his back to him, a man of a great height, in a long dark-blue coat. He knew, before the man turned, who it would be. It was young Stane's father.

A few minutes later Judith noticed that Georges was not at her side. She had been absorbed by the incidents of the last bout, and when she saw Watson beaten she felt, as Georges had felt, that there was some personal omen, intended for them both. That was not like her. She realized it herself, but these last weeks had tried her. Yes, she wished she were older and wiser and, in general, more patient. She wished that she were not so easily excited – excited by just anything, a piece of silk, a cloud in the sky – and then by a man hanging! It was then that she saw that Georges was not beside her and, at once, apprehension seized her as it always did now. It seemed to hover over her like a black bird – yes, and the sky white behind the bird, the Tarn dead white and all the bracken dead.

Watson was walking slowly towards her, pulling on his coat. She had to speak to him.

'Next time, Charlie,' she said, smiling.

'Aye.' She could see that he was bitterly disappointed. She was not sure that there were not even tears in his eyes.

'I'll whack him – great oaf!' he said, half to himself, half to her. She realized with a quick sharpness of perception that he had done it all for her, all from the first to the last. She put out her hand and it lay in his hot one, damp and sweating from the tussle.

'I'll back you, Charlie Watson, against all the world.' And yet, although she was so grateful to him and friendly, the truth was that she was scarcely aware of him.

Over and over again she was saying: 'Where's Georges? What's he about? Why did he go without telling me?'

She turned and ran down the hill. Pushing open their door, she saw a strange sight. A giant old man stood looking at her. He had long white hair that fell to the blue collar of his long heavy coat, and he had a white beard, like the cleanest, most shining wool. Above his beard a sharp pale nose and two pale-blue eyes. All down his long blue coat were round brass buttons, and he wore tall boots that gaitered him to the thigh. He was so white and clean that he seemed to be wrapped in some mask-like covering, and Judith had the odd sense that with a gesture he could throw off all of this – the hair, beard, face, clothes – and that he would be then a thin naked old man, sharp like a sword.

Another odd thing was that at once she knew him. She did not need to hear Georges' voice:

'Mr Stane, this is my wife. Judith, this is poor Mr Stane's father.'

She remembered always her sudden resentment that Georges said 'Poor Mr Stane.' There was weakness and cowardice there. She would never have said 'Poor Mr Stane' had a thousand of his fathers been there!

She went forward, holding out her hand.

'How are you, sir? Will you not sit down? You must be weary after your walk.' She saw at once that the old man liked her and that, very strangely, she liked him. It was always Judith's way, her life through, to know in the first instant whether she liked or disliked anyone.

The old man sat down. Georges had not moved from his place, standing against the wall, and Judith did not look at him. Rather she was compelled to notice everything about old Mr Stane, how, with solemn, dignified, cautious steps, he moved to a chair; how he slowly sat down, spreading on either side of him the long heavy skirts of his coat; how he put up his hand and smoothed his white locks, pinched his white nose, then, very carefully, as though he were dealing with something extremely precious, laid his hands on his immense knees. It was then that she was struck with his great strength. His hands looked as though they could wring the neck of an ox.

'Mr Stane,' Georges said, 'took a chaise to Keswick and walked from there to see us.'

'Aye,' said the old man. 'I was drawn like. My heart is aching for my son, madam, and your husband was the last to see him. It was a terrible accident and God's will. But he was all I had in the world.'

He spoke with very little accent in a soft mild tone. Then he went on: 'Whoso casteth a stone on high casteth it on his own head. He that worketh mischief, it shall fall on him, and he shall not know whence it cometh.'

Her heart beat wildly. He knew then? He had come here for some kind of vengeance? But he looked up and gave her a smile, so gentle, so friendly, so amiable that she could only smile back at him.

'The Scriptures, madam,' he said, 'have been a comfort to me all my days.'

'Yes,' she said, not knowing what to say. 'And now you must have some food.'

'Thank you kindly, madam. I could enjoy a bit of food. Although I like a walk, you understand.'

'Mr Stane, Judith,' Georges said, 'will stay here with us tonight.'

'Thank you kindly,' the old man answered, pinching his nose. 'I wouldn't mind.'

He smiled on them both, then sighed a deep heavy sigh.

TUMBLE DOWNSTAIRS

OLD STANE stood, as he liked to do, the blue skirts of his coat spread, before the fireplace.

Judith sat on the window-ledge, peeling potatoes from a large 'kist' on her lap, looking out of window at the gold smoke of the bracken that rolled in a low cloud up and up above the thin splintered blue of the Tarn. A late October afternoon, quite still, without a cloud in the sky, and the running everywhere of water, crystal clear.

Within the room, too, everything was sharp and clean; Judith, her lithe figure like a cut jewel, the flames of the fire like painted laths, old Stane's beard like the white of an egg, his blue coat without a spot, his long strong hands washed, you would say, with pumice-stone. Cleanest of all his long nose, always like the nose of a mask.

'Well, madam,' he said, 'I swore that my son should become a great man. I had myself sold fish with my feet bare on the White-haven cobbles, and the Lord thought it well for me to do so. My wife, ma'am, died in childbirth. She was a good woman, although with impulses not entirely Christian. When the Lord took her I accepted my rebuke that I could not have made her more godly, and I offered my son, even as Abraham offered Isaac a sacrifice to the Lord—'

('Young Stane,' thought Judith, 'a sacrifice to the Lord!' She could see his face, mean and ambitious, and his hands as they moved towards her . . . if she had allowed him—! She shuddered a little.)

'But as Abraham with Isaac, so with myself and my son. The Lord did not at that time demand the sacrifice. He knew His own good time . . .'

Oh, when would he stop! She thought that in these last weeks he had managed to creep into her very being. She would never be rid of him again. He had done nothing but hang about the house. He never went farther than the steps beyond the door. He was always there. At night they could hear him move his great body in his bed, yes, although there were a thousand doors between themselves and him! He ate but little, drank only water, spoke to no one save Georges and herself. He was quite silent if they were not there. Sometimes he would talk to them, some-times only look at them. He would stare and stare over his long nose.

He had little movements that made her long to scream out. One was when he laid, slowly and almost sacramentally, his thick heavy hands on his thick heavy knees. Then he would stroke his beard with a purposeful meditation as though he were wondering whether, with a quick jerk, he would not tug it off and show it to be a disguise. He would raise a hand as though he would give a blessing. He was always gentle, kindly and patient. She liked him behind her terror of him. Had he not been young Stane's father she might have been his friend.

As it was he must go – and as soon as might be. But Georges would not let him go. He was fascinated by him as the rabbit by the snake.

Two days before this, almost hysterical with irritation (for it was absolutely against her character to be passive in this manner), in their room at night she had attacked Georges.

'Tell him to go!'

'I cannot.'

'Why not?'

'This is the least I owe him.'

'You owe him nothing! Georges, tell him to go!'

'You don't understand . . . So long as he wishes to remain he must.'

She could have shaken him until his head rolled on his shoulder.

'Georges, wake up! You are dreaming. You killed the man in self-defence. He would have finished you. He wished to. Well, then. The old man has no right over us.'

'I cannot tell him to go.'

'Then I will.'

'Tell him. You will see. Nothing will happen.'

'But what *is* it? What spell has he laid on you?'

'No spell. I cannot do otherwise.'

'But is he to be here with us always?'

'So long as he wishes.'

'But he makes you miserable. He reminds you always. If he went away you would forget.'

He came to her, put his arms round her.

'In this you *are* a child. You are too young to understand. It is not because I think I was wicked to kill Stane. I've done many worse things. But I'm not the same man since I did it. I feel that I must confess it to someone. Then it will be over.'

'But you have confessed it – to me.'

'You are part of myself or you have grown to be. We are both in this – as though you had been in the boat too.'

She stood up straight beside him, like man standing by man.

'Well, I shall tell him to go.'

And so, on this golden afternoon, she did.

She was not afraid to tell him; her earlier fear of him seemed to leave her as she spoke.

'Mr Stane,' she said, coming quite close to him, 'when will you be leaving us?'

He didn't answer: he was pulling at his beard.

'I ask,' she said, smiling up at him, 'because I may have a guest. Mr Francis Herries. He has written that he may be coming.'

The old man's nose seemed to probe into her, tickling her skin. As a fact he was bending down towards her.

'When you have no place for me,' he said, very gently stroking his beard and almost, it seemed to her, drawing her into the meshes of it, 'I may reside in the village. It is a pleasure for me to be near your husband, who was so good a friend to my son.'

She was on the verge of crying out: 'He was not good to him. They hated one another.' It was one of Mr Stane's peculiarities that he seemed to draw out of you your most secret thoughts.

He smiled on her very affectionately as he added:

'I am an old man, madam. The Lord has seen fit to take everything from me. These, your husband and yourself, are, it may be, the last affections of my life.'

After that what could she say?

That night they lay awake hearing him walk his room. It was a heavy soft tread like an animal's. They heard him get into his bed at last. Then there was only an owl's cry.

They clung together that night like children.

'Georges, let us run away.'

'Where?'

'Anywhere. London. Paris.'

'He would come after us.'

'Georges, I *must* help you. I must! I must! I'm not a fool. This is a ridiculous thing, to be hemmed in by an old man.'

He sighed, holding her very closely.

'It matters very little. I'm happy because now I love you. Judy, Judy, I love you so.'

'And I love you more and more.'

'But how can you when there is so little in me to love? I have never treated you well from the beginning.'

'Georges, I shall never love anyone again. That is true. I know it absolutely. This is for all my life long.'

He stroked her hair. That, at least, he had loved from the very beginning.

'Judy, if we could be rid of this I know now what we would do. I could settle here now, I wouldn't wish to move. I would farm with Watson. I have lived out all my restlessness. We would have enough. Perhaps you would have children. If only we could be rid of this!'

'But we can, Georges!'

They were whispering as though the old man in his room could hear them.

'He must go, and then you will forget it all.'

'What did he say when you spoke?'

She did not answer.

'Did he say he would go?'

'No.'

'You see.'

'Oh, but I shan't be beaten by an old man.' Her voice rose. She dropped it to a whisper again without knowing that she did so.

'Judy, I love you! I love you! I love you!'

'Oh, Georges, I love you so! It has come at last, both of us loving one another – both of us.'

'Yes – both of us . . .'

'It is very seldom that two people love with the same strength.'

'I did not know that I could love anyone for long. You have made me by being so good.'

They heard the old man in the other room rise from his bed. The boards creaked. They were silent, their hearts beating the one against the other.

But it was on that night that they both had terrible dreams. Georges dreamt that he was being hanged from a tree that was covered with white moss, and in that last moment before death the moss was alive with worms. Judith dreamt of a white horse that, plunging through dark water, leapt up the black hills beyond, and that, as it leapt, her father (she had never seen him, but she knew that it was her father) ran and jumped on to its back, calling to her to follow. But she could not, because Georges was struggling in the water and she trying to save him. The white horse vanished, a star fell from the sky into the water, and Georges was drowned.

In the dim musk-like shadow of dawn she waked and found Georges sleeping at her side. In her relief she laid her hand on his bare heart and felt its steady beat. Then she looked in his face and saw that he, too, was struggling in dreams.

She brushed his dark hair back from his forehead, kissed his eyes, stroked his breast, gently as a mother her child.

In the morning, however, all her sentiment was gone. They must be rid of this old man. The weather had changed. The sky was a fury of wind and rushing cloud. The clouds ran like messengers, and the sun struck like a whip on the hills, slashed and was gone. The bracken changed in an instant from dun to fire, from fire to sullen death. The clouds, after racing the sky, suddenly gathered into heavy bales of wool and then slipped down, enclosing Watendlath in mist. The rest of the world was shut away. Judith, in spite of her common sense, began to lose her wits, for now she, too, was conscious of a terrible impulse to catch the old man by the beard and tell him everything.

'Yes. It's true. I don't know whether you think it or not, but Georges killed your wretched son, and he deserved it. Now will you go?'

She had never felt any urge like this before. It was exactly as though someone were whispering in her ear. Their nights were broken. They were afraid to sleep because of their dreams. The old man stayed by the house, and they found that they, too, stayed there also. Charlie Watson was away in Carlisle. She did not seem to want to speak to anyone. She never went into the Ritsons' kitchen. The low wet clouds seemed to shut them off, the three of them, from all the rest of the world.

Judith sewed, cooked, sometimes walked to the Fell and looked down to Rosthwaite. That was the farthest she went. Georges sat, walked to the door and looked out, sat down again. It was as though they were both held by a spell. It could not, of course, continue like this. But what would happen? Old Mr Stane seemed to be perfectly content. He talked much and always about himself and his son. He gave no trouble, stayed for the most part beside the fire.

'You may be sure that I appreciate your kindness. The Lord will not suffer a sparrow to fall to the ground . . . My boy would have been wealthy had he lived. He had a fine head for business. Aye. Aye. All that I had, but it is the Lord's will, and His mercy must be great in our eyes . . . But it is a grief to me that he should have perished in foreign waters. Your husband, ma'am, did all that he could, but it was beyond human power to save him. I know that. For an old man it is a hard blow, but it will not be long before the Lord will take me to Himself . . .'

Nevertheless he did not give the impression of great sorrow, but rather of intent watchfulness. He watched with his nose, and when he stroked it with his thick slow finger it was as though finger and nose were communicating together.

One afternoon the rain came. It fell in hard relentless torrents. The country was blinded as though a hood had been drawn over its eyes. That night in the war of water and groaning trees Georges caught Judith's hands and told her that he could hold out no longer. He must tell the old man and be damned to him.

'When I have told him, I can take him by the neck and shove him from the door. He can take what revenge he pleases.'

For a moment she thought that perhaps this would be best. Then she saw what it would mean. Georges would be arrested and hanged. She told him that that would be the end of everything, of herself as well as of him.

'Well, maybe that would be best. Anything's better than this. He is strangling us as though he had a cord around our throats, and he knows it.'

She had a wild notion that they should start out then and there, run for their lives, on and on, reach some foreign country – China . . . Even as she said it she knew that it was hopeless. He had strangled all her energy.

On the next night the rain had ceased, and a cold pale stillness lay over everything. They sat around the fire, and Mr Stane told them about his home, his possessions, his clothes, his Bible, his intimacy with God as he had done a thousand times before. There never was such an egoist.

'The Lord giveth and the Lord taketh away . . .'

Georges sprang from his seat by the fire, stood up against him, front to front.

'I killed your son. I killed your son. I threw him into the water

and watched him drown. I hated him and hate him yet ...
Now be damned to you both ... You and your son ... both of
you.'

It was as though the words had been spat out and then
returned into him again. He put his hand to his throat. Judith
rose with a startled cry. She came close to him, as though to
protect him, so that they were all near together. In the silence
she heard the owl's cry that had been haunting her for weeks.

At last, after this great pause, old Stane slowly lifted himself
up from his chair, stood above them, then with his white hand
pushed them, breaking through between them.

He looked at them, nodded his head.

'I knew it ... a long time back. I wanted confirmation from
your own mouth. Bloody murderer of my son—'

'Well, he had been bent on my ruin for years. He wished to take
my place.' Georges panted the words. 'It was an old feud
between us. We hated one another from the beginning.'

Old Stane nodded his head. 'Aye – you hated him.'

'Now go!' Georges cried. 'Call in the Justice. I shan't run
away.'

He seemed like a man liberated. Judith went to him and put
her hand on his arm.

'We shan't run away,' she repeated.

But Stane did not move. Georges felt such a sickness of the
sight of him, a sickness that involved himself, his deed, the whole
world. He would never be free of all this until Stane was gone.

'Finish it,' he said, and went up the stairs.

Everything happened then with great swiftness. Georges had
reached the upper landing, when old Stane turned and was
after him. For so heavy a man he moved quickly, as though someone very young and vital were concealed in that bulk.

He was at the stairhead in a moment. Georges turned to face
him and they stood close together as though in amity.

Stane shouted:

'I came for this! ... I came for this! Down you go,
murderer—'

His arms shot up, he hugged Georges close to his heart as
though he loved him, lifted him like a baby, then hurled him
away from the stair, over to the floor below.

He waited, looking down, then rushed down the stair, bent
for a moment over the huddled figure, passed out through the
door.

* * *

It had happened in a flash, as lightning strikes a house. Judith had not stirred; now, liberated, she ran to Georges, frantically, crying she knew not what, knelt down beside him.

His head was bleeding and both his legs were bent beneath him. He was quite conscious and he looked at her and smiled.

'My back is broken . . . he has done for me.'

'No. No—' She lifted his head and placed it against her breast.

'There's nothing to do, Judy, my darling. I'll be gone in a moment. The old devil was strong . . .'

She tried to be clear-headed and wise. This was the crisis of her whole life, something for which she had been always preparing. Her hand was soaked in the blood from his wounded head, but she could think of nothing save his eyes, which stared into hers as though they would never let her go.

'I must fetch someone. They shall ride into Rosthwaite . . .' She did not know what she said.

'No. Don't go. Don't leave me. Soon I shan't see you.'

She began to cry.

'. . . It is just . . . Now we had come to love one another. Ugh, I can't speak. I am swimming in water . . . Sinking. Hold my eyes, Judy. Oh, Judy, darling, how I love you!'

'And I you, Georges. Always. Oh, Christ, for help. Someone to help . . .'

'Nothing to be done.' His head sank deep against her breast. His voice fell to a whisper.

'I love you – for ever—'

His hand touched hers and he was gone.

Part III

The Bird of Bright Plumage

FAMILY PAPERS

Letter from Judith Paris to Francis Herries, Esq

22, WESTBOURNE PLACE, LONDON,
16th of May, 1800

MY DEAREST FRANCIS – Dinner is over, Emma has gone out
to visit a friend, the candles are properly trimmed and now is the
time to do what I have for several days pledged myself to – write
a proper and informing letter. You know well by this time, dear
Francis, that I am never as informing as I would wish to be, but
on this especial occasion I have real news for you – for, what do
you think? I was actually present at Drury Lane Theatre last
night when the poor King was shot at by a ruffian and had a most
providential escape from death.

Mr Ross, with whom Emma has on several occasions acted
at Drury Lane, had given her two tickets and, as you may well
believe, we were all agog for we were promised that the King
and Queen and all the Princesses would be present.

Now fancy the event! Scarcely had the King entered the box,
before he had taken his seat and was yet bowing to the audience
(myself and Emma were on the floor and had a most excellent
view of it) when a wretch in the pit not far from us aimed at the
poor King with a horse-pistol and fired.

You can imagine the sensation! Everyone was screaming. It
was fortunate that there was not a panic. The King alone was
calm, for he turned, said some words to an attendant, took his
seat quite tranquilly and sat out the entertainment which was
She Would and She Would Not and James Cobb's *Humourist*.

It was terrible to see the people throw themselves upon the
wretched would-be assassin, who was pulled over the spikes
and hurried across the stage. Sir William Addington examined
him in an adjoining apartment.

After a while up went the Curtain and we all – on the stage
and off it – stood up and sang 'God Save the King'. Emma was
crying like a child and I must confess that my own eyes were wet.
Princess Mary fainted twice they say, but Princess Elizabeth
was most brave and we could see how the Queen nodded to the

Princesses that they should keep up their spirits.

They say today that the name of the man was James Hadfield and that the King was indeed lucky, for one of the slugs from the pistol was found only a foot to the left of the royal chair. The affair is the more mysterious it seems, in that only that same afternoon during his attendance at the field exercises of the Grenadier battalion at Hyde Park a Clerk in the Navy Office was shot while standing only a few feet from the King. It was thought at the time to be an accident but now it looks otherwise.

What times we live in! The whole world is disturbed and the wretched Revolution in France has been, I am convinced, the cause of it. Gold is scarce they say, and I know from my own experience how scarce food is. Everyone is complaining but nothing is done and many well-informed persons fear that we are on the verge of Revolution. Well, after all this public news you will wish to hear something more personal.

This is now my second year with Mrs Dudeney and her children. I go to her house in Mecklenburgh Square at nine every morning and am there until six, save for Saturdays and Sundays. I take my dinner with them and often drive out with Mrs Dudeney or her sister Miss Chalpaine.

I must confess that I have grown attached to the children. They are good little things, even a trifle too virtuous, for you know, dear Francis, I never care sufficiently for those I can completely rule.

Poor Mrs Dudeney misses her husband very sadly and this that we have in common should draw us closely together. But something holds me apart from everyone, even from Emma. It is as though my heart were indeed quite dead and, although time has now passed, I live in a dream. It seems to matter nothing where I am or what I do. My whole movement is external. I speak of this to no one else save yourself – even Emma has no notion of it but thinks that I am well recovered from Georges' death.

But oh Francis, I am not! Something has died in me for ever. That condition of living when one existed only for another is gone never to return.

That catastrophe was a dream. Hunt though they did high and low for old Stane, he was never seen again. Was he imagined by Georges and myself? I sometimes think so. But it is not that I cherish any illusion about Georges. He was neither strong nor faithful; I loved him as he was – not as a Perfect Being, whom, in fact, I should have detested. Forgive these sentiments. You are the only one with whom I ever share them.

Emma has now abandoned the Theatre or possibly it would be more truth to say that the Theatre has at length abandoned her. She is a strange Creature, quite devoted to me until some man crosses her path, when she is for a while like a schoolgirl. She has still her Charms and is less stout than formerly and as good a woman as ever was known.

Our apartment here is pleasant and looks out to a Square with Trees. There are sparrows, a man with a clarinet, a Poodle that walks every morning in the Square and an Artist up the stairs who quizzes me at every opportunity.

Write soon and tell me all about dear Uldale. Is the Museum still there at Keswick and have there been any Balls? Give Deborah my greetings and nod to every stream, hedgerow and little hill in the neighbourhood. Do the clouds still dance above Skiddaw? How I wish that I were there! – Your loving

JUDITH

Francis Herries, Esq, to Judith Paris

ULDALE, *14th of June, 1800*

DEAREST JUDITH – I was delighted indeed to have a letter from you, for it was several months since I had heard and I was beginning to feel some anxiety. When I saw you last year in London you had not been sufficiently with Mrs Dudeney to know how you would find her, and it is very gratifying indeed to discover that at least she is neither a bore nor a bully.

I cannot quite accommodate myself to the necessity of your earning a living in this manner, but quite honestly, dear Judith, I do not feel that it would be altogether wise for you to live with us while Deborah is here, nor would you yourself I think wish it.

Deborah is the best of women and the most kindly of sisters, but she must rule domestically any place where she is and will brook no rival. You also as you admit have a certain ruling capacity and when Greek meets Greek—!

Moreover, remembering Georges still as you do, work is I do not doubt the most helpful of Panaceas, and I know that you are of the greatest value to Mrs Dudeney and her family.

You do not say in your letter whether you have seen Brother Will. I hear that he is with every week a man of greater wealth and more important responsibility. I am told that they are to take a house in Mount Street (my information is from Bournemouth). I hear also that Christabel is no more in love with a grand life than she ever was, poor thing, and has in fact never recovered socially from the unhappy and now historic Ball.

Will will have no dealings with me and breathes fire and slaughter against his Bournemouth relations. Is this not foolish? But Will was always as filled with himself and his affairs as an egg with meat, and an insult to his wife is a snap of the finger in the face of the Almighty.

Nevertheless Will prospers and I do not. He is the other side of the Herries blanket from ourselves, dear Judith, and I think all the interest in our family's history must come from that, that men like Will are being for ever disgraced and made anxious by men like me. We break in upon their solid plans as a horse-thief breaks into their gold. So also on their side they break in upon our dreams. Where, I must ask myself, wandering among these fields and hills, do the two worlds join? Who may bring them together? Last week I rode up Borrowdale to Stonethwaite and wandered for an hour about the little overgrown court and garden of Herries where my grandfather and your father dug for so many years the hard and ungrateful soil. A shepherd, Wilson, now has it and lets it go as it will.

It was almost as though your father were at my elbow. I had forgot him but my father so frequently spoke of him that it is as though I had known him. I have only one memory of him, a tall gaunt black man with a scar on his face, riding up the white road to Uldale. I must confess to you that I was miserable enough that hour in that garden. All has gone wrong with me of late. Deborah's little sociabilities, the neighbours, their tea parties, cards and small festivities I can take no interest in. My writing such as it was has failed me; even my reading has little power over me. The country seems to me on the verge of ruin, the country people seething with discontent, the towns no better, a crazy King on the throne and a Prince – you do not need me to say anything there.

But you know what it is, dear Judith, that drives me. I am a man now of forty years and should be past such madness and should be master of such folly – but rather I am sunk in it deeper than before. Every breath I draw, waking or sleeping, seems to drag me to Bournemouth. They tell me that she is more beautiful than ever. She should be indeed now in the full flower of her loveliness. I hear also, and this has possibly given strength to my madness, that young Beaminster, the Duke of Wrexe's eldest son, is crazy for her. What a match for her that would be! But if anyone in our age is fitted to be a Duchess it is she! What a triumph for the Herries family if it should be so! I hear too that she is both proud and kind beyond ordinary measure – and truly in every grace and virtue she is over all others …

I will not burden you more with this. You ask whether Skiddaw stands where it did. Indeed it does. This is a perfect month for this country. There is a spot by Portinskill bordering the Keswick Lake where I love to be. The trees are now young flames and when the water is like glass they burn in their reflections. Then a breeze ruffles that glass and the fire is suddenly in the sky carried on the breast of a cloud. Were she with me here to see this beauty I know that I could win her to love me. I know it, Judith, I *know* it! But what is the value of such vain dreams? If you should hear anything of young Beaminster being at Bournemouth or of their meeting in Town, pray let me know – Your loving

FRANCIS

Miss Jennifer Cards to the Hon. Angela Painter

GROSSET PLACE, WILTSHIRE,
September 2nd, 1802

MY DARLING ANGELA – Forgive this odious hand for I cannot find my own pen and all the writing-tables here are filled with birds' nests and bones for the dogs. I speak with the utmost literalness for you cannot conceive the disorder in which Maria Rockage loves to confuse everything. But I have told you of this odd Place before and there is no need to make a repetition save that it is truth itself that there is a Basin on the floor of my bedroom at this instant to catch the drops from a crack in the ceiling, for it has rained for twenty-four hours without ceasing and every room in the Place runs with water. Not that we any of us are disturbed in the slightest degree. We are all True Britons in this respect and discomfort is part of our Birthright. There are but three of us here at the moment, Rockage, Maria and Phyllis, twenty last week and quite pretty in a milkmaid kind of style.

I fancy that she is the principal cause of my invitation here, for she had her Coming Out last Season and then must Go In again for they haven't a Penny amongst them and can make no sort of Show — while I, they suppose, have everyone in my Handkerchief from Mrs Fitzherbert downwards. They fancy too that I can give the Child some kind of a 'ton', but I am too amiable on the one side and too lazy on the other. And indeed she is not so bad in a simple kind of way.

But you know, dearest Angela, of what it is that I would write. Have you seen Beaminster since his return, have you spoken with him, if so did he mention me and what is his attitude now that he has seen China and all the Indies? Perhaps he has brought back with him a young Chinese Woman and I will not care if he has. But will I not? What is my mood? Upon my word it is hard to tell. How perverse is the world! Here am I, thirty-two years of age and still Single. And yet I have had every Element in my favour, have no aversion to Matrimony. At least I have told Beaminster a thousand times that I do not love him and would marry him only to be a Duchess. I like him at least sufficiently to be honest with him and as you know have refused him a hundred times. But now, time passes. It will not be long before I am a Withered Hag. What is Love, Angela? I swear I have never known it. My cousin, Francis Herries, swears that it is the Toothache of the Soul that no dentist can cure. I can only say then that my Teeth have no need of a Doctor. But why are the Virtues and Qualities of men so obstinately dissipated? There is Francis himself, the best and happiest of company, but having nothing better than a small Place in Cumberland where it rains inordinately. There is young Stephen Hailes whose every breath showers gold pieces but he is so gross in his feeding and thinks of nothing but Horses. There is Beaminster (and I would adore to be a Duchess), but he whines through his Nose like a Parson and cracks at the knees.

And many another all of whom you know, dearest Angela. I'm not boasting that I tell you this, but only that I may remind myself of my Vast Age and how my Opportunities are slipping over me.

There is talk still everywhere of the Peace and it is the fashion only to hasten to Paris. Rockage has heard that Charles Fox is on a visit to Bonaparte and that Mrs Fox is for the first time publicly acknowledged.

I shall be soon returning to Bournemouth for Wiltshire rusticity is softening my Wits. Moreover there is shortly coming here little Judith Paris whom you have seen I fancy in London. Maria has an odd Affection for her. She is a quaint thing whose

French husband was killed some years back in a brawl in the North, since when she must be a Governess or Companion as he left her without a Penny. She is, as you will remember, an Oddity, being but a few feet in height and with hair of coarse flaming red.

Maria vows that she is a Noble Creature. I am not myself prepossessed too strongly in her favour as she supports the Will Herries part of the Family in that ridiculous squabble of which I have often told you and over which we have so frequently laughed together. In any case I prefer my Nobility over two foot and a quarter!

Write soon, dearest Angela, and relieve the Anxiety of Your loving Friend,

JENNIFER

Francis Herries, Esq, to Judith Paris

ULDALE, CUMBERLAND,
14th of September, 1802

DEAREST JUDITH – I am following my letter of yesterday with this brief note that I may enclose this silver chain and cross. Last night rummaging in some old drawers, I came upon some effects of my father's, a packet or two of letters, a book or two, a riding whip, this Chain and a small silver Box. The Box was the one of which he had often told me, decorated with the Picture of girls dancing round a Maypole and gentlemen hunting. It was given him when a Child by a Pedlar. The Chain also he had spoken of, and it seems that your Mother's Mother bequeathed it to your Father for some Service he had one time done her.

The Chain then is by right your own and it pleases me greatly that I have discovered it, as also the silver Box by which I know my Father held considerable store.

I have no further news than that of yesterday – Your loving

FRANCIS

Judith Paris to Mrs Will Herries, of 48 Mount Street, London

GROSSET PLACE, WILTS,
December 3rd, 1802

MY DEAR CHRISTABEL – It was most kind of you to write to me. I was most grateful. I have been here now for two months and have as yet no regrets at having left Mrs Dudeney. Phyllis is a charming girl, modest and intelligent, with a sense of fun that enables her to see the Ludicrousness of much in her home and her Parents, and yet in no way impairs her Love for them.

They are indeed Lovable and yet most truly there is also something of the Ludicrous! Had you but now seen Carey peeping over the banisters, his nightcap nodding above his eye-brow, his nightshirt flapping at his bare ankles, shouting for Doggett, the man, because he heard that the sow had but just now littered! Indeed this is no place for early rising, for even now I was downstairs at ten o'clock to find such a confusion in the breakfast room, fender huddled two yards high, into the middle of the room, chairs, tables, shovel, poker, tongs anyhow, carpet thrown back, dust everywhere, dogs everywhere, bees-wax, rubber, brush, broom, mop, pail, and before a cheerless grate Maggie the girl on her knees. All the doors on this house have rusty refractory doorlocks of which the hasp invariably flies backward, all chimneys smoke, going to bed the candle at once goes out with a whiff and a stink in the passage and you break your shins at every step, all the corks break and drop in fragments *inside* the bottles, all keys are lost to all drawers, room after room (there are dozens of unused ones) is piled with broken bricks, scattered chisels and hammers, battered trunks mildewed with neglect. No proper alliance is formed with any butcher, carrier or baker, no salt-cellars have their spoons, no knife its proper fork, every snuffer to every candlestick tilts off and drops its contents on the carpet, every bell-rope breaks, or if it rings, brings the wrong servant, every scissor pinches without cutting . . . and so on, and so on! Dear Christabel, I could con-tinue this for an hour!

Into this chaos it is hoped that I shall bring some kind of order, and indeed I see a good ten years' work in front of me. But after all these are my own people and not strangers, and as I see Maria in an old silk Negligée padding around, her slippers flapping on the carpet, dogs sniffing at her heel, and that kindly amiable smile on her face, knowing that she loves me (as indeed I believe that she does), I must love her in return.

All this must seem terrible to you in your smart Mount Street Mansion, and you can understand what it must be to myself who have, as you know, a Passion for cleanliness, but I have no longer Energy to direct my own path and take what comes. Affection seems to me everything just at present.

Your beautiful Enemy, Miss Jennifer, was staying here in

the summer. They report her proud, matter-of-fact, worldly, not over intelligent but kindly and not conceited. They were rather relieved though, I fancy, at her departure. They say that she has any number of times refused Lord Beaminster and that now he, after a visit to the East, is paying attention to Lord Garrison's girl, but I do not know what truth there is in these rumours.

Has Will still the same implacability about Francis? The Monynghams have been here. I dislike the name and am glad that Carey's father after being Lord Monyngham became Viscount Rockage – a far handsomer title!

What of Pomfret in Kensington? I hear that he has been ill and that James, the monster, is biting his thumb till he can be Baronet. Like his grandfather Raiseley, whom Will's father always so thoroughly hated, I never cared for James.

Love to all in Mount Street and if Mrs Dudeney pay a call, as I fancy that she may, pray be kind to her for my sake – Your loving

JUDITH

Francis Herries, Esq, to Judith Paris
(Portion of letter only)

ULDALE, *Jan. 6th, 1805*

... You know what it was that I read in the *Gazette*. And so she has surrendered! Well, it will become her to be a Duchess although I hear that he is sadly spindle-shanked and a dull dog. I will think no more of her. I feel stronger now that the blow has at length fallen. I must build my life on a sounder bottom.

One agreeable thing has occurred. A Mr and Mrs Coleridge have for some time past lived at a Keswick house, Greta Hall, and now he is joined by another poet, Mr Robert Southey, whose sister-in-law he had married. I have met Mr Southey and find him a most agreeable person of immense learning, but no haughtiness of manner. Mr Coleridge is an extraordinary man who lives for the most part in other worlds than ours. He is often absent from Keswick and, so gossip says, is on no very easy terms with his wife, but the Southey family is excellent and very friendly towards myself. I am even stirred once more to attempt something with my pen. But more of this later ...

William Herries, Esq., of 48 Mount Street, to Judith Paris

48 MOUNT STREET, LONDON,
Feb. 20th, 1805

DEAR JUDITH – You must forgive the brevity of this letter. I am but now returned from the City where I was consulted in certain important matters having no indirect connexion with His Royal Highness's affairs. Your enquiry on Carey's behalf concerning his City Investments I will prosecute further and send you information when I have it.

The Budget of two days back causes some concern especially the extra 6*d* per bushel of salt which will I imagine greatly hamper the curing of bacon and ham, but on the whole things might I consider be worse.

Have you heard how Jennifer's engagement to Lord Beaminster prospers ? I can only say that I pity the foolish fellow from the bottom of my heart. He little knows the Tartar that he has taken to his bosom. After dancing round him for years she has condescended to be his future Duchess without I fancy intending him any return. He will discover his mistake in time. I must however admit that the Match is a fine one for our Family.

There is considerable anxiety in the City about the King's health. Stocks fluctuate accordingly. Christabel would I know send her love were she conscious that I was writing. She is lying in her room; she had a slight stomach affection today.

Pray give my regards to Maria and Carey. I am pleased to learn from Christabel that you find your stay with them agreeable. I must confess that I have little love for the Country save for our own Northern portion of it, which however for family reasons of which you are well aware I am little likely to see again.

With kindest regards, dear Judith, I remain – Yours most sincerely,

WILLIAM HERRIES

Judith Paris to Francis Herries, Esq

GROSSET PLACE, WILTS,
Feb. 25th, 1805

DEAREST FRANCIS – I hesitated whether to write after I had seen the news, but I feel that it would not be friendly on my

part did I not tell you of my sympathy. She has made her choice
and that she can prefer a marriage without love because of its
Social Splendour is only proof to me of her unfitness for any
marriage with a finer man.

Put her utterly out of your Heart, dear Francis. I do not doubt
but that you have done so. I pity her for her unwise decision,
for where there is no love there can be neither companionship
nor respect. So at least I feel. I wish that I were with you. I
myself have often a longing for the pressure of your hand. You
remember how as a Child I loved you and how I would watch at
the window for hours to see if you came. As it was then so is it
still, save that I am a woman now and have learnt something
of life and know what it is to be alone.

Do not fancy, however, that they are not all goodness to me
here, for indeed they are. I have brought some discipline
into affairs here, but the real trouble is lack of means. Poor Carey
has no mind for business and he cannot keep more than one
thing in his head at a time.

No sooner is he distressed by the loss of a silver spoon than
he is told that a dog has the Eczema, and some woman is up from
the village to beg something of him, or Squire Somebody or
Another has ridden over from Somewhere and must have a Bed.

The Guest Room is always in disorder, there are rats in the
wainscot and a window-pane is broken. Still time passes and I
am tranquil, refusing to lament over milk that is spilt or a fire
that has died. Only maybe the fire is not dead and burns the
more fiercely because no one perceives it . . .

We have had a Visitor this last week and a pleasant one,
Warren Forster of Alnwick. You recollect that he is the Grandson of Mrs Dorothy Forster who used to visit at Keswick. He is a
man of some thirty-five years and has been visited by incessant
misfortunes. When a child he was kicked by one of his father's
horses and has been slightly lame ever after.

He has also, I fear, some affection of the Heart. In addition
to these things his wife to whom, as I understand, he had been
some four years married, last year abandoned him and ran away
to America with a theatrical gentleman and has never since been
heard of.

In spite of these visitations he is a man of great Character and
much tenderness of Heart, never complaining and always
cheerful. Maria dotes upon him and I must confess that I myself
have a warm Friendliness towards him. I can see you smile at
this point, and prophesy me a second husband, but that will

never be – Georges remains with me as though he were yet living. I must go now as I hear Carey calling me – Your loving

JUDITH

Francis Herries, Esq, to Judith Paris

ULDALE, *November 9th, 1805*

DEAREST JUDITH – By now you must be aware that Jennifer has broken her engagement. Scarcely had the glorious news of Trafalgar reached us and we were in the midst of waving flags and hanging lanterns, when I received a letter written by herself informing me that she had broken off all relations with Lord Beaminster. She begged me to come to Bournemouth and you will not be surprised to learn that I am catching tonight's coach at Kendal.

I will write from there – Yours in haste,

FRANCIS

Judith Paris to Mrs Emma Furze

GROSSET PLACE, WILTS,
Dec. 8th, 1805

MY DEAREST DEAREST EMMA – Late though it is and mean and drunken my candle, I am scribbling a hurried word to you to tell you what I have only myself this evening learnt – that my dear Francis was married to his Jennifer secretly in London three days ago. I have only had the barest word from Francis acquainting me with the fact and that they have already set off for Cumberland. As I sit in this large bare room with the wind howling down the chimney and the mice scratching in the wainscot, it is hard not to be melancholy. How, how can this end? Only badly, I fear. She has but accepted him on the rebound from her trouble with Beaminster. She does not love him and even though she did, could never endure the remoteness of our Cumberland country. I can see that they will move to London and poor Uldale fall into the tea-party chatter of Deborah's domination. And yet I have heard that Jennifer does not love London either and that that is one of the first causes of her quarrel with Beaminster. You know, dearest

Emma, that yourself and Francis are now the two human beings whom I love the most deeply and for Francis this affection has existed from my earliest childhood. He has been always a little remote from life and interested in notions more than persons – always, that is, until this passion seized him. He is one of the noblest of men, but reserved in the expression of his feeling. She must be proud and selfish, accustomed to adoration and her own way. What *can* come of this but disaster? I have heard, too, that she is lazy and idle and will sit for hours admiring herself in the glass but this, I confess, comes from Will Herries who detests her.

Where are you now – at Colchester or Nottingham? Is Mr Edwardes the Knight at Arms that you fancied and is the care of his two little girls as entertaining as you had anticipated? There are times when I am tempted once again towards London and Mrs Dudeney. She would welcome me with open arms back again any while.

Only my affections hold me here, for try as I may I cannot bring any order into the Place. This Country is at its worst in the Winter, all muck and mist, so unlike my own beloved Cumberland, where the Winter is the best, for the hedges sparkle with frost, the hills are powdered with snow and the air smells like wine.

Here, at Grosset, the Country is low and miry and one must walk in high, hard-bottomed fields not to be knee-deep at every step – one is like a frog kicking and sprawling through a welter of water.

My candle is at its last drunken nod and I must go to bed – Your most loving

JUDITH

Mrs Cards of Macklin House, Bournemouth, to her daughter, Mrs Francis Herries, of Uldale, Cumberland

(*Portion of a letter*)

MACKLIN HOUSE, BOURNEMOUTH,
June 8th, 1807

MY DEAR JENNIFER – Your father has requested me to say that we are both anxious at not having had news from you for so long a period. You must really, my dear daughter, try to oblige your loving father and mother more frequently in this respect. It is not kind to continue any sort of grudge against your father because he did not in the first place approve of your marriage. A year and a half have passed since that event and he has become as you know reconciled to it. He wishes only for your happiness and welfare and you know well that there is no human being on the face of the globe for whom he cares as he does for you. You know that it is our wish that you should lie-in in Bournemouth and I have written to Francis asking him his own feelings in this matter.

I have not much News for you. The talk is only of the Princess, whose behaviour since the return of her Champion, Mr Perceval, into power, has been, they say, outrageous. At a Ball at Mr Hope's she was truly a sight if eye-witnesses are to be trusted. Her figure is now as round as a drum and she paints monstrously. Her conversation is so wild that she seems often like a mad woman and she is not ashamed to be seen anywhere with her boy 'Billy Austin'. The Prince has broken entirely with the old Whigs and his hatred of Grenville and Grey is fanatical. Sheridan rules him in everything and in your father's opinion is nothing but mischievous.

The London dresses are now so tight that it is almost impossible to walk in them. In my old-fashioned eyes the *robes en Calecon* are quite shameless, all the outline of the figure being clearly seen beneath them. Very often there is nothing but a thin petticoat beneath and that is sometimes omitted. The skirt is now in two pieces, a third piece sewn in diagonally as a lateral gusset . . .

Francis Herries, Esq, to Judith Paris

ULDALE, *Dec. 7th, 1807*

MY DEAREST JUDITH – I wish you to be the first to know that last evening at seven-thirty of the clock Jennifer was delivered of a fine boy. They are both doing well and my happiness is beyond measure. I am convinced that now with a child in the house all will go well.

I will write later at greater length – Your loving,

FRANCIS, Father of John Herries

Judith Paris to Francis Herries, Esq

GROSSET PLACE,
March 29th, 1808

DEAREST FRANCIS – This is the first sign of Spring this year and so I write to ask you whether you are yet living or have changed into a Leprechaun or one of the Borrowdale Cuckoos ? What I would give to see Keswick Lake or Newlands Valley or the Moor above Uldale on such a day as this – for at home the skies are ever changing and streams are running and the bracken is popping while here even on this Spring day all is Languid and barely stirs.

But do you know, Sir, that of late you have very gravely neglected your Half-Aunt or whatever is my true Relationship to you ? It is now some six weeks since I had any word from you and I am feeling very gravely neglected. Two Nights back I had a Dream about you and I awoke distressed, thinking that you had called to me and I could not go to you. Do pray write and tell me how you are and how Jennifer is and little John. I am uneasy in my mind.

At this especial Moment it is necessary that I should write to calm my Feelings, for this morning has witnessed one of my most celebrated Tempers. I fear I give vent to them more frequently than of old, whereas it should be the other way. This morning I stamped and shouted like a Fishwife. I think I had some reason though, and you shall judge. It was over young Carey, who is at home just now and doing no good here. He should have gone for the Navy, as was originally intended, instead of this foolish notion that he should superintend his Father's estate. For that he has no more gift than his poor Father has, nor has he his Father's sweetness of nature. He is a thick heavy Oaf as I had the pleasure this morning of telling him, for I had but just, urged by the sweetness of the Spring sunshine, directed the clumsy Maggie to the proper cleaning of the Drawing and Breakfast Room when in Carey must come, knee-deep in mud, cracking a whip and followed by four huge dogs so that he breaks a China Ornament kissing Maggie (not knowing that I was present) and sets the dogs after the cat, crying 'Halloo! Halloo!' and riding the Chairs with all his lanes and bogs clinging to them.

I treated him to a pretty Scene and then, when he laughed, boxed his Ears. Although he is twice my height that flummoxed him and while he stared I told him all I thought of him, that he was a selfish good-for-nothing nincompoop living on his Father's Bounty and doing nothing but chase Foxes and set the Dogs on the Cats. And I fear, although I did not tell him so, that he does worse than this with the Girls in the Village and thinks it all Fine Sport.

Well, in upon this comes Maria, who thinks him the Paragon of all Wonders. He went off in a Sulk calling me a fine collection of names, and Maria was altogether at a loss for she loves me and thinks I can do no wrong. But I am sometimes deeply weary of this life here, dear Francis. There is something in me that aches for Cumberland, even though there are scenes there that I could never have the Courage to revisit. This is not my place nor are these in truth my people. But where is my place and where are my people? Like my father before me I have no Home and yet I am truly a domestic creature and could not live except for the affections of those of whom I am fond.

Warren Forster has been here visiting again and we are become the greatest of friends. I think his lonely situation touches me – not that we are melancholy together but rather laugh for most of the time.

Pray write to me soon and tell me how little John fares. In your last letter you mentioned that he was suffering with a Colic.

Francis Herries, Esq, to Judith Paris

ULDALE, *June 10th, 1808*

DEAREST JUDITH – I have not written frequently of late because I have not been in the merriest of spirits – nothing specific but only a Malaise that is, it seems, difficult for me to shake myself free of. But now I have two Items of News that I must give you. One is that Jennifer will be lying-in again this November. We hope that this time it may be a girl. She is well and seems to have no fears of the event. I am afraid that she sometimes finds me a Dull Dog.

My second Item is that Sister Deborah is engaged – to a Squire Withering of Summerhays by Carlisle. As Deborah is now forty-six years you can fancy that this event was most unexpected but Withering is of her own age and has already been twice married. He is a jolly red-faced Ox, whose interests are entirely bucolic, but he will I think suit Deborah well, for her desires are as you know of an exceeding Sociability, and now she may entertain the Neighbourhood to her heart's desire.

Her relations with Jennifer have been, as I have hinted to you before, of an armed friendliness and I doubt whether there will be many tears shed on either side at parting.

The Cotton Riots at Manchester have been I understand of a serious nature, houses have been broken into, managers burnt in effigy and many rioters lodged in jail. The People are making themselves more and more felt and I must admit that they and their Cause have increasingly my Sympathy. Jennifer is an Aristocrat of the Old School and would have every Rioter burnt at a public Stake – Your loving

FRANCIS

I am becoming good Friends with Mr and Mrs Southey and frequently visit them.

Mrs Francis Herries of Uldale, Cumberland, to
Mrs Judith Paris, at Grosset Place, Wilts

ULDALE, Nov. 10th, 1809

DEAR JUDITH – You will I fancy feel some surprise at receiving a letter from me, but indeed I would have written sooner had we not all been so occupied with the Jubilee which for my part I am most thankful that it is safely over. You would not, however, have recognized your little Keswick. We had grand Fireworks above the Lake, an ox roasted whole in the Market Place and many other Diversions.

It is not however of the Jubilee that I wish to write to you. I am Laziness personified and to write a Letter is always an agony to me so I will come sharp to the point.

It is this – that both Francis and myself wish that you should come and live with us. It is plain enough that Francis should wish it – he has always wished it – and therefore I write myself that you may believe in my own independent desire for it. In honesty I discover that, since the departure of Deborah, the two children and the management of the House are more than I can properly sustain. But beyond this I will admit that I consider that it will be of advantage both to Francis and myself that you should be with us. I have grown unaccountably sluggish of late and so I fancy has he. In addition to these things I have a real wish that you should love me – something that may at this

present seem to you quite impossible, but juxtaposition and a
Good Will may work wonders. – I am, Your sincere friend,

JENNIFER HERRIES

Judith Paris to Francis Herries, Esq

GROSSET PLACE,
Nov. 15th, 1809

DEAREST FRANCIS – I have but now received a Truly Extraordinary Letter from Jennifer which I have answered as honestly
as I may. You doubtless know of it. But what am I to say?

Of course I wish to come to you and Uldale. I have wished
it all these years when I have been in sober truth a real Exile
from my own country. I have developed a fondness for Carey
and Maria and Phyllis. I would leave them perhaps for no one
else in the world, but you have always been – save for Georges –
first in the world to me and I would go anywhere to serve you.
Also it is a Happiness to think that I must have the Care in
some part of your Children.

But does Jennifer truly wish me to come? Have you not
pushed her into that Letter? I must know this before I give any
Answer. I had fancied that she had in her Heart no affection
for me. I am myself not easy, love to dominate where I am, am
often in terrible Rages and am haunted by the past. But you
know this, dear Francis, and you know your wife. It seems to me
that if I come and things go ill I may imperil all our Happiness.
Yet the House at Uldale calls me like a living person. I cannot
refuse if you assure me that it is Jennifer's wish as well as your
own. – Your loving

JUDITH

Francis Herries, Esq, to Judith Paris

ULDALE, *Nov. 19th, 1809*

DEAREST JUDITH – Come. It is Jennifer's wish most certainly.
Things are not too Happy here. You can help us to understand
one another. Come – Your loving

FRANCIS

Judith Paris to Mrs Emma Furze

(Portion of a letter)

GROSSET PLACE, WILTS
Nov. 29th, 1809

... If you can meet the Coach I shall be most happy. Farewells here are of a quite Tragic Description. Even young Carey weeps down the Barrel of his gun.

Oh Emma to what Adventure am I going? My Life is built on that piece of ground. I have tried to shake myself free of it, but how fruitless was that effort I now know as I feel the excited beatings of my Heart. It may be that I am committing the supreme Folly of my Life ...

ULDALE AGAIN

'LET US WALK up the hill,' Judith said to Francis.

They got down from the chaise and allowed it to draw slowly ahead of them. She put her arm through Francis'.

She was not going to tell him how frightened she was. This scene so amazingly familiar to her, the trees bright and bare so that the winter sun seemed to be shining in the heart of their branches, the thick soft carpet of leaves, the fresh sharp air with a breath of approaching snow in its stillness, all these were the friendly accompaniments of countless old winters. Soon, at the turn, the first houses of the village would appear, the blacksmith's, the little house with the round bottle-green windows, and beyond them the first comfortable shoulder of the moor. All so familiar that they were part of her own blood, and yet her heart was beating with an almost agonizing apprehension.

She wished now that she had not come. Oh! how she wished it! She had been safe there in Wiltshire, safe even though she had not been alive. Now the pain was sharp as when the blood returns to a limb that has been numb.

At once, on her first sight of Francis in Keswick, she had been sure that he was not the same. She had seen him before he had seen her; he had stood in front of the inn, slim and dark, slapping his thigh with his whip, looking sternly out into a forbidding world.

She had instinctively drawn her shawl more closely about her and shrunk back as though she would prevent him from seeing her. He had kissed her, put his arm about her, given her a hot drink, seen to her baggage and, through the drive out of Keswick along the familiar Carlisle Road, had been infinitely kind. It had been her own fault that she had been so helplessly constrained. He did not know that with every step Georges was approaching more closely to her. Georges, Georges . . .

But that cowardice she had foreseen, and with every strength in her character she had beaten it back. Then, in place of it, as they turned away from the Lake into the heart of the woods, the thought of Jennifer increasingly possessed her. Why had she come? Jennifer did not want her. She *could* not want her. She had yielded to Francis' entreaties, and now she thought that Francis did not want her either. It was true, in fact, that for Francis, too, there had been a little shock. When he had last seen Judith she had been a girl; now she was a woman, and, with that exceptional sensitiveness that was his curse as well as his blessing, he felt, at first sight of her, that she had become a woman whom he did not know.

This resolute, solid little person almost hidden under her shawl and pelisse, her small white face looking out at him from her rose-coloured bonnet with such seriousness, was very different from the fire and impetuosity of his own familiar Judith. He had good reasons – there had from the first been many – for doubting the wisdom of this experiment and now he suffered a sudden panic, foreseeing every kind of trouble and even disaster. He had, Heaven knew, enough already!

So, while they rode, a silence fell between them. Then, as they started on foot up the hill, she stopped, laid her hand on his arm, looked up into his face.

'I am frightened, Francis,' she said. 'I feel as though I cannot go on.'

'I am frightened also,' he confessed.

They looked at one another. Then she laughed, and it was as though a screen were rolled away, the old Judith of all his life was back again.

'Do you remember once when your father beat me and I climbed out of the window?'

He nodded, smiling.

'I thought then that I could never be frightened at anything. I am wiser now . . . I am frightened of Jennifer.'

It was he now who put his arm through hers, drawing her close to him. They marched now steadily up the hill.

'There's no need to be,' he said. 'You can do so much for Jennifer, Judith. And for myself as well. We are in a tangle. You must clear it.'

'Do you think she will like me? Because if she does not – I can do nothing with anyone who dislikes me.'

'You must make her like you,' he answered. 'Everything hangs on that. She is proud, she has been spoilt by much admiration, for which she does not really care. She *could* be happy here. You can make her so.'

'Are you yourself happy?' She stopped again, looking up into his face.

'I, my dear?' He shrugged his shoulders. 'Have I ever been happy save for a moment or two? But I love her very dearly. I am not a wise man,' he added, lowering his voice as though he were speaking to himself. 'I have never been wise all my life. I killed my father. My mother hated me. It is not natural that I should be more fortunate with my wife.'

'I have come into a pretty business,' she thought. 'This will not be easy.'

But they had found one another again. Her resolution, obstinacy and common sense were all active now that she realized that there was something to be done. The dusk had fallen when they reached the house. She could see it only as a white ghost. The lights in the hall confused her, and it was a moment before she could realize that Jennifer was greeting her. Then she was almost shocked by Jennifer's beauty. It was a woman of forty who confronted her, but age here had nothing to say. Jennifer's loveliness came from her superb richness of colour and form. Her hair was dark with the darkness of clouded fire, when the flame is imprisoned by black shadow. Her skin had warmth in its ivory softness. She was very tall, a height that was emphasized by her high close dress with its waist just below the breasts, but her body was moulded by her maturity to a perfect fitness. She stood, her head up, her lovely neck and arms bare, save for a thin Cashmere purple shawl, as though she were receiving a deputation of loyal subjects. Only her eyes were a little sleepy, heavily lidded.

Judith had never in her life before felt so small, so insignificant. It was as though she were a servant coming for a place. She was weary, too, crowded about with old memories, homesick for she knew not what. But it was not her way to be beaten.

Only, as on so many other occasions, she wished passionately that she were taller.

The thought in Jennifer's mind as she bent down to kiss her was: 'Well, I need not be afraid of this little thing.'

Jennifer moved into the little parlour that was thick, for Judith, with pressing memories. She recognized at once grate-fully that it was not changed. That was Francis' doing. But also, with a flash of intuition, she realized that Jennifer must be lazy. She would have altered things if she had had a mind for that. Here was the old spinet with the roses on its lid, the music-box with the King in his amber coat and the Queen in her green dress; there was the carpet with the pictures of the Battle, the leaping horses and the cannon firing. For how many years had it been there – and yet it looked even fresher than in earlier days. Best of all, here was the China wallpaper with the blue and white pagodas, the bridges, flowers and temples.

Jennifer helped her to take off her jacket and bonnet.

'You must be weary.'

'Oh no, thank you'; but she was. She sat down on the old brown sofa that was covered with a pattern of red leaves and little rosy apples. Francis had gone to see about the horses. She and Jennifer were alone.

'Did you have an agreeable journey?'

'Yes. The weather was fine. We had only one storm before Kendal.'

'You must rest now and take your ease. Life is very quiet here.'

Judith thought: 'She talks as though I had never been here before. I knew it before she did.' She was in that nervous state of weariness and loneliness that can rouse, very quickly, the Devil, but she had already faced the Devil so often in her life that it was easy to say to him now, as she did, 'Lie down!'

She smiled. She could not help it. Jennifer was so very beautiful.

'What lovely hair you have,' Jennifer said.

'It is sadly tumbled.'

'No, but you will want to go to your room. I will show you.'

They went up the staircase down whose banisters Judith had many times slid. That was something at least that Jennifer had never done. Jennifer moved upwards like a queen.

'I hope you will like this room,' she said, throwing open the door.

Oh heaven! it was Mrs Monnasett's room, the room where

once she had crept up to the bed and touched the cold body, searching for the little box . . .

'I trust that you will be comfortable here,' Jennifer said, staring with her sleepy eyes about her. 'If you need anything pray tell me.'

'I have known this room,' Judith said, also looking about her, 'all my life.'

The two women looked at one another – one swift appraising glance – and at once Judith knew it was going to be a battle.

'She is going to let me be happy here,' she thought, 'if I do what she tells me.' Then there was the further thought: 'You've never done what anyone told you – except Georges.'

But she was so weary that she could have cried if she had been a woman accustomed to crying. She was not.

'Thank you, dear Jennifer,' she said. 'You are very amiable.' She knew that Jennifer was thinking: 'I can manage *this* little thing.'

For several years after Georges' death the terrible time had been the night. If she slept, one horrible dream after another swept over her; if she were awake, loneliness and remorse weighed down her heart. Loneliness because Georges was not there, remorse because again and again she asked herself whether she might not have done something to prevent the calamity. Why had she not driven the old man from the house, driven him, with whips and scorpions? How was it that she had submitted to his presence so passively? It was as though he had cast a spell.

What could she have done? What? What? She tormented herself day after day, night after night. Then, as the years had passed, quiet sleep had come back to her. She was not one to bewail the past. She had her new life to make. But during the years in London and Wiltshire there had been no life. It had been as though she had walked in her sleep. Now with one step into the lighted hall tonight, life had swept back to her. Contact was made again.

She woke in old Mrs Monnasett's four-poster and looked about her trying to penetrate the darkness. It seemed that she could. Georges was alive again and at her side, and said with his old reckless impudence: 'Soon we'll have this house in our hand.'

So, leaning her head on his breast, she went happily to sleep. In the morning she met the two children, John aged two, Dorothy aged one, in the charge of a fat beetle-browed woman, Mrs Ponder. Judith knew at once that this was a bad, ill-disposed servant who was resolved to defy her. John was a square-made, sturdy child with the high Herries horse-bones and light blue eyes that reminded her of David. There seemed to be no nonsense about him at all. Dorothy was small and dark and nervous. She hid herself in Mrs Ponder's dress.

Judith loved children and had a swift power over them, perhaps because she was herself little and was amused by small things that seemed, however, to her important.

For John the only thing that mattered on that day when Judith first saw him was that Matt the stableman had made a ship for him and would take him later to the Tarn to sail it. As soon as he discovered that Judith also wished to see the sailing of the ship, she became part of his world and was never again outside it. He did not as yet talk a great deal, but expressed his emotions with wriggles of the body and small stern frowns.

'Pray, ma'am,' said Mrs Ponder, 'do not permit the child to be a worrit.'

'I care for children extremely,' answered Judith quickly, looking straight at Mrs Ponder's black eyebrows. 'To be quite honest, I do not think I can live without them.'

'That is very well, ma'am,' said Mrs Ponder, who was a woman of one idea at a time. 'But he must not be a worrit.'

Dorothy was another matter. Baby though she was, she was already nervous, suspicious and reserved. Mrs Ponder was her only haven. When Judith came near to her she screamed, which pleased Mrs Ponder very much indeed.

Indeed everything that occurred on this first day after Judith's arrival contained the signs and portents of the struggle – a struggle that involved the fates of all of them, and of many more besides them – that was to come. The prophecy of the walk up the hill had been a correct one.

Snow fell all day, snow most unusual for that time of the year, soft, feathery, gentle, at first not lying, then, as the day sharpened, lying with a silver radiance over all the world.

It always seemed to Judith afterwards that she gathered in her complete and final knowledge of Jennifer in that first winter afternoon. They sat after dinner in the parlour, drinking their tea, the two of them one on either side of the fire, where the logs crackled and hissed, the only sound save the gently whispering clock.

Jennifer sat very straight, working at a piece of silver embroidery. Erect, her splendid body, with its soft rounded arms, its swelling breasts, its crown of dark, slumbering hair, gave an

odd impression of being on guard. Often Judith was in the future
to notice that Jennifer's body seemed to have a life apart from
the brain that directed it. Jennifer's brain, she was to discover,
was not active. It moved very slowly from point to point and
there stayed obstinately without stirring. It was not an animal
brain at all – something quite other – but her body was entirely
animal, wanted only to be cared for. That was why, perhaps,
Jennifer was not conceited and minded nothing at all when her
body was admired; why, too, men had deserted her at the
moment of crisis.

But if she was not conceited she was intensely proud. She
had all the pride of a woman who has no imagination, the most
fundamental pride of all because the owner of it cannot look
outside and make comparisons. Her pride had its origin in the
fact that she was a Herries (though but a portion of one), and
in fact that she had a father and mother who thought her perfect.

She did not admire herself because they thought her perfect,
but admired *them* for that reason, and her pride was all the
greater.

There were things that Judith, as she sat by the fire on that
first day, wanted to know. First, how so gloriously beautiful a
creature, who might (so Judith, rather simply and very modestly,
thought) have had all London on its knees, could stay year after
year in this little distant country place; secondly, whether or no
Jennifer loved Francis; thirdly, why Jennifer had asked her,
Judith, to come.

Before the hour by the fire was over, Judith had discovered
the answer to the three questions. First – Jennifer liked the
country better than the town because Herries were of more
social value in the country, because she had always lived out
of London and was a woman of habit, but in chief because
she was lazy. The country demanded less energy than the
town.

Second – she did not love Francis in any sense that Judith
understood the word. But – she was lazy. That might explain it.

Third – she had asked Judith because, after Deborah was
gone, there was too much to do. A housekeeper was impertinent.
Judith, to whom, in Jennifer's judgement (she repeated this
several times), Francis was quite devoted, would please Francis
and keep him quiet. In short she had invited Judith because – she
was lazy.

'Pray come nearer to the fire. It is monstrously cold.'

'Thank you. And is Deborah comfortable with her Squire ?'

'I believe so indeed, as much as one may be comfortable in this world.'

She raised her slumbering eyes, lifted her white hand on which a great ring with a deep crimson stone glittered, to shield her face from the fire, and said: 'Are we to be friends, Judith?'

Judith bent forward, giving her glance for glance.

'I trust so. It is my own most earnest wish.'

'You will be on my side sometimes?'

'Your side?'

'Yes. You were not on my side in that most unseemly quarrel in London many years ago.'

'I was then quite unformed . . . And Christabel was then my friend. You were not.'

'Yes, we were young then. I wonder. Is it wise – do you think – that we have met again?'

Judith answered gravely. 'It is for yourself to decide.'

Jennifer's body became more active. You could see the life stirring through it, as still water is suddenly moved by a breeze.

'Are you passionate?'

'I beg your pardon?'

'Are you passionate? With that hair you should be. I hear that you have a temper that can be monstrously roused. I should like to see it.'

Judith laughed.

'There is time enough,' she said. Moved by a quick impulse and because she wished always to be friends if it were possible (she could be an enemy very easily if that was wanted), she went over to Jennifer, bent across her chair and kissed her. To her own surprise Jennifer put up her arm and with her soft warm hand drew Judith closer, kissing her again.

'It is by far more comfortable to be friends,' she said.

But was it Jennifer's body that had kissed her – or Jennifer?

That evening Jennifer, Judith and Francis sat in the parlour. The little clock with the china dairymaid struck. Jennifer rose stretched her arms, threw up her lovely head. Her eyes were almost closed. She seemed to be tasting some delicious food or smelling a marvellous scent.

'I am sleepy. I shall go to bed.' She moved, slowly, majestically to the door. She turned towards them, showing a sleepy smile. She yawned.

'Goodnight,' she said.

After a little silence Francis said: 'I am so happy that you are here, dear Judith. Jennifer likes you already.'

'Do you think so ? I am afraid that at first I shall be needlessly troublesome. In time things will settle themselves.'

'Is it strange to you to come back here ?' He looked at her with eyes of deep affection. Now he had regained his old Judith. It was true that on the outside this was almost a middle-aged woman who sat near to him, a woman, too, who had known the most bitter unhappiness, who had suffered years of the harshest loneliness, but there was there also the child with the light of humour in her eyes, with her pugnacity, eagerness and acceptance of adventure.

'Strange ?' She looked into the fire. 'No. But, Francis, with what passion I love this house. I had not forgotten it – no, not a table nor a chair, not a print nor a carpet, and the garden, the high wall, every branch of every tree. But I had not known that I would be so touched by it, nor that it would lead me on into the country beyond it. *My* country . . .' She laughed. 'Perhaps it will be wisest in me to check my feelings while I can; I am determined against too much enthusiasm. In an old woman it is an absurdity.'

'An old woman!' he said fondly. 'Why, Judith, you are not changed.'

'No,' said Judith. 'When I was in my room this evening after dinner and pressed my nose against the pane, standing a little on my toes, just as I did when I was a child, I could see nothing but the snow falling through the darkness. Nevertheless, the country crowded about me – Scarness, Bowscale, Calva, Blackhazel, Mungrisdale.' She said the names like a spell. 'And so leading to Watendlath, which I must face if I am ever to have any peace here. On the first fair day I shall ride over to Watendlath.'

'Why, Judith,' he said, 'you are a poet.'

'Part of me is a poet, and the other part, I fear, most unpoetical.'

He sighed and stretched his long, thin legs to the fire, rubbing his hands in his hair. 'I also. Part poet, and the useless part, the only part for which I have any care. We are a strange family. It seems that the Dreamer must always destroy the Man of Deeds, and so either way you fail. Your father let the practical go and was called a madman. My own father was ultimately all practical and faded spiritually away. Will had always been for the practical – he has never known a conflict and is become a money-bag. There is Reuben who has rejected the practical and is saved, maybe, by his Maker. And you and I, Judith – our fates are yet undecided. But it would be a subject for an Epic, this

Herries struggle, with a changing England behind it. Which
is real ? Is there a soul ? Are we for ever to be exiles from our true
country ? All my life I have been like a man wandering down a
road that leads nowhere.'

'You should ask Mr Southey these things. He is a poet.'

'I have asked him. He is sure of his destiny. His answer is
in his books and his family. I never knew a man more confident.
But his brother-in-law, Mr Coleridge, has more genius, and so is
more lost . . .' He drove his fist on to his knee. 'Judith, I must
lose myself in something greater than myself. That is the only
answer.'

'And your marriage ?' She asked at length the question that
had been hovering between them all day.

'My marriage is a failure, a damnable pernicious failure. How
could it have been otherwise ? Jennifer never loved me. She has
never loved anyone. When she dismissed Beaminster she was
frightened of her old age and she liked me better than the others.
So she took me. And she has done her best with me. But there
is a devil of selfishness in her. In a country life some sort of
selfishness is, I conceive, a necessity. I also am selfish. But our
selfishnesses – hers and mine – do not coincide.'

He stopped. Then went on eagerly, 'Judith, I say these things
because all our lives we have been frank with one another, but
also since you must live here you must understand what the
situation is.'

'Yes,' she said. 'What is the situation ?'

'I am as crazy for Jennifer as ever I was. She has a terrible
physical spell over me. In a while you will feel it right through
the house – the spell of her body. I care for her, too, in other
ways; I have a great tenderness, sometimes an almost unspeak-
able longing to make her happy. And so long as she is comfortable she is happy, but let her comfort once be disturbed and the
whole house is wretched.

'She is pure Herries, the unimaginative practical sort. Had
she energy she would be the feminine Will of the family, turning
everything to practical profit, but she has none and she wants
none. She does not love me but she loves no one, not her parents
nor her children. But she is proud of everything that is hers,
myself as well. She will quickly be proud of you if you serve her.
If you do not—'

'Yes – if I do not ?'

'She will fight you until you do. And she has many strange
weapons . . .' He went on after a pause. 'I had thought when I

asked her to marry me that what she would not be able to endure
would be the quiet and silence here. That she would be restless
here, want people that would entertain her, admire her. But that
has been the slightest of the trouble. She has settled here like a
cat by the fire so long as she is comfortable.'

'Then why,' asked Judith slowly, 'did you ask me here? If
she is comfortable . . .'

'I had to have you, Judith. I had to. It is turning me mad, this
life here. It is not that I have not much to do. I have learnt much
of the estate. I have grown a wise countryman. Things are
prosperous here. I buy land, sell cattle. So far I have conquered
my dreams. But I love her and despise her. I love her and despise
myself. I know that she does not care for me, that my children
do not care for me. I am in touch with no one here. And therefore I had to send for you. For the last three years I have had
this longing, but beat it down. Now it has been too strong for me.'

Judith felt her heart leap. She had loved Francis all her life
and at last her reward had come. He needed her and had told
her so. This was perhaps the first moment of true happiness that
she had had since Georges' death.

But she showed no emotion.

'Yes, but if we care for one another – brother and sister as
we are, although, Francis, I am in reality your aunt, you know –
what will Jennifer say?'

'There we must be on our guard. I do not know how it will
affect Jennifer. If she is against it she will use every weapon
to be rid of you.'

'She thinks,' said Judith, 'that I am a meek little thing. I
saw it in her eyes tonight. But I am not. Francis, now that I have
come, I cannot go again. Nothing can turn me out. I am resolved. This is my country, my home . . . even if Jennifer hates
me.'

'You have no true realization,' he said slowly, 'of Jennifer's
obstinacy.'

But she was astonished at herself. She felt rising in her breast
a resolved determination on power. That other self – not the self
that at her window behind the falling snow had in the gloaming
traced every rise and fall of the fell, the peaked line of Skiddaw,
the thin haze of the Scottish hills; but the self that had conquered
Georges and these last terrible thirteen years, this obstinate self –
was moving her forward to this new conquest.

She would make them all love her, Jennifer, children, servants,
even the dogs. But – if they would not love her – then they should

obey her. But for Francis she felt an infinite tenderness. She
got up and knelt in front of the fire by his chair. She did not
touch him. She would never again kneel by a man to embrace
him. That had been for Georges alone. But she turned to him,
looking at him with so much sweetness that his heart was comforted as it had never been since the day of his marriage.

'Francis,' she said, 'in the way of love I shall never care for
any man again, but in the way of ourselves, of all our lives, I
love you most dearly. And I will win a victory here.'

He was about to put a hand to her. He stopped and listened.

'Hush,' he said. 'I thought I heard a door opening.'

But there was no sound. The door was fast closed.

PAYING A CALL ON MRS SOUTHEY

OPENING THE DOOR of her bedroom on a fine July afternoon,
intending to prepare for her visit to Mrs Southey, Judith stood
frozen to the wall.

In the far corner of the room could be seen the broad, ill-
shapen back of Mrs Ponder, its calico covering spread to its
utmost as she bent over the drawer of the little spindle-legged
escritoire near the window. In these drawers were Judith's
papers and personal odds and ends – old letters, legal documents,
programmes of dances and concerts, ribbons and faded flowers.

Most of these were now scattered about the floor while Mrs
Ponder, in furious haste and grunting like a pig, burrowed even
deeper.

'Yes,' said Judith. 'Good afternoon.' She had always hated
the woman; from the very first she had detested her, and now
there was such a rage beating in her throat that she had a most
childish impulse to rush across the room and seize the woman by
the neck and shake her head off.

Mrs Ponder's back jumped, then straightened itself; then
Mrs Ponder's pasty-faced, beetle-browed countenance turned
round, terror braced by defiance appeared in it.

'Yes, Mrs Ponder?' Judith said again, her voice small and
quivering in her anger.

'I was straightening things, ma'am,' the woman answered in
her sulky, deep-toned voice, 'helping to keep your drawers tidy.'

'You are not paid, I think, to keep my drawers tidy.'

Mrs Ponder was recovering her self-command. She had thought that she was safe enough, had just time enough. What ill luck that the little soft-footed, prying thing should come creeping up five minutes too soon! Oh well! she wasn't going to be put down by this red-haired leftover of a thief and a vagabond. She knew what she knew.

She put one hand on her hip.

'Excuse me, ma'am. I cannot say I am sure what I am paid for and what I am not paid for, only to do my duty, I should suppose.'

'And is it your duty to decipher my personal letters?'

'I do not know what you mean, ma'am, by deciphering. I was intending for the best.'

'You are very obliging, but it is a dangerous precedent, Mrs Ponder, as I think you will find. Leave this room! It will not, I trust, be long before you leave this house.'

The woman came forward. She was half of a mind to have her say. It was a year and a bit since this French Madame (for Mrs Ponder, like many another, confused facts when she wished to) had come to the house interfering and disturbing. She, Mrs Ponder, had hated her from the first. She would like to say now all the things that she knew and had picked up from gossip. What was she after all? The daughter of some road gipsy who had married a thief killed in a cheap scramble. If it were not for the Master, poor silly fool, she would not be here another day, with her red hair and standing on her toes to make herself taller! Mrs Jennifer didn't want her, that was plain enough. And then she was alienating the children. The little boy had never been the same since her coming . . . Mad she was, going off bareback with no hat on her head all the way to Caldbeck! Mad, as her rascal of a father had been, so she had heard, before her.

All these things Mrs Ponder would have liked to say, but there was something about Judith, something both in her rage and her dignity, that frightened the woman against her will.

She was about to go through the door when Judith stopped her: 'Why did you do this? For what were you looking?'

'I, ma'am? Looking? . . . Why, for nothing, I assure you.'

'Nonsense. Of course you had some purpose.'

Judith stepped forward, and Mrs Ponder, thinking she was going to strike her, retreated.

'No. I would not touch you. You are a bad servant. You have always been one. You will leave this house in the morning.'

'That is for my mistress to say.'

Yes. It was true. The woman was right. But Jennifer would not hesitate. After such a thing as this!

'I cannot understand what it was that you wanted. Pray inform me.' The disgust in Judith's eyes was more insulting than the anger. Mrs Ponder would not quickly forget it. But, for the moment, it would be better to withdraw. So she withdrew.

After she was gone Judith sat in her chair considering. They were to go to take tea with Mrs Southey at Greta Hall, she, Jennifer and Francis. She had come up to put on her bonnet. But she must speak to Jennifer before they went. She could not calmly join in the social amenities of the Southeys while this was raging in her breast. To break open her drawer and read her letters! There were packets of letters from Georges there ... Oh, it was monstrous, it was impossible! The insolence of the woman. But she would go at once – that was one good thing. The affair would have a good issue, for the woman had been always impossible, and now there would be a fine reason for her dismissal. Jennifer would not hesitate. Of course she would not. Judith's heart seemed to stop a beat. Jennifer was so strange a woman. They had been friendly enough during these twenty months. She had been delighted for Judith to take the house in her hands; she had given her free rein. But Judith knew her no better than on that first evening.

She could not any more now than then say whether it were War or Peace. The time had gone so swiftly; there had been so much to do – the house to order, the servants to watch, the children to care for, Francis to make comfortable, new neighbours to know, and sometimes – twice or thrice – strange sudden expeditions into the mountains, to Watendlath, to Newlands, once so far as Ennerdale, when another life altogether had stirred and moved, a life that was not dead, although it was given so little freedom. The time had gone, Judith had even been happy because of Francis, because of the children, because the neighbours were kind, and chiefly because this house and the little village and the Moor were all hers. From Iredale to Caldbeck, from Threlkeld to Mungrisdale it was hers. And so, because of all these things, the central situation, the pivot upon which everything else turned, the relationship between herself and Jennifer, had never been examined.

But it had been growing; all the while it was growing. As she sat there, beside her bed, looking at the dove-grey bonnet that lay upon it, she suddenly shivered. *What* was Jennifer thinking? Had Jennifer? ... And at the very suspicion of that thought, she, to whom honesty and cleanliness and fair dealing were the first rules of life, sprang indignantly from her chair. Oh no! that was monstrous ... Monstrous ... But she must go, at once, *at once*, and speak to Jennifer.

So down she went, and the first thing that she saw was the fat, handsome, sensuous face of Captain Fernyhirst in the hall. Captain Fernyhirst lived near Caldbeck. He had bought, only last year, old Uncle Tom's house, Stone Ends. He had a pale, ill wife there and two lanky children. And he was an admirer and friend of Jennifer's.

He was a fine upstanding man with a broad back and stout legs. His eyes were too small, his nose a trifle too large, but he looked elegant in his green coat, his hair curling above his ears, his spurred heels spread, yes, as though he owned the house and everything in it.

They were a handsome pair, a very handsome pair. He greeted Judith with the courteous patronage that he always used to her. He said something about the weather, and went. Jennifer was dressed in green and white, her lovely hair falling in thick ringlets on her bare neck. Very lovely, Judith thought, was her hair, parted in the middle of her fair smooth forehead, combed towards the sides, falling in curls that seemed to hold in their dark shadows a strange, steely lustre.

'Very lovely hair,' thought Judith, 'but I wonder whether Mrs Ponder ...' She was in fact too angry to wait, as she should have done, for a more favourable opportunity, and in that lost an important chance of commanding the situation.

Impetuously she led the way into the parlour.

'Jennifer, I must speak to you.'

'My dear ... but we are late, and Mrs Southey is most punctilious ...'

Slowly she followed Judith in.

'Jennifer, Mrs Ponder must be dismissed. At once. Tonight.'

'And why?'

'I caught her, now, five minutes back; I went to my room and she was searching my drawers. My papers were scattered about the floor.'

It was not Jennifer's way to speak quickly. It was as though slowly and with practised deliberation she sent a message through all her tall body that it must be prepared for a set of circumstances, that there was no haste required ... plenty of time.

She sat down, put her hand to her hair, looked out of window.

'Well, Judith, I must inquire. Mrs Ponder is an admirable servant. She was perhaps making tidy your effects.'

'Making tidy my effects? But who is she to make my things tidy? It is not her business. She had no place in my room. No, indeed. She was making nothing tidy. She was spying.'

'Spying? What is there for her to spy into?'

'Nothing, of course. I have nothing to hide.' Then amazement, increased by her anger, seized her. 'But, Jennifer – are you not yourself indignant? Do you understand what it is? She was *spying*! The woman was in my room, my letters were on the floor. Letters. Letters from my husband ...' Her voice broke. She was very near to tears.

'Well, it shall be inquired into. I am convinced that you have judged too hastily. It *is* your weakness, Judith. You act too immediately on the impulse of the moment ...'

'*My* fault! My fault!' Judith broke in. 'But Jennifer, I cannot understand! You appear to be blaming *me*! Do you hear what I said? That Mrs Ponder was discovered by me tossing my private papers about the floor, her hands among my effects. She did not deny it. She could not. She was most insolent. She must go ... must leave ... at once, tomorrow morning. You must tell her so. A fine thing to have in the house, a servant who opens drawers and carries her secrets, I have no doubt, to the kitchenmaids and the grooms. You cannot hesitate. Francis would insist ...'

She pulled up. For her life she wished that she had not spoken those last words. Her rage had carried her away. The very thought of the woman's ugly thick back and the packets of Georges' letters ... But she should not have mentioned Francis. Was she never to learn?

In the short silence that followed, the place seemed to fill with the summer scents, the radiant sun floated the room with shadows of gold. Some man called to his horse, wheels creaked on the road. Then Jennifer spoke:

'Yes ... It was I who asked Ponder to search your drawer.'

She looked at Judith, and Judith looked back at her. Judith's pale face slowly flushed. This was an incredible thing. It was as though the spinet had leapt through the ceiling, or the little rosy apples on the sofa had rolled like little live bullets about the floor. An incredible thing. To Judith, in spite of the many events that had been her lot, the most astonishing, the most dumbfounding of them all.

'You ... told her?'

'Yes. I wished to know what you were writing of me to London.'

'I ... to London?'

'Indeed, yes. To dear Will and Christabel, who have so true an affection for me.'

'And so ... you thought that such dishonest behaviour was in my character – that while I lived here and was your friend I would write ...' She broke off. All words failed her. The sun had died from the room, which was grey in her eyes and chill.

'But why not? We must have common sense. When you first came here I hoped that we should form a friendship, but you had other ideas. You were determined to be mistress here. You alienated my husband, my children, my servants. I was well assured that your friends in London must have the benefit of your experience. Why not? If I had had your ambitions I should have doubtless done the same.'

'You thought that? I have been here for more than a year. All this while you have fancied me indulging in such treachery; you have known me so little that you suspected *such* things in my conduct? Why, then ... why, then ... if your mind has been of such a colour, you must have hated me! ... And I thought that we were friends. For a year I have suspected nothing. And you have made your servant spy on me ...'

She was shaking, quivering with rage, astonishment, but also with a dreadful miserable unhappiness that seemed to strike deep into her very soul. All her life long, through every difficulty and distress, she had been supported always by her sense of her own integrity and the conviction that everyone thought her honest. She had not had pride in that, but it had been her comfort; whatever else went, that remained. And now – to be charged with such treachery and to be hated when she had thought that she was cared for.

Her lip quivered. If she wept now it would be a humiliation for which she would never forgive herself.

Steadying her voice she said quietly: 'I have never suffered any disloyalty to you, Jennifer, in myself or another. I had thought we were friends and so acted. You have wronged me,' and left the room.

Once in her own place any tendency to tears was gone. Tears! No, indeed! She walked the floor like a raging little animal in a cage. The letters, papers, ribbons were still scattered about, where Mrs Ponder had left them. Mechanically, without knowing it, she bent down and put them back and closed the drawers. She remained, kneeling there, looking in front of her.

Her immediate impulse was, as it had always been in every crisis of her life, to take some dramatic action instantly – to find Francis, to tell him what had occurred, without either self-defence or accusation of anyone, and then to depart – to be, as swiftly as possible, as far from Jennifer as the world allowed her. But very quickly her temper cooled. Her intelligence reasserted itself. There was more in this than a vulgar quarrel. The whole of her own past life was in it, her father, her mother; the whole of the Herries family was in it, for what she was meeting now in Jennifer was the thing in the Herries blood that her father, herself, Francis, Reuben, Georges had always been fighting – the unimaginative, calm, self-assured obstinacy and confidence.

At that she knew that she was herself now calmer. She rose from her knees and, as she looked about the room, realized something with an absolute certainty of its truth, as though someone had whispered it in her ear. Jennifer had intended this quarrel. She did not hate Judith. Hatred was an emotion unknown to her sluggishness. She had decided – perhaps some while back – that Judith made her uncomfortable and that Judith must go. Francis would never allow her to go, unless there were some very obstinate reason or unless Judith herself was provoked to it. She must provoke Judith or she must find a reason. In all probability she was smiling now quietly to herself, thinking that she had succeeded.

At that Judith flung up her head and swore that whatever occurred she would not go. This was her place, and here she would stay. She could be as obstinate as Jennifer, yes, and more obstinate.

There was a knock on the door, and opening it she found Francis there. The carriage was ready. Jennifer was ready. He was smiling, had no consciousness that there had been any trouble. She looked at him and smiled too. She was there to make Francis happy, and make him happy she would, Jennifer or no Jennifer. She put on her bonnet and shawl and went down with him.

'I like the grey bonnet,' he said.

'I had it in Carlisle,' she said, 'a month ago.'

Jennifer, in her fine green and white bombasine dress and an ostrich feather in her bonnet, stood by the carriage, the moors undulating in hummocks and pools of green on every side of her. She smiled as they came towards her.

'Dear Judith,' she said, 'what a charming bonnet!'

So it was all bonnets, and a more agreeable trio, sitting behind the immense back of Fred the coachman, could surely not be found in Keswick. Francis might complain that Will made the money and that he was a failure, but nevertheless things were very comfortable at Uldale. That land that they had bought towards Caldbeck was turning out very well, and, in spite of the unsettled times, the shares in the Liverpool shipping business were for ever improving. And, in a year, Judith had brought the house to a fine discipline. Mrs Harper, the housekeeper, a widow from Carlisle, was an excellent woman. Jennifer herself was not at all extravagant. Whatever she wore seemed to be beautiful on her. She had no great taste for entertaining. An occasional little dinner with cards afterwards, a Ball at Christmas. No magnificence even then. Ten couples at the most. Yes, new bonnets could be afforded. They were very generous to Judith or, at least, Francis was. His allowance was most generous. She had never had so much in all her life before; never been so comfortable ... Comfortable? A glance across at Jennifer on the opposite seat, and it was as though everything sinister and destructive thickened the summer air.

To be charged with such malice and deceit, to be suspected of the basest treachery ...

'They say that Mr Coleridge dislikes his wife extremely and will never again return to Keswick. He goes often, I believe, to visit Mr Wordsworth in Grasmere ... How cool the woods are! ... The Southeys always seem to me very pleasant people. Judith my dear, if the sun is too hot you must change places with me. You know that I am never disturbed by the heat.'

She was not. She basked in it, or like a great bird of brilliant plumage bathed her feathers in it, letting the light strike gold and emerald and sapphire from her loveliness.

'Edith Southey,' said Francis, 'is a very pretty-behaved child, very pretty-behaved, indeed. And little Hartley, Coleridge's boy, is most unusual. But, of course, he is growing now. He must be fifteen, at least. He is at school at Ambleside. Yes, this is a most beautiful day; the air is exceptionally warm.'

Francis was happy today. He was always pleased when he was going to see Mr Southey. That she should set her servant on to spy and then, without a tremor, admit it ... How lovely that rather selfish droop of her mouth and the faint warm glow of her cheek, and the softness of her eyes as they looked out so calmly under their heavy lids! ... The falseness! That Judith had tried to alienate the children! John loved her. That was not Judith's fault. And he was uneasy with his mother. He knew, as children always know, that she did not in her heart care for him. Or did she care? Who could tell for whom she cared?

'Look, Judith, how blue the Lake is! There is not a ripple.'

Yes, she had thought that she had got her way, and that in a week Judith would be gone. She was wrong. As they approached Keswick the air was rich with the scent of the summer flowers. July and August are the bad months for this country. There is rain, everything is heavily green without variety. But days come like this one when all the trees, larch and birch and fir and oak, are so deeply shadowed and so highly lit that fire runs from stem to stem, melting into cloud and climbing into swift eddies of green smoke. If only there are clouds in the sky the hills lie waiting to receive the shadows that slip like birds from shoulder to shoulder. The clouds have a great richness in this month, so proudly filled with white light that they quiver with their intensity, throwing paths of ghostly radiance on to the Lakes that are blue, here and there ruffled darkly like tarnished silver. On such a day the richness of the English scene, when the hay burns in the nostrils and every cottage garden has the dusky odour of snapdragon and sweet-william, is immortal. One summer's day is enough for memory to be enriched for ever.

Keswick was so small a country town that in the summer its gardens dominated all the rest. Greta Hall is at the entrance to it from the Carlisle side, and once they had crossed the little bridge they were almost there, but Judith could smell the flowers mingling with the soft friendliness of the cut hay that lay on the open fields.

She could see the peace of the town, the farmers' carts, Mr Probus the Apothecary standing at his door enjoying the sun, two young ladies laughing as they came out of Mrs Gray's, the bonnet shop, old Mr Fordyce the Antiquarian, who was said to sleep half the year on the Roman Wall, with his snuff-coloured wig and old-fashioned breeches. As the carriage turned up the drive she thought: 'It will take more than Jennifer's insults to drive me away from this.'

This was Judith's first visit to the Southeys. Mrs Coleridge and Mrs Southey had been to Uldale. They were quiet, comfortable women; certainly Mrs Southey was a comfortable woman. About Mrs Coleridge one could not be so sure; there were lines of discomfort about her mouth, restlessness in her eyes. You could see that they were sisters and had lived for most of their lives together.

Yes, the house was charming, a nursery garden on the right as they climbed the hill; then you could see an orchard with plum trees and apple trees behind the house. They were admitted by a cheerful motherly-looking woman, who conducted them into the parlour on the left of the passage. They waited in the parlour, gathered together in a kind of attitude of defence as people are when they are awaiting their hostess.

This was a charming room, with a large green shaped like a horse-shoe in front of the window. The room was comfortably furnished with old furniture, shabby but friendly. There were pictures on the wall – one really dreadful painting of a staring doll-like Mrs Coleridge.

Mrs Southey came in. There were greetings all round, words about the splendid weather, about the hay, the crops, being tired, not being tired, being hot, not being hot. But they must all come upstairs to Mr Southey's room. That was where tea would be. So upstairs they all went.

Oh! this was a wonderful room, so light, so well-proportioned, so airy! And the views were fine. Were the views not fine? They were indeed. The room had three windows. The large one that looked down upon the green and the flowerbeds and away to the Lake and the mountains, the two smaller ones whence you could see the lower part of the town.

The room was lined with books, and there were splendid volumes bound in vellum lying in heaps on the floor. And the family portraits on the wall; before long Judith knew who they all were – Mr and Mrs Southey by Downman, little Edith Southey and little Sara Coleridge by that fine artist Mr Nash; the other three Southey children, Kate, Isabel and Bertha, also by Mr Nash.

Much good furniture, Mr Southey's writing-table piled with books and papers, a screen, a desk. The room was decorated in quiet dignified tones, the curtains of French grey merino, the furniture covered with some buff colour. A noble room, the room of a poet, lit now with the summer sun, and all the summer sounds mingling beyond the open window.

It was, in fact, Mr Southey himself who showed Judith the portraits and then some of his books. At first she thought him a little alarming with his dark hair, his grave features, the dignified, rather remote way he had of moving, a little as though, she wickedly fancied, he were carrying the offertory plate in church. He was at first the official host, cold and ceremonial. He held up his head as though he knew it was a fine one; she thought

that he certainly was aware that he was an important personage.
She fancied, too, on their first arrival, that he had thrown an
impatient glance or two at his writing-table, where his papers
lay, as though he wished his visitors very far away. And he
certainly had no idea as to who she was; he took care to give her
no name lest he should be in error. She thought that he had
difficulty sometimes in seeing her at all and would have spoken
with the same grave courtesy if she vanished; he would not
know that she had gone.

And then, when they moved to the large window, he became
entirely another person. When he spoke of this country, this
country that she loved as dearly as he, his voice thrilled, his
face was lit, his black hair flung back.

'You know it is hard for me to speak of these things. When I
first came to Keswick I assured myself that I should never
settle down without a violet – no violet and no nightingale. But
now I have long forgot those losses. My brother Tom was settled
in the valley of Newlands, and I would not like to confess to
you how we have been, the two of us, our childish behaviour.
And now with my own children there is no stone or leaf of Walla
Crag or Watendlath that we do not know.' (Watendlath – a
quiver at the word touched her and fled.) 'And with my books –
my books. Are you yourself a bookworm? If so you see in front
of you the most impassioned of your clan. Let me show you—'
He waved his hand and, eagerly walking to the bookcase, began
to pull out volumes for her. 'Have you been ever in Portugal?
Do you know Portugal? What! you have never seen Cintra! . . .
And is Verbeyst an unknown name to you? Verbeyst of Brussels.
He has three hundred thousand volumes. Do you know what it
is to open a chest of books? What are you going to find? . . .
No, let me show you this – *The Revelations of St Bridget*. See,
not only are the initial letters illuminated, but every capital
through the volume is coloured . . . Fuller's *Church History* . . .
Is not Sir Thomas Browne a favourite with you? . . .' A small
tortoiseshell cat came and rubbed its back against his leg.

He was quivering now like a boy. His hands shook, his face
was all smiles. Then ruefully laughing at himself: 'Ah, I am for
ever making collections. It is foolish, is it not, for who will read
them if I do not, and they arrive more swiftly than even I can
peruse them. Time! Time! Why are the days not twice as long
and the nights four times. Come, I must not weary you, but I can
see that you have a fancy yourself this way. You have a fancy,
have you not? you have a library? I hope that you have a

library.' He smiled at her so friendlily and his eyes were so kind that she wished that they could be examining books for ever.

At tea, seated in a half-circle, Mr Southey, Mrs Coleridge, pretty Edith Southey, Mrs Southey behind the tea-table, they were all very gay. Judith had often noticed that when at parties Jennifer was present, everything went well. People were delighted with her beauty. Shadows and shapes of loveliness seemed to radiate from her passivity and composure. Then, being so beautiful, people assumed that she would be haughty and proud. But when she was anywhere, the first thing that she did was to secure her comfort and, as she was always the most beautiful person present, she was always the first to be offered a seat, food, drink, whatever it might be. So, assured that she had all that she needed, she was as amiable as anything, listened with apparent attention to everyone's stories (although Judith suspected that she never heard a word of them). There was, however, always a sense of thunder behind the calm. When suddenly out of her comfort she might, Judith thought, snap something in her fingers, even as on that old historic occasion she had snapped Christabel's fan.

But on an afternoon like today's she was entirely at her ease. She had had a fight and, as she thought, won it. She had been increasingly uncomfortable during the last six months; now that cause of that discomfort would be removed. Then the weather was hot, which she greatly preferred. Then the Southeys were reputable people; she had herself never read any of Mr Southey's long poems, but she knew that they were generally respected. What she liked was for the Herries to be gracious and condescending to families that were worthy of graciousness. The Southeys, she thought, were really worthy. Then Francis was happy here; he could here indulge his ridiculous passion for literature; and, although she only cared as to whether he were happy or no because when he was unhappy his sulkiness made her a little uncomfortable, yet, in warm weather like this, she preferred that everyone should pass a pleasant hour.

And lastly there was that little pushing nonentity Judith, who had been this very day told her place and at whom therefore it was agreeable, once and again, to look.

All in all, Jennifer that afternoon was very comfortable at the Southeys'. There would come a day when, looking back, she saw that warm, quiet afternoon as the beginning of all her trouble.

Mrs Southey was the conversational one; Mrs Coleridge had a

tendency to peevishness (which you could understand, Jennifer lazily pondered, if it were true that her husband was always away from her and was a slave to opium . . .).

'Are you partial to evening visiting?' Mrs Southey inquired. 'I must confess that we are not. Mr Southey has so much work in the evening and the roads are so often floated by the rain. Not that I think this is a rainy district in reality. It is only that it seems very hard when it does come down. Does it not rain hard sometimes, Mr Herries? I have never seen such hard rain anywhere.'

Mr Southey, who was offering cake and bread and butter with a graciousness that almost demanded the accompaniment of music, answered with gravity: 'It is the rainy hours that give us the opportunity for all our reading. Is it not so, Edith? Or rather, in my little girl's case, the writing out of charades and riddles into our book. Come now, Edith. Confess. How many charades have you copied in today?'

'None at all, Papa. I have been in the town with Mama.'

What Judith liked in him, she thought, was the warmth of his affections. As he spoke to his daughter his eyes looked on her as though he would surrender the world for her sake. And, as she knew, there was his boy Herbert whom he loved even more dearly.

'That is what my friend Wordsworth will never do. Copy a charade for a lady. No, he bows and regards her sternly and slips out of door and takes a walk. Are you acquainted with Wordsworth, Mrs Herries? The greatest man alive in England today. Yes, indeed, the greatest man in England, as the world will see one of these times. There has been a young man in Keswick this last winter, a Mr Shelley, with his wife. A most unusual young man. I have told him that when he is as old as I am he will grant the truth of my prophecy about Wordsworth. He, too, wishes to be a poet. We are all poets these days, Mrs Herries . . . Well, he is an unusual young man. Just what I was myself in '94. What it was hard for him to understand was that you may have Five Thousand Pounds a year and yet be a good man; I fancy that there are many young men like him today. The Revolution in France is responsible, you know. But I set him upon a course of Berkeley. That should do him good. He does not realize as yet that a man must put a bound upon his desires and work within them . . . Dear, dear, how sententious I am becoming! Pray, Mrs Herries, another of Mrs Southey's tea-cakes. They are quite famous in the neighbourhood, you know. John Wilson declares there are none like them even in Scotland, which is the land of tea-cakes.'

'Yes,' thought Judith. 'But will Francis be on my side? He must not know. He *shall* not know unless Jennifer herself tells him. And I believe that she will not.'

She had a horrible sense that the battle now would be underground, that no one henceforth would tell anyone anything, and that was so against her own character that it was as though she must twist her whole soul to conform to it.

'For my part,' Mrs Coleridge was saying, 'I would never encourage anyone to marry. There can be so many blunders in matrimony. Although, to be sure, young people must marry. 'Tis only natural for them.'

It was now that Judith saw enter the room a very extraordinary being. This was a boy of some fifteen or sixteen years of age; he had a small restless body dressed in clothes too young for it, the short blue cloth jacket, the white trousers and open frilled shirt of boys junior to him. Dark hair strayed untidily over his forehead, but his eyes were the strangest part of him, burning with intelligence and yet at the same time lost, as he gazed about the room, in a kind of abstract wonder. He saw them all seated about the tea-table and smiled, came towards them, stared at Jennifer as though he were mesmerized, then, pulling himself back with a jerk, nodded, still smiling, and stepped away to the farther part of the room.

'Nay, Hartley,' said Mrs Coleridge, 'you must wish Mr and Mrs Herries good day.'

He came back to them with an odd stepping dancing movement as though he scarcely touched the floor. Then he stood there, shook hands, seemed as though at any moment he would break into laughter. What was amusing him? It was to Judith exactly as though he had sprung through the wall, coming from another world. He was no resident in this one. All his real life was elsewhere, and as she watched him she became restless. She wanted to get up and run away from all of them – to Watendlath, maybe, find the old house, sit with the Ritsons by the great hearth and hear the lambs bleating beyond the window; then to pass into that other room and to stand watching that staircase, to see again that old man with the white beard as he turned to the stair. Georges would come in, wait beside her as he often did, take her and lift her, pressing her backwards against his breast. Oh, after all these years, after all these years . . . Was she never to be rid of it? If the battle were joined now between

Jennifer and herself, it was also joined between the one world
and the other. It was almost as though Georges were beside her
fighting Jennifer.

All this disturbance had come from that strange boy there,
moving away again, flitting now here, now there, regarding no
one and regarding everyone, humming (she fancied, although
she could not be sure) some tune to himself. They had all
moved away from the tea-table and so she found herself encountering Hartley. He was standing on one foot, one ankle
curled around another, and staring at Jennifer. He greeted
Judith as though he had known her all her life. Children often
did so because she was small and independent.

'That is the most beautiful lady, ma'am, I have ever seen,'
he said.

Jennifer was being shown books and manuscripts now by
Mr Southey.

'Yes,' said Judith. 'You are Mrs Coleridge's boy?'

'Yes, ma'am; there are Derwent and Sara and I. I go to a
school at Ambleside. Mr Dawes is the Master.'

'And what do you learn there?'

(It was the strangest thing, as though behind this outward
talk they were conducting a quite different conversation. As
though he said to her: 'I have just been with Georges and he told
me . . .' It was the boy's air of being not yet awake, of suffering
under some enchantment.)

His eyes were never still, nor his feet. He looked at her with the
most engaging friendliness.

'Oh, they try their best to teach me, but I cannot learn any
of the ordinary things. I shall dream of that lady for weeks and
write stories about her. She shall be the Queen of Ejuxria.'

'Where?'

'Ejuxria. It is a country that I discovered many years back.
She shall be the next Queen. Oh, ma'am, what a grand Queen
she will make.'

Oh yes, she will, and her servants will go spying in the drawers
of her Ladies-in-Waiting, reading their letters, undoing the
faded ribbons . . .

'Do you like to be here?' she asked him.

'I like to be everywhere. It is all the same, for if a place is
ugly one can make one's own picture of it, can one not, ma'am?'

How odd it was to see this small child, with his restless, unexpected gestures (so that he would crack his fingers or move
three steps on one foot as though he were playing hop-scotch,

or swing his little arms above his head), a child like none other
that she had ever seen, and feel that she had so much in common
with him. She felt no awkwardness. He understood her absolutely. His smile was the most bewitching part of him; it
embraced and included her in his own delight.

'And what will you be when you grow up?' she asked
him.

'I shall be nothing,' he answered, twirling round on one foot.
'I shall never grow up, I should think. I cannot learn the things
that help one to grow up, and I know such a number of things
that one must not mention. I have a secret name for everything.
What is your name, ma'am?'

'Judith – Judith Paris.'

'Judith – I shall call you Florindascantinopolis. One day I will
show you where Ejuxria is.' Then he added quietly: 'And now
I must go and do my Greek lesson. And then we are going to
play cricket – when the others come back from the Lake.'

Yes, they were going. Farewells were being said. Goodbye,
Goodbye . . . How warm it is! Is it not warm!

'Yes, the laurels are in great profusion here – but the kitchen-
garden is not really too extensive. So beautiful at Uldale! So
fine a view of the Scotch Hills . . . But certainly we will come . . .
very much obliged . . . too kind of you . . . Goodbye. Goodbye.'

So they rode home.

'Most agreeable people,' Jennifer said. 'When you are in
London, Judith, you must read Mr Southey's poems. They are
all the thing in London.'

'London!' Francis cried. 'London! But Judith is not going
to London.'

'No. I am not,' said Judith.

The two women looked at one another. Upon Jennifer's fine
smooth white brow a small, a very small frown appeared, the
first, Judith thought, that she had ever seen there.

'Of course not,' said Jennifer. 'But we cannot expect Judith
never to wish to leave Uldale.'

'I am very happy at Uldale,' Judith said, smiling at Francis.
'You are so very good to me.'

But afterwards when Jennifer had gone upstairs, slowly,
majestically, like a green and white swan floating upwards, to
take off her bonnet, Judith had a desperate, almost choking need
of reassurance. She caught Francis by the broad lapels of his

coat. He paused astonished. He was always shy of demonstrations, she knew. She looked up into his face and he saw that her eyes were filled with tears.

'Francis, you do want me here, do you not?'

'Want you!' He put his thin firm hand on her small one. 'Why, I will never let you go!'

She nodded and said in a low voice: 'I am glad. I wished you to tell me so.'

He added kindly, holding her hand more closely in his: 'You have altered everything here. The servants, the children all love you. And the best of it is Jennifer has grown so attached. I have never known her trust anyone so before. She relies on you completely. I cannot thank you sufficiently.'

'I am glad,' said Judith, moving towards the stairs, 'that you are pleased.'

GONE TO EARTH

ON A LOVELY October afternoon a post-chaise drew up outside Fell House and from it stepped a little short man in a brown hat.

He wore a dark brown 'carrick' with many capes, breeches of a light grey and very smart and shining top-boots. He was something of a dandy. He opened the gates, walked up the tiled path and pulled the bell-rope. He walked with a slight limp.

There was complete stillness round him. The thick, gold leaves of the trees in the garden, the little heads of amber chrysanthemums, never stirred in the blue air. Only the pigeons rustled in a flock above the pigeon-house at the sound of the bell, then settled again.

While he waited he sniffed the sharp beauty of the autumn weather and savoured the great spaces surrounding him on all sides. The edges of the hills were clear as though they had been cut out of paper. He could hear the sheep cropping on the moor beyond the garden wall.

A manservant opened the door and he inquired for Mrs Paris. He was shown into the hall bathed in sun, then after a pause into the parlour, where he stood holding his hat and looking anxiously at the door.

A moment later it opened and Judith stood astonished. Then she ran forward holding out both her hands.

'Warren!' she cried.

He laughed and was so glad to see her that his little grey eyes, bright and restless like a bird's, twinkled with pleasure. He had not seen her for four years.

'You are not changed in the least,' he said, holding both her hands in his.

'Why, of course not,' she said, leading him to the sofa. His limp made her seem protective towards him. 'And why should I be?'

'I have thought at times,' he said, looking at her very closely, 'from your letters, that you were.'

'In which way?'

'Oh, more serious, more grave.'

'I am a most serious person,' she said. 'You have never granted me that sufficiently.'

She was enchanted to see him. He was exactly what she was needing, an easy, good friend who cared for her, who was outside all the increasing perplexities and complications of this house and her position in it.

'But why are you here? And where have you come from?'

'I have been in Keswick a week.'

'In Keswick a week and only just come!'

'I had some business there and I would not come to see you until it was concluded.'

'But why not?'

'Because it concerns you.'

'Concerns me?'

'Yes. Wait an instant until I have seen you. I have been looking forward so impatiently to this moment.'

He was holding her hand a little harder than she wished. Very gently she withdrew it. He must be her friend, nothing more. But her *friend*! She had never in her life wanted a friend so badly as she did just now.

His face was very charming, ugly because the nose was too large and the mouth too small, but eyes and mouth both were wrinkled and lined with kindliness and humour. His looks had also that sense of strain common to everyone who has had a life of pain and ill-health. But he did not appear a weakling. His body was broad and sturdy, and he was alert and active save for his limp. He was now forty-three years of age.

'Well, what is your great news? I can tell that you are bursting with it.'

'Yes. You may not care for it when you hear it.'

She was quickly apprehensive; recent events had made her so.

'I had thought that you might have got wind of it.'

She suddenly knew. Of course! he was to be married. She was disappointed.

'I know – you are to be married!'

He looked straight into her eyes, so that she dropped them.

'No ... not yet,' he answered quietly. 'Nothing like that. Will has bought Westaways and I am to be manager of the estate.'

She drew back, erect with amazement.

'What!'

'Yes; Will has bought Westaways. The purchase was concluded last evening.'

Westaways was the house that old Pomfret, Raiseley's father and David Herries' uncle, Francis' and Will's great-uncle, had had built for him between Keswick and Crosthwaite Church. It was called Westaways because it was one of the best examples of the work of an old crazy genius of an architect who, a hundred years ago, had lived in Keswick. It had been built for Pomfret and his wife at great expense and it was a beautiful house. When Raiseley had moved with his wife, Mary, to London, he had sold the house to a Colonel Grant, who, however, had infrequently resided there. Six months earlier Colonel Grant had died in Spain and there had been much local speculation as to its next owner.

Will had bought Westaways! Will was coming here to live, eight miles from his brother with whom he was not on speaking terms! Will was coming back to Keswick. Will with his money and pride and scorn of everything outside London! Will! ...

'Oh no, no!' she broke out. 'It is impossible! Westaways and Will! Will and Keswick!'

'I know. But it is so. I have concluded the purchase myself.'

'And he is to live here?'

'He will come up occasionally. I fancy that Christabel and Walter will be here more frequently. She has not been well of late. Young Walter loves the country. He is mad on horses.'

'How old is Walter now?'

'Twenty-one. He was born in '92. He will make as good a business man as his father. But different. He loves power even more than Will. I never saw a young man so arrogant. He must have his own way in everything.'

'But I cannot believe it. It is incredible. Does he mean to be reconciled with Francis? He will not find it so easy.'

'No. I am afraid not. He is very bitter against Francis, and young Walter carries on the feud.'

'Then—' Judith waited. Suddenly she cried: 'Oh, he is coming here to show off! To triumph over Uldale! I see it all. Oh! it is shameful, shameful! With his money he thinks that he will humiliate Francis!'

'Remember,' Warren said, 'Francis married Jennifer.'

Judith could not grasp it. The change in everything that it would make, the unpleasantness, the rivalries, jealousies, personalities! The difficulties for herself, a friend of Will's and Christabel's as she was. She could not cut herself off from poor Christabel. That would be a disloyalty that no one would command in her . . . but how otherwise was her life with Francis and Jennifer to be possible, difficult as it was already?

In her perplexities she burst out: 'Warren, you should not have taken this. It is going to lead to nothing but hatred and ill-feeling—'

He nodded his head.

'Perhaps I should not. I hesitated, I will confess, but there was one thing that decided me.'

She said nothing. He went on.

'That you were here.'

'Oh no, Warren, please—'

He persisted.

'No, you have to hear me. I came to say this. From now we shall be living near to one another, and I do not care what you or any other may think. For four years I have tried to conquer my love for you, but it will not die. No, listen . . . listen . . . please do not send me away! No, Judith, please – please!'

She had risen and stood there looking at him: 'Warren, it is quite useless. You know that it is. We settled that four years ago. We were to be friends. You promised it.'

'I know, I know,' he answered. 'And so I intended it to be. But I cannot command it, try as I may. It is the last of my life. I shall have no more. My life has been always broken, everything has failed in it. This too will fail. I see that it must. But I am compelled to tell you.'

As she looked at him she longed to be kind to him, to give him anything that he wanted. What she had always desired, what she would always desire, was to give people what they wanted. And for seventeen years now no one had wanted anything very much. At Grosset it had been a carpet brushed, a window mended, a consoling word to Maria, a humorous word

to Carey, and here it had been comfort for Francis, who after
all was not comforted.

As she looked at Warren whom she liked so greatly, who was
so courageous and bore pain without flinching, who never made
complaint, she longed to give him anything. But how could
she? She did not love him. He wanted passion, and she had no
passion left for anyone in the world. And then it was absurd;
she was thirty-nine.

'Dear Warren,' she said gently. 'I care for you very greatly.
With Francis here you are the best friend I have. But love – love
of the sort that you mean, I have none for anyone. It is true
although it may sound fantastic, but I love Georges after all
these years as dearly as I did when he was alive. Is that false,
a sentimentality? I think not. Or, if so, I am myself deceived.
And then I am so old. I am near forty.'

He got up and stood beside her, but did not touch her.

'Yes, I know everything. Nothing has altered since we talked
at Grosset. You are not old to me. Besides, I am not myself
young. There is nothing to do – I did not ask you to do anything.
But I could not come here to live and not show you that there
is no change in my feeling. I shall not do anything but what you
would wish.'

He kissed her hand, gave a little bow, and limped away out
of the room. She heard the carriage rattle off down the road.

The light was failing, and the little room was shadowed with
yellow dusk. She stood there, her hand on the lid of the spinet,
looking at the dim garden and the white road beyond it. Her
head whirled. Will coming to Keswick! Will only eight miles
away! Will and his family hanging over Uldale and flicking
Francis' sensitiveness, Jennifer's pride, with every hour that
passed! Oh, but it was impossible! The situation was impossible!

The door opened, and Jennifer came in.

'Who was that who was here?' she asked. She was wearing a
dress of deep crimson that fitted very close to her body. She
walked wearily. During the last months Judith had seen that
something was distressing her, something that had nothing to
do with her comfort. A curious perception of life was slowly,
slowly waking in her. One could see it tremble in her like a
faint flutter in a white sky before dawn. Her battle with Judith
continued, but this was not the cause of her disturbance. It was
from some other direction.

'That was Warren Forster.'

'Warren Forster? Why did he not stay?'

'He had a piece of news—' Judith hesitated. This same news was going to shake Jennifer's placid laziness as nothing else could do. Judith longed to see that shaken; in part Judith hated Jennifer as she had never hated anyone before. But, beyond that, there was something further. Jennifer's anger would include Francis' discomfort. They were all included in this.

'Well,' Jennifer said slowly. 'Cautious little Judith. You *are* cautious, are you not? With your own plans and purposes—'

She always, now, when the two of them were alone, tried any kind of irritation that seemed to her clever, but like all unimaginative women she could only think of the taunts and teasings that would goad herself if someone applied them. Quite different ones would be needed for Judith.

'No, I am not cautious!' Judith answered, smiling. 'But this is rather astonishing news that Warren brought. Prepare yourself for a shock.'

Jennifer, who was standing, drawn to her full height, looking out of window, had her mind only half on Judith's words. She was watching or waiting or listening . . .

'Well, my dear? What is your great news?'

'Will has bought Westaways at Crosthwaite and is coming to reside there with Christabel and the family.'

Judith had her reward. Jennifer turned; her eyes for once were wide and awake, her beautiful mouth open, her whole body stung to attention.

'What? What do you say?'

'It is true. Warren has just completed the purchase. He is to be Will's bailiff.'

At that same moment Francis came in. He had been riding and looked immensely handsome in his many-caped coat. His face was splendid now, very sharp and set, thinner than it had ever been; his whole body was drawn fine and alert.

'Francis? Do you hear? It is impossible, fantastic. Oh, no . . . he cannot . . . he would not dare. No, no. There must be a mistake.'

It was astonishing enough to see Jennifer pacing the room, her head up, waving her arms, in a flurry of agitation.

'Judith, what is it? What's amiss?'

'Only that Warren Forster has been here and has told me that Will has bought Westaways and is to come there with Christabel.'

'Will! Bought Westaways!'

'Yes.'

Jennifer turned sharply upon Judith.

'You knew of this. You had heard of this already. You knew this was coming.'

She was so frantically disturbed that for once she forgot the caution that she always kept before Francis.

He at once turned to her. 'Jennifer! Certainly Judith did not know—' He stared at her as though he were seeing something new.

'Well, then,' she cried, tossing up her head and moving towards the door, 'it is at least just what Judith would have. Her dear friends, Will and Christabel, next door. No one can wonder at her pleasure.'

Before she went, her voice shaking with rage, she said to Francis: 'You have brought me to this – to be humiliated before that City merchant and his chicken-faced wife, but I shall not sit under it patiently, you shall see.'

When she was gone he put his arm around Judith and drew her down in front of the fire.

'You are sure of this?'

'Quite sure.'

'Warren himself came to tell you?'

'Yes.'

'And of course you had not an idea of it?'

'Why, no – of course not.'

He sighed deeply, leaning his head on his hand, looking into the fire. He was still wearing his heavy coat. She slipped it off his shoulders.

At last he said: 'Will is doing it only to humiliate me. He could have no other purpose.'

She tried to reassure him. 'No. Why should you take it so? After all this is his home. He lived here all his childhood. He must care for it. He will come to make friends.'

Francis struck his knee with his hand, his favourite gesture when he was excited.

'Never, never. He hates me and Jennifer too. And besides – if he wished to be friends I would not agree. He has insulted Jennifer in every way, and now it only needs this—'

She said what she could, but what was there to say? It was quite true. She knew that there was only one reason why Will had bought Westaways.

Then quite suddenly Francis asked her a surprising question. Dropping his voice a little he said:

'Judith, has Fernyhirst been here this afternoon?'

'No. Why?'

'Oh, for no reason. I wondered. He seems to ride this way frequently.' After another pause he asked her: 'Why did Jennifer speak to you like that?'

'Speak to me?'

'Yes, in that manner – unfriendly, angry. Is she offended with you?'

'Sometimes a little.'

'I have thought lately—'

After a while he said: 'Everything is turning wrongly. I feel as though some great misfortune were coming.'

She must get away. That, when she awoke the next morning, was her first and most dominating impulse. This was no new passion for escape. It had been constant with her all her life long. She was for ever wanting to escape – but never in the end escaping! That might be the just epitaph on her tomb were she ever to have one! Now she was going to escape almost exactly as she had escaped to Tom Gauntry's out of the window all those years ago after David Herries had beaten her. Only now she would not escape out of the window!

No one in the house seemed astir. It was as still as the lovely October morning around and above it. She left a note for Francis, laying it on his table in his study. She went round to the stables and brought out Peggy, who whinnied with delight at her approach.

Peggy was a small and very strong mare that Francis had given her, a brown mare with a most human expression, for she could look wicked and evil at the approach of Jennifer and most affectionate and engaging when Judith was near.

As she turned the corner at the bottom of the hill, leaving the house and the village behind her, her spirits rose with every clatter of Peggy's hoofs. She had told Francis that she would be a night away in Watendlath; but now she thought that it would be very pleasant were she to extend the one night into two. She wished to wipe Uldale and everyone in it out of her mind, yes, even Francis.

For two days she would not be the woman of Uldale, but someone quite different – the woman of Watendlath.

As her spirits rose she was like a girl of twenty instead of a woman of almost forty. Peggy, who was also, by mares' standard, a middle-aged female, became a very conscienceless child, pricking up her ears at sounds of birds and rustlings in the trees, although she knew that they meant nothing at all, and

striking the stones of the road with an especially youthful gaiety
because this piece of freedom was quite unexpected and the
thing that most of all she enjoyed.

Judith was once more reminded with especial clearness of that
evening when she had climbed out of window and ridden to
Tom Gauntry's. It seemed only yesterday, and she remembered
how lively she had been, swearing in good strong Cumberland
at the men in the road. It was as though nothing of any importance had occurred in her life between that ride and this, except
Georges. And yet she was middle-aged, riding off like a girl.
Something very ridiculous about that, but then she often found
herself ridiculous! Women rode on horseback very much less
than they had done when she was a child. They went now
sedately in chaises or barouches; it was quite a common thing
now to go to Edinburgh or even to London, whereas in her girl-
hood it had been quite an adventure.

And how formal and careful in these days the women of her
age were! Mrs Osmaston of Troutbeck (very far from sedate
her old mother-in-law had been!), Mrs Worcester from Threlkeld, Alice Sandon of Keswick and Mary Robertson of St
John's in the Vale, Mrs Southey, Mrs Coleridge – all stout,
careful, sedate women who would never dream of riding on
horseback from Uldale to Watendlath!

The matter with her, Judith, was that she was a trifle vulgar
and common. It had always been so, always divided her from
people. She had it, she supposed, from her mother. How enchanting it would be to see her mother appear suddenly now
out from the hedge, with her hair about her face, her gay ragged
clothes, her wild behaviour!

'I am your daughter,' Judith would say, jumping off Peggy,
and then they would sit down in the hedge together and talk
about everything. Judith would show her the silver chain that
Francis had sent her; she always wore this under her clothes.

'Come away with me,' her mother would say. And away at
once they would go for ever! No question of a real escape then!

She had never been a proper lady; even Francis, she suspected, found it so. That was why she had been so easily
friends with people like Georges and old Tom Gauntry, Emma
Furze, Charlie Watson, who were not ladies and gentlemen
either. If only she had looked a little different! – here Judith,
in spite of herself, sighed. To be so small, to have such un-
important features – and now she was a little stouter and her
hair had lost some of its lustre.

She could not understand how Warren Forster could be in love with her! Nobody had ever been in love with her for her looks; Georges had only come to love her through propinquity. But that was her greatest triumph, the triumph of her life!

But to return to the vulgarity of her nature, that was the reason, no doubt, of her struggle with Jennifer. Jennifer detested anyone who was not a lady. She had hoped that Judith was a lady, and then, when she found that she was not ...

Well, Judith could not help it. She was not to worry her head on this beautiful morning about Jennifer. She bore Jennifer no kind of malice – only why was she, Judith, in that house at all? Some part of her was always dragging her back into Herries affairs. She did not want to go back. How splendid it would be if she could stay in Watendlath for ever – then her real life would begin!

She would not go through the town, but took the bridle-path at the back of it, along the lanes under Skiddaw until at last she joined the path that led up to the stream above Lodore.

Here at a clearing between the trees she was compelled to stop Peggy and watch, for a moment, the storm that struck the Lake. It had been, when she left Uldale, a perfect October morning, without one cloud to mar the pale delicate blue. But, with the dramatic splendour that makes these skies the most wonderful in the world, a rolling black cloud, like a great funnel of smoke, had rushed over from the sea, pouring over Cat Bells and Robinson like the issue of a conflagration. The Lake was yet blue, the hills still gold with their burnished bracken. But this cloud hurried with the gait of a drunken man. It had been a funnel of smoke, but now, even as Judith watched, it swung outwards as that same drunken man might wave his cloak in a gesture of defiance. Then it spread with ferocity, eating up the sky, frothing at its edge in spumes of grey vapour, its black heart catching a purple light, the stain of blackberries.

It ate the sun. The Lake shivered and fell into a trembling agitation of tones and circles; the hills, that had been so bright, raised their heads; they seemed before Judith's eyes to increase their stature, and shadowed gulfs of purple rent their sides. Around her still the bracken was gold, the sun beat upon her face. Then with a quick whirr of wind the raindrops fell. The woods sighed. Where, only a moment before, there had been gentle stillness, there was now a sibilation like the whisper of a thousand gossips.

Soon the rain was falling as though a huge bowl had been

opened over her head, but already, above Robinson, a thin line
of gold cut the black wedge; light, mysterious and lonely, fell
on one of the small islands and lit it with an unearthly glow. The
black cloud began to break.

This moment's storm seemed to mark her passage from one
world into another. As she moved on up to the road above
Lodore, she felt that all her other life was closed to her, and she
was so happy that it was absurd to think that she had ever been
otherwise.

It seemed a moment later that she was in the Ritsons' kitchen.
What a welcome she had! She had been to Watendlath three
times in the last two years, but only for very short visits. She had
not slept a night there, and, on one occasion, Francis had been
with her. Now she *was* to sleep a night there, maybe two, and
she was quite alone. With all Cumbrians, when, after long years,
much silent watchfulness and infinite caution, they decide that
you may be trusted, the fidelity and affection is all the more
fervent because of the earlier testing. But Judith was quite
unique in the lives of the people of Watendlath. Her appearance,
her history, her marriage with its extraordinary end, her long
years with the 'Grand Folk' down South, her character with its
odd mixture of fiery temper and great patience, of humour and
seriousness, of youth and old wisdom, half a lady, half anything
but a lady, her character honoured them by being both so
strange and yet so ordinary. In a way they took her quite for
granted now after all those years with them, but in another way
they never took her for granted. They were never sure what she
would do next. And, in addition to all these things, most of them
loved her (there are always grumblers everywhere who do not
love anybody) because she made them laugh, because she washed
dishes and scrubbed floors, because she was interested in everybody and everything, because she could talk the broadest
Cumberland and often did, because she knew as much about
sheep as anyone, because she could lose her temper with a man
like any good woman, because her rascal of a husband (they had
always hated Georges) neglected her, because she continued to be
fond of him long after he was dead, because she had no pride
and someone in one class was the same to her as someone in
another, because she was shocked at nothing that they did,
whether they were dirty, mean, lecherous, drunken, cruel,
spiteful (and at times as with all other of God's creatures they
were one or another of these things), because she was a plain-
looking little woman but also unusual, so that you always looked

at her twice – but chiefly they loved her because they trusted her, which, with a Cumbrian, is first and last the principal thing. She kept her word; her heart was warm; she was not 'stuck on herself'.

Old Man Ritson had died two years back, his daughter-in-law last year; now Tom Ritson and Alice shared the farm. Tom had married a girl from Cockermouth, a simple little woman who was a good cook, and Alice had married young Roger Perry of Thunder, who was so thick through, broad across and short of leg, that he resembled the small stone wall above the Tarn. He had a round red freckled face and was a very silent man. However, he liked Tom Ritson, loved Alice, had three small boys who rolled about the kitchen floor like little ninepins and was excellent with cattle and sheep. The Ritsons were now a very happy household.

They all rushed at Judith, even the three small Perry boys, who had not the least notion as to who she was, but, like puppies, felt that she was part of a good and friendly world. Alice was perhaps the best pleased of them all. She had an almost re-verential love for Judith. Although now a quiet pale-faced woman who went about her work with little comment, she saw further into character than did the others. She understood a little of what Judith's feeling for Georges had been; he had not been for her merely the foreign rogue and rascal that the others had thought him.

As Judith sat down beside the huge open fireplace, realizing with deep pleasure that all the busy life of the kitchen was going on around her just as though she were not there, the men stumping in and out, the women in their clogs clattering about, baking, working at the butter, going after the chickens, shooing geese out of the doorway, looking into the sunny yard to see whether the men were coming for their dinner, Alice Perry quietly watched her. She was anxious for her, thinking of what none of the others would consider – for Judith had not slept the night here since the night of her husband's death; more than that, she had never since then entered that room. Alice knew that now, this time, she would enter it.

Then, just as the men came clattering across the yard, hungry and thirsty, Charlie Watson rode in on his horse.

'It's Charlie!' Alice cried. 'Charlie Watson!'

Judith ran to the door and then out to meet him. He jumped off his horse and stood there, his legs spread, his mouth twisted in that strange, shy, almost angry smile so peculiarly his. It was as though he said: 'Well, it's a foolish thing to feel this pleasure and one is an idiot to set one's affections on anything but a sheep – still, I can't help myself.'

It was a year and a half since she had last seen him. He had stoutened, but otherwise was little changed from the man she had met on the road from Rosthwaite seventeen years ago. His skin was as clear, his teeth as white, his colour as ruddy, his body as strong – and his tongue as silent.

'Aye. 'Tis good to see ye. Lookin' fine.'

Then they walked into the kitchen together.

While they were all eating, Charlie sitting among the farm-hands and with one small Perry on his broad knee, she watched him with exceeding pleasure. She knew from all that she had heard in the last year that he was growing to be a very important person, not only in that neighbourhood but beyond, as far as Ravenglass on one side and Mardale on the other. One thing for which he was becoming famous was his fighting the cause of the farmers against the cattle-dealers. In those days, when there were no railways and few newspapers, cattle-dealers did much as they pleased, naming their own prices and seeing that they got what they demanded.

He was already beginning to buy cattle himself at fair prices, and sending them to Liverpool. At present only in a small way; it was, later on, to become a famous thing. Then he was a great arbitrator in all local disputes. His scrupulous fairness, his even-ness of judgement, made him ideal for the settling of boundaries, squabbles about sheep and cattle, even domestic troubles. He was himself growing wealthy, but lived always in the simplest fashion on his farm. Although he was older now he was still a great wrestler and player at any and every game. She had heard also that he refused to marry, laughing at every suggestion. Many liked him but he had no intimates; he seemed to prefer to be alone. He liked her, she knew, but she could not flatter herself that she knew him. She was even at times afraid of him.

But now as she sat there watching the October afternoon fall behind the kitchen windows, hearing all the sounds that she loved, sheep slipping like a flock of anxious old women up the path, water being drawn from the well, the soft crooning song of little Mrs Perry as she rolled the dough on the long kitchen table, the screeching of the turkeys on the field above the farm, her own fear gathered about her. Because she knew that she was soon to do that of which she was most in the world afraid. The first time, after coming up from the South, that she had ridden over, she had intended to force her will, but Francis had been with her and that had been her excuse. The second time Alice Perry had been sick, and that, she told herself, had been her excuse. But today there was nothing to prevent her.

Her pale face grew weary and strained. Her hands were clenched on her lap. She answered Mrs Perry's chatter without an idea of what she was saying.

Then she nodded her head as though something spoke to her, commanding, and she submitted. She got up and went out into the yard. Watson stood there speaking to Perry. She nodded to him, and he came across to her.

'Charlie, will you come with me?'

He seemed to know at once what she meant and walked off with her without another word.

The distance was nothing, but at the door she hesitated.

'I have never been inside – since it happened.'

Gently he put his hand through her arm.

'Come in,' he said.

She felt as though she were leaving everything living behind her. The air was suffused with a purple dusk, and she turned back to see the Tarn one blaze of fierce white light. The hills seemed gigantic. She heard, exactly as though she were leaving them all for ever, all the sounds of life, the animals, the human voices, the running water; then they went in together.

The room that had once been her sitting-room was used now for lumber, and one end of it was piled with sacks. An old kitchen table, rickety on three legs, was in the middle of the room and on it stood a large swinging mirror whose glass was cracked. The glass reflected the staircase. Some hens were rooting about on the floor. The place was dusky, but everything was as clear to her as though flooded with sunlight. And everything had happened yesterday, that night, only a few hours ago.

'Old Mr Stane stood there in front of the fire. Suddenly Georges went up, as close as to touch him, and cried out: "I killed your son! I hated him! I killed him, I tell you, and you can do what you like." Then he went up the staircase and the old man ran after him and caught him and threw him down. Then he ran down the stairs again and went out. I saw that Georges was dying. There was nothing to be done – nothing at all. But before he died he caught my hand and he told me he loved me. He died at once. There was nothing I could do. No one could have helped. It was too late.'

'Aye,' said Charlie. 'It must have been terrible for you.'

She began to cry, hiding her head in his coat, holding to him, and he put his arm round her. He stood looking over her into the cracked mirror.

At last she whispered, so faintly that he could scarcely hear her: 'This is my home . . . I shall never have any other.'

She cried on, then went and sat upon the stairs, looking all round at everything, taking every piece of it into her so that she need never fear to come again. And he stood gazing at her and knowing that she had altogether forgotten him.

They stayed so long without moving that the hens grew bold and scratched in the dirt at their very feet.

GHOSTLY IDYLL

BUT, AS EVERYONE knows, just when Fate seems to have a fine bouncing climax in his hand he shakes his head, changes his mind (which is not nearly so settled a one as people seem to think) and puts the climax back into his pocket again.

It was so with Judith now. She came back from her two nights in Watendlath happier than she had been for many a year. She had slept in her old room again. Whether she had truly slept or no she could not say, but, without either sentiment or nonsense, it had seemed to her that Georges kept her company. Therefore, she returned to Uldale in a state of great happiness. She settled down into all the Uldale affairs again as though she were for a moment pitching her tent there. Very soon she would be back at Watendlath. Nothing should keep her. But everything kept her. It was to be months, and then even years, before she saw Watendlath once more. Members of the Herries family never escape so easily as that.

Her time now at Uldale was difficult, and it was the difficulties that kept her. Feeling that she must stay, she did not dare go even for an hour to Watendlath lest it should keep her for ever and her duty be broken. The first difficulty was Jennifer. Strange! Can one be so secret a woman without being secret at all? For although Jennifer had now her mysterious preoccupation that caused her to twist her brows and bite her thumb, yet she was not really secret. She was wondering, Judith knew, whether to go further with Fernyhirst.

Judith suspected that Jennifer was moved, as a woman stirred by a man, for the first time in her life; that she was as uncomfortable, bewildered and disturbed as a child wakened up from a deep sleep by sunlight. She was finding one discomfort after another press in upon her. Always before she had been able to deal with discomfort. Now she could not. She had told Judith to depart, but she had not departed. She had tried to make Francis a convenient figure in her life and nothing more, but of late he had begun to frighten her. She had told Fernyhirst to cease to make love to her, and he had not ceased. She had told herself to be indifferent to him, but she was not indifferent. Even with Mrs Ponder she was beginning to be uncomfortable, for Mrs Ponder now was often insolent. Even with her children she was not comfortable, for they were growing and insisted on having lives and personalities of their own.

Because of all these unsettled discomforts Jennifer was at last beginning to live. Her eyes were no longer half closed. She was often alert, as though she were listening for some sound.

One thing for which she was listening was the arrival of Will and Christabel at Westaways; but the months passed, one year closed and another year opened. Still they did not come.

Warren Forster, who was often at Uldale, although Jennifer disliked him and showed it, said that This, That and the Other prevented them ... They would come ... Surely they would come ... A pity ... He had endeavoured to persuade Will to alter his mind. Westaways was not the house for him. But Will was obstinate. He did not know why he was so obstinate.

Francis, however, knew; Francis was an altered man. Biting, sarcastic, silent, even with men of his own mind, like Southey, he appeared to have lost all his sweetness.

'He's gone sour,' said Fernyhirst to Jennifer, and he stretched his broad chest and pinched his strong neck with a smile of satisfaction. It was a long business, this siege, but she was the handsomest woman in the country and it was a fine occupation for a dull country life. It could have but one end to it. He was an extremely patient man, as his training of horses and dogs (for which, in the North, he was famous) showed.

Worst of all, Francis had now shut himself away from Judith. If he spoke his mind to her he must speak of Fernyhirst, and that he was resolved not to do. He was now entirely alone, even as his grandfather and namesake had been before him. He was going the same road.

It was on a winter morning towards the close of '14 that family history took a stealthy step forward. Young John Herries, aged now seven, was the cause. He was a very typical Herries child, square and strong like his grandfather, rather sensitive, but with a more plentiful allowance of humour and less sentiment about his father than David had had about his.

In fact at this time he had no sentiment about either his father or his mother. His mother he quite honestly disliked. He knew that she did not care for him. He hated to be embraced by her. In his father he was more truly interested; but this was a bad period for anyone to be interested in Francis. John saw him as a thin, severe, august figure moving about the place giving orders. He admired his father, but was happier when his father was not present. For Dorothy, his sister, he had a feeling of mixed contempt and protection. She cried a great deal, and she clung to Mrs Ponder, whom he, John, without extenuation or limitation, detested. No, he thought very little of Dorothy.

His whole heart was given to Judith, and had been ever since she had gone to the Tarn with him to sail his boat. He was very tenacious of ideas and affections. He loved Judith because he trusted her, because she talked to him like a human being, because she did not mess him about with embraces, because she was always so clean and neat (he was already fastidious about these things), because she thought the things in which he was interested important, because she considered the things funny that he considered funny. He treated her as he would have treated another boy who was a friend of his (he had no boy friends). He never gave any sign that he was glad to see her. He would look at her, a little frown gathered between his eyebrows, and he would ask her opinion. When he was going to laugh, the laugh came first in his eyes, which would be twinkling with merriment while the rest of his face was quite grave. He liked to rub the flat of his hand up and down the side of his breeches. Another pleasure was to put on a sudden very deep bass voice which was supposed to be an imitation of Mrs Ponder's.

'Boney's coming to eat you!' he would say out of his boots. It was her favourite threat, but instead of fearing he would chuckle with laughter.

He would walk up to Judith with great gravity and say, with his chin sunk into his neck so as to bring out his deep voice better: 'Boney's coming to eat you!'

It was John on this winter morning who made history. Judith

had dressed and was ready for the day. She came out of her room on to the landing. On this landing the rooms of both Jennifer and Francis opened. Stairs led up to Mrs Ponder's sacred chamber and attics; stairs led down to the main hall. Standing there for a moment before she descended, Judith thought of all that she had to do. She looked what at that instant she was, a very competent housewife, with keys at her waist, a green apron, and a spotless lace cap on her head. She had much to do: there was Mrs Harper, there were the kitchen-maids, there was the dairy. Mrs Birket and some London friends of hers were coming to supper and cards ... She heard then, from a large ancient cupboard that had stood for many a day in a corner under the stairway, strange sniffs, and then – a most startling sneeze.

Opening the cupboard door she beheld an odd sight. Seated on the dusty floor was John, absorbed in the feeding of a large, and, it seemed, very greedy brown rabbit.

'Why, John—' she cried.

He jumped to his feet, catching the rabbit by its long ears. As always, in any situation, now or ever, he stood his ground, but he was very red in the face and his cheeks were marked with dust. The rabbit squirmed in terror.

'Oh, but, ma'am,' he said in his husky confidential voice, 'I was intending—'

She could see that he was really frightened. But why? She could not think that there was anything very terrible in feeding a rabbit ... But why a cupboard? Why this furtive secrecy? She asked him. He stepped out of the cupboard, holding the rabbit in his arms.

He dropped his voice so that it became even more husky.

'You see, ma'am, Mrs Ponder had forbidden me to keep it. Yesterday. You see,' he dropped his voice yet lower, 'she has an exceptional distaste for rabbits. She ordered Jim to have it killed, and so I have been hiding it in this cupboard—'

'But why did you not tell your father?'

'Why, ma'am, he says that I must do as Mrs Ponder orders. It is only,' he whispered, coming very near to her, 'for today. I have found a place in the field—' He broke off. She realized that he did not want her to know where the hiding-place was lest she should be inconvenienced by questions. She whispered back to him, smiling:

'My indulgence shall be given. I shall tell no one.'

Greatly relieved, he went back to the cupboard.

S–P

She remembered something in her room that she had forgotten, and, for a moment, was back there, opening and shutting
a drawer. Before she had reached the door again she heard a
clamour. A woman's voice, muffled as though she were endeavouring not to be overheard, but so passionate that it shook
the air. Hastening out, she was horrified to see Mrs Ponder,
her face all black eyebrow, hurry across the floor and, with a
vindictive gesture, fling open the window and throw the rabbit
out. John gave a cry, then stood there, his face twisted with
anguish. Not seeing Judith, Mrs Ponder threw herself upon the
boy and, in a convulsion of passion, dragged him by the hair
towards the stairway. She moved so swiftly in her rage that she
had knocked his knees against the lowest step before Judith
could move. Then she was stopped by something else, for Francis
had come out. Mrs Ponder heard him and stayed. She let John
go, and he, as though driven by a sort of wild fury, uttering little
sobs, his eyes staring, ran past them all down the stairs.

'What is this?' Francis asked.

Judith had once heard him described by one of the ladies of
the neighbourhood as 'a pleasant gentlemanlike man'. He had,
she thought, never deserved the description less than at this
moment. To speak in the terms of the author of *The Italian*, he
was 'cold fury nobly seething'. Mrs Ponder felt this, and for
once in her courageous life was alarmed.

'Not at all, sir. Nothing, I mean. Master John has been
disobedient.'

He moved towards her as though he would strike her. Judith
remembered that she had once done the same. Mrs Ponder
appeared to have that effect on her critics.

He drew up and, looking at her as though she should, were
he magician enough, change into a rat at his feet, said:

'You will leave this house within the morning.'

And she, recovering some of her confidence, answered, as
once before she had answered Judith:

'That is for my mistress to say, sir.'

It happened then (for this landing was as public a place as
that generally chosen in the theatre for intimate confidences)
that Jennifer came from her room, looking very lovely in some
loose garment of a rosy shade and a white cap with rosy ribbons
covering her dark hair.

'Well, Ponder—' she said, and, seeing Francis and Judith,
stopped.

'This woman,' Francis said, 'will leave the house today.'

Judith then saw Mrs Ponder give Jennifer a very strange look.

Jennifer said: 'Why, what has she been doing?'

'She has been in a bestial temper and has dragged John by the hair.'

Mrs Ponder folded her arms as much as to say: 'You have not the smallest chance of moving me.'

'And what has John been doing?' Jennifer asked.

'If you please, ma'am, he has been most disobedient. He had concealed a nasty filthy rabbit in the cupboard, and after my telling him that of all filthy animals and filled with diseases, and my doing all for the best, ma'am, as I always do—'

'She had thrown the rabbit,' Judith broke in, 'out of window and was beating John against the stair.'

It had been better, as usual, if she had not interfered.

Jennifer, looking only at Francis, said: 'Mrs Ponder was in the right if John disobeyed her.'

'I have said what is to be done,' Francis answered, his face cold with disgust. 'The woman goes today.'

'I shall do what I think right,' Jennifer answered.

They looked at one another, a strange long look. His unspoken words were: 'She has the command of you. You do not dare to let her go.'

But he would have no scramble before servants.

At the top of the stairs he said again: 'She goes today,' and went down.

Mrs Ponder began: 'I assure you, ma'am, I had no thought but for the best. I would always do my duty—'

But Jennifer returned without a word into her room.

This little scene, so swift and so impromptu, was to have a deep and lasting effect on all the persons concerned in it, but on the life of Judith most of all.

After it the house was as silent as a valley in the moon. The winter day was sharp and sunny. The hedge sparkled with crystal and the lawn was laced with silver frost. A very fat robin at the parlour window sang. He was the only live thing. Francis rode out. Jennifer stayed in her room.

Judith went about her work and felt very lonely. What would happen? Would Mrs Ponder go? Whatever happened she had for a long time to come lost Francis, who would now keep more within himself than ever, and John, whose look of terror and anguish as he ran down the stairs she would never forget. Meanwhile the rabbit lay, with its back broken, on the stones below . . .

While she was in the storeroom, marking in a book the jams, jellies and preserves while Mrs Harper, a small thin woman like an amiable radish, chattered along, she thought impatiently: 'I cannot endure this much longer. I can't stay in a house where nobody cares for me.' Although she was forty years of age she was as childish as that. But perhaps what she really meant was that she needed to be close to somebody, close in affection and sympathy. This house today was a prison.

So that when, an hour later, Warren Forster arrived on horseback, her reaction from that early morning scene was terrific. She had never before been so glad to see him. Had it not been for that early disturbance she would never have gone riding with him, and had she not gone riding with him everything in later Herries history would have been different.

As it was, she did not care. She was reckless that day, reckless through exasperation and a longing for someone who was not angry, was not hurt, was not deceitful.

Warren, his little figure so dapper on his large horse, was not angry nor hurt nor deceitful. He was enchanted to see Judith, who was kinder to him, more responsive to him, than she had ever been. The house was quite still. She looked around her and found nothing alive in it but the robin. The air was filled with distress and anger. So she gave the robin crumbs, took Peggy out of her stable and rode off with Warren.

Often, when afterwards she looked back upon this eventful day and tried to see how one step had so determinedly led to another, it seemed that it had all been planned. But it was not in reality so. Nothing was planned. They just rode into the cold and crystal air.

At first they talked lightly of general things: of how Napoleon had tumbled down at last; of the quarrels among the Allies at Vienna, and the clever man that Talleyrand was; that it looked as though France, Austria and England would soon be fighting Russia and Prussia; of Napoleon's exile on Elba, and whether he would be there for the remainder of his days. They talked of those things, but they did not really care any more than their descendants would care for similar figures and intrigues. Napoleon, Talleyrand, the Czar of Russia were as remote from them as they rode along the Cumberland lanes as figures on a Chinese screen. They talked about affairs in England: of the King and the Regent, and the high prices and the uncertainty of everything and everybody; of how the world was changing as it had never changed before; of how interesting it was to live in a time of transition, but also how unsettling; of how there were no great figures in the world any more, no great literature, although Mr Wordsworth's poems were pleasant and *Childe Harold* had some fine writing (and was it true that Lord Byron was both so beautiful *and* so wicked? Judith asked), just as their descendants afterwards would talk. Warren said that Will Herries said that trade was going soon to recover and that everyone would be wealthy again, that there would be wonderful new industries, and that everyone would soon be living in towns because the country was too dull.

'That would be a pity,' said Judith, looking about her at the grey hills, their tops scattered with snow like sifted sugar. 'There is nothing so beautiful as the country.'

'I think so also,' said Warren, looking at her. He was madly in love with her that day. He was never to know why his love for Judith was so much fiercer and more sharp than any other emotion of his life, his greatest happiness and his greatest distress.

It had been so from the first moment of his seeing her at Grosset, although that had not been a good occasion, for it had been a stormy wet afternoon and she had been standing in the hall rating a servant when he came in. Her voice had had a sharp and dominating note in it, as though she were telling all the world to go to Hades. The fire in the hall had been smoking, there were dogs all about the place and one of Maria Rockage's garments hanging up to dry. Judith had turned on him like a cross, exasperated child and had been anything but gracious. So perverse are men, and so beyond all rules is love, that he had liked her the better for her mood. He preferred, perhaps, women who were of the ruling kind. Then as he came to know her more truly he found that, although she wished to dominate, she could be led by her affections almost anywhere. She could not indeed be led to love him, but would do almost anything for him out of kindness.

He was a man of great courage, humour, and spirit, and his pains, physical and other, had taught him patience. So he waited for a long time, and at last he had his reward.

They had no plan of direction, but they rode through Keswick (where Judith did a little shopping), then out, above the Lake, to the Grange Bridge and on into Borrowdale.

'My father lived her,' Judith said, 'all his life. They could not persuade him to move away. His house tumbled about his ears, but he died in it and I was born in it. Here,' she waved her whip to a broad bend of the little river, 'they drowned a witch. My

father went before them all and took her out of the water and
carried her away.'

The trees, bare above the chattering river, had a rosy edge
to them in the cold air. The top of Castle Crag played with little
wreaths of mist that crowned its head with a thin light, behind
which the black rocks gleamed. His hopes began to rise, he
knew not why. She was so friendly today. There seemed to be a
new current of intimacy running behind her words. He did not
know that he was indebted to a rabbit for his happiness.

'Would you have an objection,' she asked, 'if we paid a visit
to that old house of my father's where I was born? I have not
for a long while visited it. There is only a shepherd there. It
must be bare and deserted.'

They turned off the road and across the little bridge.

In the little graveyard near here Georges had been buried, and
here her father and mother had died.

The house that stood behind a little courtyard, defended by a
rough stone wall, seemed quite dead against the pale blue sky.
It had been, Warren thought, two houses; on the right it was of
some height, with latticed windows and a gabled roof. From this
attempt at grandeur it fell away to a low rough place that had
what seemed to be farm buildings attached to it.

But all was now in utter desolation. As they led their horses
in through the gate, shabby and broken, their feet struck the
rime from the stiffened grass. Birds rose in a whirl of agitation
from the thin stems of the bushes; a large white cat with malevo-
lent eyes slunk across the fast disappearing stones. Yet it was a
scene of great beauty. Rosthwaite Fell and Glaramara in farther
distance rose above the fields in purple grandeur. Water ran
in silver skeins down the rocks, and its tumbling was the only
sound.

Warren had got down from his horse to lead it in, and now,
standing in front of the old door, he cried, 'Is anyone here?'

There was no answer. They heard some animal stamping in a
byre close by. They pushed the door back and entered.

A musty odour of decay, straw, animal dung, met them, but
they persevered and, climbing the stair, found themselves in a
large room.

This, it appeared, was the place where the shepherd was at
home. A sort of couch made from boxes, and a decayed chair
that had great arms from which the stuffing protruded like a
disease, had been arranged with cushions and a blanket before
the wide stone fireplace. There were remains of a meal – a loaf,

some cheese, a plate – on the table that was the only other piece of furniture there.

Judith stood looking about her. 'It is strange,' she said. 'It is as though I had lived here. I know where everything was. There are the marks on the wall yet where that picture hung. It was a picture of an old man of Elizabeth's time. It hangs in the house at Uldale now. When I was a small child he terrified me. Here they would sit, my father and mother, before the fire, and up-stairs they died and I was born.'

'Ugh! It's cold,' said Warren, shivering. 'We will not stay.'

'We will make a fire,' Judith said. 'Why not? Perhaps we will bring their ghosts back with the warmth.'

He was eager to do anything that she asked. They climbed the rickety stairs, rotten now with holes, creaking at every step, into the upper storey. The rooms here were pitifully small, but had a more human air, for one of them was plainly used for sleeping by the shepherd and his wife.

'It was here I was born.' Judith stared about her. 'Uncle Tom has often told me. How he was riding through the snow and heard an infant crying. He came up here with all his dogs, and in the bed my mother lay dead, in a cradle myself, and on a chair the old woman asleep with drink. And in the next room my father dead. So he picked me up in his arms and rode off with me home.'

Warren would have wished to come close to her and put his arm around her. She looked so small and by herself. But he did not dare. In the next room they found a pile of logs. They carried some down and made a great fire in the open hearth.

They sat down near to it, close together, warming their hands. The house was filled with her father and mother. Georges seemed there too. Only dead people. And for that reason, because she could not get at the dead and her heart was so moved that she longed to be kind to the living, almost without knowing that she did it, she laid her hand on Warren's knee, and then, when she felt it throb in response, she did not care to take the hand away again.

It was the first demonstration that, unurged, she had ever made to him; after a little he, as though he were moving moun-tains or the heavens would fall, laid his hand on hers.

'The fire makes me sleepy – the fire and the cold air.' She took off her riding hat and shook her red curls about her face. 'Warren,' she said, 'you look most solemn. Well, I should also feel solemn. Perhaps I do, but I have often noticed that when-ever I feel most solemn I want to laugh.' She went on talking as though she would cover the emotion that she knew he was feeling. 'This house, deserted as it is, is better than Uldale just now. Everyone is at odds there, and I am weary of trying to make them better. I want a life of my own, Warren.'

'Come away with me, then,' he said.

'But that would be no life of my own. Since Uncle Tom carried me out of this place in his arms I have been for ever mixed with the lives of other people.'

'You can go to a nunnery,' he said laughing. He came a little closer to her. The fire was burning with splendid energy and roaring up the chimney.

'No. I am mixed with other people because I want to be. I am not such a coxcomb as to suppose that I am inhuman. I am inquisitive; I must know just what their lives are, and then I must tell them what they ought to be. And yet I wish to be by myself. I am only happy in one place, and that is Watendlath.'

'Are you not happy now?'

'I shall soon be warm, and then, when I am, I will tell you whether I am happy.'

He put his arm around her; she did not move away. Why should she if it pleased him? And he was alive. His heart was beating against her breast. She was tired of anger and disappointment. Her heart ached to be kind.

She went on talking. At last he said (his hand was trembling under hers):

'Judith, I love you every day more ... What shall be done about it?'

In ordinary times she would have checked him, but now – what did it matter? Was she not too particular in guarding herself? After all, was she so important? She had only in all her life been important to one person, and that was to Georges, and even to him for only a little of a time. How much she was making of her life, considering herself this way and that way, when in reality she was nothing. The mother of no one, the lover of no one, scarcely the friend of anyone ... She was not pitying herself – rather laughing at herself – with a little interest and tenderness, because she knew herself better than she knew anyone else.

So she let him hold her hand, then tenderly kiss her cheek, then with great gentleness stroke her hair. The trembling of his body touched her infinitely. Warren, who had faced so many things with such courage, needed her now to help and befriend him.

'Oh, Warren!' She liked him close to her, the fire was very

pleasant, and figures, friendly figures, seemed to be in the room. 'It is so long since Georges died. I wish I could let him go in peace. I shall not be a free woman until I can be friends with everyone and yet be independent. Does it make you happy to be sitting here, the two of us beside the fire?'

'Desperately happy.'

'I want you to be happy.'

Why not? Oh, in God's name why not? There was Reuben's bear, and the boy hanged on the gibbet, and Georges thrown down the stair, and John's rabbit . . . Why not be kind while one may? So soon it is all over and nothing done, no kindness remembered, no indulgence or charity. She thought, looking into the fire and feeling perhaps the figures in the room gather more closely about her, that she had never been charitable enough. If this life had a purpose (which she gravely doubted), it was for us to learn charity. A dangerous lesson, because the more charitable we became the less free we became, and this desire for freedom was becoming with her a passion. But the bear danced in the Square, the rope swung on the gibbet, Georges lay with his back broken, little Hartley Coleridge was a prisoner, the rabbit was flung out of window, Warren had a bad leg, and his wife had left him, and he loved *her*, poor man – although why he loved her she couldn't conceive.

'I have never been happy until now,' he said, resting his head on her lap. It seemed as though Georges, and the child that she had never had, and maybe her mother and father whom she had never seen, were all represented in that little damaged body holding her as though she were its only hope.

She smiled, looking out above his head. Why should she be so proud of herself? Why should she not be kind? Why should she not give anything she could that would make him happy? She sighed, touched his cheek and then surrendered, giving him all he asked—

WILL HERRIES DINES AT EASTWAYS

SHE KNEW EARLY in February that she was to have a child For some time she had been happy, and, when she was certain of this new circumstance, it was as though life beat up in her like a released fountain.

For years after Georges' death there had been no life, then slowly, slowly it had returned, always finding its source in Watendlath. Now she was going really to live again, and all she had to do was to fight for her freedom. That she had not yet secured, but she would secure it now that the child had come to help her.

She was beginning at last to understand something about life. A woman is made for the love and protection of someone or something else; this is the mainspring of her nature. But in order to employ this love and protection at its fullest she must be free of any bond that is simply a tyranny without love. All the women around Judith at this time were so bound – it would be generations before they would begin to be free – and Judith would have been held in the same way had it not been for the lives and natures of her father and mother whom she had never seen or known. The whole history of being a Herries is learning to be free.

She took things as they came. What was coming was her child. What was also coming was Will Herries to Westaways. What was also coming was some decisive crisis between Francis and Jennifer. And it seemed that all these things were arriving together.

Since the ride to Borrowdale, Forster had seen Judith less frequently. He was shy now and uncomfortable, for he had never realized so sharply that Judith did not and could not love him as at the moment of her surrender to him. He did not know that she was to have a child, but he did know that, on that day, she did not surrender to him but to her memories. She had begun by wishing to be kind to him, and then had recalled the voice and movements of a man who was dead. That hour had been filled with ghosts.

So, although he loved her with a fire that really ate into the very nerves of his small and ailing body, he came to visit her less often and, when he was with her, saw her as someone always just beyond reach.

She was resolved that he should not know about the child. It did not seem to her that it would be Forster's child at all, so filled had the ruined house been with others on that winter afternoon.

Passionately she wished that it should be born in Watendlath, in that room where Georges had died, but her practical mind saw beyond the sentiment of that desire. That her child should be born in Watendlath would involve too many others besides herself – the Ritsons, Charlie Watson, Jennifer, Francis . . . She must go away, and the child must be born with only herself for its guardian. She did not know at present where she would go or what she would do.

There were more immediate necessities, for, in this same month, on a gusty evening of February 1815, Will Herries with his wife, his son and a vast deal of impedimenta arrived at Westaways.

On the morning after his arrival Judith and Francis had a talk.

Francis looked a man twenty years more than his real age. He was so thin that his facial bones, always prominent in the Herries fashion, gave shadows and lines to his cheeks and eyes. His dark, thick hair emphasized his pallor. He looked a man with his back to the wall. Judith knew that, besides his trouble with Jennifer, he was in great distress about the condition of the people around him. The long years of the French wars had brought hunger and unhappiness everywhere; in the agricultural parts of Cumberland and Westmorland, where life was largely self-supporting and where the narrow and remote valleys led to seclusion, the pinch was not so severe as in many parts of England, but in the last twenty years industrial life was beginning to make itself felt, a new phenomenon, and towns like Kendal, Whitehaven, Cockermouth knew something that was close to starvation.

He, who had been always on the side of the people against privilege, of the rebel, the under-dog, found himself now a rich man with a fine house and a body of servants. He would like to give away all that he had, but he was not free – he had a wife, children, dependants. More than that he saw that this new growing England did not want his charity. He was held to be an aristocrat, and to be responsible for taxes, bread prices and all the other evils. Of his class he found no one in sympathy with his ideas. The squires and landholders round him thought that a sign of encouragement to a poor man meant that the poor man would rule, as he had been doing in France. The French example was before every eye. So Francis was once more alone, as all his life he had been. But he was not only alone – he was inarticulate. He had the great misfortune of seeing the justice of both sides. He, who had once proclaimed exultantly the fall of the Bastille, now feared any kind of revolution for his own country that he loved so dearly.

Until now there had been no riots in Cumberland, as in the

Midlands and the South, but only a week or two ago rioters
had burnt some ricks and stable buildings of Osmaston's, and
he himself had received several threatening anonymous letters.

If only, Judith thought, he would speak to me, say frankly
all that was in his mind, as he used to do. But it was years now
since he had been honest with her. Silence had grown upon him.
He was shut up within himself.

But now today he began frankly enough.

'Judith,' he said at once, 'I want you not to avoid Will and
Christabel because you are living here.'

That, unfortunately, produced a feeling of irritation in her –
all in a moment when she had intended to be so kind and understanding. She was suddenly tired of the lot of them – Francis,
Jennifer, Will, Christabel, all of them.

'What do you wish me to do, Francis?'

'Why . . . to go to Westaways . . . when you wish . . . as often
as you prefer.'

'And Jennifer?'

He shook his head impatiently.

'What has that to do—' He broke off. 'I often think you hate
Jennifer.'

She sat down, suddenly weary.

'Oh no – hate? – oh no, dear Francis. Perhaps I am a little
tired. What would you say, Francis, if I went away altogether?'

'Went away!' His thin pale face was aghast. He put his hand
up to his forehead in a movement of bewilderment.

'Oh no! You to desert us! It would be shameful!'

Then she was angry. There was the implied right here that
had always irritated her in him, as though, if he decided that she
was necessary for him, why, that was reason enough for anything. It was not selfishness but rather an obstinate preoccupation with his own ideas.

Her anger gave her the opportunity to say some things that
had long been in her mind. She looked up at him, and part of
her thought, 'Oh, poor Francis, how weary and despondent
he looks!' But the other part thought, 'How insensitive he is!
I have endured this long enough.'

'Listen, Francis. I am going to say one or two things. One is
that I have been here for over five years and have been a failure.
Yes – don't protest – it's true. I have been a failure with you.
Do you know that you have not spoken out your heart to me for
three years? No, not once. I have loved you all my life. You are
the only friend I have beside Emma and Reuben, whom I never

see nor hear of, and one other. But of late you have shown me no friendship. You have never thought of me at all, never inquired how I did nor how things went with me. You have been filled with your own troubles. I have been the housekeeper here. Good enough.

'Then I have failed because Jennifer hates me. Oh yes, she does! When I first came she was too languid to hate anyone. But now she is not languid any more and is perfectly capable of hatred. Do you know that when I had been here a year or so I discovered Mrs Ponder searching my drawer for my private letters? No, you did not know. But I begged Jennifer that Mrs Ponder should depart. Mrs Ponder did not depart. Later, *you* ordered that Mrs Ponder should depart – but Mrs Ponder is still here. I have not failed with the children – John loves me, I know, but even that has been an added aggravation to Jennifer. Yes, although for five years Jennifer and Mrs Ponder have done all that could be done to make me miserable (and I am not happy, you know, when people near me dislike me), I have stayed because I love you and I love your children. Or no – maybe there is too much sentiment in that. If I am strictly truthful, I have stayed in part because I like to make people do as I wish. I have stayed even because Jennifer has wished me to go. I have stayed, perhaps, because I would not be defeated by a fat snake like Mrs Ponder.

'But you, dear Francis, have never given these things one thought. You have not asked yourself whether I were lonely or unhappy. In fact, I am almost frantic for my freedom. There is a place but a few miles from here where I could be happy for ever. But, although it is so nearby, I do not seem to be able to reach it. My father, by all that I hear, was the same. But he was not a complacent female as I am.'

She smiled up at him then, feeling quite friendly again now that she had said her mind.

But he, in a voice of horrified disgust, said:

'Mrs Ponder searched your private papers. You told Jennifer of it and yet Mrs Ponder stayed?'

'Well, but *you* told Jennifer about the rabbit, and yet Mrs Ponder stayed.'

She wanted then to rise and throw her arms around his neck, so terribly unhappy did he look.

'You are right,' he said at last. 'Dreadfully right. I have been most fearfully to blame.'

Then, of course, she repented of having said anything. She

did not want to add to his distresses. What she *did* want, however, was to be free of them all and to have her life to herself!

She went on quietly: 'You see, Francis, I am the only one in this house who is friendly with Will and Christabel. What complications will come now from my being here! I cannot abandon Christabel, who was so good to me in London. And of course I cannot abandon you! I think it shameful of Will to have come here, and so I shall tell him, but I shall be a shuttle-cock between the two houses. I am nearly forty-one years of age, and that is too old for a shuttlecock!'

'You say you cannot abandon Christabel and you cannot abandon myself – but a moment ago you were implying that you wished to be free of all of us!'

'And so I do.' She shrugged her shoulders. 'And so I will. I am for ever promising myself. Tomorrow – the day following . . .'

She had risen and, instinctively, they came together. He drew her to him and they exchanged a long embrace, the first of real intimacy for years.

'Judith,' he whispered, stroking her cheek, 'do not leave me, I beg you. I beg you. I am unhappy. No one understands—'

She thought of the child alive within her, and then she was so happy that she thought humorously, 'Was ever a woman in so many complications? But this is living – every moment has excitement.' At that instant she was so much a child that she could have sat down at the spinet and strummed any discordant noise. For she loved Francis to love her. Never mind if she could not be free just yet. Time for that! She *loved* Francis to love her. He had not for so long!

'Oh, Francis, I love you!' she murmured. What would he say if he knew that she was to have a child, she who was, he thought, so faithful to Georges' memory? Well, so she was. But Georges would be glad for her to have a child. Then she could not have Francis back again without at once wanting to manage him. She drew him down on to the sofa beside her, holding his hand. She wanted at once, without delay, to make him happy! Somehow to make him happy! Her eyes were so glowing with life and eagerness and vitality that she did not seem like a small, round, middle-aged female in a grey spencer, but rather she was the daughter of a gipsy, telling fortunes.

She held his hand lightly.

'Now listen, Francis. Here is what you must do—'

And at that moment Jennifer came in.

They were both silenced. They had nothing whatever to say. Jennifer, brilliantly attired, stood there and looked at them. She was dressed for going out.

Francis thought, 'She is going to meet Fernyhirst' and was at once miserable.

Judith thought, 'I really hate this woman at last.' But did she? There was something *ignorant* about Jennifer, as though with all her beauty, her husband, admirers, children and the rest, she had never learnt anything about life at all. Just as you pity a selfish, wilful child because of the trouble that is in store for it, so Judith pitied Jennifer. And where you pity you cannot hate.

She was dressed in a crimson spencer with long sleeves that she wore open. It was lined with white fur. Over it she had a delicate Cashmere shawl and under it a long, tight-fitting dress of grey. On her head was a tiny crimson bonnet, close-fitting to the head, decorated with an upright ostrich feather. Her low boots, ankle high, showed the beautiful elegance of her little feet.

Remarkably, at this critical moment – for it was the only one at which the three of them together discussed the Westaways situation – scarcely a word was said.

Jennifer, looking at Judith as a bird of Paradise might look at a sparrow, said:

'So I hear that Will has arrived at Westaways. You know, Judith, that your visits there will inconvenience us in no way whatever. Pray visit there when you feel inclined.'

Judith got up and, simply because she knew that it would annoy Jennifer, rested her hand on Francis' shoulder.

'Thank you, Jennifer,'

Mrs Ponder was in the doorway. 'Fred is there with the carriage, ma'am,' she said. She gave her two enemies, Francis and Judith, a dark look. Yes, she had stayed there although they had told her to go. And she would stay so long as she pleased.

Jennifer, her head high, her ostrich feather nodding, swung her way out.

When the door had closed, Francis said: 'Judith, do you think? . . .' Then he stopped.

'And now,' said Judith, pointing to the sofa, 'I will tell you what you must do, Francis—'

The first occasion on which Judith dined at Westaways was on a wild, stormy afternoon in March. She was generously allowed the closed barouche by Jennifer, who was for ever making attempts to suggest that Judith was a sort of poor relation. (And indeed was she not just that in reality?)

'Dear Judith, I pray that you may have an entertaining evening. Do not encourage Christabel to call on us here.'

'I am sure that she will not wish to,' said Judith.

Jennifer looked at her closely. Was she beginning to suspect the child? Then Jennifer was clouded by a glance of apprehension. She looked back to the stairs as though to be sure that no one was there.

'Judith,' she said. 'If they talk scandal of me at Westaways – as of course they will – even though you dislike me, well, I am Francis' wife.'

'Scandal?' said Judith. 'What scandal?'

'There is always scandal in a country neighbourhood.' She looked most beautiful in the candlelight. Her dark ringlets gleamed on the soft orange texture of her Cashmere shawl.

Judith smiled, compelled by that beauty to which she was always surrendering wherever she saw it.

'How little even now you know me,' she said.

But as she climbed into the dark carriage she stubbed her shoe against the step. In the dark she nodded to herself. 'I cannot *endure* these people!' It was as though her mother, puzzled and bewildered at Herries fifty years earlier, had spoken.

But it was a most interesting evening. Judith stepped, in a moment, back into her old place. There was James, son of Pomfret and Rose, great-grandson of old Pomfret, who had built the house; he was a short, stubborn-looking fellow of thirty-six, very silent, and, everybody said, waiting for his father to die that he might succeed to the baronetcy. There was Montague Cards, in whose London rooms the famous arbitration had once taken place. He was now forty-eight, looked as though his cheeks were painted and wore most affected clothing. He spent as much of his time as possible in staying with relations free of charge. He planned to remain at Westaways longer than Will had any idea of. Carey Rockage, now sixty, was a splendid old fellow, wearing loose garments that seemed to have been made for someone else, most absent-minded but always finding something interesting and amusing to entertain himself with. Maria was now an old woman of sixty-one and looked like a haystack on wheels. She moved with a kind of rolling motion. She had peculiar habits; she would whistle to herself or, at table, make little pellets of bread and flick them about. She was so untidy that no one of her garments seemed to belong to any other. Her hair was white and she wore a lace cap, none too clean and set rakishly at an angle. For Judith, who had such a passion for cleanliness, her untidiness was an agony. She found herself, before she had been at Westaways ten minutes, running after Maria, picking up her handkerchief, fastening a button, tying a ribbon.

Will Herries was not greatly changed, save that he was a wealthy man now of forty-five, and so had swollen in importance. Not physically swollen; he was as thin and stiff as a water-pipe, and he spoke like Moses delivering the Ten Commandments to the people of Israel. Christabel also was now a middle-aged woman, dressed better than of old, and was not so deeply terrified of functions and ceremonies.

She was, however, one of those people whose anticipation of catastrophe spoils every occasion. And expectation of disaster attracts it as surely as mountains attract rain.

Walter was now their only remaining child, his sister having died some years previously of smallpox.

Walter was terrific. He was, Judith thought, the largest young man she had ever seen. Horselike as all the Herries were one way or another, he resembled a charger for whom no general, how-ever famous, could ever be grand enough. He had all the splend-our of bone and muscle united to a supreme self-confidence and determination. He was the absolute symbol of Herries, blood, bone, and soul, all mingled together, engaged upon the same pursuit. He was neither dour nor aloof like his father. He laughed often, and his laughter, Judith thought, must make the inner confines of Borrowdale quake. His chest was the broadest, his legs the thickest, his neck the strongest, his arms the most muscular that she had ever seen. Set in all this splendour were very small eyes that had a strange meditative stare, even when he was most jolly. Later in the evening she was to perceive how instantly he could change from pleasure to business. She decided that he would become the most important of all the Herries family, and she was correct in her prophecy.

Already he dominated everyone there. He wore a huge stock, a vast purple coat and immense trousers, just then coming into fashion. His hair was a dark curly brown, and he had a snuffbox as big almost as a band-box.

He ordered the servants, arranged the details of the party as though he were master of the house. Two years previously he had married Agnes Bailey, daughter of a rich City merchant. She was not present this evening because she was expecting very shortly her first child. So Walter, roaring and laughing, informed Judith, adding that if the child were not a boy he would let his wife know of it! She was a little bit of a woman, he informed Judith, whom he could slip easily into his pocket. He spoke of her with all the pride that the Herries feel for any woman who had been wise enough to marry one of them. As always, when she was with anyone of great height, she was embarrassed by her own smallness. But she soon recovered. He at once chaffed her.

'Why, you are the pocket Venus!' he cried.

'Oh, Walter!' cried Christabel. 'Pray, pray—'

But Judith laughed.

'How much brain is there in all that muscle, Cousin Walter? I've seen bullocks at a fair—'

He thought that immensely good. She found that he laughed at almost everything. She rather liked him. After the restraints of Uldale this was rather refreshing. She discovered very shortly that it was he who had persuaded his father to come to Westaways. He was all for carrying on the family feud, partly from rancour and scorn of Francis, partly from pride and physical good health. And he had never been in Cumberland before, although it was his home. Of course it was his home. His grandfather had been the best fighter in the district, and his father had been born here. That was enough for him. She saw that he was determined to get Uldale into his hands before he had done.

She was happy at once when she saw how greatly pleased Christabel and Maria were to see her. Then speedily also the light of battle was in her eye. For she perceived that they were all there, that everything was done, to impress her. She was the spy from the enemy camp, and the intention was that she should return and tell them all at Uldale that they had no chance, that they had better surrender at once, pack up and go. Well, she was going to tell them nothing of the kind. She was fond of Christabel, but she loved Francis. Poor Francis, growing old now, with nothing to show for life at all save his children, who did not know him. Yes, she was on his side, and so she would let that great hulking elephant of a Walter know before the evening was over.

The house she had never been inside before. She knew well its charming exterior; she had often walked and ridden past it, its roof covered with rosy tiles, the beautiful wrought ironwork, the door with the fluted columns and the delicate fanlight.

Within it was by far grander than Uldale, with the pillared hall, and up the wide staircase to the grand saloon that had been decorated by old Westaway himself. The subject of the decorations was Paris awarding the apple, and there were three fine, plump, rosy goddesses. In this fine room, glittering and gleaming with the candlelight and the swinging splendours of the glass candelabra, they were all gathered. Soon they went down to dinner.

Judith was seated between Walter Herries and his father, who, his back erect, his thin neck raised like a hen's, should have commanded the assembly. He did not. Walter praised the food, guaranteed the liquor, chaffed old Maria, scolded and commanded the servants.

At the last moment Warren Forster slipped in and, with a nod and a smile to them all, took his place.

'You have nothing, I wager,' Walter said to her, 'like this at Uldale.'

Judith looked about her: a very grand room with a massive fireplace, the table piled with food, perfect organization.

'I prefer Uldale.'

'You prefer Uldale? But, come now, Cousin. I may call you Cousin? What can you prefer? There is no space at Uldale, no light—'

'No light! We have all the light in the world!'

'Well, well – so has a barn. I know what I know. You shall have your Uldale.'

She looked at him with great calmness.

'You have come here, Cousin Walter, to crow over Uldale. Well, you shall not do it for me. I am old enough to be your mother, Cousin Walter, and there are one or two things I shall teach you before we are done.'

He looked at her with admiration. He liked her. He had heard that this little woman had spirit. What was she? Born in a barnyard out of a gipsy? No matter. She had pluck.

'Is Jennifer as lovely as they say?'

'She is very lovely.'

'I would go a long way for a beautiful woman. But Francis, now – he is vexed, is he not, at our taking Westaways?'

'He has other things to think of.'

'Ha, ha! ... I warrant he has, and there will be more before long. Jennifer insulted my mother, you know ... in a public place too.'

'That is an old story – and there are two sides to it.'

'Not so old that I have forgot it. And you would smack my face if there were cause, Cousin Judith. By gad, I believe you would too.'

'Certainly,' said Judith gravely, 'if there were cause.'

'Well, I drink your health, Cousin. We are to be friends.'

'I am in the other camp,' she said, smiling at him.

'It will be all one camp one day,' he answered her.

She heard Will saying with great gravity:

'I have heard my father tell many a time how as a small boy he came to this house. It was your great-grandfather Pomfret, James, who had it then, you know. Yes, and he sat there with my poor grandmother – she died shortly, poor thing – and stared and stared. For it was a grand house to him. He had never seen the like of it. And there were all the things in the room that are here yet. I will show them to you afterwards, Maria. We had them in London and brought them up with us. Out of the parlour window the fountain with the bird that has been here from the beginning. The screen with the gold work on it, the clock with the sun and moon. We had them in our London house. You must have seen them often, Maria. But what frightened my father – he was only a small boy, you know – was his great aunt Maria, sitting there with a spaniel on her lap. He often told us children of it. She had a wig with flowers and a hoop as large as a tent, a black patch on her cheek, and her fingers covered with jewellery. She was born in the year of the battle of Naseby, you know. So here we are back to the battle of Naseby.'

Will, Judith thought, was quite human all of a sudden. He was so proud of being here, back in his rightful place. Yes, she understood him and sympathized with him. Then he looked at her, as though he would say: 'Here we are, you see, and we shall remain.' Then her cheeks flushed. So would Francis remain *and* his children. She would see to that while she had breath left in her body. (Odd that only an hour or two ago, in the carriage, she had wanted to be free of the lot of them! Now she was in the very middle of the battle, and glad to be!)

More and more food appeared. (They had not dinners like this at Uldale.) More and more wine was drunk. James began, in his stubborn determined way, to talk of the present discontents. He had nothing good to say of anyone – King, Regent, Parliament, Army – but the villains of every piece were the working classes. Oh! these working classes! What was it they wanted, the dirty dogs? Why were they *never* content? They complained of the price of food. Well, let them work harder and earn more. They said that their homes were not fit to live in! What did they expect? Palaces?

Nearly everyone joined in. At Manchester and at Liverpool there were disorders every day. Of course it would be right enough now that Napoleon was safe in Elba. But would it be? Someone said that we would be fighting Russia next ... Wars were endless. One led to another. And while there were so many wars, of course trade would be bad ... At the word 'trade' Will lifted up his sharp blue-tinted chin and told them all what he thought about Trade.

Money would be in the towns – Birmingham, Liverpool, Manchester ... This new machinery ... The country would be a dead place in another thirty years. Cotton? Had any of them thought about cotton? Well, he had. India and the East were all very well, but wise men were turning their attention to home products. Now that Napoleon was shut up and the Allies were in Vienna ... In another thirty years there would be no country in England, no *true* country.

Why, when his grandfather had come first to Keswick his father, as a little boy, had ridden into Borrowdale on horseback as though you were riding into China. His father had often told him. Why, nothing on wheels had ever been seen in Borrowdale a hundred years ago, and now he wouldn't be surprised but that one day they would be driving carriages with steam. He looked at them all grimly, just like an angry and emaciated Moses.

'They'd better look out,' he seemed to say, 'or they would have the surprise of their life!' For a brief moment he dominated all of them; even Walter disappeared.

Old Maria Rockage, on his other side, listened to him and thought what nonsense he was talking. She had drunk some wine – not her customary habit – and her head was a little fuddled. To tell the truth, she was homesick for Grosset. Oh yes, she knew that this was all fine, with the fountain in the garden, and the painting of the naked women upstairs and all the shining candles. Everything was very orderly, the servants moved most quietly. There was enough food to feed the village at Grosset for a week (and that when all the countryside was starving!), but she wasn't really comfortable here. She didn't care for that big shouting Walter, and Will wasn't kind to Christabel, and the large four-poster that enshrouded herself and Carey at night was not truly a *friendly* bed, and she missed her children; even though Carey the Younger *was* fond of doing nothing, she would rather have him than this hulk of a Walter, and Phyllis was a *sweet* child . . . She began to feel very melancholy indeed. A tear fell into the goose on her plate. Then she looked up and changed a smile with Judith.

She felt better. What a pity that Judith had ever left them! They had all been very happy together! And now she heard the strangest things about Jennifer. Judith surely was not happy there. But the child (for although Judith was over forty, Maria thought of her as a child) *looked* happy. She had grown stouter. What a sensible woman! Grosset had been in pieces ever since she had left them! And it was neither nice nor kind of Will to come here simply to triumph over Francis, all because years ago Christabel had slapped Jennifer's face. Not that she had ever liked Jennifer, beautiful though she was. And they said that Francis was most unhappy . . . It was not as though he were a boy any longer . . . He must be fifty-five or so, and had done nothing with his life, poor man . . . She piled up little pellets of bread beside her plate.

Behind the wall of talk and laughter they were moving on their secret ways. Will was stiff with triumph. This was a grand dinner. He would show brother Francis at Uldale . . . Christabel longed to have a real talk with Judith. She wanted that somehow, in one way or another, they should understand at Uldale that she was not their enemy . . . In her heart she would rejoice to have a reconciliation with Jennifer.

Walter was hot and thick and turbulent with the pride of life. He saw himself as a conqueror. Of what? Of whom? It did not matter. James had in his heart contempt for all these country bumpkins, the grand Walter included. The old-maidish bachelor with the painted cheeks was enjoying the food and the wine. Here was the place for him! He would stay . . . one month, two, three? Old Carey was thinking of a dog of his, Pluto, who was as game a dog . . .

Warren Forster, who had scarcely spoken, sat, his eyes secretly fixed on Judith. Judith, placed so demurely there, once in his arms while the logs crackled in the stone fireplace. Judith, the passion of his whole life . . .

And Judith herself began to wish to escape. She felt unwell, some great uneasiness at her heart. She *was* in the camp of the enemy! It was as though she could foretell in some secret way all the consequences that were to come out of this move into Westaways, a move made from vanity and vainglory. She had sympathized with Will, but now she felt that he was there only that he might snub Francis. And as for his son! He seemed to be more overbearing with every minute that passed, as the room grew more heated, the food more grossly devoured, the wine more carelessly drunk, the lights more brilliant. He seemed to grow and hang over her in a vast imposing shadow. He had drunk great quantities of wine, but it had not affected him. Will's speech was already clouded, poor old Carey was waving his glass with uncertain hands, Monty Cards was calling for a song in a shrill high tone, James scowled ... It was time for the ladies to be gone.

They rose. Walter got up, bowed, then kissed her hand.

'Adieu, Cousin Judith!'

His purple coat with its high collar strained across his tremendous shoulders, his stock seemed scarcely to confine the muscles of his neck – but his eyes were very small. She looked up at him, glance to glance. What she would give for a few more inches! But his little eyes closed before hers. In a majestic procession the ladies left the room.

Upstairs, seated beneath the rosy goddesses, Christabel at once drew Judith aside. From where Judith sat, under the swinging glittering glass on the gilt sofa, she could look out through the curtains that were not yet drawn, to the Lake darkening now in the gathering dusk. Its bosom was shaken with trembling; its surface was crossed with paths of pale opalescent light, and one rosy shadow hung on to the green skirts of the hill. It moved Judith most strangely to see how the Lake was trembling; however, in another moment she was looking about the room and thinking how she would arrange it were it hers. That cabinet would be best in the corner and the large clock with the marble pillars ...

'And so, Judith,' Christabel was saying in that hushed anxious voice of hers, while old Maria nodded her head, jumped awake and then fell off again, 'you must understand that I have no animosity. Bygones must be bygones.'

'No, you have no animosity,' said Judith, nodding her head and swinging her legs as well as she could in her long gown (for the sofa was a trifle high). 'Of course you have none, dear Christabel. But what of Will and Walter?'

'Oh! yes!' Christabel admitted, her brow wrinkling with anxiety. 'Should not the curtains be drawn? It is almost dark. Ah, here comes Wiggins with the tea – I am half afraid of Wiggins. We brought him from London. Monty found him for us!'

Judith looked at Wiggins, who was almost as mountainous as his master, Walter. Poor Christabel – to be crushed among all these huge men! But she would like to have the managing of Wiggins. He would be child's play beside Mrs Ponder.

'Yes, Wiggins. Here, if you please. You understand, Judith, that men look upon these things quite differently. Walter regards it as a sort of a game. He does indeed, and he is very chivalrous about any insult to myself ... And Jennifer *was* rude to me, you know ...'

'So long ago!' said Judith scornfully. (Yes, and the spinet would be better nearer the window. What a lovely pattern of flowers and leaves on its cover! And then you could have the sofa ... Sofas were still rare and this was one of the finest Judith had ever seen.) What a lot of money Will must be making! Well, it was what he had always wanted ...

'At least,' Christabel went on, 'you will not leave me, dear Judith. I must see you sometimes. I must indeed. It was my only comfort in coming here. You must not hate me because Jennifer does!'

'Hate you! Dear Christabel!' Touched as always by any appeal to her affection, she leaned forward and kissed Christabel's dry cheek. 'Alas, I hate nobody! Hatred is so difficult to sustain. Even Mrs Ponder—'

'Who is Mrs Ponder?'

'An odious female.'

'And Jennifer?' Christabel looked to see that Wiggins was gone and Maria fast asleep. 'They are saying very odd things about Jennifer, Judith.'

'What things?'

'Is there not a Captain Fernyhirst? And they say that Francis—'

'I suppose Walter brings you this gossip,' Judith broke in indignantly. 'Remember, Christabel, that I love Francis more than anyone in the world. I will not hear a word against him—'

'No, no,' Christabel cried, frightened of offending Judith. 'It is only that it is common talk—'

'There is always common talk,' said Judith. 'In every country place they talk.'

She was thinking: 'Well, there you are, now it has all begun. Christabel is different already, sniffing out things about Uldale. And soon Jennifer will be saying things about Christabel.' She saw Walter on a huge horse riding deliberately past Uldale and making rude gestures, mocking the smallness of the place

and the bareness of the garden. Oh! it would be impossible!
She had an impulse to rise there and then and run for her life.

'Indeed, she did shortly run, but not before she had heard
some astonishing news. The door burst open; all the men were
there, Walter in front of them. They were shouting and crying
out. Old Maria woke up, Christabel thought the house was on
fire, Judith wondered whether Walter's wife upstairs was suddenly delivered of a child. But no! Walter was roaring out:

'What do you think? What do you think? Boney has escaped
from Elba! Escaped from Elba, by God! He's in Paris, and the
French are with him to a man! Esthwaite has looked in to tell us.
There's news for you! Boney escaped from Elba! Whoop!
Whoop! . . . What a fellow! By gad, I admire him! Escaped from
Elba, by gad!'

They were all in a frantic excitement, even James, and Monty
Cards was crying out like a woman:

'He'll be in London yet! We shall all be French before the
year's out.'

Judith, standing by herself, beside the window, felt the news
run inside her like wine. That marvellous fat little man, whose
corpulent shadow had hung over them, almost all their lives
as it now seemed, had done it again! Yes, it was wonderful. He
was a wonder. She could see, looking through the haze of the
candles, all Europe in a hurry and a scurry, hastening like ants,
hither, thither, everywhere. Stiff and conceited Talleyrand, and
the sentimental weak Russian, their own mountain of flesh, the
Regent, the old mad King, all the bourses and the shops and
the theatres, the country lanes, cottages, mountains, lakes – all
suddenly quivering again under the shadow of that little indomitable monster!

The others in the room had for the moment forgotten her.
They were all talking together; in the doorway Wiggins and
another manservant stood listening.

Bonaparte free again! You could hear the cry from China to
Peru! Well, if Napoleon could free himself so easily why should
not she?

The news and a sudden glimpse of Warren Forster's anxious,
pale face (even in the excitement he did not forget her) made her
almost mad with eagerness to get away. Away! Anywhere . . .
To have her child somewhere by herself. No Herries. No relations or duties or scandals. Napoleon had done it. She had as
strong a will.

Moved by an irresistible impulse she was out of the room and

S–Q

had slipped down the stairs. They were not thinking of her. She felt as though she had the energy to escape down the road just as she was, and in a moment she would be in Paris! Well, why not? Anything to escape. However, she found her bonnet and shawl, ran out into the garden, and then in the courtyard at the back discovered Fred. She told him that she wanted the carriage. At once! At once!

While she waited for him she smiled up at the stars that were beginning to break into the sky.

If Napoleon had done it she could! And it was as though the child in her womb laughed its approval.

JUDITH IN PARIS

THIS TIME JUDITH escaped some distance; she ran from Westaways to Paris.

In June the battle of Waterloo was fought and Napoleon's escape was concluded.

Judith told Francis and Jennifer that she would take a little holiday. She was going to stay with Emma Furze in London. Jennifer was kind to her and kissed her goodbye. Judith did not know whether she was aware of the increase in her figure or no. No one else seemed to notice anything. Francis was grave and reserved again. All he said was:

'It is not for long, Judith. Have you sufficient money?'

'Yes, thank you . . . No, it is not for long,' she answered him. She did not know whether she were lying or no. It might be for ever.

But John made a scene. Quiet as he usually was, on this occasion he made a scene. He cried himself into being sick and scratched Mrs Ponder's cheek. Then, two hours after Judith's departure, he ran away. He was found on the road to Bassenthwaite in a hedge, fast asleep . . .

On a very hot summer afternoon, in the middle of the Café des Mille Colonnes, sat La Belle Limonadière, dressed in crimson velvet and covered with jewels, serenely looking down on her hundreds of clients, like an empress, but very accurate in the change that she gave to the waiters. Spread before her were dozens of portions of broken sugar, five or six pieces in each portion, arranged in little silver saucers like wine-funnel stands. This was the remnant of the respect for sugar induced by the period when Napoleon closed Europe against English commerce. There were at this moment no sugar basins in Paris.

La Belle Limonadière, although perhaps her best time was now over, was indeed a brilliant creature. A contemporary – a gentleman certainly to be trusted – describes her as having a complexion of Parian marble. He goes on (his letter is in the Herries' archives): 'Her black hair and eyes were in striking contrast with her complexion. The usual aids of colour to the cheeks were not forgotten, but quite what the French call *au naturel* – a word merely meaning something less artificial than the last stage of artifice. *La Belle* has an air and expression of great good nature; and, what most amused me, a most solemn attitude of correctest propriety. Nobody presumes to address her without previous formal presentation, and it is found impossible to give any coffee orders to her majesty except through the medium of a gentleman-in-waiting!'

To Judith and Emma, sitting almost under her nose, this brilliant, black-haired, crimson-clad creature was infinitely fascinating. They could not take their eyes off her! She reminded Judith a little of Jennifer, only that she was not so beautiful. She always afterwards seemed to Judith to be the symbol, the decorated figurehead of this strange Paris adventure – to have the colour, the audacity and also the sordidness and under-ground thunder of this fantastic Paris scene. During all that followed in these exciting weeks, La Belle Limonadière was marching just in front, the presiding deity of this affair.

On this especial afternoon she was very gracious to a noble-looking gentleman (plainly not a Frenchman) who sat with some friends near to her, eating an ice and smiling up at the queen's throne. This gentleman, someone confided to Emma, was no other than Mr Walter Scott, the famous poet. Judith looked at him with all her eyes, and loved him at once for his grand high forehead, his eyes beaming with kindness under their shaggy eyebrows, the courtesy of his mien. He was like a very noble sort of sheepdog. When he got up and, limping on his stick, passed down the hall, she felt as though all were indeed well with this strange world, which was neither so fantastic nor so threatening as she had thought it.

For although she was greatly enjoying it all she was also rather frightened. For one thing they had not very much money, she and Emma, for another she was not very well, she who had

always been so strong and so healthy. And then she was taken
with strange waves of homesickness, wondering whether Francis
were in health, whether the meals at Uldale were served properly,
whether John missed her and what the clouds were doing to
Skiddaw.

However you cannot, as she was for ever discovering, both
have your cake and eat it, and this was most truly a fascinating
scene. Paris was now a hotch-potch of all the nations of the
world. This splendid hall, mirrored all round, divided by fluted
Corinthian pillars, made the company seem innumerably
multiplied. Here were English officers, then Highlanders with
their plumed bonnets, now Prussian hussars, and again Bruns-
wickers in their sombre uniforms. The French ladies, in their
walking dresses and in high-crowned, plume-covered bonnets
and shawls, were attended by their beaux, who were as gay,
lively and noisy as though there had been no revolutions, no
devastating wars, and as though their country were not at the
moment occupied by the triumphant foe.

But how dazzling this scene, thought Judith, and how
unreal the figure of the strange crimson hostess, her figure,
solemn, correct, almost austere, multiplied in all these mirrors, herself entrenched with peaches, sugar and nosegays of
flowers!

Beneath all the gaiety and sparkle you felt that the ground
trembled. The English were popular, but the Prussians were
hated. She saw on every side of her the Prussian arrogance.
She had heard that when Wellington had protested about some
outrageous piece of conduct, Blücher had replied: 'Yes, but
remember – the French were never in England.' The very
fact that the French found it so difficult to submit to the domination of a people whom they had so long despised, caused those
people to be more arrogant. In the cafés their behaviour made
Judith, who, when the English were not in question, was, because of Georges, more French than the French, tremble with
indignation. And the whole public life of the French, so that
they seemed to be never at home but spent their whole time in the
cafés, the theatres, or on the boulevards, made this trouble with
the Prussians the more prominent.

But then, as she by this time thoroughly realized, the French
themselves were scarcely, as yet, disciplined. They had not
suffered a revolution in their country so long a while for nothing.
The French boys in the street, for instance, were insolent
beyond belief, and she and Emma were for ever encountering

both men and women who seemed to them like dangerous animals just let loose from their cages.

She found evidence enough of it in the lodgings; they were in the rue Vivienne. They had two rooms in the apartment of Monsieur and Madame Dufresne. Little M. Dufresne, thin as a stick, with a funny black toupee and a tiny black moustache, had suffered some terror in his earlier years from which he seemed to find it impossible ever to escape. His chief pleasure was in animals, so that he had in his room a cockatoo, a monkey, three dogs, two cats and a tortoise. For animals he had, it would seem, a very special gift, but for human beings no gift at all. His wife, on the other hand, was a large brawny woman, whom Judith could well imagine knitting in front of the scaffold while the tumbrils rolled up. Her great muscular arms were always bared to the elbow and she had a deep bass voice like a man's. They were a pair who led their own lives – they interfered with neither Judith nor Emma in any way, but at night one could hear the thick, low rumble of Madame's voice through the wall; it seemed to threaten every sort of vengeance.

However, here they were in the Café des Mille Colonnes and enjoying every moment of it. For Emma, indeed, this stay in Paradise was simply heaven. She had her darling Judith to look after and care for, and there rolled all around her the very life that Fate should have designed for her. She was now a woman between fifty and sixty, handsomer than she had ever been, for her figure, tall and majestic, had thinned, and her grey hair, her sparkling eager eyes, her vitality attracted attention wherever she went.

She was more ready now to be spectator than actor, but the sight of almost any man stirred her blood and excited her curiosity. And had ever a city in the world's history been so grandly filled with splendid men as was Paris at this moment? Glorious men, and most especially the Highlanders, who, in their intriguing costume, simply had the French ladies at their feet!

She was always on the move, for ever seeing the sights. They went to the Opera, saw the King, a most benevolent-looking gentleman, the Emperor of Austria and the Duke of Wellington. They witnessed a ballet in which some of the performers were dressed as Highlanders, and heard the building ring with cries of '*Vivent les Ecossais!*' – a glorious moment. There were constant processions, and one morning they saw pass no less than thirty thousand Russian soldiers. They went to the Théâtre des

Variétés and saw 'Jean Bool' most amusingly caricatured. Best of all, perhaps, were their visits to the encampment of the English troops – the 95th Rifles, 52nd Light Infantry, and 71st Highlanders – in the Champs Elysées. This was one of the sights of Paris and immensely Emma enjoyed it. The world seemed only to exist to provide handsome military forms and fine ladies to gaze upon them.

She would, in fact, have known perfect happiness had it not been for a certain anxiety about Judith. Judith had been the one constant and unchanging devotion of her life. She would never have claimed for herself that she had a constant nature. She had not one herself, nor did she, any longer, expect constancy of others. She knew, she said, human nature too well.

But Judith was changed. You must expect it, of course. Judith was over forty and the child coming. It was no light matter to have your first child when you were over forty. But there was more in it than this. In the first place, Emma could not understand Judith's devotion to Georges. No, she certainly could not! It was true that Georges had never really liked her, but it was not that she was prejudiced. She could never have fallen in love with Georges herself; but one of the things that life taught one was that everyone must have, and be permitted to have, their own taste!

No, but Georges had not been good to Judith; he had been a thoroughly worthless, selfish fellow; and here she still was, after all these years, adoring him as though he had been a paragon!

But she was filled with contradictions. She adored Georges' memory, but some other man was father of her child. She had always seemed to Emma one of the most virtuous of women, possessing in fact a virtue that poor Emma herself could never hope to command. And yet she had apparently given herself to a man for whom she did not greatly care, simply from an impulse of kindness. Emma herself was kind, but she was also passionate, even now when she was nearing sixty. But Judith was passionate only in relation to Georges. And how ironical that she had offered all that love to Georges, who was never to give her a child, but that now, when she was almost past child-bearing, a chance moment with someone whom she did not love should accomplish everything! But life was like that. Emma herself could remember . . .

Beyond her nostalgia for Georges there was a deeper nostalgia, and this Emma could not understand at all. For it seemed from Judith's brief and broken confidences – Judith talked very little about herself even to Emma – that she thought that could she only get away to Watendlath, leave for ever all her Herries relations, and hide herself in the hills for the rest of her days, all would be well.

'Surely then,' cried Emma, 'in heaven's name, go! You are your own mistress!'

But that, it seemed, was exactly what Judith was not. She was for ever being dragged back into Herries affairs.

'But you are not so weak!' cried Emma.

'But don't you see,' Judith answered, 'it is a struggle inside myself. And one day it will be too late. I shall be compelled to choose, and shall make the wrong choice. And then I shall be inside the Herries for the rest of my days. And the worst of it will be that I shall like it – and I shall have lost all my real life for ever.'

Not that Judith often talked like this. But she was brooding, Emma knew, too much within herself. If Emma made a fool of herself, which she often did, she burst into a rage or a flood of tears and it was all over. But Judith took things to heart. And then of course you did brood when you were having your first child. Poor women! What a time they had! And then Emma would see a Highlander pass by, with a great swing of the haunches, and be glad indeed that she was a woman!

On this particular afternoon Judith was in the highest spirits. They came out into the Palais-Royal, chattering and laughing. Judith was full of Mr Walter Scott – what fine eyes, how kindly an expression, how interesting his limp made him! Emma had never read one of his poems – they looked so very long – but she was prepared to find anyone noble whom Judith thought to be so.

The Palais-Royal was a place of enchantment. Under the hot afternoon sun it glittered and glowed with its life and splendour. It was a little city in itself. In shape an oblong quadrangle with piazzas completely around it, a garden planted with rows of trees, laid with gravel, with flowers and grass plots enclosed. Under the piazzas were countless shops, far more brilliant, as it seemed to Judith and Emma, than the shops of London. On the ground floor, coffee-houses and restaurants; on the principal floor upstairs, coffee-houses, gaming-houses, exhibitions; higher up again, what a Herries traveller of the period calls in his Journal 'the abodes of vice and profligacy'. (This is from the Journal of Rodney Herries, the very pious younger brother of James, who in middle life took orders, and was ultimately Archdeacon of Polchester.) He goes on: 'The attics are inhabited by filth, misery, and crime, in endless variety and in a manner that renders it much safer to take that fact on hearsay than on actual reconnaissance. I should have mentioned,' he piously continues, 'that below the pavement are places much corresponding in character to the attics, though many of them are only cheap cafés, traiteurs, or pastry-cooks, of fair respectability.' He ends in a passage of particular eloquence by calling the Palais-Royal 'This immense gangrene'.

It was for Judith wonderful in all its mingled life, its wealth and poverty, fine ladies and scoundrels, triumphant soldiers and washerwomen, ordinary quiet Frenchmen and ruffians almost in rags, clerics and flower-sellers, tourists and solemn officials. They had been in it so often, Emma and she, that she wondered why it seemed today to have some special significance for her.

She stood for a moment under the burning sun, jostled on every side, trying to define her impression. She was being reminded of something. The broad space around her seemed to narrow. The dazzling sunlight on the white walls darkened. She was suddenly chilled. The movement was frozen. She heard a voice in her ear: 'No, madam, I fear the crowd is too great . . . Yes, he stole from his master's till . . . a butcher . . .'

She caught Emma's arm. 'Let us go home, Emma. We must rest before this evening.'

'Why, my dear, you are pale. You are unwell.'

'No, but I was reminded of something.'

Afterwards, in the dark little room in the Rue Vivienne, she said to Emma:

'Emma, I am sure that something will happen to us in the Palais-Royal. I shall not return there.'

And Emma thought to herself: 'It is beginning. These fancies that women get at such a time!'

She made her lie down, and sat beside her, telling her lively improper stories of her own past life. Through the wall they heard the odd plaintive chatter of M. Dufresne's monkey. It chattered like a child, then broke into an angry scream. Then the dogs barked. Then could be heard the deep menacing rumble of Madame Dufresne.

Their window was open because of the heat, and from far below them came the rattle of carriages, the crying of wares, the distant dreamy cadence of a band. In the air was the smell of Paris, the scent of carnations, the tang of baking bread, the hot touch of the iron trellises before the balconies, the sniff of crumpled paper, dry almost to burning-point. Judith was almost asleep. Once opening her eyes, looking at Emma, she said: 'I saw a boy hanged once in London. I thought of it today.'

'I know; you have told me of it often,' said Emma composedly. 'What is a hanging? You are too sensitive, my darling.'

'Perhaps I shall die when the child is born.'

'Nonsense. Nonsense. Die! I never heard such folly!'

'I know how cool it is now up Newlands, and how the breeze blows above the turf of Maiden Moor ... I rode once, but only once, with Francis to Hawkeshead, and then up the hill to where the two little tarns lie. Oh, Emma, you never saw a thing so quiet and so cool when a great white cloud floats overhead and Fairfield and Helvellyn watch over you ... Oh, how hot it is, and how sorry I am for Monsieur Dufresne's monkey ... Madame Dufresne will murder us one night in our beds. She hates us for Waterloo. And she will hide our bodies in that vast cupboard with the creaking door. I am sure there are rats in the wainscot ... Emma I *know* that something will happen to us in the Palais-Royal, and that great woman with the black hair and the crimson dress will sit above us and watch us torn to pieces while she arranges pieces of sugar ... I wonder how Francis is, and whether he has that blackberry preserve that he loves. They are always forgetting to have it on the table unless I am there ... I wonder if you can see the Scottish hills clearly today, and what they are doing at Westaways ... That crimson woman has Jennifer's air ... Jennifer would be fine in a café with mirrors multiplying her ... How I wish I knew Mr Scott! He has stayed, I know, with Mr Southey. Francis may have met him ...'

She dropped away to sleep while Emma, her eyes full of devotion, watched her and listened to M. Dufresne's monkey.

That evening they went to the Tivoli Gardens. Judith, after a long sleep, had recovered all her spirits and was ready for any amusement. Here there was plenty. They had quite agreed that the place could not compare with Vauxhall for size and splendour; but the summer evening was so lovely, the crowd so diverse and so intent upon enjoyment, that it was impossible not to be merry. There was a great crowd on this especial night, for it was said that the King and the Duchesse d'Angoulême were to be present to see the floating of an illuminated balloon. Emma had said that the Duchess would not be there, because she was so devout that she considered all amusement harmful. In fact no Crowned Heads were present, nor could they persuade the

balloon to rise, although a great many people paid five francs
to stand within the ropes to see it do so.

There were all the regular diversions. One of the principal
of them was to guess who were French officers; for in spite of
Blücher's order that any discovered should be at once appre-
hended and treated as prisoners of war, Paris was filled with them.
Then there was the gaiety of going around in a circle – the gentlemen on wooden horses, the ladies in chairs – in order to carry
off with a small sword a ring hung out upon a post for the purpose; or you might get into a boat and ride about on a small
artificial pond scarcely larger than the boat; or you might watch
Mlle Sachi, elevated sixty feet on a tightrope; or there were the
fireworks, *quite* as good as Vauxhall; or you might simply laugh
at the costume of the French ladies, which seemed to Judith
and Emma very ugly, with the high headdress, the hair drawn
tight from the temples and forehead over a coif, or hid with a
high-crowned bonnet covered with feathers, no perceptible
waist, but a loose robe hanging like a sack from the throat to the
ankles, carefully collected about the wrists, and a shawl worn
three-corner-wise. Emma and Judith thought these styles most
absurd and laughed together a great deal.

However, the grand feature of the Tivoli, as of every other
place of entertainment in Paris, was the dancing.

Everyone formed a circle round the dancers, who did everything possible to be as widely observed as might be. One
gentleman was pirouetting round on his wooden leg and vastly
enjoying it.

Soon a grave French gentleman with a square black beard
invited Emma to dance, and, old though she was, she eagerly
agreed, giving Judith a nod and a wink and setting off into the
middle of the ring as though she were not a day more than twenty.

Judith was tired and sat down on a little wooden bench. The
green of the trees was as brilliant as fresh paint under the
illuminations, and between the leaves the evening sky showed,
soft and delicate and tender. She loved to see people happy, to
hear their cries of pleasure, to see the children running, to watch
the sturdy simple faces of the English soldiers as they walked
about in pairs, gravely considering the French girls, to catch
the quick coloured flash of the fireworks, blue and green and
red, above the dark water of the little pond . . . She was tranquil.
She was waiting for the delivery of her child. She felt at peace
with all the world; she owed no one a grudge. When she
thought of how hazardous and desolate had been her entrance

into the world she was fortunate indeed to have had so full and adventurous a life. When her child came she would see that it had all that she could give it. Poor Warren! She thought of him with warm kindliness and affection. She was glad that he did not know what had happened to her.

She heard a familiar voice say 'Judith', looked up and saw Warren Forster standing in front of her.

At once she cried: 'Oh, Warren, how ill you look! Sit down. Sit down here beside me!'

That was at first all that she could think about. He did look very ill. His sharp face, always strained with the memory of past suffering, was grey and haggard. He was so frail that, although when she began to think of all that his being there in Paris would mean, she would be intensely aggravated, she wanted now to put her arm around him and protect him. He sat down beside her. She patted his knee. He thought as he looked at her: Had she any idea of what his finding her meant to him, of what burning dizzy happiness it was to him to look at her small child-like face with its honest eyes, its rather sharp ironical mouth, its clear smooth brow, the whole energy of her sturdy compact body, the independence, courage, humour that her poise always implied? No, she did not know. Had she known she would not have had the heart to leave him without a word.

'Well, Warren. What are you doing in Paris?'

'I have been searching for you for a whole fortnight, every day, all the time—'

'But how did you know that I was in Paris?'

'Francis told me.'

'Francis! – but he did not know my address.'

'No; that is why I have been searching for a fortnight. I have been looking everywhere. I had a feeling that today I should find you.'

'But what did you want to find me for?'

'Oh, Judith, you should not have left England without telling me! That was not kind of you. And the other also was not kind.'

'What other?'

'I know everything. Jennifer told me ... Yes. I went one day to Uldale. I had not seen you for three weeks. I must see you, so I went to Uldale. Jennifer was in a temper. She had been furious. When I stood in the hall, asking for you, she leaned over the stair and said, quite loud, anyone could have heard,

' 'Judith has run away because she is going to have a child!" '

'Oh!' cried Judith. 'Did she ?'

'Yes. And so I then at once understood everything. How could I have been so blind, so selfish ?'

'So now they all know,' said Judith slowly. 'Well – it does not matter.'

'I was crazy with anger at myself. All these months and I had never thought! I went to Francis and demanded to know where you were. All he could tell me was that you were in Paris.'

'Poor Warren,' said Judith, patting his knee with her gloved hand. 'You look so very unwell.'

'So then I went to Will Herries and said that I must be permitted a holiday. He made some demur, but Walter said that it would be right. It did not matter. Walter is staying at Westaways through the summer. So then I came to Paris.'

'But why do you look so ill, Warren ?' she asked again. 'What have you been doing to yourself ?'

'It is my heart – nothing at all. I have been so anxious about you. Oh, Judith, you should not have gone without saying anything to me!'

'Why not ? It was no one's affair.'

'No one's affair! It is my child as well as yours. And I love you so. Ah, let me say that once again. For a whole fortnight I have been searching for you. I deserve to be allowed to tell you that I love you. And now you are going to be mother to my child. That is so wonderful that I cannot believe it is true.'

'It is true enough.' She sighed. Here she was – caught again! But he looked so unwell that she could think of nothing else. She would take any trouble now, when he looked so unwell, not to hurt him. She began to be very practical.

'Now listen, Warren. I am here with a friend – Emma Furze. You have heard me speak of her. We are in lodgings in the Rue Vivienne together.'

'I am in an hotel near the Palais-Royal.'

'Near the Palais-Royal. Very good. Then tomorrow morning—'

'Oh, not tomorrow morning!' he broke in. 'I have been two weeks looking for you. Allow me to stay with you for a little while this evening.'

'Our rooms are very small.'

'I do not mind what they are. I must see that you are comfortable. You must have better rooms. You must allow me—'

'Nonsense, Warren. Everything is very nice where we are.'

A moment later Emma arrived, very heated. She smiled at the square-bearded gentleman, who bowed significantly, as though they had agreed on a further meeting, and went away.

'Oh, such a charming man! And he speaks perfect English! He is a Professor of Languages, and his wife has been dead five years. He has a—'

'Emma, this is a friend of mine from England. Mr Warren Forster.'

So this is the father of Judith's child, thought Emma, this little pale insignificant man!

She was inclined to be resentful, because he had provided all this trouble for Judith, but when she saw how ill he looked her heart was melted and she was as eager as was Judith that he should be comfortable.

They hailed a carriage and drove to the Rue Vivienne. Oh, dear! thought Emma, how he does love her, poor man! For he continued to look at her as a dog looks at its mistress, a fashion that always irritated Judith, who thought that everyone should be equal.

Warren insisted that he should pay the carriage. That Judith permitted him. Then they went through the courtyard, climbed the dark and smelling stairs.

In the close little sitting-room Warren said: 'What is that?'

'It is the monkey and the cockatoo in the next room.'

Emma was very tactful and went away. She knew that they would want to talk to one another. There were only two chairs. He insisted that Judith should take the larger. So she sat there, her hands behind her head. She felt her child move beneath her heart, her child and his. He sat very erect in the stiff-backed chair, leaning forward, his thin fragile hands tightly clasped together.

'Oh, I am so glad that I have found you!' he said. 'If you knew how happy it makes me. And that you are to be the mother of my child – that is the proudest thing that has ever happened to me!' Then as he saw that she was going to speak: 'No, don't say anything yet – pray, pray do not. I know that you do not love me, that you have never loved me. But you have given me such great kindness, and now that we are to have a child, I do not know – I do not know—' He broke off, twisting his hands nervously together. He looked up at her, smiling like a child asking a favour. 'It is a bond.'

But that was exactly what she would not have it. How was she to be honest with him without hurting him?

'No – Warren. I must be free. I am bound to no one, and the

child will not be bound either.' She got off the chair and came to
him and stood close to him. She put her arm round him, and he,
like a child with its mother, bent his head against her.

'You know, Warren, I have told you before. I have only
touched life deeply once. I have only once loved and I never
shall again. At that time I was so young that I did not know
that that would be the only time. But I could not have valued
it more highly even if I had known. And at the end when he was
dying and said that he loved me ... No, no,' she broke off,
her hand trembling on his shoulder, 'that was my real life. Nothing, my dear friend, has been quite real to me since. And I
came to France because I wished my child to be born in Georges'
country, and if I have been unfair to you, forgive me. I did not
mean it—'

'No, no,' he broke in, 'never unfair. You have been only good.'

He bent forward and kissed her. She went on eagerly:

'We will make you comfortable, Emma and I. We will all be
together. I was wrong, Warren dear, not to see you more frequently in England. That was most reprehensible, but now we
will make you well. We will all be so happy together—'

For he looked so ill, poor little man. He had sunk against the
hard back of his chair. His fingers clutched her hand. His face
was the colour of ash. His lips were purple.

'Yes ...' he murmured. 'I am ill ... my heart ... In my
coat ... drops.'

She rushed to his carriage-coat that he had flung off when he
came in. In a pocket she found a little bottle. He murmured
directions. She thought that he was going to die. There seemed
nothing so important in all her life as to save him. Little by
little he came to himself. His lips were less blue. He even smiled
a timid nervous smile.

'The pain,' he murmured. 'The pain is very terrible.'

'Oh, you must remain here!'

She knelt by him, stroking his hair, holding him close to her.

'Are you better? Are you better now?'

'Yes, I am better now.'

'Of course, you must remain.'

She thought what she could do. One of the beds must be
moved out of the other room. She and Emma could sleep
together. Reassuring him that she would return in a moment
she went out to find Madame Dufresne, and behold that woman,
who had been so fierce and so sinister, was now the very soul
of kindness.

Emma also was there. All together they moved the bed. Then alone Judith helped Warren to undress, as a mother her son. She gave him one of her own nightdresses. Very small and wan he looked lying there, never taking his eyes from her face. The doctor had been sent for.

She sat down beside the bed, sewing at something for the child.

She could hear very faintly the street noises. The candle flickered and threw great shadows on the wall. He put his hand out, took hers and kissed it.

'Now, now ... you are to sleep. That is what you are to do.'

But she bent forward, leaned over the bed and kissed his forehead. He closed his eyes as though in an ecstasy of happiness. She continued quietly to sew, to listen for the doctor. She felt the child move in her womb. How strange life was! That she should be sitting here in Paris, waiting for her child to be born, Warren in bed in her room!

How strange, incongruous, foolish and touching! She felt a strong pride as though she had her hand on life, a mettlesome steed, restive under her touch, restive but obedient!

PALAIS-ROYAL

'SON ALTESSE LE PRINCE DE BENEVENTO!'

'That is Talleyrand,' whispered Emma, who was in so frantic a state of excitement that the feather in her head-dress wobbled like a live thing.

Oh! thought Judith, how I wish they were all here to see us – Will, Christabel, Walter, Pomfret, Rose, Maria, Carey, Francis, Jennifer and the children, John and Dorothy. How they would adore it – the brilliant colours of the uniforms, the flash of the decorations, the silks, satins, shawls, diamonds of the ladies!

It was not Judith's natural disposition to want to show off, even to the members of her family whom she disliked most; but this was one of the great Balls of History!

How was it that they were there at all? Well, Warren had encountered (on the first day that he was able to go out after his recovery from his heart attack) a business friend of Will's, a Monsieur Rakonitz of the famous Viennese jewellers, and he knew everyone: had supped with Blücher and shown rubies to the King of Prussia, and sold a bracelet to Fouché. He had suggested that he could find three tickets for Warren. In all probability he had some deal with Will in hand, or wanted Will's influence for something. In any case, he was a grand jolly fellow, with a big beard and his hat cocked on one side. Then, unlike so many men with their hats cocked on one side, he had remembered his promise, and Warren had had his tickets.

So here they were, as merry and excited as three children. Judith was very near her time, and, in consideration of her age and that this was her first child, it had been wiser of her perhaps not to have come, but she could not resist it. She could never refuse to have fun, nor could she refuse to be kind to anyone, and she knew that Warren's evening would be nothing were she not there with him.

Not so Emma. She was devoted to Judith; but whether Judith were there or no she would enjoy herself. Her purple gown, her splendid turban, gave her a fine dramatic air, as of a prophetess given to acting tragic roles at occasional moments. This was her pose while she remembered, but when she forgot she was simply a tall jolly libertine, ready to smile at anything and eager for every kind of attention, with a heart that Warren, who did not really like her, described as 'incredibly open'.

Judith stood beside her, insignificant in the white gown that hid her figure, a little, very ordinary, middle-aged woman, but to Warren more magnificent and splendid than any one there.

They stood against the wall under a huge galaxy of candelabra, and Warren told them who everyone was.

Talleyrand was an old, powdered, old-fashioned gentleman. He might have been any card-playing, gently-flirting, fussy-about-his-food-and-his-bottle, old gentleman – one of the milder, politer Herries, Judith thought. But when you looked at him more closely (and they had an excellent opportunity, for he stood near to them, smiling, bowing, his sharp eyes ceaselessly darting now into this face, now on to that stubborn back, now beyond the other ingratiating desire for recognition) you could see an elaborate calm, a dangerous mildness . . .

'*Le Duc d'Otrante!*'

Fouché, the villain of the piece, the super-policeman, sly devil, malicious tyrant, admirable teller of indecent stories . . .

'*Sa Majesté le Roi de Prusse – leurs Altesses Royales les Princes Royaux de Prusse – le Duc de Mecklembourg.*'

The Prince of Orange, pale from his recent wound, Lady Castlereagh, General Alava, the Prussian King, plain, kindly,

stout, melancholy, the princes his boys, also melancholy ... Oh
yes, it would be agreeable to have Francis here, *dear* Francis
whom, now that one was away from him, one loved as deeply
as ever ... he would enjoy this and would look so distinguished
and for a moment would forget Jennifer ... and oh! if Jennifer
suddenly entered how startled everyone would be! What a
wonderful entrance she would make, moving lazily like a queen,
ever so slightly smiling in her consciousness of the great beauty
that she was, and Talleyrand would bend his little figure forward
and inquire of Lady Castlereagh, and Fouché would turn his sharp
eyes, and the Prussian King would stroke his melancholy cheek.
Yes, Jennifer should have been a queen in some country where
everyone admired her, where there would be little work ...

And then followed the great thrill of the evening. An important body of officers and aides-de-camp, a rather aged, not
very interesting officer at their head, and the announcement:

'*Son Altesse Sérénissime – le Prince Blücher.*'

Everyone pushed forward to stare at him, and then what a
moment! halfway down the salon, Wellington moved forward
and, meeting with smiles, the two great heroes shook hands.

But for Judith even that was not the final climax, for, just
behind her, she heard a voice say 'Look at that – a few weeks
ago those two men delivered Europe' – and, half turning, saw
standing quite close to her, whom but Mr Walter Scott?

His expression was one of rapt and intense fervour. His eyes,
from under their heavy eyebrows, glittered with emotion. She
thought there were tears in them. As he leaned forward, his
high-domed forehead rising into an odd peak, his strong
shoulders set, the nobility of his mouth speaking of all the kindness (and yet firmness and stiff obstinacy too) that a Scottish
gentleman is capable of, she felt that she *must* speak to him,
wisdom, folly, or no.

'It is not wonderful to be present at such a moment?'

He turned and saw a modest, stout little body in a white
gown. As he greatly preferred modest and simple people to any
other, he smiled like a brother and gave a little bow.

'It is indeed, madame.'

He turned his eyes back to Wellington and Blücher. She did
not venture any more, but she pulled Warren away to a little
distance and whispered in a voice husky with excitement:

'I have just spoken with Mr Walter Scott.'

She was so happy and Warren was so happy that they were
united in this hour more than they had ever been. For some weeks

she had been looking after him, and he had needed her so; she had grown as a sister, as a mother, fonder and fonder of him. And he *was* someone to be fond of. She had not known that he had so tender and gentle a nature, one so honest and sincere. And in knowing him better she perceived a new and a better side of the Herries character, something more generous, easy, and kind. Francis had had that strain, Maria and Carey had some of it, even Pomfret and Rose. If only their wretched ridiculous family quarrels did not obscure it!

She said to Warren one day:

'Although you are but *quarter* Herries you are the *right* quarter! You are what we all ought to be!'

He flushed with pleasure.

'You can say that when yourself—'

'Oh no, I am all wrong. I shall turn into the most awful old woman if I live. Always grab, grab at people, and they will all run – and then I shall blame them and not myself.'

So tonight they both forgot Emma (who was quite capable of entertaining herself) and wandered about in blissful excitement together. Every once and again, laying her hand on his arm, she would say: 'Are you certain that you are quite well? You feel nothing? You are sure?'

And he would answer radiantly: 'I am too happy to feel ill.'

His features were very pale, she thought, but otherwise he had filled out again. His body was sturdy and firmly set once more.

They saw many interesting things. They saw a portrait of Napoleon resting against the wall, the stern fixed eyes gazing out upon this scene that emphasized his defeat. They saw in the ante-chamber of the great supper-room Wellington himself slip across to a small supper-table and join Lady Castlereagh and Mr Scott. They were all very gay and merry, Lady Castlereagh indeed screaming like a peahen.

They themselves went out into the gardens, where long supper tables were laid and hundreds of people were supping. They sat down at a table under the trees from which lights were shimmering. Everywhere there was a flood of noise like the sea, multitudinous voices, laughter, knives, forks, plates, the popping of corks, the rhythm and pattern of the distant band.

'Oh, Warren, I feel as though something wonderful were going to happen with the birth of our child. Will it, do you think? Am I cheating myself? I have not been so happy since I was with Georges. You know I came to Paris because of Georges, do you not? You are not angry, are you? Because now I am so glad that you came. I wasn't glad at first. I was so *sickened* of Herries. All quarrels and temper, and no one caring for anyone. I wanted to be rid of it all. But now you are yourself, dear Warren. We are splendid friends. I care for you so much. I am glad that it is your child. Is it not ridiculous that it cannot be always like this, you and I and the child? I don't *want* to go back to all the Herries character. It will catch me up, and I shall like it and become a managing, *nasty* old woman, and be too old to know that I am . . . You must save me from that, Warren.'

He put his hand on hers. 'You are so good, Judith . . .'

'No, I am *not* good. I have never done anyone good. Emma said that the other day, and that when I met her first she was drunken and lost. But Emma would never be lost. She has too great a vitality. And I did Georges no good either. But now perhaps, if I choose rightly and stay outside the Herries family—'

'You must eat some of this chicken,' said Warren. 'This chicken is excellent.' Then added inconsequently: 'I have not long to live. Another attack like that last one will finish me. But I want you to know, Judith, that you have given me the happiest days of my life. I did not know I could be so happy . . .'

'Yes, is not this chicken excellent? It would be nice to have Francis here, and Maria—'

'Ah, now you want others—'

'No. It is beautiful as it is. But I want everyone to be happy tonight. Imagine! All the Kings eating chicken only a yard away! And I spoke to Mr Scott and I heard the Duke say "Damnation". Would it not be funny, Warren, if I suddenly had my baby here on the grass, in a corner under the tree? And then we would ask Mr Scott to be its godfather. I do hope that it is a boy. What shall we name him? Some new name. Not a Herries name, like Francis or Pomfret.'

She sucked a chicken bone, holding it in her fingers.

There was a '*grimacier*' entertaining a crowd on the lawn away from the tables. At his side were the long windows flooded with light, phantasmal figures moving within, beyond him; behind him shadows pooled with dancing candleshine, and into the pools figures moved with white, excited, laughing faces. The King of Prussia's two boys were there, laughing at his antics. He was a long cadaverous man and wore a sheepskin cap. He made the most extraordinary faces, pulling his chin down, wrinkling his forehead, closing his eyes. He imitated the English, did a Highlander making love to a French girl, 'Jean Bool' and his wife eating at a restaurant, Napoleon running from Waterloo, Mlle George singing a song.

Judith began to laugh.

'He is so clever. Is he not clever? Oh, Warren, see – look what he does with his cap! Is not that marvellous?'

She laughed till she cried. They stood close together and then hand in hand, while Emma, in another part of the garden, told a stout Frenchman how comic he was; and Fouché took the leg of a chicken in his fingers and cracked the bones with his teeth as though they were so many condemned criminals.

Then came the fearful day, never to be forgotten by Judith as long as she lived, September 4th, 1815.

On the early afternoon of that day they walked, the three of them, to view the site of the famous Bastille. At first they had all been in the highest spirits. Judith had, in the last few days, been feeling almost incredibly weary, but heavy though her body was, her heart was light. Since the day of the famous Ball she had known a new relationship with Warren, a deeper intimacy. They were now like brother and sister; she could care for him, watch over him without any falseness on her side or irritation on his. On these days he poured out everything from his heart, talked and talked as though he could never tell her enough, and she loved to listen. It was all thrilling and exciting to her as though she had shared in it. Emma, occupied with many romances of her own, left them much to themselves.

Then, early on this morning of the Fourth of September, Judith awoke in a panic. She lay on her bed, feeling the child kick in her womb, wondering whether it were a bad dream that she had. Some figure seemed to be in the room with her, now it was young Hartley Coleridge twisting one leg round the other, now Reuben, now young Stane, and now, more definitely, La Belle Limonadière from the Palais-Royal with her black hair and crimson dress, arranging the lumps of sugar.

The figures faded as the light in the room grew clearer. There was no one there. The panic remained.

They started to walk in the afternoon, but it was very hot, and they called a carriage. Little light silver clouds flecked the sky, the buildings were pigeon-colour, the air full of the scent of flowers, there was the echo of bands, distant as though from behind closed doors.

They crossed the bridge of Austerlitz, drove gently along the boulevards and then came to the site. Here they got out, dismissed the carriage and walked about, seeing, from every angle, where the famous attacks of 1789 had been made. For Judith this was an event of poignant memories. She could see now David advancing across the bright shining grass of the Uldale lawn to meet Francis, then the talk, the quarrel, the uplifted stick. If David had lived, had Sarah not 'gone crazy' ... Ah well, what was the use of that kind of memory? Every link in the chain must be there; she would not be here now had she not ridden over to Stone Ends and struck a small boy because he loved her hair; she would not be the woman she was had she not rescued Reuben's brother in Cockermouth, had she not ...

She dragged herself wearily after the other two (how tired she was, how hot the day, how heavy the child within her!), but she smiled when Emma, who was being very dramatic over the Revolution, turned to her; she put her hand through Warren's arm, and was interested in everything.

What they especially were interested in was an immense wooden shed, in the middle of the site, and a half-finished colonnaded tower of freestone. This was enclosed with a wooden paling and had a gate. Inside the gate on a stool was sitting a slim, pale-faced, elderly woman, one of whose cheeks had a painful twitch. Her eyes were sad and staring, as though she were looking for something that she could not find. She was clothed very decently with a shawl over her thin shoulders.

She begged them to enter and see the 'Elephant'.

'The elephant?' said Warren. 'Pray, what elephant? This is not the *Jardin des Plantes*.'

But it seemed that Napoleon had determined to erect a huge fountain on the Bastille site that its waters might wash away the memory of the awful events that had occurred there. This fountain was to spout its waters through the trunk of a great elephant. The melancholy woman, her eyes staring far beyond them while she spoke, pressed them to enter. Judith did not want to go; she did not know why, but she did not want to go.

However, Emma was all for seeing everything, so in they went.

The model was built of clay, indurated and whitened, exactly in figure and size what the bronze was intended to be, and it stood at the tremendous height of sixty feet. It had been intended that it should be placed on a stone pedestal and that then the water should pour out of its trunk into a succession of basins all round.

The woman, in a dreary unhappy voice, said that the English intended to finish this work, so she had heard.

'They have a number of other things to finish first,' said Warren laughing. But nothing at all seemed to amuse the woman.

She asked them gravely, as though she were accusing them personally:

'What have *you* done with the Emperor?'

'He is in charge of the Allies.'

'Will he ever return?'

'Never! . . . Never!'

'*Tant mieux! Mais l'Eléphant!*'

For some reason this huge white towering beast affected Judith with nausea. It looked so bare, so savage, so revengeful. With its great trunk it seemed to be ready to catch them, throw them up, and then, when they had fallen at its feet, riotously trample on them. In the hot quivering summer air it appeared to move, there was life in its vast body. The woman became more sinister, her cheek twitching, her hands moving; they would be prevented from escaping and the elephant would pursue them, trumpeting, within the palings. The air was so close that it was stifling.

She felt that in a moment she would be hysterical.

'Quickly. I cannot endure it. It is horrible. It is moving, cannot you see that it is moving?'

'Why, Judith—'

'No, no. I must get out. I cannot endure it.'

In a moment she would be laughing and screaming. She ran out into the street.

They followed her, wondering what the matter was.

'No. It is nothing. The heat was terrible. And the elephant . . . its trunk . . . And the woman hated us. Could you not see? Of course, she hated us.'

They sat down at a little table on the boulevard and ordered coffee. Judith was surprised to discover that she was trembling.

'But did you not feel it? I cannot understand why you did not. The elephant was alive. Oh yes, I know . . . But it *was* alive. In another moment . . .'

She drank her coffee, feeling that she had been too foolish for anything. She to give way to nerves! So that when they suggested that they should go to the Palais-Royal, although she hated to do so, she agreed.

Arrived there, they sat at a little table beneath a wide awning and watched the scene. The ladies with their high hats, their long sumptuous dresses, some of them with canes, all of them painted, vivacious and, it seemed, without a care in life, smiled at the men as anglers throw their baited hooks. The shops glittered, the sun shone down relentlessly; the moving crowds were like players in a game where something has to be found, now suddenly hurrying forwards as though the scent were 'hot', now hesitating, halting, the scent lost.

Judith's uneasiness increased. It was the heat, it was the noise, it was the smell of hot iron and dried dung and clothes. The long stretches of the square shone like glass. Some toy balloons, red and green and yellow, were floating like swollen puff-balls in the air. In one place a *'grimacier'* held a little crowd, throwing on and off his headgear, changing his coat, dancing, bending backwards. Nearer her there was a Punch and Judy, and from within the little coloured box came the sharp rasping cry and the quick bark of the little frilled dog.

It seemed to her that everyone was hostile, and this was not all her imagination, for at this time in Paris, behind the gaiety and laughter, all nerves were taut, no one knew what was to happen next, no one could trust his neighbour. There was great hostility to the Prussians. French officers in disguise were everywhere waiting to pick a quarrel. One of the means was to sit in a public place with your feet stretched and trip up a Prussian. Duels were fought every day. Two Prussians had been murdered the night before in a dark street behind the Opéra.

Judith sat there wondering what was the matter. She was not exactly ill, but felt a deep apprehension. Was her time imminent? Perhaps she had best go home, but she did not wish to spoil Warren's pleasure. She knew that he would insist on going with her.

She looked at him while he talked to Emma; how fond she had become of him, what good companions they were! She liked to be fond of people, especially when they were not weak and yet did what she advised. The pleasantest people in the world were the selfish ones who were also kindly, so that in the middle of their selfishness they thought of you and did something for you. Unselfish people who were always eager to do something for you were so irritating . . .

A group of French people, eagerly laughing and talking, came out of the restaurant behind Judith and, not noticing her, bumped against her and almost knocked her chair over. She felt her heart leap, the shops and chairs and coloured clothes danced before her eyes. She could not drive that horrible white elephant out

of her mind. It would not surprise her to see it come trumpeting
and trampling, the crowd running before it. She would not be
able to move; she would be held in her place as one is in a
nightmare. Something had warned her not to come to the Palais-
Royal.

Then she noticed sitting near to her a young Prussian officer,
quite alone. He had large melancholy eyes and was little more
than a boy. He stared out into the pageant with unseeing gaze.
What was it? Was he sick for home? Was he thinking of someone he loved and wishing that she were with him, wondering
what he did there?

Warren turned to her smiling. He was watching the 'Punch',
laughing at the little dog. Always after she would remember
every detail of the next few minutes. A tall very handsome lady,
in a high green fur hat, was leaning across her little table, gazing
into the eyes of a stout frog-faced gentleman choked by a huge
stock. Some band was coming nearer, the music grew louder
and louder as though a door were opening. Two more crimson
balloons floated into the air; a small poodle, ridiculously naked,
ran forward into the crowd, lost, and a shrill feminine voice
cried 'Dédé . . . Dédé!' It heard the voice and eagerly ran back
again.

Emma was exclaiming: 'But the air was so ravishing that I
could not endure to return, so I waved my hand and he came,
running, such ecstasy painted on his features . . .'

Then everything happened in a moment. The band just
entered with a blare of sound, someone laughed, the lady in
green pinched the gentleman's chin . . .

A young Frenchman with a black moustache and sharp
beady eyes moved against the chair in which the young Prussian
was sitting; a glass fell with a clash, the Prussian was almost
tumbled from his seat. The Prussian started up, his hand on his
sword. The two faced one another. A pistol-shot cracked; the
young Prussian, his legs bent oddly beneath him, lay huddled
against the iron legs of the table.

At the sound of the shot the sky seemed to swing, the buildings
to bend forward.

Everyone came out running from the restaurant. There were
shouts and cries. Two officers in Uhlan uniform approached
the Frenchman.

Judith saw him struggling with them. She was quite near to
him, and could observe how, although his face was white, he
expressed a rage that was like a mad cat's. He repeated, in a

shrill treble voice, over and over again the word 'L'Empereur!'

He pushed back the men who were attacking him, turned with a swing of his body and looked straight into Judith's eyes – without of course seeing her, but, in the fiery meeting of sun, sky, roofs, and floor that seemed now to whirl in a wheel of flame before her, she saw the face of the hanging boy from London.

She felt herself now, just as she had done then, sick from a kind of claustrophobia, the crowd shutting her in. She had lost sight of both Emma and Warren. She was alone, as she always seemed to be in every crisis.

Then the young Frenchman, brushing his cheek with one hand, as though a fly had bothered him, flung out the other, and again a pistol-shot crashed like a stone flung through glass.

At that it was as though the Palais-Royal had been a plate in a second tilted forward, spilling its contents downwards into some abyss. The screams and shouts were detached. One shout was deep like a drum, another was shrill like the knock on a high gong.

Judith, struggling to escape from chairs and tables, saw Warren endeavouring to push through an absurd clump of bodies that clung together like plants in a storm. Behind them the whole Palais-Royal, still tilted, swarmed with figures as unreal as puppets worked by strings.

He called 'Judith! Judith!' He beat the bodies in front of him frantically aside with his arms. He reached her, fell against her. Horses were rising. A horse, mounted by a soldier, came charging through fallen furniture. Glass fell with a crash. A dog barked, and on that bark she caught Warren in her arms, for his face was purple. He could not speak. He dropped limp against her, so that she stumbled to the ground.

Kneeling there, her arms around him, she saw that he was dead, heard a bell ring just above her head, saw the horse (shaped like an elephant) go charging into the sun.

A wave of pain caught her, so frightful that some other person broken to pieces inside herself screamed. Everything was black.

She sank down on a descending shaft of pain. She slowly mounted again, to find that she was quite clear-sighted, was lying on a hard, dry sofa, her head on a pillow that smelt of cheese. She hated the smell, but also the row of lofty shining mirrors that reflected again and again the long room with empty tables, chairs piled high.

Somewhere in the distance shouting fell against the mirrors and died on the floor. She felt the sweat tumble into her eyes, wiped it away, and saw a vast Emma towering above her.

'Warren is dead,' Judith murmured.

A little stout man with two chins, who seemed also to smell of cheese, advanced to her. She saw that he was greatly agitated. A big silver ring trembled as his hand trembled. She heard him say:

'A screen! A screen! . . . Where is a screen!'

Then she had one more absolute moment of clear vision.

Warren was dead. Her child was being born. She would die also, and history would repeat itself, for even as she had been born at the instant of her parents' death, so now would her child be born of their death.

The little man leaned over her. She saw the silver ring tremble. A cascade of pain hovered in the air – but before it broke over her she screamed out, 'I will not die! . . . I will not die!'

'It is a boy,' said the doctor to Emma, quarter of an hour later.

They were bringing the bodies of the wounded into the restaurant and laying them in the shadow where the room was coolest.

Part IV

Mother and Son

THE HILLS

WALTER HERRIES rode up the hill from Hawkshead one fine summer's evening to get some air before spending the evening with his friend, Squire Thistleton, at High Grange. He had come over from Grasmere more swiftly than he had intended, having already eaten his dinner with the Bordens there, not wishing to invade High Grange before nightfall. Squire Thistleton's lady bored him most desperately: stay the night with Thistleton he must, for he had important business matters to discuss with him, but be bored by Mrs Thistleton he would not. Although he was so genial, for ever laughing at the jokes of others, yes, roaring and slapping his vast thigh at them, yet, like all very self-centred men, he had a watchful eye. If he must suffer at the jokes of others there must be excellent reason for it. He did nothing at all without an admirable reason. Immense in build though he was, he was not yet corpulent for his twenty-eight years. He looked exceedingly handsome in his green riding coat as the white horse picked its way carefully up the rough stone-strewn path. The summer is the worst time of the year in which to see this country: the naked blue sky does not suit its shape and size; the hills dwindle beneath the sun; the green carpet of field and brow has neither shade nor variety. But tonight fragments of orange cloud floated across a blue so faint as to be almost without colour, and the hills were so clearly outlined that they forced themselves, dark rocks of a mysterious country, out of a sea with no ripple.

Walter had no eyes for scenery; he left that to the romantic writers, now ever more numerous. But, pausing on the brow, and looking down to the left where the waters of Coniston lay bronzed and still, he felt all the pride of one who owns a fine property. For he had come now to feel that he, and he alone, possessed the whole of this charming and fruitful land. It was a natural and happy evolution of circumstance. He was at this moment well beyond his own actual territory, which was not as yet a very large one, but he felt himself to be so infinitely the most important person alive in the combined counties of Cumberland and Westmorland, and what he felt himself to be, that he was.

It was now over three years since Will Herries, his father, had departed back to London. He was to be seen very seldom at

Westaways. It had been made clear to him (Walter has assisted in the demonstration) that the City was the place for him. For one thing, there was nothing in life so pleasant for Will as the making of money, and although now much of his wealth had its richest foundations in Manchester and the Midlands, London was inevitably the heart of affairs. For another, Walter had helped him to perceive that, although Cumberland society did not object to wealth, it still objected to the City. The time was coming when a City man, granted that he had retired and had pocketed plenty of gold before retiring, would be admitted into good company, but that time was not quite yet. Moreover, Will had no intention whatever of retiring. He was now only fifty years of age and in excellent health. Business had never been so interesting as now when it was beginning to rouse itself, in the promise of so much fresh industrialism, out of the depression that followed the French Wars. The chimneys of the Midlands were gallantly smoking, and Will must be there to see that they were properly supplied.

Walter's ambitions were quite other. He disclaimed now all connexion with business. With his handsome person, his geniality, his ruthless selfishness, his happy disregard of the interests of any but his own, his fine place (but he already felt Westaways far too small for him) and, above all, his almost insane pride in the Herries name, he was excellently placed to dominate his country world. The men and women around him, he would say, had judged of Herries by the miserable specimens hitherto offered to them. *He* would show them what a Herries really was. Indeed, his earlier scorn of Francis and Jennifer had by now grown to an irritated and festering hatred. He would never dominate this country properly until Uldale and its occupants were wiped from the face of the land. They had not a chance against him; Francis weak and idle, Jennifer dull and scandalous. Only in their children could they rival him. At that thought, which constantly peered up at him out of the dark recesses of his mind like a malicious stinging animal, his whole body would tremble. For, in the spring of 1815, his wife had presented him with twins, a boy and a girl, and the boy was a weak and ailing cripple. Moreover, his wife would give him no more children, and, unless she died, Uhland must be his only son.

In his disgust at the puny and deformed baby he had not cared what they called him, and Mrs Herries, moved perhaps by the increasing wave of German Romanticism, or hoping, it may be, that the child thus named might make some escape from the

Herries nature, had had this outlandish fancy. The boy was Uhland, marked in this way, as in all others, from the common kind.

And Francis' children, John and Dorothy, were healthy and strong. Elizabeth and Uhland – John and Dorothy. He was beset by the contrast.

The horse moved forward. He turned down the hill to the two small pools that lay, in blue translucent stillness, under the dark guardianship of the wood. Behind the trees Helvellyn and Fair-field kept sleepy tolerant guard.

The day had been hot; their purple shadows slumbered.

There was perfect stillness all about Walter Herries as he sat on his horse and looked into the pool. There were other little things that had exasperated him today. He had been slowly riding by Grasmere Lake when he encountered that crazy old poet, William Wordsworth, and his mad sister as they walked along.

Walter, with his accustomed geniality, had stopped his horse to speak to them, as a king might to his subjects. Everyone knew that Wordsworth as a poet was a mock and a derision, and his sister, Dorothy, was as mad as a hatter. Wordsworth wrote poems about donkeys and daffodils. He was a joke to the neighbourhood, and that little sister of his, with her shabby clothes and fiery eye . . . And yet, speaking to them with all courtesy, he had been in some way rebuked. The comical pair! Wordsworth was going fishing; his sister said something about a bird on a tree. They did not seem at all gratified that he had spoken to them.

'Good day to you, Mr Herries . . . Good day to you,' Words-worth had said, as though he were impatient to be gone, and his sister had wandered about the road, following some bird with her glittering eye . . . Oh, mad, mad both of them! But mad or no they should have been impressed by his greeting.

Another vexation had been a queer one. As he left home that morning little Uhland, five years old, had limped to wish him farewell. He had felt a sudden pride in his heart at sight of him. Proud of that white-faced bony little cripple! But it was pride that he had felt; he had been moved; he had bent down to em-brace him. That was an absurd emotion – although, after all, when all was done, the child *was* a Herries . . . his only heir . . . In spite of himself he sighed, rested his hand on his great thigh and looked about him, breathing-in the sweet-scented summer air.

At that same moment there rushed past him, out of the wood,

the most astonishing figure, a small naked child. It was a boy, and, straight in front of Herries' horse, he splashed into the pool. Another moment and he was swimming vigorously, tossing his head and uttering cries of delight. The pool was deep – the two pools would be a fine small lake one later day – and this midge of a boy, screaming like a little shrill bird, dived, appeared a moment later at the pool's edge, and then sprang out, dancing about and waving his arms in front of Herries' horse.

The horse, alarmed by this unusual adventure, reared, and Herries, in anger, snapped his whip, catching the child's bare leg. The child laughed and plunged into the pool again; a moment later a peasant woman appeared at the wood's edge, then ran down to Herries.

'What are you doing, whipping a baby! Have you nothing better—'

She broke off. They had recognized one another. This woman was Judith. She was dressed like a peasant in some rough material of red and green. On her red hair she wore no covering. On her bare feet she had wooden shoes. She stood, her small body set, her little face grinning.

'Why, Cousin Walter, I did not know that it was you . . . It is a long time since we met.'

So it was. Years and years. He had not set eyes on her since that night in '15, when she had dinner with him, and they had heard of Napoleon's flight from Elba. None of them had seen her. She had been living in the hills with her bastard child. She had gone back to her origin.

'Well, well. Cousin Judith.' He took off his hat.

'Yes, and don't you whip my son or I shall have something to say.'

She was laughing, and he felt that in some way she was mocking him.

'Your son?'

'Yes. Adam, Adam, come here!'

The child seemed to spring from nowhere and stood, naked and dripping, by the horse. Yes, this would be her child. It would not be a day more than five, born in the same year as his own. He saw, with satisfaction, that the boy was ugly. The small body was brown with sun, the hair – that lay thick and matted above his eyes – jet black. He had a short snub nose and a large grinning mouth, a strong sturdy body, but the legs and arms were too long. Yes, an ugly and common-looking child. He did not seem to feel cold, but Judith drew him to her, put her green shawl over him and her arm around him. He leant against her, wet as he was. She did not seem to care.

'This is Mr Walter Herries, a relation of ours,' she said to him.

How strong and sturdy the woman seemed! She must be between forty and fifty now. What a queer pair they made.

At that he recovered his self-command which, for a moment, he seemed to have lost. He leaned lazily towards her, resting one hand on his hip. The horse shifted a little and, bending down, began to pluck the grass. The stillness was exquisite. A cloud, like a bronze chrysanthemum, jagged at its edges, floated over the wood and darkened, like a hand, the little pool.

'Where have you been all these years?' he asked her, friendly and patronizing.

'You know well enough.'

What clear bright eyes she has! he thought, and wondered whether there were specks of dust on his clothes. His hand moved down the lapel of his coat.

'And when will you return to civilization?'

'It is quite civilized enough where I am.'

'Have you seen Francis and Jennifer lately?'

'Francis has come to see me at Watendlath.'

'Well, I must be off to my supper.' He looked at the infant, and the infant looked back at him. 'So your name is Adam, young man?'

The child grinned up at him, looking at him fearlessly.

'Adam Paris,' he said. Then he added most unexpectedly: 'I could make your horse jump more if I tried.'

'You try – that's all!' said Walter, suddenly angry again.

'Now you leave the child alone, Cousin Walter,' said Judith. 'He is not afraid of you nor of anything else in the world. But I will give you something to be afraid of if you touch him with your whip.'

He had a sharp consciousness (which he was to recall one day) of the force and vitality of her personality. Whenever he encountered her she compelled him to remember it, small though she was. While she was away he created, if he thought of her at all, his own picture of her as an insignificant sort of poor-relation-governess. But when he was with her it was another matter. And now he suddenly thought: 'I had forgotten *her*! Suppose that she should come back to Uldale!'

However, all that he did was to be gracious again. He took off his hat, bowed, invited her to bring her boy to see them at Westaways.

Judith was not ungracious. She always returned courtesy for
courtesy. 'Yes, I will come one day, Cousin Walter. I hope Mrs
Herries is well.'

'Oh yes. Well enough.'

Then Walter rode away, his figure for a moment gigantic at the
top of the bend against the soft glow of the milk-white sky.
Judith, her hand in her son's, started along the little path that
skirted the pool. Adam was wrapped up entirely in the shawl;
the end of it trailed on the ground behind him. He danced along.

'What a fat man!' he said.

'That is your Uncle Walter.'

'In truth my uncle?'

'Near enough.'

'I could have made his horse jump.' He skipped a few paces
and nearly tumbled. But she did not move to catch him nor did
she ask him whether he were cold, as any other child would
have been.

'Was the water agreeable?'

He wrinkled his nose like a little dog. 'I can smell the fire
burning.' He shouted and cried aloud with happiness. The shawl
fell off him, and bare as a young foal he ran towards the wood.
Judith walked soberly after him. She was thinking deeply about
Walter.

A small nondescript dog ran out to meet them. This was a
mongrel dog who, coming from nowhere, had attached himself
to them. He first ran eagerly towards Adam, moving awkwardly
on legs that were longer than they should have been, but with
eager excited joy. Then, just before he reached Adam, it occurred
to him that he might not perhaps be so popular as he had hoped,
so he crawled on all fours, dragging himself along with a bright
supplicating eye.

'Dog! Dog!' Adam cried, and picked him up and ran into the
wood, hugging the animal to his bare stomach; the dog's tail
wagged in an ecstasy of happiness.

Just inside the wood a bright fire was burning, and on the
other side of the fire sat a stout man in black, reading a book,
and with an absentminded hand once and again stirring with a
stick the pot that hung over the fire.

Adam, who was now almost dry, flung himself, dog and all,
into the stout man's lap.

'Uncle Reuben, a fat man on a horse tried to whip me, but he
could not. Can we eat now?'

'You must dress yourself,' Reuben said, putting his book down and reaching out to a pile of minute clothes near to him.

Adam stood up on Reuben's thighs, putting his hands round Reuben's neck. Reuben clasped him round his small naked body, holding him lest he should fall.

'And who was this fat man?' he asked, moving his face a little; the small dog, when he saw what Adam was doing, was trying the same with the addition that he would lick Reuben's cheeks. The fire threw a shining colour on Adam's body. He seemed to be surrounded with a nimbus of light.

'Mother said he was my Uncle Walter ... Can we not eat now?'

He jumped suddenly off Reuben's thigh and had scuffled into a shirt and a pair of diminutive blue trousers. His legs were bare.

'Mother, can we not eat now?' He ran towards Judith, who stopped to look into the pot.

'Whom do you think I have seen?' she asked Reuben.

'I know. Adam told me.'

He spread his black riding coat for her and she sat down, leaning her head against his knee. She looked up and could see the dark fans and wheels of the trees flecked with cool shell-white sky.

'Yes, Walter. After all these years. He looked huge and mightily satisfied. Do you know what he said to himself as he looked at me, Reuben?'

'No.'

'Here is slattern Judith and her bastard ... Adam laughed at him ...' She pushed Walter away for a moment and went on: 'You had a grand meeting this noon. The grandest I've seen.'

'Yes, praise the Lord!'

'But Reuben, you talked more of political things than religious. You were trying to make them discontented.'

'They are discontented already. They have been starving for years and now their masters will bring in machinery and they work in the dark like slaves.'

Judith shook her head.

'No. Not here. They are farmers and shepherds. There is no discontent in Kendal or Keswick.'

'No, but a little way out – at Whitehaven, Cockermouth ...'

She looked up at him and put up her hand. He took it in his.

'I like it better when you talk about God. Although I do not believe in Him I like others to. At least . . . believe or not . . . I haven't the wits to be so certain. But I like to hear you speak of Him. You bring Him so close. You are so sure of yourself now, Reuben, and yet as kind and good as ever you were. I had rather people were kind than anything else. Yet I detest a fool, and so many kind people are half-witted.' She let herself run on, looking up and seeing that a little evening breeze moved, as a tiny boat moves on a pond, through the trees. She looked down and saw that Adam was playing with the dog.

'Reuben, are you still bothered with women?'

He laughed. 'No. I am too old.'

'Nonsense. You are not sixty. When did they cease to torment you?'

'I will tell you. It was in Kendal some ten years ago. It was in the wintertime and I had been preaching out on the hills. It was perilously cold, and in the inn after supper a large red-faced girl invited me to her room. Then, to be warm and to be comforted by someone (for I was much alone at that time) I went into bed with her. And she had but just blown out the candle when I saw the Lord, a young man in silver armour standing on the floor. The fire shone on him and he was glorious. He cried to me, "Reuben, the pleasure is not worth the pain." And I answered "Nay, Lord, I was so cold." And he came to the bed and touched my forehead with his hand. I lay by the girl all night but neither of us was harmed.'

'And do you truly think it was the Lord?' asked Judith.

'Who else could it have been?' said Reuben.

'No, no one else.'

'Well, then—'

'But maybe you were already asleep—'

'Not before embracing the girl. No. It was the Lord. I have seen him in such armour at other times too—'

'And women are nothing to you since then?'

'I like women,' he said. 'But the temptation is over.'

'What are your temptations still?'

He answered gravely, counting on his fingers. 'One, I am a coward; two, I am greedy; three, I like a warm bed; four, I tell tales; five, I hate the Methodist preacher at Cockermouth; six, I am lazy – I can sleep all day—'

She interrupted him. 'Look up. There is a red cloud like a crimson bird that Georges once had, hanging between two trees.'

But it was one of Reuben's defects that natural scenery meant nothing to him. Any human thing, but a tree, a cloud, a mountain – nothing. The pot was boiling. Judith commanded the whole situation. The three of them and the dog sat and had a splendid meal.

'We will go up the hill and see the sunrise as you promised?' Judith asked.

'Yes,' Reuben said, but in spite of himself he yawned behind his hand.

She had an impulse to be cross, as she always had when things were not to be as she wished them. Then she conquered her crossness. She had been expecting for months this evening with Reuben. About twice a year they spent a night together. Once before they had ridden up into the Langdales and seen the sunrise. And now he was sleepy. His head was nodding. It had been a grand meeting and must have wearied him, but she had been looking forward passionately to a long talk with him. It was so seldom now that she could talk with her own kind, and tonight, most especially, she wanted his advice, for she was about to pay a visit to Uldale again for the first time since her return from France. She was taking Adam with her. The sudden vision of Walter had been like an omen. She was not frightened, but she needed help and only Reuben could give it her. And now Reuben was sleepy. Only Adam was not. He was dancing about with the dog, eager for the next adventure now that his hunger was satisfied.

Reuben turned round, knelt on the grass and said his prayers. Then he leaned against a tree-trunk and in another moment was asleep.

'He's asleep,' said Adam, laughing.

The night was so warm and the scent of the trees so comforting, the uncertain flicker of the fading fire so bewitching that, standing there, she felt that she was under a spell.

She was in magnificent health because of the life that she had been leading since coming to Watendlath, the life of a peasant, harvesting, digging, helping with the sheep, riding off with Watson for a whole day on the fells, ploughing for hours through the quagmires at the top of the Fell after a lost or strayed lamb – and always in perfect content. That was the life to which part of her temperament entirely responded; but the other part would not have been content had she not had Adam. Adam now was her whole life, her soul, her body, her past, her future, her God and her destiny.

She had been waiting always for some such passion as this. Her love for Georges had possessed her, but it had not been

returned until the last and, say what one may, a love that is not
returned is only half a love.

Moreover, although she had not known it, she was a woman to
whom motherhood was the only possible complete fulfilment.
Her love for Georges, her affection for Reuben, Francis, Maria,
Warren, Emma Furze, Watson, had been in its impulse maternal.
But they had not been her own. Now she had something that
was her own, and anyone watching her might have been frightened of the fiery, possessive, passionate element at the heart of
her love for her son.

But she was not a fool. She kept her love in control as yet. And
Adam was not at present difficult. His mother was his companion;
he knew none other as good. He loved her quite naturally without
thinking of it. He was independent but warm-hearted and, at
present, he had no feeling that she threatened his liberty. There
was as yet no cloud on his sky. The first five years of his life, two
in France, three at Watendlath, had known no blemish. She had
been able to give him all he wanted, because when Warren's will
was read it was found that he had left her all his own small means
— not much, but enough for her needs. The boy was of amazing
health, and, so long as he was not shut up in a room for too long,
asked for no attention. He trusted everyone as a puppy trusts
everyone before his first betrayal. He was fearless, truthful and
gay, the three best things a small boy can be. He would defend
his mother against anyone or anything; he was obedient so long
as she did not hamper his liberty. Once, for some small crime,
she had locked him in a room; he had broken the window and
disappeared until nightfall. She understood that because she had
once climbed out of a window herself.

Their relationship was, at present, perfect.

Now as the light faded and the stars came out she tried to
persuade him to sleep. She would not wake Reuben. She would
walk up the hill and see the sunrise by herself. But she almost
hesitated to speak because the silence was so glorious, broken
only by the running water that is to be heard everywhere in this
country, the gentle friendly crackle of the burning wood as it
fell into crimson embers, the occasional movement of the horses
behind her.

Adam, too, seemed to feel the silence, for he stood without
moving, his legs spread, looking up.

'Now you must sleep, Adam.'

He shook his head, not saying anything.

'Oh no . . .' He looked at her, smiling. 'There's the moon.'

And there it was, sailing very calmly with a sort of smiling conceit between the trees.

She knew that he wouldn't sleep. 'Come. And we shall see the sunrise.'

So he took her hand and they started off, the small dog following. Adam was never very talkative. To be out at night was no very new thing to him. They left the little wood behind them and started to climb. They were now on the open moor. The Langdale Pikes, Fairfield, Helvellyn were beyond, and across Yewdale loomed the hump of the Old Man. The light about and around him was diffused as though shed by the multitude of stars. The pools of shadow, neither brown nor grey, lay below them like lakes of sleeping water. Fairfield and Helvellyn were marked with crags and precipices like the tearing made by some giant's fingers. How black, how black the hills against the luminous sky! A little higher on the moor and they were suddenly staring into the moon's face. They could see now the two little pools which seemed to blaze with moon-silver among the surrounding vapour. No wind stirred; somewhere some sheep were moving and the air was warm like the breath of a flower.

They sat down against a gigantic boulder; the stones around them rose in that moonshine like monolithic sacrificial monuments. As they sat in that stillness the hills seemed to approach them. Helvellyn, always a beneficent hill, leaned towards them, Fairfield embraced them, the pools below smiled at them. Somewhere in that wood Reuben was lying against a tree snoring with his mouth open. Adam curled in against Judith's side, the little dog curled in against Adam.

With her arm around her son Judith sat staring into the moon. She did not often think of the past, but tonight it came crowding towards her, figures issuing from the hills, events stealing up from the mist – the day that she had looked at Mrs Monnasett and David had beaten her, the moment when she had seen Georges' mother, the night of the fireworks when Will and Francis and Reuben had talked, the escape of Reuben's brother, David's stroke and death, Sarah's passion – and then all her life with Georges, from the first week (what a baby then she had been!) to the last awful scene with Stane's father! And then the dead quiescence of the years at Grosset, the semi-life with Jennifer and Francis, Will's coming to Westaways, the friendship with Warren leading to the drama in Paris – drama of death, drama, thank God, of life.

She did not believe in God, but she did feel tonight that every

event, every character, had led her to this – this question that
was now the dramatic crisis of her whole life – which world was
she to choose, the world of Uldale or the world of Watendlath?

She had thought that it was settled. Only a month or two ago
she had said to Charlie Watson that her Herries life was finished
for ever; she would not leave Watendlath until Adam was grown.
Then he should choose for himself, but she would remain.

She had thought that it was settled. Then came a letter from
Francis. He implored her to come to Uldale. He gave no reasons.
She was to come, if only for a night, and bring Adam with her.
The most touching thing was that Jennifer had scrawled at the
bottom of the page: 'The two of us need you.'

Well, she would go, but only for a few nights, only to show
them that she was out of Herries affairs for ever. But was she?
The invitation had stirred her. She wanted to see Uldale again –
the dairy, the housekeeping, the servants. She was sure that it
would be in a mess. And Jennifer, John, Dorothy . . . She was
too proud to come to see them, after all the scandal about her,
without an invitation . . . but if they asked her . . . For a brief
moment Watendlath had seemed small, shut in, her domination
there a poor thing, even her beloved Charlie a rough ignorant
farmer . . . Then she had been ashamed, and in a day or two her
true nature had recovered itself. For she knew that this was her
true nature, the nature that she derived from her mother, the
nature that outlawed her from the Herries blood.

Had she not written to Francis and said that she would come
she would now have refused his appeal. But she had given her
word.

Then the sight of Walter Herries this evening had revived all
the struggle again. How proud and conceited he had been! It
was thus, seated on his horse, gigantic against the skyline, that
he remained for her, and, at the thought of him, her whole proud
obstinate passion for dominating returned.

It was thus that he meant to wipe out Francis and Jennifer,
John and Dorothy. She saw them helpless and cowering under
his whip. She knew suddenly why Francis had sent that letter
to her. How amusing to return to Uldale – she, the outlaw with
her bastard boy – and fight Walter, make Adam – illegitimate
though he was – head of all the Herries! Her heart beat triumph-
antly; she drew her arm more closely about him; he was sleeping.

She looked up at the stars as though to defy them. And the
answer came back without question. 'Here is your country. Here
is your place.'

But why? All the rebels were killed or disgraced. Georges had been murdered, Warren killed, Francis humiliated, her father an outcast, Reuben – well, Reuben talked more of social things now than of God. What of the bear, the boy hanged, young Hartley Coleridge? She was not sentimental about outlawry, but it seemed that if you fought against the laws of the House – if you broke the windows, rushed downstairs with no clothes on, rang the bells in the belfry, refused the common food or drink, brought the mongrel dog into the parlour – they all together, with one loud cry, threw you into the street; and then, how were you better?

For three years in Watendlath she and her boy had been outlawed; and how was she better?

'You *are* better,' the little dog, the cherry-faced moon, the scar like a sword on Helvellyn's flank answered her. 'You have never been at peace before. *This* is your world, not the other.'

But she was practical and not given to hearing voices. To beat Walter, to dominate all the Herries, to place Adam at the head of them. He would have, she was sure, all Will's genius for money, all Walter's physical strength, all Francis' brains . . .

Which way was she going? Her whole life led to this crisis – or so she fancied, as we like to fancy that there is a line and a course and a climax, when it may not be so at all.

She remembered the way that the hens scratched in the room when she had first returned to it after Georges' death, the elephant in Paris, and that woman bending over, searching among her letters, and Adam trailing in the shawl, Reuben licking his fingers after the meal from the pot . . .

Perhaps there is no line, only a gesture here, a leaf falling, the sheep huddling up the path outside the farm. But there was Adam . . . She was responsible for the life that he would have. Would he be like Charlie Watson, blowing on his fingers for the cold, or Will sitting in his counting-house, or Walter at the head of his table, or Francis waiting for his wife's lover and pretending not to see? . . . No, not that. Adam, even now, was as brave as a lion. Poor Francis . . .

But before she fell asleep she was aware that the decision that she would make must affect many lives, much Herries history. She knew what she could do if she tried. She had never as yet tried with her whole heart. She had always been divided. Her son had united her. She saw him, as her eyes closed, reaching up with his hand, catching the stars and joining, with the light that streamed from them, her divided heart.

She woke to see one bright bar of gold above the ridge. The edge of the bar sparkled and quivered. Behind it a fleet of tiny pink clouds trembled, hovered, then merged into a fan-shaped shadow of rosy light.

She bent down and kissed Adam. 'Wake up,' she said, 'and see the sun.'

He looked up, rubbed his eyes with his knuckles, then jumped to his feet, caught her by the hand and pulled her to a higher ridge of the moor.

Little winds, little fingers passing over an instrument, blew against their faces. The sky was beyond depth, without end, but was flecked now with fire. Thick white mist lay like water beneath them, but this soon was touched and lightened, thinned; the rocks and the spear-tops of the trees rent and tore it. They, too, caught the gold, and Helvellyn was, as though it had rolled its shoulder towards the light, purple.

The mist broke everywhere, and the sky was showered with flecks of gold. The cloven mist streamed down the hills like rain. Light was everywhere. The valleys ran with sun.

'Now I'll race you!' Adam shouted, and started tearing down to the little wood.

JUDITH RETURNS TO ULDALE

WHEN JUDITH STOOD again in the so-familiar hall at Uldale she was deeply excited. It was her nature to be excited, and that nature had not changed although she was forty-six years of age.

A stranger would have seen only a little ordinary pale-faced, middle-aged woman, bewildered perhaps by the sudden light, dressed in bonnet and shawl, faded but scupulously clean, holding by the hand a very small, rather ugly boy. No romance there. Nevertheless the situation was romantic, for Judith was returning to the home of her childhood, after behaviour so scandalous that it should have ostracized her for ever, holding her illegitimate child by the hand – and she was there by invitation! She would not, she proudly assured herself, be there in any other way!

Her emotions were mixed and confused: she could never enter this house without a hundred memories crowding upon her, but it was characteristic of her that the first thing that interested her was that there were signs of neglect and untidiness everywhere. She saw that at once, and her fingers itched to put everything to rights.

For a moment the only person who greeted her was the very decent woman who opened the door. She knew that her ancient enemy, Mrs Ponder, had been dead now three years of a fever. She gave the woman a quick friendly glance.

'Thank you,' she said, smiling.

Then her very next move, instinctive, almost unknown to herself, was to step forward, still holding Adam by the hand, and put a picture that hung crooked on the wall straight again.

'That's better,' she said.

It was an old picture that she knew well, of a huntsman leaping a little ditch. She gave it a friendly little pat.

Then Jennifer came out from the parlour. 'Judith! I didn't know—' she cried; but even then she came forward a little slowly, a little lazily, as though she were but half awake.

She was not as handsome as she had been; she was middle-aged now, as Judith was, but she was still a very remarkable woman, carrying herself with the same old dignity and grandeur, and her hair, untouched with grey, was of the same superb darkness. She was wearing a coloured bodice of orange over a white skirt. The orange sleeves, puffed and slashed, were very fine. But Judith saw at once that the dress was a little slatternly, and that her cheeks were painted. Her eyes, too, were weary, not with quite the old affectation of sleepiness. There was real fatigue, disappointment, unhappiness there.

She towered over Judith and the little boy. She bent down and kissed Judith.

'Is this Adam?'

'Yes. This is Adam.'

She kissed him, and he returned the kiss with fervour. She was quite the most beautiful lady he had ever seen, as this was the most beautiful house he had ever been in. He stared at the wallpaper with its Chinamen and castles, at the silver candlesticks, at the broad staircase, at the tall grand lady with the wonderful orange sleeves. From that first moment he and Jennifer were friends.

'Here is Francis! Francis, Francis, Judith is come!'

Francis was coming down the stairs, and Judith, looking up at him, felt a shock of dismay. He had been over to Watendlath to see her a year ago, and she had thought then that he looked old and ill, but now – how thin he was, how tired he seemed; he was an old man, and yet he was not more than sixty!

In a way he was more handsome than he had ever been. His extreme thinness suited him; his high collar, frilled shirt, and dark blue trousers showed his figure to the greatest advantage.

Judith was proud of him and deeply sorry for him; she longed to put her arms around him and mother him. He took both her hands in his.

'Judith, this is famous! . . . After all this time! And is this Adam? How do you do, Adam?'

'Very well, I thank you, sir,' said Adam in his shrill piping voice that was apt to end in a squeak.

They all laughed to relieve the tension of the meeting. There was a bustle about the baggage.

Judith went out into the dark garden. Charlie Watson had driven them out from Keswick. He leaned over and held her hand. For a moment she clung to his touch. All Watendlath seemed to be personified by him.

'Goodbye, Charlie,' she said, raising herself on tiptoe. 'We shall soon be back.'

'I am not so sure about leaving you.'

'Nonsense.' His face was close to hers. She let her hand rest for a moment on his rough coat and thick strong arm.

'Watendlath is not far away.'

''Tis a world away,' he answered her gruffly, and at once drove off.

She went back into the house. Her thought was, before everything, of Adam. He must go to bed. They had left Watendlath early that morning and, wild with excitement, he had been awake at four. Then, too, putting him to bed would give her some excuse to be alone a little before coming down.

On the landing they met the two children. John was now thirteen and Dorothy twelve. John was oddly like his father in face, but would be broader and thicker in body. Judith knew that he had a most charming character, kindly, affectionate, loyal – a little weak perhaps, a little dreamy like father and great-grandfather before him. How strange! John's great-grandfather had been her father! She thought of it as she kissed him. Dorothy was good-natured, obedient and conventional, something like her Aunt Deborah, fair-haired, at present plump, at the moment conscious of her 'pantalettes', which were only fastened with tapes above her knee and gave her much anxiety. Such things were always to make her anxious.

Both children were delighted to see their Aunt Judith as they had always called her. Life at home had not been too pleasant of late; now that Aunt Judith had come it would be more gay.

They were exceedingly interested to see Adam. He was at once at his ease with them. He was always at his ease with everyone, because he trusted everyone.

He threw off his little riding coat, letting it be where it fell, and showed John how the horse that Charlie Watson was driving had thrown up its head and snorted, but in the middle of this exhibition he was excited by the sight of the room where he and his mother would sleep. He had been too young during those first years in France to notice or remember things, and since then the farm at Watendlath had been all that he had known.

Certainly the room at the Keswick Inn today had been grand, but that had been a public place with men drinking and a man playing a harp, and there had been a dog with a lame leg. This was *his* room and his mother's!

He ran round and round it, shouting cries of joy. For Judith it was strange enough. For, once again it was her old room, the room where Mrs Monnasett had died.

'I thought you would wish to be in the same room,' said Jennifer, standing in the doorway.

It was indeed the same room! In all these years the wallpaper had not been changed. Still there were those blue pagodas, there was the tallboy that had seemed to her as a baby so infinitely high, over the bed the blue tester hangings and overlay, the bed itself with the columns fluted and reeded and so charmingly carved with acanthus leaves. There Mrs Monnasett, with her yellow face, had lain, the candles flickering in the breeze, her lips fixed in a sardonic smile ... The room of all Judith's life. Nothing had occurred. Only yesterday she had bent forward to find the little box ...

'I will leave you,' said Jennifer. 'Come, children. Aunt Judith will soon come down.' There was a new note in Jennifer's voice, as though behind her words she was pleading for something.

But Judith now could think only of Adam. She undressed him and washed him. He would hardly keep still. She held him naked in her arms and kissed him. He lay back against her watching the leaping flames of the fire. His small dark head against her breast (he was quite suddenly sleepy), he asked her questions.

'Is that gentleman my uncle?'

'Yes, dear.' Impossible to explain now why and how he was not!

'Was my father like him?'

'No; your father was not so tall nor so old.'

'This gentleman is very, very old.'

'No. Not truly. He will not appear old when you know him.'

'Is that boy called John?'

'Yes.'

He yawned a huge yawn.

'I like him . . . ' Then he added, blinking his eyes at the fire: 'Is the beautiful lady his mother?'

'Yes.'

'But he called her ma'am.'

'Many boys and girls call their mother ma'am and their father sir.'

He thought about this. 'I cannot call my father sir because I haven't one, and I have never called you ma'am.'

'No, and you never will,' said Judith resolutely. She put on his shirt and carried him to the big four-poster.

He looked so small in it that she laughed. Then they both laughed. The touch of the cool sheets woke him up again and he rolled all over the bed. Then he lay still, watching her with wide-open eyes while she changed her dress, washed her face and hands, brushed her hair.

'This is a very grand house,' he said at last.

'Yes. I lived in it when I was a little girl, younger than you are.'

But the strangeness of it! In that bed, where her small son was lying, old Mrs Monnasett had once lain! She looked at him, her heart bursting with love, but her voice was quite severe when she said:

'Now go to sleep, Adam. Are you hungry?'

He could not be. He had eaten a tremendous dinner at Keswick.

'Yes, yes. I am! I am!' he cried, although until his mother had mentioned it he had not thought of it. But how wonderful he thought her in her evening dress! The colours of her gown were rose and lavender grey, and she had a turban with a plume of feathers.

When she bent down to kiss him he hugged her and pinched her nose, a favourite game of theirs.

'If I do not eat soon I shall be asleep,' he answered, grinning at her. Yes, he was ugly as proper standards went, but she would not alter him by a hair's breadth.

'Do I look fine?' she asked him.

He nodded and watched her with all his eyes until she was out of the door.

But she did not feel fine at supper. They had dined at three in the afternoon but she at five in the Keswick Inn, so they were hungry and she was not. It seemed very natural that Jennifer should enjoy her food. However severe the crisis her appetite was strong.

Judith was strongly conscious of her clothes. That was not like her, but for three years the rose-lavender dress and the turban had lain in a box under the stair at John Green House. Fashions had changed. Evening dresses were shorter and had a padded 'rouleau' at the bottom. Waistbands were directly above the hips. Nevertheless, although she was in fashion, Jennifer was not smart. She looked as though she had put on her clothes in her sleep. Jennifer was untidy, Judith was dowdy; that's what they were. Francis was the grand one, seated gravely at the end of the table, his head thin now, as though carved of a fine stone. The ruffles at his neck were of a peerless whiteness.

Their talk was stiff and awkward. They spoke of general affairs. People were still discussing the Cato Street business, although it was eight months since its occurrence. Judith noticed at once with what feverish excitement Francis spoke, as though ignorant desperadoes like Thistlewood and Edwards were in every town, hiding down every lane, concealed in every corner.

She noticed, too, that when he went on in this exaggerated sensational strain Jennifer's lips stiffened and her eyes were scornful. She looked at Judith once, as though to say: 'You see now what he has come to. Can you wonder if I despise this man ?' and Judith thought again that there was an appeal for help there.

Matters became even more personal when they discussed the Coronation that was to be celebrated in the following year, the King's efforts for a divorce, and the Queen's eccentric behaviour.

Francis, who had been drinking, Judith saw, very much more than was his habit in the old days, broke into a demonstrative, emotional defence of the Queen. The King was a blackguard; he did not care who heard him say it. He was surely old enough now to say what he pleased. Besides, everyone knew what the King was. It was disgraceful that the country should have to suffer under such a man. And the poor Queen – well, she had been, perhaps, a little imprudent at times. She was eccentric, emotional. But who had driven her to her eccentricities ? Brougham was a hero. He would drink to Brougham. They must all drink to Brougham. Judith noticed then Jennifer's irritation. She saw that such scenes as these were part of every evening's programme. Jennifer, looking across the table at Francis scornfully, praised the King, said that he had been much calumniated. At least he was no prig nor Methodist. For her part she liked a jolly fellow, a man who knew what life was and lived it to the full . . . not a half-alive pedant who skulked about the house . . . She stopped abruptly. Then smiled at Francis.

'I am fortunate,' she said softly, 'to have a husband who strikes the mean. Judith, do you not think that Francis is looking well?'

'Very well,' said Judith, and she put out her hand and touched his. He looked at her with a glance that had in it so much of apology and unhappiness that her heart was wrung.

The food was badly cooked and warm when it should have been hot. The meal dragged on interminably. No allusion was made to anyone's private affairs. At last they sat there in silence while the candles trembled and the old clock ticked like a miser counting his money.

What was the matter with the house? There was more in this than the relations of Francis and Jennifer, more than Jennifer's infidelity, more than Francis' self-disgust. An air of apprehension was everywhere. She had detected it, even in the faces of the two children.

When at last they got up to move into the parlour, Judith thought of Watendlath with a longing that was almost irresistible. She had an impulse to run out into the dark cool garden. She would be closer to the hills there and would hear water running somewhere. She felt the touch of her hand on Charlie Watson's strong arm. Oh, there everything was so simple, so happy.

In the hall she stopped for an instant to hear whether there was any sound from Adam. No, he would be sleeping quietly. She was comforted again.

In the parlour the three of them sat like images. The outburst was soon coming, but until it did they must be silent. Judith herself was affected by the stillness that was so vocal. Seated with her back to the window she had a sudden fancy that Walter Herries was standing outside, watching them, peering in. It was all that she could do not to get up and see.

Then Jennifer rose, said that she was going to bed, kissed Judith and went out, her eyes half closed, yawning a little, just as she had used to do.

'Well, Judith,' said Francis.

'Well, Francis.'

He got up with a quick impetuous movement and came to where she was sitting. He knelt down by her chair, put his arms around her, rested his head on her breast.

'Oh, I am so weary, so weary,' he murmured.

She thought of the time when she was a baby and had adored him, when David had whipped her, and she had not cared so long as Francis loved her. She smiled a little wryly above his head. Poor Francis!

Then to her distress he began to weep. He seemed to be completely broken down. He wept as though all his control must be abandoned or he would die. She had never seen Francis cry. She could not bear it.

'Oh no, Francis. No . . . No, no!'

Then at last he looked up at her, his cheeks stained with tears.

'Forgive me, my dear. It is many years since I wept last. I am not given to weeping. But seeing you come back tonight, after all this time, the same, so familiar, the only friend I have left — it has been too much for me. Truly, Judith, I am desperate. I don't know which way to turn.'

'Now sit here beside me.' She motioned to a place on the sofa. 'Let us talk over things quietly. They are never so urgent when one talks over them quietly. We will discuss everything just as we have always done.'

He came and sat beside her.

'But you are going to stay now that you are here, are you not ? . . . You are not going away ?'

'For a few days. Of course, we will stay for a few days.'

'For a few days ? Oh, but that is nothing. Judith, you must live here again — for a while at least — you and your boy . . .'

'Live here ?' She laughed. 'Francis, do you not realize that I am now a scandalous person ? I have had a child out of wedlock as everyone knows. With Jennifer and the children—'

'Scandalous!' he broke out. 'We are all scandalous now! Yes, I will say anything tonight. I have held myself in long enough. Jennifer has been that man's mistress for years now — quite an old family affair. As soon as I am away at Kendal or Carlisle he comes here, and everyone knows it. Everyone knows it, I tell you. It is the common joke! Walter sees to that . . . And all these years I have done nothing. I, the fine Francis who started the world with such grand ideas. I have done nothing, nothing at all.

'I have skulked in corners, taken his hand, offered him drink, while he makes my wife a common whore . . . Oh, my God, my God, I am the most despicable man on this earth, the most despicable and the most unhappy!'

She tried to calm him. He was trembling from head to foot.

'She hates me. She despises me. And, God forgive me, I love

her yet. It is because I love her that I have been able to do nothing, because with my cursed nature I have always seen two of everything. She never loved me. I forced her into marriage. Why should I have denied her all opportunity of love?'

He caught her hand.

'Judith, do you remember that Ball all those years ago, the Ball when Jennifer broke Christabel's fan? Of course, you do. It all started from that. It has all come from that. You remember that I was talking to you when she first came by! How lovely she was that night! Do you remember? Catherine de' Medici with the collar of pearls and her white neck and the crimson dress? Her excitement at the Ball – do you remember? . . .

'And after – the meeting in Berkeley Square. Do you remember? When I sat in the window and it was so hot and the scent of the lilac came up from the street. I sat in the window thinking of Jennifer, and then do you remember how I broke in upon Will and how angry he was? Our separation dated from that.'

Did she not remember? And how, a moment after, Georges stood there in the doorway, Georges in his brown suit, spent and done? . . .

'Before that,' Francis went on eagerly, 'everything had been well – for all of us and for the country too, I think. What a good old country it was when I was a child, so quiet and so cosy! Everyone drank ale, and there was "oat clap bread", and no one came to disturb us. The children would help in the spinning or drive the sheep on the fells. Everyone was happy together. But now there are visitors peering and fingering, and in the towns children of six and seven years work in the dark, and the machines have come to take the bread out of men's mouths. The sky is blackening with smoke, we have a King too drunk to sit on the throne, and class is against class . . .'

He broke off. 'No, by God, what do I care for the country any more? There was a time when I cared. Did I not kill my own father and cause my mother to hate me, because the Bastille fell?'

He laughed bitterly, striking his knee with his hand.

'But now what should a cuckold think of his country – a cuckold plain to all his neighbours, and any who do not know of it kind Cousin Walter will tell them of it.'

She tried to calm him. He was so dreadfully excited that she thought that at any moment he might raise the house.

'Dear Francis, the country is well enough. This is a time of transition, and such times always seem hard to those who are in them. There is a grand new world coming . . .'

'And I don't care if there is!' he interrupted her. 'You can have your fine new world! If I could but get my fingers round dear Walter's large throat!' He stopped himself with a tremendous effort. 'You see how it is with me tonight, my dear. I am excited at seeing you again. For you are the only one I have left, the only one who understands me. I killed my father. My mother hated me. My brother and wife hate me yet. God knows but my children hate me too. But I ask for no pity. It is all my own doing. You and I, my dear, are misfits; and to be a misfit in the Herries family is to be slain.'

'We are neither of us slain,' she said, looking up at him quickly. 'It is perhaps true that we are misfits. But it is the misfits, I fancy, who give the value to the world. What would the Herries family be without us? A dull, poor lot. We are the ones who understand and because we suffer have charity. We can see into both worlds. We travel into strange countries where the others cannot go, and bring back the news.' She laughed. 'I am turning very poetical,' she said. 'It is not my ordinary fashion. But I must tell you, Francis, that if I am a misfit I am a very happy one. And so may you be too if you will. I am certain that Jennifer does not hate you. She must be long weary of that other affair. All will soon be forgotten . . .'

'Forgotten!' he broke in. 'Not with Walter Herries there! Ah, you do not yet know the villain of the piece!'

'Walter?' she asked. 'What can he do?'

'What can he do? What has he not done? He hates us, has always done, because, firstly, he says Jennifer insulted his mother, secondly, he must be king of the castle here and wants no other Herries round, and, thirdly, he has a deformed son, and my children make him mad . . .'

'But he can do nothing.'

'Do nothing? He can do everything. He is my perpetual enemy and has been these five years. He is so proud that he will burst his skin one of these days. He has all the neighbourhood in his pocket.'

He calmed himself that he might give the value to his words. 'Do you know what for five years he has been doing? There are spies all around me, and every small action of mine is repeated to him. It has been so for five years now. Fancy to yourself what it would be if a good friend of yours, who had known you well for a long while, drew a caricature of you in a book, using all your external habits, your tricks of speech, your eccentricities, and then, with a diabolic cleverness, twisted them all to mean and sordid motives ? You would be yourself bewildered. You would say yes, that it was true; you had done this and that, you wore your hair so, you laughed thus, and like all men you had your weaknesses, your follies. Was this perhaps a true picture ? And if you saw it as partly true how much more would others, who know you but externally, judge of your true self ? And you would begin to doubt yourself and to suspect every movement, every gesture. I tell you, Judith, that my neighbours here who have known me all my life long take rather Walter's picture of me now than their own. There is nothing goes on in this house that he does not know, nothing that he does not use . . .'

Yes, he would be like that. She knew instinctively that what Francis said was true. She felt, even here in the warm safe room, the force and danger of his overbearing vitality.

But she answered firmly:

'Listen, Francis. No one can traduce you but yourself. Even your bitterest enemy knows that a satire is a satire. Its very exaggeration must make him consider the opposite. One is alone in this world. No one knows one save oneself, and then it is only a glimpse of the truth that one has. Forget Walter, and if you cannot forget Walter fight him!'

She jumped to her feet.

'I could fight him! He should have enough of his spying and traducing if I got at him!'

'Yes, yes,' he cried eagerly. 'You must stay, Judith. Remain here. With you to help me I can be another man. Although I am old—' His voice faltered. 'Sixty is an age . . .'

She had had enough. She was infinitely weary. Francis' request that she should stay gave her a sudden flick of terror. She did not want to stay. She must get back to Watendlath. She and Adam safe in Watendlath, away from all these Herries . . .

She kissed him.

'Goodnight, Francis, dear. All will come right.'

But as she climbed slowly the stair she thought, in spite of herself, 'But how *could* he not have challenged Fernyhirst ? How *could* he let it go on as he has – all these years ?' But she was weary to consider it further. However, her evening was not yet done with. As she passed Jennifer's door a voice called her.

She went in.

Jennifer was sitting on her bed in her shift, her long white legs dangling to the floor. Her room was in a disorder. Clothes were flung about the floor, drawers were pulled open, the curtains were roughly drawn, a lamp by the bed was smoking to the ceiling.

Judith closed the door.

'What has he been saying?'

'Oh, it is so late!' Judith sighed. 'Dear Jennifer—'

'No, I must know.'

'He has been saying nothing, only that he is unhappy—'

Jennifer put out a long white arm and drew Judith to the bed.

'I am unhappy too! Oh, so dreadfully unhappy! It is all his fault. I hate him . . . I have hated him for years. Why was I such a fool as to marry him? He has been speaking to you of Edward.'

'Edward?'

'Fernyhirst. But that is all finished. Finished long ago. I hate him too.'

Judith looked at her, and again her tiresome maternal impulse that was for ever preventing her real action interfered. But what was she to do? This poor, tired, aged woman! And once there had been that brilliant happy girl, radiant with beauty and success, in the crimson dress, the collar with the pearls?

But she had still lovely legs and feet! How different might Judith's own story have been had she had such wonderful feet and ankles! She put her arm round her, but how she longed for her bed!

'Francis spoke for the most part of Walter!'

'That devil! He is determined to ruin us, Judith, all of us – my poor children—' and even then, when she should have wept, she yawned, kicking her feet a little, looking at her silver slippers. And in that yawn Judith saw once and for ever exactly what she was. She was true Herries. She had no imagination, none whatever. Had she had any she would never have married Francis, never have lived in Cumberland, never have suffered an intrigue with Fernyhirst, never have stayed here for years, doing nothing, understanding nothing, seeing nothing! And it was against the Herries in her that Francis had beaten in vain! Had she been of an age it was Walter that she should have married. They would have suited one another to perfection.

It was from that moment of comprehension that Judith's complete domination of Jennifer began.

'Dear Judith. You are such a consolation. There was a time when I was jealous of you. I know how shockingly I behaved. You need not tell me of my behaviour. But now I would do anything for you – and Francis too. It is the one point on which we are agreed. You must stay for a long, long while.'

Judith smiled and shook her head.

'I am an abandoned woman, Jennifer – myself and my little bastard. We do not belong to good society any more.'

'What foolishness! I am sure that an illegitimate child is nothing. Everyone is so free in these days. And I am as bad as you. Everyone knows about Edward. Certainly you must stay.'

'I have grown unused to society. I am a peasant, digging and ditching, watching the sheep. You cannot think how strange these clothes seemed to me tonight.'

Jennifer, looking at her naked legs with approval, answered:

'I am sure that is a very good costume. But we are two old women. What does it matter what we wear? My legs are still fine, although there is no one who cares any more. Nor do I wish there to be. Love is the most wearying thing I know.'

Judith said goodnight.

'Then you will stay?'

'For a day or two at least.'

'No, for always. The children worship you, and little Adam is a love.' She stood up in her shift that fell in folds to her silver slippers. For a moment there was something genuine and touching in her fine eyes that looked out above her painted cheeks in a true and human appeal.

She said what Francis had said:

'You are my only friend.'

Judith undressed and lay down beside Adam. She stared into the dark. She *would* not, no, she *would* not be caught by these two. She *would* not come back into these Herries affairs . . . But they were so alone. Francis had no one – Jennifer only her brother, who was a fat careless bachelor in Bournemouth. Both Prosper and Amelia were dead.

But she *would* not be caught . . . She seemed to hear beyond the window the water of Watendlath. She could see the Tarn lying in ebony silence under the stars. The sheep were pressing up the road, the cows were to be milked; here came Tyson, his arms loaded with hay for the cattle. Armboth touched the stars . . .

She was near to tears; she was so homesick.

She was too old, too settled in her quieter life to take up these quarrels again. Ah, but Walter, riding his white horse, striking at Adam with his whip . . .

With a gesture of protection she stretched out her arm and

drew Adam to her. He was deep in sleep but he grunted like a little pig and nestled into her side.

ROUND OF THE MOON

THE HOUSE WAS bathed in sunlight and ladders of dust quivered in the air. No room had been swept for months; the kitchen was a disgrace; the dairy – ah, how beautiful it had once been with its gleaming cleanliness, the stone floor like a mirror – and now! In the stables there were but three horses, two of them fit for little but to drag the carriage at a funeral pace along the rocky, uneven roads.

Judith swept through the place like a whirlwind. Mrs Quinney, the housekeeper, Martha Hodgson, the woman who had opened the door on Judith's arrival (she was cook and maid both), Doris, a stupid country girl, and Mr Winch, the thin cadaverous little tutor, were, in addition to Bennett the coachman and Jack the stable-boy, all the servants. Very different from David's day, different even from Jennifer's early day, but Judith must make the best of it. And make the best of it she did. In no time she had them all at her call, all save Mr Winch, of whom more in a moment.

She summed them up instantly. Mrs Quinney was lazy, greedy, gossipy, weak, amiable, gossipy, greedy and lazy. Martha was earnest, plain, silent, faithful, opinionated and earnest. Doris was little, if anything, removed from the beasts of the field and like them was hungry, obedient, and responsive to overtures of love from the opposite sex. Bennett had always reminded her a little of her dear Charlie. She liked him because of that. He was stouter, less intelligent, had far less personality, but was a man – that is, he was a Cumberland man and therefore silent, suspicious, obstinate, faithful and courageous.

Jack the stable-boy pleased her best of all. He was only a lad and had come from the depths beyond Mardale, but he had the makings of a grand gentleman. He, from the first, would do anything for her.

There they were, ready to her hand. For years they had been neglected. Francis had scarcely spoken to them, Jennifer had let them do as they would. Before the week was out the house looked a different place, the floors shone, the silver glittered, the food came hot to the table, the horses trotted, Caesar the dog barked at night when he heard a strange step, the spiders were broomed away, the carpets were dusted, the grass of the lawn was cut, a dead cat was removed from the Gothic temple, a mouse was found in the chaise, chrysanthemums, bronze and orange, lighted the parlour, the drawers in Jennifer's bedroom were tidied, Dorothy had fresh ribbons to her dress, and the holes in John's stockings were mended.

Judith was to stay only a day or two. It was nearly Christmas before she had the house entirely to her liking.

Then, one winter's day when the sun like a swollen red penny rolled between shifting orange clouds over Skiddaw, she looked out through the bottle-green glass of the parlour window and saw Mr Winch creeping round the corner of the house towards the stables.

Creeping he was. His thin lanky body was bent almost to all-fours. There was a moment when in actual fact he knelt on the path and looked ludicrous enough in that position.

Abruptly round the corner came Francis, his head bent, his arms behind his back, and almost stepped on Mr Winch, who was diligently brushing his trousers. Francis said a word to him and came on, lost in thought as he always was in these days.

Now what had Mr Winch been doing? With her accustomed impetuosity Judith had disliked him from the first moment of meeting him, and, it is to be feared, for no better reason than that his hands were damp. Afterwards there were other reasons. Whence had he come? He had been in the house for four years and yet both Francis and Jennifer were exceedingly vague about him. He had tutored Lord Somebody's son once somewhere; he said himself that he came from Warwickshire; Jennifer disliked him and behaved as though he were not there. Francis talked to him on a day, and then on another day disregarded him. It seemed that he taught the children something. John at least said that he did. Judith disliked him increasingly, and the more she disliked him the more obsequious he became. His appearance was most certainly not prepossessing, for his narrow grey eyes were so placed that you could not be sure whether he had a squint or no, his suit was always a shiny black and he was for ever blowing his nose.

This vision out of the window woke Judith to life. She had been alive indeed all these weeks, engaged on a business that she adored, but the house had swallowed her. She had not seen outside its affairs. Except in one matter, and that was the emotion that never left her, night or day, her love for her son, Adam. She was suffering for the first time in her life from jealousy.

For Adam, when he had been in the house two days, fell in love with John. He was in love so completely and absolutely that he forgot his mother altogether. For five years she had been everything to him, and now she was, in the flash of an instant, it seemed, nothing to him at all. Of course it was not so. It was simply that he was at the age when he could not think of two things at the same time. He had never, as yet, in his life had an older boy for companion, and he found it simply enchanting.

John was kind, amiable and easy. He had not had in these last years a happy life. The house had been smoky with unhappiness. The two children had been quite neglected. He had followed the hounds at a time, but then the horse had been sold. He went out shooting rabbits with Bennett. He witnessed an occasional wrestling or cock-fight. But he was 'soft' for his time. He hated cruelty of any kind. It made him sick. It was hard to say at present what he cared for. He was not a student like his father, he did not roam the country. He liked to stay at home, work in the garden, read stories. Although he was no student he could read tales and poetry to himself by the hour. He would sit curled up in a corner somewhere and pray that he would not be noticed. He had always detested Mangnall's *Questions* and Butler's *Guide to Useful Knowledge* – for such things he had no use whatever, but Goldsmith's *History of England* he devoured in all its four volumes because of the thrilling detail in it. Then there was Vicesimus Knox's *Elegant Extracts in Prose and Verse*, then *Marmion*, *The Lay*, the Waverleys, *The Parents' Assistant*, *The Fairchild Family* and, secretly, obtained from some of the Forresters who lived in Bassenthwaite, many volumes of the Minerva Press, *The Mysterious Hand*, *The Demon of Society* and the rest.

He read, he dreamed, his life was intensely solitary. It was an amazing thing for him when this ugly baby, so fearless, so interested and so happy, came into it. The two great characteristics of Adam Paris, then and always, were his interest and his happiness. In later years he was to exasperate many persons by these two qualities, for most human beings quite naturally call extensive interests selfishness, and happiness complacency.

John had not known much happiness yet in his life, and few persons had cared very actively whether he were happy or no. He was shy of his father as his father was shy of him, and afraid of his mother. Dorothy was a girl. Mr Winch was nothing. Only

Bennett was his friend, and Bennett had never much to say. Now this small boy came and worshipped, thought him a god, believed everything that John told him, trusted him utterly. Soon they were inseparable.

Adam did not forget his mother, but she was always there, while John was something new and showed him everything that he wanted to see.

When Judith realized that she was jealous she was amazed at herself. She liked John and trusted him; Adam could not be with anyone better. But her jealousy would not let her alone. She showed it to no one, but something told her that the first stage of her life with her son was over. She would never again have him so completely her own as she had had him during those first five years. She was alone again. It seemed to be the one lesson that life was for ever teaching her. Alone she was; alone she must ever be. She did not yet realize that it was the lesson that every other human being was also, with exasperated tears and helpless gestures, learning.

The fire of her love for Adam burnt her heart, it seemed to her. She stood listening for him. She called softly, then louder, then louder again. At last he would appear at the stairhead or at the stable door, John beside him. She would smile and wave to him and go away.

At night she had him. He would dance into bed, ask her one question after another on the wonders of the past day, and then instantly fall asleep. Then her time came. She would fold his small body in her arms and, with his head against her breast, would tell him how she loved him, how he was everything to her, how he was all that she had, how she loved him as no mother had ever loved her son, and the shadows of the fire would leap ironically on the wall and Adam would breathe softly in his sleep, lost to her even then.

But he was not really lost to her. In the depth of her being she knew it and was comforted. Meanwhile the discovery of Mr Winch on all-fours on the garden path woke her to important issues.

Having the house now tidied and disciplined, she was aware that, in spite of herself, Walter Herries' shadow was hanging over her as it was over the others. Not so grimly perhaps, nor so tragically, for she still maintained to herself with all her energy that her stay here was only temporary and that in another fortnight – after Christmas for certain – she would be free, in Watendlath, of the pack of them, never to return. She was not very sensitive as to her social position – she had never been sensitive – but she was aware that the visitors to Uldale in these last months had all regarded her with a very lively curiosity, and she thought that, behind their politeness, there was a kindly ostracism. They did not, she was aware, invite her to their houses, but that might have been as easily because of Jennifer's scandal as her own.

Only good, kind Mrs Southey invited her. She went with the secret hope that she would see again that strange boy Hartley. But Hartley was not there. None of the children were present. Mr Southey was very kind and a little distant.

Of Walter himself and his family she had seen nothing. The two households were cut off from one another as though they were as remote as China from Spain. But, rightly or wrongly, she heard the loud voice and saw the broad back of Walter behind everything and, in spite of her own good common sense, began to catch something of the superstition that Francis and Jennifer had of him – as a sort of malicious devil, horns on his head, hoofs instead of feet, and an eye in the middle of his back.

Seeing Mr Winch, one thing at least became plain to her: Mr Winch was Walter's spy. Assured of that, she was, in a moment, alive to a whole blazing bundle of circumstances, as suddenly bright and crackling as though she had seen it burst into flame before her eyes.

On looking back afterwards it appeared to her that everything and everyone sprang into action from that moment when she saw Mr Winch on all-fours. It was, in any case, very soon after that day that some of the worst and unhappiest moments of her life confronted her.

The awful day opened for her quietly enough. It was a fortnight before Christmas, and in the morning the sky was a bright shrill blue, the tops had a powdering of snow and the roads were hard with frost.

Adam was to go on some grand Christmas expedition into Keswick with John and Dorothy. She accompanied them, riding her own sturdy little mare, Phyllis, that she had brought with her from Watendlath. She thought that after she had seen them safely into the town she would ride on into Borrowdale and have a glimpse of Herries again. She had woken that morning with her head full of Warren. She could not tell why. She had not thought of him, she was ashamed to confess to herself, for months. But now, without warning, he had returned as the dead do unexpectedly return.

They had an agreeable ride into Keswick, passing many enchanting things on the way – a pedlar, a blind man with a trumpet, two drunken men fighting, a flock of sheep and a herd of cows. Adam had had his eyes and nose pressed to the windows of the chaise and was asking questions as fast as he could breathe, not waiting for any answers. The vast broad back of Bennett bobbed up and down on the box outside, the inside smelt of straw and mice, and Judith tried to feel no jealousy as she watched John holding Adam that he should not fall.

Then she rode on into Borrowdale. The road was still wild and uneven and unfit for a carriage, although carriages often used it, for it was the thing now to tour the Lakes and see 'the horrid precipices' and 'the thunderous waterfalls' that had so terribly frightened Mr Gray. Today, however, Judith had the scene to herself. Not a human being did she see, save an old man gathering sticks in a field. The Lake embraced the blue sky with a little tremor of excitement, and very lovely were the reflections of the snow-sprinkled hills in that blue water, hill-tops trembling like shadows in a swaying mirror.

The village of Grange was dead, and when at last she came to the Herries house, that was dead also. As before, when she had been with Warren, no one was there, but there were the remains of a meal on the table and a crumbling fire in the kitchen.

She sat on the old mildewed couch in the upper room for a while. Here she and Warren had sat ... how long, long ago! Had they not sat there that day Adam would not be sucking lollipops (as she was sure that he was doing) in Keswick at this moment. Once again she asked herself why she had surrendered to Warren? For love of Georges' shadow? – and then with a sharp pang she realized for the first time how swiftly Georges was now fading from her mind. All the pain of losing him was gone. She did not miss him any more! Adam had taken his place.

She was not a sentimentalist. Facts were facts, and Georges, who had always wanted everyone else to be happy so long as he himself was not uncomfortable, would be glad. But Adam! She stood before the dead stone fireplace and pressed her hands before her eyes. Her passion of possession was terrific. She must govern it, guard it. Adam as he grew must be free. Looking into darkness, seeing into the future, she was afraid of herself.

The house dripped with damp and was of a fearful cold. She listened. Were there ghosts about? No; today Adam had slain them all. Father, mother, husband – one crick of her son's finger and they were fled.

She visited Georges' grave, then stopped at one of the cottages in Rosthwaite and ate and drank there. She knew every man, woman and child in Rosthwaite. It needed all her control not to push Phyllis up the well-known track. She was so near to Watendlath that, had Adam been with her, she must have gone – and then never have come down again! It was just over her head! If she listened she could hear Mrs Ritson calling and Molly the cow lowing for her calf!

She would not come this way again. It was dangerous. But she would not need to come, for in a fortnight Christmas would be here, and directly after Christmas she and Adam would leave Uldale for ever.

She started homewards and saw that the weather was changing. She looked back and beheld how over Scafell and the Gavel great black clouds were climbing. They were piling up as though out of a vast vat. The blue sky above her head seemed to tremble in anticipation of its destruction. The clouds had a sort of boiling rage and fury in their blackness. She turned on her horse to watch as though at some show or pageant. Then she saw a small white cloud, like a puff of smoke from a cannon, spring above the hill and start to fly from the enemy. The little white cloud spread across the blue, and the black clouds pursued it. She could almost hear them roaring in their fury. 'I hope it will escape! I hope it will escape,' she could fancy the bare trees around her, that were all beginning to tremble, saying. But of course the little cloud had no escape. The vanguard of the black army put out an ebony feeler, as an octopus might do, and the little white cloud was instantly swallowed. The landscape around her went dead as though a hand had struck it. The trees were shaking violently. A drop of rain smacked her cheek. She whipped Phyllis up and ran for it. By Grange she was caught. The rain slapped the earth like a woman beating a carpet. The drops danced on the ground with exultant joy. There was an empty outhouse off the road opposite the bridge. Pulling Phyllis after her, she ran in – and found Walter Herries filling the little place with his bulk!

They were at first very polite. His eyes twinkled with amusement. The noise of the rain on the roof was so loud that they had to shout. Then, quite suddenly, she sprang in.

'Walter Herries, you should know that shortly I intend to wring the neck of your shabby little spy and throw him into the stable.'

'My spy!'

'Nasty Mr Winch.'

He laughed, throwing his great head back and slapping his thigh.

'Cousin Judith, come and stay at Westaways for a little. Food and drink are better than at Uldale.'

She looked at him contemptuously.

'I would marry Mr Winch sooner than sleep under your roof.'

'I am not inviting you to share my bed, Cousin Judith.'

She flushed.

'That was worthy of you,' she said. 'But remember you cannot touch *me* anywhere. It may be in the end I can harm *you* the more.'

He seemed contrite. 'I said a dirty thing. For once you see me ashamed. Make the most of it.'

She looked at him with a quiet inspection that made him, she saw, uncomfortable.

'I believe I could be your match if I cared, but I have done with all the Herries affairs. I never was in truth part of them and I never will be. But you must understand that I have loved Francis all my life, and something will come of your persecution of him.'

They had to shout, and there was something very ludicrous in that. In spite of herself, and although she was feeling exceedingly angry and had never hated him more, she smiled. He smiled too.

'I think we could be very good friends,' he said.

'Never! Never!' she answered passionately. 'I hope very much I can do you some harm before I die.' Then, to her great vexation, she smiled again, for a little trickle of rain, coming in from the roof, fell down his cheek and made him look absurd.

'Why do you persecute Francis? It is a very small game and not at all worth all the energy you put into it.'

'Jennifer insulted my mother,' he said like a sulky schoolboy.

'What! You are going back all that way – because years ago at a stupid Ball Jennifer broke your mother's fan?'

'They can leave Uldale and go elsewhere. Francis is doing no good there. Jennifer is the countryside scandal. They do the Herries name harm.'

'The Herries name! And what good do *you* do the Herries name?'

That touched him. He started up.

'By God! I do the Herries name more good than your rascally father, or *his* miserable puling grandson.' He grew calm again, came near to her and would have taken her arm had she not moved away.

'Now listen, Judith. I have but begun. I am a young man, strong and healthy. I shall wipe your Uldale family out as though they had never been. I have wealth and power, but nothing at all in comparison with what I shall have. I am here for ever – I and my son after me.'

'I have not seen your children,' she said quietly.

It was cruel of her. She touched him there. His stout red face grew more crimson. For a moment she felt almost kindly towards him.

'Never mind,' he said, so low that she scarcely caught the words. 'My son has one leg that is shorter than the other, but he will have a head-piece that Francis' boy will one day fear.'

'So you carry the feud into a later generation,' she said scornfully.

'Not if they leave Uldale. Let them go South. I will not bother them.'

'I see!' She looked him in the eyes. They were now very close together and she could smell the stuff of his handsome brown riding coat.

'Had I not other plans for myself I should like to stay and fight you, Cousin Walter . . . I, too, have a son, you know. His father was Herries, even though distantly.'

'Yes. Poor Warren.' He laughed contemptuously. 'An illegitimate Herries, my dear.'

'But Herries blood,' she answered.

He caught her arm then, whether she liked it or no.

'We should be friends, Judith. We are of the same sort.'

'But we are enemies, Cousin Walter,' she answered. 'Good, sound, rock-bottom enemies. Good day to you.'

The rain had almost ceased. She mounted Phyllis and rode away. It was nearly dark when she reached Keswick, but the sky had cleared again. There were a few stars already and a fine frosty tang in the air. Soon there would be a grand full moon. The thought of the moon stayed her. There would be plenty of light to ride home by if she returned later. Francis had gone to Cockermouth for the night on a piece of business and she shrank from an evening quite alone with Jennifer. There was nothing more dreary, for Jennifer would either yawn and say nothing, or seek to abuse Francis, when Judith must stop her, or retrace the by now desperately familiar path of her affair with Fernyhirst, her weariness of him, the unfairness of everything and what would Judith advise her to do?

When Francis was present things were better, but without

him – no, she could not endure it! Moreover, she was herself tired. She was not so young as she had been. It had been a long ride to Borrowdale; the visit to Herries, the encounter with Walter had for the moment exhausted her.

So she stepped in to see the only two friends that she had now in Keswick. They were a quaint pair, Miss West and Miss Pennyfeather. They were one of the scandals of Keswick, and about them Keswick was never weary of talking. They lived in a very small house in Main Street, next to a smithy. They were indeed an eccentric pair, devoted, original, entirely indifferent to public opinion, clever and sarcastic.

Miss West dressed as near a man as to be no matter. She wore a powdered wig and a coat with brass buttons. It was said that in the evening in her parlour she wore trousers. She drank and, it was rumoured, smoked a long clay pipe. She had a thin dried face with a long nose and very bright keen eyes. Miss Penny-feather was very feminine, round and plump, pink and white. But she was even more sarcastic and cruel than Miss West in a quiet soft way. In reality they were neither of them cruel, but gave much in charity. They hated men and would not, it was said, have one in the house. They liked Judith greatly and would have seen much of her had she wished it. She liked them also, but was not in Keswick sufficiently.

She knocked on the door, was admitted by their little maid Betty, and found them by the fire in the parlour, Miss West reading to Miss Pennyfeather from one of the novels of Mrs Cuthbertson.

They were enchanted to see Judith.

Miss West threw Mrs Cuthbertson on to the floor, crying in a deep bass voice: 'This is Stuff!'

Then they had supper off cold chicken, rhubarb pie and cheese and, after that, played cards very frivolously. Miss West told some scandalous stories about the curate of Crosthwaite, about the wife of a coal-merchant who had recently come into money and set up his carriage, and a French poodle owned by the eccentric Mrs Mason, a widow. They all laughed very much and Miss West imitated the Crosthwaite curate looking for his hand-kerchief in the middle of his sermon.

When Judith at last departed she wondered what had hap-pened to her lately. It seemed so long since she had last laughed with real abandon.

Phyllis was thinking of her stable and under a full moon trotted with enthusiasm. It was late. The Crosthwaite Church struck the hour of eleven as they turned into the Carlisle road.

As she went along she was happy and confident. 'Three old women! Never mind. We know how we can enjoy ourselves without the men – and I stood up to Walter. I enjoy standing up to Walter. I shall do it again.' She would tempt Miss West and Miss Pennyfeather up to Watendlath after Christmas. They were great riders. They should stay a day or two with her at the farm. They would enjoy the Ritsons . . .

When she reached the house it was five minutes to twelve by the round-faced clock above the stables. The moon shone with such brightness that the whole world of hill, fell and dead white road was recreated into unreality. The stars were fiery – all else was icy cold and like a dried bone in colour.

She put Phyllis into her box, patted her nose and then, almost startled by the sound of her own steps on the cobbles in the still world, crossed over to the house.

She let herself in and with soft tread went straight to her room. The stair was flooded with moonlight.

She lit the candles and, with one raised in her hand, went over to see that Adam was sleeping. With his cheek on his hand, his mouth a little open, he looked so entirely hers and hers alone that she gave a little gasp of happiness, put down the candle and sat on the bed-edge gazing at him.

She blew out the candle, drew back the curtain and let the moonlight spread a pool of liquid shadow about the carpet. She did not feel sleepy. She was immensely content. She sat at the window looking at the frosted slope of Skiddaw, the friend of her life.

She was thus idly watching and had listened to the clocks tell the half-hour when, muffled by the window but sharp on the frosted road, she heard the hoofs of a horse. She bent forward and saw, to her amazement, the horse stop at the gate and a heavily-cloaked rider, whom she quickly knew to be Francis, dismount. Francis! Here! Now! She stood up, her hand at her heart. Something told her at once that there was trouble. She saw him open the gate and lead the horse round to the stable.

Driven by some instinct, unreasoning but imperative, she softly went from her room on to the landing, and, as she did so, at the same moment Jennifer's door opened and she appeared, in her nightdress, her ringlets about her shoulders, a candle in her hand, and on her feet her silver slippers.

'What was that?' she said, her finger to her lip.

'Francis is returned.'

'Oh, my God!'

Even as she breathed that they heard the outer door of the house open. Jennifer seized Judith's wrist. She never spoke, but pushed Judith into her room.

Six candles were blazing, a table with wine and the remains of a chicken was near the bed, which was tumbled and in disorder, and Fernyhirst in his shirt and trousers, his shirt open at the neck, his rather long grey hair untidily over his forehead, sat sprawling in a large crimson chair.

'What is it?' he asked, looking up; then saw Judith and his mouth stayed open. She thought that she had never seen a more unattractive creature, purple-veined, double-chinned, with a heavy stomach and thick unwieldy legs. Her disgust with both of them was so intense that for a moment it covered everything else. That they should thus – these two elderly lovers – have been philandering in the room next to her sleeping son seemed to her a foul thing. That Jennifer should thus have gone back on her word—

But beyond her personal sense of affront she knew at once there was something more important. Francis must not find them there. He must not. And once this hateful discovery of hers was passed she would see to it that Fernyhirst came to the house no more.

But they remained, frozen into silence. The room seemed chilled by an icy wind from the cold world outside although the fire blazed in the grate. They waited, the two women standing where they were, Fernyhirst sitting up in his chair.

Jennifer only whispered once: 'He always goes to his room.'

They heard nothing, for the door was closed: then, as though the house crashed about their ears, the door opened and he stood there.

Judith saw at once from his face that he had known what he would find. Instantly he flung himself across the room and fell upon Fernyhirst, pulling at his shirt, beating his face with his hand and crying:

'At last! At last! ... You bloody rat ... You whoring, filthy ...'

Jennifer ran to them, pulled feebly at Francis' coat and screamed. The table with the chicken and wine fell over, making a terrible crash.

Judith ran in among them.

'Francis! Francis! Listen! ... Be quiet! Be still! The house must not hear, it must not wake ... Francis! Francis!'

Francis seemed to hear her, for he stopped clawing at Ferny-hirst and walked away, trembling from head to foot, his breath coming with a strange shrill sob.

The scene indeed was very quickly over, for Fernyhirst, silent and, it seemed, unmoved, rose, felt the blood that trickled on his cheek, put on very calmly his waistcoat and coat, picked up from the chair his hat and riding coat and walked to the door.

There he turned and, looking at Francis, said heavily, 'You shall answer me for this.' He seemed not at all disturbed, and even looked at the decanter on the floor as though he had half a mind to pick it up. Then he went out.

Francis came forward, and, speaking very rapidly and, Judith thought, as though he had made up his speech in his head before-hand, addressed Jennifer, who was now sitting on the bed and crying very wildly.

'I go now,' he said, 'and I shall never return. Thank God I have seen the last of you ... I shall attend to your lover ...'

He stammered, as though he would say something to Judith, but suddenly hung his head and went swiftly out of the room.

He dragged his horse out of the stable and clattered up the road in pursuit of Fernyhirst, who was but a little ahead of him. He had but paused to take two rapiers from the corner of his room – the small room behind the parlour that was cluttered with guns, fishing-tackle, books, papers, swords and these rapiers. No one had touched them for many a year.

As he rode he did not feel the cold; he was rather bathed in a damp heat that was also dry, so that, although his forehead was wet with sweat, his hands had no moisture. That afternoon, walking along the street in Cockermouth to see some fellow on a land transaction, he had been touched on the elbow by a ragged man with a black patch over one eye, who had given him a dirty piece of paper. On this was scrawled in a rough unfamiliar hand: 'The Captain is with your wife tonight and don't leave till morning.'

Reading it, he walked on mechanically until he was almost out of the town without knowing it. He was no longer Francis Herries – that weak, lily-livered creature was gone for ever. He was a fiery man of action, but cautious withal, a crafty vengeful devil, murderous in intent, brilliant in device. This sly fiery devil waited until night at the Cockermouth inn, sitting in a room there, with a plate before him, but not eating. Once and again he held scornful converse with the pitiful Francis, who was imprisoned in a cage and could not get out.

'Let me out!' cried Francis.

But the fiery devil only grinned, while his hand trembled on the table and his eyes were blind.

Later he found them just as the dirty piece of paper had said, and now he was going to kill Fernyhirst.

He came upon him a quarter of the way to Stone Ends. He rode past him at a gallop and then turned and faced him. There was bare moor on either side and the moon cynically observant. Everything was as bright as day, and the smoke from the horses' nostrils clouded the air.

'Off your horse, Fernyhirst,' Francis said. 'We will finish this here.'

'Let me pass, you blackguard,' Fernyhirst cried. But he was a coward at a pinch, had always been. He did not know whether Francis had not a pistol. He climbed off his horse and began blustering.

Francis showed him the rapiers.

'We will fight here and now,' he said.

'This is monstrous,' Fernyhirst said. 'No seconds. No arrangements. I protest. I refuse—'

'We will fight here and now,' Francis repeated.

Perhaps it occurred to Fernyhirst that here would be a good opportunity to teach this puling husband a lesson, for although a coward he had been a skilled duellist in younger days, and the rapier was his favourite weapon. He knew, too, that this business would be scandalous if he let it go on. The quickest over the less said.

His hesitation swung to bluster.

'If you wish it,' he said scornfully. 'You are a poor husband, Herries, and poor husbands always make shabby fighters.'

Herries said not a word.

They drew the horses up the moor and over the ridge to a hollow where they could not be seen from the road. They fought in their shirts, although the cold was intense. Francis was a good swordsman, but it was years since he had had any practice. He fought in what was known as the Neapolitan style, with straight arm and straight back, his knees bent. Fernyhirst fought with a flourish, sweeping his rapier in the air. He knew instantly that Francis was a good swordsman, and cursed his own lack of condition, for he was fat and had been drinking heavily that same night. The scene was strange enough. Sheep came up the moor and stood bewildered. The two horses cropped the grass, and across a cloudless sky the full moon proudly sailed. The hills cut the sky sharply in the frosty air and seemed to bend their brows in attention.

They fought for a while without advantage to either side; then suddenly Francis, lowering his rapier a little, pressed upon his enemy. Fernyhirst retreated a step or two, then Francis made a short lunge in tierce. Fernyhirst backed again, but, after some clever feints, came forward and himself began to challenge Francis.

This extra exertion told on him. His breathing distressed him, and soon two moons circled in his vision, swinging about the shining length of Francis' weapon. Was he to be killed? In this bitter air with no witness? A sudden fear of Francis' intensity caught him. He lunged, his breath coming in pants, but he could not find Francis' body. Everywhere that stiff wall of steel met him. His legs were trembling, the ground rocking. The fear of death, of imminent and dreadful death, leapt at his throat like an animal from the moon.

He gave a yell that made the sheep scatter down the slope, turned and fled for his life. Panting, he flung himself on his horse, threw the rapier away from him and rode off as though all the Furies were beside him.

And Francis stood under the moon without moving. This had been the creature to whom for all these years he had surrendered his wife.

The agonized bitterness of a self-contempt that now would never find a cure stole slowly, quietly down upon him.

Gently his head bent; he went towards his horse.

FRANCIS IN LONDON

Spring 1821

FROM THE WINDOW of his little lodging off St James's Street Francis could see a pale green sky floating between the clouds of two smoking chimneys, a curricle waiting outside the bow-window of Ashton's, the hosier's, and a very elegant dandy picking his way through the puddles as though his life depended on the dryness of his boots. Both before and behind him spouts, charged with the rain that the flat roofs had collected, were pouring out their floods. He had navigated one. Now he paused before the other as though collecting all his resources. Soon the lamps on the little elevated posts that dotted the street would be lighted. The sun was almost set. One star, freshly washed, so bright it was, by the recent rain, hovered in the green sky. So agreeable was the spring air that Francis had his window open. He could hear the rattle of the carriage-wheels on the cobbles of St James's, could smell the damp and soot and sea-coal and the cooking that was going on in Mrs Morland's room downstairs.

In his melancholy depressed mood, to watch the dandy gave him some occupation. The man in his light pantaloons (surely his calves were padded!) his absurdly exaggerated hat, his ridiculous collar *à la guillotine*, his monstrous waist (he was wearing beyond question Cumberland corsets), seemed scarcely human.

As he paused, looking at the water-spout, raising first one foot and then another, Francis, in spite of his dejection, could scarcely forbear to laugh. Then there hurried past, his coat up to his ears, a little man with a pile of books under his arm, who, Francis fancied, might be Mr Lamb, to whose house his friend Daintry, the water-colour painter, had one evening taken him. Francis thought, for a wild moment, that Mr Lamb might be coming to pay him a call. Why not? He had been most pleasant to him, talked to him of old plays and actors, asked him whether he had thought of playwriting, had appeared to be interested, had inquired his address . . . but no, it was not Mr Lamb. Of course not. No one ever came to visit him.

The green sky faded, the old lamp-lighter whom Francis knew so well by now, with his funny step that was a kind of dot-and-carry walk, passed down the street. Francis closed the window, drew the curtains, lit the candles, went to the table, drew out his papers; he was writing an article on Malthus which he hoped (very faintly) that the *Evening Chronicle* might look upon kindly. He wrote a few lines and threw down his pen. It was no good; the thing was a farce. He sat there, his head between his hands, muttering to himself that the end had come.

He had taken of late to talking to himself, for indeed he had for the most part no one else to talk to. Mrs Morland told Morland that the poor old gentleman was wrong in his head; she hoped he would do no one a mischief. Morland, who was a coal-merchant by trade and as kind-hearted as any man in London, shook his head and said that he thought that Mr Herries had lived too long in the country. He had lost touch with the Town. 'London's a big wild place these days, Maria, and not good for a gentleman who has no friends seemingly and is accustomed to country fields.' This was perhaps true. Francis *had* lost touch with the Town. He had been here now for nearly five months. After the wretched farcical fight with Fernyhirst he had ridden to Penrith, slept the night there and taken the London coach on the following day.

He had found rooms with the Morlands, and for a week or two had fancied that he might begin a new life. He had written a brief letter to Jennifer, saying that he would never return, but that proper provision would be made for her and the children. He had sought out some of his old friends, avoiding, however, any possible contact with any Herries relations. His principal success here had been with his old acquaintance, Samuel Rogers, who, only a year or two younger than Francis, welcomed him with the warm kindliness and good heart that that crabbed old poet hid under his sneers and oddities.

He welcomed Francis to his famous house in St James's Place, with its view of the Green Park, its collections of prints, its Etruscan vases. Here Francis could have found exactly the society suited to his taste, and many happy contacts might have come of it. He had real literary feeling, could talk excellently when he was in the mood. He had, however, developed an almost crazy spirit of suspicion and self-detraction. It seemed to him that everyone must know of the disgrace and misery that weighed so heavily upon him. No one knew and no one cared; but, after a few visits, some fancied slights, some momentary irritations on the part of old Rogers, he slipped away and hugged his loneliness. He had thought that writing would be his great recourse. He thought that now at last he had the freedom and independence. But always his own wretched thoughts broke into his imagination and shattered it.

He walked mile upon mile of London streets, but here, too, he was unhappy, for the old London that he had known was gone or going. The stucco of Mr Nash was rapidly covering with its pallid cloak the red and brown and grey of the earlier houses. A passion for building seemed to have sprung upon the town, and the suburbs were eating fields and lanes and trees as fast as they could be devoured. This was a busier, more serious London than he had known, and it seemed to have no place for him. Everywhere new shops were opening, no one appeared to have leisure any more, all were thinking of making a fortune or seeing some new invention. Housebuilding, experiments with machinery, expeditions to America, a visit to Paris and back, a tour on the Continent – all these were everyday adventures. It was a world in which he was lost. He was altogether a lost man; he had no foothold anywhere any more. On the little ink-stained desk near the window lay a pile of letters from Judith unopened. He had not read one of them; he did not dare to. She would implore him to return, would tell him of John and Dorothy, of himself and, worst of all, of Jennifer.

The awful thing, the poison that in his loneliness devoured him, was that he still loved Jennifer. He loved her as ardently and as hopelessly as at the beginning, yes, as madly as on that first occasion when he had seen her at the Herries Ball. The thing that had ruined him, apart from his own indecision of character, was that his love had never been returned. That had not been Jennifer's fault – she had been honest with him – but from that misery of tantalization he had died. For now he was as good as dead. Had he once captured her he would have found, likely enough, that the thing captured was neither interesting nor valuable, but he had been able neither to catch her nor leave her, neither to admire her nor despise her, neither to fight for nor against her; she had completed the ruin that his own miserable weakness had begun. As he sat there he did not pity himself nor curse himself. He did not feel that he was altogether to blame. He was a piece of pottery in whom the potter had carelessly set a flaw.

He might be, as Judith had said, one of the hopes of the Herries; but they had been too strong for him and the hope was lost. From the very beginning he had been frightened of Will's efficiency, a rebel against his father, acquiescent in things as they were, a slave to his mother's melodrama, subservient again to his wife's lazy indifference. The Herries had beaten him every time. He might have been a success in any other family. Judith alone had understood him. Judith . . . dear, darling Judith . . . so kind, so wise, so brave, so friendly and true . . .

He got up, made a step towards the desk. He had almost those letters in his hand. But no, he must not. If he read them he would return and there would begin that wretched half-life, with Walter's spying and bullying . . .

Walter! He called the name aloud as though he were challenging it. He could see that swollen, red-faced, confident boaster . . . There was a knock on the door. Mrs Morland looked in.

'A lady to see you, sir,' she said.

'A lady?' He turned back, smoothing his hair that had grown too long and tumbled over his forehead. His heart beat nervously, as it did now when anyone approached him. There was

a pause, and then who should come in? Who but old Maria
Rockage?

He was so greatly surprised that he could not speak, but could
only stare at her with his mouth open. She was an odd enough
figure. She must be, he thought, nearly seventy. She was
wearing a black, rather faded costume of a fashion quite ten
years earlier, all in one piece, tied with a band of ribbon immediately under her ample breasts. Her shoes were muddy and
she had a black poke-bonnet. Her face wore its accustomed
expression of anxiety, nervousness, kindliness and assurance.

Her nervousness was for the actual moment, her assurance
for her general state. But, as always, kindliness was the pre-
dominating note. As a matter of fact, she was not so old as
Francis thought her – she was sixty-six – and she felt a great
deal younger than that.

'Cousin Maria! . . . But I never expected . . . Pray come in . . .
I am delighted . . . But how did you know my lodging?'

She smiled at him with great beneficence.

'Mr Rogers told me. Carey and I were at a party in St James's
Place the other evening, a very fine party . . .' (The odd thought
came to him that, in spite of her Methodist proclivities, she was
ever going to parties.) 'I had Phyllis and Carey with me. Literature and the Arts . . . And then Judith wrote to me. She begged
me to search you out. She is so greatly distressed—'

She was looking at him, and biting the fingers of her worn
gloves, and putting up her hand to pat the hair under her
bonnet, and screwing her mouth round in a strange way that
she had. What a funny old thing she was!

He cleared the papers away and sat her down at the table. Of
course, he said to himself, she was looking around her and seeing
how shabby everything was. She would tell Will and Christabel,
and everyone would know. How was he certain that she had
not come to spy out for Walter? She had but recently been staying at Westaways. Tiresome old thing! And then, to his amazement, he saw that tears were trickling down her cheeks! When
he saw that, it was all that he could do not to cry himself, so tired
and wan and miserable he was. She began to chatter with little
gulps and stammers.

'Francis, we have never known each other very well. We are
almost of an age. I fear it is an impertinence my coming like
this and intruding on your privacy. But I had to come. The Lord
told me to come; and although I know that you think me foolish
about my religion, still we are both old people now and can be

tolerant about one another. I have not come to interfere in any
way, dear Francis. Indeed I have not. But I could not bear to
think of your being all alone and away from Jennifer and your
lovely children – although I have never quite agreed with
Jennifer, yet she is no longer as young as she was neither, and
the pomps and vanities of our life fade away, leaving us often
much alone. I know, although I have the best husband in the
world and dear Carey and dear Phyllis, I know what it is to be
lonely and have only the Lord to depend upon—' She broke off
and looked at him with mild kindly eyes, beseeching him not to
be rude to her.

She smiled at him over her handkerchief, a watery but en-
couraging smile. He wished to be kind – but what was he to say?

'Dear Cousin Maria, this is very good of you. I fear I have no
hospitality to offer you.'

'Oh,' she broke in, 'I want nothing. I want nothing at all, I
assure you. Too good of you – and your room is very cosy, very
cosy indeed. And right on the street, so that you have people
passing. I always say that if you have people passing you cannot
really be lonely. Always something going on – a carriage accident
or a fire or a Punch and Judy. I would go anywhere myself to
see a Punch and Judy. Carey is for ever laughing at me for it.
"Why, Maria," he says, "I believe you'd run down the street if
there were a Punch and Judy about" – and I believe I would, you
know. So very amusing . . . One never tires . . .' She broke off
and then said abruptly: 'And when was the last time you heard
from dear Judith?'

'I haven't heard,' he said in a very low voice, 'for quite a
while.'

She put out her gloved hand and laid it on his.

'Francis,' she said, 'go home. Think of your dear children.
Forgive Jennifer and go home. We must all forgive one another.
I am certain that Carey and I have forgiven one another a hun-
dred times. Go home, Francis.'

He caught his hands one within another and looked straight
in front of him.

'I cannot, Cousin Maria. I cannot. You do not know—'

She came closer to him, putting her hand on his arm.

'No, of course I do not know, but I cannot endure to see you
looking so unhappy. We are not young any longer, Francis, you
and I; and when we are old it is not at all easy to be alone. No, it
is not easy. Carey and I miss one another if we are apart a day.
What will you do here in this lodging alone? Come to us at

Grosset for a while if that will assist you. And then go home. Jennifer means very well. She means very well indeed. She had a selfish upbringing. Poor Rose never had a notion of how to bring up a family. She is the mother of your children, Francis.'

He was deeply touched. Her sincerity and true longing to be good to him were beyond any question. But he wished that she would go. No one could help him any more. He smiled at her and laid his hand on hers.

'Thank you, Cousin Maria. You are exceeding kind. But I must shoulder my own troubles. What you say is very true. We are growing old, and nothing is of very much importance any more. Thank you, Cousin Maria, but indeed I must stand on my own feet.'

There was something in his face that told her that it was so.

She hesitated, stammered, then broke out: 'Well, then – would it trouble you . . . You would not laugh, I am sure . . . but it might be a help to you. The Lord is always nigh. If I offered a prayer . . .'

Her eyes gazed at him with the eager moisture in them of a puppy begging for a biscuit.

'Certainly, Cousin Maria. It is good of you—'

At once she knelt down on the floor beside him and, her bonnet falling back a little from her head, her gloved hands clasped, prayed.

'Oh Lord God, I pray Thee to look down on this Thy servant who has been sore troubled and in deep distress. Thou knowest what are our faults and failures, but there is in Thy heart an infinite patience and an all-preserving Wisdom. Take this Thy servant into Thy care and show him the way that he may find once again those whom he best loves and be restored into their company. Thou knowest what is best for him, and Thy will be done. In the name of Thy Son who was crucified for us on the Cross and whose Divine Example we would eternally follow. Amen.'

She waited a moment, her head between her hands, then she rose. There was thick dust on her black gown, but she did not notice. She stroked her nose with her hand.

'And now I must really be off,' she said briskly. 'Phyllis and I am to spend a little evening alone together. We are reading *The Task*. Remember, pray, Cousin Francis, that we are most eager to have you with us at Grosset, if you care to come. You have only to send us word. Yes, we shall all be delighted to see you.'

She bent and kissed him on the forehead; then murmuring

something to the effect that she did hope that it was not raining, she gave him a smile at the door and went out.

He sat on, lost in thought. In what was he lost? The candles flickered, the shadows leapt on the wall, carriages rumbled beyond the window, steps hurried by, voices rose and fell, but he was engulfed in his sense of utter disaster. Good old woman! She had wished to help him, but it would need more than Maria Rockage to help him now.

At last he rose, found his hat and coat and went out. He walked up St James's Street and into Piccadilly. He did not know why he was walking nor whither, but it seemed to him that a figure was at his side, keeping pace with him, murmuring in his ears: 'This is your farewell to the world. Soon, when the lights have dazzled your eyes sufficiently, you will return into your dark house.'

In the nervous state in which he was, it seemed to him that there was a babel of sound all about him. The lamps were lit, but there was still a great deal of traffic and business, and the fine spring evening after the rainy afternoon encouraged everyone to be out. London, although it was so rapidly growing in size and energy, had still something of the village about it. In this central part at least there was much recognizing of acquaintances, the cheerful intimacy of shopmen who knew their customers and, only a yard away, big houses, silent squares with lawns and gardens, the grandeur of the great mansions on the Park, footmen standing on doorsteps, coachmen from the boxes of their carriages looking down upon this world as though they commanded, shopmen filling their doorways, their legs spread, their noses sniffing the fresh evening.

To all this Francis was a stranger; he passed like a shadow, hurrying nowhere. At every moment something occurred to infuriate him. For some while a cart accompanied him. It contained it seemed, a thousand iron bars that rattled and rumbled and screamed above the cobbles. A drunken sailor, rolling by, ejected a shoot of tobacco and missed his shoes by an inch: an odour of meat seemed everywhere; the hackney coaches rattled his brains to pieces.

Infuriated by the noise, but still, as it seemed at him, driven on by this companion at his side, he turned up a side street hoping to find quiet, but first on a doorstep a footman was practising 'Paddy Whack' on a small fife, execrably out of tune, a headlong butcher's boy rushed by uttering a shrill cat-call; in a room just above his head there was a dancing lesson being held. The window was open and he could hear the 'One – Two – Three' and then 'Now then – Left – Right', and the shrill discordant wail of a fiddle . . .

Despairing of freeing himself from all these miseries, he turned back, found Piccadilly again and ventured into Mr Hatchard's bookshop; there would be silence, the friendliness of books, the courtesy of good Mr Sumner who, although he looked like a prize-fighter, had all the delicacy and sensitiveness of one who knew Byron and Scott and Coleridge, and had often, under Mr Sheridan's direction, supplied the Prince, in earlier days, with the best literature.

So Francis stepped in – and there was old Mr Rogers!

Yes, old Mr Rogers, the very last man in the world whom he wished to see. Nor was he alone. He was attended by a stout thick-set young man, badly dressed, with an untidy neckcloth and a very supercilious air.

Mr Rogers gave him a finger and introduced him to his friend.

'This is Mr Macaulay, who is at Cambridge and soon will be having the world at his feet. Come, come, Macaulay. You know you will. You know you will. You are as confident of it as I am.'

The thickset untidy youth raised a pair of very remarkable piercing eyes and began to talk with great eloquence and volubility. It was clear that he did not suffer from shyness.

Francis meanwhile hated the confident young man and hated Rogers. He was sure that they were mocking him; indeed, that everyone in the shop was mocking him. It was true enough, perhaps, that Rogers was not over-pleasant, because he had gone out of his way to be kind to this fellow who, of late, had treated him casually.

'Well, Mr Herries,' he said in his sharp restless voice, 'it is well met and farewell, for I am shortly taking a sister and niece with me on to the Continent – Switzerland and Italy. I have been trying to persuade Tom Macaulay here to accompany me, but he has better things to concern himself with . . . Well, well, Mr Herries – good day to ye. Good day to ye.'

The loquacious young man had already forgotten him and was talking eagerly to Sumner about a book that he held in his hand. Sumner also (who was, as a rule, so courteous) had not noticed him. In a tumult of irritation Francis left the shop. So Rogers had had enough of him? Even Sumner did not care to speak with him, and so old and insignificant was he that an untidy young man from Cambridge could turn his back on him.

It was true enough. He was old and shabby. He had no place in the world any longer.

At the corner of St James's Street he met a man whom he slightly knew, an effeminate bore, and this fellow would not let him go, but with one finger on his coat must, in a shrill piping voice, talk about the coming Coronation. It was all that anyone was thinking of, it was the finest and grandest the world had ever seen, no expense was to be spared, and they said that the Queen, poor thing— At last Francis broke away. As he hastened down the street he fancied that the man was looking after him, wondering what madness had taken possession of him. Well, he was mad if they liked. He had no place in this absurd world any longer – this absurd, monstrous crazy world.

When he entered his little room again and lit the candles once more, a sense of disgust took him. What a mean little place it was, with its smell of soot and cooking food! How grimy and foul the world had grown!

He went into his little bedroom, filled his basin with water, stripped, washed from head to foot, put on clean linen and another suit. Then he returned to his table, took out paper and pen and began to write:

DEAREST JUDITH – You have all your life forgiven me for my many faults and failings; once again – and this is the last time that I shall ask you – you must forgive me. For many weeks your letters arrived here and now they are lying in a pile on a table near me unopened. For it is only a part of my general weakness that I have not opened them. I did not dare, for I know that if I had done so you would have tempted me back. But I must not go back, dear Judith. Were you not so noble and generous to me you would be honest with me and tell me what I know well to be the truth – that I must never come back again. You have known me all my life long and once when you were a baby you loved me. Perhaps you love me still, for your heart is so generous that it can pass over all weaknesses and all mistakes. But I myself cannot pass them over. In these last weeks I have learnt to face myself and to see what is there. You will think that there is too much self-pity in what I have written, but it is not so. I have never pitied myself. I have had every chance to make something of life and I have thrown every chance away.

When I was a young man and you were a child I used to talk to you about all the things that I intended to do. I had great faith in myself, and because I have none any more is not a reason for pity, but rather for acceptance. I have failed everyone – my father, my mother, my wife, my children and my ideals.

I think that there are other men in like case. Men of our time have some of them been unfortunate because they have lived in an age of transition. The Great Time was behind them. The Great Time is coming again – but some of us have had our faith taken from us and have not been given, or have not found, a new one. I thought once that all men would be free now. I thought once that the poor man would have Justice. But the poor man is more a slave than before, and we are all of us in prison. I cannot write clearly; I see everything darkly, but I know that for myself I took the wrong path.

I am writing this only because you must not, *you must not*, dearest Judith, take the wrong path also. Return to your own life, take your boy, have nothing to do with the fortunes of our family. For such as you and I there can never be any happiness in Herries affairs. They are ruin and damnation to us. They deprive us of all that our souls need. I have been no good friend to you. I have not given you assistance when you sorely needed it. I have left you alone when you were most lonely. In this as in everything else I have betrayed myself. But now I am speaking truth from the heart. Your life is not with Will and Walter and Jennifer and the rest. They are strangers to you and you to them. Because I married a stranger and, God help me, love her now as dearly as I ever did, I have worked my own Destruction.

I know that you will be good to Jennifer and my children, but they are provided for, and *you must not stay with them.* Be true to yourself. You know well enough what you should do . . . Go back to Watendlath. I can see the light over the hill, hear the streams running . . . the streams running. My hand shakes. Tell Jennifer that I love her, I love her, just as I did . . . as I always . . . Embrace the children. John will be a fine boy . . . and your Adam. Go back to the light over the hill. There is so terrible a noise in this town. Dear Judith, think of me kindly, but better to forget me. I could not find a Balance. I was always fearful of Action. God be with you, but there is no God – none for me. Nothing . . .

He broke off; his pen rattled on to the table. He sat there for a long while, his head buried in his hands. Then he got up, folded the letter and addressed it. He went to the window, pulled back the blind and looked out. Two ladies were talking, laughing. A little dog came sniffing up to the lamp-post. Another dog saw him from the other side of the street and came slowly across. A boy, carrying some parcels, stood idly and watched them.

Francis went to the drawer of his little ink-stained desk and took from it a pistol.

He crossed to the mirror, cracked and seamed with age. He saw with great clearness the faded green paper, the print of the fight between Gully and the Chicken, the copy of Drayton's Poems, that he had been reading, on the table. Then he put the pistol to his mouth.

Mrs Morland, fancying that she heard someone tumble or the distant firing of a gun or the collision of two carriages, went to her window and looked out. But no: in the street there was nothing to be seen but two ladies laughing together and the cautious intimacies of a Newfoundland and a King Charles.

MONEY

'WILL YOU NOT come in and pay us a visit, Cousin Judith?' Walter Herries asked. He was standing at the high pillared entrance to Westaways. The wind was blowing with a kind of innocent child-like caprice and turning back the leaves of a giant beech to a duller chillier gold. Judith, with Adam beside her, felt the wind tugging at her big velvet-lined feathered hat. Her hands were warm inside their muff. Her face for once was rosy; the sharp air, the wild sky, the scudding fragments of blue and the harp-like swing of the wind across the bare fields, the ridges of snow on the brown range of fell, all exhilarated her.

Moreover, it was four days before Christmas and directly Christmas was past she was returning with Adam to Watendlath – yes, for ever and ever!

She had passed Watendlath as she had done a thousand times before, walking from Crosthwaite to Keswick. The carriage was in Keswick for the day; Jennifer was paying visits and after their three o'clock dinner at the inn they would drive home.

It was now midday. The Crosthwaite Church clock had but just told the hour. She had intended to take Adam to show to her friends, Miss West and Miss Pennyfeather. The last thing that she had expected or wished was to be caught by Walter Herries.

Westaways looked gleaming and polished in the wet windy sunlight. On the eastern corner there were ladders and men working. Walter was for ever doing something to the place.

'Do come inside now, Cousin Judith, and taste a glass of sherry.'

She knew that he had a family party for Christmas – Will, Christabel, old Monty Cards, Rodney, the pious second son of Pomfret and Rose from Kensington, old Pomfret himself and his ancient old-maid sister Cynthia, and best of all, Maria's Phyllis with her husband, Mr Stephen Newmark, and two of their children; Phyllis had been married in 1818 and had already three babies!

It was Phyllis whom she would like to see; Christabel too, Will even. But she shrank from the crowd of them, all gathered in the parlour, talking scandal, most of it of the family order. In she would march with Adam, and Will's neck would tighten in its collar, and fat, over-decorated, 'Regency' old Pomfret would wink at her (she could bet on it!), and silly kind old Monty would stroke his powdered cheek while his corsets creaked, pious Rodney would look down his nose – only dear Phyllis, untidy like her mother, with some of the Grosset disorder clinging to her, only Phyllis would really welcome her, would be enchanted to see her. She had a curiosity, too, to behold Phyllis' husband, Mr Stephen Newmark. Maria, in letters, had informed her that he was a very fine man indeed, a wealthy religious landowner from Warwickshire. Wealthy *and* religious – not a very promising combination!

There was the other temptation, too, that this was her last opportunity for spying out Westaways. Was it not absurd, perhaps, to say that, when Watendlath was only a mile or two away? But Watendlath was more than a mile or two away, it was a world away. As poor Francis had said in that last despairing letter.

Strange to pass from the thought of that letter to that great brilliantly-coloured body straddling there in the gateway! But, looking at him, she suddenly wondered whether he were not already a trifle old-fashioned? The thought gave her a malicious pleasure. He was certainly over-dressed for the present times, with his billowing stock and its jewelled pin, his claret-coloured coat with the exaggerated waist (he was corsetted – and what immense corsets they must be!), the fawn-shaded pantaloons fitting so tightly over the calves. There were rings on his fingers. And yet he was a man! Do Walter all the injustice in the world, but you could never name him effeminate. He was the prize bull of the stock. Already, young as he was, there was a purple tinge to his cheek, but his eyes were hard and clear and his mouth firmly and confidently set.

'Come inside and drink a glass of sherry with us, Cousin Judith.'

She looked up at him from under her broad-brimmed hat with that air of humorous impertinent defiance that they seemed always to use to one another.

'I have Christmas shopping and calls to pay. Have we not, Adam?'

Adam, who was holding a little toy whip, had never taken his eyes from Walter since he had first seen him.

'Why, young man, you have some clothes on at last, I see.'
'Yes, sir.'
'And how old are you since I saw you last?'
'Six, sir.'
'Six, are you? Well, your mother shall bring you in out of the wind. Not too young for a glass of sherry, are you?'

'Of course he is, Walter. A glass of sherry indeed!'

'Why, I was drinking sherry before I was weaned, and look at me! Come along in! Come along in!'

So Judith went and Adam also, his eyes still following Walter's back as though he had never before seen anything like it.

She knew that he had been doing things to the house, and when she stood in the hall her astonishment was vivid at the changes that he had made. Everywhere were riches. On the wall facing the front door a great piece of purple tapestry showing Diana hunting, on either side of the door pieces of sculpture, one of a Pan playing his flute, another of a stout naked goddess drinking. (What, oh, what would Maria Rockage say to this paganism?)

At the stairhead, over the door of the saloon, was a sumptuous painting of a French king (Louis XIV perhaps) dining with his ladies, and, beside the door, a silver pedestal with a black bust of some Roman Emperor – and Walter, as he walked slowly up the stairs, gave the impression even in his backview that it was he and no one else who had wrought all these splendours.

They were gathered about a blazing fire in the saloon – Will, Christabel, Monty Cards, Rodney and his father, Phyllis, Carey her brother, and a thin upright man with a hooked nose who must be her husband, Mr Newmark.

As Judith crossed the long shining slippery floor, holding Adam by the hand, she felt that both herself and her son were midgets. She was not frightened but she could feel their intense interest as they all turned towards her. She was helped by Adam's absolute confidence. He nearly tripped and fell as he bent his head back to look at the gods and goddesses in their brilliant nakedness. He feared no one.

Christabel and Phyllis rose with cries of pleasure to greet her. Everyone made a display over Adam. Pomfret (still a very gay and brightly set-up dog in spite of his years) was the most pleased with him. He took him between his knees and looked into his ugly little face with a very lively interest. He asked him questions, and Adam, in his funny high voice, answered them all instantly.

Judith, sitting with her hand in Phyllis', thought: 'This grows grander every month. Up, up, up. And at Uldale we go down, down, down! Never mind. The battle is not ended yet ... Yes, Adam is ugly. His mouth is too large by far – but he charms everyone ...' That strange pang at her heart again! He charms everyone! He always will – and I shall be left ... 'But I *wish* him to charm everyone, to be happy and honest and brave as he is now – always.' And then, following quickly on this, cutting across the self-sufficient tones of Rodney, who would be one day Archdeacon of Polchester and patronizer of the very Black Bishop, came this thought:

'In ten days we shall be in Watendlath, eating food with the Ritsons, and Adam will be mine, mine, mine!'

She could almost hear the sheep shuffling with the noise of the rustle of leaves across this shining floor. She could see the sun strike the flint in those rocks until they shone like spearheads, dulling the painted goddesses. 'Oh, if anything should hinder my reaching there! But nothing can, now surely nothing can!' It was as though she were planning to get as far as China!

They were still discussing that now so wearily worn topic, the Coronation and the Queen's beating on the Westminster doors. Will, who was strangely aged now and thinner than ever, so that he looked like a stork standing on one leg and protecting his nest (only his eggs were money-bags), was all for upholding the Crown.

'What we want,' he said with his usual air of delivering judgement, 'is stable conditions. To counteract the lower classes.

Relax, and we shall have another Peterloo ... But the country is recovering its Balance. I am glad to be able to say that the country is recovering its Balance.'

Everyone looked greatly relieved. It was pleasant to hear from Will, who must know, that all was well.

Adam was passed round from hand to hand. They were all kind to him although he was a little bastard. But Judith knew that it was for the moment only, and that her presence made them uncomfortable, yes, even poor Christabel, who was restless under the eye of her lord and master. The thought came to her as she saw Rodney's eyes meditatively resting upon her: 'Oh, if Adam could grow into the master of them all, rule the pack of them! He could. He has even now twice their spirit ...' But she was going to Watendlath, and Adam with her, leaving the Herries behind them for ever, and Adam would be a farmer like Charlie Watson, and one day he would come down into Keswick, driving his sheep, and he would encounter Walter's children in their fine carriage, and the coachman would shout to him to clear his sheep from the road ... And after Adam would return, riding up the road to see the Tarn shining with the evening sun, and he would call to his dog, and the fields would smile up at him, the hills look kindly down ...

'Well, my little friend,' said Rodney Herries to Adam (he spoke as though to a little black child newly rescued from the heathen), 'and what is the game you enjoy the most?'

'To cut men out of wood,' said Adam with complete assurance, but his eyes wandering a little. 'I have cut Mr Noah and the Duke of Wellington and Mr Winch.'

'Very praiseworthy. Very praiseworthy indeed,' said Rodney, looking, however, bewildered.

'He is commencing,' said Judith, 'to carve figures. He has a true disposition towards carving.'

'Yes,' went on Adam eagerly, looking at everyone with an enthusiastic smile, 'and I colour them also. And Bennett gives me the wood. He says—'

'Hush, Adam, hush,' said Judith, drawing him towards her. He came to her, but with one last look round him and pointing at old Cynthia Herries, Pomfret's sister, who had a nose like a door-knocker:

'That old lady would be very fine for cutting.'

His manners, Judith could see them deciding, were not at all of the best, but what could you expect when his mother? ...

Then Walter came forward.

'Judith, you must see my improvements. Forgive me for taking you away an instant. I must show you the improvements.'

She knew that he wished to speak to her alone. She had known it all the time. The drama of the scene, the implication of it all, had been rising in her with increasing force. Poor Francis was dead, Jennifer bewildered, like a woman lost in a wood, the children helpless – and this power, this force, destructive and remorseless, hung over them. And something told her that she was the only one whom Walter feared; it had always been so. And it might be that she was the only one whom, of all that company, Walter respected.

She looked back and saw that Adam was safe with Phyllis' arm around him. Then she followed Walter out.

He preceded her into a little parlour off the saloon, a room so small that, when he had motioned her into a red morocco chair and himself stood, with his legs straddled, in front of the fire, the two of them filled it. There was nothing in the room save a Chippendale cabinet on which was a bowl of Christmas roses. They were full-blown and wore that look of patient expectancy that precedes death.

Walter began at once:

'Judith – how long will you remain at Uldale?'

'I cannot see that that is any business of yours, Cousin Walter,' she answered sharply. She had retained her white fur muff, and her fingers in it clasped one another with self-congratulation. What was it in her that made her love a battle? She was at the moment perfectly happy, all her faculties widely awake, her eyes on the rich panelling, the Christmas roses, and the brilliant person of Mr Walter Herries.

'No business of mine,' he went on. 'Well, perhaps not. And yet because I have a regard for you, Cousin Judith, I would wish you out of Uldale. That place and all in it are doomed.' He said this, a little swell of importance rising in his great chest.

'Really! That is exceedingly interesting. And by whom are they doomed, pray?'

'By myself.'

'Are you so powerful?' He was, she reflected, like a giant schoolboy fallen from some star where everyone was twice as big as nature.

'I am indeed,' he answered. 'And growing more powerful every day. It is my father's wish that our family should be the chief figures in this country. Natural enough, when you think of it. He was born here, and his father lived here till the end of his life. He has developed an affection for the place.'

'An affection so deep,' interrupted Judith, 'that he never comes near it save on Saints' Days and Festivals! No, no, Cousin Walter,' she went on, 'there are the two of us alone here, and we may be frank. I belong to this country far more than you ever can. My mother may not have been of the country, but at least for generation upon generation my ancestors have lived and thieved here, stolen cattle and ladies only too ready to be stolen. I love this country, and so will my son after me. I love it because it is dark and full of storms and rains every other day, and smells of bracken and sheep and cow-dung. But you have none of these reasons. You love it because you wish to impress it, and I can tell you, Cousin Walter, it is not so easily impressed. What have you got? You have one thing – money. Nothing else. You are not especial clever that I have heard; you are too stout to be beautiful; you are a bully of those weaker than yourself; you are as conceited as a peacock. I am almost old enough to be your mother, Walter. In fact, in Eastern countries I believe I might have been – so forgive me for my frankness.'

'Go on,' he said, smiling at her.

There were moments when she thought that she rather liked him. Hatred would make everything easier.

'Very well, then, I will. You have nothing but money. At Uldale they have much. Poor Francis, who took his life because he had so much more perception and understanding than you, loved this country with all his heart. He made an unhappy marriage. Oh! I am not blaming Jennifer. There was a time when I hated her, but it is hard to hate anybody long. It was not her fault that she could not love him. Now that is all over, and there are two very fine children who are *not* doomed, dear Walter, however much you may say it. They have more right to this country than you have. Money can't beat them, and don't you think it.'

Walter nodded.

'Very well, then. We know where we are. You have said nothing, though, of the scandals that we have all suffered for years past. It may be foolish' (again his immense chest swelled), 'but if I am proud of one thing in this world it is of being an Englishman and a Herries. I have as much right as yourself to any part of England, Cousin Judith, even though your ancestors *were* cattle-thieves. How agreeable has it been to us, do you think, that for years past, under our very noses, we should have a Herries who is too weak to challenge his wife's lover, who allows adultery any day or night under his roof; a woman so lost to shame that she receives her lover in the room next to her children; a man so lily-livered that he challenges that same lover, and then before the duel is fought runs to London?—'

'I do not believe that,' Judith broke in, her eyes flashing. 'We have only the word of that miserable oaf whom everyone knows for a coward—'

'Yes; and what about Uncle Francis for a coward, who let such things be year after year?'

'And who are you,' she broke in hotly, 'to be so virtuous? How have you treated *your* wife all these years? And what of milkmaids in Keswick and loose women in Kendal? Do you suppose that you are so sacred that no one talks of you?'

He threw his head back and laughed.

'I am no hypocrite, Cousin Judith. Nor are you. I am as other men. You had your little come-by-chance in Paris. But I have not allowed my wife a lover, nor have you blown off the top of your head with a pistol. But come . . . that is not the point. You may say that there is no power in money. But I say there is. And more. Money is going to be powerful in England as it has never been before. I am no such fool as I look, Judith. In spite of my size I have a trifle of my father's brains. But the long and short of it is just this. They must leave Uldale. It is my obsession that they should. I hate Jennifer, for she was rude to my mother; but beyond that they are a blot on the Herries name. I will pay them a good price for the house, but they must quit this part of the country!'

'Never!' cried Judith, springing up. 'Never! Never! Never!'

'Now come, Judith. Why should you care? What are they to you? You loved Uncle Francis. Good. I have nothing against it. But he is gone. Jennifer is a dull, heavy, stupid woman. You have never liked her. What is all this to you?'

'It is this to me! These are Francis' children. You would bully them out of existence. Well, you shall not.'

'What will you do to prevent it?'

'Never mind. You shall not.'

He shrugged his great shoulders.

'It may be true that I am a bully,' he said slowly. 'I hate the weak. They have no place here if they cannot stand up for themselves. You are the only one whom I admire, and you have put yourself out of court with your little bastard. Not that I have anything against bastards; but you are a little public with yours, are you not? It was worth seeing just now the way that prig Rodney's nose curved down his cheek. So leave them alone, Judith! Be quiet with your boy in some place and we will be good friends. But leave Uldale alone.'

It was on the edge of her tongue to tell him that he need not be disturbed, for in ten days she would be in Watendlath and free of him for ever. But she did not speak. As she faced him the dominating part of her longed to oppose him, to fight him, and beat him, to defend John and Dorothy, to show him that the little bastard was not so negligible as he pretended. She *could* fight him! And what a fight that would be!

Meanwhile there was Watendlath. She almost sighed as she turned away and saw a smooth white petal of the Christmas roses flutter to the ground.

'Good friends?' she repeated. 'Not if you touch Uldale.'

'Well I *shall* touch Uldale,' he said, moving towards the door. 'I have told you. And now, come up and see the children. Bring your boy with you.'

But at the door she paused.

'This is not a game, Cousin Walter.'

He stood over her.

'No. I have told you. It is a chapter in family history.'

'What have you ever done,' she asked scornfully, 'to be so proud of our family history?'

'*Non mi ricordo*,' he answered in the phrase that had been the popular catchword ever since Majocchi's evidence in the Queen's trial. He was determined to be amiable.

But, with her hand on the door, and with a passion that in these days she rarely showed, she burst out: 'I tell you, Walter, you must leave Jennifer and the children alone'; and he, smiling, murmured lightly that popular epigram:

> *Most gracious Queen, we thee implore*
> *To go away, and sin no more;*
> *But if that effort be too great,*
> *To go away, at any rate.*

They looked into the saloon and found Adam diving into old Pomfret's pockets and producing treasures – a gold snuff-box, some seals and a small watch set with diamonds. The old man was watching him with delighted pleasure, and Judith at once forgave him all his pomposities, sensualities, infidelities to Rose, every other crime or weakness.

Adam came at once running when she called him. He turned

when he was halfway to the door and waved his hand to the figures at the fire. Pomfret and Christabel waved back. Phyllis got up from her chair.

'Are you going up to see the children ? You shall see my babies too.'

Judith knew how deeply intrigued they all were. What had Walter been saying to her ? How much part did she play now in family affairs ? She knew that Will was regarding her with secret alarm. She had always been a signal of danger to him, representing everything that was lawless and unsanctified. And she had been always Francis' ally. Perhaps he thought now of that old scene in Monty Cards' house when Francis had defied him . . . lured by Jennifer's beauty . . . Well, he had never been lured by anyone's beauty, and he was glad of it. But this pain in his leg was vexatious. This Northern air did not suit him. He was truly well only in the City. But she knew by this time that she was in the camp of the enemy and, as she went out of the room with her head up and trying not to slip ignominiously on the polished floor, her hand went quietly to the silver chain, her father's, that she always wore beneath her clothes.

So the four of them went upstairs, Walter leading. It was a fine high room where the children were. Almost a hundred years ago old Pomfret's children, Raiseley and Anabel and Judith, had sat there, the girls with boards down their backs to keep them straight, learning their Latin. But much had been done to the room since then. The windows were fine and high, with a great view over the Lake and Scafell, and the Gavel grouped handsomely at the end of it. The waves were running across it now as though in a race, and the woods by Manesty were black as jet.

Inside the room everything was warm and cosy – a great fire roaring, a decent-looking elderly woman sitting beside it sewing. On the carpet Elizabeth, one of Walter's twins, was playing with Phyllis' two babies; Uhland, the other, was sitting on a small chair by himself, his face absorbed as he pulled the hair out of the tail of a painted wooden horse.

Many, many times afterwards she was to look back to this moment when she first saw Uhland. (Poor child, that he should be burdened his life long with so outlandish a name!) How characteristic that he should be sitting gravely by himself pulling something to pieces! But, at the moment, she felt nothing but pity. He had already, although he was but six years old, the face of an old man, the high forehead lined and the corners of the mouth bitter, and those strange grey penetrating eyes. His legs were dangling over the chair, but she noticed immediately that, absorbed as he was, at once, when he heard someone enter, he drew them up so that no one should observe their inequality. His body was too small for his head; his hands, she saw, were very beautiful, and, later, when she had reason to know how proud he was of them, she was interested to remember how quickly she had perceived them.

What followed touched her deeply. Walter, in his magnificent claret coat and resplendent pantaloons, hurried forward to his son, caught him up in his arms and held him close to his breast. The child seemed unmoved. His face did not change. Only one hand rested on his father's big one. Walter kissed him many times, oblivious of everyone else there.

'You must say How do you do?' he commanded him, and brought him to Judith. The child's cold grey eyes rested on her and, she fancied, with an expression of instant dislike.

'How do you do, ma'am?' he said in a small, remote voice. She bent forward and kissed his cheek, which was chill and dry. It was odd to touch that pallid, small face and feel Walter's great red one just above it. Walter took him back to his chair and, kneeling on the floor beside him, talked to him about the horse.

Walter had shown no attention to his daughter Elizabeth. This was a charming child with fragile, delicate features and pale flaxen hair.

She glanced once at her father as though she would have liked his attention, but she did not seem at all unhappy; she talked eagerly, made friends with Adam, played games with the babies, who already, Judith thought, bore, both of them, resemblance to Mr Newmark.

After a little while they came away, but Judith saw that, as they left the room, Uhland stood up and gazed after them with an almost frightening intensity.

Judith, with Adam holding tightly to her hand, walked into Keswick. Even the road was alive with the stir of Christmas, but she moved for some while with unseeing eyes; she had a sense of danger – as though did she let Adam out of her sight for an instant Walter would get him.

The touch of his warm little hand in hers comforted her; but that was not enough. In one hand she held her muff, but with the other arm, had it not been so public a place, she would have encircled him that he might be the more secure.

He meanwhile had observed everything and had a hundred

questions to ask. Why did no one wear any clothes in the pictures? Why was the floor so slippery? Who was the old gentleman with the diamond watch? The little boy upstairs had one leg longer than another. Why was the big man who had tried to hit him with the whip so red in the face? Why ... Why ... Why? ...

Then suddenly he was aware, with the perception that came from their long-continued intimacy together, that she was disturbed and wanted his help. He always knew when she needed him, although he might not understand what it was that she needed. Even at the time of his greatest intimacy with John (he was as deeply devoted to John as ever, but the novelty was gone) he would look up and run off to find her, although he could not himself tell why.

She walked more slowly. She wanted him to understand something.

'Adam, would you wish to live in a house like Uncle Walter's, so grand and rich, with everything you could need?'

He put out his tongue at two small boys who were mocking him from the hedge, then he applied his whole intelligence to the question.

'I would like that rocking-horse,' he said at last.

'Yes. But besides——' Her step was slower. So soon she would be in Keswick, and there would be Jennifer and gossip and the outside world. At this moment she felt for him so overpowering a love that it was as though she were saying goodbye to him before he departed to America or the incredible South Sea Islands.

'Besides – would you wish to live there – always?'

'Would you come and John and Dorothy and Bennett, and might I cut things?'

'No. We would not come.'

He considered it.

'I should *like* the rocking-horse,' he said slowly. 'But *of course*, you would be in the house.'

'No, I would not.'

'But you will be everywhere I am always.'

'No.' She shook her head. 'No.'

He laughed, for the two little boys were running along in the hedge making faces at him, and one of them, not being able to see in two places at once, fell down.

'The boy fell down,' he said, screwing his head round to see better.

She stopped at the little stream that was now coffee and now a froth of foam.

'Listen, Adam. I wish you to hear this. No one will ever love you as your mother does now. No one can take you from me. No one. We will soon be in Watendlath with Charlie and Mrs Perry again. I could make you a fine man in a grand house, and everyone would do what you say, but I am going to make you a farmer like Watson, and when you are in the road with your sheep, the carriage that you should have ridden in will order you to clear the way. You will be walking and you might have been riding. You will be rough and poor and you could have been grand and rich.

'But we will be happy, you and I and Charlie and Alice; but the little sick boy will be rich and powerful, and you will be poor and nobody.'

He did not mind at all. He was looking to see a fish jump in the river.

But she put her hand under his chin and looked into his eyes.

'I want you to remember this, because all my life I have been making this choice. You cannot understand now, but one day you will look back and perhaps be angry with me.'

He knew that she was wanting him to understand something, so he screwed his forehead into a hundred wrinkles and did his best.

'Would you prefer that you were Charlie Watson or big Uncle Walter?' she said.

He laughed at the thought of being Uncle Walter and, then and there, puffed out his cheeks, swelled out his chest, and began to strut about. Then his face was grave. He turned, looking back down the road.

'If he hits me with his whip again,' he said, 'I'll *beat* him.'

The change was so swift that she was astonished.

'But you like Uncle Walter,' she said. 'He was very kind to you.'

'Why does the little boy have one leg bigger than the other?'

'He was born like that.'

His mind seemed to jump.

'It's Christmas! It's Christmas!' he cried, and began to run down the road in front of her. She walked after him. He turned back to meet her.

'Boneyparte was beat at Waterloo, Mr Winch says,' he remarked very gaily, dancing about. Then catching her hand again and dragging her along he shouted:

'And I will beat Uncle Walter when I am bigger!'

He ran, pulling her hand, calling like a song:

'And I love you better than everybody – better than John, better than Dorothy, better than Bennett, better than Jack, better than—'

But even as the litany continued, something caught his attention, a goat dragged along by a cord, and a very small girl in charge of it. He pulled his hand away and ran on to see this phenomenon, but as he ran he chanted in a high absent-minded refrain:

'Better than Bennett. Better than Jack. Better than—'

And she, feeling that it was an omen, followed after.

MOB

JUDITH IN A state half sleep, half wakening, heard a voice say: 'Dig deep here. The deeper you may dig the richer the loam.' She recognized that she had a choice either to stay in that square of country, hemmed in by hills, and dig down and down – for what? treasure perhaps – or to fasten to her shoulders a pair of very elegant gold wings and fly the country over, but, of course, be for ever on the surface. She had to make a choice, and she made it without hesitation. With a sense of great relief and satisfaction she shouldered a spade, and as she did so saw the pair of wings be drawn up on a gold wire through the dark sky.

With confused notions of Mrs Radcliffe, a novel that the night before she had been reading, *The Last Step; or The History of Mrs Brudenal*, Rousseau's *Confessions*, and *Isabella; or The Rewards of Good Nature*, she woke to see the thin January light covering the floor with a sort of pale mildew and to realize that Adam, having thrown off the clothes, was sleeping upside down with his feet on her breast. She turned him round, heard him sigh happily in his sleep, and staring up at the bed-hangings, thought: 'He— She— It was right. She must dig and remain faithful to the—' To what? That question woke her. She realized that the crisis of her life had come.

How often before it had seemed to be upon her – when David had beaten her, when Georges had married her, when old Stane had robbed her, when Jennifer had insulted her, when Warren had kissed her, when Adam had kicked his way out of her, when

Francis had called her back to Uldale, when Francis had written
a last letter to her, when Walter had challenged her – but now
at last the crisis had truly come, for today she must make Jennifer
realize that within a week she was positively and for ever de-
parting and that no prayers, no beseechings could alter her
resolve.

She moved restlessly on the bed as she thought of it. No
wonder that she had woken early with this in front of her!
Again and again in the last year she had attempted the break; but
first there had been poor Francis alive, and then there had been
poor Francis dead, and then Jennifer had kept to her bed for
weeks, and when at last she had been driven out of her bedroom
had refused to attend to her affairs, refused to see Mr Bertram,
the solicitor from Keswick, refused to do anything unless Judith
were there to force her to do it.

During the last three months it had come to this. Again and
again she had said:

'Well, Jennifer, I will do this for you' (speak to Mr Winch or
Bennett, or talk business with Mr Bertram, or write to London
about some shares or discuss with Mrs Quinney the fare for the
coming week). 'But you had far better yourself, you know, for a
week after Christmas I am off, and you will have to manage it all
then.'

'Oh, a week after Christmas – besides, you will change your
mind.'

'I shall not change my mind.'

After the discovery of Fernyhirst (who had never put in
another appearance), Francis' refusal to return, and then his
suicide, Jennifer's sluggishness had swallowed all the rest of
her. Once she had been lazy because she was proud; now she
was lazy because she was humiliated. She tumbled into a slattern
over whom Judith had absolute command. Judith had seen her
as lovely girl, proud and overbearing wife, self-satisfied mistress,
betrayed beauty (her attitude after Francis' departure), and now
she was humble, but yawning, slattern. Poor Jennifer! Parents
who had adored her too deeply to educate her or to force her to
anything that she avoided had begun her ruin. Her lazy and stupid
indifference completed it. She cared now only for her food, an
occasional fine gown, and sometimes to dress Dorothy up and
take her into Keswick. (But when there always fancied that she
was insulted, and returned in a state of indignation and confused
panic.)

She went to bed of an evening ever earlier and earlier; the

time would surely come when she would never rise at all.

She had, however, one increasing terror, and that was of Walter Herries. He had assumed now quite gigantic proportions for her. He could do, she was convinced, any horrible thing that he chose. He was bent on her destruction. And in that last she was perfectly correct.

Poor Jennifer! She might have been, Judith thought, a brilliant, successful beauty at an earlier time. She was born too late for her period. Like many of her contemporaries, she was the victim of a transition world.

She would, however, now be forced to action. When Judith was gone, Mrs Quinney, horrid little Mr Winch, kindly but saturnine Bennett, would do as they pleased. And then John would grow and take his place. He was now fourteen years of age and as nice a boy as you could find – gentle and kind, thoughtful for others, but manly also; more resolute in character than his father. He was reticent; no one had ever known what were his real feelings about his father's suicide, or how much he knew about the scandal in the house. Judith suspected that he had suffered with intensity. She fancied, too, that he had a sort of irritated pity for his mother. . .

But John against Walter? That was the only thought that gave her obstinate departure a touch of treachery.

Today she must tell Jennifer that the matter was final, and, three days from now, she would be safe with Adam in Watendlath.

It was a kind of fate, as things developed, that before mid-day she should encounter Watson.

He stopped his horse by the Uldale gate. He would not come in. She came out to him.

Why did her heart beat so when she saw him? She was not in love with him. She had never been. He was a fine thick figure of a man, but it was not his figure that made her heart beat. Did a shadow pass? Behind him the hollows under Skiddaw filled like wine in a jade bowl – but it was not the hollow valleys. He did not love her, or at least had never given her reason to think that he did. They were two elderly people now, she nearing fifty, he over sixty. Was it their friendship and mutual trust that made her heart beat? But when she put her hand in his all the nonsense was over. He never had much to say. She had many things to do and could not waste precious time standing there in the cold.

Besides, after three days, she would be seeing him six times a week! There was a joy! It was so intense that she burst out:

'Now there's no need, Charlie, to keep me in the cold. I am busy this morning – and in three days I shall be in Watendlath, for good.'

'Truly, you're coming?'

'Truly, I'm coming.'

'Aye, but you've said it so many times . . .' Then he added, smiling, speaking his broadest, as he did when he was happy: 'I willn't believe tha, not without thou'll swear 't.'

'Oh, I'll swear it. In three days.'

'Aye, I'm glad!'

This was too much emotion for both of them, so she asked him what he was doing so early in their direction. He could give no connected account of himself, mumbled something about visiting for an account in Caldbeck, but she was aware instantly that he was troubled and had come to tell her something. He talked on about agricultural distresses – the old grievance of cash payments, the abundant harvest of '20 that had led to over-supply, the wet autumn of '21 that had destroyed the crops, the new contemplated Corn Law, Huskisson's speech in the House of Commons, all uninteresting enough to her with the wind driving down the road in icy gusts. Then at last he came out with:

'There's trouble about.'

'Trouble?'

'Aye. They burnt Squire Forrester's ricks last night over at Deddon.'

'Who did?'

'Oh, some of t'wild lads and men with no work, and others egging them on!'

'Poor Mr Forrester!'

'Aye. 'Hope they'll hev a long wait in gaol. Well, I must be moving. 'Tis true you're coming in three days?'

'Yes – true enough. And never going away again. Adam is to be a farmer like yourself, Charlie.'

'Reet.' He smiled a tremendous smile, his teeth as white and perfect as they had been twenty years before. 'I'll gang down and mak' all ready for [him.' He gave her one of his long protecting looks as though he thought she was only safe when he had his eyes upon her; then he lifted his hat and rode away.

All day she remained troubled. Charlie was so cautious that

you had to guess from one spoken word the twenty that he had intended. But the remark about Forrester's could have no application to them. No one would want to burn *their* barns. Nevertheless she knew that this was a day of fate. She set back her shoulders as though a shadow had warned her that before nightfall she would need all her endurance.

In any case, without any shadowy whispers, she needed all her endurance for her talk with Jennifer. All her life she had detested scenes, but she was aware that Jennifer fell into them and out of them as easily as she washed her hands. A scene there would be – but it would be good to have it behind her, and, although there would be, in all probability, three days of silence and sulks, after that – liberty!

She chose her time well – six o'clock in the parlour, following an excellent dinner, the curtains drawn, Jennifer languidly – with a painted hand-screen to shade her face – before the fire, thinking of her food and the handsome flock-gauze gown that she was wearing.

'Jennifer,' said Judith. 'I think that you should realize that in three days Adam and I will be gone.'

'Oh dear,' Jennifer, stifling a yawn, answered. 'Not this evening, Judith, pray. You are for ever speaking of going. "Jennifer, tomorrow I am going – the day after tomorrow I shall be gone, Jennifer," but, thank Heaven, it is only a bagatelle like Mr Hume and his grey top-hat.'

Judith sighed. This would be indeed a tiresome affair.

'This time it is no bagatelle. It has been one often enough. I had intended to go a year and a half back, and I have remained on and on until I do not wonder that you hesitate to believe me. But this time it is true and certain.'

'But you cannot go in three days. Mr Bertram is coming from Keswick next Wednesday.'

'Well, it will be practice for you in something you will have to do very often – talk business with Mr Bertram.'

'Oh, but it is absurd! Of course I cannot talk business with Mr Bertram.'

'Really, Jennifer. A woman of your age and unable to talk business.'

Jennifer smiled and put her hand on to Judith's arm.

'Oh well, you do it so very much better than ever I can. You are made for business, Judith. Why, only last Tuesday—'

This would be interminable. She rose from her chair and stood between Jennifer and the fire.

'I am very serious. You *must* understand. I am going to Watendlath in three days' time to *live*. This was always temporary – my stay here. You have been very good. I have been happy here; but it is not, it has never been, my real life. I have been running away from this house since I was a baby, since I can remember, and I am for ever returning to it. Now I am running away for the last time.'

Something in Judith's grave serious gaze, something in the determined set of her small body, caused Jennifer to put down her screen and move her head uncomfortably.

'It grows wearisome, Judith, this everlasting talk about Watendlath. What you should want to go to the place for at all I cannot conceive; but if you *must* go – for a visit, to see your farmers and their wives – well, I cannot prevent you. Only, pray return as soon as may be.'

Judith stamped her foot with irritation.

'Jennifer, listen! I am going to Watendlath in three days and I am not returning. I am *not* returning. Now, do you understand?'

'You will leave me?'

'Yes, yes, yes. I have told you a hundred times.'

'Leave me?' The screen fell to the ground. Her big blue eyes widened, her hand began to beat on her dress. 'Leave us? Oh, but, Judith, you cannot! You cannot indeed!'

The note of terror was there. Jennifer was awake to reality; fright was the only thing that awoke her. Judith was suddenly compassionate. She put her arm around the large trembling woman:

'Listen, Jennifer. I have been trying to escape from this house ever since I was a baby, and I am now a woman of middle age and *still* I haven't succeeded! From the house, not from Francis or you or John. I have never been permitted to lead a life of my own. When I was with Georges I was devoured with love for him, so that I was not myself. Now I have Adam, and Adam shall not lead this false life, nor will I any longer.'

But Jennifer did not understand a word of it. She had no imagination, and she saw only things that concerned herself.

'False life? But this is not a false life here.'

'No,' said Judith, striving to be patient. 'The tables and curtains and chairs are real, but it is a false life to me, nevertheless, occupied with fears and ambitions that do not matter. You see, Jennifer, I am only half Herries. My mother was a gipsy. And even that Herries half is wild. You know what my father

was. So now I am going away where there are no Herries, and
I shall take my son with me.'

But Jennifer had not heard a word of it. Slowly, while Judith
was speaking, her brain had been taking in this fact – that Judith
was going away and that she would be alone and defenceless.

She gripped Judith's arm and cried out, her body trembling
again and her cheek white where it was not painted.

'No, no . . . you are going away, to leave me and my children
to Walter Herries! You cannot . . . You must not!'

Now the terror was real enough, and the strange thing was that
Judith felt it also. She looked for an instant at the darkened
window-pane. She had been troubled all day. She was, in her
final resources, alone in this house with this crying, hysterical
woman. Of course Walter could do nothing, nor did he wish to.
He was at this moment kneeling on the nursery floor embracing
his pale little boy. Nevertheless . . .

'Now, Jennifer. Come, this is absurd. Walter can do nothing.
You have Walter Herries on the brain. Everything is well here.
There is money enough, you have Mr Bertram in Keswick,
you have most devoted servants, John is growing a fine boy.
You cannot wish me to stay here and cosset you for ever. Besides,
I am blown on. Everyone knows that I have an illegitimate child
and that poor Warren was its father. What good can that do you ?
You will discover when I am really gone that it is much better so.'

But Jennifer, in full realization now that Judith meant what
she said, was past all control. She clung to Judith, holding her
with a frantic grasp.

'What can you mean ? You cannot be so cruel. You were never
cruel even when I was stiff with you in the old days. Walter is a
devil. You have seen it for yourself. All the scandal about me
everywhere is his doing. He will poison my children and—'

'Jennifer, don't be so absurd.'

'No, but it is not absurd. I am certain he will poison all the
water here before he is done. I see him at every turn. I dare not
walk out unless I should see him. I am quite alone here. I have not a
friend but you. Everyone hates me. Walter sees to it that they do.
He is everywhere whispering . . . If you go, Judith, I shall kill
myself and then you will have to come and see to my poor children, my poor deserted children. I know that Walter forced
Francis to kill himself. I am sure of it. He wrote him a letter or
something, and only because years ago I broke his mother's
cheap little fan. Oh! how I wish that I had never left my
dear father and mother. There has never been anything but

unhappiness since I left Bournemouth. But I will not be alone in this house . . . If you go I kill myself . . . '

'Come, come, Jennifer. You must not be so foolish. You are like a child.'

Jennifer was now in floods of tears. She waved her hands, beat with her feet on the ground and behaved like a madwoman. Part of this was stupid and lazy histrionics, but part of it was the true bewildered apprehension of a slow, but not evilly intentioned, woman who might, had she married a rich warm husband in a safe comfortable place, never have been exposed. It was because Judith knew this and by now understood her so well that she was touched.

'Come, Jennifer. Come upstairs and lie down.' (Always the recipe for Jennifer's distresses.) 'We will talk quietly. There is nothing for you to be so distressed over. Nothing at all. You have an obsession about Walter. He can do you no harm. Come and lie down.'

She surrendered as though hypnotized. Judith led her away. On the stairs she said:

'Well, but you were only laughing at me, Judith. You are not going away?'

Judith patted her shoulder.

'You will see in the morning it does not look so terrible. After all it is only a few miles. I shall be close at hand.'

But when at last Jennifer had been laid down and petted and quietened and she, Judith, stood in the still hall with the clock ticking the only sound:

'Phew!' she said to herself. '*That* was something.' But she was resolute. Nothing now could turn her. However, half an hour later she had to suffer another attack. There was a knock on the parlour door and John appeared.

He looked at her shyly. Of late she had noticed in herself a certain embarrassment which she was for ever trying not to show him. Was she not going to desert him? A look that he had of his father, although he was more firmly built, a look of delicate sensitiveness and courtesy, deeply touched her. Then there was his love for Adam.

He had fair hair, blue eyes, a very white skin and a proud mobile mouth. His worst fault was his modesty and his lack of self-assurance. Perhaps the unhappy history of his parents had encouraged that. She knew that his sense of honour was so scrupulous that decisions, their rights and wrongs, were often an agony to him.

'John,' she said. 'Come in.'

He came in and stood near her, twisting and untwisting his hands.

'Aunt Judith, Mother is crying. She says that you are going away.'

'John, dear, come here,' Judith said, drawing him to the sofa where so often she had sat with his father. He sat close to her, very erect, his thin white hands resting on his knees. She looked at him and loved him dearly. In that one look the foolish childish jealousy that she had had because Adam loved him too vanished altogether.

'I want you to understand. Adam and I are going away because it is best for you all that we should. I have managed everything for too long here. I am a managing old woman, you know. I cannot see a thing without wishing to arrange it. Now you are growing into a man, and this is your position, not mine. And then—' she hesitated for a moment, 'you know that I was not married to Adam's father, and people gossip. So – it is better for me to go.'

He gave a small gulp in his throat, staring into the fire.

'Yes, Aunt Judith.'

'You do understand, do you not?'

It was harder than she had expected.

'Yes, Aunt Judith ... But will you never come back any more?'

'You and Dorothy will come to visit us – only we shall be farmers, you know.'

'Yes.' He hesitated, then said: 'You and Adam are my best friends. I know Mr Winch says that I am not one that others can like very much—'

'What does Mr Winch say?' she burst out indignantly.

'Oh, he means it very well. And it is true. I like to be by myself unless it is someone I understand. And I do understand you and Adam. So – if you go—'

And then to her utter dismay he broke into tears, hid his head in his hands and sobbed most bitterly. She put her arms around him (a thing that she seemed to be doing to everyone today). He leaned against her for a little, then looked up, deeply ashamed and rubbing his eyes with his knuckles.

'I never cry,' he said. 'I don't know why now ... Mother was so unhappy ... and she is afraid of Uncle Walter. She says that if you go he will destroy us ... and I am not very old yet ...'

'John, John. Listen to me. Uncle Walter can do nothing to

you. You are here to care for your mother and sister. You are on guard over them. There is nothing to fear, and Adam and I will only be a few miles—'

She was interrupted by a loud banging at the door, a furious, impatient knocking.

They both started up, and she was never to forget that John put out his hand on to her arm as though he intended to begin, at once, to guard her from danger.

The knocking was repeated, more impatiently than before. She hurried out and opened the door. There was a figure against the dark, and then as he moved forward she saw who it was – it was Reuben.

'Reuben!' she cried, astonished. Then she saw that he was in the very greatest agitation. He closed the door behind him. Mrs Quinney was coming towards him.

'Quick, Judith,' he said, 'I must see you alone.'

She drew him into the dining-room, something in her saying: 'This is what you have been expecting all day long.'

When the door was closed she caught his arm. 'Reuben, what is it ? I thought you were at Whitehaven.'

There was perspiration on his forehead, and his breath came in gasps until he was calmer.

'Have you not heard anything ?'

'Heard anything ? No, of course not. What is it ?'

'I have ridden as swiftly as I could. I got away only in time ... My own men ... My own people ... They would not listen to me. They knocked me down, threw things at me. I tell you, Judith, they have thrown me over and it is because I have deserted God. I have been drawn more and more into earthly things, politics, money ... and now—'

He was incoherent, staring about him; scarcely, it seemed to her, recognizing her at all.

'No, but, Reuben, what *is* it ? Please, please ...'

'Yes, you are right. I scarcely know what I am saying. Listen, Judith; they are on their way now to burn this place down. I had dinner in Cockermouth and it was there that by chance I learnt of it. Holroyd, Atkinson, Bell, Wood – no, but of course their names mean nothing to you. There is a mob of them on their way now. Someone had put them up to it. They have been out of hand the last month. Last night some of them burnt Squire Forrester's ricks ...'

'Yes, yes, I know. But why here ? We have done nothing.'

'No. No. I don't understand.' He wiped the sweat from his

forehead. 'It was about Jennifer – some vastly improper things that they were saying.'

'Jennifer ?'

'Yes – and Fernyhirst.' He seemed to waken then to the sense of the urgency. 'No, but no matter. They can be only a mile or so away. A good hundred of them. What are you going to do ? What have you here in the way of servants ? '

He stood staring about him. Then he went on quickly: 'Someone should ride for one of the Magistrates. Mr Fox at Holtby is the nearest. He is old but courageous. Only last year he wished to have me whipped off his grounds. Is there anyone can go ? He should be there in an hour.'

'Yes. Jack. He's a brave boy. He'll go.'

She seemed to be transformed. This was a situation that she could understand. No tears and vapours and horror of some vague unknown danger. Something definite.

'We must have all the servants in' – and from that spoken word until the end of the affair she was in absolute command. She went out into the hall and found John and Mrs Quinney there, wondering.

'John – will you do a thing for me ?'

'Anything,' and she knew that he too was glad that action had come at last.

'Go up to your mother. Sit beside her bed. Read to her. Anything. She must be kept quiet and tranquil in her room for the next hour.'

He gave her one look, asked no questions, and went.

'Now, Mrs Quinney, I want all the servants. Everyone. In here. I have something to say to them. Will you fetch them, please ?'

Mrs Quinney went. Judith returned to Reuben.

'Reuben, you must have something to eat and drink.'

He nodded. He was sitting down and in his eyes was a look of utter dejection. Once again she was carried back to that day when she had given succour to his brother. The same incident – the same command. She brought him bread and meat and ale, and he ate and drank eagerly.

'But I cannot understand,' she repeated. 'Why here ? Why Jennifer ? Jennifer has done no one any harm but herself, poor thing.'

'Oh, they are mad. They have been so for months – indeed for years. This is only a little sequel to Peterloo, and there will be many another before all is done. But the wretchedness of this is that it is I who have been urging them to it . . . Oh no, not here, of course, nor to any violence. I have preached peace, but of late I have been filled with their material harshness and have forgot their souls. You yourself saw it when we were at Hawkshead. You spoke to me of it. And now today they would not listen to a single word from me. Bell and Holroyd are the worst. And only a year back Holroyd would have done anything for me.'

The door opened and they came in: Mr Winch, Mrs Quinney, Martha Hodgson, Doris, Jack Turner, Bennett.

At the sight of Bennett Judith's heart warmed. With his broad thick bulk, his utterly unperturbed air, his kindly protective eyes (just as Charlie Watson was protective), he would be the man for her now.

They stood in a group together, Mr Winch, with his pallor and nervous shifting eyes, a little apart from the others.

'Listen!' she said, smiling to reassure them. 'Mr Sunwood has ridden on to tell us that some rioters are on their way here from Cockermouth. It seems they mean mischief. Well, they shall find us ready for them. Jack, I want you to take Peggy and ride off at once to Squire Fox at Holtby. He is a Magistrate. Ask him to come as speedily as possible. You should be back with him in two hours. You know his place ?'

Jack nodded.

'Well, go then. Be as quick as you can.'

With another nod he was off.

'Fred' (this was Bennett), 'have we any firearms ?'

'There's two guns and an old pistol. I don't know if 'tis firing yet.'

'Good. Get anything you can. So soon as we hear them we will make the whole house dark. Do not disturb Mrs Herries or the children until we must. It should be an hour or more yet before they are here. They may not come at all. Now, Mrs Quinney, Martha, Doris, no fuss, now. At the worst it is only a few rough boys and men. Mr Fox will be here as soon as they – that is, if they come at all. You be quiet in the back of the house, will you ?'

They smiled and nodded proudly. They were Cumbrian women and not lightly disturbed. Nor were they garrulous. They showed no agitation at all. Bennett remained alone with Judith and Reuben.

'Dusta think,' he asked, 'there'll be many of them ?'

'A good few, I reckon,' said Reuben.

'Aye,' said Bennett slowly. 'T' height of wickedness. And

they'll suffer.' Then he added: 'Foreigners likely.' That was his principal sentiment – that he was shocked. He did not know, as he was often fond of declaring, what had come to the country. However, he was really only unhappy when he was puzzled as to which way he should act. It was the fear of his life that he should act the wrong way and look a fool. Happily in this present case his duty and his pleasure were clear.

He went off to the stables.

Reuben looked at her admiringly. This was how he liked to see her.

'Judith, you should be the Captain of a pirate.'

She laughed. 'Perhaps they will not come after all, Reuben.'

'Oh yes,' he said. 'They will come.'

'Let us go out and listen.'

They went into the garden and then on to the road. Then up on the moor. It was a fine night now, with a thin moon and quivering sheets of dim smoky stars. On the ridge of the moor the frosty air stung. Hills and valleys lay, under the deep shadows of the moon, in up-and-down disorder like a quilt shaped by the limbs of a recumbent giant. They listened, but there was only the thin whistle of the wind, smell of earth and sheep and rabbits, and the peaceful sleeping land.

'Maybe they will not come.'

'Oh, they will come. Not a doubt of it. Holroyd shouted filth at me; I had lost all touch with him. Do you remember one night when I came to Watendlath and Georges asked me about God? I was in touch then. It was as though I had Him under my cloak; but the world tempted me again, and I lost Him. First, when I was a boy, it was my fear of being a fool; then it was women; then I climbed over that and saw God as plainly as I see you; then their politics tempted me, and I lost Him. So I lose them as well.'

'You have done a good, kind thing coming to tell us, Reuben. God will be pleased with that. For myself, if there is a God, I will be grateful one moment and defy Him the next. It is no use to be always on your knees.'

She was talking to cover her own fears. She was thinking at that moment only of Adam. Her heart was wild with fear for him. Had she not been ashamed she would have snatched him out of bed, caught him up in her arms and run away with him out of the back door. When she was in the house and there was plenty to be done it was one thing, but out here in the cold and silence quite another. An owl hooted. A little wind pulled

at their feet. The anaemic moon was enveloped by a thin cloud
of gauze, and the world was veiled.

'Hark! Can you not hear something ?'

She caught his arm. They both listened. The breeze rose and
fell; a church bell from a great distance could be heard echoing
the half-hour. On the wind for a moment there seemed to be
the crack of horses. But it died.

'No. That was the church clock.'

They listened again. It seemed as though all the landscape
were listening with them.

'Yes. I am certain I hear something.'

She stood close to him. He put his arm around her. The
breeze came up the slope again and the moon rode out, her light
stroking Skiddaw's shoulder.

'Yes. Listen. Listen.'

Then above the beating of their hearts they heard it beyond
any question, the strike of horses' hoofs on the winter road.

'Quick! Quick! Back to the house!'

They ran down the fell, along the road and through the gate.
As Judith turned in she saw a figure come out of one of the
village houses; the black shadow stood looking down the hill.
It was beyond doubt now, a clatter of horses, laughter and
voices.

She ran into the house and up the stairs. First she went into
Jennifer's room. It was in darkness. John came towards her.

'She is asleep.'

She went to the bed and shook Jennifer's shoulder.

'Jennifer! Jennifer! Wake up!'

When she was awake she told her as quickly as possible.

'Now, Jennifer, it is nothing. Only some drunken boys. But
you must stay here. Don't move from here. It will be soon over.'

'Drunken boys ? . . . But what do they want ?'

'Reuben is here, and Bennett has a gun, and Mr Fox of
Holtby is coming over.'

'Oh dear. Oh dear . . .'

But she had no time for Jennifer's 'Oh dears!'

'John, you remain with your mother. Adam and Dorothy
had best be here as well. I will bring them.'

When she went into her own room her heart for a moment
failed her. Adam was lying, his head on his arm, fast asleep.
She woke him, wrapped him in a blanket so that he looked a
young bewildered Indian, and told him quietly:

'Adam, there are some noisy men in the garden. If they shout and throw stones, it is no matter. Mother is here and Bennett and Mr Winch and Uncle Reuben. You stay with John, darling, in Aunt Jennifer's room.'

He nodded his head, yawning and rubbing his eyes with his knuckles. 'Where will you be ?' he asked.

'I shall return very soon. Now, go to John, darling.'

'Can't I see the men throwing stones ?'

'No. Not now. Be a good boy.'

He was always a good boy if his mother thought that it was serious. He saw that she thought that this was serious, and obeyed. She took him into the next room, saw that Dorothy was also there, and Jennifer sitting up in bed and asking John questions. She gave Adam to John and left them.

When she came downstairs another world had already burst upon them. The house was in darkness, save for the candles in Jennifer's room. The women were in the kitchen. Bennett and Reuben, each with a gun, were in the hall. They all three moved into the parlour.

She looked between the curtains and almost cried out at the scene. At least a hundred men, women, and boys were gathered in the road, dark and shadowy in the moonlight, but some of them carried torches whose flames, leaping in the wind, jumped from shadow to shadow. About a dozen men were on horseback.

She recognized at once a number of villagers among them. Since Francis' death the men and women of the village had held aloof from Jennifer, whom in fact they had always disliked.

There was the strangest contrast between the black silence of the house and the shouts, laughter, cries that came from the crowd. She saw that one of them, a long thin bearded man on a white horse, was their leader.

'That is Holroyd!' Reuben whispered to her. The crowd moved backwards and forwards as though stirred by some impetus within themselves. Through the closed window she could not hear what they were crying. White faces leapt into torchlight and out again. Arms rose and fell. Suddenly the gates swung back and they all tumbled pell-mell into the garden. Then there was a pause and silence. They stood transfixed, as though a spell had been cast on them, staring at the house.

That was queer – to stand behind the curtains with that familiar room all about her, to look out and see that multitude, faces like fish-scales in the moonlight, all still and waiting. All for no reason! These were familiar things, the furniture, the

walls, the pictures, and yet these strangers had the impertinence
to break through the gate, to trample on the garden, to insult
the shadows of David, of Francis, of Sarah – perhaps to frighten
the spirit of her own son, Adam! A furious indignation began
to rise within her.

The silence cracked. A stone was flung and smashed through
the parlour window, missing Judith by a breath.

'Take care!' Reuben whispered, pulling her back.

The throwing of that stone released them. They all began to
shout at once. More stones were thrown. Figures were running
down the lawn, others towards the stables. Meanwhile the thin
man with a beard sat motionless on his horse.

'I must go out to them!' Reuben said.

'No. No. They will throw stones. Wait—'

'No. I cannot wait.'

He went out. She heard him open the door of the hall, and,
before he shut it, a roar of voices reached her, like a sudden ripple
of thunder. What had she better do? Her impulse was to go with
him. The parlour door had closed, but now it opened to show
the meagre black figure of Mr Winch, who entered with a lighted
candle.

'Blow out that candle!' she ordered him sharply.

But he could not. He stood there, his mouth open, his eyes
shifting from place to place, the candle shaking in his hand.
He was in a sweat of terror. Indignantly she snatched the candle
from him and blew it out, saying:

'No one will harm *you*, Mr Winch. Your place is with the
children upstairs.' She heard him slip away.

From the intervals where the curtains were not drawn the
glare of the torches, falling and rising, lit the room – the coloured
top of the spinet, the crimson chair, the sofa with the red apples.
She could also hear now through the break in the window that
the stone had made. Reuben's voice came across to her, and it
seemed that they were listening:

'. . . and if I had done so you might have charged me with a
fault, but for many years now I have had only your interests
at heart. What others could I ever have had? Have I not given
my whole life to your friendship? . . .' She lost it again. Then
it returned. '. . . and this house has never harmed you. It has not
starved you as some have done, nor ill-treated your children
as some have done, nor thrown you out of employment like
some. But even though it had, this would not be your Court of
Appeal. Violence of this sort has never won anyone any good,

and well you know it. Cruelty to women and children has never been our Cumberland way . . .'

'A little too much of the orator,' she thought. '*I'd* speak to them!'

But he was not to speak much longer. She caught the words: '. . . and be for ever ashamed of as dastardly an action . . .'

Perhaps someone was stirring up trouble from the road. In any case, there was a sudden rush from the rear of the crowd, shouts and screams, and someone threw a lighted torch, whirling through the dark until it fell with a hiss on the lawn and lay there blazing. The man on the horse made as though he would ride on to Reuben and so past him into the house; but, in spite of his furious movement, his voice was sharp and controlled as he cried:

'Enough words, Sunwood! Back to the stables, lad. And we'll see them blaze!'

'Shall I fire? Shall I fire?'

Judith heard a voice in her ear, and putting out a hand felt Bennett's breast and his heart beating like a clock.

'No . . . Wait, Fred. Oh, the devils! I cannot endure this. And with the children upstairs. Oh, when will Mr Fox come? I must go out to them! I cannot endure this here!'

'No, no, ma'am. Stay where you are!'

'No. I must go.' She tore herself from Bennett's hand and ran from the room, he following her. She could never quite clearly remember afterwards what occurred in that outside pandemonium. The air was cold and yet the heat seemed intense. There was smoke in her nostrils. Reuben was shouting. She saw that his forehead was bleeding, and that seemed to loose a fury inside her. She never knew what she cried, but she drove into the middle of them; then, nearly stumbling over a mounting-block by the door, she climbed on to it.

'Be ashamed of yourselves. Attacking women and children who have done you no harm. Go back to your homes, you bullies . . .'

The ineffectiveness of her words enraged her yet more. They swept past her and around her, not even seeing her, shouting, some of them singing, the horses rising in the moonlight like white seahorses. Then, as though it were a banner unfurled, a shuddering, quivering flame leapt up into the sky from the stables. The fire lit the whole scene; all faces were white, the house like a black wall with the pale glass squares of the windows. A woman's cry came from inside the house.

'The horses! The horses!' Judith cried, and began to push and fight through the mob, who, at sight of the fire, seemed dimmed and quieted as though they sank from the scene. Some man struck her in the breast. She turned, gasping for breath, and saw Bennett behind her, his gun raised.

'You shall have it then!' he cried, and fired.

Holroyd on his horse half turned, raised an arm, shivered and slowly fell. Reuben sprang forward, was for a moment illuminated by the fire; a shot rang from the road, and he too jumped as though, with arms lifted, he would touch the moon, and collapsed on the horse-steps.

The two shots, the crackle and gesture of the fire, the riderless horse plunging, seemed in a moment to change the scene. Men and women all turned. They fled through the gate.

A woman, her hair loose, turned and shouted in a shrill broken voice: 'Curse you . . .' and something more about Jezebel and vengeance.

Then panic had caught them all, for they were flying down the road – horses, men, women – the white moonlit stretch was black with fleeing figures . . . Then, save for Reuben's huddled body on the steps, there was nothing in the garden. Only the flames of the stable chattered, hissed, rose and fell as though they were busy with their own private important business.

Judith, with Reuben's head in her lap, looked desperately around her.

'Quick, quick, Fred. Someone fetch Doctor Borden from the village. He'll be hiding in his house. Tell him' (her voice was fierce and bitter) 'that it is safe now. He must come. The women must get buckets for the fire . . .' She caught sight of some slinking figures in the gateway. Villagers who, now that the riot was over, had crept out. 'Force them. They must help. The house must not burn.'

Bennett answered. 'The house is safe. It is only the outside sheds. The fire is burning itself out. Oh, Mr Reuben, are you hurt, sir? Are you hurt?'

'He's dying, Fred.' She bent over him. His eyes were open, looking at her. He smiled.

'Goodbye, Judith. I did my best.'

She knew that he was dead. Her hands were soaked in blood. She stared out above him to the quiet sky and the stables lit by fire. She felt a hand on her shoulder and looked up. It was Mrs Quinney.

'He is dead,' she said quietly. 'Help me to carry him in.'

THE CHOICE

REUBEN WAS BURIED five days later in Ireby Churchyard. As
Judith drove in the carriage, away back to the house again, she
was so weary that the whole world was quite unreal.

A great crowd had been at the funeral. Men and women had
come from all parts, for Reuben was in general much beloved,
and the riot, the disorder, and his death had made the greatest
possible stir. Nothing else was talked of. Holroyd (who had
only a flesh-wound in the arm) and Bell were in Kendal gaol;
other arrests were expected to be made.

All of this could do poor Reuben very little good; but Judith
was aware as, a lonely little black figure, she moved through the
courtyard gate into her carriage, that she was surrounded with
sympathy. She had known already that Uldale village was
properly ashamed and anxious to make amends. She did not
care. Reuben was gone – and, very soon, oh, very, very soon, she
would be away from them all, safe with Adam in Watendlath.

It was a most curious day, she thought, as she drove up the
road. For three days and nights there had been unceasing rain,
and as, night after night, she had lain awake the rain had seemed
to shroud her in as though it were weaving for her a great suit
of silver armour, and in this she could live, safe and protected,
for ever after.

But this rain in the valleys had meant snow on the hills. They
were more thickly covered than they had been for many years.
Today the landscape was shrouded in mist. There seemed to be
three veils, one upon another, and these were always shifting.
The middle veil was faintly radiant and orange in colour, for it
held the sun, sunlight enfolded and shrouded. The farthest veil
was of a very dim blue, cold, with snow in it. The first veil was
almost transparent, of the thinnest gauze.

All the land moved in mystery behind these veils, for it was
the land that appeared to be moving as the veils shifted. Everything was on the edge of discovery, but nothing was clear,
only the stones under your feet, trunks of birch and larch and
oak at your hand. In the corner of a field leaves were burning,
a blazing fire in smoke.

So, sitting in the carriage, only half awake, in this shrouded
world, it did not seem strange to her that the forms of her four

friends, all dead from violence, should be sitting beside her –
Francis, Georges, Warren, Reuben – one of whom she had
loved and still loved, one the father of her son, two the friends of
her lifetime.

They none of them, she thought, looked at her with any
reproach. She had in a way been the cause of death in all of
them – at least she had been in the minds and hearts of all of
them when they died. But, unsentimental as ever, she did not
intend in any way to reproach herself. She had been honest with
them all, and she knew that they wished her well. They had all
died fighting – Georges fighting discipline, Francis his own soul,
Warren convention, Reuben fighting his way back to God.
They had all, in fact, been fighting Herries one way or another –
if you took Herries for fact against fancy, as she did.

However, she was too weary to do more than smile upon
them and assure them that they need not look at her with such
anxiety. She and her little son were on the very point of escaping.
The Herries would not get her, try as hard as they might.
Nevertheless, she knew that when she was alive again she would
discover that the unfair savage death of Reuben had placed something hard and bitter in her heart that had never been there
before.

When she had taken off her bonnet and cloak, washed her face
and brushed her hair, she thought that she would finish the
thing once and for all. Jennifer was down in the parlour looking
at the mist that trailed past the window. A small block of wood
had been placed where the stone had crashed; they would come
very shortly from Keswick and mend the window. Indeed, very
little damage had been done: two windows broken, a shed or two
destroyed – that was all there was to show for the flaring torches,
the flaming sky, the shouts and curses and Reuben's death.

Jennifer looked very fine in her black gown. There was no
paint on her face, and her magnificent black hair gave her today
some nobility. But the shock of that night had done something
to her. She was more properly controlled than she had been for
years.

'There is a letter come for you,' she said.

Judith took it and saw that it was from Emma Furze. Emma!
As she read it her heart glowed. And then, when she found that
Emma was in London, was well and happy and gay, and wished
to come up and spread some of her happiness around the Watendlath farm, it was as if the sun had broken into the room. She

should, indeed she should. In another week Judith and Adam would be there. Then there would be Emma and Charlie and Alice Perry . . .

'Were there many at the funeral, Judith dear?' Jennifer asked. Judith told her of the funeral.

Jennifer nodded to all the details.

'I am glad that I did not go. I am very unrestrained at funerals. And I do not know that I shall ever have the courage to go out again. Do you not know what they were calling . . . some of the women? . . . Doris heard them. "Jezebel." One woman wanted to burn me in the stable.'

'Nonsense, Jennifer. You must not think of it. They are very kindly disposed to us. They are ready to do anything.'

'To us? To you, you mean. So long as you are here we are safe. But I want to tell you. I have been thinking deeply and I see how weak and wretched I have been. I am terribly ashamed. And I mean to be a help to you, Judith, in the future as I have never been. And to John and Dorothy too. Yes, I am most wretchedly ashamed, and John, that evening, was so brave and so good. I am sure no boy of his age anywhere is so brave. You will find, Judith, that I shall be quite another woman—'

'Well, that is excellent,' said Judith cheerfully. 'It is what I have always told you, Jennifer. You have been frightened by shadows.' Then she went on more gently, but with great firmness. 'Next week Adam and I are going. My mind is quite made up. You will find everyone here as kind as possible – everyone in the village. Eager to make friends.'

'Oh no,' said Jennifer in a voice so low that Judith could scarcely hear her. 'Oh, please Judith – it will kill me if you go away.'

They had had it out already so many times. There was to be no more discussion of it. But as she bent to kiss Jennifer's cheek she had an appalling sense of weakness.

Oh, let her waste no time! Let her slip out now, this moment! Jennifer was harder to resist now that she was so quiet, and there was John who had been so brave and Dorothy who, on that awful night, had been so good to Adam, telling him stories. As she kissed Jennifer and felt the cold touch of her hands she cared for her as she had never done before.

Another moment and she would surrender, moved and softened as she had been by the funeral. She would surrender and be lost, all hope of her happiness gone! She murmured something and hastened out, almost expecting to find Walter

Herries barring the door of the house with his huge body, defying her to escape.

But in the hall, instead of Walter Herries, she found Mr Winch.

'May I speak to you a moment, madam?' he said.

'Yes, Mr Winch,' she said. She had a new gravity. She had noticed it herself. She did not dislike it so long as she was in Uldale. It would not do at all for Watendlath. She led the way into the small room that had been Francis'. Mr Winch, very pale, his hands clasped, his head up, looked at her.

'Well, Mr Winch?'

'I thought I should tell you ...' He hesitated. '... I wish to resign my duties here.'

She felt a relief. It would be easy to find some far better tutor, someone who did not go down on his knees on the gravel path. Indeed, had she had her way he would have gone long ago. Jennifer had some weakness for him. He read Minerva Press novels to her.

'But why?' she asked. In spite of herself she was scornful. 'Have the rioters been too much for you? You remained safely in the back of the house for the greater part.'

'I know,' he stammered. 'You must despise me – and rightly. But you do not know all. If ...'

Then to her amazement he burst into sobs, threw himself down to his knees, held up his hands.

'Mr Winch!' she exclaimed, stepping back, thinking he must be out of his senses, that the fear of the other night had unsettled his wits.

'No, no. Listen to me. I have been miserable for a very long time, and this terrible catastrophe, with the death of Mr Sunwood, has destroyed me. I was his murderer.'

'You!' She could have laughed at the little figure in the shiny black with the rather grubby hands. But his distress was real, his fear was real. She saw that this was a matter of importance.

'Please rise,' she said. 'Please get up. You cannot be Mr Reuben Sunwood's murderer, for I myself saw the shot fired that killed him.'

He was sobbing. He buried his head in his hands.

'I cannot speak to you unless you get up.'

He rose. He composed himself. His head bent a little, as though he were making a confession, he went on:

'No, not in positive fact his murderer. I did not fire the gun. But in everything else – Mrs Paris, ever since I came to you I have been spying upon everyone in this house. Mr Walter Herries of Westaways has paid me for that odious business.'

'I know it,' she said quietly.

'You knew it?'

'I saw you one day on your knees in the garden spying on Mr Francis.'

'You knew it and you did nothing?'

'I did nothing because, once I knew it, you were safer than someone I did not know.'

He went on a little more confidently.

'I have no excuse. None. I did not need the money. All my life I have avoided shabby actions. But Mr Walter Herries had a strange power over me. He could do anything with me that he pleased. I do not urge that in my defence; there is no defence. But so it was. He overtook me one day walking to Keswick and from the first I was his slave. I brought him news of everything that happened at Uldale – everything. It was I who found a man that should carry the note to Mr Francis when he was in Cockermouth, telling him that Captain Fernyhirst was here that night.'

'You did that?' He thought she would strike him and he moved back, but she had not stirred.

'Yes, I. It was Mr Walter Herries' plot, entirely arranged by him.'

Her face was so terrible that he could not look at it. He turned away.

'Yes. And so with everything here. Every day he had news. It was he, by my agency, who brought the rioters here.'

'Yes,' she said (but she was not addressing him). 'I understand.'

'He intended, I think, only to give you a fright. I was in Cockermouth and saw Holroyd and Bell and the others. They were given money. There was to be no real damage to life or property. But they had drink on that afternoon. They went further than they intended.'

'Yes,' she said. 'They went far.'

'I have been very miserable ever since I have been here. Again and again I have gone to him to tell him that I would do his work no longer but when I saw him . . . I cannot explain . . . He had a power . . .'

He was trembling.

'Forgive me,' he said. 'I must sit.' He sat down, his head so bent that she could scarcely catch his words. 'Again and again I have tried to say to you that I must go. Something prevented me. And at the beginning of this week when I knew what was in hand I was in hell. I could not sleep nor eat. A hundred times I was on the edge of breaking it to you. But his presence seemed always behind me. I thought that he would kill me if I betrayed him. He has often said, in his jolly laughing way, that he would. But he did not mean it to be murder. I did not intend . . . But it is too late. You may give me up to the Justice, Mrs Paris. You may indeed. I would be happier . . .'

'You!' She turned to the window. Francis and Reuben both killed by Walter!

Her stomach was sick. Her knees trembled. She also sat down, but with her back to him. For a long while there was silence. Could she bring the thing home to Walter? She half turned, as though she would speak, but turned back again. No! there was no help there. He would have seen to it that nothing could be carried to him. Who would believe a creature like Winch? Walter's power! . . . And suddenly she saw him, as though he were there with them in the room, vast, blazing with colour and jewels, laughing, but so bent from conceit and arrogance on his purpose that nothing was too terrible for him, too mean, too cruel. And yet he was a jolly man and loved his son even as she loved hers. She got up.

'Pray go away, Mr Winch,' she said. 'Go away in the morning. What is due to you will be sent to you. I would be happier not to see you again.'

Without a word he got up, and, head still bent, went out.

Very slowly she went upstairs to her room. No one was there. She looked out. Behind the mist the moon of five nights ago was now full, but it was like a flat stone ridged with light and wrapped in wool.

She had been caught. Now she had no doubt. She could not go. She had been able to defeat everything but this. Now a hard determined anger such as she had never felt had come and would abide. Francis . . . Reuben . . . killed by that laughing man. How could she now leave Jennifer and John and Dorothy defenceless?

Oh, but the other life! Watson was expecting her. In the Ritson kitchen Alice at this moment perhaps would be speaking of her. And her home, the room where Georges had died. And Adam to be a farmer, to grow up knowing nothing of this world of money, deceit, jealousy, unkindness. The Tarn, wrapped in mist, would be waiting for the moon to break. Or,

perhaps, there was no mist there tonight and the slopes of the
fells, snow-clad, glittered.

'I cannot . . . I cannot . . .'

She turned, possessed by some strange madness, pulled
drawers open, found a box beneath the bed, began, on her
knees, to cram it.

Adam came running in. He was shouting and dancing.

'Jack says there will be a new barn. They will begin tomorrow, and the windows—'

He stopped, seeing what she was doing. She shook her head
as though the battle were hopeless. Once as a little girl she had
climbed out of window, but now – to leave them, Jennifer weak,
John, Dorothy, so young, to that determined remorseless
purpose . . .

'They are doomed, you know,' Walter had said, and even as
he said it, he was aware that he had killed Francis, was planning
this.

She got up from her knees and went to the window again.
As she looked the moon broke the mist. Skiddaw started up in
dazzling white. Like a white rose, like a glorious white rose from
heaven, she lifted her head, and the mist sank to lie in waves
across the valley.

She looked and she wept. The tears blinded her. She said
farewell.

She came and sat down by the bed and drew Adam to her.
She had command of herself.

'Tell me something,' he said. 'Tell me about Uncle Tom.'

It was his favourite story. While her mind was fiercely working
on her future, hers and his, mechanically she went on with the
familiar words:

'Although it had snowed so bitterly Uncle Tom got off his
horse because he heard the baby crying, and he rode over the
little bridge—'

'Don't forget the dogs! Don't forget the dogs!' Adam
cried.

'Yes. They were all there and they followed him solemnly
over the courtyard and into the house. And they went up the
stairs. And they went into a room, the dogs sat down by the
door, the old woman was sleeping—'

Oh, who was moving in the hills ? What Rogue was wandering,
calling for her, telling her that here was her home ? The dry
bones of the dead were alive. They were calling for her, those
two old ghosts, and she could not come . . .

She had now complete command of herself. She drew him closer.

'Adam, I want you to listen. You may not understand, but do you remember that one day going to Keswick I talked to you about being a farmer?'

'Yes,' he said. He drew himself up very straight because she was reposing a confidence in him and he was proud. He stood up straight with all the pride of a very small boy, that pride that is perhaps the small boy's most lovely quality.

'Now everything is changed. I have had to make the most important decision of my life – a decision for you also. You and I are to fight, Adam. I had thought that it would all be quiet and at peace, but now we are going to fight.'

'Who will we fight?' Adam asked with great interest. 'Uncle Walter?'

'You are too young to understand, but later you will see that I could do nothing else than this. We have to be very strong, you and I, and very wise, Adam. We will beat them all, and you shall be the head of them. No, you cannot understand now. But you must trust me.'

He threw his arms round her neck. She was small, and it was easy for him to draw her head down; he could kiss her and lay his cheek against hers. Now, if she wished to fight someone, he would help her. He thought that perhaps she was sorry that she made him stay in Aunt Jennifer's room when they came to burn the stables. Now, this next time, he would go with her and help her.

While he hugged her, her pride was rising. Her pride, her deep and unchangeable hatred of Walter Herries. In that hour the second half of her life began.

She got up. Now she would take command. A fierce bright delight flowed in her veins. She would make Adam the master of them all. Walter's boy . . . She saw him in his little chair, his deformity, his old, pale face, and the big man kneeling at his side. She caught Adam to her, kissing him passionately. Adam should be King.

With her head up, as though she already commanded a kingdom, she stepped downstairs.

She opened the parlour door. Jennifer was standing at the window. When she heard the door open she turned. She looked and saw a short pale woman in a plain black gown. But she saw also a woman on fire with determination, with pride and an almost fanatical purpose.

'Why, Judith!—' she began.

'All is well,' Judith said quietly, coming forward and stroking the red apples of the sofa. 'I shall not leave you, Jennifer, It is better I remain.'